AFTERSHOCK

BY

LILLIAN O'DONNELL

THE BIG FOOTPRINTS

BY

H. R. F. KEATING

FILMI, FILMI, INSPECTOR GHOTE

BY

HAMMOND INNES

Published *for the*
DETECTIVE BOOK CLUB ®
by Walter J. Black, Inc.
ROSLYN, NEW YORK

THE DETECTIVE BOOK CLUB®

Printed in the United States of America

AFTERSHOCK

BY
LILLIAN O'DONNELL

Author of Leisure Dying *which featured Detective Norah Mulca-haney, Lillian O'Donnell here introduces Mitzi Anholt, agent for New York State's Victims/Witnesses Agency. It is set up to help the victims of crime with money, etc. Mitzi goes way beyond her job and gets herself right into the middle of pregnant Faith Tully's case. She is the widow of a well-known hairdresser with a fashionable clientele, and also is the prime suspect as his killer. Mitzi gets herself into some very tight spots, of course, taking the reader with her step by step right to the end.*

G. P. Putnam's Sons Edition   **$7.95**

THE BIG FOOTPRINTS

BY
HAMMOND INNES

Two groups of people in Africa—the killers of wild animals for food etc. and the preservers—are deadly enemies. The chief animal they are struggling over is the elephant, an important source of food and ivory. Due to drought, there is no need for the usual culling of the herds, but determination pro and con leads to murders of man and beast. Hammond Innes is always very well informed on the background and people he writes about. Thus he is able to show how the resolution of the struggle grows out of the situation in a most realistic way.

Alfred A. Knopf, Inc. Edition   **$8.95**

FILMI, FILMI, INSPECTOR GHOTE

BY
H. R. F. KEATING

Faithful, modest, little Inspector Ghote is carried away with a splendid dream of life for himself in the film world of India when he is called in to solve the murder of a star. Alas, when he uncovers the murderer he is a sadder and wiser man about the movie world, as well as his chances of cutting a glamorous figure in it.

Doubleday and Company Edition   **$5.95**

AFTERSHOCK

BY

LILLIAN O'DONNELL

Published by special arrangement with G. P. Putnam's Sons

Chapter I

Saturday A.M.

It was a thin scream; the empty street and the night silence briefly nurtured it, then it was sucked up between the high-rise buildings like smoke up a flue and wafted away across a starless sky. It was a scream of anguish rather than terror, as though the woman who gave vent to it already knew that the situation was hopeless. Yet she persisted.

"Help! Help! Oh, God, somebody help me!"

Soft rain, no more than a soggy mist, muffled her impotent cries as she sought to penetrate the dark houses and the consciousness of the sleepers inside.

"Help me! Please, please, won't somebody help me?" she moaned, and the moan turned into convulsive sobbing, a retching of despair, the beginning of a dirge.

None of the lights in the surrounding buildings came on, though there were people who heard. Her screams lodged in their memories and would echo later to disturb other nights. For now they were dismissed: by some as the ravings of a drunk—it was just before Christmas, the season for drunks; some rationalized it as one side of a family quarrel and wished that people would do their fighting indoors. In apartment 5C of the Riverview House on Eighty-second Street one man threw aside the covers, slipped out of bed quietly, so as not to disturb his wife, and padded to the window.

But he had awakened her. Or the screams had. "Oscar? What are you doing?" she demanded fretfully.

"Nothing. Go back to sleep."

"What are you looking at?"

"There's a woman down there screaming."

Rena Beinecke raised herself up on one elbow and waited. "Well? Can you see?"

He was looking down on a wire-fenced parking lot adjacent to his building and extending to the corner of First Avenue. Newly installed vapor lamps bathed it in a bright, shadow-free glow. He could see between the cars and even a portion of the avenue as well as most of his own block, except for a few feet along the building line beneath his window.

"She's just standing there screaming," he reported. "I can't see another soul."

"God knows what she's high on," Rena Beinecke commented, torn between pity and disgust.

Abruptly, her husband reached a decision. He strode back to the night table and fumbled under the lamp for the switch.

"What are you doing?" his wife cried in alarm.

"I'm going to call the police."

She grabbed his arm. "Don't put on the light! Are you crazy? If there's anybody out there, if anybody is making that woman scream like that . . . we don't want him to know where the call came from."

"I can't see to dial in the dark."

"Just call the operator. No, wait . . ." Rena Beinecke got out of bed and ran barefooted to the window, where she pulled the cord that closed the blind. "Okay."

Her husband turned on the light, and just as he did so, the screaming stopped.

In the middle of the sudden brightness, blinking sleep-swollen eyes, Oscar and Rena Beinecke silently consulted. In unspoken accord she turned out the light again and together they crept to the window to peer through the slats.

"She's gone," he whispered.

"Thank God." His wife sighed.

"Maybe we should call anyway?" he suggested, uneasy.

"Why? What's the point?"

"Well, just to report . . ."

"What? What are we going to report? We didn't see anything but some woman standing in the rain screaming. We don't know why she was screaming. She could have been a nut. Probably was."

"Still . . ."

As his assurance ebbed, hers grew. "Do what you want," she said, knowing that she had won. Then for good measure she added, "You know what'll happen: the police will get everybody in the building out of bed and keep them up for hours, for the rest of the night." She glanced at the luminous dial of the bedside clock and gasped. "You know what time it is? Quarter of two! We have to get up at six. If you call the police we can forget about any more sleep tonight."

Beinecke stifled a sigh. "You're right, Rena, you're right. You're always right."

"Well, don't blame me. It's not my fault," she complained. "I'm not the one who had to get an early start. If we'd booked on the afternoon plane like I wanted . . ."

Beinecke slid into bed. He pulled the covers up and turned over on his side. His wife droned on in the dark. Oscar Beinecke stopped listening.

No use to go on screaming, Faith thought. Nobody was going to come out, or open a window, or do anything. Nobody gave a damn.

Rain beaded her dark hair, rain and tears streaked her pinched, sallow face. No use. Faith Tully raised a fist and shook it at the dark windows. Folks up here didn't care for nobody but themselves! Fury and frustration staunched her anguish, then it gushed forth again, more devastating for having been even briefly assuaged. The pressure building up inside her was so great, causing actual physical pain, that Faith thought she must open her mouth to relieve it by another round of screaming. She couldn't afford the time. She rocked to and fro keening softly. God, oh God, help me! Tell me what to do.

A phone. Of course. She had to get to a phone.

Vaguely, she recalled having seen a couple of those new pedestal-type booths back on Second Avenue. She ran. She ran up Eighty-second Street past rows of crumbling and somehow sinister tenements, not bothering to skirt the refuse that spilled from overflowing cans and plastic garbage bags, unaware of the startled rats that scampered out of her way. She ran till her breath came in searing gasps and the stitch in her side was so sharp she wouldn't have been surprised to discover that she was cut and bleeding. Finally, she reached the corner.

Where were the phones?

There were no booths on the corner or anywhere up or down the avenue as far as Faith Tully could see. Was it on Third she'd noticed them? Or on some side street? She couldn't wander around searching. Hadn't there been a bar? Yes, there it was. Closed. At least the big neon sign overhead was out. It couldn't be closed; it couldn't. Somehow, she found the strength to run those last few feet to the plate-glass window. It was dark inside, all dark. Flattening herself against the glass, she tried to peer past the counter and tables with the upended chairs. There was a dim light all the way at the rear: she could just barely glimpse it. She ran around to the door and pounded.

"Hello! Hello? Anybody inside? Please, let me in!"

She grasped the doorknob with both hands and shook. The whole door rattled in its frame, but there was no other sound, no response.

What she'd seen was only a night-light.

The rain was coming down harder now, but Faith wasn't aware of either the wet or the cold as she searched up and down the avenue. The traffic lights went through a cycle: green, yellow, red, then green again, casting their auras on pavement and buildings. She spotted a car turning the corner of Eighty-sixth and heading toward her. She ran out into the middle of the road to flag it down.

Windshield wipers sweeping at a fast rate, the driver could just make out a woman in a long bedraggled skirt and a jacket, no hat, no coat, the rain streaming off her. She loomed into his headlights, a nightmare of red-rimmed eyes and bloodless lips and a tangled mass of black hair. He had to cut the wheel hard to avoid hitting her. Drunk, he thought, and sped by. Ugly to see a woman drunk. Young, too. And pregnant. Shame, lousy shame.

Faith watched him pass. She was close to exhaustion as she began the slow trek up the next block to Third. Plenty of action on Third Avenue: all-night movies, amusement arcades, bars, restaurants. Lots of folks milling around, she encouraged herself as she stumbled on her way.

Faith Tully never made it to Third Avenue. Halfway down the block she was picked up by a passing patrol car.

*   *   *

Officers Quinlan and Boucha observed the woman at approximately 1:55 A.M. She was trudging through the rain: no umbrella, hatless and coatless, long skirt soaked and dragging at her ankles. They approached from the rear, and when they pulled over, they could see that she was in partial shock. She was not even aware of their presence; they honked the car horn and she didn't hear, only kept moving doggedly ahead.

Dry and warm in the patrol car, the two officers looked at each other in resignation. Quinlan, in the passenger seat, sighed and opened his door. "Ma'am?" he called. No answer. There was nothing for it but to get out.

"Ma'am?" he repeated, stepping in front of her and looking directly into her face.

Faith Tully blinked a couple of times before she took him in, realized who he was and that her search was finally over. "Oh, thank God! Thank God, you're here, Officer. Gene, my husband, he's been hurt . . . shot. He's lying out in the street. I've been trying to find someone . . . I've been trying to get help. . . . Please, come with me. Please. Hurry."

"Where? Where is he?" Quinlan asked.

"This way. Come on, I'll show you. Come on. Hurry." She tugged at his elbow.

"Get in the car, ma'am; we'll drive. It'll be quicker." Disengaging himself, the policeman now took her arm and drew her toward the backseat.

"Just exactly where is he, ma'am?" Tony Boucha, the driver, asked.

"This way, between First and Second avenues. Just outside the parking lot. You know the parking lot?"

The ground which it had taken Faith Tully nearly eighteen agonizing minutes to cover was now traversed in seconds. Though it lay in the shadow cast by the front row of parked cars, the two officers spotted the prone figure almost as soon as they crossed the intersection of Second Avenue. The man was lying motionless, yet the officers did not immediately leave the car and go to him. They pulled up a few yards short and reconnoitered. Tony Boucha and Reed Quinlan were young, but they had already learned caution. The woman's condition suggested that her distress was genuine and that the man on the sidewalk just outside the parking lot fence had been shot as she claimed, but they were wary of an ambush. Fake calls for assistance had become all too prevalent, luring too many police officers to let down their guards and then be shot. They looked up and down the street; they scanned the dark windows and apparently empty doorways.

To Faith Tully this last delay seemed only callous. It was more than she could bear. She threw open the rear door of the car and jumped out, running to the body on the pavement.

"Gene, Gene, I'm here. . . ." She stopped abruptly, for a split second frozen in horror and then screamed, "My God! My God! What's happened? What've they done to him?"

Quinlan leaped out just in time to grab her before she could fling herself on top of the victim.

"Look at him, look at him . . . look at his poor face . . ." she wailed.

He looked as though he'd been pistol-whipped and stomped. His face was a bloody pulp; there was dirt tracked across his jacket and shirt.

"He wasn't like that when I left him. What happened? What happened? He was lying on his stomach, facedown . . . I covered him with my raincoat . . . I covered him. . . ." She was sobbing convulsively now and at the same time struggling to get out of Quinlan's restraining embrace and down to the battered figure.

"Call an ambulance," Quinlan shouted to his partner while trying to hold on to the nearly demented woman. "Please, ma'am, would you just please stand aside and let me look at him?" Instantly, Faith stopped fighting. Reed Quinlan got down on one knee beside the victim. After a few moments he rose and leaned in the open window of the car. "Forget the ambulance. Call homicide."

Though he'd whispered, Faith Tully heard.

"No!" she shrieked.

Quinlan made a dive, but this time he couldn't stop her. Faith Tully literally flung herself on the body of her husband. "You mustn't do that," he pleaded. "Please, ma'am, get up. Please. You shouldn't touch him." He reached down, intending to help her to her feet.

"Give me a hand, Tony," he yelled. "She's passed out cold."

Saturday P.M.

Mr. Creedy wore his usual sweet smile. Some called it dumb; they said Mr. Creedy had nothing to smile about. It made them resentful, even angry, that a man with so little in life should be so constantly cheerful. It shamed them. Since obviously they were much better off, it robbed them of the right to complain. If he had known what they were thinking, Mr. Creedy would have been surprised. He was aware, of course, that he wasn't like other people, that he was below par. His speech was labored and his movements jerky and uncoordinated, but he could take care of himself—that was the main thing. He even held a job. He worked for the Parks Department. That is, he had, up until six months ago.

Simon Creedy had been proud of that job, of the work that he was able to perform. He hadn't minded walking around with his spiked stick picking up bits of paper and putting them into his gunnysack, or sweeping the paths, or shoveling snow and scattering salt over the ice in winter. He didn't consider it demeaning—what he was doing was keeping the park beautiful. Later, when he was promoted to assistant gardener, when he could dig and plant, he was so proud that he would come on his day off to watch over his shrubs and saplings. If the children were abusing the new plantings, he would chide them gently, and they didn't laugh at his halting speech. He gained confidence, and so his disabilities were less apparent.

Early retirement had more or less been forced on him. He bore no grudge. He understood that it was because the city was broke. He had his pension. He could still walk in the park and watch over his plants and talk to his friends, for over the years the wiry little man with the shuffling gait, the liquid brown eyes, and the steady smile had made many friends among the visitors to the park as well as the workers. He could still visit with his buddies in the Mineral Springs House, which was a kind of headquarters for the maintenance people around the Sheep Meadow area. They wouldn't let him help out, though, not even to rake leaves, because that would be taking the work from somebody else. Simon Creedy understood that, too, but he desperately needed something to do. He could feel himself slipping, knew that his speech was slurring, that he walked unsteadily. He needed an interest. He knew that no one would hire him, so he decided to work for nothing. He would be a volunteer.

When he presented himself to the Home Assistance Agency, Simon Creedy smiled that same sweet and fixed smile, and the social worker hadn't the heart to turn him away. Isabel Pallo allotted him the simplest tasks, chores a child could do, and he did them willingly. He was completely trustworthy; he never missed a day, was never late. Finally, he was raised to the status of part-time worker and was even paid. So as it turned out, Simon Creedy did have a lot to smile about—he had found people worse off than himself and was able to help them. At age sixty-one, retarded and retired, Simon Creedy was visiting the indigent aged, helping them clean themselves and their homes, buying their groceries, giving them their medicine, doing the odd, dreary, sometimes dirty jobs that had to be done. It didn't matter if he was slow and clumsy; his charges were slower and clumsier. He had infinite patience. He sat for hours on end with them; he talked to them, though often they hardly knew what he was saying. He was their friend.

Every Saturday night Mr. Creedy treated himself to a bottle of Christian Brothers sherry, medium dry. By careful management, at the rate of one glass just short of full per day, the bottle lasted the entire week. Tonight he was late getting to the liquor store, and tonight of all nights according to the people who were so much smarter than Mr. Creedy, he had no right to be smiling. He had just been to the funeral of one of his very special charges. Sol Jacobson, ninety-one years old, had passed away peacefully in his sleep. Though Jacobson had been a loner, between them Mr. Creedy and Isabel Pallo had rounded up a respectable crowd for the funeral. Sol Jacobson had not gone to his grave unattended.

The bell tinkled as Simon Creedy stepped across the threshold of the Red Coach Liquor Store. "Good evening, Mr. Walsh," he greeted the proprietor.

Jerry Walsh was at the cash register. He appeared startled. "We're closed," he snapped testily.

Easily hurt, Mr. Creedy flinched. "I'm sorry I'm so late. You see, I . . ." He started to explain about the funeral, but he sensed that Walsh was not in the mood. "Couldn't you just let me have my usual? You don't need to wrap it or anything. I'd really appreciate . . ." His voice faded as it so often did when he was upset or uncertain. Mr. Walsh was usually so nice.

"I told you we're closed."

Tears sprang into Mr. Creedy's weak eyes.

"Go on, give the old man his bottle."

Up to then Mr. Creedy hadn't even been aware that there was another customer in the store. How could Mr. Walsh be closed when he still had a customer? Mr. Creedy puzzled over it. And if he was closed, then how come he hadn't locked the door? Mr. Creedy was going to ask about that, but the proprietor had already got the sherry down from a shelf behind the counter and was handing it across. Creedy fumbled for his wallet, but Walsh waved him off.

"Pay me another time."

"It's on the house," the customer said.

Both spoke at the same time.

More bewildered than ever, Simon Creedy looked from one to the other. The customer seemed like a very nice young man, maybe twenty-five or so. He had on a nice, neat suit and a striped tie, and he had a neat, short haircut—well, what passed for a short haircut nowadays. He also wore those big dark glasses that were so popular—Mr. Creedy couldn't understand why people wore dark glasses indoors. But what right did this nice young man have to be making decisions for Mr. Walsh? Suddenly, Simon Creedy was frightened.

"It's . . . all right. I have the m-m-money right here." With shaking hands, Creedy extracted a five-dollar bill and took a step forward to lay it on the counter. As he did so, he saw the gun in the young man's hand. "Oh," he said. He stared at the gun as though mesmerized and his entire face began to twitch uncontrollably.

"Nuts!" the robber muttered. "Sorry, old man. Now that you know what it's about you gotta stay. Get over there, out of the way." He gestured with the gun. "Now you stand over there nice and quiet and you won't get hurt. Come on now, move it."

Mr. Creedy was willing; he was anxious to do as he was told, but now, suddenly, in this moment of crisis, all the years of medication, training, exercise, and self-discipline, all failed him. His legs refused to function. He couldn't take even a single step. And when he tried to explain this helplessness, all he could produce was a series of gutteral, unintelligible sounds.

"I said, move!" the nice young man snarled.

Mr. Creedy literally could not. Exasperated, the robber simply shoved him to one side. Creedy slipped, his arms flapped wildly as he tried to maintain his balance and failed. He went down, hitting his head against the corner edge of the counter. It was a stunning blow.

Sunday P.M.

They gained confidence as they moved along the train from one subway car to the next. There were about half a dozen of them, boys in their early and mid teens, and they started boisterously but innocently shoving and roughhousing among themselves, transistors blaring, while the other passengers eyed them askance and were careful to stay out of their way. As the IRT Number 2 lurched going around the bend toward Fulton Street, it threw Jojo Schaufuss off balance and sent him careening across the aisle, to land in the lap of a middle-aged housewife. They were both startled, but no more than that. Jojo would have got right up again if it weren't for his friends' shouts of glee.

"Hey, Jojo, she's not bad. Give her a kiss," they urged. "Give her a feel, Jojo."

The woman flushed and looked around anxiously to the male passengers who squirmed and averted their eyes. The gang laughed uproariously, punched and pounded one another in delight.

"Go on, man. Show us, show us what you can do, man."

"Hey, you want it dark, Jojo? You like it better in the dark?" One of the boys swung his transistor radio—it was stolen, so he could get another if he ruined it—at an overhead light and shattered it.

A woman whined softly. The others in the car were too frightened to do even that.

"Hey, man, you want it dark?" The others took up the chant. "You want it dark, man?" Another light bulb was shattered.

Jojo was a big boy, tall, with plenty of weight on him, but he was only thirteen. If the housewife was afraid, he was embarrassed. His dark skin glowed like smoldering coal. "Ah . . . she ain't my type."

They howled at that. They swung around the poles in the center of the subway car like maniacs. "Sorry, lady. Better luck next time!" they sang out, ready to pass on.

But Robert Deacon was not ready. He was very much aware of the sag in his right-hand pocket caused by the new "piece" he'd just bought. You could get just about anything up there around 126th Street. At first, Deke had been nervous, not knowing whom to approach. But he got the feel of it fast. You just kind of walked around, and after a while buyer and seller sensed each other—it was like they could see into each other's heads. Weird. Exciting. Deke felt proud. He spoke with the confidence of the gun.

"So which one is your type? Which one do you like, Jojo?"

"Ah, Deke . . ."

"Look 'em over."

It was an order, and Jojo knew it. He made a show of considering. He walked slowly down the center aisle, and as he passed each woman she cringed.

The bright lights of the station platform broke the spell. The train stopped. The doors opened. Nobody got on. They were in the heart of the financial district and it was Sunday night. It would have been a miracle for anybody to be getting on.

One man tried to get off.

"Where do you think you're going?" Deke demanded.

"This is my stop."

"Yeah?" Deke's hand slid to his pocket and he fondled the piece nestled there. "Stick around; you don't want to miss the fun."

The man hesitated. Hissing, the doors started to close.

"Sit down!"

It was a command, and the passenger obeyed it.

He hadn't even needed to show the piece! Deke gloated inwardly, a thin smile stretching his pale lips. "So, how about it, Jojo?" he asked jocularly. "Which one do you like?"

The train gathered speed.

"Ain't none of 'em my type, Deke."

"No? That's too bad. I guess we'll just have to try the next car."

The relief was palpable, but nobody stirred or even dared to breathe too heavily till the gang moved on. The passengers watched anxiously as the youths tugged and yanked at the recalcitrant doors between the cars while the train pounded along the tracks with a clatter and clang of metal on metal.

Seeing how scared they all were gave Deke a real high—and an idea. A real, cool idea.

"I'm sure you won't mind making a contribution to console old Jojo for his disappointment," he announced, his gaze sweeping the seated passengers. "Here." He took off his bright red knitted cap and tossed it to the woman into whose lap the young black boy had inadvertently fallen. "Go ahead, honey; you take up the collection."

While she passed the hat, Deke fingered the gun in his pocket, but he still didn't need to show it. Nobody refused to put something in; most of them were eager.

By the time Deke and his boys reached the fourth car the train had pulled into Wall Street, the last stop in Manhattan, and was hurtling through the tunnel under the East River toward Brooklyn. The prankish parade had turned into a march of terror. Deke strode at the head of his gang exacting tribute from the cowering riders. When the door of car number four was yanked open, the people inside were no more aware of what had happened in the car ahead than the occupants of cars three and two had been. The noise of the advance was more than covered by the roar of the train, and certainly no one had any occasion to look from one car into the next. So when the gang burst through, the passengers of car number four were taken by surprise just as their predecessors had been.

Ramon Lara sat at the far end, eyes closed, half dozing. He'd really put out that afternoon, run his ass off. It was the money that mattered, naturally, but he couldn't help gloating over the victory too. He'd taught those hackers a little respect! He'd reminded them who he was, reminded them that under the gray hair the old man still had plenty of "smarts." They'd been all over him with congratulations. Oh, sure— afterward. Afterward, half the club tried to buy him a drink. Actually, he'd accepted a couple more than he should have, but what the hell, it wasn't every afternoon he could stir up the juices to play like that. And it wasn't every afternoon he could clear five hundred and twenty bucks!

Ramon Lara was a professional tennis player, had been for close to thirty years. In the days when he had been at his peak, the game was the stepchild of professional sports. There were only a handful of playing pros, as opposed to teaching pros, and there weren't many of those. The playing pros barnstormed around the country, giving exhibitions in clubs and hotels, competing in tournaments among themselves in which the top prize money was maybe fifteen hundred dollars. Most of them learned to hustle to keep alive. Now that the game was a big-money proposition, now that kids nobody ever heard of were dragging down a hundred thou a year, Ramon Lara was over the hill.

Sure he was bitter; how could he help it? Even his name didn't mean much anymore—he'd never reached the heights of a Pancho Gonzales or Jack Kramer; none of the big sporting-goods companies were fighting for his endorsement; he wasn't even getting job offers from the clubs— that is, not the kind of offers that would enable him to hire a couple of eager young guys to stand out in the blazing sun for eight to ten hours a day and do his teaching while he supervised. Ramon himself was no teacher; he didn't have the patience. He was a playing pro, always had been, so now the hustling was all that was left. And even there he wasn't in the big time—no Bobby Riggs. What Lara did was hang around the clubs and work himself into the kind of game where he could make a side bet or two—say, five, ten, twenty bucks, whatever the traffic would bear.

Today had been fantastic. A business executive, a shrewd operator except where his tennis prowess was concerned, had challenged an ex-Davis Cup player and a well-known playwright ranked class A to a match against himself and Lara. Lara had partnered the executive to many victories, but not against players of this caliber. The whole club was laughing because the tycoon was a loud mouth who had finally overmatched himself. On paper he and Lara didn't have a chance. Lara played the fool along with his partner and offered to cover all bets. He had plenty of takers.

He'd got good odds, naturally. If they'd lost, he wouldn't have been able to pay off. He would have been barred from that club at least and the word would have spread that he was a welsher. But he hadn't lost. It had been close. A real cliff-hanger. A lot better than most of the matches they put on TV, Ramon Lara thought bitterly. Nevertheless, he would have preferred it if it hadn't gone to a tie-breaker in the third. He shuddered when he thought how close they'd come to losing.

"Wake up, Pops."

He felt a hand on his shoulder. Somebody was shaking him. Lara opened his eyes. "What?"

A black kid, a big, black kid loomed over him; he was holding a red knit cap that bulged with money, watches, assorted jewelry. Beside him, a white youth pointed a gun.

"Come on, Pops, you're holding up the parade. Put it in the hat."

"Put what in the hat?" Lara was awake now and completely sober.

"What's the matter with you, Pops? You blind? You dumb? Put your money in the hat like everybody else," the white boy commanded.

"No."

"What?"

"I said, no."

It was the "Pops" that had got to Lara, triggered his anger, and reminded him that he was dealing with children. Punk kids. "I worked hard for my money and I'm not handing it over. You go out and work like I did."

Deke's gray eyes narrowed; he thrust out what he had of a chin; the hand that held the shiny, new gun shook slightly. "I'm telling you for the last time, Pops, put your money in the hat. And the watch too. It's a nice watch. Take it off and put it in the hat."

The watch was an Omega; Ramon Lara had won it in the New Hampshire State Men's Singles the year before he turned pro. That was a long time ago, when he was young.

"No."

The noise of the train as it sped under the river was an assault on the ears, but as far as the terrified passengers of car number four were concerned, there was only silence. The gang had stopped laughing and clowning and were now closed in behind their leader forming a tight half-circle on Lara. There were just too many of them, he thought, unless somebody came to his aid. He glanced around surreptitiously. Forget it. Nobody was going to risk his skin for a stranger. If he could hold the boys off till they got into a station— Was it his imagination or was the train actually slowing down?

He reached a hand under one knee, feeling for the pair of tennis rackets lying sideways on the floor and against the seat. He still used the old-fashioned wooden presses so that they were extra heavy. The two swung together should deliver an effective clout. "The first one that tries to lay a hand on me is going to get his head cracked open," he warned and brought up the pair of rackets like a club.

Definitely, the train was slowing, Lara thought. He could feel it. Though he didn't dare shift his gaze, he could tell from the darting glances of those passengers within his line of vision that the train was coming into the station. Deliberately, still holding his rackets ready, Ramon Lara stood up. Jojo Schaufuss stepped aside; after a second's hesitation, one by one the others did too, and the circle around the tennis player was broken. The train stopped. The passengers rose en masse and rushed for the opening doors.

"Come back!" Deke yelled. "Nobody leaves! I said, nobody leaves. Come back or I'll shoot."

They only pushed more frantically to get through the doors, shoving against one another, stumbling, some of the women sobbing, some screaming.

Deke raised his new gun, aimed, and fired. The bullet hit the last man trying to get off the subway car. It hit him in the spine and he fell forward, his arms and torso on the platform but his legs still inside the train. The sound of the shot echoed and re-echoed in the underground chamber driving everybody in the station to cover, whether or not he'd been on that fateful ride. When it died away at last, it was a very long time before anyone moved, or so it seemed, though it couldn't have been very long because Deke was still inside the car and the doors were still open. He was the first to act. He bounded over the fallen victim and out to the platform, then through the turnstile. His gang followed. Nobody showed any inclination to stop them. The whole troop passed the ticket booth and was making its way up the stairs to the street before one of the passengers thought to hurl himself against the train door to prevent it from closing on the injured man.

"Stop the train!" he yelled. "Somebody help me get him clear."

Now there were willing hands. More than enough. They seized him by the shoulders, others by the legs, and lifted him across the threshold to the safety of the platform.

Ramon Lara moaned. "My legs . . . my legs . . ." He clenched his teeth biting back the pain, but the panic inside would not be quelled.

Dios mio! Santa Maria Virgen! he exhorted silently. Preserve for me the use of my legs!

Three crimes. Three victims. An ordinary weekend's violence.

Chapter II

"The victim's got a right to know what he's got going for him! It may not be much, but he ought to be told. He's entitled."

Smiling, blue eyes bright and clear almost to transparency, eager as a politician for votes, Mici Anhalt never missed a chance to plead the cause of the victim—to an assistant DA, a police officer, a civilian, anybody who would listen.

Having pinned her quarry, she would make her case. When a crime is committed, the police are concerned in apprehending the perpetrator and clearing the case from the books. The courts are out to provide a fair trial for the accused. In theory it's all done on behalf of the victim; in practice the victim is all but forgotten. It's only recently that workers in the field of criminal justice have begun to address themselves to the problems of the victim and to set up certain services to assist him. The services are useless unless the victim is aware of them. Mici Anhalt wanted to make sure he was aware.

The public did not appreciate the extent of the victim's ordeal. It was generally assumed that once he was rescued and the perpetrator caught, it was over. Lately, some of the ignominies suffered by victims of rape after the attack and during the filing of the complaint and the trial period has been publicized. However, most people did not realize that, while not as horrendous or degrading, the distress continues for the victims of other crimes, too, and for the witnesses. Mici wanted the public educated both on the victim's problems and on his rights, and she was not shy about approaching even important personages to accomplish it.

At an ecumenical St. Patrick's Day dinner, for which her supervisor had passed on a pair of tickets he couldn't use himself, Mici Anhalt approached Police Deputy Commissioner Alan Champlain.

"Commissioner, don't you think the victim should know that somebody is willing to go to bat for him? That a staff worker will call his boss and vouch that he's not calling in sick on Monday morning because he's got a hangover, but because he really did get mugged on Sunday night? Or if he's unemployed, that the staff worker will explain to his unemployment office that he can't make his regular reporting date because he has to appear in court? Doesn't he have the right to know that there is financial assistance available if he needs it?"

It was not unpleasant to be propagandized by Mici Anhalt. To begin with, she was an extraordinarily pretty young woman, tall, slim, with naturally wavy red-gold hair, which she wore loose at shoulder length, and those blue eyes quite startling in their clarity—the deeper one looked into them, the clearer and paler they appeared till finally the color was gone completely. More important than her looks was her enthusiasm; she was thirty-two and enthusiastic as a teenager. It suffused everything she did and it was catching. It captivated men and turned some women who might have resented her good looks from adversaries into allies, even friends.

"Wouldn't it make sense for the police officer at the scene to inform the victim of his rights in the same way he informs the criminal?" Mici added, and then delivered the snapper. "Doesn't the victim have rights with the criminal?"

That sobered them all and Commissioner Alan Champlain was no exception. "I'm convinced, Miss Anhalt. Unfortunately, I don't determine procedure. I will drop a word where it may do some good. That's a promise."

Mici also knew when to quit. She and the commissioner shook hands vigorously. "Thanks for listening, sir."

Mici began charming the opposite sex early in life. Her first conquest was her paternal grandfather, and she accomplished it from her cradle. László Anhalt had been an officer in the hussars serving Franz Josef, Emperor of Austria-Hungary. Later he, his wife, and son had become refugees from the war-devastated and revolution-wracked homeland. For him, the baby girl was a symbol that his blood would flourish in the adopted country. The name selected for the infant was Maria Ilona, but in that first glimpse of her, in that moment of pure joy while the women stood around cooing, tears filled László Anhalt's blue eyes, blue as the baby's, and he bent down to whisper, "Ah, Mici, Mici . . ."

According to purists, Mici, pronounced Mitzi, is a Hungarian endearment applicable to any female, something like "honey" or "sweetie"; others insist it is the diminutive for Maria. Either way, it stuck. Before she was walking, Mici's grandmother, Szoka, who had danced for the old emperor at the palace of Schönbrunn, proclaimed the baby perfectly formed and possessed of all the graces requisite for a prima ballerina. Mici did, in fact, train for a professional career. For two years she had danced with the Joffrey Ballet. She was good, but not good enough. What was lacking was not technique but commitment. Her heart wasn't in it. Dancing didn't seem important. During the company's summer residence in Seattle, she drifted into volunteer work in John Kennedy's presidential campaign. When Robert Kennedy became attorney general, she was surprised to be offered a job in Washington. She loved the ballet, and continued to take classes regularly, but it was no longer her vocation.

When Robert Kennedy was killed, Mici Anhalt left Washington. She was twenty-four; she'd lost some illusions, but not her dedication to the cause of criminal justice. She went to New York, and applied for a job at the Vera Institute of Criminal Justice, an acknowledged leader in the field. She got the job and stayed with Vera for eight years, spending four of them working for the revision of the court system with regard to victims and witnesses.

Then the Law Enforcement Assistance Administration gave the Vera Institute a grant of $144 million for a one-year demonstration project to assist victims and witnesses, and the Victim/Witness Assistance Project went into effect. The area selected for the trial period was Brooklyn.

It was Mici's responsibility to send out the disposition letters informing each victim or complainant of what the decision had been in his case. Incredible as it had seemed even to her, many complainants never learned the ultimate results of their cases. The reasons were varied:

the defendant might be charged with a previous crime and answered to that so the current complainant was not called on to appear. Perhaps the defendant plea bargained and the case never came to trial at all. Even if the defendant went to trial and the complainant appeared in court, he still might be unaware of the judge's decision. In contrast to the clearly spoken pronouncements of the judges on television or the stage, the sentence might be rendered in such private tones at the bench that the complainant sitting humbly at the back of the room simply didn't hear it.

And until the Vera Project nobody bothered to tell him.

In spite of that, the operation might seem rudimentary to the average citizen. After all, what is so innovative about constructing a reception area in the Criminal Courts Building where people who are called to appear in a case can wait in reasonable comfort and safety? What's so great about putting in chairs and a coffee machine? Isn't it only rational that there should be an information clerk available to answer questions and direct people to the proper courtroom? Isn't an alert system, which makes it possible for the victim and witness to remain in his own home or office till needed, or in the police officer's case on active duty, instead of hanging around drafty corridors day after day— isn't such a system just plain common sense? Yet these things did not exist till the Victim/Witness Project in Brooklyn initiated them.

In other boroughs of the city, victims and witnesses still wander through dirty, overcrowded halls of dirty, overcrowded courthouses, with no idea where they should go and no one familiar with their cases to inform them. Many lose heart and either fail to report altogether or else fail to return when postponement follows postponement with no end in sight.

Hard as Mici had worked in the planning and implementation and with all her enthusiasm for the project, she became restless. Even her occasional sessions in the highly charged atmosphere of the Notification Center or the ECAB (Early Case Assessment Bureau) were not fulfilling. Dismayed by her own reaction and trying to analyze it, she came to the conclusion that she was looking for a more direct contact with the people involved—a one-on-one situation.

She took her time looking for her next job and finally found what she wanted.

On Monday morning of the week before Christmas and the day after the shooting of Ramón Lara, it was snowing lightly. Mici Anhalt came out of the subway at City Hall and crossed the street. She stopped at the coffee shop on the corner for a couple of their pastries, then she entered the New York State Office Building at 270 Broadway. She was thinking of a white Christmas with the family in Connecticut and New Year's with Danny and his parents in Miami. That was why she was coming in early, to get her work cleared up so she could take the time off with an easy conscience. A glance at the indicator showed that the elevator was up on the tenth floor. As usual, Mici was too impatient to wait.

She sprinted for the stairs and made it to the second-floor landing without even breathing hard. She was delighted at this evidence of added stamina. It was all due to the new partner dance class in which she'd enrolled this season, to all those lifts and *grands jetés*. She'd never felt more fit. Turning the corner of the main corridor, she entered the door marked CRIME VICTIMS COMPENSATION BOARD.

Mici Anhalt was one of ten investigators for the board's New York City office.

Though she'd been working here for six months, the cheeriness of the place always struck her when she came in. The main room was large, with floor-to-ceiling windows that not only let in plenty of natural light but overlooked the open space provided by City Hall park with a view of City Hall mansion and the municipal building beyond. Except for the deep-blue wall-to-wall carpeting, it was furnished in government functional, yet the atmosphere was informal: Mici had sensed it on her first visit, the day of her job interview. Certainly one reason for it was those big windows and the vista they offered—at this moment a Christmas-card scene of fat snowflakes drifting lazily around the ugly old mansion—but the main reason was the friendliness of the people who worked there.

"Mici?"

That was the supervisor, Adam Dowd, calling from his office.

"Yes?"

"Can I see you for a minute?"

Quickly she shrugged out of her shearling-lined coat and hung it on the rack. Without bothering to check the mirror, she brushed the melting snowflakes from her damp hair and one from the tip of her perfectly straight nose, and hurried to the coffee machine, where she drew two cups, fixing the supervisor's the way she knew he liked it—hardly any milk but with three teaspoons of sugar. Purse tucked under one arm, a container of coffee in each hand, there was only one way to carry the paper bag with the pastries: in her mouth. She had to kick the supervisor's door open.

"I figured it had to be you," Dowd began. Then he looked up and smiled. "You look like a Saint Bernard."

Mici walked over to his desk, leaned forward, and opening her mouth let the brown bag fall on his desk blotter.

"Whatever turns you on."

Adam Dowd laughed aloud. His tired eyes sparkled. Then he opened the bag and looked inside. "Say, are these some of those great *krapfen* your grandmother bakes?"

"Sorry, Adam, I didn't get home this weekend. These are just ordinary jelly doughnuts from the coffee shop downstairs."

"You bought two? How come you knew I'd be in so early?"

"Oh, I figured."

Adam Dowd was in his late forties, a family man whose two sons were too grown up to be living at home and whose wife was drinking because she didn't know what to do with herself now that they were gone. He was a man who kept his troubles inside, who was not made bitter by them but rather more understanding when dealing with the troubles of others. Adam Dowd was that rarity—an idealist in a bureaucracy. He was that greater rarity in the criminal justice system—a believer in the inevitability of justice. Dowd maintained that everybody got caught. By that he meant that everybody got punished. Specifically, it was his tenet that street criminals (for those were the ones he and the staff dealt with most frequently) who strike and flee inevitably paid by either getting shot or knifed by one of their own, or OD-ing on drugs. These small fry got so little in their forays that they had to go back for more, repeating the offense over and over so that justice, in one form or another, had to catch up. Pressed, Dowd would admit that perhaps perpetrators of major, well-planned and executed felonies might escape, but for them there was the ultimate retribution. Adam Dowd believed in heaven and hell.

He was a big man, with a beak nose, balding, and developing a paunch. Any description of him was bound to start, "You'll like Adam Dowd . . ."

In Dowd, Mici had found a superior who treated her as an equal. Mici, the supervisor had found a very special kind of investigator, one who could relate to the needs of the victim while keeping in mind the financial situation of the state; one who could help the victim to laugh as well as to cry with him; one who knew when to be tough. Mici Anhalt was compassionate, but was not about to give the store away. The Crime Victims Compensation Board was, after all, a state agency.

"Ever hear of Ramón Lara?" Dowd asked when they were both settled. "Used to be a pretty good tennis player. Runner-up in Forest Hills one year. That was when the top players were all amateurs. I saw that match. Bunch of us from Princeton went. That was a while ago, of course."

"Mm . . ." The investigator bit into her jelly doughnut, licked some grains of sugar from her lips. "About the time of Bill Tilden and Helen Wills."

Dowd glared with mock outrage. "Not that long ago. Make it Jack Kramer and Pancho Gonzales, okay? That Lara was some competitor. Not much to look at on the court—bandy-legged, awkward, bouncing and tumbling after the ball—but he never missed. His opponents learned to take him seriously, and audiences that started out laughing ended up applauding." He paused. "Ramón Lara was shot on Sunday night."

She nodded. "I read about it." All the investigators read the newspapers very carefully: you never knew which of the reported crimes might cross your desk. "Was he badly hurt?"

"Slug lodged in his spine. They got it out, but . . ." He shrugged.

"Is that his claim?" Mici indicated the form on the desk.

"Your friend, Roz, delivered it personally."

Mici's eyebrows went up. Roz Pell and she had worked together during the planning of the Victim/Witness Assistance Project and Roz was presently assigned to the complaint room of the Brooklyn Criminal Courts Building. If she thought that a complainant had suffered an injury that made him eligible for compensation, she would so advise him. If he needed assistance to fill out the form, she would supply it, and then she would mail the form in for him. But for her to hand-deliver . . .

"It seems that a gang of about six or seven youths were running the length of a subway train terrorizing and robbing the passengers," Dowd briefly reviewed the crime. "They took money and valuables from maybe forty people before they shot Lara and left the train at Clark Street. As it happened, a pair of transit police were waiting on the opposite platform and they gave chase. They apprehended two of the youths and the leader, one Robert Deacon. Unfortunately, at that point all the witnesses had disappeared."

Mici groaned.

He met her look. "The only one left was the victim, Ramón Lara, and he was unconscious. They took him to the hospital and he was operated on. He'd barely come out of the anesthetic when he was shown mug shots and made a positive ID. He also signed the complaint."

That explained it. Roz Pell was rabid on the subject of responsibility. She had nothing but contempt for those who evaded it, but would do anything to help people like Ramón Lara.

"Mrs. Pell explained that this is a real hardship situation," Dowd continued. "Lara has no money, no insurance, no steady job."

Mici took it in stride. "How about Medicaid?"

"Probably not eligible. He's got an assortment of odd, undefined jobs —sells space in various tennis publications, represents one of those air-bubble construction companies that put up plastic domes over tennis courts and swimming pools. He's not indigent, but he hasn't any regular income either."

"And the kind of medical treatment he's going to need won't come cheap." Mici held out her hand for the form. "I'll get right on it."

"I hate to stick you. I know you're trying to get out from under so you can go South, but everybody's got such a heavy load. Ordinarily, it wouldn't hurt for the claim to sit for a few days, but your friend was insistent."

The investigator's blue eyes sparkled and one corner of her generous mouth lifted mischievously. "And, anyhow, Roz suggested me for the job."

"It is your kind of case."

"No sweat, Adam; I've just about cleared my desk." That wasn't strictly true, but a couple of hours on Thursday night would make it true. She took the claim from the supervisor and glanced over it. "Seems straightforward. Shouldn't take long to check out."

"Just notice that his wife signed for Lara," Dowd cautioned. "Evidently, Lara was asleep when Mrs. Pell went over there. You'll have to get his signature."

"Sure. No problem."

The shades were drawn in Ramón Lara's hospital room. The first thing Mici noticed when she put her head around the partially open door was the flowers. They were everywhere; their colors glowed in the semidarkness; their scent hung heavy in the enclosed space; they were an indication that the tennis star was not forgotten. Lara himself was propped up in bed in a sitting position but appeared to be dozing. Mici took a moment to study him. He was older than she had anticipated; his coarse, black hair was heavily streaked with gray. One section over the left eye had gone completely white, and his face was scored with lines deep as knife cuts. His color, which by his heritage and his occupation should have been a glowing mahogany, was instead the sad yellow of the invalid. She had expected Ramón Lara to be handsome, and he was not, but there was a somber dignity in the triangle of his face formed by high cheek bones and pointed chin that was characteristic of his Aztec heritage.

The door blocked Mici's view of the rest of the room and she didn't know there was anybody else there until the woman came forward.

"Yes? Can I help you?"

She was a sun-streaked blonde, very attractive, with a round, full face, the kind of face age touches lightly, almost reluctantly. She'd done her part by keeping herself fit. She was tall, at least five-nine or -ten, large boned and athletically hard. In fact, she wore her good health—shining hair and clear skin with the same flair she wore the stylish turquoise pantsuit. Probably, Mici decided, she was in her early forties.

"Mrs. Lara? I'm Mici Anhalt from the Crime Victims Compensation Board. It's about the claim. . . ."

Diane Lara put her finger to her lips and, casting a warning look in the sleeping man's direction, nodded toward the door to indicate they should step outside.

"What claim?" Ramón Lara demanded, startling them both.

"Your claim for nonreimbursable losses that you may suffer as a result of this assault, Mr. Lara," Mici replied. "Under a grant of the Law Enforcement Administration, the State of New York is empowered to pay victims of crime for medical expenses and loss of earning power not otherwise covered." She smiled warmly. "In other words, Mr. Lara, we want to help."

"I didn't file any claim."

She usually got a warmer welcome, at least in the initial interview. Later, because the procedure was slow—it took over four months before a disposition was made—the claimant might become eager, even abusive, but she had never before met someone who wasn't interested in recouping some of his costs.

"The form was filled out on your behalf by Mrs. Pell from the Vera Institute—"

"I don't want charity."

"Assisted by your wife and signed by her," Mici concluded.

Diane Lara didn't deny it, but she didn't affirm or explain either.

"Well, we withdraw the claim. Tear it up, Miss . . ."

"Anhalt."

"Tear it up, Miss Anhalt. Forget about it. We don't want it."

His wife frowned. "Would you excuse us a moment, Miss Anhalt?" Her eyes were on her husband.

"We don't need it, *querida*."

"We need any help we can get," she corrected, holding on to her composure. "I haven't wanted to bother you, but the bills . . . you have no idea, Ramón. I don't know how we're going to manage."

"We'll find a way.'

"Will we?

"We always have."

Tears welled up in Diane Lara's eyes, but Mici thought them tears of frustration. Her mouth was stretched into a thin, hard line, and the frown on Diane Lara's brow was well grooved.

"We've always found a way," her husband repeated. "Haven't we, *querida*?" He was forced to prompt. "Haven't we?"

"It's different this time." Deliberately, Diane Lara looked down below his waist.

And despite herself, so did Mici. She couldn't help but contrast the well-muscled development of his upper body with the inert shape of his legs under the blanket. In her imagination they seemed already atrophying. She wondered whether the tennis star knew how serious his injury was. Obviously, his wife did. Mici waited for her to offer him some encouragement. What she did, again with pointed deliberation, was to shift her gaze.

If he hadn't known before, he did now, the investigator thought, and rushed to fill the ugly moment. "I never had the pleasure of seeing you play, Mr. Lara, but my boss saw you at Forest Hills. He says you were terrific. I'm looking forward to seeing for myself—very soon."

He met the challenge firmly. "An athlete's life is short; mine has already lasted longer than most. I have other resources. I have friends." He gestured around the room at their tributes.

"Flowers are cheap," Diane Lara almost sneered.

He cast her a withering look, and she said no more.

Mici got up. "It's your decision, Mr. Lara."

"No, no, don't go, Miss Anhalt." Mrs. Lara had flushed a deep, unhealthy scarlet; her eyes bulged; she was at that moment far from attractive. "Ramón, we're entitled to the money. They're not going to give us anything we don't have coming."

"That's correct, Mr. Lara," Mici backed her up. "We are not a charity or a welfare organization. Accepting compensation does not brand you as a pauper. Naturally, there are certain conditions for eligibility and limits to the amount of cash we can disburse. I think you'll agree that both are reasonable."

"Such as?" he was wary.

"We don't duplicate coverage. In other words, we don't reimburse you for costs covered by your own insurance, but if your bills exceed your own insurance or your company's insurance, then we pick up the tab and we continue after your insurance runs out. We put no time limit on the length of your treatment. Salary loss is handled in the same manner: we don't pay for the first two weeks you're out and after that we make up the difference between your regular income and any benefits you may get from your employer, workmen's compensation, and the like. We try to make you whole again, Mr. Lara. You could say that's our motto."

"I don't want people poking around in my private affairs."

Mici spread out her hands, palms up, in a gesture of helplessness and smiled a one-cornered smile. "We're a government agency, Mr. Lara, and we are spending the taxpayers' money and we have to account for it, so we're bound to get a little nosy, but we try to cause the claimant a minimum of embarrassment. I'm not a talker, Mr. Lara. If I should inadvertently stumble on something really juicy—I promise to keep it to myself."

Lara's response to the attempted joke was to turn to his wife. "You want me to do this, *querida*?"

"Yes, Ramón, I do." Her face was soft, her eyes melting as she went over to the bed, took his hand in hers, and raised it first to her lips and then to her cheek, where she held it.

"Very well then. What must I do, Miss Anhalt?"

"Just sign these papers." Mici rested her briefcase alongside him on the bed, laid the forms on top, and handed him a pen.

Ramón gave his wife a long, appraising look, then gently withdrew his hand and took the pen. Quickly he scrawled a signature, almost illegible but legal. As soon as he had done it, he fell back against the pillows, closed his eyes, and let the pen roll from his fingers.

Diane Lara leaned over and kissed him. Then she handed the papers and the pen to the investigator.

Chapter III

Ed Stiebeck didn't mind the graveyard shift. It was quiet, not much action—the main reason why detectives on the twelve-to-eight duty had been reduced to a skeleton crew. That also meant that nobody got stuck with the tour too often. Not that it mattered to Ed Stiebeck; his routine was flexible; he could come and go as he pleased, sleep and eat when he wanted, didn't have to answer to anybody. There were no strings on Ed Stiebeck. He had been married once, a long time ago, and it was not an experience he cared to repeat. Four and a half months it had lasted before they broke up, with mutual relief. Not that he blamed Jill, but he didn't consider himself at fault either, thinking back, which he did as seldom as possible, he had few memories to cherish and plenty to forget. In fact, as the passing years eased the throbbing pain of the experience, he wondered how he had ever got sucked into the marriage? What had he seen in Jill? He couldn't remember loving her. He became wary of women. His emotional life was limited to one-night stands and these were decreasing in frequency.

The bitterness spread to his job. In the early days Ed Stiebeck had been as dedicated and idealistic as anybody. He hadn't known any better. Those memories of his naïveté were not as hard to dwell on and brought a bittersweet smile to ease the dour set of the detective's mouth. Reality had come up from the pavement and smacked Ed too hard and too often. He'd had to make the accommodation between what should be and what actually was. He'd had to accept the system. You couldn't buck it; only fools tried. Ed Stiebeck was no fool. He considered himself a good cop; he did his best, knowing that he wasn't going to get any thanks for losing sleep or missing meals, and that flouting authority got you a kick in the pants. He no longer agonized over revolving-door justice; that was a problem for the courts. He took the long, wasted hours in courthouse corridors as a matter of course: if that was the way the city wanted to utilize the time of a detective first grade, it was their money and his overtime.

Detective Stiebeck considered that he was a lot smarter now than when he joined the force eighteen years ago. He didn't know that the disillusion those years had brought was etched into his face. His friends could have told him, though they didn't know it was graven into their faces too. Neither Ed Stiebeck nor the men he worked with, played squash with a couple of times a week, shared beers with, ever asked themselves if they were happy.

Ed Stiebeck made good time getting to the scene; at that hour the streets were just about deserted, another advantage of working the graveyard shift. Of course, everybody else made good time too. Guys from the DA's, forensic, the ME's people, they were all there ahead of him. Can't win 'em all! Stiebeck thought and shrugged it off. Grimacing because the rain had become a downpour and he'd just had his car washed, he pulled up at the end of the line of official vehicles. As he did so, an ambulance pulled out.

"What the hell?" he muttered to himself. "Boucha!" He'd spotted the patrol officer from his own precinct. "What's going on?"

"That's the victim's wife, sir," Boucha replied. "She fainted when she learned her husband was dead and the intern couldn't revive her. She's also pregnant, so they're taking her to emergency."

Stiebeck pursed his lips. He couldn't have talked to her anyway. He shrugged that off too. There were plenty of other things to claim his attention. "So what's the scoop, Boucha?"

The officer consulted his notebook. "The victim's name is Eugene Tully. He lives at 973 Park."

The detective's eyebrows shot up. "That's the Regency Towers. Pretty fancy place. His wife mention what they were doing over here?"

"No, sir. Like I said, she fainted before we could interrogate her. We got a driver's license off the body, so I figure maybe he was over here to park his car." With a nod Boucha indicated the lot. "It's not far from where he lives."

"Far enough. Besides, the Regency Towers has its own garage." Stiebeck let his gaze wander over the area back of the chain-link fence.

"Maybe there's no space available?" Boucha suggested.

"Hm. We'll see. How about money?"

"He had one hundred and nine dollars in his wallet."

So robbery was out, Stiebeck thought. "What else?" he prodded. "How about the wife? You sure the faint wasn't an act?"

"Not according to the intern," Boucha reiterated. "We picked her up near the corner of Third. She was wandering around in a daze. We put her in the car and drove her over here. As soon as we pulled up, she jumped out of the car and ran to the body. She said—" he consulted his notebook once more "—'Oh, my God, what've they done to him? He wasn't like this when I left him. He was lying on his stomach, facedown. I covered him with my raincoat.'"

Stiebeck pushed his lips out as he considered. "What time did you pick her up?"

"One-fifty-five."

Stiebeck nodded sagely and pointed inside the parking-lot enclosure to the caretaker's hut and the sign that was illuminated by a single naked bulb. "Closes at midnight. What would Tully be doing here nearly two hours after the place closed? Unless you think he was shot at midnight? Which makes quite a while for him to be lying around without somebody stumbling over his body and reporting it—aside from his wife, naturally."

"I didn't notice the sign," Boucha admitted.

"Never draw a conclusion until you have all the facts, Boucha." The detective gave the patrolman a patronizing wink. Six months on the force and they all thought they were detectives, he decided as he turned his attention to the body.

Assistant Medical Examiner Ray Pollis was still conducting his examination. While he waited, Stiebeck made his own observations. The victim was indeed lying faceup, if you could call what was left of it a face. A tan raincoat that might be either a man's or a woman's lay partially under him, lining side showing, that appeared to confirm the wife's assertion that his position had changed, but whether he'd turned over himself or been turned over was something else.

"So what's the scoop, doc?"

Ray Pollis looked up at the detective and nodded noncommittally. As a man who'd made his own compromises, he could hardly criticize Stiebeck for having done the same. He just didn't particularly enjoy facing his own image. "Shot in the back, beaten around the face and head, probably with a pistol, and stomped in the rib area. Can't say which was the direct cause of death till the autopsy."

"That still doesn't tell what he died from, the bullet or the beating."

Touchy, damn touchy, Stiebeck thought and turned his back on the ME and did a walk around the body. Swollen, bruised and bloody, almost unrecognizable, the face could tell him little. Hardened as he was, one look was enough even for Ed. He concentrated on other things. The blond hair, bright and shining except where blood had run into it, was cut in a bowl shape, without part, and hung down to the brows. The eyes were fixed by death in permanent amazement as though Eugene Tully couldn't believe what was happening. Under the circumstances, age was hard to gauge. Still, from his build—tall, thin, lanky as a schoolboy, and from the firmness of his chin, and the clear smooth flesh of his hand (Stiebeck was very big on reading age from hands), Eugene Tully figured to have been between twenty-five and thirty. He was wearing a midnight-blue velvet evening jacket, exquisitely tailored, evening pants of the best fabric, and those black patent-leather evening pumps one hardly ever saw anymore. Stiebeck himself dressed casually, but he paid plenty for his clothes—except for his car, what else did he have to spend his money on? Ed knew good threads when he saw them.

He examined the hands more closely. Not merely youthful, they were almost lasciviously well cared for. Tully could have been a model, dancer, fashion designer, faggot. Or a combination. Of course, he was married, but nowadays that was no guarantee a guy was straight. Stiebeck's lips curled with distaste. On a personal level, he had nothing but contempt for those who straddled the sexual fence. As far as it concerned the investigation, once a man was revealed as gay his associates were usually easy to trace and it was a good bet his killer would be among them.

Ray Pollis snapped his medical bag shut and got his feet.

"How about time of death, Doc?"

Pollis hesitated. "Within the last couple of hours."

I could have figured that myself, Stiebeck thought. It had to be after the lot closed at midnight or the attendant would have been a witness and before Boucha and Quinlan came on the scene at one-fifty-five. Pollis was always real cautious about committing himself. Though the official photos had already been taken, Ed now made his own sketch of the body, its position and its relation to the parking lot and the street. It was lying between the entrance to the lot and First Avenue, head lying west toward Second. Finished with that, he next considered the surrounding buildings, it seemed incredible that all the activity, including ambulances and police sirens, hadn't awakened anybody. On the other hand, people in New York were inured to noise; they did not rush to their windows unless a charge of dynamite went off directly underneath. Didn't want to be disturbed. They'd be disturbed in the morning, Ed thought, every one of them. The lieut would want the whole area canvassed. Was this one worth getting the lieut out of bed for, Ed wondered. He decided it wasn't.

Lost in thought, he wasn't aware of Ray Pollis at his elbow.

"I noticed an all-night luncheonette on Third. Personally, I could use some coffee. How about you?"

"Sorry, Doc, have to get with the paperwork. You know how it is."

Pollis had never before made such an overture to the detective and he didn't really know why he had done it this time. Maybe because it was such a lousy night, maybe because it was too late to go back home and try to get some more sleep, maybe because at the moment he needed the companionship of somebody who was in the same lousy line of work. Maybe he wanted to make up for his earlier testiness.

"Yeah, sure."

Stiebeck had reacted automatically and now he was sorry. "Doc," he called. But Pollis was already in his car.

Stiebeck shrugged. Some other time, they could get together some other time. He was only vaguely aware of having snapped another frail link to life outside his work. Some other time. He put it out of his mind and turned to watch as the body was strapped to the stretcher and hoisted into the morgue wagon.

He concentrated on the MO. Shot, beaten, stomped. Overkill? No, two different styles suggested two different perpetrators. Two different people had tried to kill Eugene Tully. Of course, only one had succeeded.

MAN GUNNED DOWN OUTSIDE PARKING LOT
Dies While wife Screams For help.

Ugly headlines. Lieutenant Nelson Dicker deplored them. Not that they were pejorative as far as the police was concerned. On the contrary, Nelson Dicker saw in the story a chance to make the department look good. But they had to move! They had to break the case fast, while the story was still fresh in the public's mind. Precious hours had already been lost.

Ed Stiebeck squirmed while the lieut made it very clear that he did not appreciate the detective's consideration in not disturbing his beauty sleep. He should have been called. Dicker also questioned Stiebeck's priorities. What the hell was he doing at the parking lot at seven A.M. instead of the hospital? the wife was the key to the whole thing, for God's sake!

Finally allowed to speak, Stiebeck explained that he'd called the hospital and been told that Mrs. Tully would not come out of the anesthetic till late morning. That was why he'd gone over to interrogate the parking-lot attendant.

It eased but did not erase the scowl on Dicker's brow.

Stiebeck further explained that the parking lot seemed an unlikely scene for the murder and assault, or vice versa. It bothered him.

So what had he found out?

Ah, not much, Stiebeck was forced to admit. Tully did have a car and he did park it on Eighty-second Street. The attendant was new and all he could say was that Tully rented space on a monthly basis. The car, a snappy white Jaguar, was in the lot at the time of the interview. The attendant did not remember seeing it come in the day before, but he went off duty at four P.M. Maybe the car was already there; maybe it wasn't. There was no time ticket used for regular customers, just a decal on the side vent.

"That's it?" Dicker demanded.

No sir, he'd examined the interior, Stiebeck continued. He'd found a maroon leather train case fitted with combs, brushes, electric curling iron, and a hand dryer. The business cards tucked into the pocket of the lid cover told it all. Stiebeck handed them on to the lieut.

EUGENE TULLY
SALON CHERI
BY APPOINTMENT

A hairdresser! Dicker snorted. A whole morning wasted to find that out? Stiebeck would have been better off to have been sitting in the hospital corridor waiting for Mrs. Tully to wake up, like the reporter who had written that story. The lieut sighed aggrievedly. One thing they could be grateful for was that the reporter, though persistent, had not been smart; he had not asked the one really pertinent question. He shared a moment of fleeting satisfaction with Ed, then gave him a good, hard look to make sure he knew what that question was.

"Where was Mrs. Tully when her husband was shot? Was she with him? If not, what was she doing out in the street in the pouring rain at one fifty-five A.M.?" Stiebeck recited.

"You got it." Dicker nodded. "Now be sure to get the answer before anybody else does."

Though he had developed emotional detachment, Ed Stiebeck was not an insensitive man. He simply did not permit himself any emotional involvement with victim, suspect, or anybody connected in any way with any case. He regarded those involved like pieces on a chessboard to be manipulated this way and that till the winning combination was found. Yet he could not suppress pity when he learned at the hospital that due to the shock of discovering her husband and the particular way in which she hit the pavement when she fell, Mrs. Eugene Tully had lost her baby.

He was shocked when he saw her. She was young, eighteen; he knew that from the hospital record, but she looked old and wizened, anything but pretty. Her heart-shaped face was pale and pinched, her hair a lackluster black tangle against the white pillow. Her eyes, large and heavily fringed by long lashes, were dulled by the effects of the anesthetic.

"I'm sorry to disturb you, Mrs. Tully." Stiebeck had introduced himself and explained his errand with a gentleness that was unusual for him. "I'm very sorry about your loss . . . losses. . . ."

A tear rolled down the young widow's cheek, but she disdained to wipe it away. "I want you to find Gene's killers."

That was two surprises at once, and Ed wasn't sure which hit him the hardest: her use of the plural or her cold vindictiveness. "Did you say 'killers,' Mrs. Tully?"

"I did. I saw them a week ago. I don't know their names, but I'd recognize them if I saw them again."

Fantastic. "A week ago?"

"Exactly. One week ago Friday night."

Despite himself a chill passed over the detective at the combination of southern speech along with the ruthless determination.

"We were coming home from the picture show, Gene and me, and we spotted this bunch of girls ganged up on another girl, much younger— say, maybe ten or eleven. They were trying to take her bike from her and she was holding onto it and crying. They were hitting her and kicking and yelling. Gene got real upset. I wanted him to stay out of it. I begged him not to interfere, but he wouldn't listen. Said they was only kids. I couldn't stop him."

Her eyes filled, but she would not let the tears fall. "He crossed the street and broke it up. He handed the bike back to the little kid and sent the others on their way. But they were mad. Oh, boy. They used all kinds of bad language—I mean, bad. Threatened him. Gene only laughed."

At that, her voice broke. She took a moment to pull herself together and then resumed with the same bitter control as before. "We walked the bike over to the lot where we kept the car. Gene had trouble with it; there was something wrong with the front wheel. Anyhow, he got it over there and put it into the trunk. He drove me home first, then he took the child home."

Stiebeck waited. "That's it?"

"Yes."

"You really believe that these girls—How many were there?"

"Four."

"How old? Take a guess. You say you could recognize them if you saw them again, so you must have some idea of their ages."

"Fourteen or fifteen."

"You think they . . ." He hesitated because he didn't want to upset her by being explicit. "You think these girls killed your husband over a bicycle?"

"I know it."

Stiebeck stifled a sigh. It was no news that there were girl gangs all over the city. No news that the girls were as vicious and cruel as their male counterparts, often more so. Assuming the provocation to have been sufficient, why wait a week? To organize the attack? For the right opportunity to get Tully alone in a deserted place?

"Can you describe the suspects?"

"I'll know when I see them," she repeated stubbornly.

"How about the child your husband rescued and then took home?"

Faith Tully frowned. "A little thing, brown hair in pigtails, brown eyes. She had on one of those down-filled jackets, you know . . . they make everybody look fat. She had a thin little face."

"Your husband drove her home, so he knew where she lived. Didn't he tell you when he got back?"

"No."

"Didn't you ask?" Stiebeck could not hide his disbelief.

"He wouldn't tell me."

The detective just shook his head. "I'm sorry, Ma'am. I don't want to upset you, but I really don't understand that."

"He wouldn't tell me because I wanted to contact the police. It seems the bike didn't belong to the child, after all. It was stolen."

"Stolen? From whom? The girls that were trying to get it back?"

"I don't know. I don't know. Gene wouldn't tell me. He wouldn't tell me the child's name or address because he knew I'd pass it on to the police. He said it was over and done with and forget it."

Stiebeck tried it another way. "How long after your husband dropped you off at home was it before he got back?"

"Maybe half an hour."

And what did that tell him? There was no way of gauging the distance Tully had driven unless you knew the speed at which he'd driven and the length of time spent at the child's home. Forget it. His frustration mounted.

"About last night, Mrs. Tully, were you and your husband out together?"

"No. My husband was working. He's . . ." She caught herself. "He was a hairstylist. One of his clients was giving a very large reception and he had gone to her home to do her hair."

So that was why he had the kit in his car. It suggested that he'd been using the car that night, at least till he'd finished that particular appointment. "Did he make such house calls frequently?"

"A couple of times a week. He had a lot of clients."

He'd have to, in order to be able to afford a Jaguar and live at the

Regency Towers, Stiebeck thought. "How late would he normally get home from these appointments?"

"Depended. Like, if he was doing Madame Florescu's hair—"

"The opera singer?" Even Stiebeck had heard of her.

Faith nodded. "When she was in New York, Madame Florescu wouldn't let nobody but Gene touch her hair. He'd go over to the opera house before the show and fix it for her. Then he'd stay to fix it after the show for whatever party she was going to. A lot of times he was invited to the party too. Everybody loved Gene."

"Did you go with him?"

"Sometimes . . . before I got too big and clumsy." She'd answered matter-of-factly, then, remembering, looked down at her now flat belly.

Stiebeck would have offered comfort if he'd known how, but it wasn't within his investigative repertoire, or even within his emotional capabilities. He did the only thing he knew: got back to business. "Who was Mr. Tully's client last night?"

"Helene Kalb."

Senator Seymour Kalb's wife, one of the Beautiful People. Tully sure did have important clients, and a plain, little nothing wife. "Did he stay on for that party?"

The plain little wife nodded, evidently without rancor. "He didn't want to leave me alone, but I insisted. It was a chance to make new contacts." She paused, then added almost involuntarily, "He was supposed to come home for dinner."

Ah, now they were getting to it, Stiebeck thought, alert to every nuance.

"When it got to be nine o'clock and he hadn't come home, I called the Kalb residence and spoke to him. Seems the senator had been delayed getting in from Washington, so it would be a while longer."

Ed Stiebeck scowled. It was natural enough not to want to leave before the senator showed, he thought. Or was it that Tully was having too good a time?

"He said I shouldn't wait dinner; I should eat and go to bed. He knew I had to get my rest."

Looked more like Tully was having too good a time to go home, the detective decided.

"So I did go to bed, but I couldn't sleep. I never could sleep till Gene got home. Around eleven, or a little after, I called again and Gene said he was just leaving."

"I see."

"So I got up and fixed some coffee for us and waited. I waited till one o'clock and then I called the police."

"You what?"

"It doesn't take two hours to get from Sutton Place to here!" For the first time she showed her agitation. "I thought the police would help.

The operator said I should wait a while longer; then, if Gene still hadn't come home, I should call and they'd check the hospitals."

Routine procedure.

"The operator said probably Gene had stopped to have a couple of drinks." Her voice broke. "Gene doesn't . . . didn't . . . drink."

No need to ask, she was about to tell him exactly what both he and the lieut wanted to hear.

"I hung up, I threw on some clothes, and rushed out. I was going to cover the whole area between here and the Kalbs' residence, but I didn't need to. I found him right off, first place I looked: the parking lot. He was alive. He'd been shot and he was bleeding and unconscious, but he was alive! I know he was. I screamed for help, but nobody came. Nobody opened a window. Nobody looked out. Nobody . . . nobody . . . nobody . . ." She stared past the detective, remembering, seeing not him but the dark, closed windows, and her eyes were filled with hate.

He should have asked her right then whether there was any indication that Tully had been beaten. He also should have got an estimate of the time that elapsed between her leaving the body and being picked up by Boucha and Quinlin in the patrol car. He couldn't bring himself to do it, not now. He reached over and patted her hand awkwardly, then abruptly got up and walked out. As he was closing the door behind him, he heard low sobbing.

Good, he thought, it would do her good to cry. Before he could pull the door shut he was galvanized by one shrill shriek of pure madness.

"Nobody . . ." was an indictment.

CHAPTER IV

Christmas wasn't much for Ed Stiebeck; he had to work. But then Christmas was never a particularly joyous occasion for the detective because it was one of the few times during the year when he couldn't justify his aloneness even to himself. This was not the first Christmas he'd spent on duty; working made it easier and he was honest enough to admit that. However, this particular holiday was the exception: he wished himself anywhere but at his desk, even at home in front of the TV with his holiday turkey in a half-warmed TV tray on his knees. At least at home he wouldn't have been harassed by her constant telephone calls. It was getting so he cringed each time the phone on his desk rang. He'd ended by telling the operator not to put her calls through. And that, he now saw, had been a major error because here she was in person coming through the squad-room door.

She couldn't have barged in on him if he'd been at home. Or could she?

He groaned inwardly, but got up politely, offered her the chair beside his desk, and waited until she was settled before sitting again himself.

"What can I do for you, Mrs. Tully?"

"You can answer your phone when I call."

She wasn't really homely, Stiebeck thought, but she sure had a talent for looking her worst. Black was a terrible color for her, made her skin look sallow, but of course she had no choice but to wear it since she wanted to advertise her mourning. She could have picked something with some shape to it, though, and a little style instead of that loose, wrinkled cotton, ethnic job she had on. The mink jacket was expensive, a beauty, but on her it looked like it came from a thrift shop. The less said about the dusty suede boots the better. Her husband had been a talented and much-sought-after hairstylist who associated with glamorous, elegant women, but apparently none of it had rubbed off on Faith Tully. By now Stiebeck knew her history. Faith Goss was born at the outer edge of Appalachia; her family was still there, dirt farmers, probably moonshining on the side. Before Tully married her she had never been out of her hometown. Stiebeck was also well aware that blood feuds still raged in those mountains and would be part of Faith's heritage. According to her lights, she was probably behaving with considerable restraint.

"Mrs. Tully, I've told you over and over that I'll contact you as soon as there's anything new. Anything at all."

"It's been a week."

"I'm sorry. We're doing the best we can. We don't have much to go on."

She gasped. "I've told you who did it. Those girls."

"We have to find them!"

"You just have to find one. The child they were picking on. She'll tell you who the others are."

"We're working on it."

"No, you're not. You're just sitting here."

He clenched his teeth. Sighed. "Mrs. Tully, yours is not the only case I'm working on. Everybody wants results. There are only so many hours in the day."

"I knew it! I knew it. You can't be bothered. We're not important enough, Gene and me."

"That's not true."

"Sure it is. Sure. It's the God's truth and you know it!" Her voice rose in accusation. "Why aren't you out this minute ringing doorbells, asking questions?"

"Fifteen detectives canvassed the neighborhood around the parking lot the day after your husband died, Mrs. Tully."

For a moment she was mollified, but it didn't last. "How many are out looking for those girls?" she demanded. "Fifteen? Ten? One?"

Stiebeck squirmed. He looked around uncomfortably. There were only about half-a-dozen men in the squad room and so far none was paying particular attention. They would all be though if he let her go on. "Where should we look, Mrs. Tully?"

"Where? Well . . ."

"We don't know where to look, Mrs. Tully. Please, try to understand. You gave us a very vague story." He didn't elaborate, or tell her just what the lieut thought of her story. "We've checked with the juvenile authorities. They don't know of any girl gang in this neighborhood."

"They could have come from another neighborhood."

"Right. Which one? It's a big city."

"So you're not even trying."

"I didn't say that. We're doing our best." Stiebeck was, in fact, embarrassed, but not by her accusation. He couldn't explain to her the actual status of the case. No way. All he could do was continue to make excuses that obviously she wasn't buying.

"Why don't you go home, Mrs. Tully? Go back to Keyser, to your folks. Try to forget all this."

"Forget? You'd like that, wouldn't you? That'd suit you just fine, wouldn't it? Well, I'll tell you something, Detective Stiebeck, I'm never going to forget. Never. Never."

Now he'd riled her for sure. "You've had a terrible shock and you're probably still not physically—" He shouldn't have wandered into this area but now that he had. "You need rest and care. Let your folks look after you. It's the best thing, believe me."

But she wouldn't be soothed. She got to her feet. "I'm never going to forget that my husband was shot and lay dying in the street and nobody helped. I'm never going to forget that he was beaten and stomped while I went looking for help."

She made the announcement without hysteria, in a voice that was flat and hard and audible to every man in the room.

"The pain will pass," Stiebeck murmured, very much aware that now they were watching and listening.

"You bet, when those girls are caught. And I'm never going to rest till they are caught. I don't want sympathy, Detective Stiebeck. I don't want excuses. I want results."

Stiebeck felt himself grow hot. "Will you please sit down?" he hissed.

"What for? You either can't or won't do anything for me. So I'll find someone who can."

At this point he should have been relieved just to get her out of there, but in spite of all good sense he made one last try.

"Leave it alone, Faith. Go home."

Lázló Anhalt fled Hungary when the revolution broke out, immediately after the end of World War I. His first action on arrival was to find a place to put down his roots; he took what he'd managed to salvage from the family fortune and bought the old, Federal-style house in Darien, Connecticut. When his son, Paul, Mici's father, married, he brought his American wife, Margaret, to live there. There Mici was born, and there, three generations lived under one roof in deep affection. Mici loved the old place with its white shingles and green shutters, its polished oak floors, gracious halls, and odd, secret nooks. Though she did not really expect to live there when she in turn married, she was sorry not to continue the custom. Her children would be deprived of the sense of security and heritage she'd had.

She went home for Christmas, eagerly as always. Christmas was on Saturday, and on Sunday she'd intended to fly down to Miami to join Danny and his parents. But she hadn't been able to conclude the investigation on the Lara claim, so she was going to have to postpone the trip. The anticipation of having to call and tell Danny hung over her all of Christmas Eve. She knew he wouldn't take it well, and he didn't.

"Ah, come on, Danny, it's only a couple of extra days." At this point she was playing it light. "I'll be down Tuesday night at the latest. Probably Monday. Listen, I'll take my suitcase to work with me on Monday, that way as soon as I get through I can head straight out to the airport and get on the very next plane. Okay?"

Danny continued to talk. "I figured we'd cruise over to Freeport. It wrecks the whole schedule."

"Who needs a schedule? Why don't we just float with the tide?" He didn't answer. She kept trying. "We'll sail a little, swim a little, sun a lot. . . ."

He remained silent.

"I'm disappointed too, you know."

He picked up on that, fast. "Then why do it? You've told me a hundred times that it takes over four months to process a claim. So what difference is one day more or less going to make?"

"One week," she corrected. "If I don't see this Mr. Hoguet on Monday, then I won't see him till I get back from Miami the following Monday, right? When somebody's waiting for money to buy groceries and pay medical bills, one week makes a hell of a difference."

"I don't see why you couldn't have talked to this Hoguet on Friday."

"Because he was out of town. I explained that," Mici replied patiently. "So I'll be down on Monday night. Tuesday at the latest. Okay, Danny?"

Long pause. "Suit yourself." He hung up.

Of course, he called back almost immediately. Of course, he apologized, told her to call him from Kennedy when she was leaving, that he'd be waiting for her call and would meet her on arrival.

Mici felt as bad afterward as she had before.

On Sunday night, instead of stepping out of a plane and into a balmy southern night, she got out of the train at Grand Central Station, trudged up the ramp to Vanderbilt Avenue lugging her suitcase, and emerged into driving rain and sleet. As usual in any kind of bad weather, cabs were just about unavailable. After nearly ten minutes of dashing back and forth from her shelter out to the curb, Mici thought she had one. So did a well-dressed, middle-aged man on the corner. They raced each other for it, and he won. Mici was left standing ankle-deep in the icy water of the gutter.

Cabs weren't any easier to get the following morning. Mici had re-packed her suitcase with summer clothes and now had to haul it down to the office via subway. By the time she arrived, her right arm felt stretched by several inches. Once she set the suitcase down beside her desk, she just couldn't pick it up again. She'd have to leave it, even if it meant coming back after the interview to get it.

Sports Enclosure, Inc., had a prestigious address, 30 Rockefeller Plaza, but the office itself, though elegantly appointed, was small; as far as Mici could tell, the reception room and the room opening off it comprised the entire suite, and the girl at the front desk the entire staff. It could be just the New York branch, but from the manner in which Hoguet received her, Mici thought it was more likely an expensive front for a shoestring operation.

"So sorry I wasn't here on Friday, Miss Anhelt."

Lawrence Hoguet pumped her hand and genially led her forward to place her in the client's chair. He was a short, plump man, who, despite the extra pounds, exuded an aura of good health and energy. At the moment he was flaunting an obviously recently acquired tan. "I sneaked away a little early for the holidays," he admitted with a touch of boastfulness. "Of course, it wasn't all pleasure," he added. "We put in a bid for one of our installations in Bermuda. I went down to give it a little push. They get a lot of rain down there and most of their existing courts don't have the kind of drainage we insist on when we build. By the way, did you know that we build courts as well as put up the air bubbles over them?"

"No, I didn't."

"Oh, yes, yes, indeed." He stepped around her chair to his desk and sat down. "We also do your lighting, outdoor as well as indoor. We can provide all your accessories down to ball machines, nets, posts, you name it. We're equipped to do your complete installation. By the way, would you care for coffee, Miss Anhalt? My secretary can—"

"No, thanks, Mr. Hoguet."

"We don't do pools. But if you should want a pool, we are connected with a very good, very reliable—"

"I'm not here to buy anything, Mr. Hoguet."

"Oh? I understood that you're a friend of Ramón Lara's."

"Not exactly."

His charm ebbed. "Just what is it you want, Miss Anhalt?"

"Did you know that Ramón Lara had been shot and severely injured?"

"My God! No, I had no idea. I hadn't heard. When did this happen?"

"A week ago Sunday."

"Oh? I was down in Bermuda, as I told you. I'm so sorry. I really am very . . ." For a moment his mouth hung open. "How serious is it?"

"The bullet lodged in his spine."

He turned pale. "That's terrible, terrible. What about his legs? Can he . . . will he . . . walk?"

"We don't know yet."

He sighed heavily. "Listen, Miss Anhalt, I'm a little short right now." He reached for his wallet and thumbed through it fingering the bills. "Here's twenty. If you need more, just give me a call."

"I'm not soliciting funds, Mr. Hoguet."

He looked both relieved and wary. "What then, Miss Anhalt? What's your business?"

She handed him a card. "Mr. Lara has filed a claim. According to the information he's given us, he's a vice-president of this firm."

"Yes, that's right. Ramón is Vice-president for Public Relations. Un . . . what's this Crime Victims Compensation Board?" He was puzzling over Mici's card. "I never heard of it."

"It's part of a program to assist victims of crime. Fourteen states have it and New York is one of them. In fact, New York and California are pioneering the concept."

"Marvelous."

"About Mr. Lara . . . we understand he doesn't draw a regular salary, but we would like to know his average yearly income as a basis for computing his benefits."

The president of Sports Enclosures, Inc., frowned over the vice-president's plight. He leaned back in his chair. He gazed up at the ceiling. He sighed. "I'm afraid that Ramón's position is mainly honorary. Of course, if he brings in any business, if he should be directly responsible for getting a contract, then naturally he would get a commission. So far, unfortunately, that hasn't happened."

"I see."

"Does that mean he doesn't qualify?"

"I merely collect the information, Mr. Hoguet."

"You have to understand that Ramón's income comes directly from playing; he doesn't teach. He earns money by partnering somebody who wants to be able to say he played with the famous Ramón Lara and is willing to pay for the privilege. Sometimes there's money bet on these matches and Ramón often bets on himself. He usually wins too. I don't suppose you can base benefits on that."

Mici didn't comment.

"What's he going to do if he can't play anymore?" Hoguet asked. "He needs his legs to earn a living. That ought to be taken into consideration."

Mici agreed and intended to make a strong presentation on that basis, but she knew that there was no provision in the law to compensate for loss of earning power. She got up.

"I feel bad I had to go and spoil it for Ramón," Hoguet said as he came around to join her.

"You were obliged to give us the information."

"I know that Ramón will understand I had no choice, but Diane, she'll blame me. She'll tell everybody I fixed it so Ramón wouldn't get any benefits." His mouth formed into a round, wet pout. "I don't suppose . . ." He looked hopefully at Mici.

"We don't reveal our sources."

He was relieved, but only momentarily. "She'll find out. That woman! She's so protective of Ramón. It's really ludicrous. She's worse than a wife, a thousand times worse. She's an absolute virago when it comes to anything about Ramón." Noticing Mici's raised eyebrows, he stopped. "Didn't you know?"

"They're not married?"

"Oh, God! I've done it again. I thought you knew. I naturally assumed —Hell!" He kicked at an imaginary fleck on the carpet.

Watching him, Mici wasn't sure whether he was as upset as he seemed, or whether he hadn't actually let the information slip out on purpose. Perhaps to counteract the anticipated attack from Diane Lara? "What is Mrs. Lara's legal name?"

"Ah, she was Mrs. Hersheimer, Hirschhorn . . . yes, Hirschhorn. Look, Miss Anhalt, does it matter? I mean, they might as well be married; they've been together for ten, twelve years, as long as I've known either of them. Everybody accepts them as married. She's stuck to him and he's stuck to her through thick and thin, and believe me, it hasn't been easy for either of them. The way I heard it, she had a pretty nice life before she met Ramón. She was married to a big hardware man in Detroit, lived in Grosse Pointe with all the socialites. Ramón came through one summer with a troupe of touring pros and played the local club where the Hirschhorns were members. Well, you know, these things happen all the time. Everybody figured that when Ramón and the troupe moved on, that would be the end of it. Only it wasn't. Diane left her husband and her beautiful house and all the comforts. She just walked out. At least there were no children, though she probably would have abandoned them too; she was that infatuated."

He paused, perhaps expecting some comment; when none was forthcoming, he continued, "She trailed after Ramón from tournament to tournament, from exhibition to exhibition. After a while it looked like Ramón might be settling down; he got himself a cushy spot as resident pro in Southampton and Diane took over running the pro shop for him. Evidently, she was prepared to accept his romancing his lady pupils as part of the job, but the board of governors was not: they asked him to leave. So it was back to the gypsy life, except that by this time there was a whole new batch of young, strong players, and Ramón just couldn't compete. Now that tennis has zoomed to such a fantastic popularity, Ramón is too old to cash in."

"You're sure they never married?"

Hoguet shrugged, "As far as I know, Hirschhorn refused to give Diane a divorce."

"Anthing else you should tell me?"

Hoguet flushed under his tan, making it look as though he'd had an extra hour's sun before he came to work that morning. "It won't make any difference, will it? Their not being married, I mean? It won't have any bearing on Ramón's claim?"

"It's a little late to worry about that, isn't it?" Mici asked. "However, don't concern yourself, Mr. Hoguet. We will judge the case on merit, not morals." She gave him her best and brightest smile before flouncing out.

CHAPTER V

The subway doors closed. The train gathered speed; it slowed and stopped; people got off, people got on. Mici was oblivious.

Was it because they were not legally married that Ramón Lara had been so reluctant to file and sign the claim? Nowadays society was so tolerant that it hardly seemed a valid reason. Of course, Ramón and Diane were not exactly of the now generation; in their day, shacking up was called "living in sin." Quite a difference. As she'd indicated to Hoguet, Lara's morality and life-style had nothing to do with the validity of his claim. That was based on the extent of his injuries and length of time he remained out of work. So forget it. But Mici couldn't forget it. She had her own moral problem: should she include the information in her report? Might it prove subconsciously prejudicial in the ultimate disposition? She recalled that she had promised Ramón Lara that if she came upon some "juicy tidbit"—her own words—she'd keep it to herself. She'd been joking, but that didn't change the promise. She was so deep in thought that she almost rode past her stop. The doors were closing when Mici realized where she was and made a lunge, threw her weight against them, and forced them open enough so she could squeeze through.

Adam should be told, she decided. An illuminated clock on the station platform showed that it was just five minutes to twelve. She'd have to run for it if she wanted to catch the supervisor before he left for lunch.

Entering the lobby, Mici cast her usual quick glance at the elevator indicator and, as usual, opted for the stairs. The starter grinned as she sprinted past him.

"Gotta keep in shape, Charlie," she threw over her shoulder.

He just shook his head.

Mici pulled up short in front of Dowd's door. Closed. She panted more out of disappointment than the exertion. She frowned. The closed door meant that the supervisor was in conference, probably with one or both of the board members. The New York State Crime Victims Compensation Board consisted of five members directly appointed by the governor. They headed the various regional offices; the New York City office being the busiest was allocated two members, Mr. Cornelius and Mr. Weyerhauser. It was one of these two men who studied the reports compiled by the field investigators, read the supervisor's advice and comment, and made the final decision on each claim.

"How long has he been in there, Mrs. Jarrett?" Mici asked the supervisor's secretary.

"Too long. I'm going to have to pull him out." Frances Jarrett reached for the telephone.

That meant Adam was not with either of the two board members; even Jarrett wouldn't have dared to break that up. "Great."

"Oh, no, you're not going to see him now. I'm sorry, Maria Ilona, but it's out of the question."

Mici stifled a sigh. The secretary was fifty-one. She'd worked for the compensation board since its inception and felt she ran the place. It was almost true. Nobody resented it. She was like a strict but kindly schoolteacher, and because she treated everyone the same, including her boss, nobody resented that either. In fact, they liked it. So did Mici; only she couldn't get used to be called by her full name.

"I only need a couple of minutes, Mrs. Jarrett," she pleaded.

"I'm sorry, Maria Ilona, that's it. He's due at the city council, and if he doesn't leave right now, he's going to be late," Jarrett scolded, and instead of picking up the telephone, pushed back her chair and bustled straight over to the closed door.

Definitely Adam didn't have either Weyerhauser or Cornelius in there with him, Mici decided, and fell into step behind the secretary.

She knocked and opened the door. "Sorry to disturb you, sir." Jarrett was at her most deferential when she was most disapproving.

Dowd knew it but chose to ignore it. "I was just going to buzz, Fran. I want . . ." He spotted Mici in the background. "Come on in, Mici. Yes, Fran, yes, I haven't forgotten the council meeting. I'm on my way. You call and tell them I've just left." He countered her look of outrage with, "Do it, Mrs. Jarrett."

All Mrs. Jarrett could do was toss her head as she stalked off.

"Mici, I want you to do me a favor."

"Adam, I have to talk to you."

"Not now, I've got a job for you."

"I'm trying to catch a plane!"

Quick phrases overlapping till the last brought the supervisor up short. "Damn. I forgot." He grimaced. "All right, all right. Never mind. I'll put somebody else on the case, Houghton or somebody, but for now just come in here and take over for me."

"Sure."

He gave her a quick smile of thanks as he ushered her forward to introduce her. "Mrs. Tully, this is Miss Anhalt. Miss Anhalt is one of our top investigators. She'll help you with the form and answer any questions you may have. I'll leave you in her capable hands." Dowd smiled genially and a bit guiltily at both of them as he scurried out.

Left alone, the two women slowly measured each other.

Mici had read about Faith Tully of course. The papers had played up her story to the melodramatic hilt. What Mici now beheld was indeed a woeful figure—a young woman, couldn't be twenty yet, who had lost both husband and baby within hours of each other. She appeared to be still partially in shock, unable to cope on either an emotional or a practical level.

Faith Tully saw a pretty girl, real pretty—bright, full of pep, sure of herself. She was like those improbable career types on the TV, self-satisfied, smug.

"You in a hurry too?" Faith turned the question into an accusation.

And because she'd hit so close to the mark, Mici was flooded with guilt. "No, Mrs. Tully, I have plenty of time for you," she replied and determined to take time.

Faith Tully remained skeptical.

"Mr. Dowd really did have a very important appointment," Mici assured the claimant as she went around to sit in the supervisor's chair. "He wouldn't have left unless he had to." She picked up the partially filled-in form on the desk. "I see the crime is still under investigation by the police."

"That's what they say."

"Then it is still under investigation." Mici passed on to another topic. "I also see that Mr. Dowd has marked this as a possible Good Samaritan claim."

The girl looked blank.

"When someone has the courage and compassion to go to the aid of a person in trouble and is injured or killed himself as a result, the law gives him special consideration," Mici explained. "For example, a homicide victim's widow who receives benefits under the Good Samaritan provision will get more money and for a longer period of time. Naturally, which category your claim will fall under depends on the results of the police investigation. It will be up to them to decide whether your husband's death is directly attributable to his helping that little girl who was attacked and abused. It may take some time, but I don't think we need to wait in order to—"

"I don't care about the money," Faith Tully interrupted. "I didn't come here for a handout. I came for help."

"What kind of help?"

The mountain girl's dark eyes glittered in her cadaverous face. "I want Gene's killers caught."

"Of course." Very much aware that privileges of birth and education insulated her from the others pain, Mici chose her words carefully. "But we don't do detective work. Our concern is for the victim. We try to help the victim cope with the aftereffects of the crime. We want to help the victim, or in the case of a homicide, the victim's family to recover and resume as normal a life as is possible under the circumstances. In other words, we want to help you."

"All I want is justice!" the widow proclaimed.

"An eye for an eye?" the investigator asked.

"Yes!" She was defiant.

"Vengeance?"

"Redress," she corrected.

The blonde sighed. "You've come to the wrong place. We're not vigilantes."

"Where can I go then? What can I do? I have no money for a private detective, and the police aren't even trying. The detective on the case as good as admitted it." Sensing Mici Anhalt's doubt, she grew vehement. "He acts like he doesn't believe me, like he thinks I made up the whole story about Gene and those girls. But it's true. I swear it. Every word."

"Why shouldn't he believe you?"

"Because he can't find the girls, that's why. If I'm lying, then the girls don't exist and he's off the hook. But I'm not lying. Why should I lie?"

"I don't know."

"Then you tell him, Miss Anhalt, please. Go and see Detective Stiebeck and tell him you believe me. Do that much for me, do that for me at least."

Again they assessed each other, and each one knew that she had been wrong in her first judgment. Mici realized that far from being adrift, the young widow from Appalachia had set herself a ruthless course. Faith Tully could see that the claims investigator was neither shallow nor antagonistic and might even be a friend.

"Just because Gene did women's hair doesn't mean . . . there was anything wrong with him." Mrs. Tully flushed slightly. "Being a hairstylist is a job like any other."

"Of course." Mici hadn't expected this deviation.

"My own family sneered," the girl continued. "First, when he came up here and got himself a job and started sending money home, oh, they were for him then all right. You bet. He was a good old boy then. A fine boy who didn't forget his folks. When they found out his job was fixing ladies' hair, that was different. They laughed. All the lazy, no-good bums laughed and made sly jokes. Even his own people was ashamed, but they went on taking his money. There wasn't nothing wrong with his money, you bet. My pa didn't want me to have nothing more to do with Gene, even ordered me to stop writing to him. Then one day Gene came home in his beautiful white car, carrying presents for pretty near the whole town. Like a prince, he came. He wanted to marry me, and when he laid down the cash on the table for Pa to pay his debts, then Pa stopped laughing and gave his blessing." She paused, her eyes misted. "We went to Miami Beach for our honeymoon.

"I never saw nothing like that Fountain Blue Hotel . . . never in my whole life. And when we came up to New York, Gene had a whole beautiful place fixed up new for us. I never saw nothing like that neither, except on the TV. I never dreamed I'd live in such a place." Her memories were too much. She could deal with the present, but the memories overcame her.

Silently, Mici went over and put an arm around the girl.

"I hate them, I hate them all!" Faith Tully cried out. "If it hadn't been for them, Gene'd still be alive. He knew what they was saying behind his back and he was ashamed—for me. He only interfered in that fight so that the story'd get back to Keiser and I could hold up my head. As if I cared what they thought back home. I didn't care. But I never told him I didn't care. I never told him . . . I was too embarrassed to talk about it."

It didn't seem to Mici that breaking up an argument between some teenage girls, no matter how vicious they might have been, would impress Faith's mountain kin. At this point, though, it was academic. She let the young widow cry a little longer, then put an end to her tears with a brisk announcement.

"I'm sure that Detective Stiebeck does believe you, Mrs. Tully, and is doing everything he can, but I'll just make a note here for the investigator who handles your claim to see him and get a progress report from him."

"I thought you were handling my claim."

Too late Mici realized the damage: the girl had started trusting her. "I'm just filling in for Mr. Dowd on the original interview. He'll assign a permanent investigator."

"I thought you were an investigator."

"I am, but I'm not available."

"I see. You're passing me on, right? On to the next one, who'll pass me on to the next—"

"It's not like that."

"First it was Detective Stiebeck who couldn't be bothered, then Mr. Dowd, now you. I'm pretty dumb, I guess; I learn hard, but I really did think you were different, Miss Anhalt. I really did think so."

Mici felt awful. "It's not that I don't want to handle your claim, Mrs. Tully. I can't. I'm going out of town—today. Actually, I shouldn't even be here now; I was supposed to leave last night." She wasn't getting through. She tried once more. "My boyfriend's expecting me in Miami. I'm going on vacation."

"Oh, you're going on vacation!" The sarcasm was heavy. "Why didn't you say so! You couldn't possibly postpone your vacation."

Wrong again. All wrong. Insensitive, stupid. How could she have said it? Mici berated herself. "Please, Faith."

She drew herself up. "Mrs. Tully, if you please. Forget it, Miss Anhalt.

You go on your vacation and have a good time. I can look after myself. I'll get what's mine, don't you worry." She started for the door.

"Faith!" Mici called in a sharp tone.

Curiosity made her stop, though pride would not permit her to turn around just yet.

"Do you know what the temperature in Miami Beach was this morning?" Mici asked. "Twenty-nine degrees! Who wants to go south in that kind of weather?"

The rest of the day was all downhill.

Adam didn't get back from his city-council meeting till nearly three. "You still here?" he commented when he saw Mici neither expecting nor waiting for an answer.

"I'm not going." She fell in behind him and followed him into his office. "Faith Tully wants me to handle her claim, and I've agreed, if it's all right with you?"

He grinned. "Got to you, huh?"

"Adam!"

"No, ma'am. No, I don't, I swear I didn't bring you in on purpose. I was looking for Houghton; you know that. I intended to put Sam on it, but you just happened by at the opportune moment." His eyes were dancing. Then he became serious. "I'm glad you've called off your vacation. There's so much—"

"Postponed, not called off. Postponed till next week."

"Sorry." The supervisor shook his head. "If that's what you want to tell Danny, okay, but I can't spare you next week. You know what it's like after the holidays."

Of course. The crime rate soared on weekends and holidays. The longer the holiday period, the more crimes committed. And after the crimes came the claims of the victims. At the office it would be the busy season. That most of the claims would be disallowed didn't lessen the work load that much. A large percentage of holiday crimes were the result of family quarrels—too much togetherness. The victim would be either related to the perpetrator or have provoked the incident: either way it meant automatic disqualification. Explaining to a distraught, perhaps prievously injured person that he was not eligible for compensation required tact and firmness, and the reactions varied from reasonable to hysterical to actively aggressive. Nobody in the office looked forward to the postholiday period, and Mici had known that Adam wouldn't be able to let her go.

The truth was that, difficult though the period might be, she didn't want to miss it. Refusing a victim compensation didn't mean refusing sympathy, and very often that was what the victim was really looking for. She'd asked Adam for the time so that she could honestly tell Danny that she'd tried and been turned down.

Reaching Danny was the next problem. She tried his apartment, then the marina, then finally had to leave a message with Danny's mother. It was not the ideal way to pass on the news.

"Danny will be so disappointed," Mrs. Best murmured. "And so are we, dear; we were looking forward to having you with us. We're very fond of you, you know."

"Thank you, Julia. I'm disappointed too. It really can't be helped. I'm sorry to disrupt your plans, yours and Jake's."

"Oh, don't worry about us, dear. We understand. You're a career girl, and we admire you for it. I'm afraid Danny sees it differently."

"I wish he wouldn't."

"So do we, dear. We're on your side. We hope you can bring him around."

"I'm trying, Julia."

"I know. Thank you, dear." There was a suspicious quaver in Julia Best's voice. "I'll tell Danny to call you tonight. Will you be home?"

Julia and Jake Best were darlings, Mici thought, but they had spoiled their only son. Equating money with love, they'd lavished both on Danny from boyhood into manhood. Even now realizing their mistake, they couldn't stop. How could Danny understand Mici's sense of responsibility to her job when he had no sense of responsibility himself to anyone or anything? Now his mother and father were looking for her to undo the damage. She wondered whether it wasn't already too late.

"Sure, Julia. Tell him I'll wait for his call."

Next Mici called the precinct and asked for Detective Stiebeck. He'd come on duty at four, she was told. She left her name, stated her business, and asked that he return her call. When she hadn't heard by five, she called again. Detective Stiebeck had stepped out for a few moments. She was tired; she wanted to go home; she managed to hide her exasperation. "Tell Detective Stiebeck I'm waiting to hear from him."

"Maria Ilona?" Fran Jarrett stuck her head in the door. "There's a Mr. Creedy here. He was injured in a liquor-store robbery. Okay to send him in?"

Mici grimaced. "Ah, Mrs. Jarrett, I was just going to leave in a few minutes. Can't you give him to somebody else?"

"You're the only one who's not busy."

"You've got to be kidding!"

"You cleared your desk."

"So I could go on vacation. Have a heart."

"He's a nice old boy. A little light upstairs"—Dowd's secretary tapped her temple significantly—"but sweet. I don't think it was all that easy for him to get over here."

"Well, if he's penetrated your hard heart—"

"Good girl." Frances Jarret turned and waved Simon Creedy in.

Age had dehydrated him; his skin was alabaster pale and he appeared to be shrinking inside his clothes. He paused on the threshold to orient himself and gave Mici the tentative and ingratiating smile of a stray dog that is used to being kicked. She felt a physical stab of compassion as he shambled into the room, moving unsteadily, shaking slightly, but she made no move to help him—it might be an offense. When he got right up to her desk, then she rose and held out her hand.

"Hello, Mr. Creedy, I'm Mici Anhalt."

He took her hand and his smile became less anxious.

As he settled himself, she scanned the information Frances Jarrett had left for her.

"Well, Mr. Creedy, you certainly walked into that liquor store at an inopportune moment, didn't you?" One thing Creedy had not needed, she thought, was a knock on the head. "How do you feel?"

"A little shook up, I guess."

"That will pass." There was a covering letter from a Miss Isabel Pallo at the Home Assistance Agency. "I see you were doing part-time work caring for old people in their homes—visiting them, running errands, keeping them company."

"Yes, ma'am. But they say I can't do it anymore. They say I'm not fit."

"I'm sure that's only temporary, Mr. Creedy. You'll get better, and when you do, you'll be able to resume the good work you've been doing."

"Thank you, ma'am. You're nice. You're a real nice lady. I like you." He gave her his usual sweet smile.

"Thank you, Mr. Creedy. I think you're nice and I like you, too." For a moment they basked in each other's approbation. "Well, now let's see. The incident occurred over two weeks ago."

"Yes, ma'am."

"Who referred you to us?"

"Miss Pallo. At the agency."

Not the police, not anybody from the DA's, not even the doctor who had examined him to determine the extent of his injuries! Referral was so haphazard, Mici thought with considerable bitterness, so much left to chance. "Well, you found us, that's the main thing. Now let's see what we can do to help." She went back and read the claim form more carefully. "Did you fill this out yourself?"

"Miss Pallo did it for me."

"That's all right," she hastened to assure him. "But you do know what's in it?"

He nodded.

"According to this, your medical expenses—that is, those outside your regular treatments, those that are a direct result of the commission of the felony—are being taken care of through Medicaid. You also have a pension, but you're looking for reimbursement for loss of income from your part-time job while you're laid up."

"Yes, ma'am. I understand."

"Good. Meanwhile, if you have any questions, or if you need anything, don't hesitate to give me a call, okay? Here's my card with my name and my number."

He studied the card, then very carefully brought out a cheap, worn wallet, selected the proper compartment, tucked the card inside. Then, carefully and methodically he returned the wallet to its place. "You're a nice lady, Miss Anhalt. A real nice lady."

Simon Creedy was slow and maybe he wasn't too bright, Mici thought, but he sure had a great smile.

The interview had refreshed her. She tried Detective Stiebeck once again and, when told that he still hadn't returned, decided to pay him a personal visit on her way home.

The suitcase packed with her vacation clothes seemed larger and clumsier than ever. And heavier. Just the thought of hauling it back up on the subway made her arm and her back ache all over again. If she didn't take the suitcase home now, it would sit there all winter! Mici sighed and hefted it. How could a couple of bathing suits and some shorts and shirts weigh that much? She didn't know how she managed to get on the train with it. From the glares of the other passengers—she'd managed to hit the peak of the rush hour—she had no right to have brought it on. Hanging on to the overhead strap with one hand and struggling to keep the bag out of the way, she managed to drop it on somebody's foot.

"Oh, I'm sorry. I'm terribly sorry."

She snatched her bag up off well-polished boots, let her eyes travel to tight jeans and a sweater—no jacket, no coat . . . in December! He was a real *macho* type. She'd met them before: they thought treating a woman as an equal meant they could insult and abuse her. Mici braced herself for the inevitable nastiness and got ready to parry. Instead, the *macho* type stood up.

"Take my seat."

She flushed at having been so wrong. "Oh, no, thanks. I'm okay."

"Take it. I've been sitting all day."

While they argued, an old woman with a shopping bag and a harried expression slipped behind them both and with an audible grunt of triumph took the disputed seat.

Mici and the man in the sweater and jeans looked at each other in dismay, then both started to laugh.

"Sorry," he said, in a voice that passed for a whisper in the roaring, charging subway train. "She looks like she needs it worse than either of us."

Though they were jostled and pummeled by the crowds getting on and off, by the train's lurching, by the fierce competition for seats that was renewed at every station, they didn't continue the conversation. As the train pulled into Fifty-seventh Street, the young man nodded.

"This is my stop. Better luck next time." He waved and was swept away with the mob fighting to get out to the platform.

He hadn't tried to pick her up, or get a feel, or anything. Who says New Yorkers can't be friendly? Mici smiled to herself.

Though she'd never been in the Nineteenth before, Mici knew her way around a police station. She'd dealt with cops and usually got good cooperation. Most cops she'd met had plenty of compassion, and when they learned what her job was, they were glad to help every way they could. There were always the exceptions, naturally: cops who resented anything that suggested even the possibility of adding to the reams of paperwork that every case entailed, or who were harassed by the work load into permanent irritability. Which kind would Ed Stiebeck be? According to Faith Tully, the latter.

By the time Mici Anhalt walked into the squad room, the weight of the suitcase was making her list to one side. She set it down inside the door and then looked around. Nobody paid any attention to her.

"Detective Stiebeck?" she called out in a good, strong voice.

A man at the far end of the room looked up. He was perhaps in his late forties. His dark hair was threaded with gray, his face long and narrow, features rough-hewn. He was one of those ugly-handsome men that some women find irresistible. Mici was willing to bet that he wasn't married. She left the suitcase where she'd set it and went over.

"I'm Mici Anhalt."

He just barely raised himself out of the chair. "Oh, yes. I got your messages—all three of them."

She could have retaliated by asking why he hadn't called back, but smiled instead. "Then you know how eager I am to talk to you."

"You should have waited for me to get in touch, Miss Anhalt. You could have saved yourself some trouble."

Not a good start, Mici thought, but kept smiling. "As long as I am here, do you mind if I sit down?" Without waiting she ensconced herself in the available chair. She was really more tired than she'd realized.

"What can I do for you, Miss Anhalt?"

If he had received her messages, then he knew. "I'm handling Mrs. Tully's claim for compensation. I've read all the newspaper accounts and I've talked to her, of course, but I need to know the status of the case presently."

"There's nothing new."

"The situation is somewhat special," Mici explained. "Mrs. Tully is applying for benefits under the Good Samaritan provision. We have to know—"

"You can forget that. I think I can safely say that Mrs. Tully does not qualify for Good Samaritan compensation." Ed Stiebeck hesitated, thoughtfully reached for a crumpled pack of cigarettes buried under some papers, and lit up without offering one to his visitor.

Mici wasn't offended; she could see that he was using the act of lighting up to study her and make a decision.

"It begins to look as though Mrs. Tully won't be eligible for any kind of compensation."

She felt a constriction around her heart and a cold chill creeping over her. "Why not?"

"I'm sorry, I can't tell you that."

"Come on, Detective Stiebeck, we're both government employees; we're supposed to cooperate. If you know something that affects Mrs. Tully's claim, you've got to tell me. I'm not going to blab it around and spoil your case."

He frowned. He took a deep breath. "We have reason to believe that Faith Tully killed her husband."

Chapter VI

"You're kidding!"

Mici Anhalt was shocked. The color drained from her face, her translucent blue eyes clouded.

"Hardly," Stiebeck replied huffily.

"I can't believe it!" Mici insisted. "According to the officers who picked her up, she was wandering through the streets in the rain looking for help for her dying husband. She'd been screaming for help, but nobody answered her screams."

"That's what she said. That's the story she gave. Suppose she wasn't looking for help. Suppose she had just shot her husband and was fleeing the scene?"

Mici gaped at him.

"Nobody heard her scream," Stiebeck pointed out. "The neighborhood was thoroughly canvassed, believe me."

"Did anybody hear the shot?"

"No."

"There you are!"

"The shot could have passed as a backfire. The point is we know there was a shot; we have a dead man to prove it."

Mici refused to concede. "As long as you can't prove she *didn't* scream—"

"How can you prove a negative?"

"Every account of the events that I've read described Faith Tully as confused, disoriented, severely agitated when she was picked up by the patrol car."

"She'd be all of that if she'd just committed murder and walked right into the arms of a couple of police officers, wouldn't she?"

He was right. Faith Tully's actions could be interpreted either way.

Mici bit her lip. "The only thing I can say is that if she is guilty, then she's also pretty resourceful. She came up with a story that covered all the eventualities and she came up with it fast."

"I'll give you that." Stiebeck nodded. "She looks like a poor, helpless waif, but back of that thin little face and those great big eyes there's one tough lady."

"We're all tough ladies, Detective Stiebeck, big and little, plain and pretty, only till lately most of us have been afraid to let it show." As an investigator Mici had never before handled a situation in which the claimant was also suspect. She had asked Faith Tully to go over the events of the night of the murder, so now she opened her purse and consulted the notes she'd taken.

"Mrs. Tully says that she called the precinct, this precinct, on the night of the murder to report that her husband was missing."

"Unfortunately, the call wasn't logged."

"The desk sergeant doesn't remember the call?"

"The call never got to him," Stiebeck explained. "It was taken by the civilian telephone operator. You have to understand procedure, Miss Anhalt. To start with, we don't accept missing persons complaints for anyone over the age of twenty-one. We assume that a person over twenty-one is an adult and so free to come and go as he pleases."

"Well, sure, but what if he's missing as a result of an accident or an assault?"

"Right. We do check out the accident and hospital reports. But according to Mrs. Tully herself, when she called her husband was unaccounted for for less than a couple of hours. Well now . . ." He shrugged. "The operator advised her to wait a while longer and then if he hadn't showed to call back."

"And the operator doesn't keep a record of such calls?"

Stiebeck shook his head.

Mici considered. "Faith Tully wouldn't know that. She'd be afraid to claim that she'd called the precinct if she hadn't actually done it; she wouldn't want to be caught lying."

"Have you had legal training?' Stiebeck asked, studying her with the beginning of real interest. She was pretty, much too pretty to be taken seriously.

"I worked for Vera, but that's just common sense."

"Okay, I'll give it to you straight, Miss Anhalt. Faith Tully says that a week before the murder, as she and her husband were going home from the movies, they saw a group of girls beating up another, younger girl. Actually, the fight was over the younger girl's bike."

"I know. I know all that. She told me. She also—"

"Wait. According to Mrs. Tully, those girls threatened to get even with her husband. Still according to her, they were the ones who ambushed Gene Tully Friday night, shot him, and while she was running through the streets looking for help, finished the job by stomping and beating him."

"I've heard worse than that about girl gangs."

"Who hasn't?" He looked straight at Mici. "The thing is, Mrs. Tully couldn't offer any kind of lead to the girls. Her husband took the little one home, but she doesn't know either the child's name nor her address. Claims her husband refused to tell her because she wanted to report the incident to the police and he didn't want her to. Do you buy that?"

"If the bicycle was stolen—"

"You don't sound as positive as you did. Okay, leave it for now. How about the time lapse between the original incident and the alleged revenge?"

"They were waiting for the right opportunity."

He pounced on that. "How did they know where to wait? They didn't know Tully's name or address or where he parked his car or even that he had a car."

"The little one told them; they made her."

"And they hung around night after night waiting?"

"Its not inconceivable."

"It's unlikely. The point I'm trying to make, Miss Anhalt, is not that Faith Tully made up the incident, but that she embellished it, enlarged on it, dramatized it."

"You mean she's using it as a red herring."

The detective nodded. "I think there was an incident, very innocuous, but that it suggested to Mrs. Tully how she could kill her husband and put the blame on someone else."

"No."

"According to the autopsy report it was the bullet that killed him. Since the shooting and the beating came so close together it's difficult to state absolutely, but he may well have been already dead when the beating was administered. No, I just don't see a gang doing it like that. It doesn't make sense. The gang would have no trouble subduing him and they would want him to feel every blow. Their purpose is both to injure the victim and debase him—it's a high for them. They get no high if the victim is unconscious." Stiebeck paused. "Maybe if they were interrupted during the beating, then they might shoot him to finish him off, to prevent him from identifying them. But the shooting first . . ." He shook his head.

"You're saying that Mrs. Tully shot her husband, and then when he was dead or dying, beat him to make it look like the work of a gang?" Mici summed up. "I can't buy it. Absolutely not. Maybe that's how it was done, but she didn't do it. It's too cold-blooded."

"Every premeditated murder is cold-blooded."

"She was carrying his baby," Mici cried out. "You're making her into a monster."

"I deal with monsters every day, Miss Anhalt."

For that, she had no answer. "Tell me why. What was her motive?"

"Jealousy. You've seen Faith Tully; you can't call her pretty. Not ugly either, just nondescript. But Eugene Tully was something else. He looked like . . . a sexy choirboy. And he was in a business that brought him into contact with very elegant, very glamorous, very rich, and self-indulgent women."

"But he married the plain, nondescript girl from his hometown," she reminded him. "He went back and literally bought her from her father."

"So maybe she had no reason to be jealous, but she thought she did and it's the same thing. Anyhow, we don't have to prove motive."

"You do to me!" Mici flared. "Okay, okay, let's pass motive for now. I'll grant you opportunity, but how about means?"

"We're working on it. Look, Miss Anhalt, I know that you feel a lot of sympathy for Faith Tully, and so did I at first, but it fits." He sighed. "It all fits."

In spite of what he said, Mici got the impression that Ed Stiebeck wasn't really satisfied with the case he was making. It encouraged her to continue her challenge. "It's theory. You've got nothing tangible to back it. You haven't got any more to back your version than she has to back hers."

"I'm sorry to disappoint you, Miss Anhalt, but we have." Ed Stiebeck folded his arms and leaned back, with considerable satisfaction. "We've traced the girls."

"You traced them? How? How did you trace them?"

Her reaction was gratifying. Stiebeck preened himself. "We traced the bike."

Mici, who had begun to think that he was completely devoid of emotion, was delighted by this indication that he was human enough to be proud of himself. She stoked his vanity. "How did you do that?"

He didn't quite smile, but the dour lines running from nostrils down to mouth were almost erased. "Mrs. Tully mentioned that the bike's front wheel was damaged. Well, there was no reason for her to lie about a detail like that. So, I figured that if the wheel was out of line it would have to be repaired and I canvassed the repair shops. Simple."

"Terrific. Really, terrific." She meant it. "And so?"

"Nothing. It seems the kid, Arlene Meyer, the one Eugene Tully befriended, bought the bike from another girl, Judy Caniglieri, for fifty dollars. When Judy's parents found out, they were naturally furious. The bike cost a hell of a lot more. Okay. So they ordered Judy to return the fifty and get the bike back. Only Arlene wasn't about to give it up. She claimed the bike belonged to her, that she'd bought it fair and square. And that's what the argument was about. There was a little pushing and shoving, but strictly kid stuff. The next day the two sets of parents got together and straightened it out. Nobody was mad at anybody."

"That's it?" Mici asked.

"That's it." He watched as the investigator returned her notebook to her purse. "Don't feel too bad, Miss Anhalt. She conned me too. I've been in this racket a long time, a lot longer than you, and I've made it a principle not to get involved, but I fell for her act. It was a damned good one."

"Too good, if you ask me," Mici replied. "Why keep demanding that you find her husband's killers? Why accuse you of not trying hard enough? She should be delighted to have you give up. She should keep her mouth shut. All that ranting about revenge . . ."

"So, she doesn't know when to quit." Stiebeck shrugged it off, but that last scream of Faith Tully's as he closed the door of her hospital room reverberated in his memory. He shrugged a second time and still could not be rid of it.

Mici was watching him very closely. "Are you going to arrest her?"

"Not yet. We don't have enough."

"You sure don't."

"We'll get the evidence."

"Want to bet?"

A corner of his mouth twitched in what might just possibly, finally have been a smile. "You give up hard, don't you?"

"You give up easy."

His lips tightened. "It's not up to me which way an investigation goes. I'm a detective. I'm at the bottom of the chain of command. I do the legwork; I go out and get the information; I don't evaluate it."

"Who does?"

"The brass."

"Like who?"

"The lieut. Lieutenant Dicker."

"So Lieutenant Dicker is the one who's decided that Faith Tully is guilty." Suddenly, Mici felt a lot better.

"I didn't say that. I never said that."

"But you buy it?"

Stiebeck reddened. He was furious with himself for having given her the opening. Twice within the last couple of days he'd made the mistake of trying to be honest! This one was using her good looks the way the other used her helplessness; he would never have opened up with a man. He jabbed a bony finger at Mici.

"Now you look, lady. We don't go around railroading people. We don't put a hand on anybody till we have reasonable evidence of guilt. I've been square with you, but if you say that I told you the lieut is trying to pin this thing on Mrs. Tully or on any other specific person, I'm going to call you a liar right to your face, Miss Anhalt."

"Call me Mici."

"This is no joke."

"I know it, Ed. I just wanted to be sure where you stood. I have no intention of quoting or using anything you say against you."

The irony was lost on him. "I stand where I'm told to stand."

"But you believe Faith Tully. I know you do."

"I did believe her at the beginning, yes; I told you that. She got to me. Her grief seemed genuine. Now I realize why. She'd lost her baby, and it was the baby she was mourning, not her husband."

"Is that the way Lieutenant Dicker rationalizes it?" Mici asked. Then added gently, "Don't you have an opinion of your own?"

"Okay, Miss Anhalt, that concludes the interview." He picked up the stub of the cigarette from the ashtray and, unaware that it had gone out, stuck it into his mouth. He turned to the typewriter on its separate table and began pecking out something, anything. "I've got nothing more to say to you."

"I have something more to say to you. Mrs. Tully has put in a claim for compensation. You've thrown doubt, considerable doubt, on her eligibility, but you haven't offered proof to discredit her. So it's up to me to conduct my own investigation."

He stopped pretending he was engrossed with his typing and stared at her. Then deliberately, he mimicked her.

"You're kidding!"

"Hardly."

"You can't conduct your own investigation!"

"It's my job, remember?"

"Ah, come on, Miss Anhalt . . . Mici!" He was smiling now, openly. "It's one thing to check out a victim's claim, look at his bank balance, talk to his insurance company and his employer, but it's something else to track down a killer."

"Certainly. I absolutely agree."

"Well, then, no offense, you're a real smart lady and you're probably very good at what you do."

She matched his smile. "Thank you. I am."

He laughed out loud. "You've got plenty of moxie."

"Chutzpah," she corrected.

He chortled, then grew serious again. "We can't have civilians messing around in police business. You could get hurt."

"I'm not a civilian, and I won't get hurt because I'm not going after the killer. No, thanks. I'm just going to prove that Faith Tully is telling the truth. That is within my province." She got up. "And don't waste your time complaining to my supervisor because he'll back me up." She slung her handbag over one shoulder. "And if you want to inform 'the lieut,' that's okay. I don't want either one of you to say later that I went behind your backs."

"We won't say that."

"Good. And thanks for your time."

She marched across the room to the door, where she'd left the suitcase.

She bent down and when she came up, Detective Edward Stiebeck was holding the door for her.

"You'll let me know how you're making out?"

She gave him her nicest, most impish smile, the right-hand corner slightly higher. "I'll keep you informed. My pleasure."

"If there's anything I can do . . ."

"I won't hesitate to call on you."

He grunted, then abruptly reached out a hand and took the suitcase from her. "I'll help you find a cab."

It wasn't till she got home, laid the suitcase on the bed, and started to unpack her summer clothes that Mici thought about Danny. By then it was after eight-thirty. Had he called already? Probably. Well, he'd call again. She set about preparing dinner. Though she ate alone, Mici enjoyed cooking. She always prepared a full meal and ate it at a properly set table. While the lamb chops were broiling, she poured herself a glass of beer. Summer or winter, it was the one alcoholic drink she really enjoyed.

Having eaten and washed up, she watched the ten-o'clock news. Danny was probably sulking, she thought, waiting for her to call him. She really should; she owed him more than a message through his mother. But much as she wanted to talk to him, to hear his voice, she dreaded the inevitable pleading, arguments, accusations. She went into the bedroom, sat on the edge of the bed, and stared at the phone. She couldn't say she hadn't been warned about Danny, right at the start.

"He's no good for you," Roz Pell told her on the very first night she met Daniel Emerson Best.

She hadn't taken the warning seriously. "I like him," she'd replied. "I really think he's a great guy. I don't know when I've met anyone I've liked so instinctively."

Mici had been having dinner with Roz and Charlie when Danny Best dropped in. He claimed he wasn't hungry and then proceeded to load up his plate. They hit it off right away. By dessert he was asking her for a date.

"Don't go out with him," Roz persisted. "Don't even start. Sure, sure, he's charming, marvelous sense of humor, handsome, got plenty of money . . ."

"Who did he murder?"

"Okay, okay, you're laughing now, but you won't be laughing later. What I'm trying to tell you is that you can't have a lasting relationship with Danny Best. He's not the type."

"Terrific. I'm not looking for a 'lasting relationship.' Come on, Roz, I'm just going to date the guy a few times."

"Why bother? Why waste even one evening? Date somebody who's got something to offer, somebody with a good career ahead of him, steady, reliable. Charlie was just telling me there's a new man in his shop." Like all happy newlyweds, Roz and Charlie kept trying to fix up their friends.

"Oh, Roz, I appreciate your concern, honestly, but don't worry. I really have no intention of getting serious."

But she had come to care for Danny Best . . . too much. She knew he cared for her, too; she couldn't feel as she did about him unless the feeling were reciprocated. Her grandfather said that Danny didn't have a sense of his own worth, that he relied on his money, or rather his parents' money, for his sense of identity. They had different sets of values. Mici sighed and picked up the phone.

The phone rang a long time. She visualized Danny's luxurious thirty-six-foot cruiser, *Sandpiper*, bobbing gently at anchor in its berth at the marina, its lights reflected in the still water. The marina was small and out of the way. It catered mainly to locals who took charters out early for a day's fishing and brought them back, discharged them, and sent them to do their partying elsewhere. The sound of the ringing phone in his salon would be heard on the dock and as far as the marina office. If Danny were anywhere around the marina, he would hear it; of course, he might be home with his parents. She was just about to hang up when the ringing stopped.

"Hello?"

"Danny. It's me."

"Mici! Hey, Mici! How are you, kid?"

Her heart sank. He'd had a few, quite a few.

Then his tone changed, became eager. "You coming down? You going to make it after all?"

"No. I can't. I'm sorry."

"Oh. So why did you call?"

"I just wanted to tell you that I'm sorry."

"Okay. So you've told me."

She knew it was useless to try to reason with him when he was in this condition, but having made the call she had to try. "I'm sorry, darling, I really am. I wanted to come. I was looking forward to it."

"Yeah? So then why aren't you here?"

"Something came up. This girl—her husband was killed. She has nobody to turn to."

"You in social work now?" he sneered.

"It's my job. If you'd ever held a job yourself, you'd understand," she retorted.

"I understand all right. I understand that you're staying up there because you want to."

"Danny . . ."

"What's the point of denying it?" Disappointment combined with resentment almost sobered him. "You're not the only investigator in the place. You could have turned the case over to somebody else, but you didn't. So, you want to be there more than you want to be with me."

"No."

"No? Fine. So then when are you coming down? Tomorrow? Next week? The week after?"

"I don't know."

"Ah . . ."

He sounded almost pleased, as though he'd expected her to say just that and was now vindicated. Mici had known that they were heading for a showdown, but somehow she hadn't expected it to come like this, by long distance. Maybe it was best. If they'd been together, they would never have been able to keep their hands off each other. In his arms, she certainly wouldn't have been able to say what inevitably had to be said.

"Maybe we ought to forget it." Then she spoiled it by adding, "For now."

"Maybe we ought to just forget it," Danny said, and hung up.

He did not call back.

Chapter VII

Salon Chéri read the brass plaque at the corner of the elegant townhouse, then underneath HOUSE OF BEAUTY.

As she mounted the stairs to the red lacquer door, Mici admired the way the brownstone had been restored, with respect for its residential origin and nothing except the discreet plaque to indicate its commercial present. Inside, the true nature of the establishment was more openly admitted. Whatever the layout had been originally, the ground floor was now one spacious foyer, mirrored and tiled, dominated by a huge horse-shoe-shaped desk over which presided a gaunt, model-type blonde whose natural beauty was distorted by too much makeup. At Mici's entrance she raised what was left of her eyebrows in polite inquiry.

"I am Maria Ilona Anhalt." She used her full name, rolling it out with aristocratic hauteur.

The receptionist was cowed. She consulted the day's chart, then dissolved into professional charm. "Oh, yes, Miss Anhalt. Mr. Randolph is waiting for you on the second floor." As Mici started for the curving marble staircase, the receptionist cleared her throat. "Ah . . . you may take the elevator, Miss Anhalt, behind that screen."

Upstairs, the treatment was, if anything, even more supercilious. Mici wasn't exactly a stranger to such establishments as Salon Chéri. In the days when her parents paid the bills she'd frequented them regularly. Mr. Randolph met her at the elevator, holding the door for her as she stepped out. Looking her over, he knew instantly that she was playing in a lesser league now and he was subtly telling her that he knew and at the same time transmitting the information to the others. His manner was impeccable as he escorted her across the floor to a private cubicle and his ministrations would be superficially faultless, of that Mici was certain.

If she weren't familiar with real courtesy she probably wouldn't have been aware that she was being snubbed.

It rankled. Nobody likes to be put down; the real damage, however, lay in the fact that if Mr. Randolph didn't accept her as a rich client he would not be likely to gossip with her. If she'd just wanted facts and figures, she could have shown her credentials and gone through the salon books, but Mici was after intangibles—what Eugene Tully had been like, how he lived, who his friends were . . . in a word, gossip. What better place for gossip than a beauty salon? And what better way to get it than to pose as a customer?

She had hoped for a large open room where she would have the opportunity to study both the operators and the patrons. Instead, she caught the merest glimpse of the customers and not much more of the stylists. The stylists were all men, all young—say, in their twenties. Variants of her Mr. Randolph, they were tall, slim, with unbelievably flat, almost concave stomachs and no hips. They were uniformly pale of face and wore their hair in a variety of sleek styles just short of shoulder length. They were dressed in expensively tailored three-piece suits with nipped wrists. That was all she observed before she was ensconced in her own cubicle and the curtains closed around her like hospital curtains a dying patient. Her coat was taken from her by two minions, both female. They scurried about silently while Mr. Randolph assessed the client's needs. As he felt the texture of her hair, soft, silky, noted that both color and wave were natural, and saw that no matter which way he moved it and let it fall, the effect was becoming to her oval face, Mici knew her tactics would fail.

"What is it you'd like me to do for you, Miss Anhalt?" It was a thinly veiled challenge. It said: you don't need my services.

"I'm going to a formal dinner," she lied. "The dinner is being given by Senator and Mrs. Kalb, and I thought something more sophisticated . . ." She waved her hands, deprecating the casualness of her hairstyle.

There was just a flicker of interest in Mr. Randolph's eyes. "Mrs. Kalb is one of our most loyal clients."

"It was Mrs. Kalb who suggested I try Salon Chéri," Mitzi purred. "She told me to ask for Mr. Eugene."

Unaccountably, Mr. Randolph lost interest. He now had Mici's hair gathered together in one hand and was desultorily draping it around her head like a swatch of silk.

"Terrible what happened to him. Terrible." Mici dangled the bait.

Mr. Randolph was only interested in her hair.

"You must all have been deeply shocked."

"Deeply shocked," Mr. Randolph echoed and at the same moment spun Mici's chair around so that it was angled sideways and, stepping on a lever, tilted it back so that she was in a prone position. The shampooist appeared and began operating the faucets.

"If you'll excuse me, Miss Anhalt."

Before she excused him or not, the spray had drenched her head, and Mr. Randolph was gone, having drawn the curtain behind him. Mici closed her eyes and decided she might as well give herself up to the luxury of the treatment till he returned. But when the shampoo and the accompanying head and neck massage were completed and she was restored to an upright position, her head wrapped in a warm towel, it was not Mr. Randolph who parted the curtains and stepped inside.

"Good morning, Miss Anhalt. I am Mr. Tyrone, Tyrone Witte. I am the manager of Salon Chéri. I understand you've been enquiring about Mr. Eugene."

Mr. Tyrone was suave, elegant, and no longer young, but shrewd enough to make an asset of his age. He was tall, not stout—oh, never that—but he permitted himself the weight of maturity . . . call him, robust. His hair revealed a judicious amount of gray, and he sported a neat, squarely trimmed beard. He was perhaps forty-two or -three, an indication of what the slim, young men of the salon might aspire to become. He represented their optimum future.

"Just what is your interest, Miss Anhalt?"

"Your Mr. Randolph is a most astute young man; he saw through me. He knew that I didn't come just to get my hair done." Mici smiled disarmingly.

"Indeed."

The smile didn't work. She had intended to show her credentials and explain her errand, but his coolness suggested another approach. "Actually, I'm a writer, Mr. Witte. I'm doing a piece—"

That didn't delight him particularly. "I'm sorry, Miss Anhalt. We've had just about all we can take from reporters, police, and the whole—"

"I'm not a crime reporter, Mr. Witte." Then she had an inspiration. "It's Mrs. Tully I'm interested in."

"Oh?"

"Yes. She inspires sympathy: a young bride, a girl from the backwoods in the big city, pregnant. Within hours she loses both husband and baby."

"We all feel sorry for Faith," Witte said.

Aha! she thought, he'd talk; he'd have no excuse not to. "I have the feeling that she's lost, confused, and not merely as a result of the tragedy, but that she hadn't adjusted to the life up here."

"I think you're right."

"You know her well?"

"We gave the newlyweds a party and then they entertained us."

"What is your impression of Faith Tully?"

"As you say—unsophisticated, unspoiled, natural."

"And very much in love with her husband?"

"Of course."

"Perhaps a little jealous of him?"

"Jealous?"

"Because of his work. Because of the beautiful, glamorous women with whom he came in daily contact. Wouldn't that be natural?"

The manager gave her a searching look. "You'll have to ask her."

"Did she have any reason to be jealous?"

"I wouldn't know." Expertly, Witte peeled the towel from her head. "You said you were going to a formal dinner?"

Mici met his eyes in the mirror and smiled ruefully. "No."

"Ah, well, we can't let you walk out of Salon Chéri looking like this, can we?" He picked up a comb and ran it through her wet hair.

"I find it intriguing that Eugene Tully adapted to the city so quickly and so well," Mici continued. "His background is the same, was the same, as Faith's, yet where she seems to have been overwhelmed, he thrived."

Witte made no comment.

"He must have had a natural flair for this work."

"He had plenty to learn."

"Yes, of course. But he must have had a natural aptitude to become so good at it so fast."

"As a matter of fact, he did," Witte admitted with an engaging smile. "He had plenty to learn, as I said, but he worked hard and he deserved his success."

"How did he happen to come to Salon Chéri?" Mici asked. "I've wondered about that. It seems an improbable kind of job for a young man from Appalachia. Had he worked in some other salon before?"

Having combed her hair, Witte now began to section it deftly. "Eugene Tully came to us in answer to our advertisement. He had no previous experience whatsoever. We prefer it that way." Evidently, this was a subject he didn't mind discussing, and as quickly as his fingers moved, his words spilled out. "As you may know, the original Salon Chéri is in London. Its success derived from a hair-cutting technique evolved by the founder, Mr. Gregory. It became so popular that Mr. Gregory set up branches all over the world. Actually, they are franchises. That's general knowledge. A woman who visits us here in New York knows that Mr. Gregory himself is not going to be available, but she expects that whoever serves her will work in his technique. We have found that young men untainted by previous methods learn best."

"I see."

"We've also found that men have a decided flair for cutting that women do not; that is why, as you've undoubtedly noticed, we have no women doing this particular phase of the work. Perhaps an analogy with the chef of a fine restaurant would be apt."

"Perhaps."

The manager now pulled a tray of rollers over to his side and began to twirl Mici's long red-gold hair around them one by one.

"However, although we do seek applicants without experience, we do screen them very carefully. We require good background and education, some interest in the arts, and an indication of a creative imagination. Ours is a creative profession."

"You found all that in Eugene Tully?" Mici couldn't help blurting it out.

"Well, no," Witte admitted with the first trace of humor he'd shown. "However, personal charm is an asset in our business, and our Eugene had plenty of that. So we gave him a chance."

At last he'd called it a business, Mici thought, or had it been a slip? Anyhow, he'd dropped his hauteur and was more relaxed. "And he made good," she concluded.

"He certainly did, though for a while . . ." Tyrone Witte turned his hand from side to side indicating uncertainty. "As I said, Eugene had a lot to learn and I don't mean just cutting hair. We taught him, but you wouldn't believe what we started with. In Eugene we just about had a male Eliza Doolittle." The older man chuckled indulgently. "Eugene had no manners, no manners at all. Part of the job of making a woman look beautiful is to make her feel beautiful. At first, Eugene was disconcertingly honest, then blatantly obvious. Subtlety was foreign to his nature."

"But he did learn?"

"Oh, definitely. He became exceedingly popular, a credit to the salon and, if I may say it, to my instruction."

"I'm sure that's so." Mici tilted her head sideways to smile at Witte. "Tully seems to have been a sensitive person, and a compassionate one," she added. "The way he went to the aid of that little girl certainly showed compassion."

"What it shows is that he was still a country boy and didn't know any better."

"Oh?"

"He got killed for his trouble, didn't he?"

"The police aren't sure. They aren't sure just how serious the incident was."

Witte shrugged. "I suppose they know their business."

Mici wondered just how much the salon manager had heard about the encounter. "Did he talk to you about it?"

"Yes, he did. And he took it seriously, I assure you. He said the girls were vicious."

Here was corroboration for Faith's version! Mici hid her elation. "Was he afraid for his safety?"

Tyrone Witte hesitated; even his fingers paused momentarily in their work. "No, I don't think so," he decided. "I think he considered it a nasty incident and was relieved that it was over. I don't think he would have been in such a hurry to get involved on another occasion, though."

Naturally, the girls and their parents would downplay the whole thing, but Tully's interpretation was certainly as valid as theirs, Mici thought, and made a mental note to suggest to Detective Stiebeck that he discuss it with Eugene Tully's boss.

"As I understand it, a lot of Eugene Tully's work was done at the client's own home?"

"Most of our stylists take outside assignments," Witte told her. "Our clients are women who are constantly in the limelight, and nothing affects a woman's appearance so much as the way her hair looks. To such a woman the attendance of a trusted and talented stylist with whom she enjoys a good rapport is invaluable. Did you know that Sanda Florescu took Eugene with her to the White House?"

"Really?"

"Yes. Madame Florescu was invited to perform at a state dinner in honor of visiting dignitaries from the Iron Curtain countries, because she is Rumanian—"

"Yes, I know."

"Well, she insisted that Eugene accompany her to do her hair for the concert. It was a great honor for him and for Salon Chéri."

"It must have cost her plenty."

The manager winced. "She had to reimburse the salon for his time, of course."

Evidently the honor did not wipe out the bill. "I suppose that she also had to pay Eugene's travel expenses."

"Certainly."

"And tip him?"

"It's customary."

Witte's fingers flew and soon Mici's head was a bristling armature of wire rollers. He was just about finished and would be placing her under a dryer, where she'd be effectively incommunicado. Though there was still the combing out, the essence of the stylist's art, Witte might not then be in the same cooperative mood. Worse, he would have had time to wonder about her credentials as a writer. She'd better get what she could now.

"How did his marriage affect Mr. Eugene's popularity?"

"Now, Miss Anhalt, you're asking me about Eugene's personal life and his relation with his clients. How can I answer that?" He was almost jovial. "Is that within the scope of your article about Mrs. Tully?"

"Natural curiosity, Mr. Witte. Everybody enjoys a little gossip."

"Do you print gossip, Miss Anhalt?"

Tyrone Witte had characterized Tully as charming, but he had plenty of charm himself. His attitude toward the victim was that of indulgent patron toward protégé. Was it just a little overdone? Mici wondered how much jealousy there was under that façade and if she could sting him enough to make him show his real feelings. Witte was now inserting a row of clips along the nape of her neck.

"I would think that Mr. Eugene's marriage would be bound to affect his clients' attitude toward him, no matter what the relationship," Mici said. "It says a lot for Tully that he was willing to risk losing some of his prestigious clients in order to go back and marry his childhood sweetheart. It shows integrity, a solid sense of values."

Witte moistened his rather fleshy lips. One more clip to go. He held it posed between thumb and forefinger. Mici held her breath.

"He had to marry her."

She let it out in a gasp.

"He had no choice. Down there, where they both come from, they take such things very seriously."

"But, I understood that he went down with the express purpose of marrying her. In fact, I understood that Faith's father was very much opposed to the marriage."

"Who told you that?"

"Faith."

"I got my version from Eugene."

Tyrone Witte slid the last clip into place, pulled the dryer over, and positioned it above Mici's head. Before she could think of anything more to say, the heat had been turned on.

When the timer rang, it was Mr. Randolph who took her out and combed her. His tight-lipped manner barred any attempt at conversation.

When she went to pay her bill, Mici forgot everything else. Forty-five dollars for a wash and set? And she'd actually been thinking that Mr. Witte might put it on the house and she would have to insist on paying. Wow! On top of that, she'd have to leave at least five bucks for the taciturn Mr. Randolph. Mici grimaced; there was no way she could put it on the swindle sheet, no way. This little foray into detection had cost her fifty bucks. While she made out the check, Mici looked past the cashier into the wall mirror at the back of the desk. Her red-blonde hair was piled on top of her head and gathered into a tight corkscrew knot; little dumb wisps stuck out all around the hair line, front and back; she looked either like a scrubwoman or a cancan girl. Fifty bucks and she couldn't wait to get home and tear the whole thing down.

As for Tyrone Witte's version of Eugene and Faith's marriage, it didn't have to be true. She could see no reason for the manager to lie, but Tully might have lied. If Gene Tully had been performing additional, very personal services for his ladies, then he'd have to offer some kind of explanation for running down to West Virginia and coming back with a bride.

Going down there herself to the Tullys' hometown wasn't going to prove anything one way or the other. Faith's family and Gene's would each tell the version that suited them. She'd look up Faith's doctor. Mici sighed lugubriously. For fifty bucks all she'd accomplished was to pile more doubt on Faith Tully's already shaky story.

Mici was through role-playing. From now on she was who she was and she'd make the best of it. Besides, she figured that Helene Kalb was too smart to fall for anything but the truth.

According to the society columns, Mrs. Kalb was svelte, charming, and dynamic. She was not displaying these qualities for the benefit of an investigator from the Crime Compensation Board. She looked older than her pictures and tired. Maybe she wasn't up to the effort, or maybe she didn't consider another woman worth it. At any rate, she received Mici Anhalt in a small sitting room on the second floor of the Sutton Place townhouse in a markedly listless manner.

"My office." She gestured around the room deprecatingly and sat down at her desk, an ornate, spindle-legged, heavily gilded, rococo showpiece.

"Thank you for seeing me, Mrs. Kalb," Mici began, but was not allowed to continue.

"I've already made a statement to the police. I would have thought you'd refer to that."

"Our interests are somewhat different," the investigator explained. "The police are naturally concerned with finding the perpetrator of the crime. We want to help the victim of the crime, in this case the victim's widow, Faith Tully."

Helene Kalb considered, then decided to display some of the charm for which she was famous. "How can I help?"

Having decided in advance that she would be honest, as honest as reasonably possible, Mici could reply promptly. "I'm not sure. It's been suggested that Mrs. Tully might be guilty, that she might have killed her husband."

Helene Kalb showed no reaction either way. "I thought Gene was beaten up by some girl gang."

"The police have not been able to prove that allegation." Mici didn't mention that they had all but disproved it; honesty didn't require her to be so explicit.

"If Mrs. Tully is guilty, then surely she isn't eligible for compensation, is she?"

"No, ma'am, she wouldn't be," Mici very carefully corrected.

Helene Kalb waited. "You will get to the point, won't you, Miss Anhalt?"

Mici obliged. "Jealousy has been put forward as a possible motive for Mrs. Tully's having committed the crime. Eugene Tully may have been having an affair with one of his clients."

The dark eyes widened. "Me? You don't mean me? You can't possibly!" She began to laugh. "The senator will be so amused." She laughed a little more. "The senator and I are happily married, have been for twenty-four years. That's a very long time, and in all that time neither of us has felt the need for any other partner. But if I were looking for a lover, I have a very wide field from which to choose, a very distinguished list of candidates. I am not so hard up that I would have to get myself a shampoo boy for a stud."

Mici had not expected that kind of bluntness from Seymour Kalb's lady. "He was a shampoo boy?"

"Don't they all start that way?" The lady shrugged and chose another attitude. "Of course, Gene was an absolute genius with hair. *Fantastique.* I absolutely depended on him. When he stopped making house calls, I was completely *éeperdue.*"

"He stopped? When?"

"When he first returned from his honeymoon. The little bride objected." Her lips formed a moue of pity. "She wanted him home nights. Of course, it was only natural, charming, and I understood, but it was not convenient. I told Gene that he could hardly expect me to fit into his schedule and run down to the salon for the privilege of having him arrange my hair. If he didn't find it *agréable* to come to me in my home when I required him, he could forget about my custom altogether. Wonderful as he was, he was hardly the only hairdresser in the world, or even in New York."

"So he resumed his house calls?"

"I was very generous with Gene, not that he wasn't worth it. He could hardly afford to lose me."

"He did resume?"

"My dear Miss Anhalt, you know he did. You must know that it was on his way home from our reception that he was murdered."

"I understood he was a guest."

Her face froze. "He came to do my hair." The smile fought its way back. "Gene was always welcome to stay afterward if he cared to."

"May I ask what time he left?"

"I really don't know, Miss Anhalt. There were over one hundred people here, very important people, friends of my husband's, members of the UN, dignitaries in all branches of government . . ."

"Yes, I understand. Perhaps—"

Helene Kalb had had enough. "I really don't know what more I can tell you, Miss Anhalt, and I do have a luncheon appointment."

I really don't know what more I can ask you that you would answer, Mici thought. "May I speak to your butler?"

"Fulton? Fulton is our houseman. Yes, of course, speak to whomever you like."

There was a light knock on the door and a man walked in. Mici recognized him instantly from his pictures.

"Sorry, darling." Senator Kalb planted a kiss on his wife's cheek. "Fulton didn't mention you had a visitor."

"Miss Anhalt is just leaving."

"Oh?"

Seymour Kalb was even better-looking in person. About sixty, lean, fit, his rugged face had the healthy color of a man who spent plenty of time outdoors, but the lines around his thoughtful, gray eyes suggested an intellectual. As he turned those eyes on her, Mici felt the full charge of his attention course through her like an electric current. Call it charm, charisma, or plain old sex appeal, it was irresistible. Maybe after twenty-four years it had gone stale for Helene Kalb, maybe the senator dispensed his charm elsewhere and his lady had been driven to seek consolation with Tully, but at the moment Mici only knew that she found the senator devastating.

Seymour Kalb extended his hand and gripped Mici's. "Please don't hurry off on my account."

His wife broke it up. "Miss Anhalt is investigating the Tully case on behalf of the Crime Victims Compensation Board."

"Is that so?" It increased his interest. "You're doing good work down there. We're in the process of passing a federal law to assist victims of crime. I suppose you know that? Under it the state will be reimbursed fifty percent of what it pays out. In essence, that means you'll have more money to work with."

"Yes, sir."

Mrs. Kalb had stopped trying to shove Mici out, so now they stood around smiling at one another. Well, she thought, here was a marvelous opportunity to further the cause.

"It isn't money we need the most, Senator."

"I never heard of a government agency that didn't need money."

"What I mean, sir, is that we need to have the public know about us. Rather, about the program. All the money in the world isn't going to help if the victim doesn't know it's available."

"What do you suggest?" Kalb's smile was encouraging.

"The victim should be informed of his right to compensation in the same way a criminal is informed of his right to be silent and to have an attorney—by the police."

"Seems logical. Of course, then there would be many, many more applicants, and you would in turn require a great deal more money."

"True." She smiled.

"Also, its a local decision; it can't be legislated in Washington. On the other hand, I do have some influence at the city level. We'll see what can be done." He held out his hand and this time it was a parting handshake.

Mici floated down the marble staircase and out the front door of the townhouse in a euphoric daze. Senator Kalb was an influential man and if he really kept his word . . . wouldn't that be something? Not till she reached the corner of York Avenue heading for the bus stop did the investigator realize that she hadn't spoken to the houseman. Should she go back? Would it be an intrusion on the luncheon party the Kalbs were giving? Mici decided she could see Fulton at another time.

All she'd wanted was to find out what time Eugene Tully had left the party on Friday night and if he happened to mention where he was going. Also, if he'd been using his car.

Probably Detective Stiebeck had already asked.

Sanda Florescu had presence. On stage, she was exciting; at close range overwhelming. Mici had always admired the diva. She had seen her in *Tales of Hoffman* playing all three of the heroines, singing them magnificently and acting them with verve and as much variety as could have been provided by three individual performers. Now, meeting her in the sun-filled living room that overlooked Central Park, Mici Anhalt felt swamped by her energy.

She had only to state the reason for her visit and Madame responded as though on cue.

"Ah, my poor Eugène, what a tragic end!" Sanda Florescu exclaimed, giving the name a French pronunciation. The rest of her speech was accented only slightly and the accent was not so easily recognizable. Mici dubbed it as European. Madame continued, "One reads about such atrocities every day, of course, and deplores them, but one is not touched —here." She tapped the ample area of her bosom. "Not until it happens to someone close."

She was a voluptuous woman with broad features, not photogenic, but striking on stage, and flaming red hair. She was wearing a flowing djellaba of violet silk, and the contrast with the mass of her hair was stunning. Tears shimmered in her green eyes and her wide mouth quivered slightly. She was playing a scene; Mici knew it, and was lost in admiration while at the same time not doubting her sincerity.

By contrast, Doru Florescu was so unimpressive that Mici wasn't aware that the star's husband was present until he spoke.

"When Madame says that Eugène was close to her, she means in a professional sense, of course."

"Of course," Mici echoed. She knew about Doru Florescu, as did everyone interested not merely in opera but in headline personalities. Doru was his wife's manager. He had nurtured her talent and subjugated everything to her career, divorcing his first wife and giving up his own business. Mici knew before she saw him that he was a nondescript, short, balding man with a pot belly and that the whole world marveled at the strength of their ties. Sanda Florescu clung to this undistinguished little man with a fierce loyalty that the celebrity watchers found close to incredible. Now that she saw for herself just how ordinary Doru Florescu was and how magnificent the prima donna, Mici marveled too. And admired.

"Madame feels a warm rapport for everyone who works with her, from members of the company to stagehands and wardrobe people. Even tenors," he added with a shy smile.

Mici laughed louder than the gentle joke required.

"We consider everyone connected with a performance, whose skills contribute to the final effect, an artist and a friend. We loved Eugène for his talent, but we knew little about his personal life," Doru concluded.

Having permitted her husband and manager to make the statement, much as he might have during a press interview, Madame now took over. "But you've heard talk, eh, Miss Anhalt?"

"Well . . ."

"You've heard stories, eh? About me and a certain baritone? Perhaps about me and the new Armenian conductor? So you think, maybe her hairdresser, too? Why not? He was a good-looking young man. Quite beautiful, in fact."

"I did wonder."

"Of course." Sanda Florescu's laughter trilled. "That is part of the image, Miss Anhalt. We nurture it, Doru and I, to titillate the public. Would they be interested to know that after a performance I am too spent, both emotionally and physically, to do more than have a light snack, perhaps a glass of champagne, and go straight to bed? I don't think so. They want to hear about orgies. Unfortunately, one's offstage performance has to be as exciting as the one onstage to hold the public's interest. As it is, people find it difficult to understand our placid life together." She looked at her husband. "Because they lack devotion in their own lives they cannot understand it in ours. Putting me on the level of their own needs, they assume that I'm unfaithful."

She went on. "It is a popular misconception that sex embellishes the voice, colors it. Shall I tell you what sustains the voice? Rest, diet and practice, practice, practice. As for the aura, the bloom they talk about— that comes with the applause. When an artist hears that, when the house gets to its feet in acclaim, that love from across the footlights is what nourishes the art. As for the other kind"—she held out her hand to her husband who came over and took it—"I have never lacked for it and I know that I never will.

"But I do enjoy playing the game. I like to be surrounded by attractive men; isn't that better than being surrounded by ugly men? I like sexy men and sexy books and sexy movies. I like to flirt. It's fun, it's good for the ego, keeps a woman on her toes. But beyond that, I don't play games."

Her green eyes were fixed on her husband, and he raised her hand, turned it palm side up, and kissed it.

Mici felt as though she were intruding until she reminded herself that this woman was used to displaying her emotions, and her husband was accustomed to watching while she did so.

"Do you think Mrs. Tully might have misunderstood your relationship with Eugene?" She almost pronounced it the diva's way.

"I made certain she would not." Sanda Florescu frowned and then paused to clear the lines from her brow. "I invited her to a performance of *La Fille du Régiment*; I thought that would be within her understanding. Oh, please, I don't mean to belittle her intellect," she hastened to explain. "But it was her first opera, and I wanted her to enjoy herself.

Afterward, when she came backstage, I did my best to draw her out, but it wasn't easy. The poor child was painfully shy."

Mici could well imagine that Faith Tully had felt eclipsed. "It was nice of you to go to all that trouble."

"Not at all. It was selfish. I didn't want to lose Eugène. He had told me that now he was married he wouldn't be available outside the salon— not for the theater or special concerts or out of town, least of all that. I wanted his bride to be satisfied that our relationship was absolutely professional."

"And was she satisfied?"

Madame shrugged. "There was no more talk about Eugène not being available. In fact, he dressed my hair for the television taping of *Traviata* on the very day he was killed." Her voice broke slightly.

"How long did the taping last? I hope you don't mind my asking?"

"Why should I? We worked until . . . about eight that night." She glanced at her husband for confirmation.

He nodded.

"How long did Eugene stay?"

Again Madame looked to Doru.

"Normally, he would have seen Madame through the entire session, but he had an evening appointment to attend Mrs. Kalb, so we excused him at about six," he replied.

"And what did you do after the taping was completed?" Mici asked.

The star answered. "It had been a very exhausting day. We had dinner with a few members of the cast, then came back here for a nightcap and then to bed. It couldn't have been later than eleven when we retired."

"It was just ten before eleven," her husband offered. "I remember because I had to get up very early the next morning and I set my alarm."

At ten of eleven Gene Tully had been very much alive and enjoying himself at the Kalbs' reception. Mici got up. "May I ask just one more question? What will you do now for a hairstylist?"

"Ah . . ." Sanda Florescu sighed. "We were in fact just discussing that, Doru and I. You must not think us unfeeling. Probably, we will go back to Tyrone, Tyrone Witte. He does not have Eugène's flair, but he does have a certain elegance of his own."

CHAPTER VIII

There was cheerful solicitude from nurses, interns, and the other patients on the floor as Ramón Lara was made ready to go home, but it was subtly different from the bustle that surrounded the usual release of a patient. Though he didn't show it, the tennis player was acutely aware of it. As for Diane Lara, her jaws ached from smiling; she was afraid that if she ever unfroze that smile she wouldn't be able to hold back the tears. What she wanted more than anything at this moment was to go somewhere by herself, close the door, and just bawl, yell, scream out the unfairness of it! Well, there would be time later, plenty of time. For now, having packed Ramón's bag, she went around saying good-by to people whose names she didn't know and about whom she didn't care just to keep herself busy while the nurse helped Ramón dress. He hadn't wanted her around; he had been curt about it. At home, of course, he'd have to accept her help, he'd have no one else, but then there wouldn't be anyone to witness his dependency.

And yet they were lucky.

The doctor had talked to them both at the same time. Each one needed to be reassured that nothing was being held back, and this was Dr. Clarence Rudel's way of doing it. According to Dr. Rudel, Ramón had had a narrow escape. A slight deviation in the path of the bullet and he would have been permanently paralyzed from the waist down. Rudel didn't dwell on what might have been but on what was or, with diligence and determination, could be. Lara could walk again. It would take work, hard work, progress would be slow, but the prognosis was favorable. While he would need help to function, Diane would be taught how to provide it. She would also be taught some simple massage to keep his leg muscles from atrophying.

Dr. Rudel did not mention whether Ramón Lara would ever play tennis again. Neither Ramón nor Diane asked.

So, finally, Ramón was dressed, transferred from bed to wheelchair, his bags packed, his bills paid, courtesy of his friends in the Association of Tennis Professionals who had taken up a collection. The secretary of the association handed the check to Diane because he knew about Ramón's pride.

"Play it by ear," he told her. "If you don't want to tell him where the money came from, don't. Whatever you think is best. We leave it to you."

"He should know that he has friends," she replied. "But maybe not right away. When he's feeling better, when he's starting to get around . . ."

But Ramón demanded to know. "How are we getting out of here?"

"We'll get a cab."

"You know what I mean. How are we going to pay the bill?"

She explained hesitantly, then winced in anticipation of the tirade.

"That was nice of the guys," he acknowledged. "They owe me, of course," he added, "but it was nice just the same."

Diane breathed a sigh of relief. She hoped that now they would get out of the hospital without Ramón getting upset, but just as they were leaving, as the orderly helped Ramón into the taxi and was folding the rented wheelchair and placing it in the front with the driver, a student nurse in her distinctive striped jumper, all bouncy curves and no brains, came dashing down the steps.

"Oh, Ramón, Ramón, I'm so glad I caught you!" She was breathless; her eyelashes fluttered coyly. "I won't say good-bye, just *arrivederci*. We'll be seeing you soon, real soon."

Diane could have slapped her. Her stomach tightened into a hard knot and the pain shot through her. Dumb, dumb, how could she be so dumb as to remind Ramón of what everybody else had so very carefully been trying to make him forget—that he would have to come back. That the ordeal was far from over. That he was going home to recover from surgery but then he would be back for extended therapy. Somehow Diane managed to take time getting into the taxi and to place herself in such a way as to block Ramón from the student nurse. Much as the girl deserved it, Diane did not want Ramón to snap the girl's head off. It would ruin Ramón's mood and he'd stay irritable for the rest of the day.

Ramón didn't say a single word. He waited till she had no choice but to settle in her seat, then he leaned across her.

"*Arrivederci*, Patty. I'll be looking for you."

He waved and smiled. He actually smiled. Diane could hardly believe it.

"Aren't you going to shut the door?" he asked, then gave the driver their address in a firm voice that indicated he had taken over.

After that, they were silent for the rest of the ride, but it was not an uncomfortable silence. Ramón appeared withdrawn, thoughtful, and perhaps a little tired, which was only natural, considering the excitement of leaving the hospital and the exertion involved. A couple of times Diane stole a glance at him. He was so thin; his jacket hung pathetically loose and his proud face was shrunken. She no longer let herself even glance down at his legs. Once or twice, Diane was on the verge of speaking, of saying something, anything, but she was afraid to destroy Ramón's composure. To offer hope when she had so little would have been dishonest and he'd know it; to offer false cheerfulness would be an admission that she had no hope. So the silence became a refuge, as it had been so often before between these two. Then, unexpectedly, Ramón reached over and put his hand over hers and left it there till they reached the dingy, yellow-brick apartment building in the Cobble Hill section of Brooklyn.

As the cab pulled up, the front door opened and Hans Ritter, the superintendent, came running out. Just before leaving the hospital, Diane had called Mr. Ritter asking him to be on hand to help her and the taxi driver transfer Ramón to the wheelchair and then into the building and the elevator. There was no way around it; Ramón was obliged to accept that much help. Now, as she saw the array of neighbors assembling, she felt a cold anticipation of the worst. Evidently Hans Ritter had spread the word, and she had most insistently warned him not to do that. She suppressed a sigh of dismay. Half the neighborhood had turned out.

Ritter hurried forward, opened the taxi door, and as he helped her out, explained softly. "It was in the papers that he was coming home, Mrs. Lara. I tried to stop them. I told them he'd be tired, just like you said."

"Don't worry about it, Mr. Ritter." The damage was done. Looking back into the cab, she tried to indicate to Ramón with a gesture of both hands palms out that she'd had nothing to do with the demonstration and that she deplored it. Again, he surprised her.

"The chair's up front, Mr. Ritter, if you'd be good enough to give the driver a hand and set it up!" He smiled at his neighbors; he waved. The short trip across the sidewalk became a triumphal procession. He shook hands; he seemed to know everybody's name and greeted them all and thanked them all for their concern. When they got him upstairs and into the apartment, he made no bones about needing Ritter's help to transfer to the bed.

"I'm kind of tired; I think I'd like to rest. If you could just give me a hand, Mr. Ritter?"

And then at last and inevitably they were alone in the small, shabby apartment. Diane stood uncertainly beside the bed. No need to draw the blinds; they were on a narrow court and the whole apartment was always in shadow.

"Anything I can do for you?"

"Yes." He pointed through the open door at the bookcases in the living room. "Clean the trophies; they look terrible."

It had always been one of her pleasures to keep the collection of his trophies shining, but since the shooting and the uncertainty about his ever playing again, she hadn't known what to do—keep polishing them or store them away out of sight? She'd ended up doing neither.

"Oh, Ramón . . ."

"*Querida.*"

He held out his hand to her, but before she could take it, the telephone rang. It was on the night table, but he indicated she was to answer.

"Hello? Oh, yes, Mrs. Pell, of course I remember you. . . . yes, he is. We just got back this minute. . . . Well, he's tired. I don't think this is really a good time. . . ."

"What? What does she want?"

Diane waved for him to be quiet. "You're checking to make sure we received the subpoena? I don't know; I haven't seen today's mail yet. I'll have to go down. . . . When is the hearing? . . . That's only two days from now. I don't think he can make that, Mrs. Pell. It's much too soon. . . . Yes, I know it's important, but . . . I realize he's the only witness. . . ."

Ramón tapped her shoulder. "Give me the phone."

She pulled back and covered the mouthpiece with one hand. "No. Let them postpone it, Ramón. They can do that. Why not? They can do that much for you."

"Give it to me. Give me the phone. If you don't, I'll just call her back."

Reluctantly she put the receiver in his hand.

"Hello, Mrs. Pell? This is Ramón Lara." His voice was strong, assured. "Yes, I am much better, thank you. It's good to be home. Now about this hearing . . . oh, it's the grand jury. Well, can you provide transportation? . . . There's a van? Good. Then you can count on me. . . . A line-up? No, it wouldn't be too much. . . . Not at all, Mrs. Pell, thank you." He hung up.

"You've already identified his picture," Diane objected. "You'll see him in court. Why do you have to pick him out of a line-up?"

"They want to make double sure it's him, and so do I. I have to do this. I have to get that lousy kid. I'm sorry, but I don't forgive him. There's no pity in my heart. None. He had his fun; now he can pay for it. If it's the last thing I do in this world, I'm going to see that he pays for it." Color surged into his face; his eyes blazed with the determination with which he'd faced his opponents on the court in the days when he'd been a winner. Long ago. Gradually, the energy generated by desire for revenge was spent, but in its place there formed a deep tenderness for the woman beside him who remembered those days and still cherished him, though they were long gone.

"Sit down." He patted the edge of the bed. "Now," he said when she was settled. "We've always managed somehow, haven't we? We've had rough times, but we've always pulled through. Haven't we?"

"Yes, Ramón." The tears brimmed in her eyes.

"We'll pull through this time."

It was too much. She had been so determined not to let him see her cry, but she couldn't hold the tears back. She bit her lips and still the tears rolled down. "I'm sorry, Ramón. I'm sorry. . . ."

"Cry, *mi vida*, cry. It will do you good. But when you're through crying, call that woman—what's her name? At the compensation board?"

"Miss Anhalt?"

"Yes. Call her. Tell her I want to talk to her. She was so eager to give us money, let's find out when we're going to get it."

All day Diane had been waiting for release; all day she had been waiting to shed her tears, but she had not expected that she would be crying out of relief and, yes, out of joy.

Tears are not kind even to beauty, and Diane required constant vigilance, rest, and exercise to maintain an illusion of it. The tears undid all her work. Ramón reached for her, pulled her to him so that her ravaged face was hidden against his shoulder, then he could remember her as she had been, a pretty young matron, rich, a little spoiled, coyly resisting his advances. It had been a challenge to break down her resistance.

He pressed his lips to her fading blonde hair. "It's going to be all right, *querida*. I promise you."

For once Mr. Creedy wasn't smiling. If anyone had stopped to ask him what was wrong, he would have replied that he had a headache. After all kinds of tests, the doctors had concluded that Simon Creedy had suffered merely a mild concussion and had advised rest. But the headaches were getting worse. He awoke in the morning with a band of pressure around his skull; as the day progressed, the pressure increased. It eased only when he went to visit his former charges. He wasn't supposed to be working, but he didn't consider it work; these people were his friends, and anyhow, he wasn't getting paid. Then somebody snitched—the field worker who had replaced him, probably—and Miss Pallo found out. She had been very angry about it; she'd shouted at Mr. Creedy. Remembering made him wince and the throbbing in his head became more painful, almost unbearable. She had scolded him as though he were a child and had absolutely forbidden him to continue. After the outburst, she'd calmed down enough to explain that the decision wasn't hers, that it came from the agency head. It wasn't a matter of Mr. Creedy's not being able to carry out his duties, but that they were afraid he would injure or overexert himself. The agency couldn't be responsible. No matter what assurances he offered, Miss Pallo remained obdurate. It was a matter of policy. They couldn't take the risk. She was sorry, but she had her orders. She'd said a lot more, about how everybody liked Mr. Creedy, how he'd be missed, and about how his job would be waiting for him when he felt better. The old man didn't even bother to listen to that part. Miss Isabel Pallo was still talking when he walked out of her office.

The park was bleak and chill. Mr. Creedy felt the damp cold right through his quilted jacket. Though the Christmas snows had long since disappeared from the streets and paths, some vestiges still remained on the grass and around the bases of sheltered shrubs; the lowering sky portended more snow to come. Climbing a slight rise, Mr. Creedy looked out across the Sheep Meadow. Empty. There was only that nice silver-haired woman with the two miniature poodles, one black and one white; he recognized her from her walk as well as from the dogs. She was a regular. She spent at least a couple of hours in the park every day, and though he didn't know her name, he knew the names of the dogs: Pinocchio and Shakespeare. Today, though, Creedy didn't feel like conversing with a civilian; what he wanted was to sit for a while in the warmth of the Mineral Springs House and rap with his old buddies. He tried the door; locked. Only three-thirty and everybody was gone? Then he remembered that it was New Year's Eve; well, they'd sneaked out early. Why not? Creedy sighed. If old Sol Jacobson were still alive, they would have spent the evening together, played chess, shared a bottle of sherry. Mr. Creedy hadn't bought any sherry since the incident. He wasn't going to get any for tonight either. Just passing a liquor store made him nervous. Knowing it was useless, he tried the metal door once again, and while he stood there not knowing what to do with himself, he heard the yapping of dogs and a woman yelling. He ran in the direction of the noise. He turned the corner of the refreshment stand just in time to see a couple of boys throwing stones at the two poodles.

"You stop that!" he shouted. "You leave those dogs alone!" From a pile of dead branches recently pruned and waiting for collection, he selected a thick, gnarled limb and ran toward them.

Simon Creedy wasn't exactly sure what he would do when he reached the boys, but they didn't wait. They fled. The blond woman was down on her knees, circling the two dogs with her arms and consoling them.

"Oh, my poor darlings, my little angels, don't be frightened. The boys are gone. The bad boys ran away." Then she looked up. "Mr. Creedy, I can't thank you enough. I don't know what would have happened if you hadn't come along. I can't thank you enough."

"That's all right. I'm glad I was here, really glad. Are they okay?" He indicated the poodles.

"Yes. Thanks to you, yes."

Suddenly Mr. Creedy gasped and pointed to her forehead. "You're bleeding. You've been cut. You're bleeding."

She put a hand up to feel, then regarded her bloodied fingertips in puzzlement. "I didn't even realize."

"You should see a doctor."

"It's nothing."

"You never know," he insisted. Then he had an inspiration. "You could put in for the doctor's fee. Did you know that? Did you know that here's a place that helps victims of crime. Crime Victims Compensation Board, it's called."

"I'm not exactly a victim of a crime."

"Of course you are. They're so nice down there; you have no idea." Mr. Creedy warmed to the subject. "If you want, I could go down and get one of their forms for you to fill out. Would you want me to do that?"

"I really don't think it's necessary, Mr. Creedy. Look, the bleeding has nearly stopped."

"I have to go down anyway to find out how my claim is coming. I could just as well pick up a form for you."

"If you're going anyway . . ."

"Yes, I am."

"Well, it's very kind of you."

"My pleasure." Mr. Creedy was smiling his sweet smile once again. He didn't even think about his headache; he wasn't even aware that it was gone.

Chapter IX

"Methinks the ladies do protest too much—both of them,"Mici paraphrased.

It was the next morning. She was sitting in the supervisor's office and they were sharing the coffee and jelly doughnuts that were becoming a ritual for these early-morning consultations. Dowd was weary and depressed; the New Year's Eve celebration had turned into a disaster. His wife had passed out at the club party, simply slid off her chair to the floor. Dowd, with the help of the club manager, had carried her out while the members clucked false sympathy that masked censure. New Year's Day had been spent listening to the litany of Elaine's penance and watching as she became progressively gloomier at the realization that he wasn't going to let her get to the booze—not that day, not while he was around to stop her. It was a relief for Adam Dowd to get back to the office, to be looking at Mici Anhalt's pretty and intense young face.

As for the investigator, New Year's Eve had been nothing great, but not bad either. Roz and Charlie had a few people over, and Roz, having found out that Mici and Danny had broken up, provided a young lawyer from Legal Aid for Mici. Clyde Lauer turned out to be less grimly career oriented than most of Roz's candidates, and Mici found herself liking him. He made a mild pass at her when he took her home, but he wasn't hard to discourage. He called the next day. They went skating at the Wollman Rink in Central Park and had an early dinner together. The whole thing was very low key, the scene so different from Miami, his manner so different from Danny's, that she almost forgot what she was missing. She was grateful to Clyde Lauer for the absence of stress. Undoubtedly Roz had given Clyde a rundown on her situation and warned him not to push, and that was why he'd turned down her invitation to come in for a nightcap. Not that Mici intended jumping into bed with Lauer, but she liked to make her own decisions. A little talk with Roz was in order.

Right now she was concerned with bringing Adam up to date on the Tully case.

"In her own way each one of them, Mrs. Kalb and Madame Florescu, was very anxious to convince me that there hadn't been anything between her and Gene Tully, and that as far as she was concerned, Faith Tully had no cause for jealousy."

"Do you think that Tully was having an affair with either or both?" Dowd asked.

"Who knows? What bothers me is the interval immediately after Tully returned from his honeymoon. It seems he informed clients that he couldn't see them privately anymore, that he would be available only during business hours at the salon. They both mentioned that."

"Sounds like he was trying to break off."

"But when they told him, both of them, that he could either continue as before or they'd get somebody else, take it or leave it, he changed his mind."

"Couldn't afford to lose their business?"

"That's their version," Mici said.

"I suppose it seemed odd to Faith Tully for her husband to be attending his clients in their homes at all sorts of hours."

Mici sighed, "According to the salon manager, Tyrone Witte, Tully married Faith because he had to."

Dowd's lips formed a silent whistle and his eyes asked the obvious question.

"I talked to her doctor," Mici replied. "She was eight months pregnant. They were married six months ago."

No comment from Dowd.

"That doesn't mean Gene Tully didn't love her. Would he have tried to break off with his special clients if he didn't care?"

"Maybe she demanded it."

"I don't see that girl demanding anything; she was absolutely besotted with Tully. Besides which, I don't see Tully giving in to any demand if he didn't want to."

For a while they just drank coffee and nibbled at the oozing pastry.

"Have you passed the information on to Detective Stiebeck?" the supervisor asked.

Mici was completely absorbed in not dripping jelly on the desk. When she had carefully wiped her mouth, she answered, "I figure he already knows."

"Well, just in case he doesn't, you better tell him."

"I really don't see that it has any bearing. What does it matter whether or not Gene Tully was forced into the marriage? Faith loved him; she wanted to marry him. I know that for sure. She loved him and was carrying his child. You can't ignore that. How could she kill him when she was carrying his child?"

"They could have quarreled. She could have been provoked beyond her endurance."

"Then why did she scream for help?"

"Because as soon as she'd done it, she was sorry."

How many things had he himself said and done and then instantly regretted, Dowd pondered. Even yesterday he'd said things to Elaine, harsh and unforgiving words that he would have taken back even while they were on his lips. Physical violence had been the next step; he'd actually had to hold himself back from striking her. Shame flooded over him. It could have happened that way for Faith Tully. If it had, he could understand and pity her, but he could not condone her trying to shift the blame to a group of innocent girls.

"We don't know that she did scream," he reminded Mici. "Nobody heard her."

She gave Dowd the same answer she'd given Ed Stiebeck. "Then why doesn't she leave it alone? Why does she keep demanding action? The police were willing to let the whole thing slide."

"I don't know. I can't explain it. What I'm concerned about is our part, our official attitude. We have to cooperate with the police. We cannot withhold information."

She nodded. "I'll call Ed."

"You're not following me all the way, Mici. It's easy enough to call Detective Stiebeck and advise him that Faith Tully was pregnant before she got married. It doesn't really prove anything about her guilt. But suppose you come up with something, real evidence, against her?"

"I won't."

Dowd gave her a long, hard look. "Leave it to the police."

"All they're doing is trying to prove she's guilty."

"Oh, come on. I don't buy that."

"They're doing a number on that girl, Adam, believe me. Stiebeck as much as admitted it. She's the only suspect they've got and they're not even looking for anybody else. I don't expect to find the killer; I'm not looking for the killer. All I'm trying to do is to direct the attention of the police toward somebody besides Faith Tully."

Dowd finished the last of his pastry, drank the lukewarm dregs of the coffee, and wiped his mouth with the paper napkin. Then he collected the debris and dropped it into the wastebasket. He did it all with deliberation because he didn't like what he had to say next.

"I don't know how much farther I can let you go with this."

Mici's clear blue eyes widened. She'd had full confidence that Adam would support her and she was not only surprised but deeply disappointed. Then she realized that the supervisor didn't like it any more than she did. The decision had obviously come from Dowd's superior, Roger Cornelius. Could Mici offer Dowd any justification for continuing the investigation that he could pass on to that higher authority? Something valid enough so that Cornelius could in turn justify it to the other members of the board? If necessary even to the governor?

"We really should not be interfering in a criminal investigation," Dowd murmured.

Interfering! The word stung. Cornelius' word, she assured herself. "I'm not interfering. I told Ed Stiebeck exactly what I intended to do, and he made no objection. None. In fact, he didn't take it seriously. He laughed. He had a really good laugh over it."

"He doesn't know you like I do."

A slight smile twitched at the corners of Mici's mouth. Her tongue flicked out and in again. "I expect to have the last laugh," she admitted. "We're investigating Faith Tully's eligibility for compensation, right? If she killed her husband, she obviously can't profit from her crime."

"Agreed. But she's not under arrest. And as long as she's not under arrest, we have to consider her innocent and treat her claim the same as anybody else's."

"Being under suspicion is prejudicial to the disposition of her claim."

"No."

"How can it help but be? No matter how hard Mr. Cornelius tries to ignore it, no matter what effort he makes to be fair, how can he forget the police suspect her of murder?"

Dowd refused to discuss it any further. "She has recourse. If she doesn't think the finding is a fair one, she can appeal to the full board. Anyhow, any finding is a long way off. By the time the claim reaches Cornelius' desk the whole question may be academic. The case will undoubtedly have been resolved." He knew it wouldn't satisfy Mici. "I'm not telling you to drop the whole thing, simply to proceed along routine lines. Make the usual inquiries. Who knows what may turn up?"

She accepted that. What choice did she have? "I'll go back to Salon Chéri and talk to the manager. I suppose Tully's salary was minimal and that he depended largely on tips. . . ." Her eyes lit up; a smile formed and grew. "Pretty hard to estimate tips. I'd have to talk to his clients again, wouldn't I? Now, Adam," she forestalled his objection. "According to the IRS, tips are income."

"Sure, but who reports them?"

"Aha! Did Tully report them? That's one of the things we should find out." She got up.

"Hold it. Wait a minute. I'm not through with you yet. How about the Lara case?"

"Oh." She sat down again. She hadn't mentioned the uncertainty of the Laras' marital status. "That's another toughie."

"I hear he's home."

"Yes, and making good progress physically and, it seems, emotionally too. Roz says he's being very cooperative. He attends every hearing, waits around the courthouse for hours without a word of complaint, never gets irritated at postponements—in other words, he's the ideal complainant."

"Good." It pleased Dowd that the tennis champion was fulfilling his expectations.

"According to Roz, the DA isn't going to accept any plea bargaining on this one. He figures all the jury has to do is take one look at Ramón Lara in the wheelchair and they'll vote for conviction. The only thing worrying the DA is that Lara may appear too vindictive. He really wants to see that kid put away."

"Who can blame him? Once the jury learns that he will probably never play tennis again . . ."

"He may never walk."

They stared at each other.

"It's going to be a long process for him to learn to take care of himself," Mici said. "At the moment, he's almost completely dependent on his . . . wife. The doctors are talking about sending him somewhere like the Kessler Institute over in Jersey so he can get psychiatric counseling as well as physical therapy."

"I thought his attitude was improving."

"It is. Very much so. But he's so focused on the coming trial and getting the hoodlum who shot him that he's not thinking beyond that. Right now it fills his whole existence. But what's going to happen when it's over? What is he going to use for motivation then? What's he going to do for a living? At the Kessler Institute they could help him make the adjustment and channel his abilities as well as his thinking."

"What's his financial status?"

"Pretty much as you figured at the start," Mici replied. "He's got all kinds of connections and all kinds of titles: vice-president of this, member of the board of that; name on the letterhead but not on the salary sheet. He gets paid if he brings in business, but evidently he hasn't been bringing in business. He's in the unfortunate position of not making enough to live on, but too much to qualify for Medicaid. That's another reason he should go to the Institute. As long as he's home, Diane has to to be there to take care of him. If he were at the Institute, she'd be free to get herself a job, maybe teaching tennis. I understand she's a pretty fair player herself."

Dowd's eyebrows went up. "So it looks like we'll be going light on the salary reimbursement, but heavy on the medical."

"I think so. There's something else . . ."

The phone on the supervisor's desk rang. He answered. At the same moment, the outer office door opened and the first wave of clerks and investigators poured through. Adam Dowd waved Mici off: the regular business day had begun.

When she got back to her own office, Mici found Simon Creedy waiting.

"Well, hello Mr. Creedy. How are you? Are you feeling better?"

His eyes lit up; he smiled his shy smile. "Oh, yes, ma'am. Yes, Miss Anhalt. A lot better. I slept just fine last night. Soon I'll be able to get back to work."

"That's marvelous. That's very good news. Did Miss . . ." It took a couple of seconds to come up with the name. "Did Miss Pallo say so?"

Creedy's smile dimmed. "Not exactly. She says I should rest a while longer."

"Maybe that would be best," Mici agreed, her mind still on the Laras, wondering if she should simply send a memo about them to Adam. "If you went back too soon, you might have a relapse." No, she decided, a memo was not adequate. She set the uncertainty aside and gave the old man at her desk her full attention.

"I'm afraid I have no news about your claim yet, Mr. Creedy. As I told you, it takes a considerable time to process, but I'm sure it's going to be fine and there won't be any difficulty in getting it approved."

"Oh, that's all right, Miss Anhalt, I didn't come about my claim." Sitting there in his ragtag assortment of clothes, a thrift-shop ensemble, Simon Creedy beamed. "I came for a friend, a very nice lady, almost as nice as you, Miss Anhalt." He bobbed his head up and down for emphasis. "I know her from the park; I've known her for years. She has two lovely little dogs, a black one and a white one, and she walks them every day, rain or shine, summer and winter. Never misses. Yesterday, some boys threw stones at the dogs and at her."

"That's terrible." Mici was sympathetic. "And she was injured? Seriously?"

"Her forehead was cut. She was bleeding. The dogs were yapping, but they're too little to scare anybody. I yelled at the boys; I told them to leave her alone. Then I got myself a big stick and I chased them away."

"Good for you, Mr. Creedy, good for you. That took a lot of courage. I'm sure your friend was very grateful. Is she too severely injured to come in to the office herself? I assume she's going to file a claim."

"Yes, ma'am, she is, but I told her I could pick up the form for her. Wasn't that all right?"

Something about the way he said it bothered Mici. What was it? She decided not to press the old boy. She opened her drawer and got out the papers. "Have your friend fill this out and she can mail it in if she wants to."

"I'll bring it in."

"You don't need to bother." She was on the verge of explaining that one way or another, sooner or later, his friend would either have to come in, or if she were not ambulatory, someone would have to go to the hospital or her home and interview her. Seeing Creedy grow anxious, she let it go. "That would be very nice of you."

"Oh, it's no trouble. I'm glad to do it, Miss Anhalt. I like to help people."

He was radiating happiness. As the day progressed and she looked back on it, Simon Creedy's pleasure seemed the only bright spot.

Mici rang the young widow's doorbell shortly after lunch.

"It's real nice to see you, Miss Anhalt, real nice. Come on in." Faith Tully's pinched, anxious face eased into a smile.

"I thought you were going to call me Mici?"

Her pleasure almost made her pretty. Despite the loose, black cotton thing that hung shapeless on her thin frame, despite her tumbled, lackluster hair and the gouged out dark circles under her brown eyes, there was something appealing about Faith Tully. It was her vulnerability, Mici decided. For all her fierce dedication to seeing her husband vindicated, she was personally timid; she was as appealing as a starving kitten suddenly presented with a bowl of milk.

"It's real nice of you to come calling, Mici."

"I'm here on business."

"You found out something!"

For a moment the investigator considered asking Faith straight out what she knew about her late husband's involvements with other women. One thing held her back: to ask might be to inform. If she didn't know or suspect, why spoil her memories?

"Nothing definite. I'm sorry."

She was disappointed, of course, but she tried not to let it show. "You're trying, that's the main thing. You're the only one that's trying." Despite her best effort, resentment crept into her eyes, destroyed what was left of the smile, and with it went any illusion that she was pretty.

"Have you heard from Detective Stiebeck?" Mici asked.

"Him?" She sniffed deprecatingly. "Not a word."

Considering the line Stiebeck was taking, that was just as well. Of course, Faith didn't know that. "I need some information about Gene's financial situation," Mici told her. "Where he banked, what kind of investments he had, life insurance...."

"He never talked about such things."

"He must have kept records."

"Everything like that would be in his desk, I guess."

So now Mici sat at the modern butcher-block-topped desk in the chrome and leather living room of the Park Avenue cooperative, trying to make sense out of Eugene Tully's finances.

"We never talked about money," Faith explained apologetically but also with a shy pride. "Gene said he didn't want me to worry my head. He set up charge accounts for me everywhere—the supermarket, the hardware store, Bloomingdale's. Told me to go ahead and get whatever I needed. He paid the bills without a word. He never complained. Never said I was spending too much."

Except that he hadn't paid the bills, Mici thought. There they all were in the deep bottom drawer of the desk, along with receipts, bankbooks, statements, contracts, salary vouchers, in no kind of order or system that she could discern. He had bought the apartment six months ago, just before he and Faith married, and already he had fallen behind in the mortgage payments. He had paid for the furnishings, but he owed on car payments. At least one minor mystery was cleared up: Tully was parking in an outdoor lot eleven blocks away because he simply couldn't afford the garage in his own building. She'd have to tell Ed. What interested Mici even more than the extent of Tully's indebtedness was the wild fluctuation of his bank balances. One day his checking account would be down to less than fifteen dollars and on the next up to over five thousand. His savings account also showed abrupt deposits and withdrawals of large sums. Where did these sums come from? No matter how appreciative of his skills the ladies might be, their tips would hardly run to four figures, not for the usual services.

"Did Gene gamble, play the horses, anything like that?" Mici asked.

Faith didn't think so.

"How are you making out now, Faith? I mean, what are you living on?"

"I have the charge accounts."

"Yes, I know, but those bills are already overdue. How are you going to pay them?"

The answer was a surprise.

"Ty's helping me out. Tyrone Witte, over to the salon? He was a real good friend of Gene's and he's paid up the biggest bills and given me a little cash to be going on with."

Tyrone Witte made light of the whole thing. "I'm just making sure she's got food in the house."

"She says you're paying her bills," Mici insisted.

"All right, I paid the maintenance on the apartment. If I hadn't, they would have thrown her out. It's not a gift. I expect to get the money back."

"I hope you will."

"Why not? Gene made good money. Once the estate is straightened out . . ."

"He seems to have spent everything he made and more. That's what I'm here for, Mr. Witte, to find out just how much Eugene Tully made and how he made it."

"How? I've already told you that most of it came from tips and that there's no way to estimate the amount."

"I'm not talking about tips, Mr. Witte. I'm talking about three, four, five thousand dollars at a time."

They were sitting in the manager's office, a small, oppressively over-decorated room whose red damask wall covering was almost obliterated by gilt-framed photographs of celebrities, most of them women and all inscribed with affectionate sentiments to "Ty" or "Tyrone."

"In talking with Madame Florescu, I learned that she had been your client before becoming Gene Tully's." Mici indicated the display. "Now I see that Helene Kalb was also one of your clients. How many others did you lose to Tully?"

"None. These ladies were my clients before I took over the franchise. When the salon became mine, I had less time for private clients, and as certain ladies were extremely demanding, I passed them on to the operator I thought would serve them best. It was Eugene."

"You taught Eugene Tully everything he knew. You passed on the cream of your clients. Now you're helping his widow out of your own pocket. You and Gene Tully must have been very close."

"Close? How do you mean, close?"

"Friends, close friends."

He thought that over. "I don't understand what you're after, Miss Anhalt. First, you come here posing as a client, then you claim that you're a journalist, now you're supposed to be some kind of investigator."

"Not supposed to be, I am, Mr. Witte. I'm sorry about misleading you before, but you can be sure of me now. I showed you my credentials."

"All right, you did, and you said that you were looking into Eugene's financial situation. Fine, but now suddenly you're prying into matters that are totally unrelated."

"Are they unrelated?" Mici fixed her clear blue eyes on the elegant Mr. Witte, with his perfectly trimmed beard and meticulously shaped and brushed eyebrows. Not a muscle of his face quivered. The only suggestion that his composure might possibly be disturbed was an unnecessary adjustment of the sleeves of his expensive burgundy velvet blazer. "You're not obliged to answer, Mr. Witte."

"I know that, but if I don't answer, you'll think I have something to hide."

"That's true," Mici admitted. "However, I'm not a police officer. What I think doesn't matter."

He frowned. Maybe he sensed Mici Anhalt's sympathy, maybe he just felt like unloading and she happened to be there. Whatever the reason, he bowed his head, covered his face with his hands, and remained so for a few moments. "Eugene Tully was a beautiful young man, but he was not gay, if that's what you're trying to find out. It might have been better if he had been, for his wife, anyway."

"What do you mean?"

"I think you know." Again he adjusted the jacket sleeves so that just the right amount of cuff showed. "He was a womanizer, the worst kind; he debased and degraded women. People think that all male hairdressers are gigolos." He shrugged, lost interest in the shirt cuffs, and looked straight at the investigator. "Sometimes it's true and sometimes it isn't. They don't usually play one infatuated woman against the other."

"Are you talking about Madame Florescu and Mrs. Kalb? Are you saying that they were bidding against each other for his favors?"

"I cannot name names, Miss Anhalt. All I can tell you is that their gifts kept getting larger and larger."

"If he was that shrewd, how did he get trapped into marriage?" she asked, accepting for the moment Witte's premise on both subjects.

"He outsmarted himself." The older man couldn't help showing a trace of satisfaction. "He went back home for some occasion, an aunt's funeral, something like that. He didn't care a damn bit; it was a chance to show off to the home folks, to let them see what a big shot he'd become. And he couldn't keep hands off the local talent, including, naturally, the old girlfriend. He couldn't bear the thought that any girl, particularly a simple, backwoods innocent like Faith, could resist him. And, of course, he finally got her, but he was accustomed to the smart ladies in the big city and he expected that she'd taken precautions. Only she hadn't."

"He must have known how her people would react. He must have known they'd insist he marry her."

Witte shrugged. "As it turned out, the marriage was very useful to him. It gave him an excuse to withhold his favors. Drove the women frantic."

"You knew what was going on?"

Removing an impeccable handkerchief from his back pocket, Witte dabbed at his face, lingering over the beard. "I warned him. I threatened to fire him, but he just laughed. He told me it was none of my business. He said if I interfered he'd leave and take half the salon's clients with him—legitimate clients, women who did not see Eugene outside but who were ardently devoted to him and wouldn't let anyone else touch their hair." He sighed. "We're not doing all that well here, Miss Anhalt. These things go in cycles: one day you're in and you can't handle all the business; the next day . . ." He laughed bitterly. "The next day you have a struggle scraping up the rent money. If Eugene had walked out, taking his clients with him, we might just as well have closed our doors."

When she had asked Sanda Florescu who would be doing her hair now that Tully was gone, the star had answered that she would probably go back to Tyrone Witte. If the other women felt the same way, then not only was Salon Chéri rid of an embarrassment while still retaining its clientele, but Witte himself was restored to the position of favorite that he'd enjoyed before the younger, handsomer man had usurped it, for she didn't for a minute buy Witte's story of willingly transferring his most illustrious customers. Was that motive enough for murder? For all his deprecations, Mici couldn't believe that the salon was doing all that badly and that Mr. Tyrone himself wasn't making a more than adequate living from it. Salon Chéri was still one of the most prestigious establishments of its kind, and as its head, Tyrone Witte's position in his own limited world was enviable. He would not let it go without a struggle.

"Besides," he added, "it is not my responsibility how clients conduct their personal affairs."

It was a strong motive, Mici decided, but if Witte were actually guilty, would he have literally handed it to her?

"Do you think Mrs. Tully knew what was going on?"

"No, I don't. I'm not saying she's stupid, but women a lot smarter were taken in by him. Shrewd women, out for their own advantage, lost all sense of reality and all sense of values when dealing with Eugene. As for the little bride, she was living in a fairy tale come true. The only decent thing I can say about Eugene is that he didn't disillusion her. In fact, he seemed to be getting a kick out of keeping her up there in the clouds. Probably it was a game with him, a novelty, pampering his wife, showing off his life-style to her, the luxuries he could afford. Game or not, I think he made her happy."

If Tyrone Witte had committed the crime, would he have missed the chance to point suspicion at someone else?

"Of course, it couldn't have lasted," he continued. "Sooner or later Eugene would have got tired of the game, bored with it. When that happened, he wouldn't even bother to lie about what was going on or pretend that he was sorry. He'd go to the other extreme: he'd flaunt the affairs, torment his wife with the details, humiliate her by reminding her that it was the proceeds of the other women's passion that fed and clothed her."

Ugly. Witte had conjured up an incredibly nasty image.

"She's lucky," he concluded, "only she doesn't know it. She's better off without him, much better off. Somebody did her a favor."

"I don't think she appreciates it."

"She will. Except for the baby, of course. That was the real tragedy, losing the baby."

His regret and pity seemed genuine, yet while championing the young widow, he had subtly laid the basis for doubting her innocence. Mici didn't know what to make of Tyrone Witte, but she was sure of one thing: he was not as guileless as he tried to appear.

At least two women had been vying for Eugene Tully's favors. He had lived on their obsession; it had inflated his pocket and his ego. Both women were his superiors, intellectually, financially, and socially, yet Mici could accept their apparently total subjugation. She'd had a friend, young, attractive, intelligent, who'd committed suicide because the married man with whom she was in love refused finally to leave his family for her. Not an unusual story. Even in these days of women's lib a man could still make a woman degrade and debase herself for love. Actually, Mici mused as she walked out of the salon to Madison Avenue, Diane Lara was a case in point. Look at the way she had thrown away her husband, home, social position. But she was lucky. Ramón Lara was a decent man who had honored his obligation and stuck with her.

Mici had already made up her mind that Faith Tully had not known about her husband's other women, but did they know about each other? Did either Sanda Florescu or Helene Kalb know that she had a rival and did she know who that rival was?

CHAPTER X

"I have no idea where Eugene got these large sums you mention; it wasn't from me. I paid him the standard fee. I can't speak for his other clients."

Sanda Florescu puckered her wide, generous mouth to show she was displeased. She'd already made it clear that Miss Anhalt's second visit was inopportune. They were leaving for Dallas in the morning to fulfill a concert engagement, Madame informed her. They were in the midst of packing—she'd waved a graceful hand toward the bedroom and Mici could see that it was, in fact, a maid who was actually performing that tiresome chore. But she nodded sympathetically.

"Do you happen to know any of his other clients?" Mici asked.

"If I did, I wouldn't tell you," the diva replied with uncharacteristic tartness. "I wouldn't want to subject anyone else to the kind of embarrassment that I am undergoing at this moment."

"I'm sorry, Madame Florescu; I'm just trying to get some information."

"I told you everything I knew on your first visit."

Leaning back into the depths of the caramel-colored velvet sofa, Sanda Florescu held center stage, as was her custom. She raised her arms and rested them along the sofa's back to display the butterfly-shaped silk sleeves of the day's costume, another djellaba, this one of varying shades of blue. The singer seemed tired and therefore older, and though she was still larger than life, her glamour seemed somewhat diminished.

"I should take offense, Miss Anhalt, but I won't. I thought I had made the situation clear to you; evidently I must explain once more. Just once more. I do not *pay* for anyone's attention. Every person who works for me, directly or indirectly, from stagehands to fellow artists, I consider a colleague and a friend. I enjoy giving my friends gifts, from time to time and according to my mood. I gave Eugène many things—cuff links, ties, a gold cigarette case—because it pleased me to do so."

"How about money?"

"Never." She took the bluntness in stride.

"Having his name linked with Sanda Florescu was worth more than cash to a young man who wanted to make a career," Doru Florescu remarked.

As usual, the diva's husband was sitting off in a corner, inconspicuous but alert to his wife's interests. "Many a young artist has flourished because Sanda's interest focused the public's attention on him. I'm sure that being the hairstylist of Madame Florescu, accompanying her to the White House, paid off handsomely for Eugène." He got up and came out of the shadows. "And now you really must excuse us, Miss Anhalt. This is my wife's rest period. As for myself, I have a great deal of work to do before we leave in the morning. In any case, neither of us has anything more to say."

At his look Madame rose obediently, albeit gracefully, nodded to Mici, and with silken robes flowing around her, withdrew into the bedroom. When she was gone, when the door was firmly shut behind her, Doru Florescu indicated that he would see Mici out. He not only accompanied her to the door but out into the hall. He stopped at the elevator, but did not press the button.

"My wife told you the absolute truth, Miss Anhalt; she never gave Eugène money. I did." His plump, pale face glistened. "I gave him three thousand dollars. To stay with her."

Mici stared. She didn't know what to say.

"If I told you that I paid to get rid of him you wouldn't have any trouble understanding that, would you?"

"No."

He swallowed. He was sweating profusely. "I intended that to be the end result, but I wanted Sanda to be the one to break off the affair. I wanted her to be the one to get tired of Eugène and to drop him as she'd dropped all the others. I wanted her to kick him out." He paused, took a deep breath. "I'm a realist, Miss Anhalt. I look in the mirror and I see an ordinary man, fat, losing his hair, whose only distinction is that he's married to a magnificent woman. Miss Anhalt, I know that my wife needs . . . other interests, and that her relationships are not always platonic. That is a convention between us to make it easier for both of us when one of these affairs ends. And they do end. Sanda comes back to me each time and comes joyously because I give her something the others do not—unselfish loyalty. I accept the situation and I'm always waiting."

"Eugene Tully disturbed the pattern."

"Exactly. He was not satisfied with the usual benefits of being linked with Sanda. All that business about his bride not wanting him to take outside work—ridiculous! He wanted to be paid for his favors. Can you imagine? The audacity! The gall! Sanda Florescu, La Straordinaria, the toast of three continents, paying a pipsqueak hairdresser!"

"Why didn't you tell your wife?"

"And humiliate her? I preferred to pay."

Mici sighed.

"You don't believe me?"

"It's . . . far out, Mr. Florescu."

The plump little man frowned, then took the plunge. "He not only threatened to dump Sanda, but to leak it to the gossip columns that she indulges in kinky sex."

"That's blackmail!"

"It's libel," he corrected. Having brought it out into the open, Florescu's agitation subsided considerably. "Ugly as it was, the threat didn't have much more than nuisance value. I mean, nowadays who cares? We could have sued him if we wanted to dignify the rumor. That wasn't what disturbed me. I was worried about the effect on Sanda. What would it do to her image of herself? She is not merely a superbly skilled artist, she is a glorious and self-confident woman. When she walks down to the footlights, the house is hushed and expectant; she mesmerizes not merely by the technical brilliance of her voice but by the magnetism of a woman who knows herself to be desirable and coveted." His rotund face glowed with that inner vision. "Would the sordid gossip that Eugène might engender shake her self-confidence? Would she feel soiled? Could she regain her pride? Could she walk out on that stage and face that packed house?"

"How many payments did you make?"

"One, just one."

"You must have known he wouldn't be satisfied with one."

"I was buying time. I was hoping Sanda would get tired of him."

"Or that somebody would get rid of him for you?"

"Somebody did. I can't say I'm sorry."

"Suppose Eugene Tully hadn't been killed?"

"I would have thought of something," Florescu assured her. "I may not look like much, but I'm not stupid, Miss Anhalt. Ask around and you'll discover that I made Sanda what she is today. When I found her, she was a utility singer, playing bits and jumping in when somebody better got sick. Her voice was not properly placed. She was pretty, but fat, and she lacked style. I got her the best voice coach in the business. I put her on a diet and bought her a wardrobe. I paid for her debut: bought the gown, hired the hall, paid for the publicity—launching a concert artist does not come cheap. I've managed Sanda's career from the start and I scratch for every penny and for every advantage now as I did then. I can

promise you that I was not going to let a hick hairdresser turn into a
leech and bleed us for what both of us have worked a large part of our
lives to earn."

"Would you have killed him?"

"Perhaps."

Florescu gritted his teeth. "First, I would have told the little bride. I
would have told the sweet Faith just what kind of man she'd married, if
she didn't already know." Now he pressed the elevator button. "She, of
course, was at the scene at the time her husband was killed. I was here,
in my own home, asleep beside my wife."

"I'm sorry, Miss Anhalt, but both the senator and Mrs. Kalb are in
Washington. They will not be back until the end of the week."

Perhaps Helene Kalb had dubbed Fulton a "houseman" because she
deemed it too ostentatious for a man in the public's service to be employing a butler, but it seemed to Mici that Spencer Fulton was performing
all of a butler's duties and surely his aplomb would have done credit to
any of his legendary models.

Perhaps Miss Anhalt would like to speak to Mrs. Kalb's secretary, the
houseman suggested. Mici declined and wondered if she might just have
a word with Fulton himself—the style was catching.

Gravely, he led her to his small, comfortable office off the main entrance hall.

"I wonder, Fulton, if you remember what time Mr. Tully left the house
on the night of the party?"

"I'm sorry, Miss Anhalt, I did not see him leave."

"Mrs. Tully says that she called here at about nine o'clock and spoke
to him."

"Mrs. Tully called several times."

"Oh?"

"Three times, I believe. I was very busy that evening, as you can
imagine, but I think she called three times. The first, as you say, was
around nine o'clock; I took that call and summoned Mr. Tully to the
telephone. The second was around eleven. I took that also. I'm certain
of the time because the guests were beginning to leave and I was about
to dismiss the temporary staff."

"And the third time?"

Now the houseman frowned, less sure of himself. "There was some
confusion over that call. It came around midnight. Most of the household
had retired, and I had turned on the automatic answering device." His
raised eyebrow asked whether she was familiar with it, and Mici nodded
to indicate she was. "One of the maids, a young Spanish girl, was waiting
for her father to come and pick her up. Thinking that the call might be
from him, since he was late, she answered."

"What was the confusion?"

"Well, the girl is new; she was not familiar with the device and didn't know how to turn it off. She tried to speak over the recorded announcement. By the time I took the phone from her and turned the recording device off, the caller had hung up."

"In other words, you don't actually know it was Mrs. Tully who called?"

"Carmelita said that the caller asked for Mr. Tully, so I assumed . . . I realize now that I should not have made the assumption," he admitted stiffly.

"It was natural."

"Thank you, Miss Anhalt." It was obvious that he did not excuse himself. "Carmelita is here today, if you would care to speak to her."

"Yes, thank you."

It was a matter of punching a button on the house phone and summoning her. Mici admired the organization.

Carmelita Rodríguez turned out to be young, with the luminous look of innocence that some well-protected and strictly raised Spanish girls still have. Having introduced her, Fulton waited, obviously intending to be present for the interrogation.

Judging that he acted out of a sense of responsibility toward the girl rather than avid curiosity, Mici liked him for it. She smiled at both of them. "It's about the telephone call that you took on the night of the party, Carmelita."

The girl nodded, indicating she knew well to which call Mici referred, but she looked to the houseman for guidance in answering. She spoke when he indicated that she might. "I was waiting for my father. He was very late. I was worried. I had been ordered not to answer the telephone, but my father had not arrived and I was worried."

"All right, Carmelita, Miss Anhalt understands." It did not seem to reassure her. "So do I," he added.

That was what she'd wanted to hear. Now she gave Mici her full attention. "My father went to the wrong address. He went to this number but on the West side."

"The call, Carmelita," Fulton brought her up firmly.

"*Sí, señor.* Yes, Mr. Fulton. When I answered the telephone, I heard a voice already speaking. I did not know who it was, but I thought it could be someone calling for my father. My father's English is not so good as mine." She said that shyly, almost apologetically, as though to do anything better than her father was unthinkable and a presumption. "I studied in the school," she explained. "So I announced myself, but the person continued to speak and then another person spoke also. Then I realized that it was Mr. Fulton's voice and that it was not two people but the recording and one person and that the person was not calling on behalf of my father but wished to speak to one of the guests, a Mr. Tullee." She pronounced the name carefully, accenting the last syllable.

"You're sure of the name?"

"*Sí señorita.* Tullee. I am sure."

AFTERSHOCK

"Did you ask who was calling?"

"*No, señorita.* I said that everybody has gone home. I said there is nobody here but the family, and the family has gone to bed. I said the party is finished. Then Mr. Fulton comes and takes the telephone from me."

Mici thought about it. "But the caller was a woman?"

"Oh. I think so. *Sí.* I think so."

"Are you sure?"

Carmelita Rodríguez hesitated. She sought Fulton's guidance. "It is important?"

"Very important," he told her.

"Mr. Fulton's recording and the other person were speaking at the same time. It was difficult to separate them. I cannot be sure. I am sorry. It was confusing."

Mici sighed and looked to the houseman.

"As I said, I took the phone from Carmelita just in time to hear the receiver click as the caller hung up."

Mici relaxed. "It doesn't matter. The voice is on the tape. May I hear the tape?"

"I'm sorry, Miss Anhalt, I couldn't take that responsibility. You'll have to apply to the senator or to Mrs. Kalb. I'm sure you understand."

"Of course." She turned back to the maid. "Just exactly what did this person say?"

"She . . . the person asked for Mr. Tullee."

"And you said?"

"Everybody has gone home. The family has gone to bed. Except for the senator and he is out."

"Out?" Mici repeated as the import hit her. "The senator was out?"

She replied matter-of-factly. "I saw him myself going out the back door perhaps ten or fifteen minutes before."

Fulton intervened. "The senator often enjoys a stroll along the river before retiring."

"It wasn't a particularly pleasant night for strolling," Mici pointed out. "It was pouring rain."

"The senator enjoys every type of weather."

Mici let it go. "What time did he return?"

"I have no idea, Miss Anhalt. As soon as Carmelita's father arrived, I locked up and retired. The senator has his own key and does not require me to wait up for him."

She'd get no more out of Spencer Fulton, Mici knew, and the girl had no more to tell. So she smiled at them both once again, thanked them, and was about to leave when she thought of one more point for Fulton.

"Obviously, Mr. Tully came early to do Mrs. Kalb's hair. Did you happen to notice whether he came in his own car?"

"Yes, he most certainly did." The houseman pursed his lips and there was no doubt of his disapproval. "Senator Kalb had obtained a police permit to close off this street to traffic and use it for parking for his distinguished guests. There were many UN dignitaries, government personages, and the like. As it was, there was insufficient space for their vehicles and many had to be parked on York Avenue. Since he arrived early, Mr. Tully availed himself of one of the choice locations. I spoke to Mrs. Kalb about it and said I would suggest to him that he move the car, but she said to let it go."

"I see."

"Mr. Tully had little regard for anyone but himself."

And that, Mici thought as she left the Kalb townhouse, pretty much summed up Eugene Tully.

The city was enjoying a January thaw, an exceptionally mild spell of springlike weather. Fresh, salty breezes lured Mici over to the East River Drive, where she leaned across the railing at the top of the embankment and looked out over the scintillating water below. Between the road and the water there was a strip of park. Had Senator Seymour Kalb been walking down there the night of the murder? Or had he walked uptown to Eighty-second Street and the parking lot?

According to the autopsy report, Eugene Tully had been killed between the hours of twelve midnight and two A.M. This was further narrowed by known circumstances: the parking lot closed at midnight and the attendant had left about fifteen minutes later; Faith Tully had been picked up by the patrol car at one-fifty-five A.M. If she had discovered her husband, say, ten minutes earlier, that put the time of the shooting at between twelve-fifteen and one-forty. If her story was true, and Mici's entire investigation was based on its being true, the beating occurred between the time Faith left her husband and the police brought her back in the patrol car, that is, between one-forty and two. The theory of two killers, the second just happening along at the fortuitous moment, seemed highly unlikely. Mici thought that whoever shot Tully saw Faith coming and hid. When she left to get help he took the time, trouble, and risk to beat him up.

Certainly, it didn't suggest a gang. To begin with, a gang would not have been one bit intimidated by Faith's approach and they would have stayed to finish what they had begun. It did suggest someone who wanted to make it appear like the work of a gang.

To even speculate that Seymour Kalb could be that man was . . . well, it was beyond speculation. There had never been any gossip about the senator's lady. Mici had only Tyrone Witte's innuendos to go on and they might be simply pique at having lost a valued client. Of course, he had been proved right with regard to Sanda Florescu. Assuming then, for the moment, that Eugene Tully had also been Helene Kalb's lover, you also had to assume that the senator knew. He needn't have been as sensitive to his wife's emotional fluctuations as Doru Florescu was, but he might well have been sensitive to her depleted bank balance.

Granting motive and opportunity, and even conceding that he owned a gun and had it handy, Mici still saw one insurmountable objection to Senator Seymour Kalb's being the killer: his twenty-six years of honest public service and integrity.

She could imagine Ed Stiebeck's reaction if she even mentioned Kalb as a possible suspect. He would not be enthusiastic about investigating Mrs. Kalb, or the Florescus for that matter, husband or wife. He'd show some interest in Witte, but probably not in preference to Faith. If only she could find something to support the young widow's story, Mici pondered. She didn't doubt that fifteen detectives had canvassed the neighborhood of the murder and came up empty. For her to go back and cover the same ground was to suggest that she doubted either their efficiency or their honesty, which she did not. Besides, on her own, the job would take more time than she could possibly spare. Forget it. On top of which there was a good possibility that some people who had been home the night of the murder would be away now. A lot of people went away at this time of year, south for the sun or north to ski.

And lots of people who had been away on holiday came back!

Almost two and a half hours later, Mici also found what, or rather whom, she was looking for. She then headed uptown to give Faith the good news.

Ed Stiebeck opened the door.

"What are you doing here?" Obviously, he was not pleased to see Mici.

Why not? she wondered. And what was he doing here? She kept in place the smile she'd prepared for Faith. "May I come in?"

Grudgingly, the detective gave way. She marched into the living room and stopped short just across the threshold. The place was a mess. It looked as though Faith were getting ready to move: books had been removed from shelves and were piled on the floor; doors of cabinets and drawers of bureaus were wide open and their contents piled on chairs and tables. A man sat at the butcher-block desk going through the papers as Mici had done just the day before, except that he wasn't as neat. The man wasn't a mover; he could only be another detective.

"Do you have to turn the place upside down?" she appealed to Stiebeck as the one in charge.

Before he could offer a defense, Faith Tully came running in from the bedroom.

"Oh, Mici, thank God. I've been trying to call you. They have a search warrant, but they won't tell me what they're looking for, or what they're doing here, or anything."

She'd located the witnesses just in time, Mici thought. Faith didn't know that she was under suspicion and now she wouldn't have to learn it. "Don't worry," she counseled. "I have good news. For you too, Ed."

"Yeah?" He was skeptical.

"I did promise to keep you informed."

"Right. So?"

"So I just spoke with a very nice couple, Mr. and Mrs. Oscar Beinecke of the Riverview House on Eighty-second Street near First."

"And?"

He might pretend that he didn't know what was coming, but he knew! Mici grinned. "And Mr. and Mrs. Oscar Beinecke have been down in Miami Beach for the past three weeks enjoying the sunshine and the dog races and the jai alai. Do you know when they left? The twentieth of December at six-thirty A.M."

Tully was murdered on the twentieth. "Are you telling me that those people were already gone when the detectives rang their doorbell."

"That's how it was." Mici's eyes danced with delight.

Stiebeck's were wary. "What put you on to it?"

"Logic. Pure logic."

"Oh, sure."

"Woman's intuition?"

He nodded at that, then catching the blonde's eye smiled in spite of himself. "Okay, okay, it was smart—and lucky."

"I'll go with lucky."

They both laughed.

Faith looked from one to the other, not understanding the change of mood but encouraged by it.

Nevertheless, Ed Stiebeck was not prepared to concede victory. "So you've got a couple of witnesses. What exactly did they see?"

"It's what they heard."

"The shot?"

"No. I asked them that, but they don't remember a shot. They went to bed about eleven and they opened their windows. They like to sleep cool. Either they were sleeping so heavily the shot didn't awaken them or most probably they were vaguely aware of it but dismissed it as a backfire. You, yourself, suggested that."

"All right, all right. So what did they hear—consciously?"

Mici looked at Faith. "They heard a woman screaming. Mr. Beinecke got up and went to the window and he saw a woman standing out in the street in the rain, screaming. He did not see the body. I looked out the window myself and from that angle the shadow cast by the front row of cars would hide anything low on the pavement. Anyhow, Mr. Beinecke was on the verge of calling the police when the screaming stopped and the woman left. That was at one-thirty-five A.M. He took particular note of the time because they had to get such an early start in the morning."

"Could they identify the woman?" Ed Stiebeck was catching her enthusiasm. "Could they pick her out of a line-up?"

"Since when do you put an innocent person in a line-up?"

"That means they couldn't."

"Would you accept an identification made by witnesses five stories up?" Mici hedged. "The street was very well lit by those amber-colored vapor lamps. They saw clearly enough to give a good description. Both of them; Mrs. Beinecke got up too and went to look." Mici underscored that. "They saw a young woman—yes, I know, I asked them how they could tell she was young and they said it was an impression: the way she held herself, the timber of her voice. Anyhow, she appeared to be young; she was medium height and"—Mici cast a quick look at Faith, then, lowering her voice, murmured—"she was fat."

"Fat?" Stiebeck was confused, then he grimaced. "Oh." He'd realized that Faith Tully had been still carrying her baby.

"She had black, curly hair and was wearing black slacks and a tan raincoat," Mici continued. "She had no hat and no umbrella. Now, how many girls, young women, like that would you say were out on Saturday, the twentieth of December, at one-thirty-five or one-forty A.M. on that particular street and screaming in the rain?"

Stiebeck heaved a long, long sigh.

"Come on, Ed. How many?"

He was saved by a detective summoning him from the other room. "Can I see you for a minute, Ed?"

Faith waited till he was gone then burst out. "He thought I was guilty, didn't he? He thought I killed Gene! I just can't believe it. How could he think such a thing? How could he?"

"He has to consider every possibility. It's his job."

"It's crazy, crazy. And what is he doing here? What is he looking for?"

She hadn't really thought about it, but now that she did, Mici thought she could make a pretty good guess. "Don't worry about it. With the Beineckes backing your story you're in the clear."

"I'm afraid not."

They both whirled to see Ed Stiebeck in the bedroom doorway holding a cardboard hatbox, its cover off. "The Beineckes' evidence doesn't mean a thing, not now." He dipped his hand into the froth of tissue paper and brought out a shiny black revolver. "Belong to you, Mrs. Tully?"

Faith seemed perplexed rather than frightened. "I never saw it before. Honestly."

"Then how did it get here?"

"I don't know. I swear I don't know."

"This is your hatbox?"

"Yes, but I don't know how the gun got there," she reiterated more forcefully.

At last Mici recovered enough to object. "You don't know that's the murder weapon."

"Wanna bet?" the detective retorted.

"It could have belonged to Tully. Why not?"

"Did your husband own a gun, Mrs. Tully?"

"Down home everybody owns a gun. Not that kind, a rifle."

"Let's just say that this is your husband's gun, which he bought for protection, okay? A rifle would not be exactly suitable. Why would he keep it on the top shelf of your closet under your Easter bonnet." Again the detective dipped his hand inside the box and brought out a cream-colored straw hat with poppies decorating the crown. "Hard to get to in an emergency."

Mici stifled a groan. "You don't know it's the murder weapon." She didn't know what else to say.

He smiled. "We'll find out. Meantime . . ." From his wallet Stiebeck took out the much-worn plasticized card and began to read. "You have the right to remain silent. If you give up that right—"

"No!" Mici cried out. "No. You can't arrest her." Her eyes darkened. "Don't, Ed," she pleaded. "After all she's been through, don't do this to her. Give her a chance. At least get the gun tested first."

While they argued over her, Faith Tully stood between them stony-faced and still.

Stiebeck hesitated and damned himself for hesitating and hesitated some more. He weighed his options: if the gun was not the murder weapon and Faith Tully was in fact innocent, then to subject her to the distress and humiliation of the arrest procedure—the personal search, the mugging, fingerprinting, the whole degrading and demoralizing process—would be a shame, to say nothing of subjecting himself to the long hours of waiting around the courtroom and the paperwork . . . God, the paperwork! On the other hand, the gun figured to be the murder weapon; what the hell, it had to be. If the suspect skipped while he futzed around and waited for the ballistics report! If on top of that the lieut found out that he, Stiebeck, had failed to pick up the suspect when he had the chance . . . he must be cracking up even to consider it.

"I've got no choice," Stiebeck muttered at both of them. He took out the handcuffs.

"You're not going to put those on her?" Mici was indignant.

"Standard procedure in a felony arrest."

"You've got no choice, right?"

Stiebeck shrugged. You couldn't expect a civilian to understand. Unfortunately, this time shrugging didn't help. He wished that this particular civilian would understand. He reached for the suspect's wrist and snapped the bracelets on her.

"Could I ask her a question before you drag her away?" Mici inquired scornfully.

He winced. "Sure. Yeah. Go ahead."

"Faith, how many times did you call the Kalb residence on the night of the party?"

The mountain girl was staring down at her locked wrists as though she didn't understand.

"Faith, Faith, listen to me." Mici tried to penetrate the miasma in which the girl had subconsciously found refuge. "Faith, this is important. How many times did you call Gene at the Kalbs' on the night he was killed? Faith, how many times?"

A long sigh. "Twice. I called twice." She closed her eyes as she tried to remember. Or forget? "I called at nine and then again around eleven."

"Are you sure you didn't call again? Around midnight?"

"No. No. He should have been home by then. I was waiting for him. I was listening for the elevator to stop at our floor and for the dog to bark. The woman in 8D has a terrier. He barks whenever the elevator stops on our floor. I was listening for the dog to bark. . . ."

Mici looked up at the detective. "Someone called the Kalb residence at midnight and asked for Gene Tully. I'll lay you any odds you want that it was the killer."

CHAPTER XI

Ramón Lara was outraged when Roz Pell advised him to moderate his attitude. A surge of blood suffused his face, turning it a dark magenta; his eyes blazed, and he had to clench his teeth hard to keep from shouting his anger and his frustration. Why shouldn't he show his feelings? What was wrong with wanting revenge? He had a right to see that punk kid, that Deke, put away. Every right. Let them give him back his legs and then talk to him about compassion! He'd never get his legs back; he knew it. He'd be a cripple for the rest of his life. All that medical double-talk about therapy, rehabilitation—lies. The truth was in their eyes, which never seemed to meet his. He was entitled to redress, and he was going to get it! But maybe . . . maybe the young prosecutor was right; maybe he would lose the jury's pity. Lara seethed, but he learned to mask his inner turbulence. Lara dissimulated. It wasn't easy, but after a while he stopped tasting the bile of being forced to play a role in order to get the justice due him. What counted was that he should get it. After what seemed to Ramón Lara an interminable string of delays, postponements, and adjournments, the tennis player at last appeared before judge and jury to give evidence from his wheelchair. By that time Lara was almost calm. He told his story succinctly; hadn't he told it uncounted times? He also told it quietly, with a minimum of visible emotion, in resignation. As he was wheeled away to the back of the courtroom, he noticed that there were tears in the eyes of the women jurors and the faces of the men were grim. He gloated. That young DA had known his business.

The satisfaction was brief. Oddly enough, having simulated Christian forgiveness for so long, he now experienced the real thing.

Maybe it was all for the best, Ramón thought as he waited for the verdict. He had refused to leave while the jury deliberated; he hadn't lost interest to that extent. Maybe it had been preordained, he mused, and the kid, Deke, was an instrument of the divine will. "Dios mío," he muttered under his breath in self derision, "who would have thought that I would turn to religion in my old age?"

There was little commotion as the jury filed in. The case was of minor interest and there weren't many spectators. Only the old-timers, the regular trial-watchers who had nothing else to do, were there.

"Guilty," the foreman announced.

Having accurately predicted it, the old-timers nodded sagely and looked toward Lara for his reaction.

Guilty.

The word, the single word reverberated inside his head as though in an echo chamber, growing louder and louder till the pain of it was almost unbearable. He clasped his hands over his ears to shut it out. He grimaced from the pain.

"Are you all right?" The Victim/Witness Assistance Project volunteer leaned over and whispered close to his right ear.

He didn't hear her. He was watching the judge; the judge's lips were moving, probably setting the date for sentencing. He didn't hear that either.

Guilty. It was over.

Ramón had not wanted Diane to attend the trial. He had not allowed her to be present at any of the hearings, consultations, preparations of affidavits. From the start he'd kept her away, insisting that there was no point to her wasting time when the Vera people were so well geared to provide transportation and assistance. He'd been back and forth so many times in that van that they'd both got used to it and it was almost as though Ramón were going to an office. It had given them both a few hours of relief from the strain of being cheerful for each other's sake. Diane had even gone back to the part-time job in the fashionable ladies' tennis shop that she'd had before the shooting.

"Mr. Lara?" The volunteer repeated, looking anxiously into Ramón's pale, drawn face. She was frightened.

"I want to go home."

The van wasn't due to leave for another hour.

"I don't want to wait for the van. Just get me a taxi. I'll manage."

The volunteer knew that he didn't live far, but she had been given very definite instructions not to let him do anything on his own. "I think I better just check . . ."

"I'm tired, that's all," he assured her. And he was. "After all these weeks, hanging around, and now, suddenly, it's over. I suppose there's a natural letdown." He managed one of the old, very special smiles. "I just want to go home. Tell Mrs. Pell I'll be in touch. I'll give her a call in the morning. Okay?"

The volunteer was a plain girl, eager, strong on dedication but not much else. She admired Lara and the manner in which he'd borne his ordeal. Of course he was tired, depleted, enervated. There was no point in keeping him waiting around. She wheeled him out of the courtroom and got him down to the main lobby. There were plenty of police around to help get a cab and put Lara inside with the wheelchair up front with the driver.

"Want me to come and help get you into your apartment?"

"Mr. Ritter will be there, the super. He'll look after me. Thanks . . ." He tried to think of her name. He tried. He would have liked to thank her by at least remembering her name, by singling her out at least that much from the other plain, eager girls who had been so kind. "Thanks . . ." Sally, Jane, Ann, Mary—none of those. "Thanks, and God bless you," he said for all of them, and meant it.

As soon as the cab pulled out from the curb, Ramón Lara forgot them. He looked at his watch: three-thirty. Diane wouldn't be home till six.

The Borough Hall section of Brooklyn, the seat of the county government, is adjacent to the Brooklyn Heights section. The Heights, a prestigious residential area, is aptly named for its magnificent position overlooking New York Harbor, its breathtaking view of the lower tip of Manhattan and the Statue of Liberty. Cobble Hill, where the Laras lived, was less prestigious, though many of its long-neglected and deteriorating brownstones were being lovingly restored by young couples short on money but high on aspirations. Cobble Hill derived its name from a steep hill paved with cobblestone. Originally, the hill had been higher, but during the Revolutionary War, the British cut off the top to prevent its overlooking their position on Brooklyn Heights. It was still high enough to offer a view of the waterfront. In the old days it had been a favorite spot for sleigh-riding in the winter and for enjoying the ocean breezes on a hot summer night. Now the Brooklyn-Queens Expressway at the base made sleigh-riding too dangerous; the ocean tang was contaminated by exhaust fumes. Ramón and Diane lived a few blocks away from the base of the hill. They had no harbor view, but the area was part of urban renewal and there was even a small park that had been reclaimed from rubble. Ramón had often thought it would have been nice if they'd been able to buy one of those decaying brownstones back in the days when they were going for nineteen or twenty thousand. That wasn't so long ago either, he mused. Now the price was beyond even dreaming.

But there were no dreams left anyway, Ramón thought as Hans Ritter and the driver lifted him out of the cab and into his wheelchair. How long since he and Diane had been without even a dream to support them? He thanked the driver and paid him, but when the super started to wheel him into the building he demurred.

"It's such a nice day; I think I'll just sit outside for a while."

Ja, it was a nice day, Hans Ritter agreed. Like spring. The temperature might go to seventy, he informed Lara. Imagine, in January! He pointed across the street. "How about I wheel you over to the park?"

"I can manage. I'm getting very good with this thing."

"*Ja.*" Ritter grinned, showing an expensive array of old-fashioned gold crowns. "But it is no trouble." Without waiting for Lara to agree or disagree, the strong old man tilted the chair back on its rear wheels and eased it off the curb, pushed it across the street and into the pocket park.

When he had Lara settled to both their satisfactions, he asked, "What time should I come to get you?"

"My wife will be along soon. She can take me in."

"That is another couple of hours." Ritter frowned. "Are you sure you want to stay out so long? When the sun goes down it will be cold. As you wish, as you wish. But if you should change your mind, you can send one of the children over to ring my bell."

Ritter didn't know anything about tennis and was not really interested. To him Lara was neither a celebrity nor a has-been, just a man he liked who was trying to hang on to his self-respect. Ritter knew how that was. Not so long ago he'd had a fine position, a position of dignity and authority; he'd been brewmaster at the Rheingold brewery in Brooklyn. When the brewery closed down, there was nowhere for Hans Ritter to go. There weren't many openings in his field and he was too old to be taken on at a lower level. He became a "floating" janitor. He handled twelve buildings and did not find it demeaning to do the work to the best of his ability. So the old man was not about to do anything to humiliate Ramón Lara. On the other hand, he had no intention of leaving a cripple outside and unsupervised for two hours. Not that anything was going to happen, not in broad daylight, not on a day like this with everybody out —mothers, babies, children, and old people. Just the same, Hans Ritter intended to keep an eye on Lara, without his being aware of it, *natürlich*.

Lara watched the super disappear into the building. The old Dutchman was shrewd. Lara moved his chair a few feet forward and to the left. There. Now Ritter could still see him from the window of his basement apartment but not quite so easily as before; he would have to get right up to the window pane and tilt his head to just the right angle. Finally, Ramón could sit back and relax.

It was a rare day, he thought. It promised spring. The air was balmy; instead of the pale white light of winter, the sun glowed golden and almost warm. However, the grass remained sere; not a single crocus broke through the hard-packed earth; there was no color anywhere. Except for the sea. The sea would be blue. Ramón glanced at his watch. Time was slipping away.

His arms were strong, but he couldn't move the chair up even a slight incline, much less the steepness of Cobble Hill. As he was looking around for someone he might ask to give him a push, a teenager offered to help. Ramón gave him a dollar and had to talk him into accepting it. Nice. Nice that there were still some good kids around.

Even from the top of the hill the view was partially obstructed by warehouses, rotting docks, and freighters, but the tennis player ignored them. He looked past them at the expanse of ocean beyond. It was blue, shimmering, dazzling, and he was mesmerized by it. He sat in the wheelchair in a kind of trance without thinking about anything, not the past, or what was to be; not about himself or Diane; not about what he had been, or was now, or might have been. He felt neither satisfaction nor regret. Nothing. After a very long while he noticed that it wasn't as warm as it had been. The sun was setting and the western sky was painted in striations of orange and magenta and the blue had become electric. So he had his colors after all.

He didn't need to look at his watch. He knew that it was time.

Without so much as a sigh, Ramón Lara released the brake on each wheel, turned the chair around, and maneuvered himself off the curb and into the road. At right angles to the hill the chair teetered, off balance. Shifting his weight, Lara managed to hold it steady, then slowly, gradually, turned it in the direction of the fall line.

"Say, mister? Mister! Look out!" A woman yelled at him.

Ramón Lara paid no attention.

"Look out!" she shrieked.

The force of gravity pulled at the wheelchair.

The chair started to roll. It gathered speed. It careened down the hill, jouncing on the cobblestones. Lara leaned back and braced himself, holding on to the arms. A car coming up the street swerved to avoid him. The driver started to curse, then stared instead, open-mouthed. The pedestrians on the sidewalk froze. Horror silenced them. In fact, all sound appeared temporarily suspended as the chair plunged down toward the rush-hour traffic. Ramón Lara looked straight ahead. He could no longer see the blue water, only the steady, unbroken stream of cars speeding across his path. It would be a miracle if a gap occurred at the very moment he went hurtling through. Ramón Lara did not expect or want a miracle. In its flight down the hill the chair had become a lethal missile, and he asked only that when he inevitably crashed he might not be the cause of someone else's injury.

That last prayer, as instinctive as a reflex and more powerful because it was instinctive, was granted. Somehow the chair passed through the opposing traffic streams, struck a pothole in the farthest lane, and came to rest, a mangled coil of steel tubes and wires, around a lamppost. Lara was thrown clear. He landed on his neck and broke it.

One car stopped; another, its driver unprepared, slammed into it; the third into the second—seven in all, but without serious casualties. Then all lanes came to a halt. Before the horns could start blaring, the woman at the top of the hill who had seen it from the beginning began to scream hysterically. Her screams broke the spell and turned the sound back on.

Mrs. Salvatore in 4C chose that afternoon to have a stopped-up sink. By the time Ritter was through with it, got back to his own basement apartment, cleaned his tools and himself, and remembered Ramón Lara, the sun had sunk so low that the little park was completely in shadow. He must be half-frozen out there, Ritter thought, and decided it was time to go and get him. But when he looked from his window he couldn't see the man in the wheelchair. He went up and out to the street. Lara was gone. Everybody was gone except for a couple of boys playing ball before supper. They hadn't noticed when the man in the wheelchair had left or where he had gone.

He'd be back in the house, up in his own apartment naturally, Ritter assured himself. Of course. He'd found somebody to help him back inside. Maybe he'd managed it himself. Even as he told himself these things, the super was running back across the street. But as he rode up in the elevator to the Laras' floor, he had a sick feeling at the pit of his stomach. Cold sweat had broken out all over his body as he rang the Laras' doorbell and waited for an answer. He didn't ring a second time, but used his pass key and went inside. Nobody there, not in the living room, not in the bedroom.

Hans Ritter ran out of the building, nearly colliding with Mrs. Lara as she came. From his face she knew instantly that something terrible had happened, and of course it concerned Ramón. He gasped out the briefest of explanations, and then they separated to search the neighborhood. From their individual locations each heard the ululating shrieks of the ambulance. Diane Lara was near enough to the scene to see the chaos of cars and people. She knew what it was. She knew it was too late. She ran anyway.

Accident or suicide? At the inquest the widow cited Lara's optimism, his determination to overcome his handicap, his eagerness to join the rehabilitation program at the Kessler Institute. The verdict was accidental death. Diane Lara put in a claim with Mici for reimbursement of funeral costs and widow's benefits. She contended that the accident was a direct result of the original shooting. Mici agreed and she knew that Adam would too. If Ramón Lara had not been shot and crippled, he would not have been in a wheelchair, careening down the hill to his death. Diane Lara was entitled to widow's compensation—if she was, in fact, Ramón Lara's widow.

So Mici could no longer put off telling Adam of the doubt concerning the Laras' marital status. The supervisor then took over the interview.

He was familiar with the ravages of tragedy, but this woman, Diane Lara, was one of the strong ones, and somehow the supervisor had not expected her to be so severely affected, or at least not to show it. Her face was swollen and lumpy, probably from a night of crying; her eyes were glazed, probably from too many tranquilizers. Her carefully maintained good looks had been destroyed and it was not likely that they could ever be rebuilt.

"I'm very sorry for your loss, ma'am." Dowd was gentle. He thought that she was unnaturally on guard and wondered if that was because she was putting forward a false claim. On the other hand, the people who tried to cheat or defraud this particular office had suffered physically and emotionally and were usually in desperate straits. The supervisor was not disposed to judge them harshly.

"About your claim . . ."

"Yes?"

"Could you bring in your marriage license?"

"What?"

She didn't seem overly concerned, simply puzzled.

"Could you bring in your marriage license?"

"Why?"

The beginning of resistance. "Routine procedure, Mrs. Lara. When compensation goes directly to the victim, well, there's no problem. But with the victim now deceased we need proof that you are legally entitled to his benefits."

"Proof?"

There was now definite antagonism. Dowd cast a glance at Mici and got to the point. "It has been suggested to us that you and Ramón Lara were not married."

"That's a lie!" The blood rushed into her face.

"Then I apologize for causing you this embarrassment," Dowd said. "If there's been a mistake—"

"Damn right there's been a mistake," Diane Lara snapped, head up and defiance clearing the dull mist of the drugs out of her eyes. "Damn right! Twelve years Ramón and I were together. Do you think two people stick together for twelve years if they're not married?"

"I couldn't say."

"Well, they wouldn't."

Dowd sighed. "I'm very sorry, but we don't recognize the status of a common-law wife."

"Nobody ever questioned us before. Nobody. This is an outrage! We behaved decently, never caused trouble, kept a low profile. Why should anybody raise the question now? Why now? Are you trying to hold back on paying me? Is that it?"

"We are anxious for you to get everything you're entitled to," the supervisor assured her.

"All right, who says we weren't married? Who told you?"

Dowd looked pained but said nothing.

"I demand to know. I have the right to know. I demand to confront whoever said it. Let him say it to my face. Whoever he or she is, you bring that person in here and—"

Mici broke in quietly. "All you have to do is bring in your license, Mrs. Lara."

Diane Lara ignored her. "I'm going to sue whoever started this rumor."

It was Dowd's turn again. "I sympathize with your feelings, but it's such a simple matter to resolve."

"No. No, I'm not going to bring in the license. Why should I? I don't see why the burden of proof should be on me."

"If you intend to file for compensation—"

"Suppose nobody had said anything about the legality of our marriage, would you still have required me to bring in my marriage license? Would you demand to see it? Make it a condition for processing my claim?"

"The charge has been made."

Frustrated, Diane Lara now turned on the investigator. "This is your doing. You're responsible."

"Now just wait a minute—" Dowd began.

"No, you wait. She's the one. She picked up some gossip, that's all it is, gossip. I want to know where she got it, from whom. Was it from my husband. I mean, my first husband. Was it from Nicholas?"

"No," Mici answered. "I haven't been in touch with your first husband."

Diane scowled, then decided to believe her. And, unexpectedly, she capitulated. "I don't know where Ramón kept our marriage license, but it's got to be around somewhere. I'll find it. I'll bring it in." She got up. "And when I do, I'll expect an apology from both of you." She stalked out.

Mici and Adam stared at each other.

"You think it was gossip Lawrence Hoguet was repeating to me?"

"If you'd asked me five minutes ago, I would have said no. Now . . ." The supervisor scowled. "Damn. I feel sorry for that woman. I wouldn't want to add to her trouble."

"I know." They hadn't discussed it, but Mici was sure that the doubt concerning the manner of Lara's dying had been on his mind as much as on hers.

"Do you think she has any doubt?" he asked.

"I think it's tearing her apart," Mici answered. "If Ramón Lara went to the top of that hill with the express purpose of committing suicide, he didn't do it out of despair or cowardice, because he couldn't face the life that lay ahead of him. He did it for her. He did it so that he wouldn't be a burden on her. He knew she couldn't walk out on him, so in essence, he walked out on her."

Yes, Dowd thought, there were certain situations one just couldn't turn one's back on. There was a moral bondage stronger than love.

"He may even have been counting on her getting that widow's compensation," Mici added. "It could be one reason Diane is so determined to fight for it."

"God knows I'd like her to have it!" Dowd responded with unusual vehemence. "After twelve years of living with the man she's entitled. But the law's the law, and until we can get that one changed along with some of the others . . ." He shrugged. "You better get in touch with the first husband, Hirschhorn. The woman's going to come in here with some kind of document, and we should be in a position to either accept or reject it. The least we can do is spare her unnecessary suspense."

Locating Nicholas Hirschhorn, owner of a chain of hardware stores throughout the midwest, was no problem. He still lived in Grosse Pointe as he had when he and Diane were together. It would surely not be pleasant for Hirschhorn to learn that his wife, or ex-wife, was nearly destitute and that the legality of her present status had to be resolved before she would qualify for public assistance. It would surely be humiliating for Diane to have Hirschhorn know. Mici wished she could spare them both. She never liked writing these prying letters and usually tried to soften their tone, but on this occasion she actually took refuge in the bureaucratic jargon, saying as little as possible, trying to hide Diane's shame.

She was in the middle of it when a light tap sounded at her door and a head poked in.

"Oh, I'm sorry, you're busy. They said it would be all right."

Simon Creedy.

Mici smiled to cover her annoyance. She really did like the old boy, but he had a habit of turning up at inopportune moments.

"Come on in, Mr. Creedy, and sit down. Just give me a couple of minutes to finish this."

His presence made her keep the letter perhaps a bit more brief than she might otherwise have done. Her fingers flew over the keys. She pulled the paper from the machine, signed it, and slipped the sheet into the already addressed envelope. Then she tossed it into the OUT tray and leaned back.

"So, Mr. Creedy? Did your friend fill out the forms?"

"Yes, ma'am, Miss Anhalt. Here it is." With a flourish, the old man unzipped a cheap plastic briefcase and extracted a none-too-clean file folder, which he handed over to her. His thin, arthritic hand trembled slightly.

"And how is she coming along?" Mici asked as she took it from him.

"Oh, she's in bad shape, real bad shape, Miss Anhalt." Creedy shook his head dolefully. "You know that cut on the forehead that I mentioned? You remember I said it didn't seem like much, didn't bleed much?"

Mici nodded, but she thought that he had suggested just the opposite.

"Well, it turns out to be a lot worse than anybody thought. She's got a real bad concussion."

"I'm sorry."

"They kept her in the hospital for close to a week. She had to have all kinds of tests. I went to see her."

"That was nice of you."

He smiled his sweet smile. "She's home again now, but she's still supposed to get lots of rest."

"Of course."

"I go over twice a day to walk her dogs for her."

"She's lucky to have such a good friend."

"I like to do it. She's such a nice lady, and they're nice dogs. The black one is called Pinocchio—because he's always getting into trouble." He waited for Mici to laugh, which she dutifully did. Then he was serious again. "It'll be a while before she can come to see you. Mrs. Trent, I mean."

"That's all right. I'll stop in and see her."

"She's not allowed visitors."

"Oh. Well. There's no rush."

"That's good." Creedy settled back in the chair as though he intended to stay and visit awhile. "I feel so sorry for Mrs. Trent. She has to lie in a darkened room and she's not supposed to read or even to watch television. I offered to go into court and testify against those boys, if they ever catch them."

"We ought to have more good citizens like you, Mr. Creedy."

He beamed. Mici beamed. She wondered what else she could say to him, but he had something to ask her.

"Miss Anhalt? Could I have another one of those forms?"

"Sure. What for?"

"There's an old lady in my building got mugged coming home from the supermarket the other night. I didn't see it, but I heard all about it. They knocked her down with all her groceries. Broke the eggs, spilled the milk, sent the meat rolling into the gutter so she can't use it. And they snatched her purse with all her money and her house keys so that she had to call the locksmith and put on all new locks."

"That's a shame." Mici hesitated and then decided to anticipate. "We don't replace money or property, Mr. Creedy."

"Yes, ma'am. My friend broke her leg when she fell."

"She did?"

"Yes, ma'am. I've been doing all her shopping for her and I go over a couple of times a day to fix her meals, but there's certain things, like helping her dress and so on, that she needs a woman to do for her. She has no relatives in town, so she's had to hire a practical nurse."

Mici didn't suggest that she could have called on a woman neighbor, she let Creedy go on.

"You did say that it isn't necessary to be referred by the police or a lawyer or a doctor to qualify for benefits?"

"That's right." She handed him a form, observing him carefully as he placed it in his cracked briefcase.

"You don't mind, do you?" Mr. Creedy was suddenly anxious. "I mean, you don't mind my sort of acting as . . . as an agent for these people? Trying to help them?"

"Of course not."

His smile broke out in its full beatific splendor. "I didn't think you would." Tucking the briefcase under his arm, he stood up and shuffled to the door. "I'll get back to you real soon."

She'd been complaining that the project didn't get enough publicity, that people who needed help didn't know of its existence, so why shouldn't Simon Creedy spread the word? It wasn't exactly what she'd had in mind, Mici thought, but why not? Opening the folder, she examined Amanda Trent's claim. The form had been filled in on a type-writer, unevenly, with plenty of erasures and smudges. Neither the name of the police officer nor the case number was included. Of course, it wasn't easy for a civilian to get that information; she'd take care of it herself. Everything else appeared to be in order and properly signed. The signature was shaky, however, very shaky.

Mici frowned.

The interoffice phone rang.

Now what?

CHAPTER XII

The supervisor waved her to a chair, clasped his hands on the desk in front of him, and regarded his only female investigator with unaccustomed gravity.

"About your report on the Tully case . . ."

Oh, oh, here it comes! Mici thought.

Three nights ago she'd put a report on her findings on Adam's desk and she'd been waiting for comment. She'd also sent a copy to Detective Stiebeck as promised, though promise or not she would have sent it because he was certainly entitled to know what was going on. She hadn't heard from him either.

"I just spoke to Mr. Cornelius," Dowd said.

Mici winced. Could be that Ed Stiebeck had shown the report to his lieut. Could be that the lieut had gone over both their heads, Adam's and hers, to bring pressure to call off the investigation through Mr. Cornelius. She was stricken that she hadn't considered that possibility.

"I showed him your report."

"Oh?" She breathed easier. A little.

"Naturally."

"Naturally." She steeled herself.

"Mr. Cornelius was very impressed by the manner in which you traced the Beineckes. He considers their evidence significant."

Mici blinked. "He does?"

"Mr. Cornelius has instructed me to tell you to keep up the good work."

"He has?"

Suddenly, Dowd grinned, "I know. It shook me too. I was all set to be chewed out for letting you go ahead; I had my defenses up. Being commended really threw me."

"Wow! Oh, Adam, wow! I don't believe it."

"Believe it, but don't let it go to your head. We got lucky. The timing saved us. It seems we've been getting a bad press lately, lots of criticism about our 'means' test. They're calling it prejudicial and degrading to the victim, lacking in compassion, and a few other things along those lines.

Yet what could be more compassionate than the way we're treating Faith Tully? We're bending over backward to be fair. We're befriending a young woman, a stranger in our fair city, who is accused of the very crime for which she's asking compensation. She's actually been arrested and is in jail; yet instead of turning down her claim we're assisting her in clearing herself. No way you can call that prejudicial."

Mici laughed out of sheer delight.

"Mr. Cornelius wants you to stick with it. He wants you to give the Tully case top priority."

"Oh, I will. You can just bet I will."

"There's one provision." Dowd fixed a warning look on her. "Don't annoy Senator Kalb."

"But—"

"Or Mrs. Kalb."

"Adam, I have to—"

"You don't honestly think that either one of them killed Tully?"

She hesitated. "Well, no, I suppose I don't, but they were the last ones to see Tully alive."

"Forget it."

"The senator doesn't have an alibi. For that matter, neither does Mrs. Kalb."

"Come on—"

"Tully could have been blackmailing either or both of them the same way he was blackmailing the Florescus."

Dowd shook his head.

"They could know something."

Silently, Dowd mouthed a singled word, "No."

Mici got up. "I should quit while I'm ahead, right? Okay. I'll abide by Mr. Cornelius' rules. And thanks, Adam."

"For what? I didn't do anything."

"I know better."

There was another surprise in store for her when she got back to her office and answered the ringing telephone.

"Miss Anhalt? Hi. This is Ed Stiebeck. How are you?"

It wasn't so much that he was calling but that his manner was ingratiating.

"Fine, Ed. How are you?"

"Not bad, Mici. Not bad at all. Great weather we've been having. Like spring."

"Beautiful," she agreed. And waited with considerable amusement.

"Ah, Mici? About that report you sent me. It was certainly nice of you to do that. I'd like to thank you."

"That's okay. I promised I'd keep you informed."

"I appreciate it. I'd . . . ah . . . I'd like to discuss it with you."

Had he shown the report to Dicker or hadn't he? Was this Dicker's way of handling it? Indirectly? "Sure. Anytime."

"Could I come over now?"

Detective Stiebeck humbly requesting an audience? Not likely. He had to be acting on orders. Just the same, Mici got a charge out of it. "Now? We'll be closing in half an hour."

"Could I buy you a drink? We could talk about it over a drink."

Absolutely out of character! she gloated. "I'd love to."

"Great. Great. Uh . . . you have to come up this way, don't you? You live around here."

"It's on my way," she agreed, though it was actually ten blocks out of her way. "I'll stop by."

"Oh, no, don't do that. Don't come to the precinct!" he exclaimed. "I mean, I don't want to put you to that trouble. I had in mind that we meet someplace. There's a very nice spot, the Phoenix?"

"Very fancy," she commented.

"You don't like it?"

"Who doesn't like the Phoenix? I'll be there in an hour."

The Phoenix was very elegant and very expensive. Mici assumed that the long, well-polished bar, the small marble-topped tables, the stained-glass lamps, and the other examples of Victoriana were authentic, yet the overall effect was phony. Maybe it derived from the people who frequented the place, she thought as she entered and peered through the characteristic gloom of all bars to find the detective. Stiebeck, however, spotted her first. He got up and came forward out of the darkest of the dark corners to greet her. He smiled.

It was indeed a day of surprise, Mici thought. She also thought the smile could have made Ed Stiebeck very attractive if it weren't forced. What did he want? And why had he been so anxious to keep her away from the precinct house? She couldn't figure that at all.

He held her chair for her, ordered drinks, kept the conversation casual, and awkward, till they were served, and then, when the moment was finally at hand, didn't seem to know how to get started.

Mici was curious enough to help him. She took a handful of peanuts from the bowl and leaned back. "What's this all about, Ed?"

"You were square with me. You gave me a full rundown. I owe you the same."

He twirled his martini glass. Mici nibbled some more nuts.

"The thing is, I didn't get anywhere with those suspects you turned up."

She choked on one of the peanuts. "You followed up on my leads?"

"I couldn't ignore them."

"How about the lieut?"

He had the answer pat, prepared ahead of time. "I did it on my own time."

So Dicker didn't know. It explained why Stiebeck hadn't wanted her turning up in the squad room.

"Thanks, Ed."

He shrugged. "Like you said, we're both after the same thing."

Gravely, Mici extended her hand and he took it; their eyes met.

"Trouble is, I've drawn a blank," he said. "Naturally, I checked the alibis first. Mr. and Mrs. Florescu did exactly what they said. After the taping they had dinner with friends at the Russian Tea Room and were home and in bed by eleven. They have separate bedrooms, but on this occasion they were together. So they say."

"How about Tyrone Witte, Tully's boss?"

"Right. He likes to ski and has a place up near Big Bromley in Vermont. He started up there on Friday night and had a breakdown en route. Fuel pump failed. He stayed overnight at the Spindletop Inn, just off the Taconic Parkway. Didn't get back on the road till around eleven on Saturday. The inn is about two hours out of New York by car. No bus or train goes through there after nine P.M., and Witte was seen in the hotel bar as late as ten."

Mici nodded. The Kalbs would be next.

"Then I had an idea," Stiebeck said. "I thought maybe one of Faith's kin—her pa, or her brothers, or somebody down there in West Virginia —got wind of what Gene Tully was doing, how he was cheating on his little bride. I thought maybe we had a case of mountain justice."

Mici's eyes lit up; her heart started to pound. It made a lot of sense. "It could explain why Faith made such an issue of the girl gang. Maybe she was trying to distract you from investigating her family."

He shook his head dolefully. "Forget it. I called the chief of police down there and had him check out the entire Goss family. Everybody from the old man to the brothers and cousins twice-removed is accounted for on that night."

Mici sighed and waited for him to bring up the Kalbs.

"Want another drink?" Stiebeck looked around for the waiter.

"No, thanks."

"I'll have one, I guess." He signaled.

"Ed? How about the Kalbs?"

He frowned, took a deep breath, then looked straight at her. "If I messed with them, the lieut'd have me pounding a beat in Greenpoint, Brooklyn."

What could she expect? Mici sighed. "I've been called off too. It's not that I really think either the senator or Mrs. Kalb is guilty, but I have the feeling that there's something there, that they know something. Besides, I think the senator would cooperate if he were asked."

"Well, neither one of us is going to ask, so that's that."

"And Faith Tully just goes on sitting in jail."

"I'm sorry." He shrugged and knew it was not adequate.

"Ed, neither one of them, neither the senator nor Mrs. Kalb has an alibi," she pleaded.

"There's nothing I can do."

Mici got up. "Well, thanks for the drink . . . and everything."
"Sure you won't have another?"
She shook her head.
"I've got my car. I'll run you home."
"I'm not going home. I'm going to my class, my dance class."
"Okay, I'll drive you there."
"No, thanks, Ed. The subway's quicker. Really."

The physical exertion and the discipline of the body served also to re-
fresh Mici's mind. She was more relaxed and naturally rested after a
couple of hours of hard effort in class than if she'd slumped in a chair
to read the paper or watch TV or have a couple of drinks. In order to
perform even adequately you had to keep your mind on what you were
doing. Particularly working with a partner. It was impossible to brood
about anything else. Mechanical precision was not sufficient; there had
to be a rapport. A *grand jeté* would be spoiled if the ballerina had any
uncertainty about being caught; her partner could not be properly prepared if he had any doubt about how she would execute. The *fouettés*
were bound to be tentative if she was not certain that firm hands would
be there to grasp and hold her at the waist at the end of the combination.
The music, of course, was the link, and tonight it seemed to Mici that
both she and her partner, Paul Symes, a member of the Joffrey corps, gave
themselves up to the music and were united through it as never before.
It was highly satisfying. At the end of the session they went out together for a hamburger and a beer and tried to put into words the experience they'd shared. Paul walked her to the subway, and then each went
his separate way carrying the glow still within. For Mici the exhilaration
lasted all the way home.
There was no doorman where Mici Anhalt lived. Each tenant had his
own key to the front door, and Mici was accustomed to making sure no
one was loitering in the street or in the lobby before she used her key,
but once inside she considered herself safe. As she left the elevator on
her own floor, a man stepped out of the shadows, blocking the way to
her apartment. She opened her mouth to scream, but there was something
about the way he moved, something familiar . . . Danny!
"Oh, my God, Danny!" she exclaimed. "What are you doing here?
You nearly scared the wits out of me."
"I'm sorry. I'm sorry, sweetheart." He grinned. "Glad to see me?"
"You bet. What are you doing here?"
"You wouldn't come down to see me, so I thought, what the hell, I'll
go up and see her. I'll go on up and see my girl. Surprised?"
Her answer was to throw her arms around his neck and kiss him en-
thusiastically.
"What do you say we move the action inside?" Danny whispered,
nuzzling her ear.
She felt around in her purse for her key and couldn't find it because

she couldn't stop looking at Danny. When her fingers finally closed on it and she passed it to him, he dropped it because he couldn't let go of her. Laughing, they managed between them, somehow, to get the door open and to stumble inside. Danny kicked it shut, Mici dropped her purse; and they clung together as close as they could get.

He kissed her mouth; he laced his fingers into her hair, locking them at the back of her head, and then kissed her eyes, then back to her mouth. "God! I've missed this."

"Me too," she whispered. "Me too."

"Really?"

"You know it."

He helped her get her coat off, led her to the sofa, and pushed her back against the pillows and was almost instantly on top of her.

"Hey, hey, slow down. Hold the phone."

"Hm? What? What's the matter?"

Mici looked up into his face. He was, she thought, as devastatingly handsome as ever. The curly black hair, the blue eyes, white teeth flashing in contrast to his midwinter Florida tan—irresistible. Nearly. She pushed him away, then she sat up. "Give me a chance to catch my breath."

"Why? Why do you want to catch your breath?"

"I don't know. You're just coming on too strong, too fast."

He frowned. "You never used to complain."

"You used to have some finesse."

"You want to be romanced? You want roses and violins?"

"I want some consideration for my feelings, for my mood."

He got up abruptly, looming over her. "I thought you'd made your feelings and your mood very clear. It seems I misunderstood."

"I didn't expect you to walk in here and knock me flat on my back."

"That's a hell of a way to put it. You know, that's really one hell of a way to put it! I haven't seen you for over two months. I fly up from Miami. I rush right over from the airport. You're not home. I wait in your hallway for over an hour, and then I get criticized for being over-enthusiastic. Thanks a lot."

"Ah, Danny . . . you made me feel like I was being used."

"What's that supposed to mean? I came up here because I needed and wanted you. Not any woman, you. I thought you felt the same way."

"I do."

He threw up his hands. "Okay. We'll play it your way. We'll wait." He fumbled in his pocket for his cigarettes and lit up. He tossed the match into one of the oversized crystal ashtrays, inhaled, exhaled. Glanced at his watch. "How long should we wait?"

Mici flushed. "This is ridiculous."

"I agree. I couldn't agree more."

"Will you come here and sit down?" She patted the place beside her. "May I?"

She turned her eyes up in mock exasperation, then sighed. "I guess each of us is looking for something different. Now is probably as good a time as any to find out what."

"Say, what is this? A consciousness-raising session?" His laughter was derisive but also uncertain.

"Danny, we have to talk."

"Sure, sweetheart." He reached for her. "We'll talk all you want. Later."

"No." She didn't need to push him away this time; her tone was enough. "Sorry you had your trip for nothing."

He stared at her as though he couldn't believe what she'd said. He swallowed a couple of times. "You mean you want me to go?"

"Yes."

He continued staring. Then slowly, as though against his will, he murmured, "I love you."

She waved a hand in dismissal. "Oh, Danny . . ."

"Did you hear what I said? I love you?"

"Maybe. Maybe you think you do, but love doesn't mean the same thing to you that it does to me."

"Do you realize I've never said that before, never, to any girl? I've never pretended. I've made it a point not to—"

The phone rang. Danny glared at it and looked to Mici as though he expected her to ignore it.

She answered immediately, glad of the interruption. "Yes, this is Miss Anhalt. . . . Oh, of course. As a matter of fact, I'm very anxious to talk to the senator. I'd be glad to drop over at any time. . . ." She hesitated, just for an instant. "No, it's not too late. . . . No, I don't mind in the least. Thank you for calling." She hung up.

"Who was that?"

"Senator Kalb's secretary. He wants to see me."

"Seymour Kalb? Seymour Kalb wants to see you? What about?"

"He has some information for me about a case I'm working on. I'm sorry, Danny, I have to go."

"Now? You mean you're going over there now? Tonight? That's a hell of a thing. Why can't you see him in the morning?"

"When a United States senator calls and say he wants to talk to you, you don't say, sorry, I can't make it right now; how about tomorrow morning?"

Danny Best's blue eyes narrowed. "It doesn't sound kosher."

"Come on, Danny! Maybe he isn't free tomorrow morning. Maybe he's going back to Washington. Who knows?"

"Right, right. So you've got to go. Okay. I'm slow, but I do finally get the message. You don't love me. You don't love anybody; you only love your job. I hope it keeps you warm nights."

She made herself laugh. "Oh, darling, that's such an old ploy. Do you still get results with it?"

He left her standing beside the telephone. He snatched up his trench-coat and slung it over one shoulder, strode through the vestibule and out the front door, slamming it shut behind him without a backward glance.

Mici's cheeks ached from smiling.

There were no taxis on her street, so Mici decided to walk over to York Avenue, where she would take either a taxi or the bus, depending on which one came along first. Resolutely, she put Danny Best out of her mind and thought about Senator Kalb instead. Whatever his reason for wanting to see her, it was certainly a big break. Nobody could fault her for seeing him, not Adam, not Mr. Cornelius, or even Lieutenant Dicker, not when Kalb himself initiated the meeting.

She wasn't aware that as she came out of the building a car parked at the far end of the block started up, though the sound of the motor was raucous enough. If she had heard, she wouldn't have paid any particular attention. The light was in her favor; she saw the bus coming, and was intent on catching it. As she crossed, heading for the bus stop on the other side of York, she became aware of the car behind her, but she expected that it would stop at the light. It didn't. It raced through. One startled glance over her shoulder and she knew that it was coming straight at her. She ran. It speeded up. Somebody was trying to run her down!

She reached the sidewalk. The front wheels of the car climbed the curb. She looked around wildly. There was no doorway in which to shelter. She was trapped. All she could do was flatten herself against the building, squinting into the headlights and cringing against the inevitable.

The next thing Mici knew there was a loud crash, a clanging of metal against metal, the revving of an engine and then the squeal of brakes in the distance.

"Are you all right, miss? Are you all right?"

Mici opened her eyes and didn't see anything. Then she pulled away her hands. She was looking into the anxious face of an elderly man. She couldn't make out much about him because she was still blinded by some kind of bright light. Turning her head slightly, she realized that she'd been looking into another set of headlights—the headlights of the bus she'd been running to catch. Now she could see that the man in front of her was wearing a gray uniform: he must be the bus driver.

"Yes, I'm fine," she answered. "What happened?"

"A hell of a thing!" A hiss of bewilderment escaped through the space between his yellowing front teeth. "Never seen nothing like it. I mean, that guy was out to get you, no doubt about it. He was out to squash you up against that building like a fly." He caught himself. "Sorry, miss."

"That's okay." She swallowed hard. She felt a little sick, but she wasn't going to admit it. "I don't mind talking about it. I'm glad I'm still around to talk about it. What happened?"

"I don't know. All of a sudden I see this car come out of the side street in a hell of a hurry and against the light. I figure it's a drunk or a maniac and I go for my brakes. The next thing I know he's not crossing the inter-

AFTERSHOCK

section but making the turn and he's cutting it real narrow. I see you start to run and I get it—he's after you! I couldn't believe it, you know? For a couple of seconds there I just froze. Then instead of the brakes I stepped on the gas. I gave it all I had and went for him. If he'd got you, I was going to knock him right across to the other side of the road and into kingdom come!" With a wide sweep of his arm the bus driver indicated where the car would have landed. "As it was, I smacked him pretty good."

A murmur of approval and a light patter of applause greeted the end of the account. Mici now became aware of a half-dozen or so people gathered around her and the driver. Looking past them, she saw that the bus was empty. Obviously, these were the passengers.

"That was certainly quick thinking," she said. "You saved my life."

He smiled shyly. "Glad I happened along."

"Not as glad as I am."

The laughter broke the tension.

"Damn shame. Something ought to be done about these crazy drivers."

"Homicidal maniacs. They're all killers."

"Kids. Wild kids. Anything for a thrill. They're probably splitting their sides laughing about the whole thing."

Everybody talked at once; nobody listened.

Mici raised her voice. "Did anybody notice who was driving the car?" That silenced them.

"It all happened so fast," the driver explained.

"Was it a man or a woman?" Mici asked. He shook his head regretfully. "Did anybody make out whether it was a man or a woman?" Mici appealed to the passengers.

They argued among themselves. Finally, one voice dominated and ended the conjecturing. "How can you tell nowadays?"

She had to smile. "How about the license? How about the car? The color? Make? Anything?"

"It was big and black. A Caddie maybe," the driver offered.

The passengers backed him up on that. Big and black it was for sure.

The driver had been watching Mici. "You look kind a pale, miss. Don't you want me to call an ambulance? You could be in shock."

"I'm all right."

"Well, if you're sure— Well, I better see what kind of damage I did to the bus." Slowly, anxiously, he walked back to examine the vehicle. "Doesn't look too bad." His relief was palpable. "A couple of dents and I guess we each got some of the other's paint job, but I'm going to have to make a report. I may need you to back me up, miss."

"You can count on me," Mici replied. "I work for the state; I'll be making a report of my own. Why don't we get on the bus and we can exchange IDs."

"You're riding with us? Well, okay, if you say so. Come on, folks, everybody back on the bus! Let's roll."

For the next twenty-odd blocks Mici talked to the passengers but learned nothing new. By the time she got off at Fifty-ninth Street, she had everybody's address and they had hers. She had promised to contact them if she needed their testimony, and they had promised to contact her if they thought of anything new.

"Take care of yourself, Miss Anhalt," Gus Ittleson, the driver, said as she stepped down. Then he grinned. "Look both ways before you cross the street."

Mici waved and watched till the friendly lights of the bus disappeared.

Now that she was alone, she admitted to herself that she was badly shaken. She hadn't needed Gus Ittleson to tell her that it was no near accident she'd escaped but a deliberate attempt on her life. As she walked the short distance from the corner to the brightly lit Kalb townhouse, the block that had seemed so quaint and secure in the daytime appeared sinister. Mici scrutinized every shadow, quickening her pace till she reached the house on the run. When the door was opened at last and the bright rectangle of interior light spilled over her, she nearly cried with relief. It was all she could do to keep from pushing past the dignified Fulton and going directly inside.

"Good evening," she said, proud of her self-control.

"Good evening, miss." He didn't move.

"I'm Mici Anhalt. I've come to see Senator Kalb."

"I know who you are, Miss Anhalt. The senator is not at home."

Chapter XIII

Casting a nervous glance over her shoulder at the dark shadows from which she'd fled, Mici looked longingly at the bright safety of the Kalb vestibule.

"May I come in?"

The houseman drew back politely. She entered, and the door was closed behind her.

"I have an appointment," she informed Fulton. "The senator's secretary called me just about half an hour ago and said that the senator wanted to see me."

"Miss Kittay called you? Take a seat, Miss Anhalt." He waved her to the bench and then disappeared up the curving staircase.

Mici didn't notice how long he was gone; she was too busy trying to pull herself together. She felt cold, very cold, and she couldn't stop trembling. Reaction, of course. Delayed reaction. It would pass. What wouldn't pass was the realization that somebody had tried to kill her and, having failed, might try again.

"Miss Anhalt? Are you all right?"

It was Senator Kalb. He was standing right in front of her. "I thought . . . Fulton said . . ."

"I left orders that I didn't want to be disturbed," he explained. "Are you all right, Miss Anhalt?"

"Oh? Yes, thank you. I . . . had a close call on the way over here. A car just missed me."

"How terrible! I think you'd better have some brandy. We'll go to the library. This way, Miss Anhalt."

Senator Kalb was completely unruffled as he poured the drink and solicitous as he put it into her hand. He took none himself. He sat down, not behind his desk, but in a chair beside Mici, waiting till her color improved. "Now, Miss Anhalt, you say that my secretary, Genevieve Kittay, called you and told you that I wanted to see you here in my home?"

"The woman didn't give her name, just said that she was your secretary and that you were anxious for me to come over as soon as possible."

"And did she mention what I wanted to see you about?"

"No, sir, only that it was urgent."

"I'm very sorry, Miss Anhalt, whoever called you it was not Miss Kittay. She's not even with me. She's in Washington. Have you any idea why anyone should play such a trick on you?"

It should have been obvious; if she herself had not been the intended victim, it would have been. Coming that close to being run over tended to cloud the perceptions. "I guess someone wanted to get me out on the street."

"Oh?" For a moment Senator Kalb was puzzled. "You mean the accident? You think someone deliberately lured you outside in order to run you down? Why?"

"I'm investigating the Tully case. Someone must be getting nervous."

"I thought Mrs. Tully had been arrested and charged?"

"Yes, sir, she has." With Faith locked up, tonight's incident would at least serve as further indication of her innocence. It brought a pale smile to Mici's drawn face.

Kalb noticed it. "I take it you don't think the police have the right person?"

"No, sir, I don't."

"All right. Someone knows that you are working on Mrs. Tully's behalf and is afraid of what you may find out." His handsome face was somber. "But why should I be used as the lure?"

She hadn't thought of that, but she found an answer. "I suppose because it's been in all the papers that Eugene Tully attended your party on the night he was killed. Presumably you and Mrs. Kalb were the last ones to see him alive."

"All right. And what were you hoping that I could tell you?" The question was put mildly enough, but the gray eyes that had just a few moments ago been filled with concern were now hard and probing. Mici had some idea of how a witness coming under Kalb's scrutiny at a senate hearing must feel. "If you believed that the call was genuine, and obviously you did, then you must have had some inkling of what I might want to see you about."

She had come to do the questioning and now found herself on the defensive instead. "I assumed you had information for me."

"If I had, I would have given it to you the first time you were here."

"Perhaps something had occurred to you since."

"Such as?"

"Your party was over by midnight and all your guests had left by then. Mrs. Kalb retired almost immediately, but you didn't. One of your part-time help, the maid Carmelita Rodriguez, saw you go out."

"Ah. I went for a walk. I do that quite often."

"So Fulton says. Eugene Tully was killed sometime between twelve-fifteen and one-forty. We know you went out shortly after midnight, but we have no idea when you came back."

Though it was not an accusation, it was certainly a very strong intimation that an alibi was required. Kalb did not respond. He maintained a watchful reserve that forced Mici to lay out the rest of her hand.

"I examined Eugene Tully's finances, Senator; it's part of my job. I discovered that he made various large deposits into his bank account, lump sums of three or four thousand dollars at a time and at irregular intervals." Somewhat shaken by her own temerity, Mici was also relieved that the thing was finally out in the open.

Seymour Kalb considered. "I suppose it will not suffice you, Miss Anhalt, if I say that neither Helene nor I had anything whatsoever to do with Eugene Tully's death?"

Mici licked her lips nervously. "It must suffice me, Senator. I have no right to even be here talking to you," she confessed. "I was instructed by my superior to leave you and Mrs. Kalb alone. The detective carrying the Tully case has received the same orders from his boss not to annoy you. If I hadn't received that telephone call I wouldn't be here."

"But since you are here, you might as well give it a try, eh?"

She nodded.

"All right, you've tried."

"It doesn't bother you, Senator, that Faith Tully may be innocent? Don't you think she's suffered enough having lost both husband and child without being thrown into jail for a crime she didn't commit?"

"You're the only one I know who thinks she's innocent, Miss Anhalt. I'm inclined to accept the police judgment: they're professionals."

"But they don't know that you were out strolling alone in the rain at the time the murder was committed," Mici pointed out with deceptive mildness, blue eyes fixed on Kalb.

"Do you intend to inform them?"

"No, sir, because I doubt that they'd do anything about it, but I think the newspapers would."

The senator met her gaze. "The newspapers will not print an unfounded allegation, at least not the reputable papers."

"I'm not going to make an unfounded allegation. I'm going to tell what both your maid and houseman have no choice but to verify—that you left this house, alone, shortly after midnight on the night of the murder, that nobody knows where you went or when you came back. Actually, I'm surprised that the press has passed over your connection with this case so lightly. But I don't think they can afford to ignore this kind of information. The public appetite has been whetted; there's deep concern over the morality of public officials. At least they'll have to investigate, and we all know how resourceful a couple of dedicated reporters can be."

"This is blackmail, Miss Anhalt."

"No, Senator, it's quid pro quo. At least, that's what I thought the politicians called it."

He smiled bleakly. "Well, young lady, you're a lot tougher than I thought." He nodded several times as though mentally reviewing what he intended to say. "Very well. Some of those sums of money that you discovered deposited into Tully's account did come from my wife. She did have an affair with him. When it was over, he blackmailed her. She paid in order to protect me."

Though both his face and voice were devoid of emotion, Mici could sense his pain and humiliation.

"Helene continued to employ Tully as her hairdresser and to have him come to the house to do her hair because that was one of the requirements of the blackmail—a most embarrassing one," he commented. "Actually, the basis of the blackmail was not so much the affair—after all, the public doesn't regard such things too seriously nowadays. Rather, it was a threat to spread rumors regarding the physical relationship between me and my wife. These rumors could not be proved, but unfortunately, they couldn't be disproved either. Helene was afraid even the gossip would injure my career."

Mici nodded sympathetically; it was a repetition of the Florescu pattern.

"I put an end to it!" Seymour Kalb's distress transmuted into anger and that was an emotion he did not need to suppress. "I found out what was going on by accident. During the preparation of our estimated tax report the accountant came upon the withdrawals from my wife's account. As her explanation was vague, he came to me. She admitted everything. Naturally, I could not permit her to continue paying. We decided that the best thing would be for me to see Tully. The first opportunity was the night of our party. There was heavy fog at both Kennedy and La Guardia, so I was late arriving. I don't know what Tully expected, maybe that I would offer him a lump-sum settlement, but he didn't get it."

Kalb paused for a moment; his eyes wandering around the room. "We met here, in this room, and I told him the game was finished; there would be no more payoffs from the Kalbs. I told him he could do or say whatever he liked, tell whatever lies to whomever he could find to print them, there'd be no more money from my wife or me. I informed him that I was prepared to see my wife through any scandal and that I relied on my thirty-two years of public service to weather it myself. Then I threw him out—figuratively, of course." There wasn't a trace of humor in the remark. "I also warned him that he wouldn't be continuing as Helene's hairdresser and not to refer prospective clients to her for recommendation."

At that, he did manage a wry smile, and Mici was glad to see it.

"I won't deny that Eugene Tully's death was convenient, that I'm relieved to be spared the kind of gossip he could have spread just out of spite, but I didn't kill him nor did Helene. Neither one of us has an alibi. I can only give you my word that we're both innocent."

No trace now of that brief, fleeting smile. He looked haggard and to Mici more handsome than ever. She was deeply moved by the staunch defense of his wife.

"I wish that what you told me could end right here, Senator. I certainly will not say anything to the newspapers, but I do think that Mrs. Tully's attorney has a right to know. I'm afraid I'll have to inform him."

Kalb sighed heavily.

"I'm sure he won't use the information until all other leads have been exhausted."

He nodded.

Obviously, he was disappointed, and Mici couldn't blame him. She wished she could leave it at that and go, but there was another question that had to be asked. "Is Mrs. Kalb at home?"

He appeared surprised, then angry, and resigned in turn. "No, she isn't."

Mici hesitated; she didn't really know how to proceed.

Kalb solved her dilemma. "Helene was not the one who called you tonight and then attempted to run you down, Miss Anhalt. I've told you everything. I've been completely honest with you and I'd be grateful if you could spare my wife further embarrassment. But if you must talk with her . . . she's in Montego Bay with friends. I sent her there. I insisted that she go and get some rest. She'll be back next week."

Mici was relieved. She hoped she could eliminate the senator from suspicion of guilt in the night incident as easily as he had eliminated his wife. Surely an alibi for tonight would serve as an alibi for the night of Tully's murder, assuming, of course, that the driver of the car and the killer were one and the same.

Again, Seymour Kalb anticipated her. "I've been right here, in my study, working since dinner. I'm sure that Fulton will be more than willing to vouch for me." He paused. "Of course, I could have slipped out the back just as the Rodríguez girl says I did on the night of the crime."

"Perhaps you had a visitor? Or spoke on the phone?" Mici suggested a way of confirming his presence.

He shook his head. "My car is in the garage. At least, I assume it is. You or the police are welcome to examine it and to speak to my chauffeur." In two decisive strides he was at his desk and speaking on the house phone. "Miss Anhalt is leaving, Fulton. Please give her Alex's address and phone number and also the address and phone number of the garage."

"Thank you, Senator."

"You'll forgive me if I don't see you out."

"One more question, Senator."

"I think one more is all I can take, Miss Anhalt."

Mici bit her lip. "According to Fulton, Eugene Tully received several telephone calls on the night of the reception. One of the calls was inadvertently recorded by your telephone answering machine."

"Oh? I didn't know that."

"No one seems to be exactly sure who the caller was, even if it was a man or a woman. I thought if I might just . . ."

Kalb did not wait for her to finish. He picked up the phone again. "Fulton, give Miss Anhalt whatever she wants."

Then Seymour Kalb turned his back and left her.

There was no way Mici was going to go back into that dark street again that night, not even to walk the short distance to the bus stop. She not only had Fulton call for a cab, but when it pulled up in front of her building, she asked the driver to wait while she peered into the lobby. When she got up to her own floor she made sure the hall was empty before opening the elevator door. There was nobody there to jump out at her, not even Danny. Once inside her apartment, the first thing she did was call Ed Stiebeck.

"Somebody's getting nervous," he commented.

"Yeah, me."

"Why do you suppose he wants to get rid of you?"

"Don't ask me. I haven't a clue as to who tried to kill me or what he thinks I know. The only thing I'm sure of is that it wasn't Faith."

"Ah, well, you can't be sure of that either."

Mici caught her breath. "Why not? What's happened?"

"She was released. At eight o'clock tonight. The ballistics test proved negative. The gun we found in her apartment is not the murder weapon."

It was the news she'd been waiting for, eagerly anticipating, expecting to crow in triumph. Now she heard it with dismay. "You're kidding."

"Nope."

"Why didn't you let me know? You could have called me."

"You were at that dance class."

"They have telephones."

"You never told me the name of the outfit," he snapped back. "Do you know how many dance schools and studios there are in Manhattan? Look in the yellow pages sometime."

"I'm sorry, Ed. I'm just so upset."

"Listen, I understand. Having somebody try to kill you is no fun."

"Why couldn't you have kept her one more night!" she wailed.

"Dicker would have liked to, believe me," the detective answered. "He still thinks she's guilty."

"It couldn't have been Faith driving that car, Ed, it couldn't. I'm the only person on her side. I'm trying to help her."

"We'll know soon enough."

"We will? How?"

"Whoever went after you pulled a real boner. Of course, the poor schmuck could hardly anticipate that a bus was going to come to your rescue." Stiebeck laughed. "Now you fix yourself a good snort of something and get into bed and leave it all to your Uncle Ed."

Mici was delighted to do just that.

She awoke to a gray, dank, depressing morning, feeling gray, dank, and depressed herself. What she actually felt was hung over. Which was ridiculous on two brandies, the first at the senator's house and the second on Ed Stiebeck's advice just before she went to bed. Maybe she was coming down with something? The swine flu? At the moment, it didn't seem so terrible. The idea of just lying in bed for a couple of days and blocking out the real world was quite appealing. The truth was, Ilona Maria Anhalt admitted to herself, that she wasn't cut out for detective work. She didn't like the hours; she didn't like forcing people to reveal their secrets; most of all she did not enjoy being a target for murder. Her regular job, nine to five, routine checking of records, provided just as much challenge and diversity as she required.

As for Danny Best, who could say what might have happened if the call purporting to come from Senator Kalb's secretary had not interrupted? Maybe it was just as well. One way to forget an old boyfriend was to get a new one. Mici burrowed farther down under the blankets, savoring their warmth and comfort. Why not call Clyde Lauer and have him over to dinner? Maybe it would be a little less obvious if she invited Roz and Charlie too. They could play bridge. Clyde was most of the things Danny was not: dependable—Danny didn't think he owed anybody anything; hardworking—Danny had no idea what was involved in holding a job; considerate—Danny could be considerate but only if it suited his desires. Of course, Clyde Lauer didn't have Danny's verve, humor, joyous immersion in the moment, but then he didn't have the money that made those qualities possible. Money was Danny's crutch. Mici wondered what he'd be like without it.

Let somebody else find out.

As for the job—you finished what you started, scared or not. You didn't imagine aches and pains so you could skulk in bed all day. She threw back the covers and reached for the telephone, but it was not Clyde Lauer she called, it was Ed Stiebeck.

He was out on a case. The Tully case? She didn't ask. She got dressed and went to work.

Diane Lara's eyes were bright and her head high, but her hand trembled as she slapped the envelope down on the desk in front of Mici.

"Here. I hope this satisfies you."

Despite her final words of defiance, the investigator hadn't really expected Diane to show up again. From the first she'd had an instinct, a hunch, that Lawrence Hoguet's story was not gossip but fact and that the Laras were not legally married. The letter to Nicholas Hirschhorn had gone off days ago and there had been no reply so far. Maybe now, if this document stood up, it wouldn't matter whether he answered or not. Mici would be pleased to be proved wrong about the Laras, so she smiled warmly at the tall, aggressive blonde and picked up the envelope. When she opened it and saw what was inside she gasped.

"This is a photocopy! Where's the original?"

Diane Lara shrugged. "I have no idea. I went through all of Ramón's things and this is all I could find. What difference does it make?"

"We can't accept this."

"What do you mean you can't accept it? Why not? It's all there, all the information: names, dates, the church, witnesses. What more do you need?"

"I'm sorry, Diane. We need the original."

"Why? I don't see why."

"I'm sorry."

"Sorry won't help. I haven't got the original! I can't find it. I don't know what happened to it. What am I supposed to do? You tell me, what the hell am I supposed to do?"

Mici sighed. "I don't know. All I know is that we can't accept this."

For a long moment Diane Lara just stared at her. Frustration mottled her face. "You just don't want to give me the money. That's what it all boils down to. You don't want me to have the money," she accused. "You're trying to stop me from getting what's coming to me, what I'm entitled to by law." She was working herself into a tantrum.

"That's not so."

"Well, it's not up to you, or to that supervisor buddy of yours, either. I'm going to protest. I'm going over your heads and straight to the board. I know my rights. I'll go straight to the governor if I have to."

"That's your privilege." Mici wasn't angry; she knew that the woman desperately needed the money and, in Mici's opinion, was morally entitled to it. "If you could get this validated—" She indicated the photocopy.

"How do you mean, validated?"

"By the church where the ceremony took place. If you can get the church to put its seal on this copy, I'm sure it would be acceptable." Mici had never before come up against exactly this set of circumstances, but the solution seemed logical.

Diane Lara, however, was not enthusiastic. "How'm I going to do that? I can't afford to go way out to Detroit."

Mici was surprised. Diane had lived in Detroit when she was Mrs. Hirschhorn. She had met Lara there and run away with him. It certainly seemed odd that she should go back there to marry him. Not having really examined the certificate closely she did so now. Yes, Detroit, Michigan, Church of All Saints. The certificate appeared authentic, showed no signs of having been altered—no smudges, blots, or suspicious marks of any kind. Nevertheless, all of Mici's earlier misgivings returned. Something was wrong.

"You could mail this to them," she suggested. "They would search their records, emboss this copy with their seal, and mail it back to you."

"I think . . . I heard . . . that the church, the original church, that is, burned down. The records were probably destroyed."

Something was very wrong. "Since the church was in Detroit, I assume it was yours and not Ramón's," Mici reasoned. "Surely, some member of the congregation would remember your second wedding."

Apparently that possibility brought no cheer.

"How about one of the witnesses? That's it. We could contact the witnesses, and if one of them would sign an affidavit, that might be enough."

"Never mind." Suddenly, Diane Lara reached forward across the desk and snatched at the photocopy.

Just as quickly, Mici put her own hand over it and held it firmly. Then with her other hand she disengaged Diane's fingers and slid the paper out so she could examine the signatures of the witnesses. Only one meant anything to her, but it was more than enough.

"Clare Hirschhorn. Is she a relation of your first husband?"

Diane turned scarlet. She didn't answer.

"All I have to do is make a phone call to him or to her."

"Don't do that!" Diane Lara exclaimed. She sighed, the unhealthy flush becoming even darker. "Clare is Nick's sister."

"I see. And your first husband's sister was a witness at your wedding to another man?"

No answer.

"A wedding that took place in the same city and the same church as the first? It was the same church, wasn't it?"

The woman stood stiff and straight and mute, her jaw clamped so tightly that a nerve at her temple throbbed with the pressure.

Mici continued, "You used your original marriage certificate for this, didn't you? You blocked out the name of Nicholas Hirschhorn and substituted that of Ramón Lara." She scrutinized the document. "I suppose you had to rewrite your own name in order to make the color of the ink match. Also, you changed the date, naturally. Did you cover the original entries with a strip of paper, or did you use white-out? You did a good job." She held the paper close to the light. "Of course, no matter how good the job it would show on the original. That's why you could only bring in the photocopy."

Unexpectedly, the woman who called herself Diane Lara stopped fighting. She accepted defeat, relaxed, and her color returned to normal, or close to it. She reached for the photocopy and this time Mici let her have it.

"Does this mean I won't get compensation?"

The arrogance was stunning. "I'm afraid so."

"Well, that's the way the ball bounces."

She was so absolutely amoral that Mici could only marvel at her.

"There is one thing you could do for me. . . ."

"What?"

"I'd appreciate it if you wouldn't spread the word around that Ramón and I weren't legally man and wife."

"I won't say a word."

"Thanks. You see, Ramón had a lot of friends, and I'm sure that they intend to help me out. If they discover that we weren't married . . . well, they might feel like they're off the hook. Know what I mean?"

"Sure." Mici was sorry for her. It didn't seem any more wrong to her to dupe her friends than it had to cheat the compensation board. On the other hand, she was close to destitute and had nowhere to turn except to these so called friends. Maybe she was being realistic about how they felt toward her. "May I ask you something? Why didn't you and Ramón Lara ever get married?"

"Didn't Larry Hoguet tell you?"

"He said Hirschhorn refused to give you a divorce."

"That's right. Nick didn't believe in divorce. 'Whom God hath joined . . .' and all that jazz."

"I'm sorry. I wish— What are you going to do now?"

She shrugged. "Who knows? I'll think of something."

Mici thought she detected the beginning of a smile as Diane Hirschhorn turned and walked out.

So the Lara case was closed; at least Mici Anhalt thought so. She was surprised four days later to have Nicholas Hirschhorn turn up in her office. And not particularly pleased, since her sympathy for Diane outweighed her distaste and she considered that Hirschhorn's lack of compassion was responsible for the woman's present plight. She could hardly refuse to see him.

He was better-looking than she had expected, though she didn't suppose that looks were the reason Diane had walked out on him in favor of her tennis player. His manner was pleasant enough; there was no trace of the smugness or self-importance that most self-made men couldn't hide. It didn't prove anything. A man could be charming and also impossible to live with.

"What can I do for you, Mr. Hirschhorn?"

In his hand he held the letter she had written to him. Hirschhorn's reactions on receiving it had been mixed. To begin with, he had known nothing about the subway shooting. The incident had received minimal space in the Detroit papers. Lara's death got more space, but that was on the sports pages and Hirschhorn never read the sports anymore. The letter had not referred to these events, merely requested certain information without explaining why the information was sought. Nicholas Hirschhorn's first instinct had been to pick up the phone and contact the M. Anhalt of the letter. However, he seldom acted on impulse; it was one of the foundations of his success. In his youth, Nick had displayed a certain shy charm and a hint of gentle humor. These endearing qualities appeared to have been buried under the years, the pounds, and the money. The tall, thin, serious boy had become a burly, overwhelming personage, apparently self-contained, self-sufficient, neither wanting nor needing any kind of close emotional contact. So he did not directly call M. Anhalt, but reread the letter and then set it aside, leaving it to his subconscious to suggest the best way of handling the problem. On the Wednesday after lunch he told his secretary to book him on the first plane to New York. She got him a seat on the five-o'clock flight, and as he kept a suitcase always packed and ready at the office, he was able to go straight out to the airport without stopping off at home. His secretary thought it was a sudden decision, but Hirschhorn knew that he had actually made it on the very first reading of M. Anhalt's letter.

Now the executive carefully unfolded the letter and laid it in front of Mici. Then he sat down, though he hadn't been invited.

"I hardly expected you to reply in person, Mr. Hirschhorn." Mici was slightly discomfited.

He didn't pretend that he'd been coming to New York anyway on other business. "What's this all about?"

"The letter is plain enough." She was stung by his tone.

"If it were, I wouldn't be here," he replied courteously but no less coolly. "You ask if Diane and I were divorced and if so on what date the decree became final. Why? You don't say why you want to know. What business is it of yours?"

There was no point in arguing. "You're right, Mr. Hirschhorn, it's no longer our business. As far as our agency is concerned, the Lara case is closed. I'm sorry you've come all this way for nothing."

He regarded her for a couple of moments. "You don't really expect me to be satisfied with that, do you?" His manner changed abruptly. "Please, Miss Anhalt. This is important to me."

His anxiety touched her. "I guess there's no reason why you shouldn't know what's just about general knowledge."

"Thank you."

"We try to protect the privacy of our clients," she explained. "Since they are victims of crimes, very often sensational crimes that have been exploited by the newspapers, it isn't always easy, but we try."

"I wasn't being facetious."

She nodded. "I assume you know that Ramón Lara is dead."

"Yes." Again, had Nicholas Hirschhorn acted on impulse he would have gone directly to see Diane when he landed. Caution had dictated that he find out as much as possible about her and the situation first, and caution had been reinforced by the fact that he had not been able to find the Laras' address in the Manhattan directory. So he had checked in at the Waldorf and then headed for the main branch of the public library, where he spent the balance of the evening searching through the microfilm files of the back issues of the New York *Times*.

"I read about it in the papers."

"Well, then you know that he was severely injured, but you may not know that he applied to us for victim's compensation. Since his death was directly a result of the shooting . . ." She hesitated and decided not to delve into the murky area of the way in which Ramón Lara died. "Well, Mrs. Lara applied for widow's compensation. Unfortunately, there was some question as to the legality of her marriage."

"Could you just tell it straight out, Miss Anhalt?"

"All right. If she wasn't Lara's legal wife, we couldn't accept her claim for a widow's compensation."

He ducked his head and winced as though shying from an anticipated blow. "Why couldn't you just ask Diane?"

"We did. She insisted that she was married and that the marriage was a legal one. We asked for proof, and she brought in a wedding certificate. Unfortunately, it had been falsified."

"Oh, my God!" He passed a hand over his eyes, then down over his mouth.

There was no need to tell him that his own marriage certificate had been used as the base for the attempted fraud. Mici waited for a few moments. "Are you all right, Mr. Hirschhorn?"

He looked at her with the eyes of a man whose worst fears have been realized. "I knew it. I knew it. I kept telling myself that, no, I was wrong, that Diane would never do such a thing, but, of course, it's exactly the kind of thing she would do. Oh, God!"

Mici sensed that for Nicholas Hirschhorn to call upon the Lord in the course of ordinary conversation was a sign of great stress. "Can I get you anything? A glass of water?" She still didn't understand the reason for his great distress.

"I have to see her. I have to find out for sure. Would you please tell me where I can reach Diane? She's not in the phone book." His voice was hoarse with anxiety.

"What do you want to see her about?"

"The divorce, of course. What else? The divorce!"

"What divorce?"

"That's what I have to find out. Was there or wasn't there a divorce?"

Mici gawked. Now, she was beginning to get it. "You mean, you don't know . . . you thought. . . . She says you refused to give her a divorce."

The answer to that was a groan that shook his whole frame. "I did refuse at the beginning, when she first left me. I loved her and I believed that she'd come back. Oh, by then I was under no illusion about Diane; we'd been married six years and I accepted the fact that her feeling for me didn't match mine for her. I knew she was restless, dissatisfied, but I thought that in her way she did love me and that she did not really love Ramón Lara. She didn't leave me for him but for the fame she thought he could help her get. She thought he could make her into a champion."

"A tennis champion? I didn't even know. . . ." Mici stopped. Of course, she knew that Diane played tennis; someone had mentioned it. Obviously, she kept herself in top shape and that had to involve some kind of rigorous exercise, and what more natural than that it should be tennis?

"She never made the top; she never got a national ranking." Hirschhorn told her. "What she was, was a good club player. What she became was a tennis bum, going from tournament to tournament. Back then, ten or twelve years ago, even the top stars couldn't make a living out of it. Tennis hadn't caught the public fancy. The big tournaments were amateur events from which the pros were banned, and the alleged amateurs got expense money with more substantial payments under the table. Diane never qualified for the extra money.

"I used to blame myself," Hirschhorn continued. "It started with the house. We didn't belong in Grosse Pointe, but Diane wanted it, and I could afford it. What neither of us understood then was that simply owning the house would not make us a part of the community. It didn't open doors socially. What I didn't understand was that that's what Diane was after. She decided we had to join the country club, that it would provide our entrée. *Okay, I managed to get us in and, believe me, I had to pull all kinds of strings and make plenty of charitable contributions to do it. It didn't help. At that point, Diane discovered she had some ability in tennis. She figured that if she could get really good, then she would be sought after on the court and that would lead to general social acceptance. She took lessons; she worked hard; she worked herself up to club champion. Only she let her desire show; she was too relentless. The men didn't mind. She was attractive and a good mixed-doubles partner. But the women resented her.*

"When Lara and the troupe turned up for their exhibition tournament, she misread his attentions. He flattered her game, offered to help her with her backhand. It was a line they all used on the pretty women. The players got on the court, hit a few balls, and set themselves up for later off the court. Diane took Lara seriously. I have a feeling he was as dismayed to have her turn up and join him in the next town as I was to get home and read the note she'd left me. Lara was her ticket to fame. She would show them all. Once she was a champion they'd be eager to invite her into their homes.

"When she wrote asking for a divorce, I said no. I followed the tournament results and I could see she wasn't making it. I thought the gypsy life would pall after a while and she'd be back for the luxuries I could provide. I had a feeling that Lara thought so too. Obviously, we were both wrong. She was winning just enough to keep her hopes alive. So the next time she asked for a divorce I said yes."

Mici knew what was coming and knew that telling it would give him at least some relief.

"She offered to go out to Reno and wait out the required residency. I sent her money for her expenses and all legal fees. I didn't hear anything for a while. Finally, I received a very abject letter telling me that she hadn't been able to get to Reno after all. She confessed that she'd used the money for herself and Lara, that they'd been having a hard time financially, and she asked me to forgive her. Now things were better, she said, and she could get down to Mexico for the divorce if I was still agreeable.

"Of course, I should have known better, but I wanted to believe her because by this time I'd met someone. I was in love and anxious to remarry. I could have got the divorce myself, but I didn't want to humiliate Diane in the local courts and it wasn't exactly convenient for me to take the time from my business to go to Reno myself or the Virgin Islands or wherever. I guess you can figure the rest. Again several weeks passed and I didn't hear from her. I was getting desperate trying to locate her. Finally I did and I sent a telegram asking what was holding things up. She wired back that the divorce had been granted and the papers were in the mail. I never got them."

"You went ahead and got married anyway."

He nodded. "We have a son, seven years old. At first I kept telling myself that the papers would turn up, that somehow they'd gone astray in the mail, just as Diane claimed. After a while, I told myself that as long as I didn't hear from Diane it had to be all right. After all, she'd been the one who'd asked for the divorce. I convinced myself that no news was good news. Till I got your letter."

"Just because she and Ramón Lara never married doesn't mean she didn't go ahead with the divorce," Mici said, not really believing it herself.

"I know that, but it doesn't help. I have to be able to prove that there was a divorce, and there's no way I can do that. I haven't the slightest notion where in Mexico she might have gone for it, or even if she went to Mexico. I don't know where to start. I can't claim that my present marriage is legal." He paused and remained silent for a very long time till he added, "Not if Diane claims it isn't."

Without another word, Mici thumbed through the small card-file box on her desk, found Diane's address, copied it out, and handed it to Nicholas Hirschhorn. She didn't think he'd need it, however. She had the uneasy feeling that Diane would be looking him up first.

CHAPTER XVI

Lieutenant Nelson Dicker made it a point of honor to admit when he was wrong. That didn't mean he liked admitting it, particularly when the admission had to be made to a woman. The fact that he'd never met Miss Anhalt didn't help. Fortunately, the lieut also believed in going through channels, so when the Tully case broke, he had good reason for bypassing the investigator and contacting her superior, Supervisor Dowd. The conversation was cordial but guarded on both sides. Dowd congratulated Lieutenant Dicker and the good work of his people, and Dicker returned the compliment, thanking the supervisor for his cooperation. Neither man mentioned Investigator Anhalt directly, though she was on both their minds.

A big grin spread over Adam Dowd's face as he hung up. He got Mici on the intercom. "Can you come in?" He was so eager to share the news that he started talking before she'd even closed the door behind her.

"They've identified the car that tried to run you down. Ed Stiebeck had paint scrapings taken off the bus and the lab has made a positive identification. There's no doubt: the paint came from Doru Florescu's Cadillac."

"Florescu . . ."

"He's admitted it; he's admitted trying to run you down. What's more," Dowd paused portentously, savoring the moment, "he's confessed to the murder." He beamed on Mici. "Congratulations. You've been vindicated. Mr. Cornelius will be delighted."

Mici felt she ought to be, too. Why wasn't she? "I can't believe it."

"I can. The man's whole life was wrapped up in his wife. He was afraid he was going to lose her."

"But she'd had lovers before, plenty of them. Florescu admitted it; so did she. Well, she called the affairs flirtations, but there's no doubt what she meant."

"Maybe, but Madame liked being the dominant personality in her affairs. According to Florescu's confession, she was the one who called the tune. Not this time. Tully was different; he had something the others didn't: Madame was obsessed by him. Florescu had already paid Tully to break it off, and when Tully married Faith Goss, Florescu figured that cemented the deal. He could hardly believe it when the affair started up again. He confronted the hairdresser, who only asked for more money. He realized then that Tully would never be satisfied and he decided to get rid of him permanently."

Mici frowned.

"He's even retracted his alibi, which was, after all, not really an alibi." Disappointed by Mici's cool reception of the news, Dowd now found his own enthusiasm ebbing. "He claims that it was his custom when his wife fell asleep to return to his own room. He did so as usual, but instead of going to bed he got dressed and drove over to the Kalbs' house."

"How did he know Tully was there?"

"It was a big social event. Tully bragged about being invited."

"So then Florescu sat in his car waiting for Tully to come out?" Mici asked. "When he did, Florescu followed him to the parking lot and shot him and stomped him?"

"That's what he says." Dowd was now becoming prey to Mici's very obvious skepticism, yet he continued to present the police version. "He could hardly gun Tully down in front of the Kalbs' residence with the guests coming and going."

"Why didn't he go directly to the parking lot and wait there?"

Dowd shrugged. "Maybe he didn't know where Tully parked, or that that's where he would be going, or even that he was driving his car?"

"Hmm . . ."

"There was, in fact, no way he could know where Tully would be going or what he would be doing after the party."

"Ah . . ." Mici sighed.

Dowd's face clouded. He sought Mici's eyes and held them with his own. "Leave it alone," he counseled. "This is not our responsibility. Faith Tully has been cleared. We can now go ahead and process her claim. That's it." But he hadn't even convinced himself. "If the man is innocent, why did he confess?"

"That's the point, Adam. He didn't have to, not really. The police actually have nothing on him. He didn't even have to admit trying to run me down."

"He could hardly deny that."

"Sure he could. The police can prove that Florescu's car was used in the attempt, but they can't prove he was the one driving it. The bus driver was too intent on knocking the car out of the way, and the passengers can't even agree on whether the driver was male or female, much less make a positive ID. All Doru Florescu had to do was insist that someone else used his car."

"So he lost his nerve. It happens."

"I think Doru Florescu has plenty of nerve."

"Ah . . ." It was Adam's turn to sigh. "You think it was someone else driving the car and he knows it and is trying to protect . . . that person."

"Yes, I do."

"His wife."

"As you said, she's everything to him: a meal ticket and a living, breathing, glowing testament to his manhood. He may have created her, but without her he doesn't exist."

"You want to talk to Florescu? Now?" Ed Stiebeck gaped at her.

Mici had run him down in a corridor of the Criminal Courts Building, where he waited for the arraignment of his prisoner. Having served a large part of her apprenticeship here, she knew that as much business was conducted in these hallways as inside the courtrooms, and often the corridors were more crowded. This one certainly was jammed. Witnesses and police officers with nothing to do but wait, glazed with boredom and mired in a morass of wasted hours, leaned against the walls; attorneys, bondsmen with too much to do, who would never catch up, were running, dodging islands of people like Mici and the detective, who were having impromptu conferences.

"You ought to know better than to ask!" Ed shouted, partly out of outrage, but mostly to be heard.

"You can take me in." She raised her voice too. "We can talk to him together."

"Absolutely not."

"Come on, Ed. Would I ask if it weren't important?"

But Mici had already lost her chance. As Stiebeck hesitated, a uniformed officer peered out of the nearest courtroom.

"Hey, Stiebeck, your prisoner's attorney just went in."

"Yeah? Thanks, Haggerty." He turned to Mici. "Sorry, but that's it."

She knew that Florescu was in a holding cell at the back of the courtroom and that once the attorney went in to see him it was the signal that the case was close to being heard. If the attorney was a big shot, and certainly Florescu had called on the best, then things moved very fast. She also knew that though Ed said he was sorry, he was actually relieved.

"Could I see him after?"

"For God's sake, woman! He's made a full confession."

"Why?"

"What do you mean, why? Because he's guilty. Because he did it, that's why."

"Maybe he's trying to protect somebody."

The detective's eyes narrowed. "You're guessing!" he challenged, then asked almost plaintively. "Aren't you?"

"Have you got anything to substantiate the confession? Like, for instance, the murder weapon?"

The tip of Stiebeck's tongue flicked nervously out and around his lips. "He says he got rid of it. Threw it into the river."

"Really?"

"Well, why not? He could have done that."

"As I understand it, Doru Florescu claims he went to bed with his wife around eleven that night, the night of the murder," Mici expounded. "When she fell asleep, it was his habit to slip out of her bed and retire to his own rooms so as not to disturb her night's rest. On this occasion, he says he went back to his room but not to bed. He got dressed, got this car, and drove over to the Kalbs' to wait for Tully to come out. Now, since the party broke up at midnight, wouldn't you say that was cutting it pretty close?"

"So maybe he's wrong about the exact time he and his wife went to bed."

"Let me ask you this—did anybody see Florescu sitting in his black Cadillac while he waited for Tully to come out of the Kalbs' residence?" She didn't give Ed a chance to answer. "The Kalbs' reception was very special; they had all kinds of foreign dignitaries and important government personages there. These people arrived in chauffered limousines, and the limousines with their chauffeurs parked and waited through the evening. Also, there had to be plenty of security people around."

"Okay, okay, I'll ask; I'll find out."

"Do that. The whole street was blocked off by order of the police department, so there were probably a couple of cops on duty too. Personally, I don't think Florescu could have found a place to park within five blocks of that house."

"I'll find out," Stiebeck repeated doggedly.

"If Florescu claims he parked where he could see Tully come out the door, he's lying."

"All right, you've made your point."

"And why should he lie?" Mici bore down. "If he's confessed to murder, why should he lie about a detail? No, Ed, the whole confession is a lie. He's not telling it like it was, but like he *thinks* it would have to have been."

"You're something, you know that, Mici Anhalt?" Stiebeck muttered. "You're the one who pointed the finger at Doru Florescu in the first place."

"I never said he was guilty. I just pointed out that he was as likely a suspect as Faith Tully. You shouldn't have been in such a hurry to arrest him."

"You've got to be kidding! What was I supposed to do when he confessed? Call you up and ask permission?"

"The point is that whoever killed Tully didn't need to lurk around the Kalb residence to find out where he was going after the party. The killer already knew."

"Sure, to the parking lot to park his car."

"Why should he assume that Tully would even be using his car?"

The detective shrugged; it seemed quibbling. "Tully told him."

But to Mici the point was extremely important. "We're missing something about that parking lot, I don't know what."

"What significance? He was killed there; that's it."

"He was killed outside," she corrected. "We haven't paid enough attention to why he was killed in that particular place, and at that time. I think if we can answer that, then we will have solved the case."

"He was killed in the street to make it look like the work of the girl gang Tully had been involved with a few days earlier," he replied testily. Ed Stiebeck didn't believe in making problems where none existed.

"How about the time lapse? We decided at the beginning that Tully couldn't have been shot directly on leaving the lot because the attendant was still on duty."

"Sure, sure. He came back later."

"Why? Not to get his car—the lot was closed. Why did he come back?"

"Are you asking, or are you going to tell me?"

She was too intent on thinking it out even to note the irony. "The parking lot is between First and Second Avenue, okay? Tully lived west of the lot. If he'd been on his way home after leaving the car, he would have headed west, toward Second Avenue. But the body was found between the lot and First Avenue."

"So he wasn't going home. We've been over this—"

"Yes, he was."

"Make up your mind."

"We didn't take into account the position of the body. The important thing is the *direction* in which he was lying. He was shot in the back. Wouldn't it be natural for him to fall forward, that is, in the direction in which he had been heading?"

"Yeah. I suppose so." Stiebeck was beginning to get what she was after.

"He was lying between First Avenue and the lot, with his head toward Second. That indicates that he was coming from First and was about to pass the lot on his way to Second.

"On his way home," the detective concluded.

"Yes," Mici agreed. "Eugene Tully was finally and at last going home."

"From where? Where had he been?"

Micis translucent eyes were narrowed and her piquant face intent. "That's the question, isn't it? If we knew that— Where was Eugene Tully during the one hour and a half between twelve-fifteen, when the lot attendant closed up, and one-forty, when his wife found him dying on the sidewalk?"

"He had a date."

Mici nodded. "Yeah. And he was late. And his date got impatient and called the Kalb residence to find out what was holding him up."

"How do you know that?"

"They have a telephone answering machine and the call was recorded."

Stiebeck's eyes bulged. "I don't believe it! You mean, it's on tape? You went to the senator and the senator let you have the tape?"

"He was very cooperative."

Once again Officer Haggerty stuck his head through the courtroom door. "Say, Stiebeck, you're next."

"Yeah, yeah, coming." He waved Haggerty off, his eyes fixed on Mici. "You're saying that when Florescu went back to his own room, it was Madame Florescu who got up and got dressed and went out. That she had a late date with Tully for after the party?"

"That's what Doru Florescu thinks."

"Is that what you think?"

"Stiebeck!" Haggerty's call brooked no more delay.

In her brief career as a professional dancer, Mici Anhalt had learned that the glamour of the theater was out front. She had walked down enough filthy, garbage-strewn and rat-infested stagedoor alleys to appreciate the cleanliness of the approach to the stage door of the Metropolitan Opera House. She was not, and was sure she never would be, so blasé, however, that she wasn't thrilled to be going inside. She didn't really know what she'd expected, but it was not a relatively spacious, well-lit, fully carpeted reception area. She felt vaguely let down: it was more like an office than a theater. On the other hand, why shouldn't performers enjoy the same amenities that any office worker took for granted? Nevertheless, Mici felt cheated. She would have liked for just one moment to walk out on the darkened stage and savor the magic of the empty, waiting house. In this sanitized anteroom she was so completely disoriented that she didn't even have an idea of which direction the stage might be.

And she wasn't allowed to find out. Her name was checked against a visitors' list and she was pointed in the appropriate direction and watched to make sure she didn't wander anywhere else. Stage doormen are usually referred to as "Pop." It was an impudence to even think of this very superior security guard in that context. Meekly, Mici went where she'd been ordered.

Sanda Florescu's dressing room was small; in fact, it was cramped. Paint peeled here and there, and the small throw rug was threadbare, hardly the accommodation one would expect for a star of her magnitude. Was it an indication of the Metropolitan's dire need for funds? The only suggestion of the magic that would be created within those walls in another hour and a half was the row of costumes for the evening's performance of *Tales of Hoffman*. But in the prosaic surroundings the sumptuous dresses seemed merely garish. Even La Staordinaria herself, resting upon a kind of narrow daybed in a corner, seemed diminished. She had a damp towel over her eyes, but when she heard Mici come in, she removed it, revealing a red and swollen face. She sat up.

"I'm sorry to disturb you before a performance."

"I wasn't sleeping. How can I sleep? I'd give anything in this world not to have to go on tonight, but my stand-in has the flu. Can you imagine? The management would be forced to change the bill. You have no idea of the logistics of that." She sighed dramatically. "Besides, my canceling might make it look even worse for Doru."

The spark was missing; there was not even a sense of that tremendous and famous vitality, and Mici wondered how Sanda Florescu would get through the night's performance. If, of course, there was a performance.

"You said on the phone that you have information that could be helpful to Doru," the singer reminded Mici. "What is it?"

"Do you believe that your husband killed Eugene Tully?"

She looked puzzled. "He says that he did."

"Do you believe it?"

"Are you asking me if I believe Doru capable of committing such a crime?"

"No. Do you believe he actually did it?"

"I don't know what to believe," the singer murmured.

"The last time I was at your apartment, Madame Florescu, after you'd left us for your afternoon rest, your husband told me that Eugene Tully was the only one of your lovers who dominated you."

Madame frowned. She hesitated a long time.

"That is true. I made a fool of myself over Eugène. I admit it. I couldn't help myself."

"Mr. Florescu also told me that he paid Tully to keep him from spreading some ugly rumors."

"Rumors?" The diva shrugged. "I knew that Doru was paying Eugène."

Mici marveled that a woman so worldly could permit herself to be so degraded.

"I didn't care! I didn't care. Just as long as he stayed with me . . ." She put up her hands to her already swollen eyes.

Was she crying for her dead lover or her imprisoned husband? Mici wondered. Or for herself? "Where did you and Eugene Tully meet?" She asked casually, but having put the idea into words, Mici realized just how very important the answer would be. "Where did you go?" It could hardly have been the star's apartment, since her husband was also her manager and the apartment his office. It was not likely to have been a hotel, for Madame was well known, extremely distinctive, and ran the risk of being recognized. "Did you have a regular place?"

"His apartment."

"What?"

"You asked me where we met; we met at his apartment." She blushed. "The one he had before he married, naturally."

"Naturally," Mici repeated while her mind raced. What could have been more convenient than for Gene Tully to keep his bachelor pad and continue as before? How simple, and now that she knew, how obvious. Did he deduct the rent from his taxes as business expense, she wondered bitterly. "Where is it? What's the address?"

"Six-three-one East Eighty-second Street."

East of the parking lot? Her logic was confirmed. "You went over there the night he was killed. You had a date."

"No, I didn't."

"You were the one who went out, not your husband. When your husband returned to his own room, you got up and went to meet Tully. First, though, you called the Kalb residence to make sure he'd left."

That appeared to puzzle her. "I didn't call."

Mici dismissed that too. "When you got over to his place you found him with another woman."

The opera star sighed. "I'll tell you the truth, Miss Anhalt. I did not have a date with Eugène, but I did get up and go out to see him. I took a taxi and had the driver let me off a block away as usual. Then I walked to the corner of First Avenue. On the way, I changed my mind."

There was so little emotion and such utter weariness in the statement, that Mici wavered. "All right. You didn't go up. You knew that he had another woman up there. Maybe he told you, maybe he taunted you about the other woman . . . however it was, you knew. So you didn't go up. You waited for him to come down. You waited outside in the street from him, and when he appeared, you killed him."

She shook her head. "I went home. I went back home, I swear to you, Miss Anhalt, that I did not go up to the apartment or wait. I did walk for a while . . . till it began to rain . . ."

That made three people strolling on a lousy, rainy night.

"Suddenly I had a picture of myself, lovesick as an ignorant girl, roaming through the night. I saw what I was letting Eugène do to me and I began to feel some sense of shame. I'm not saying that I reached the decision to break off the affair at that moment, or even on that particular night, but I did find the strength not to go to him, to deny myself at least on that one occasion. . . ." Her voice trailed off.

"Too bad Mr. Florescu didn't know that."

"I could hardly have told him!" Sanda Florescu snapped with some of her accustomed verve.

"Too bad," Mici repeated. "Because you see, I believe your husband also got up in the night. Maybe he heard a sound from your room or thought he did. Whatever the reason, I believe that he looked in on you and discovered that you were gone. The next morning he read about Tully's murder. Then I came asking questions."

"*O Doammei, O Doamne!*" The star moaned. "Doru thought I did it?"

Mici nodded. "And that I suspected you. Last night he tried to run me down with his car. When that failed and the police traced the car, he decided to admit and also shoulder the blame for the killing."

"Doru, Doru! *Sa te auda Dumezeu!* That he is willing to make such a sacrifice for me!"

"He loves you."

"How can I ever make it up to him?"

"By telling the truth."

"I have told the truth."

Mici was already beginning to have second thoughts about her reconstruction, but she wasn't ready to give up. The murder of Eugene Tully couldn't have been completely impulsive; there had to have been at least enough premeditation for the killer to obtain a gun. If Madame Florescu knew about Tully's other women, then she had both the incentive and time to provide herself with a weapon. She tried again.

"Tully did have a date, but not with you. His date was with another woman. You knew of it and you meant to intercept him, but first you had to call the Kalb house to find out if he'd left." Delving into her handbag, Mici produced a small, round, red plastic box similar to the kind used for typewriter ribbons. "I have here the tape from the answering machine connected to the Kalbs' telephone. All calls received that night are recorded on it."

She got a reaction all right, but not the one she'd expected. Sanda Florescu appeared relieved. "Ah. You will not find my voice recorded on that tape."

"I don't know if you've heard of a voice print, Madame? It is now scientifically possible to identify an individual as specifically through his voice patterns as by means of his fingerprints—no matter what attempt is made to disguise the voice."

"Then I am fortunate for I did not call the Kalbs', your experts will prove that it is not my voice on your tape, even if someone has tried to imitate it."

Her face bloated, eyes inflamed, even the glory of her flaming hair dulled and lifeless, at the moment the singer was anything but La Straordinaria. Drawing from some last inner reserve, she straightened, slowly rose from the couch, crossed over to her dressing table, and switched on the mirror lights. She looked into the mirror first at her own reflection, then at Mici's.

"Once Doru knows that I am not guilty, he will retract his confession."

"That may not be enough."

The diva's eyes met Mici's and held them. "In that case I will make a confession of my own. Everything that Doru claims he did, I will say that I did instead. That should confuse the police considerably, wouldn't you say?"

"Oh, indeed yes." Mici could envision the scene at the police station, which she was sure Madame would carry through with all the dramatic gusto of which she was capable.

The diva remained thoughtful. "And if more is needed . . . well, there is that tape you seem to consider so important. Your experts will confirm that neither my voice nor Doru's is on it." There was a flicker in Sanda Florescu's green eyes as though somewhere inside her a failing battery was being recharged. She shifted her gaze from Mici to herself, stretching her chin out till the sagging jaw line was taut again.

"You've done both my husband and me a service, Miss Anhalt. We are grateful." She reached for a jar of makeup and began diligently to apply it.

"You'll have to excuse me now; I have a performance."

Cars were already lining up to disgorge the night's audience for the various theaters in the Lincoln Center complex when Mici came out of the Met's stage door. She took the escalator to the lobby, walked out and found herself in the small park fronting the Vivian Beaumont Theater. A thunderstorm with high winds and a considerable drop in temperature was predicted—a result of the unseasonal mild spell, no doubt—but there was no sign of it yet. The air was still. Strings of miniature white lights sparkled like snowflakes among the bare branches. Mici sat down on one of the benches.

She was glad that Sanda Florescu had not taken the bait. She liked the singer, admired her artistry, and would have been sad if she had turned out to be the one. So, while she hadn't trapped the killer, she had at least learned something important—the existence and location of Tully's love nest.

How naïve both she and Ed had been, to think that Gene Tully had used the parking lot to save money! He wasn't that kind of man. What did he care for a few dollars a month when he owed thousands? He wouldn't put himself to the inconvenience of parking so far from his home, walking back and forth in all kinds of weather, to save fifty or sixty dollars. He wouldn't expose his beautiful white Jaguar in an outdoor lot without a very good reason.

The reason was convenience. The lot was convenient to his bachelor pad. It was handy to the love nest.

And now the interval between the parking lot attendant's departure and the discovery of Tully's body was explained. Tully had parked his car and gone up to his pad for a late date. He had been walking home when he was shot and later stomped.

But not by either of the Florescus. Not by Tyrone Witte: he was out somewhere along the Taconic Parkway. By the senator?

If Helene Kalb was the lady Tully intended to meet after her own party, then certainly the senator was a suspect. Seymour Kalb had made one damaging admission. He had placed live ammunition in her hands, which could, if not wreck her career, certainly rock it. Not that she'd left him much choice. Still, Mici now had the same hold over Senator and Mrs. Kalb that Eugene Tully had had. Why would he have killed Tully to keep a secret that he then passed on to someone else? Seymour Kalb had no alibi in the accepted sense of time and place, but psychologically Mici considered his alibi unbreakable. And then she thought of something else. What need would the senator have to call his own home to find out whether or not Tully had left?

She felt good about that. It let him out and it let Helene Kalb out too. She might slip out after her own party to meet her lover, but she hardly needed to call him on the phone first.

A chill passed through her. Mici shivered, but not with cold. The crowd milled around her. The day's work was over; everyone wanted to forget their cares and have a good time; the atmosphere was charged with the anticipation of entertainment. Mici's prospects for the evening filled her with dread.

There was only one person left. One.

Faith Tully. The young bride become a widow. The expectant mother who lost her child on the same night she lost her husband. The mountain girl seeking vengeance and appealing to Mici for help. Had Faith Tully found out the kind of man she'd married? Hadn't her insistence on Gene's devotion always seemed a little overdone? It wouldn't be inconceivable for the bride to have discovered her beloved husband's bachelor flat and what he used it for. Both the maid and the houseman at the Kalbs' had assumed that it was Mrs. Tully who called that third time. Mici was the one who had thought otherwise. But suppose they were right? Told that the party was over and Tully had left along with the other guests, Faith would have known exactly where he'd gone and what he was doing. With Faith as the killer, it all fell into place.

Both Helene Kalb and Sanda Florescu claimed that Gene Tully had initially broken off the affair because of a promise exacted by the bride. Again it was Mici herself, in her effort to champion the bereaved young widow, who had simply refused to accept their statements. She accepted them now. Certainly Gene's breaking such a promise would have resulted in a quarrel, and given Faith's mountain heritage, the decision to take vengeance into her own hands was natural. She could have warned Gene, even to the extent of going out and getting a gun, perhaps without the real intent to use it. Then, on the fatal night, driven beyond endurance, the gun at hand, she did use it. That took care of the premeditation.

Her behavior, which Mici had been constantly justifying, now made perfect sense. Pregnant, unwanted, jealous, she waited outside in the rain for her husband to leave the other woman. And when he came out and started down the street, she leveled her gun and killed him.

Why didn't she go up to the apartment and do it there?

For one thing, she would have had to kill the woman too, and maybe she didn't want to do that. More important, she wanted to put the blame on the girl gang. To do that, Gene Tully had to die in the street.

How about her screams? There could hardly be any doubt that Faith Tully was the woman the Beineckes both heard and saw. But they might have misinterpreted her screams. What they took to be cries for help could well have been the agony of a woman temporarily unbalanced.

Afterward, her pain and sorrow appeared real because they were real. Faith Tully grieved not for the man who had betrayed her over and over again, but for her baby, for her dead baby. That was her tragedy; that was why she mourned. She had not counted on her own body's reaction to the physical and emotional stress. She had unwittingly caused the abortion of her child. Her subconscious demanded punishment, but her conscious will would not permit her to confess. The gun found in her hatbox could even have been planted there by Faith herself in expectation of its being found and tested, knowing the test would prove negative and serve to confirm her innocence. It occurred to Mici, as she looked back, that the girl had taken the finding of the gun with little emotion.

Could she have been so terribly, obstinately, and unforgivably wrong about Faith Tully? Mici asked herself. As wrong as she'd been about Diane Lara? She'd been taken in by Diane, but so had everybody else.

Even Adam Dowd. "I felt sorry for her," he'd admitted later. "I wanted to believe her."

Mici had been the only one who wanted to believe Faith Tully.

She had no idea how long she'd sat on that bench, but suddenly she realized that she was alone. The night was still mild; the lights of the park still twinkled overhead; the waters of the fountain in the central plaza splashed. The people, however, were gone. They were inside, listening, watching, for a few hours transported out of themselves. Mici wished she could be with them, but she was outside.

She opened the flap of her handbag and probed for the little red plastic box. It would give her the answer.

She got up, found a telephone, and called. She was told that Ed Stiebeck had stepped out for a bite to eat. He'd be back any minute. She left her name and destination and an urgent request that he join her as soon as possible. Then she hailed a cab and gave the driver Faith Tully's address.

CHAPTER XV

A stranger answered the door, a woman on the young side of thirty, wearing tight jeans and a loose peasant blouse. Her myopic eyes looked startled behind oversized glasses.

Mici herself was startled. And taken aback. "I'm looking for Mrs. Tully. Faith Tully?"

"Oh, yes. She doesn't live here anymore."

"She doesn't?"

"We bought the apartment. My husband and I."

Mici's stomach fell. She was too late.

"Would you like her new address?"

"Oh. Do you have it? Yes, I would. Yes, please." She had been so put off stride by not finding Faith that she hadn't even thought to ask.

"I don't really know whether she's living there or whether it's a forwarding address," the new tenant explained as she handed Mici the piece of paper. "It does look more like a forwarding address, doesn't it?"

It began: c/o Tyrone Witte.

Faith was there, but she was not pleased to have a caller. Her hair was more than usually disheveled; her face was streaked with grime and dust; her mouth sullen. Nor did she brighten when she saw who it was. She let Mici in, but grudgingly. Had she come on any other errand, Mici would have been hurt. As it was, she strode past Faith to find the living room in disarray, a pair of matched suitcases near an open closet.

"You're moving in?"

Faith nodded. "I couldn't stand the apartment. I got rid of it and everything in it—furniture, carpets, china, the works. I don't want any part of it. I don't want anything that will remind me of the past. Ty's letting me use his place till I decide what to do."

"I see."

"I've been meaning to drop by," Faith volunteered after an awkward pause. "I guess I owe you some thanks."

Mici had certainly received more enthusiastic acknowledgments. "You don't owe me anything."

"You meant well," the girl continued. "I realize you meant well. You were trying to help me."

"Yes, I was." I certainly was, Mici thought, puzzled.

"But I can't thank you for the way you did it!" Faith Tully blurted out. "I can't forgive you for the things you said about Gene. Lies, all lies!"

Whatever Mici had been expecting, it wasn't this.

"You made Gene out to be the worst kind of cheat. You made him out to be a . . . a womanizer. You dirtied his memory." Tears welled up in the widow's eyes, tears of anger and pain.

Mici was shaken. She didn't know whether to believe this performance or not. "Two women have admitted to having affairs with Gene."

"That was before we were married."

"Each one says the affair continued."

"More lies."

"Doru Florescu claims he killed Gene because he didn't break off the affair with his wife."

"Claims?"

Tyrone Witte, drink in hand, emerged from the kitchen. "Are you saying Florescu didn't do it?"

Mici looked from one to the other.

Witte smiled. "Don't be shocked, Miss Anhalt." He indicated those suitcases in the corner. "They're mine. I'm moving out." He got back to the subject. "I thought Florescu confessed."

"The confession doesn't stand up." She spoke to Tyrone Witte, but she watched Faith. "You must have known that Gene was cheating on you."

"Stop saying that."

"Why did you go to the parking lot at one-forty when you knew perfectly well that it closed at midnight?"

"I went to look for Gene. It was the only place I knew where to look. I didn't know it had closed."

"You weren't going to the parking lot. You passed it on your way somewhere else."

"I don't understand."

"You told me that you called the Kalb residence twice: once to ask Gene if he intended coming home for dinner, and the second time around eleven to ask how much later he'd be. He said he was leaving at that very moment. So you got up, made coffee, and waited."

"Yes."

"But when he hadn't arrived by one o'clock, you called the police."

"I did."

"Why didn't you call the Kalbs again? Wouldn't that have made more sense?"

"It was late."

"One o'clock isn't late when people are giving a party."

"I was embarrassed," Faith admitted but seeing that Mici doubted it, she flushed and added, "Gene wouldn't have liked it. He was already angry because I'd called twice."

That could he true, Mici thought and suppressed a spontaneous surge of sympathy. "I say that you were worried enough to call anyway, and you didn't wait till one: you called at midnight. A maid answered and told you that everybody had gone. So again you waited for Gene to come home. You waited another hour. Now, obviously, it doesn't take two hours or even one to get from the Kalbs' to your house, more like twenty minutes. So Gene had stopped somewhere. You knew where."

"No."

"You knew where he was and what he was doing. You threw on some clothes and went over."

"Over where? Where?" Faith sought Tyrone Witte's help. "What is she talking about?"

"You know, don't you?" Mici said.

"Sorry."

"I'm talking about Gene's bachelor pad. It's just a block from the parking lot, isn't it?"

He grimaced. "This is hardly the moment—"

"You know the address," Mici insisted. "It was on Tully's employment record."

"Yes, all right, I know where he used to live."

"Why did you start to give me that address the day I was in your office?" Until that moment Mici had forgotten the incident.

"That was a mistake. I'd simply neglected to cross out the old address, that's all."

Faith wasn't listening. "Gene loved me. Just me. Nobody else. There was never anybody else for either one of us."

Witte put a protective arm around her. "You're upsetting her. She doesn't have to talk to you. Please, go."

His concern for the girl puzzled Mici, had from the beginning. He had paid her bills, now he was moving out of his own apartment. "You knew that Gene Tully had kept the old place and that he was using it to entertain other women. You resented it on—"

Faith interrupted. "You tell her, Ty. You tell her how good Gene was to me."

For a moment it seemed as though the manager would do just that, then he shook his head. "I'm sorry, Faith, but I think it's time you faced the truth. If you want to live any kind of life from here on you have to admit the truth to yourself. Gene was not the man you thought he was."

"He loved me."

"He didn't love anybody."

"He married me."

"Did he have any choice?" Tyrone Witte was as gentle as he could be. Nevertheless, humiliation flooded into Faith's face. It made her bow her head and her shoulders droop. She shrugged off his protective embrace. "I'm sorry," he said. "We all knew the story before we ever met you."

"My daddy didn't want us to get married. He never liked Gene and he didn't approve of his job up here. Gene and I decided it was the only way to get him to agree to the wedding. Daddy thought he caught us, but we planned for him to catch us."

She recited it as though by rote. Did she really believe it, Mici wondered.

"Of course, my dear, of course."

Witte obviously did not.

"Gene was good to me. You saw our apartment. You saw the way he fixed it up. Everything the best. You ought to see the clothes he bought me. You can see them. Come on, come on in here and look!"

She started for the bedroom, waving for them to follow, and they did.

Clothes were spread on the bed, on chairs, some were already hanging in the spacious closet that Witte had cleared for her.

"Look at the furs, dresses, hats, and . . . things. Here . . . here . . . look here." She moved the length of the built-in compartments, pulling out drawers, running her hand through piles of filmy undergarments, colorful scarves, gloves; she scooped up costume jewelry. "Look at all the things he gave me."

Gifts to salve his conscience? Mici wondered. Did Gene Tully have enough of a conscience to bother? Or were these gifts to distract his young bride from what was going on? Had he cared even that much?

Evidently, Witte didn't think so. "Darling girl, he was playing a game. He was playing at turning an ugly duckling into a swan."

Faith bit her lower lip hard. Then she threw her head up, dark eyes blazing, and was for a few seconds not merely beautiful but magnificent. "Doesn't that prove that he loved me?"

Her confidence was impressive. In a way, it made it harder for Mici to go ahead and in a way easier. She opened her purse and produced the red box. "This contains a tape from a telephone answering machine. It's the one the Kalbs used to record calls on the night of their party. Naturally, while the party lasted, the phone was answered by one of the servants, but when the party was over and the guests left, the machine was switched on. When the third call for Gene came in shortly before midnight, it was recorded."

There was no reaction to that from Faith.

Thoughtfully, Mici hefted the little box. "I'll be turning this over to the police lab in the morning. I don't know if you've heard of voice prints, Faith, vocal spectrography, but it can identify an individual as precisely as fingerprints."

With a sudden lunge, Witte reached for the box. "Give it to me."

Mici pulled back just in time. "Why? Why do you want it?"

"She's suffered enough."

"If it's not her voice on the tape, then she has nothing to worry about. Unless, of course, you have a reason to believe that it is her voice on the tape."

"No, of course, I don't."

"Then why did you try to grab it from me?"

He sighed. "I told you."

"I don't believe you." Mici gave him a long, appraising look. "I think you know it's *not* her voice on the tape." He didn't challenge her, so she went on. "It's your voice. You made that midnight call to the Kalbs, didn't you, Mr. Witte?"

"Look, I'm sorry I snatched at the thing like that. I really was only trying to spare—"

"You were the one Tully had the date with after the party. You. Not one of his women."

"We saw each other every day at work; why should we meet at midnight?"

And that led to the motive. "He was blackmailing you."

Tyrone Witte laughed. He managed to laugh, though beads of sweat stood out on his brow, glistened in his mustache, and lay like hoar frost in his beard.

Mici had been twisting and turning, doubling back over her own track as though lost in a maze, but now she was on her way out. Instinct led, and she followed. "You had an appointment to meet Gene Tully at the old apartment after the party. The party ran late . . . ."

He sighed. "How can I convince you that you're wrong?"

"You don't have to, Mr. Witte. This will convince me and everybody else." She held up the red container. "Once this is analyzed, we'll all know."

His eyes were riveted to the box. "What time did you say the call was made?"

"Around midnight."

"Well, at midnight I was seventy miles out of New York City." He smiled, quite easily and confidently. "My car broke down on the way to Vermont and was laid up for repairs in the local garage. I had to take a room for the night at a place called the Spindletop Inn."

"Yes, I know."

"You do?"

"Are you telling me that you made that call long distance?"

He grimaced, his eyes still on the box. "All right, all right. Yes, I made the call. But as I told you, I was seventy miles out of the city."

"Fine. The Spindletop Inn will have a record of the call and the time it was put through."

"I didn't make the call from my room."

"You didn't? Why not?"

"I was restless, I couldn't sleep. I decided to go out for a walk. I don't know why I'm explaining this to you."

"You can explain it to Detective Stiebeck if you prefer." Where was Ed, anyway? Mici wondered, feeling the first touch of anxiety. She should have taken the time to stop and call in Faith's new address. But surely Ed would get it in the same way she had, and surely he would come right over. "He should be here shortly," she added.

The sweat rolled down into Witte's eyebrows, and as he shook his head it flew around him like water off a dog. "Tully demanded a cut of the salon profits. If I didn't give it to him, he was going to pull out and take his clients elsewhere. It wasn't enough that he'd appropriated the best customers for himself, taken them from me and from the other operators, now he threatened to walk out with them! With that list he could have got a job anywhere, named his own price. I had to agree to cut him in, if I hadn't it would have been the end of Salon Chéri. I was supposed to make the first payment on Friday. I stalled. I told him I just didn't have the money. It was true: I'd just paid off some bills, got socked by the IRS, and I really didn't have the cash. I told him I couldn't give him what I didn't have. He was not interested in my troubles; he told me to get it up and gave me till midnight. So we made a date at his old place. Oh, I could have taken out a loan, of course, put a second mortgage on the building—there were ways—but I'd managed finally to claw my way out of debt and I just couldn't bring myself to it. I didn't have the nerve to face him and tell him so either. I ran away. I ran up to my place in Vermont . . . to think. On the way my car broke down. Stuck in that hotel, I began to get very nervous. I began to worry about not showing up for the appointment. I thought it might make Tully extravindictive. I took a walk to think it out and decided I'd better just call and explain."

"Why didn't you call his apartment? Why did you call the Kalbs?"

"I tried the apartment first and he wasn't there."

"I see. You found a phone booth and you dialed directly, is that it?"

"Yes."

Mici sighed. "Too bad."

"What do you mean, too bad?"

"If you'd made the call from your room in the hotel, there would have been a record of it. It would have confirmed your alibi. But if you dialed directly from a phone booth . . ." She let that hang for a moment or so. "Well, I really don't think there'd be any way to verify it. There'd be no record of it, would there?"

"It doesn't matter whether there's a record or not. Don't you understand?" His voice rose to a high whine. "Don't you see? There's no way I could have got back to New York. Not with my car laid up. You can check that. You can check the garage."

"It's already been checked, by the police."

He flinched, but recovered quickly. "So there you are. I registered at the Spindletop around eight. I had dinner in the dining room, then hung out in the bar till about ten. I've got witnesses."

"Yes, I know. That was checked too."

"Nothing moves out there after ten! There are no trains, buses— . . . zilch!"

"You could have rented a car beforehand in New York."

"And driven them both out? That would be a good trick."

"You could have driven the rental out the day before, early enough so you could get a bus or other transportation back. Or you could have arranged with a local company to have the car ready for you in the hotel lot. Though that might be too obvious. Detective Stiebeck will check it both ways."

There was a low moan from the corner.

"You were the one, you," Faith Tully murmured more in wonder than as an accusation. "You were the one."

They'd both momentarily forgotten her, and now they were too tightly locked in the struggle with each other to concern themselves over her.

Witte held out his hand to Mici. "Give me that tape."

"And it wasn't Tully who was late, it was you," Mici exclaimed. "It was you. Friday night was a very bad night. What was rain here in the city undoubtedly was snow out where you were, and it took you a lot longer to get back to New York than you'd expected, or allowed for." She frowned. "You didn't want to miss him. You'd planned it all so carefully, set up your alibi, that the possibility of missing him, of having to wait all over again for another opportunity was too much. Also, if the girl gang were to look like the culprits, enough time had already passed; you couldn't afford a postponement. So you pulled up to the side of the road and called Tully."

"I want that tape," Witte said.

Mici went on. "There was no answer. You told yourself that he couldn't have left already; it was too early. You told yourself that surely he would have waited a little, but the phone went on ringing. Suppose he was late too? Suppose he'd been delayed? It was your glimmer of hope. You called the Kalbs' to find out."

Suddenly, he had a gun in his hand and he was pointing it at her.

She hadn't seen him reach for it, but there it was. She hadn't expected him to have a gun. Even if she'd anticipated that Tyrone Witte would be in the apartment, that he'd turn out to be the killer, she would not have looked for him to be armed. Ordinary citizens don't carry guns; even an ordinary citizen who had committed a murder doesn't carry a gun unless he expects to be using it. There was no way Witte could have anticipated this confrontation. She hadn't herself. All she could do at this point was back off, but at the same time she couldn't help asking, "Is that the murder weapon?"

"If I have to shoot, the police will be able to compare the slugs," he mocked. "Are you that anxious to find out?"

"No, I'm not."

"Then just hand me the tape." Gun in one hand, he extended the other.

"You killed him!" Faith cried out, and emerged from her corner. "You killed Gene!"

He replied without turning. "My dear girl, I did you a favor. One of these days you'll realize that and you'll thank me."

"Never!"

Witte risked a look. "Believe me, you will. It hurts me to tell you, but he was not worthy of you. He didn't love you."

"He did. He did."

Mici shrank back a step, then another, then one more.

"You were less than nothing to him," Witte told the widow. "He used you the way he used everybody. He was no good."

Now Mici was on the other side of the bedroom, close to the living room. Suddenly, she turned and dashed for the front door.

"Stop!" Witte yelled. "Stop or I'll shoot. I mean it."

She believed him.

"Don't make another move," he warned as he followed her out into the living room. "I'd really rather not shoot you, Miss Anhalt. I'd prefer not to, but I want that tape and I want it now."

Mici sighed, turned around, and started toward Witte, the tape in her hand as though she was about to give it to him. He took a couple of steps toward her. When they were within reach of each other, she threw the box past him.

"Faith!" she called. "Catch!"

But Faith was unprepared and missed the box. It went past her, fell to the floor, and ricocheted off the wall to land at her feet.

Witte was livid. His face twitched with the effort to control his fury; his body seethed with the turbulence of his rage. "All right, Faith, pick it up," he ordered. "Faith! Pick it up and give it to me."

She stood where she was like someone who had been unconscious and was now uncertain of the situation to which she had reawakened.

"Pick it up and give it to me," he repeated.

Faith struggled to grasp what he wanted. Then she realized what it all meant. "Pick it up yourself," she said with quiet bitterness.

For a moment Mici thought he was going to slap her. Instead he shrugged. With a quick glance to make sure Mici knew he was keeping her covered, he walked over to where the box lay and stooped.

As he did, Faith kicked it hard and sent it skittering across the highly polished white-tile floor halfway across to the other side of the room. Like a hockey puck sliding into the goal, the red box disappeared under the sofa.

Witte groaned with exasperation. "Why the hell did you have to do that?"

"You killed Gene?"

"I did it for you," he flung back. "Don't you get it? Don't you understand? I did it for you." He paused to collect himself, and when he spoke again, his tone was changed, become soft, almost caressing. "I did it because I couldn't stand what he was doing to you: humiliating you, making a fool out of you, and laughing at you while he did it. You were too good for him, too good."

Faith seemed mesmerized, and despite herself, Mici felt she too was falling under his spell. She had to tell herself to snap out of it. Don't listen, block out that silky, insinuating, hypnotic voice. Think! Tyrone Witte would not leave without the tape, nor would he risk sprawling on his stomach to get it himself from under the sofa. He could hardly keep one of them, much less both Mici and Faith, covered from such a position. For the moment he was intent on gaining Faith's sympathy, perhaps as a way of getting her cooperation. At any rate, the situation was static, but it wouldn't be long before he decided that the commitment wasn't important and that he didn't need her help.

"I couldn't stand to watch him debase and degrade you," Witte continued his grisly wooing. "If it hadn't been for what he was doing to you, I think I would have given him the money, I think I would have paid him off. I killed him to free you. You'll forgive me in time. You may even come to care for me."

Faith gasped.

Mici shuddered.

Once Witte had the box what was to stop him from killing them both? They were the only ones who knew that he was guilty; they could testify that he had admitted committing the murder. He'd think of that too, soon enough, and once he did, it would be just as easy to shoot them first and then pick up the box without any trouble at all. Without any trouble at all, Mici thought, and felt the cold prickles of real fear break out all over her body.

Meanwhile, he was getting to Faith. If the man who became Richard III could woo and win the widow of the man he'd killed even while she mourned over his bier, couldn't Tyrone Witte convince a simple, backwoods girl of his sincerity? Even now Faith's horror was tinged with fascination. She'd confided to Mici that she'd never been popular, that Gene was the only boy who'd ever paid any real attention to her. Whatever interpretation Faith chose to put on her wedding, the fact remained that Gene Tully had been forced into it. Now, to be courted like this, to be told by a suave, sophisticated, older man that he had killed for her . . . It was no wonder she was wavering. But Mici could not let her succumb. She needed Faith's help if either one of them was to get out of that room alive.

"I wonder how your current boyfriend would feel about this declaration?" she asked Witte. "I don't think he'd be very happy about it. By the way, which one is your current favorite? Mr. Randolph? I got the impression that it might be Mr. Randolph."

"Shut up."

Ah, no. Tyrone Witte did not really care about Faith: that final, nagging doubt was stilled. He'd helped her after the crime not out of love but to still a guilty conscience. Paying her bills, turning over his apartment—these were his version of the gangster's flowers at his victim's funeral.

"Oh, I'm not passing judgment, believe me," Mici assured him. "I feel everyone has the right to his own life-style. It couldn't matter less to me, but I do think that Faith has the right to know your preference."

"I told you to shut up," Witte snarled, and held the gun rigidly pointed at Mici's stomach.

Now, now was the time for Faith to make her move, now while Witte's back was to her and his attention fixed on Mici. She willed the other girl to act; she made a silent, desperate appeal, but nothing happened. Afraid to call his attention to Faith, Mici nevertheless stole a look at her.

She was still in that trancelike state. Obviously, she wasn't aware of what Mici was trying to set up. The opportunity was slipping away. Mici would have to take action herself.

"Now, Faith, now!" she yelled.

As Witte twirled to see what was happening behind him, she took a flying leap.

In ballet her partner would have been facing her and braced. She would have made a *grand jeté* into his arms to land in a classic *arabesque penché*. But Witte was not prepared, and Mici landed not in his arms but on his back. She twined her strong dancer's legs around his hips and her arms around his neck. He staggered under the impact, lurched forward, then back, overturned an end table, sent a crystal lamp crashing, and finally the two of them went down together. But though Witte had instinctively put out his hands to break the fall and though he was now on his stomach and thrashing from side to side in the attempt to throw Mici off, he held on to the gun.

Mici removed one arm from around his neck and grabbed a clump of hair that was just the right length for her to lace her fingers through. She yanked.

"Ow!" he yelled.

She was panting; she had barely breath to speak, but her mouth was close enough to his ear so that a whisper sufficed. "Let go of the gun. Let it go."

For answer, Tyrone Witte gave another heave. Then he placed his hands on the floor just under his shoulders so that he could push up to his knees. Once on his knees, even with Mici hanging on, he could aim the gun at Faith. Mici made herself go deadweight and gathered enough breath for one last appeal to the transfixed girl.

"Remember when you found Gene; the shock was terrible, but somehow you hung on, you screamed for help. This man, his killer, was there, he heard your screams. When you went away to get help . . ." she paused to fill her lungs. Witte had stopped struggling; he lay under her oddly still. Why? Was he tired and trying to regain his strength for another effort, or was he waiting for what she had to say? Was he curious? Or worried? Was he really worried about what she might say? Yes, he was. Of course, he was. And suddenly Mici knew why. What the autopsy report had not been able to confirm scientifically, her instinct did. And she trusted it. She was sure now of the events of that night, but she had to convince Faith.

"We never told you, but Gene was dead before the beating," Mici gasped. "He was dead before you left him."

The words were hoarse, barely intelligible, but their significance was reaching Faith Tully.

"The beating and the stomping weren't necessary. The blame could have been put on the gang without them. You would have been spared that second, terrible shock."

From Tyrone Witte there was only a soft sigh.

Faith's whole body jerked. The mask of her face cracked, her eyes focused at last on the inert figure on the floor.

"My baby . . . if I hadn't fallen . . ."

Witte made one final attempt. "That was an accident. There was no way it could have been foreseen . . . no way. . . ."

"You killed my baby!"

She took a step forward and brought her right foot down on the back of Witte's gun hand. Hard. She brought it down heel first, hard as she could.

He screamed.

Despite the pain, he gripped the gun all the harder.

"Let go," Faith ordered. "Let go, or I'll break your hand for you."

He uncurled his fingers and withdrew his hand.

Faith stooped and snatched up the weapon.

"You can get up," she told Mici as she released the safety catch and leveled the gun at Witte with deadly assurance. "Don't worry, it won't go off by accident," she informed him, smiling coldly. "I've been handling guns since I was eight years old, and if I have to shoot I know how to aim where it'll hurt the most."

The aches and pains of the struggle manifested themselves twenty-four hours later. Mici woke up with pains in muscles she hadn't even known she'd had. In addition, she had a nasty gash along the inner side of her right forearm where she'd been cut by a shard from the shattered crystal lamp. The arm below the elbow was swollen, possibly infected. In spite of all that, she felt fine, she felt wonderful! Maybe it was the reaction at having got through the ordeal relatively unscathed, but she had never felt better in her whole life.

They were in Adam Dowd's office, Mici, Ed Stiebeck, and the supervisor. Outside, the weather matched Mici's mood. Bright sunshine warmed the barren trees in the little park as though to console them for the storm's battering the night before; the sky was cloudless and people on the street walked with springier steps.

"When Witte pulled that gun I thought we'd had it, Faith and I. I never figured him to have a gun."

"You should have waited for Ed," Dowd observed.

Stiebeck said nothing. He was still smarting from having missed all the action. Instead of the hamburger he'd gone out for, the detective had treated himself to a good dinner. By the time he'd returned to the precinct, got Mici's message, and followed her from Faith's apartment to Witte's, it was all over. The patrol officers were there, had taken the killer into custody, and Mici and Faith were sitting side by side amid the shambles, drinking Scotch—neat.

"When I went over there, I didn't even consider Witte a suspect. It wasn't till I showed the tape," Mici explained.

"You should have known he carried a gun," Stiebeck grunted.

"How? How could I possibly have known that?"

"Because he always carried one." He had her on that at least, the detective thought, but it wasn't much consolation. "Most merchants and business people who handle large amounts of cash carry a gun nowadays, particularly if they have to make deposits after banking hours and use the night depository."

"Don't they have to have a license?"

"Sure. Witte had a license. That's why he didn't get rid of the gun after killing Tully. It was too complicated. If he got rid of it, he'd have to replace it. If he replaced it and then later on had to use it legitimately, how would he explain to the license bureau? What reason would he give for having bought a new gun?"

"He could say the old one was stolen; then they'd want to know why he hadn't notified them," Mici answered herself. "He wouldn't want to notify them because that would call attention to him. I guess it was less risky just to keep the murder weapon."

"It wasn't risky at all as long as he didn't come under suspicion, and Witte saw no reason why he should come under suspicion," Stiebeck pointed out. "Tully made a big thing out of the incident with the little girl and the bike, built up his own part in it, made himself look like a hero. Witte bought the story and decided he could get rid of Tully and make it look like an aftermath of that incident."

"And he provided himself with a pretty good alibi just in case," Dowd observed.

Mici shrugged. "He might have been better off without it."

"You would certainly have been better off not making such a grandstand play to get him to admit the telephone call," the supervisor countered with the first indication of disapproval he'd shown. "You didn't need to look into the muzzle of his gun and risk your life and Mrs. Tully's. All you had to do was have a little patience till the tape was analyzed."

"It wasn't that the call was incriminating of itself, Adam; it was Witte's lying about where he was when he made it."

"Yes, all right. You still could have waited."

"Ah, well . . ." Mitzi squirmed. "It wasn't that simple. To start with, we'd have had to get a tape of Witte's voice for comparison. I don't suppose he'd have been eager to cooperate."

"Couldn't his phone have been tapped or something?" the supervisor asked. "Once it was confirmed that Witte had rented a car a couple of days earlier and driven it out there, I should think a judge would have issued an order." He paused. "Granted the alibi wasn't suspect till he admitted making the call." He sighed. "All right, what else?"

"There's the question of the validity of voice prints as evidence, Adam. I know there's been a lot of publicity lately claiming that voice prints are as reliable as fingerprints, but that's not generally accepted in New York state courtrooms. I've researched it, and though there have been nearly fifty court decisions in state and federal jurisdictions, a voice print has been used only once in a New York state courtroom and that case was later dismissed on other grounds, so the admissibility has not yet been determined."

Dowd sighed. "Get to the point."

Mici continued to hedge. "What difference does it make? As long as Witte has admitted that he did make the call, that at one point his voice actually was on the tape—"

"At one point!" Dowd cut in.

"You mean it was erased? The tape was erased?" Stiebeck demanded.

"Ah, well, yes."

"You went in there with a blank tape?"

"You see the Kalbs' answering device is very simple; it's the type that you can buy in any department store. It has a little thing inside that records a limited number of calls, then those calls are erased and the tape is reused."

Stiebeck groaned.

"The tape isn't supposed to be removed from the machine at all. I didn't have any tape. The box was empty."

"That's entrapment." Ed Stiebeck looked sick; he felt sick. "Whether the tape was blank or there was no tape, it's entrapment."

"Oh, I don't know," she answered airily. "If you had done it, maybe. But I'm not a police officer."

"Thank God!" he muttered under his breath.

"What? What did you say?"

"I said, too bad."

Mici grinned. "You were right the first time. I'm no detective. I just stumbled on the solution.

"Oh, I wouldn't go that far."

"I would. You see, I had it figured to be Faith after all. If Witte hadn't just happened to still be in the apartment . . ."

Stiebeck relaxed. "We all need a little luck."

"That was beginner's luck." Mici lowered her eyes.

Her humility was somewhat overdone, Dowd thought, and put a hand over his mouth to hide the smile.

Ed Stiebeck didn't think so. His ego restored, he could now afford to be magnanimous. "In the crunch you handled yourself like a pro. The way you jumped Witte, that took guts."

"Thanks. Actually, that was the best damned *jeté* I ever performed." Mici took a breath. "And I hope I never have to make another one like it."

Simon Creedy was patiently waiting for her. He gave Mici his sweetest smile and seemed so delighted to see her that, instead of being righteously indignant, she felt sorry for the old man. But the moment of truth had come for Simon Creedy as it had for Diane Lara and the others who'd tried to cheat the law and get money to which they were not entitled. Mici reminded herself that catching frauds was as much part of the job as helping those who were genuinely entitled to help. So she forced herself to return the old man's smile with a stern frown. She sat down at her desk, reached into a drawer, and pulled out Creedy's claim along with the other two that he had presented, allegedly on behalf of his friends. She laid them out neatly in front of her.

Unmistakably all three had been typed on the same ancient machine. Nothing wrong with that, since Creedy had stated that he was going to help the other two victims fill out the forms. The trouble was that he'd not only filled them out, he'd also signed them. It didn't require a handwriting expert to tell that the three signatures had been written by the same hand.

"Now, Mr. Creedy," Mici began. "About these claims you filed on behalf—"

"Yes, ma'am, that's what I came to see you about, Miss Anhalt. My friend, Mrs. Trent, the lady who has the two dogs, Pinocchio and Shakespeare?"

"Amanda Trent." Mici referred to the form in the center. "She was injured by a rock thrown at her while she was walking her dogs in the park."

"Yes, ma'am, Mrs. Trent. Well, she's fine now. Just fine. And her own insurance company took care of all her bills. So she wants to withdraw her claim."

"Is that so?"

He nodded vigorously. "Yes, ma'am. And my other friend? The one who lives in my building and broke her leg?"

"Estelle Garofoli." Mici consulted the other file. "You've been going over there and cooking and cleaning for her."

"That's the one." He was delighted that Mici remembered. "Well, her sister's come from Toronto to stay with Mrs. Garofoli and look after her, so she won't be needing to hire a practical nurse after all. She's withdrawing her claim too."

"Really?"

"Yes, ma'am."

"They're both recovered, or nearly recovered, and they're both withdrawing their claims?"

The old man's watery eyes met hers. "I'm sorry to have put you to so much trouble, Miss Anhalt."

She didn't know what to make of it. Had Creedy been working a con, decided it wasn't going to stick, and was now pulling out? Or was he just as he appeared—a sweet old man with time on his hands who wanted to help people? A lonely old man who used those incidents in order to have an excuse to come back to see her and to have something to talk to her about?

Firmly, she closed the two files and set them aside. "No trouble, Mr. Creedy, no trouble at all. Anytime."

"Oh, thank you. That's really nice of you, Miss Anhalt." His smile was pure joy. "I'm so glad you feel that way because a terrible thing happened on my way over here this morning . . ."

Oh, no! Mici thought, not again.

"There was this boy, couldn't have been more than twelve or thirteen, spray-painting obscenities on a wall. It wasn't bad enough that he was defacing private property, but the words . . ." Creedy colored. "That a boy so young should even know such words! I tried to reason with him, but he told me to . . . uh . . ." Creedy looked away. "He told me to get lost."

Mici was only half listening. The old man desperately needed something to do.

"So while I was talking to him, the super of the building came out. He told the kid to beat it. He told him that he was going to call the cops otherwise." Creedy sighed. "Do you know what happened then? The child knifed him. Without a word, the child pulled out a knife and stuck it into Mr. Morrissey's chest. Before I even realized what was happening, Mr. Morrissey was lying on the sidewalk with the blood pouring out of him."

Mici gasped. Had it really happened or was it a figment of the old man's imagination? Had he actually seen it, or had he read about it in the newspaper—today's ugly? Either way, he couldn't be allowed to roam aimlessly much longer.

"Mr. Creedy, have you spoken to . . ." What was that social worker's name? "Have you spoken to Miss Pallo lately?"

He slumped in the chair. "No, ma'am."

Mici reached for the phone. "Well, don't you think it would be a good idea if we called?" She got no further. It wasn't necessary. The answer to her unasked question was in his face: Isabel Pallo had no intention of ever rehiring Simon Creedy and Creedy knew it. Had known it all along. She should have known it too, Mici thought. She pulled her hand back from the phone.

"And how is Mr. Morrissey?" Mici asked, leaning back in her chair. "How is the poor man?"

"Oh? Oh, not good." Creedy's color returned, his voice regained its vigor as he pulled confidentially close to Mici. "Not good, not good at all, Miss Anhalt. He's lost so much blood. They rushed him to the hospital, naturally, and he's had several transfusions, but more will be necessary. And you know how expensive blood is. So, I thought, if you could let me have another one of those forms . . ."

Mici already had the desk drawer open and was reaching inside.

AFTERWORD

When this book was conceived, the New York City Council had passed a resolution recommending that police officers advise a victim of a crime about his rights under the state law. All commands were notified and flyers posted on precinct-house bulletin boards. Implementation, however, was left to the discretion of the individual officer. Now, at last, the legislature has passed a law *requiring* the police officer to inform the victim of his rights in the same way that a suspect is informed of his.

New York state now regards the victim with some of the same compassion that has been lavished on the criminal.

THE END

THE BIG FOOTPRINTS

BY

HAMMOND INNES

Published by special arrangement with Alfred A. Knopf, Inc.

PART ONE

THE WILDLIFE CONFERENCE

I

It was raining, a solid tropical downpour, and the beer was warm. The supply trucks had brought it up with the food from Nairobi over the bomb-scarred gravel road I had glimpsed from the plane as we landed. We were rationed to one can each, the froth and the sweetness cloying, and the water unfit to drink. I looked at my watch. It was after ten and the night black, no chance that he would arrive now.

I lit a cigarette, perched on the crumbling parapet of what had once been a verandah, staring through the rain at the big half-circle of rooms lit by hurricane lamps and candles. The shattered glass of the sliding windows showed walls pockmarked by bullets. Some of the conference delegates were already preparing for bed, shadows in silhouette stripping off their clothes and climbing into the two-tier bunks. Others, like myself, out on the battered verandahs, talking quietly, voices subdued by the atmosphere of the place.

The night was very still, no breeze; only the sound of the rain falling vertically and somewhere the hum of a generator. The organisers had rigged lights in the dining-room and kitchens, but these had been switched off now, the power concentrated on spotlights beamed on the waterhole as though to remind us what the gathering was all about. The big circular pool showed pale and flat through the rain, but nothing moved, not even a bird. Perhaps there really were no animals left.

I had finished my beer and the mood of depression settled deeper on me. I thought of all the tourists who had sat here on this verandah, lolling with ice-cold drinks, watching for elephants and rhinos, and all the small fry that had come like shadows out of the night to drink at the floodlit waterhole. It must have been quite a place then, the Lodge so carefully planned and the waterhole like a stage set. Now the lawn was a jungle growth, the swimming pool cracked and empty, the buildings battered and fallen into decay. It would make a good opening shot, but that was all, and a wildlife conference without wildlife. . . . I stared at my cigarette, listening to the rain. It would be a dead duck, and the only reason I had accepted the assignment, the man I had come here to meet —Cornelius van Delden, who knew the northern frontier—had not arrived yet.

The voices on the next verandah were louder now: *I tell you, it's pointless. The tourists won't come back, and without tourism . . .*

You agree with Kirby-Smith then?

About culling? Yes, if it's properly organised.

And somebody else, strident and angry: *Killing, you mean. Call it by*

*its proper name, for God's sake. Shoot anything that moves, make way
for cattle. And you call that culling.*

A heavy rasping Bostonian voice cut in: *Major Kirby-Smith is a businessman, that's all. So let's be practical, gentlemen. Call him what you
like, but he's efficient and he's got the Government behind him. So I
have to tell you this, the Foundation I represent accepts that this pilot
scheme is the best deal we're* . . .

A figure appeared out of the night, dripping wet, his safari hat shield-
ing his camera. "Fabulous!" It was Ken's current word when he had something good. He had been playing around with his Leica, taking stills. "It's
the rain and the hurricane lamps, all those bunks, and the bullet holes,
reflections in pools of water." He came in under the shelter of the verandah, shaking himself like a dog and smiling his satisfaction. "I was in
black and white, of course, but tomorrow, shooting in 7252 colour—
could be difficult. The light, I mean." He went through into the room
behind me, enthusing again about the pictures he had taken, wiping his
camera before he bothered to strip off and towel himself down. "Our
roommates are on their way." His voice was muffled as he rubbed at the
dark mass of his hair. "Two CBS men."

"How do you know?"

"Karanja told me. They're coming by truck. He was posting an attendance list on the noticeboard."

"Was van Delden on it?"

He shook his head, towelling vigorously. "There was a Delden representing some American magazines. But the initial was M. There was no
Cornelius van Delden."

So he wasn't coming after all. The one man who really knew the Northern Frontier District, the man whose father had opened the route across
the Chalbi Desert to Lake Rudolf and published a book of his travels in
Afrikaans.

"Have you roughed anything out yet?"

"No." And I stayed there, staring out at the rain, thinking about the
script, convinced it wouldn't be any good and the whole thing a waste
of time now that Cornelius van Delden wasn't coming.

In the end I went inside and mulled over the agenda and the old tourist maps they had given us, sitting at the broken-legged camp table with
the hurricane lamp at my elbow. Tsavo, Serengeti, Arusha, Ngorongoro
and its crater, all those national parks and game reserves that had once
been household names, and in the north—Meru, Samburu, Marsabit. And
further north still, up by Lake Rudolf on the Ethiopian border, the least
known, most remote of all—Ileret. At dinner they had been talking about
Ileret and unconfirmed reports of game moving up through the Rift Valley to the waters of Lake Rudolf. The only real heaven left, they had
said. But none of them had known Ileret. To them it was the edge of the
unknown, all desert country and lava fields, and across the BP map, glazed
to protect its surface against the sweat of tourists' hands, some official had

banged his rubber stamp, the single word FORBIDDEN staring at me in violet ink.

The map didn't mark Porr, or the islands, only Loiyangalani and Mt. Kulal—Oasis Fishing Camp, it said. There would be no fishing camp now, and I didn't need to measure the mileage. I knew how far it was, a hell of a long way, and the whole area forbidden territory. I reached for my bag, for the map and the translation of that old book—but what was the point of reading the typescript again? I knew the passages by heart, the map clear in my mind, and who else could take me there in present circumstances? *I am retired now, but if they ask me I will come.* Well, they had asked him and he wasn't here and the Conference opening in the morning.

I leaned back, staring at the wall opposite, where a gekko flicked its tongue, feet and tail spread flat like a little jewelled brooch—the only sign of life. Ken turned in his bunk, complaining about the light, and I told him to go to hell. I was feeling angry and frustrated, the rain drumming on the roof, gushing from the broken guttering, the persistent sound of it filling the room and a trickle of water seeping in at one corner where the plaster was cracked and stained. It glistened wet in the lamplight and I was thinking of the last time I had seen the kindly, ineffective man who had helped to bring me up. Almost a year ago now, and his hand quite steady as he gave me Pieter van Delden's book and the translator's typescript of it headed JOURNEY THROUGH THE CHALBI TO LAKE RUDOLF. Tucked into the typescript I had found the map drawn on heavy parchment paper. Two days later he had been found dead in that same dingy little basement office in Doughty Street.

The gekko moved, darting its long tongue at some insect, and I remembered his words, the sense of failure—*There's nothing else of any value for you here.* Those words had stayed in my mind. Had there been a note of censure in his voice? I couldn't remember now. Probably not. He had been too mild a man, and at the time I had regarded his words as a sort of epitaph to his mismanagement of Southly Tait. When he had taken over from my father it had been quite a thriving little publishing house specialising in travel. Inflation and a changing world had killed it—and him. Or was it my fault, not his? If I had gone into the business, as they had both hoped . . .

I pushed back my chair and got to my feet. It had been a long twenty-four hours, the night flight to Nairobi, the interminable wait on the cratered tarmac at Wilson Airport—odd how habit had retained that very English name—and now the rain, the bloody everlasting rain, and this damnable dreary battered place. I should have brought some Scotch. I could hear the clink of glasses next door, the sound of voices mellowed by drink. A bottle of Scotch would have cushioned my mind against the morbid thought of his inadequacy and my own selfish determination to go my own way. Ken Stewart was asleep now. I could hear his breathing, soft as a child's, and I envied him living for the moment, for the instant exposure of his next shot, his total involvement in camera angles.

I started to undress then, wondering whether I could have breathed some life into the business. The memory of his body laid out in that funeral parlour had haunted me ever since. The rain, my own loneliness, the dreary atmosphere of this Lodge—he had been lonely, too, after my aunt's death, and I had been too busy writing scripts, launching my own company, to help him cope with a run-down business and an alien world. And now here I was in Africa trying to make use of the only thing he had left me—a map that he had asked me to return, knowing he was going to die.

Footsteps sounded on the verandah outside. I was half undressed and I turned to find a soldier holding an umbrella and two men coming in out of the rain. Their plastic macs dripped water on the tiled floor as they introduced themselves. They were both TV men, the taller of the two, Erd Lindstrom, fair-haired, blue-eyed, the other, Abe Finkel, slim, dark, and intensely Jewish. "You're representing the BBC, are you?"

"On assignment only."

"An independent, eh?" He stared at me, then gave a quick shrug. "Well I guess it has its advantages."

But I knew what he was thinking as they dumped their equipment and stripped off their plastics. "Has anybody given you a forecast? How long is this rain gonna last? It's supposed to be the dry season."

"The little rains didn't materialise, so they think this may be it and the weather out of step again."

"So we film it all against a backdrop of rain. And we were told there was a drought. That's why we trucked up. Thought we might get some shots of elephant carcases, something to give a visual point to all the talk, and the rain caught us as we climbed up out of the Rift. You been out at all since the rain started?"

"No."

"Hear that, Erd? They've been stuck in this dump since the rain started." His voice was in tune with the rain, a flat continuous monotone. "At least we got shots of the truck up to its axles, but I'm sure glad we don't have to market this one. That Karanja says nobody's seen anything since they arrived, not even the elephant who used to go the rounds of the garbage cans each morning at breakfast time. You see anything?"

"Nothing."

Ken rolled over, blinking his eyes. "I got a quick shot at a warthog, tail up and going like a little train. But the light was bad and we're using 7252—Ektachrome Commercial. If this rain continues we'd do better with EF 7241. You got any of that?"

It was Lindstrom who answered. "No, we're on Kodak 7242, and it's negative, not reversal." They were equipped with a Bolex and a Bach-Auricon. They also had the remains of a bottle of rye, so that by the time

I finally climbed into my bunk I was happily insulated against morbid thoughts.

The opening day of what was officially designated the East African Federation's Conference on Wildlife Resources dawned humid and heavy, the air reeking of wet earth. It had stopped raining, but that was about all, the clouds hanging over the Lodge like a damp blanket, moist and menacing. Breakfast was a soup-kitchen affair, tin mugs and platters on the verandahs because the dining-room roof had leaked during the night and all the tables were wet. The room toilets and showers didn't work, of course, and the area around the tin-roofed conference latrines was soon a quagmire of reddish mud. There were several women delegates and Ken made the most of their ablutions until he was distracted by the appearance of Karanja in a neat grey suit, an ingratiating grin on his face and his big ears standing out like sails. He was holding a loudhailer as though it were a bazooka.

"Guess the Minister hasn't made it," Abe Finkel said.

Karanja reached the centre of what had once been the lawn, turned to face the half-circle of rooms and put the loudhailer to his lips. "Conference delegates and newspeople please I have to express the regret of our Minister, but due to circumstances of so unusual weather . . ." The Conference, due to open at ten with a speech of welcome to the delegates by Mr. Kimani, Minister for Lands and Resources, was postponed until his aircraft could get through. It was not an auspicious start.

"Pity we can't take off for the Serengeti on our own."

I pointed to the agenda. "That's scheduled for tomorrow. Also a view of the cattle reserve in the Crater."

"It'll be scrubbed," Abe said. "The only thing of any real interest . . ."

A figure squelched on to the verandah. I didn't realise it was a young woman, not immediately, for she was tall and broad-shouldered, dressed like a hardened safari hunter in faded khaki trousers, bush jacket, and worn calf-length boots, a floppy hat on her head with an ostrich feather stuck in it. "Any of you men Colin Tait?" Her voice came deep from the throat, slightly husky.

I got up. "Yes, I'm Colin Tait."

She stared at me, a long, hard, searching look. "I'd like a word with you." And she turned abruptly and stepped down into the trampled grass, standing there, waiting. "I'm Mary Delden," she said as I joined her. "Shall we go down towards the waterhole? I can't talk to you here." She began walking then and she didn't say anything more until we had gone beyond the Lodge buildings, past what had been the VIP suite with its verandah directly facing on to the water. The long stalks of the drought-sered grass were wet with the rain, my trousers soaked by the time we stopped out of earshot. "You wrote to Cornelius van Delden."

"You're related, are you?"

She nodded. "My father." She had a dark, very unusual face, rather long with a wide, thin-lipped mouth and a determined jaw; but it was the nose that was the dominant feature, strong and aquiline. Her eyes, as she faced me, were large and of a deep aquamarine colour, the whites made whiter by the darkness of her skin. "I dropped the 'van' when I went to America. There were political undertones and as a journalist Mary Delden seemed a more appropriate name." She smiled and the smile lit up her whole face, softening the virility of it. "Anyway my mother was Italian, not South African." Then abruptly she said, "What did you want to see him about? You didn't say in your letter, only that you had a copy of *Reis deur Chalbi* and it contains new information about . . ."

"I was expecting to meet him here."

"You don't want to tell me, is that it?" She said it lightly, still smiling, but the jut of the jaw and the frosty look in her eyes betrayed a certain hostility. "Let's walk on."

I hesitated, reminding her that the Conference was due to open as soon as the Minister arrived. She gave a derisive laugh. "Nothing is going to happen today and the Conference won't start until tomorrow."

"Did Karanja tell you that?"

"Of course not. But you've looked at your agenda. Tomorrow we were all going off in the supply trucks to have a look at the Serengeti and the Ngorongoro. The organisers in America insisted on that. Can you imagine what the mood of the Conference would be if the delegates were allowed to see the plains empty, the migrating herds all dead, no predators, not even a vulture, and the Crater full of cattle?" Her voice had risen sharply. "They've been bloody lucky with the weather."

"How do you mean?"

She looked at me as though I were a fool. "It was never intended we should see the Serengeti. They'd have found some reason for the Minister to be delayed. Or the trucks would all have broken down. They'd have explained it in some way. Now they have the weather, a perfect excuse. Have you ever been to East Africa before?" she asked.

"No."

She nodded as though it confirmed the impression she had already formed. And then she began questioning me, not about the reason for my seeking a meeting with her father, but about my background. Clearly she wanted to know what sort of person I was and I sensed that she was trying to make up her mind about something. Finally she stopped. We were at the far side of the waterhole. "I don't know," she said uncertainly. "We've got time enough, all morning, but . . ." Her mouth tightened. "I think you'd better tell me what it's all about."

"I'm sorry," I said.

"You're not doubting I'm Cornelius van Delden's daughter?"

I shook my head, wondering when she had last seen him.

"Then why won't you tell me? Why the secrecy? Is it something in his past, something that happened up there at Marsabit?" She was staring at me, her eyes puzzled. "No, of course not. That book was written long before. So what makes you think he'd risk his life to take you into the NFD?"

Something swept over my head, the whisper of wings planing, and a stork landed by the water, disturbing a pair of guinea fowl. It was the first sign of life I had seen. "How did you know about my letter? Did you see your father before coming on here?" And when she didn't answer, I said, "Is he still in the Seychelles? That's where he wrote from. It's his home, isn't it?"

"Yes, it's his home now. An old planter's house on La Digue that belonged to my mother's family."

"But you've seen him, haven't you?" She must have. How else would she know about my letter? "In his reply to me he said if they asked him, he'd come. I was expecting to meet him. . . ."

"Do you really think they'd let him address a conference like this?" she demanded. "Oh, yes, they asked him. They had to. With an inter-national reputation like his . . . But he has too many enemies here. They'll never forgive him for saying that African cattle are an affront to God, that man should learn from animals how to keep the laws of nature and not plague the world with the product of his loins. Have you read his book *Man's Rage against Nature?*"

"No," I said. "But I've heard about it."

"Then how could you think they'd allow him here, when all they're interested in is grabbing more land for the tribesmen's cattle. Kit Kimani is a hard-liner as far as animals are concerned, absolutely blinkered. I don't know where Karanja stands now—he was with us in the old days at Marsa-bit—but human greed is what dictates policy and the political pressures of a population explosion which has been going on now . . ." She gave a little shrug as though she thought it a waste of time explaining the problems of Africa to somebody who had never been there before. Then, speaking more slowly and in a quieter tone, "When he landed at Nairobi airport his passport was taken from him. A South African, they said. That was their excuse, though they knew damn well he hadn't been in South Africa since he was a child and for the past three years he'd been living in the Seychelles."

"So he did come."

"Four days ago. He thought he might be able to influence the Govern-ment, not Kimani, but some of the others. He knows most of them."

"You saw him in Nairobi then? Is he still there?"

"No, of course not. The security police kept him at the airport until the following night when a flight for the Far East came in. It refuels at Mahé in the Seychelles."

So he had gone back and that was that. No chance now of discovering whether he had ever been to the top of Porr, of trying to persuade him to take me up into that forbidden area.

"Do you speak Afrikaans?" she asked.

I shook my head, still thinking about the documentary I had dreamed of, a new discovery that might have made my name and perhaps a lot of money.

"But you've read *Reis deur Chalbi na die Rudolfmeer*. That's what you implied in your letter. A map, you said. There was no map in Pieter van Delden's book. Did you invent that?"

I shook my head.

"And it was never published in English, only in Afrikaans—at Pieter-maritzburg in 1908. So how could you have read it?"

I didn't know what to say, so I kept my mouth shut.

"I think I'm beginning to understand." She was smiling, but not with her eyes. "There's an English translation, unpublished. Now, what could there possibly be in that translation that is not in the original?" And then suddenly she switched to somehing else. "You made a TV film on sea pollution. It was you, wasn't it?"

I nodded. It was the only one of my films to make the American market.

"I saw it. A very good production. But no heart."

"It was a documentary on giant tankers and the problems of oil spillage," I said, not following her train of thought. "How can a subject like that engage the emotions?" Except fear, of course. It had frightened the life out of me when I was making it.

"Technological problems. You dealt with those all right. But you didn't follow on to show what happened to the seabirds and the dolphins and the seals." She had suddenly become very tense. "But now you're here. . . . Why do you want to go into the Northern Frontier District?"

"If I could have talked with your father . . ."

"Why should he take you?" She was staring at me and again I had the impression she was trying to make up her mind about something. "You're not concerned about Marsabit and what happened to the elephants there. Why didn't you approach Alex Kirby-Smith, who has some influence with this new régime?" She paused, her extraordinary eyes fixed on me. "It's the book, isn't it—something in the translation?"

"It's time we went back," I said. "The Minister will be arriving—"

"Kimani isn't going to arrive till the evening and the Conference won't start before tomorrow." Her mood suddenly changed. "I'm sorry, I shouldn't have said that about your tanker film. Few people care about the sufferings of animals. It's just that I was brought up . . ." She hesitated, the expression on her face gradually changing, a softer, almost appealing look. "Won't you tell me what it is—this information you have?" There was a softness in her voice, too, and her hand touched my arm. "I can contact him, you know."

"How?"

But she only smiled. She was tall, about my own height, and her eyes, staring into mine, had a warmth I hadn't guessed at. "Please tell me." She was suddenly very feminine, all the hardness gone. I couldn't believe a girl could change so completely. Maybe it was the Italian blood in her, but I found her change of mood disturbing and I looked away from her, at the waterhole and the stork standing motionless, the bush running away into an endless vista of Africa, the Lodge remote and nobody near. We were alone and my own blood was responding to her warmth and the touch of her hand on my arm.

"Please," she said again, and I shook my head, not trusting myself to speak, for there was a tightness in my throat. She gave my arm a gentle squeeze, smiling at me with her eyes, her lips parted, conscious of the effect she was having. "You must tell me," she said. "I can't decide unless you tell me."

And because I thought it was just the story she was after, I said something about her taking after her mother, and that seemed to change her mood again, for she let go of my arm. "I wouldn't know. She died when I was still a child." There was a harshness in her voice as she said that. Her lips had tightened, the eyes gone hard again. "So you're not going to tell me."

"No," I said. "But if you know where I can contact your father . . ." I hesitated. "I'm not having this hashed up for an American magazine."

She laughed. "You think I'd do that?" She turned, walking slowly away from me, and the stork rose, a slow flapping of wings as it beat its way across the waterhole, but she didn't look up, her eyes on the ground, deep in thought. Somewhere a dove was droning its somnolent *do-doo-do* call and I could hear the guinea fowl chattering, but nothing else, the heat pressing down and the clouds hanging in the sky with the promise of more rain.

When I looked at her again she had stopped and was bending down; she was watching a beetle rolling a ball of earth much larger than itself out of a hollow. "That's a female dung beetle," she murmured. "The eggs are inside that ball." Her gaze wandered along the edge of the waterhole, searching. "Some animal has been here, otherwise there wouldn't be any dung to hatch the grubs." She moved along the verge until she found what she was looking for, a turd the size of a football glistening with the rain. "Phlump," she said, and laughed. "Elephants have always been phlumps in my childish vocabulary." She stood contemplating the enormous stool with a frown. Then abruptly she turned and faced me. "Can I trust you?" It wasn't a question that required an answer. She was speaking her thoughts aloud. "I think perhaps . . . But I don't even know what it is that makes you want to go to Rudolf. . . . It is Lake Rudolf, isn't it?"

I nodded. "Lake Rudolf and a hill called Porr. Perhaps Kulal."

"Kulal." She said it slowly, rolling the name out as though there were some magic in it. "I've always wanted to go to Kulal. Tembo is one of the very few men who really knows that strange volcanic mass. . . . Will you promise—" But then she hesitated, shaking her head and smiling. "No, that's no good. I'll have to trust you. Anyway, it's only for two days.

On Thursday Alex addresses the Conference, then they'll face it out in front of the cameras and everybody will know." She glanced down at the shoes I was wearing, gave a little shrug, then turned and began walking into the bush. "It's not far," she said over her shoulder. "Half an hour or so, that's all." And after that she didn't talk, walking with an easy swinging stride.

I didn't talk either, for we were almost immediately into an area of shallow swamp and it was as much as I could do not to lose my shoes. Once, waiting for me, she pointed to some tracks. "Warthogs. If nothing else survives, the warthogs will." And she went striding on, brushing past a thicket of thorn and climbing a path through rock outcrops that had probably once been a game trail. And at the top she paused and nodded towards a line of green snaking across a burned-up plain. "Down there," she said. "In that lugga."

"You mean . . ." I hesitated, feeling bewildered, and she nodded, smiling. "He's a very determined man. When he sets his hand to something . . ." She paused, then said, "He went with the other passengers out to the aircraft, but he didn't board it. He just walked underneath it and out into the night, and nobody stopped him. By morning he was into the Ngong Hills, near an old camp where he had friends." She was staring at me, and the expression on her face was very intense. "It's dangerous for him. You realise that? They might kill him if they knew he was here."

"But if he speaks at the Conference . . ." It didn't make sense. "You said he was determined to speak."

"At the Conference it will be different. He'll have the protection then of the delegates and people like us who report for the media. But out here—" She was looking at me hard. "Out here he's alone and vulnerable. You understand?"

"I shan't tell anyone," I assured her.

She nodded. "No. I wouldn't take you there if I thought that." She walked on again then, down into the plain where the acacia trees raised umbrellas of dark foliage.

Ten minutes later we were into the green belt, on the soft sand of a long-dried stream bed. There was a trickle of water flowing now, pools of it in the sand hollows, and over everything the glimmering, glowing green of growth renewed by rain. A goliath heron, standing like a sentinel, rose at our approach, its wings labouring at the air, and in a clearing beyond the red earth bank there was the bright flash of what she thought was a malachite kingfisher. The banks of sand were marked by the feet of birds. It was hot and very humid. It was also very quiet, only the soft drone of doves and the insistent bubbling call of a coucal. "The water-bottle bird," she said, and at that moment a figure stepped out from a thicket, dressed in nothing but khaki shorts. His body glistened black and his face under the grizzled greyness of a thick cap of hair was old and wizened. He had a rifle in his hand and he kept it pointed at me, while he talked to the girl in Swahili.

"He says Tembo is following the track of a kudu up the lugga. He doesn't know when he'll be back." She stood talking to the old man a moment, then she nodded, smiling, and disappeared back into the trees. We went across a smooth flat expanse of golden sand. "I'm glad that old rascal is with him. His name is Mukunga."

"A Masai?" I asked. I knew it was all Masai country here.

"No, no. He's of the Kamba people—the Wakamba. He came in last night after a thirty-six-hour trek."

"How did he know your father was back?"

"I told you, he went into the Ngong Hills. The old camp there was a poachers' hide-out. Most of his boys were ex-poachers and he knew some of them would have gone back to their old trade. So the word went out and now he's got three of them with him."

"I thought he hated poachers," I said.

"Oh, for God's sake! What do you expect? Mukunga's a hunter. They were all hunters. Killing for the pot, for survival, that's very different from killing for profit—that's what he and Alex fell out over. And at Marsabit—only one man ever tried it at Marsabit. . . ." Her voice had dropped and I thought she gave a sigh, but I couldn't be sure. She was walking a little in front of me, her eyes on the ground. "Tembo. That's what they called him. Tembo and ndovu, it's the same, it means elephant. And they're right. Over the years he's become more and more like a phlump. Sometimes I wonder . . ." She paused, half turning her head. "I suppose you think it odd that I call him Tembo, but with my mother dead I spent most of my early life in bush camps, looked after by men like Mukunga. They called him Bwana Nkubwa, the Big White Chief, when addressing him formally, but among themselves he was always simply Tembo. I just got into the habit." She gave a little laugh. "I think when you meet him—" She turned her head at the croaking of a crow, watching it settle on the dead branch of a tree. "We must be nearly there now." She had slowed her pace and was peering at the bank. "He's moving his camp each day, just in case." There was a chattering sound, a bright flash of brilliant blue. "Damned starlings," she said. "A camp, a carcase, anything at all and they tell you where it is." She was climbing the bank, pushing her way through the undergrowth. I followed her and suddenly something hard was pressed into the small of my back and a voice said in English, "No move." I stood frozen, my skin crawling and the sweat dripping between my shoulder blades.

"It's you, Mtome, is it?" She came back, smiling and her hand held out. The pressure of the gun barrel on my back eased and I turned to find a tall, thin, very black man standing close behind me. The lobes of his ears hung slackly, pierced for ornaments he was not wearing. He was dressed in a sweat-stained shirt and khaki trousers held up by a big leather ammunition belt. He grinned in embarrassment, crinkling a deep scar on the left side of his face and revealing the broken stumps of two front teeth. "Tembo not back?" she asked.

"No, Missamari. Back soon." He glanced at the cheap watch on his wrist. "Tembo gone one hour. You want something?"

"Tea would be nice. Have you got some tea?"

He nodded, smiling broadly now. "Plenty tea, plenty sugar. Not got milk. Tembo gone milk a buffalo." And he chuckled quietly at his own joke as he pushed ahead of us into a little clearing where there was a small tent and the blackened remains of a fire. Two guns lay cradled in the fork of a tree and pieces of meat hung drying in the branches. A starling perched close by, chattering and displaying the white band between its chestnut belly and blue throat.

Mtome squatted before the embers of the fire, blowing them into a glow, while the two of us sprawled on the damp ground. The fat, sleep-inducing drone of doves gave to the heavy humidity the effect of a sound track and the distant call of the water-bottle bird added urgency to my interest in the blackened pot Mtome had placed on the fire. He was talking all the time to Mary Delden in a quick, clicking tongue.

"Mtome says he was cooking for some soldiers on the edge of the Rift Valley and a security patrol came in. That's how he heard Tembo was back." Her voice was soft, almost drowsy. "It must be all of sixteen years ago since that man was brought in from a northern safari. He'd been half killed by a buff in the Samburu country close under the Mathews Range." And she added, "He's the best cook we ever had. He's also a very good shot."

I remembered the Mathews Range from studying the map. It was above the South Horr track leading to Lake Rudolf. "Does he know the lake?" I asked.

"Of course. He's a Turkana. He was born up there and he's been back to Lake Rudolf many times with my father. Kulal, too. He knows all that country."

"Yet you've never been there."

"No. I was too young. We had a permanent camp on the Olduvai and I was always left there when the safari was a long one. Later, when my father began to specialise in the NFD, the camp was moved up near Isiolo, close under Lolokwe, but by then it was time for me to go to school in Nairobi."

It was a strange life for a girl and I couldn't help comparing her upbringing with my own. And now here I was sitting with her beside a fire on the edge of a dried-up stream bed, four thousand feet up and less than two hundred miles from the equator, waiting for her father, for Cornelius van Delden, the legendary figure who had been dubbed Jumbo van Delden by the popular press. I was wondering what he was really like, this man who belonged to a bygone world of tourist safaris and game parks, who had nursed wounded elephants, lived with them in the wild, and had now walked blithely into the territory of this new black régime, camping here regardless of its security forces. I wished Ken were with me. I hadn't even a camera, no means of recording the scene, and I sat there watching Mtome as the pot boiled and he threw in the tea, thinking of the script I could write if Cornelius van Delden really did make his appearance at the Conference.

She was talking to Mtome again. "Is that Turkana you're talking?" I asked.

"No. A mixture of Samburu and Swahili. I was asking him about the scar on his cheek, which is new since I last saw him. He says he was a camel man with the Army and got shot up in the battle for Kitale."

But it wasn't his war experience that interested me. It was the fact that he had been born near Lake Rudolf. "Ask him whether he has ever climbed a mountain called Porr." And I spelt it out for her, explaining that it was on the east shore of Lake Rudolf and looked like a pyramid.

She sat up, hugging her knees. "I remember now. It's mentioned in Pieter van Delden's book." Mtome handed her a tin mug and she put it down quickly. "Is that why you want to go to Rudolf, to climb Porr?"

I hesitated. But there was no point in being secretive about it now that she had brought me here to meet her father. "It seems there was some sort of city there. Not a city as we understand it, more a huddle of rock dwellings on top of a pyramidical hill." A mug of tea was thrust into my hand and it was so hot I nearly dropped it. "Pieter van Delden thought it must be Porr. But he never got to the top."

"Then how did he know about the rock dwellings?"

"It was on the pottery he found. Broken vases, cooking pots more likely, all very primitive, and this motif of rock structures on top of a pyramid, it was repeated again and again on the sherds he pieced together."

"That's not in his book."

"No." I hesitated, wondering how much to tell her, and at that moment a voice behind me said, "Who's this, Mary?" It was a gentle voice, very deep, almost a rumble, and I turned to find him standing quite still, beside the tree with guns in it. He was watching me intently out of eyes that were pale like moonstones under the thick white brows.

"I'm Colin Tait," I said, scrambling to my feet.

He didn't say anything, nor did I after that. I was too surprised at the size of the man and his appearance, the extraordinary sense of power that emanated from him. I knew from photographs in his elephant book that he was a striking figure but none of them had been close-ups, so that I wasn't prepared for the huge hatchet face that seemed all nose in a thicket of beard and long white hair. It took me back to my childhood and an illustrated Bible that had a picture of John the Baptist preaching in the desert.

"Colin wrote to you," his daughter said.

He inclined his head very slightly, not taking his eyes off me. "Why did you bring him here? I made it perfectly clear to you—"

"He wouldn't tell me what it was about, and as there was nothing happening at the Lodge——" She gave a little shrug of her shoulders. "After you've had your say at the Conference it would be very difficult to arrange a meeting."

His hand went up to his beard, fingering it. "The Conference hasn't opened then?"

"No. It's just as you expected. Kimani has been delayed."

He nodded. "So he's not going to give them a chance of seeing the Serengeti. Pity I couldn't talk to Maina or Ngugi in Nairobi. If I could have talked to them, or spoken on radio——" He stood stroking his beard and staring at me, deep in thought. "You're a TV man, Mr. Tait. I think that's what you said in your letter. I take it you have cameras with you?"

"Back at the Lodge, yes."

"Would it interest you to film the Serengeti instead of the opening of the Conference?" He pulled a pipe from the pocket of his faded bush jacket and came forward, squatting beside me and starting to fill it from a roll pouch made of what looked like leopard skin. "Since you're here . . ." He was watching me, the cold stare of those pale eyes disconcerting.

Mtome was filling a mug from the blackened pot and I didn't say anything, thinking of the security forces out searching for him and how very alone he must feel. He took a long time filling his pipe. His hands were unusually large, strong and heavily veined, and all the time he never took his eyes from my face. Finally he said, "Apparently Mary trusts you, so I suppose I must. But to make sure, I'm offering you the chance of pictures nobody else will get." He put his pipe in his mouth, smiling at me, but the smile never touched his eyes. "Have you got the guts to take a chance and risk getting shot?"

"I've never faced that sort of a choice before."

He gave a laugh that was more like a bark. "At least that's an honest answer." He reached for the mug Mtome was holding out to him and drank it off scalding hot. "That's better." He set it down and began lighting his pipe, looking across at his daughter, not at me. "I went about two miles up the lugga, then struck out across country. Hard going and the air heavy."

"Did you find the kudu?" she asked.

"I found the carcase, or what was left of it. The noose that strangled it was still hanging from a sapling and there were the remains of a fire. Somebody else trying to live off the land. Did you see any signs of life?"

"The tracks of a warthog, also elephant droppings, about two days old."

He nodded. "That elephant will die. They're all doomed, those that haven't got out. But the warthogs, they have survival quality. Giraffe, too, I think. I caught a glimpse of two adults and a young one, but I couldn't get near them. What's left of the game in this area knows it's being hunted. Everything's very shy now. Have you seen Mukunga yet?" And when she told him how he had emerged out of the trees, he smiled and nodded. "Mukunga was at our old camp on the Olduvai when Alex began his slaughter. That's how I know what happened down there on the edge of the Serengeti. It was over a year ago, just before the start of the migration. Has Alex arrived?"

"No. Karanja says he'll be coming in with Kimani."

"I ought to have a talk with that boy."

"Karanja? It wouldn't do any good."

"No, I suppose not. He'll be changed now, like everything else. He always did enjoy the limelight. Remember when he went in after that lion? Crazy show-off little guy." There was a note of affection in his voice, the words almost an endearment. "You see him now as a public-relations man," he said, looking at me, "but when he was with me he finished up as a better shot than any of us." He shook his head and I sensed a nostalgic yearning for days that were gone. Then, turning to his daughter again, he said, "So you haven't seen Alex yet. When you do, ask him what happened on the Olduvai a year ago. Mukunga says he must have slaughtered at least fifty thousand zebra there and as many wildebeest."

"It was wartime and he had the Army to feed."

He nodded. "And that freezer plant I told you about. If the Ugandans had been smarter they would have known there'd be a war once that big freezer was completed. Why else would the Government have lent a commercial operator the cash to build such a huge plant? The Serengeti herds were doomed from that moment. No other way he could fill it." He was looking at me again. "The end of that killing was only eight months ago, so the evidence of it will still be there."

"But that was the Army. It wasn't Alex. Mukunga told me that."

He brushed her comment aside, an almost angry movement of his hand as he leaned forward, his pale eyes fixed on me. "That interest you? An ossuary of wildlife, a charnelhouse of anything up to a quarter of a million beasts."

I nodded uncertainly, not knowing exactly what he expected of me. "My assignment is the Conference," I murmured. "Anyway, I don't see how I can possibly get there." I wasn't sure how far it was, but I knew it was a lot more than a day's journey on foot.

He smiled. "That's why I asked you whether you'd got the guts."

"Tembo, you must be mad." His daughter was leaning forward, her chin on her knees and a bright gleam in her eyes. "The only transport in this area—"

"The first question I'll be asked at the Conference is what proof I have. How do I answer that if I've not seen it with my own eyes? Karanja could tell them."

"Why should he?"

"Because he has a feeling for animals. But he won't, not now, when he has his feet on the rungs of a different ladder. Remember how good he was with the elephant calves?" He turned to me. "At Marsabit he looked after my elephants for me, and elephant calves are difficult to rear. Not as bad as rhino, of course. Once when we were in the South Horr Valley—"

She laughed, tapping him on the arm. "You're up to your old tricks—changing the subject. I want to know how you're going to get hold of a truck."

"And I want to find out what this young man knows about Lake Rudolf that I don't. Now leave it at that, Mary." He turned back to me. "You realise there's nobody knows that area better than I do?"

"I realise that, sir."

He nodded, frowning and sucking his pipe. "I thought I'd been everywhere my father had been." And then he was looking at me again. "Your letter suggested it was something to do with his book. You've read *Reis deur Chalbi na die Rudolfmeer*?"

"Not in the original, only in translation." And I told him about Southly Tait and how the typescript had come into my possession. "I think it had been on my uncle's conscience, that he'd done nothing about the book. It seems he found it among a whole pile of abandoned manuscripts when he took over after the death of my parents. He only kept it, he said, because of the map, and the fact that the book itself was annotated with marginal inserts and footnotes, also several handwritten sheets stuck in with passe-partout."

"In my father's writing?"

"I presume so. It was all in Afrikaans, anyway. I've checked through the translation. The loose sheet insertions are certainly included, also the footnotes, so I imagine the margin insertions are also in the English text."

"And you brought it with you?"

"Yes, and the map. Xerox copies, of course."

"I always felt there should have been a map in the book, but probably there was no engraver in Pietermaritzburg then, or else they had no means of making a block. Does it mark his route?" And when I described it to him as best I could, he said rather tersely, "It's all in the text. If you know the country you can follow it without a map."

"But not the location of the rock drawings," I said. "Or the old sites where he found the broken pieces of pottery."

"Rock drawings?" He stared at me. "There's nothing about pottery or rock drawings in the book." He took his pipe out of his mouth, regarded it for a moment, then put it back in his mouth again and shook his head slowly. "Not my field, I'm afraid, and anyway, this is hardly the moment—"

"But the drawings," his daughter said. "An early culture, perhaps the earliest." And she passed on to him what I had told her about the motif on the broken sherds.

He listened to her, nodding absently. "I heard something about it. Leakey, I think. Young Richard Leakey—another of his theories. And there was a much earlier expedition, middle 1800s—before Teleki." He turned to me. "Anything is possible up there, but you must realise I have other things on my mind." He wasn't an archaeologist. A very early city

dwelling meant nothing to him compared to the slaughter of the wildebeest in the Serengeti or even the sprung noose marking the death of a
single kudu.

"Porr I know, of course," he said slowly, as though making an effort
to relieve my disappointment. "From Loiyangalani and the El Molo
islands it stands up out of the flat curve of the lake's east shore like a
pyramid in the desert. And if the wind gives you the chance of getting
over to South Island, then the similarity to an Egyptian pyramid is even
more marked. A lot higher, of course—over three thousand feet. It's a
trick of the light, I think, for it's only when you get near it that you
appreciate its height."

"Have you ever climbed it?"

He shook his head. "No. I've trekked all round it, along the lakeside
and by the inland route. But there wouldn't be any life up there on that
battered red-rock mass. Somebody has described it as one of nature's most
dilapidated monuments, a once-solid mountain shaken to pieces. Hillaby,
I think." He gave Mtome his empty mug to refill and said, "I find it
strange that this information should have been written into the book only
when he was seeking English publication. Is there no letter of explanation?"

"I suppose there must have been originally," I said. "But as it was
handed to me there was just the original book, the map and the translation. I did make some attempt to find a letter, but there was such an
accumulation of dusty piles of rubbish in that basement office. . . ."

"Very strange," he murmured. "He was an Afrikaner and strongly anti-
British. He lived by the Bible and his gun, a great hunter and as bigoted
as hell. It's hard to believe he would seek English publication and that he
would then include details he had not revealed in the Afrikaans original."

"Didn't he ever talk to you about it?"

He shook his head. "Not that I recall. But then he died just before
my eighteenth birthday. He was suffering from malaria and was badly
injured by an elephant he failed to bring down with his first shot." He
looked at me. "You say the additional material was handwritten and in
Afrikaans? And the original from which the translation was made is in
your possession? I'd like to see that sometime. Does the writing look at
all feminine?" And when I told him it was large and angular, he nodded.
"My mother's, probably. He didn't leave her much to live on and English
publication wouldn't have worried her, she was half German, half Bel-
gian." He smiled. "I'm a bit of a mongrel, you see." And he didn't say
anything after that, sitting there, drinking his tea, apparently deep in
thought.

It was Mary who asked me about the map. "Is the writing the same
as in the notes?"

But I couldn't answer that because the lettering was all in capitals.

"And the translation, when was that done—in your father's time?"

"No. Much later. My uncle commissioned it in 1971. You remember

Richard Leakey's discovery of a skull up by the Ethiopian border that put the origins of man about a million and a half years earlier than his parents' discoveries at Olduvai? It was a very controversial find, a lot of publicity, and Leakey aired a number of theories. One of them was that Lake Rudolf was the cradle of civilisation. According to him, it was there, and not on the Nile, that pottery was first made. In fact, he claimed that Nilotic pottery should be renamed Rudolfic." I turned to Cornelius van Delden. "Leakey also found sherds at his dig on Lake Rudolf and provisionally dated them pre-Nilotic. That was what decided my uncle to commission a translation of the book."

"But he never published it—why?"

"I did find some correspondence that had a bearing on that. It seems almost two years elapsed before the typescript of the English version was finally delivered. I suspect the fee was so small the translator wasn't greatly interested in the work."

"So it was never published."

"No."

"Just as well, perhaps." He said it so quietly that I wasn't sure he intended me to hear. And he added quickly, "No chance now of anyone looking at what he found. It's closed, all that area." He put down his mug and glanced at his watch. "Time you were leaving, if you're to get back for lunch. We can't feed you here. One warthog is all I've been able to bag so far." He indicated the strips of meat hanging in the fire's smoke. "Bush pig and posho, that's not very good eating." He smiled and got to his feet. "Maybe when all this is over and things are normal again . . ." He gave that harsh bark of a laugh and shrugged his shoulders. "When I'm back on La Digue, send it to me. Better still, come and see me. No animals there, but the birds are interesting."

He looked quickly round the camp, nodded to Mtome, and led the way down into the lugga. "Now, about tonight . . ." And as he walked with us across the sandbanks of that rain-washed river bed, he gave us instructions where to wait for the truck. His daughter did her best to find out how he was going to get hold of the vehicle, but all he would say was, "There's no problem there. It's returning it may be a little more difficult." And he added, "I plan to be at Lake Ndolo just about dawn."

He saw us to the point where we had entered the stream bed, the rock hill just visible at the edge of the plain, shimmering in the sweltering heat. "Remember, if you're seen leaving the Lodge area, or challenged by one of the soldiers, then don't come. And a convincing explanation of your absence must be given to those who share your rooms." He glanced up at the sky. "Better bring waterproofs. The rain won't hold off much longer." He patted his daughter on the shoulder. "Don't take any chances, Toto."

"Ndio, Tembo." She was laughing, I think with excitement.

He turned then with a wave of his hand. "See you about two in the

morning then." And he went ambling off up the lugga, his head swinging this way and that, alert and watchful. He didn't look back.

We went on then and I said, "He's like a caged lion. He even looks
like a lion."

She smiled, shaking her head. "No, not like a lion. Like an elephant. If
you get to know him you'll notice he behaves like an elephant, too. He
never forgets, never forgives, and nothing ever stops him." And she added,
"He's a very large man in every respect, and very exhausting, which is why
I make sure there's a lot of ocean between us."

II

The rain started again shortly after lunch, a heavy downpour as though
a tap had been turned on. About an hour later a wind sprang up and the
tap was turned off. Suddenly the sun was shining and everything steamed
in the heat. I was lying on my bunk, but I couldn't sleep, the sound of
voices a continuous murmur as delegates talked and argued, moving from
one group to another, renewing old contacts, making new ones. Ken said
it had been like that all morning, nobody minding very much that the
Conference had not opened. I could see them now, out in the bright sunlight, endlessly talking; the newsmen, too, huddled together or moving
from group to group, trying for statements from those who were interna-
tionally known.

Shortly after four a light plane flew low over the Lodge, and half an
hour later the Minister was being photographed with the Conference
Chairman, Sir Edmund Willoughby-Blair. Kimani looked very slight beside the big blond Chairman, but what he lacked in height he made up in
energy, his movements quick and full of vitality, his broad, rather flat
features alive and full of smiles.

It was on this scene that the sunlight faded, snuffed out by an electrical
storm that crashed round us for an hour or more. It was night before the
rain finally stopped and we sloshed through mud to our evening meal—
tinned stew, rice and over-cooked vegetables, tea from an urn and a can
of beer beside each place. Soldiers moved around the tables, clearing the
plates away, their faces glistening black in the light from the naked bulbs,
and I watched Mary Delden talking animatedly to a group of men at a
nearby table. No sign of nervous tension in that strong brown aquiline
face and she didn't even glance in my direction.

A Frenchman at a table by the verandah suddenly called out, "Re-
gardez! Un éléphant," and the dining-room erupted, everybody trooping
out into the night. The spots had not yet been switched on, but a young
half moon and some stars showed through ragged clouds and for a moment
everybody glimpsed a grey bulk standing motionless on the far side of the
waterhole. A cloud shadow passed across it, and when the moon emerged

again it was gone. Karanja was calling for the spotlights to be switched on, but it was too late. A big American with a Boston accent standing right beside me claimed excitedly, "An elephant. I saw it with my own eyes." And he added to the group about him, "That just goes to prove what I been saying. Things aren't as bad as that guy Winthrop would have us believe."

"Moonshine," somebody said, and there was laughter, everybody happier now that they had actually seen something.

A hand touched my arm and I turned. It was Mary Delden. "Twelve-thirty," she said. "Okay? And bring a hand camera, nothing heavy."

I nodded and she continued on past me, heading for her room.

The rest of that evening I spent on the verandah, dozing in the only chair with the Beaulieu news camera in its case beside me. It hadn't been difficult to convince Ken that we should split up in an endeavour to make good the lost excursion to the Serengeti; he would cover the opening of the Conference, using the Bolex electric H16, while I tried for some dawn shots under the guidance of somebody who knew the country. I think he guessed it was Mary Delden, but he wasn't the sort to ask questions.

The spotlights were switched off again at nine and an hour later the Lodge was silent, only a few lamps still glimmering in the dark, the moon cloud-covered, no wind and everything very still. I must have fallen asleep, for the next thing I knew there was a figure beside me and Mary Delden was whispering, "Time to go. Are you ready?" She had a Retina camera slung over her shoulder, a waterproof draped over it, and the pockets of her bush jacket bulging with film.

I nodded and got to my feet, picking up the Beaulieu and my plastic waterproof. She was already moving quietly out into the trampled grass, a dark shadow heading down towards the waterhole. I followed, keeping close behind her, feeling my way in the dark and thinking of that elephant. And if there was an elephant around, why not other beasts— rhino or lion? Wasn't this the time they came down to drink?

A branch broke under my foot. She reached back and took my arm. "Quiet now," she whispered. "There's a patrol stationed on the road a mile south of the Lodge." And she walked on, still holding my arm.

The moon was still hidden by cloud, only a faint luminosity lingering. We skirted the waterhole, leaving it to our left, and struck out into fairly open country. The going was firm, the hard gravelly soil sparsely covered with a coarse growth of stiff little bushes about knee high. Trees loomed up, dark shadows whose shapes seemed imbued with life.

"How do you think he's going to get hold of one of those Army trucks?" I whispered.

"I don't know."

"Why didn't he tell you when you asked him this morning?"

"I'm a female, that's why. He's never heard of Women's Lib."

"But he should have told you. You've a right to know what you're letting yourself in for."

"He doesn't trust women." She said it flatly, but there was an undertone of bitterness in her voice as she added, "We've never been very close, and anyway he never tells anybody what he's going to do. He's a man who acts as though there was nobody else in the world—" She suddenly froze, her grip on my arm tightening. She was staring past me, at the dark shadow of a tree that became two trees, one of them moving. Or was it a trick of the light?

She moved on quickly, then stopped at the sound of wood striking wood and a thin squeal that might have been fear or pain, or the cry of some nocturnal bird. It wasn't repeated. Instead, there was a soft gravelly sound as though something heavy was being dragged along the ground.

"He should have put it out of its misery." She was standing very still, staring after the fading sound. "He knew what they'd done."

"What was it?" I asked.

"Elephant. The same one." The moon was coming clear of the cloud now and I saw her face, tight-lipped and angry. "Rotten types!" she murmured. And after that she was silent until at last we topped a rise in clear moonlight and saw the road winding down to the lugga. Nothing stirred, the open plain an opaque emptiness bounded by rock outcrops. She stopped then, watching the road. "I think we're clear of the patrol. Karanja said it was at the top of the slope leading down to the lugga."

We began the descent and halfway down to the lugga something chuckled away to our left. There was a mewing sound, then a soft whoop. I thought it was a night bird, but she had quickened her pace. "They know," she said. "They always know." The whoops faded into the distance, lost behind an outcrop. "I don't like hyena," she murmured, staring towards the black tree shadows where the road forded the lugga, her head cocked, listening. But there was no sound now and nothing moved. Dark clouds were spreading towards us from the west, blacking out all the plain, and in a moment the moon had gone and we were engulfed in darkness. It began to rain as we reached the road and walked down it to the ford where we found a fallen tree growing out into the lugga and sat there waiting.

"Half an hour to go," I said, looking at my watch.

"He'll be ahead of schedule. He always is."

There was the whisper of a breeze here, but apart from the stirring of the leaves and the sound of the rain there was nothing, only silence. I could just see the outline of her features in silhouette and beyond her the pale line of the road climbing to the skyline. She was sitting very still, not tense, but alert, and I sensed an undercurrent of excitement in her. We were alone in the African bush, just the two of us, waiting, and I had time then to consider what I had let myself in for. The man was persona non grata, virtually on the run, and stealing an Army truck. . . .

"How far is it to this lake he spoke of?" My voice sounded over-loud in the silence.

"Lake Lgarya? Three or four hours. I'm not sure."

"And how long shall we be there?"

"Long enough for you to get your pictures."

I hadn't been thinking of that, but when I asked her what she thought would happen when we got back, she didn't answer. The silence was oppressive. Nothing in my whole life had prepared me for this and she sat there, remote and outwardly quite calm, as though this were just an ordinary safari. "Those guns," I said. "Where did he get them from?"

"I've no idea."

"He couldn't have brought them with him from the Seychelles."

"Keep quiet, can't you, and listen."

Silence again and the need to talk so urgent I had to keep a tight hold of myself. I could feel my heart thudding. I was scared, and I didn't know how to conceal it from her. Something flickered past my face. "It's all right," she said. "Only a bat." And I realised I had leapt to my feet. "You drive a car, don't you?" She sounded faintly amused. "When you're driving, you're like the zebra grazing alongside lions after a kill, you close your eyes to accidents, never admitting you could get killed, too. So stop worrying. You're far safer sitting here in the rain than driving a car along a motorway. Anyway, there isn't much left to be scared of in this area." She turned her head, looking directly at me. "Do you understand what he's trying to do?"

"I think so."

"I wonder if you do." She paused and then said, "Have you talked to the delegates?"

"Some of them."

"Then you'll have realized they're hopelessly divided. They're here at the invitation of the East African Federation. The state of the Lodge, the commissariat, everything, is a reminder that there has been a war here in Africa and many of them are more concerned with the practicalities of the moment than with what effects their actions will have on the future. In wildlife, as in everything else, there is the political element, and unless he can jolt them into concerted action . . . Are you any good with a camera?"

"I'm not a professional like Ken."

She nodded. "I'm not a professional either, but so long as our pictures are good enough to show the world what's been happening out here . . ." She paused, listening again. The rain had almost stopped, the wind increasing and the rustle of the leaves louder. "The mere threat of world revulsion may be sufficient to swing some of them. Otherwise, I'm afraid they may go along with this idea of a pilot conservation scheme. You haven't met Alex Kirby-Smith yet."

"I was told he hadn't arrived."

"He flew in with the Minister. He's seen some of the delegates already, those they know they can rely on. Today he'll be trying to convince others privately." And she added, "He always had quite a different attitude to animals. Even as a child I sensed that. He's a commercial operator. He has the same attitude to animals as a tree-feller has to a forest. They're a natural resource, a crop."

"You know him, then?"

She laughed abruptly. "Of course I know him. He and Tembo were partners. They ran a safari business together. They were both hunters then, operating under licence, fulfilling quotas. For Tembo it was a way of life. It brought him into close contact with the country and the animals. That's all he cared about. With Uncle Alex—I called him Uncle in those days"—she laughed again, a quick nervous laugh that was almost a girlish giggle—"with him it was different. It was business. He began to build up an organisation. He undertook scientific research for the Government, advising on numbers of lion, elephants, whatever was to be culled. Then he'd go in with refrigerator trucks, the lot. He had all the back-up facilities so that even the hide and the bones, every morsel of the animals he culled was put to some use. It was all very scientific and he was so bloody persuasive."

"And that was when your father and he parted?"

"No. It was before that. When I was about nine. It was shortly after my mother was killed and I remember I cried and cried."

"You liked him then?"

"Yes. Much more than—my father. Uncle Alex was a great charmer. Still is. And for a little girl—" She sighed. "Tembo, you see, has no graces. He's a tough, driving, hard-bitten man, and absolutely uncompromising."

"And on Thursday he's going to confront Kirby-Smith—"

"Listen!"

For a moment I couldn't hear it. Then, faint above the wind in the trees, I heard the sound of an engine. The skyline up the road became limned in light and a moment later the truck's headlights appeared over the rise. We went out on to the road, the lights blinding us until they were dipped. The engine slowed, the truck braking to a halt right beside us, and both the men in the cab were black. The African at the wheel sat staring at us and I didn't recognise him at first, his face ashen under the dark skin, sweat on his forehead and the whites of his eyes gleaming wildly. It was Karanja.

I thought at first something had gone wrong and he had come out to fetch us back to the Lodge. Then I saw that the other African was Mukunga and he had a rifle in his hands. A voice from the back of the truck said, "All right, Karanja. You can ride in the back now." And Cornelius van Delden climbed out over the tailboard.

"No trouble with the patrol?" his daughter asked.

He gave that barking laugh of his. "They weren't there. The rain—I thought they wouldn't be. But I had Karanja drive just in case." He turned to me. "You ride in the back. Mukunga."

"Ndio, Bwana."

"You go in the back with Karanja. Keep an eye on him."

Karanja was out of the driving seat, standing hesitantly on the road beside me, all the jauntiness he had displayed at the Lodge gone. "Mr. van Delden." His voice was high and nervous. "I think it better I walk back now. You are clear of any soldiers and—"

"You always called me Tembo. Remember?"

"Yes, Tembo. But I shall be missed. And how can I explain to the Minister—"

"Of course, you'll be missed." Van Delden's voice was harsh. "Why do you think I brought you along with me?" He put his hand on the man's shoulder. "You've got about ten hours in which to think up a good excuse for driving off with the truck. Besides, I want you to see what your people have done in the Serengeti. You, who were so good with animals. Think of Lucy, and the little toto you named Labda because you weren't sure she'd live. A big cow elephant now, but more likely she'll be dead with a bullet in her guts. That's if she's lucky. Now jump in the back and let's get going."

For a moment I thought Karanja would make a dash for it. I was standing right beside him and I could see the whites of his eyes as he looked round wildly. He was breathing quickly and I think near to panic. Mukunga sensed it too, and slipped the safety catch of his rifle. But van Delden's hand was still on Karanja's shoulder. "Come on, man. Make the best of it." He spoke quietly, as though gentling an animal, and somehow it seemed to get through to him, the tension relaxing, his body sagging in its grey suit. "Okay, Tembo." And he turned and climbed docilely into the back of the truck.

"Give me your camera," van Delden said to me. "It's going to be a rough ride."

I don't know what it was like in front, but it was certainly rough in the back. Van Delden took it slowly through the lugga, but as soon as we had climbed the further slope he put his foot down. The truck was an open one and it was empty, nothing in the back but an old tarpaulin, black with oil and soaking wet. We tried folding it so that we had a cushion to lean against. This made it just bearable so long as we were on hard gravel, but the road worsened as we drove south into what had been Tanzania. The fighting had been heavy here the previous year and there were soft patches, badly rutted, the truck slithering wildly and no weight on the back wheels. In the end there was nothing for it but to stand, gripping the handbar at the back of the cab. I could see where we were going then and brace myself as we skidded and jolted across the rutted sections, but it was hard on the legs, and my eyes streamed. "I am coming here one time," Mukunga shouted to me. "Very bad. Plenty lorries and much dust."

"With Major Kirby-Smith?"

"No. That is Mtome. Me with askari, hunting."

"With the Army?"

"Ndio." He nodded. "Very bad."

"What were you hunting—buffalo?"

"Hapana." He shook his grizzled head, his teeth white in a grin. "No, me hunt men. Me track, askari shoot."

I glanced at Karanja on the other side of me. No wonder he'd decided against making a dash for it. "What were you doing during the war?" I asked him.

"Same I am doing now, public relations." He said it quietly so that Mukunga couldn't hear and I knew he was ashamed. Then the rain started again.

After that we didn't talk. The going got rougher and it was all we could do to hang on. Once van Delden slowed, leaning his head out of the broken window and calling back. "You all right, Tait?" I gritted my teeth and said I was, but when I asked him how much further, he shouted, "Not sure. Thirty, maybe forty miles. We'll be turning right on to a minor track soon. Better hang on then." And he built up speed again, the headlights slashing the night and showing outcrops of red rock, great laval heaps of it. We crossed another lugga and he took it too fast, throwing us off our feet and nearly breaking an axle, the wheels thumping against the mudguards. Eyes blazed at us in the darkness, Mukunga's hand on my arm, his voice shouting, "Fisi." I had a glimpse of the hyena's grey ungainly body shambling clear of us as we thundered past, then we were over a rise and braking sharply as a bomb crater rushed towards us. I could see the dull gleam of water in it as the truck carved its way through low scrub on the verge, rocking wildly.

We slowed for a while, the rain teeming down and more craters. A burned-out scout car, some lorries gaping holes, then we were clear of the battlefield, driving fast again. My hat was rammed down on my head, but the rain poured in under the collar of my waterproof. I was wet to the skin and cold. Mukunga did not seem to mind it, standing beside me, the sodden khaki shirt clinging to his hard frame, water streaming from his tough monkey-like face. Karanja, on the other hand, was shivering with cold, his cheap suit shapeless, his teeth chattering. He was looking at me, looking at my waterproof, and I knew what he was thinking. Then suddenly he let go of the handbar and dived for the tarpaulin. The wheels bucked, spinning, and he was flung against the side, where he lay for a moment as though stunned.

Mukunga suddenly thumped on the cab roof, called out something in Swahili as we slowed, and then the truck swerved, a sharp turn to the right on to a barely defined track, water in ruts gleaming pale in the headlights. The wheels spun as we slithered through mud to the burned-up grass of the flat land bordering the track. We headed across country then, the wheels hammering at unseen holes. "Serengeti," Mukunga shouted to me. "Nijia nzuri sasa—road good now."

I looked round and thought for a moment Karanja had been thrown out. There was no sign of him, only the bundle of tarpaulin heaped against the side. He had wrapped it round himself so completely he was cocooned in it. Rock outcrops loomed ahead like islands in a flat lake. The first glimmer of dawn showed behind low clouds. The rain died, visibility improving. We skirted the rock outcrops and they were like pictures I had seen of kopjes in the South African veldt, and as the light strengthened and I could see further and further ahead, the plain we were on seemed endless. The clouds thinned. Ragged gaps appeared. A glimpse of the morning star low down in the west and then the sky began to take fire, the clouds all aflame and constantly changing shape, so that we seemed to be headed into a cauldron of molten lava. Even the plain was red, the wetness of uncropped grass reflecting the volcanic flaming of the sunrise and everything beginning to steam.

It was then that we came to the first of the bones. They were scattered over an area of three or four hectares, a litter of skulls, rib cages, and leg bones, all picked clean and gleaming in that blood-red dawn. I thumped on the cab roof and van Delden slowed, leaning out of the window to tell me he expected larger concentrations of bones near the lake. But as he started to drive on again, I shouted to him that I wanted to film now, while the light was this startling, flaming red.

He slowed, stopped beside a clean-picked carcase, and I jumped out, calling for my camera. "It's colour," I told him. "In this light it will look fantastic." I was excited, my mind already scripting the words, beginning to grasp what could be made of this.

I had him back up the truck, explaining that as soon as I signalled I was ready, I wanted him to drive up to the carcase, then get out and bend over it. "Pick up one of the bones," I said, "and I'll zoom in on you."

He did it just as I had suggested, and seeing him get out of the cab, the plain behind him all misted pink and his strong features picked out in a ruddy glow, even his beard tinged in red, I knew I had a subject that would make every viewer sit up electrified. But when he reached the bones, instead of bending down and picking one up, he turned suddenly, his back to the camera, and called out, "Karanja. Come here."

I nearly took my finger off the trigger, but then I thought I'd never have the light so good again and I kept the camera rolling, gradually zooming in as Karanja clambered out of the back of the truck and walked towards van Delden, who now bent down, picking up a long shin bone, holding it out for the African to see.

I moved in then, walking quickly forward, keeping them in focus and circling until I could close in on their faces. Mukunga was in frame, too, his rifle lying across his shoulder, the wizened face very clear in the growing brilliance of light. And then, as I zoomed in for a real close-up, Karanja seemed to notice me for the first time. His mouth gaped, a look of intense shock, and suddenly he covered his face in his hands. Then he bolted, running like a hunted animal back to the truck.

Van Delden turned and looked at me, still holding the bone and staring straight into camera. "You realize what you've done?" He was smiling, and on that strange reflective smile the camera ran out of film and stopped.

"What do you mean?" I asked.

"Print that picture and it's as good as a death warrant."

Mary Delden moved in front of me, her Retina held to her eye for a close-up of her father looking straight into the sunrise. I heard the click of the shutter and she said, "You did it purposely."

He nodded. "Of course. Now he's been filmed here your pictures are safe. His life depends on your cameras not being seized." He turned to me again. "Have you finished now?"

I nodded, still thinking of Karanja running scared with his hands over his face.

"Then let's get on to the lake area. We haven't much time and I want pictures of my own to show the full extent of the slaughter."

We drove on then, and as the sun rose we turned on to a track running west. A few miles further on, trees appeared to the south of us, marking the edge of the Serengeti plain. All this time we were passing scattered areas of bones half hidden in the dried-up grasses and Karanja sat on the floorboards as though in a trance, a dazed expression on his face, which was almost grey. He wouldn't stand up and hold on to the handbar, preferring to be bounced around in the bottom of the truck. It seemed he dared not look at the animal graveyards through which we were driving.

We crossed a track running south and almost immediately the wheels were crunching bone and from my vantage point in the back the plain ahead was marked with circular concentrations of rib cages like great mushroom rings. It was as though an army had fought its last battle here, falling as it stood, regiment by regiment.

The sun was already climbing up the sky, all colour gone, and when we finally stopped we were in the middle of the battlefield, the weathered bones of dead regiments of wildebeest all round us. It was such an incredible sight that we just stood there for a moment, staring at it. Then Mary Delden turned to her father. "Who did it? Not Alex. When he culls he does it properly, putting bone, hide, everything to use."

"This is wartime. The last big battle was fought up there on the edge of the plains and with their lines of communication cut—" Van Delden shook his head. "Good thing the Grzimeks can't see this." It was the Grzimeks, father and son, who had pioneered this one-time national park, had written a book I remembered—*Serengeti Shall Not Die*. "Mukunga warned me, but I wouldn't have believed it possible—such an orgy of killing." He was climbing up on the roof of the cab. He had an old Polaroid camera and as he waited for the first picture to be developed, she said accusingly, "You're going to show these pictures to the delegates and let them think it was Alex."

"He had a contract to supply the Army out of the Serengeti."

"But not like this, not killing everything."

"It got out of hand, that's all. The troops saw how it was done and the lust for killing took over." He took another picture, then turned to her. "That's his business, isn't it—killing? And now he's going north, a new contract, to feed the starving Samburu. War or drought, it's business, and there's that big freezer plant. He's got to fill it with something."

She was silent after that and I slipped another magazine on my camera, changing the lens, and took some panoramic shots, followed by some close-ups of discarded bones that had been piled in a heap.

Talking to van Delden afterwards, I gathered that in their migration the wildebeest subdivided themselves into herds of anything up to two or three hundred beasts. Sometimes the concentrations were smaller, sometimes larger, but round every concentration of these remains we found the tyremarks of vehicles that had ringed them in, enclosing them while the men in the trucks had gunned them down. I was endeavouring to film a particularly clear group of tracks to show how the animals had been panicked into a mass when Mary Delden called to me. The urgency in her voice made me turn, and then I saw it, a grey shape, almost a skeleton, covered by mangy fur.

It was a hyena, all belly and hindquarters, and it was moving towards me, the eyes gleaming and a slavering froth on the jaw. It seemed half dead from starvation; it was coming towards me so slowly, and I swung the camera, shouting at it and backing away. "Run you fool!" she screamed. I ran then and the wretched animal, which had checked at my shouts, loped after me, moving suddenly with surprising speed.

A rifle cracked. Another shot and van Delden called, "All right, Tait." I stood there for a moment, feeling shaken and my legs trembling, then I took a close-up of the emaciated hyena lying dead on its side, and another of van Delden with the rifle to his shoulder. And afterwards, as we wandered through the neighbouring boneyards, we came upon several hyenas slinking among the skeletal remains, their powerful jaws crunching up bone in a desperate attempt to obtain enough sustenance to exist for one more day. It was a depressing, heartbreaking sight, and the Serengeti plain, emerald bright now in the sun, a smiling landscape dotted with rock outcrops. Except for these last few scavenging hyenas there was not a sign of life, not even a bird, the sky empty, a blue glare with the fluffy white of clouds piled up on hills too far away to see.

"Got all you want?" van Delden asked.

I nodded, staring down at the bones spread out in the grass at my feet.

"What you've seen here," he said, "is the work of man at his most destructive. The effects of this slaughter will have been rippling out for the past six months, upsetting the fine balance of nature from the jungle to the sea and as far north as the deserts of Ethiopia and Somaliland." His pale eyes were fixed on me, almost glaring. "Get that into your script. You've got the film. Use it. The migration here was at times about a million strong—zebras, wildebeest, finally the gazelles, Grants and Tommies.

Tell people what it means to kill out great herds like that. Make them see how it affects all living things. Lions, hyenas, jackals, the bat-eared foxes, wild dog, too—they all lived off these beasts. Vultures, even eagles, right down to the ants that exist to clean up the last remains. Tell them." He checked himself then. "Karanja!"

Karanja was sitting in the shade of the truck, his head bowed between his knees. He lifted his head slowly. "Yes, Tembo?"

"Have you thought out what you're going to say to the Minister?"

For a moment I thought he had lost himself in a mood of complete dejection. But then he got to his feet and came towards us, smiling and with something of his old jauntiness. "If Mr. Tait agreed, and Miss Mary, perhaps I say I take the truck to find them, fearing for their safety."

Van Delden did not say anything, busy with his Polaroid, and Karanja turned to me. "You must say, Mr. Tait, that you and Miss Mary go to get pictures of the dawn, some animals maybe, and then you get lost. Okay?"

I nodded. "So long as they don't take our cameras."

"No. I see to that."

"And what about our film?" It would be so easy for him to have the film seized on some pretext.

"Your film will be safe." But he said it without conviction, his eyes shifting.

Mary Delden was crouched by a litter of rib cages and, still with her eyes to the viewfinder of her camera, she said to her father, "To be on the safe side I'll hand you some of my films." She straightened up and produced two cassettes from the pocket of her bush jacket.

"No need." Van Delden was waiting for the development indicator. "If this comes out all right your camera and films should be safe." He released the developing button and opened the camera. "Clear enough, I think." And he tore out the film and held it up for us to see. It was a clearly identifiable picture of Karanja as he stood talking to me, and behind him was the truck and Mary Delden crouched with her camera before a heap of bones. "Tomorrow I shall be showing the delegates the pictures I have taken this morning. Whether I include this one or not will depend entirely on you." He leaned forward, his face close to Karanja's, tapping him on the chest with his finger. "Just see that neither Mr. Tait nor Miss Mary are in any way harassed for being so stupid as to lose their way. Got it?"

Karanja nodded, his eyes rolling, his tongue licking his lips. "I see they are okay, Tembo."

It was blackmail and I couldn't help feeling sorry for the man, routed out of bed at gunpoint and forced to commandeer one of the Army supply trucks, his position, his whole future, threatened. I looked round at the endless plain, at the bones gleaming white in the hot sun, and a husky voice at my elbow said, "Now perhaps you understand what this Conference is all about—how those who have lived with animals feel." And then, with a sudden warmth that took me by surprise, she put her hand on my arm and added, "Anything I can do to help, when you come to write your script . . ." She left it at that, her gaze wandering over the plain again, and then she turned quickly away. "It's getting late," she said to her father in a tight, controlled voice.

"Yes. Well, we'll just go as far as the lake. Now we're here and have the use of a truck."

We drove on then, down the track that headed south towards the trees, and in ten minutes we had left the plain and were into an area of scrub and acacias. Here we saw our first vultures scavenging at the sodden hide of what appeared to be a recent kill. And then suddenly we were on the edge of the lake and there were flamingoes standing in the shallows, a splash of orange, and water birds swimming around unaffected by the slaughter on the plains.

We stopped then, and on the far side, on the slope above the lake, I saw a line of buildings. Van Delden got out and stood for a moment looking at them through his binoculars. "When I knew this place it had only just been built. Later a lot of people who made their names filming animals in the wild for television used it as their base." He mentioned several of them, names I had vaguely heard of. "It was partly tented, the best position camp for anybody studying the migration. But the man who ran it gave it up in the end—the Tanzanians made it impossible for him. Now . . . See for yourself. It's just a ruin." He handed me up the glasses and I saw that the buildings were roofless shells, the woodwork crumbling. Two had been gutted by fire, and behind the largest, which had the remains of a verandah, a long neck stood up like a thick pole camouflaged in black and yellow, the small head nibbling at the leaves of a tree.

"There's a giraffe," I said.

"Several if you look carefully. And a waterbuck down in the reeds to the right." His voice was very quiet, his eyes blinking, tears running down his cheeks. "It was always a good place for game. The Olduvai river is only just over there." I couldn't believe it, this hard old man weeping for the past, not bothering to hide his emotion as he nodded towards the trees sloping away to the left. "That's where we had our first base camp. All the animals moving between the Ngorongoro Crater and the Serengeti watered in the Olduvai. There were a lot of lion, and cheetah. And on the edge of the plain behind us, in the evening, when the migration was moving through, the trees would be thick with vultures, maribous, eagles—all the scavengers and predators perched there, waiting for the next dawn to pounce on the afterbirth of the night's calving and the remains of baby wildebeest killed in darkness. I used to sit out on that lodge verandah with the sun rising, hartebeest, zebra, and wildebeest grazing within yards of me." He shook his head and sighed, and I thought he was sighing for the animals that were no longer there.

"Things were different then." He glanced at his daughter, blinking his eyes, then reached up for the glasses and climbed quickly back into the cab as though to hide his momentary weakness. And when she suggesting driving as far as the lodge to get a picture of the giraffe, he said, "No. We haven't time." He said it gruffly and I guessed he didn't want her to know how the sight of the place had affected him.

"At least let me get a picture of the lodge. You and Mother had your wedding reception in the dining-hall there, didn't you?"

"Yes."

"I've never seen it. I'd like a picture."

"No." His voice sounded oddly abrupt. "The tank's barely a quarter full." He started the engine then and after a moment's hesitation she climbed in again and we drove fast up the winding track, back on to the plain. The going was harder now, the land drying in the sun, and by ten-thirty we were back on the gravel highway. He stopped there and called back to Karanja: "Do you think the Army will send a patrol out looking for you?"

Karanja hesitated, standing there beside me, a worried frown on his face. "Is possible." He shook his head, leaning down over the side of the truck. "I don't think they have the petrol. They fill up at the Nairobi barracks, you see, and only enough for supplies to the Lodge, so they cannot waste it looking for me."

"Good. Then I'll stop just short of the lugga and you can drive on from there."

After that it was all we could do to hang on, for the ruts were hardening and he was driving fast. We saw two tiny little antelope that Mukunga said were dik-dik, also an emaciated jackal, nothing else, only birds, none of them big—no vultures, no eagles, the skies above us empty and low clouds drifting in. From bright sunlight the day grew overcast, and shortly before noon we slowed by an outcrop of red rock, coming to rest at the top of a rise. Ahead of us the road dipped down to the green of trees. Nothing stirred, the air heavy and very still, a sort of brooding quiet. Van Delden got out. "All right, Karanja. You drive them to the Lodge now. And you, Tait—you get into the front with Mary. And remember, you've been lost in the bush all night." He smiled at me as I dropped into the roadway beside him. "You look tired enough, so I think you'll get away with it."

Karanja climbed slowly into the driving seat, his broad flat face tense. I didn't like it. He looked scared. And as I squeezed in beside Mary Delden he was saying, "What I do if the Army arrests them?"

"See your Minister," van Delden snapped. "And stick to your story." And he added, "Remember, I've got a picture of you down there on the Serengeti and if anything happens to them, if their film is seized, then I'll produce that picture tomorrow. You understand?"

"Yes, Tembo."

"D'you know what time Kirby-Smith is due to address the Conference?"

"No." He shook his head. "It will be in the morning, I think."

"Well, find out the exact time and pass it on to Miss Mary. She knows how to contact me." He looked across at her, his big head framed in the window, his white hair blowing in a sudden gust of wind. "See you tomorrow," he said and stood back, telling Karanja to drive on. The last I saw of him he was loping off into the bush, Mukunga behind him carrying his rifle.

"Will he really come to the Conference tomorrow?" I asked.

"Oh, sure," she replied. "It's Alex Kirby-Smith he's gunning for."

"Why?"

She shook her head. We were across the lugga and grinding up the slope behind. "Something that happened between them. That's all."

"When they were partners?"

But all she said was, "A long time ago." She was sitting very stiff and straight, her teeth clamped down on her lower lip, staring straight ahead. She was like that for perhaps a minute and then she added, as though explanation were necessary, "Their attitude to animals is so entirely different, you see. And now . . . I don't know . . ." Another long pause, then she turned to me, smiling. "Well, you've met the great Cornelius van Delden, so what do you think of him?"

I didn't know how to answer her, conscious of the soft pressure of her body against me and her large eyes glinting with laughter. "I've never met anybody like that before," I murmured hesitantly, searching for some word to encapsulate his strange, wild personality. But all I could say was, "He's larger than lifesize."

She nodded, laughing. "You can say that again. He's always been larger than life." The laughter died and she said slowly, "He's a very wild man, always has been, and he'll take chances. . . ." She hesitated, then shook her head. "I don't know any man . . . I've never met any man— his equal. Once he's made up his mind, nothing will shift him, no argument, no threat, nothing. He sets his mind to something and that's that, whatever the danger to himself or others." She turned to Karanja. "How did you think Tembo was looking?"

He glanced at her, his eyes staring. "Very strong," he said. "Very strong and like a pig's head. He does not think what he is doing to others." He knew what she had been saying and the echo of her words sounded a note of warning. My mouth was suddenly dry, for I knew I had got myself mixed up in something that wouldn't just end with him delivering a speech to the delegates. I sat there, thinking about it, and she was silent now, staring straight ahead again.

"This man Kirby-Smith," I said, trying to distract my thoughts. "You must have known him well. What's he like?"

"I was only a child."

"But you've met him since."

"Once or twice."

"Then what's he like?"

She didn't answer, only shook her head, and at that moment we rounded a bend in the road and a soldier was flagging us down, his rifle at the ready. He wore a cap rather like a kepi with the insignia of a rhinoceros sewn on to the front. "An ex-game scout," she whispered as Karanja greeted him, smiling with obvious relief. "They seem to know each other, which may help." But the man still insisted on calling his corporal, who came out of the little shelter of boughs they had built for themselves, grasping a submachine gun.

The talk went on and on. Finally, the corporal nodded, shouted some instruction to his men, and climbed into the back with the soldier. We drove on then and Karanja said, "He will take us to his captain. Those are his orders."

"Did they send out a patrol to search for you?"

"No. But they know you and Mr. Tait are missing."

"So they will not be surprised that you went out looking for us."

"Perhaps. But I am not Army, and to take an Army vehicle . . ." He gave a quick shrug, his voice uneasy. "And there is my Minister. . . . He will be very angry because I'm not here this morning. And tomorrow, when Tembo . . ." He shook his head, looking worried and the sweat shining on his face. "Miss Mary."

"Yes?"

The Lodge was coming into view, the sprawl of buildings brown against brown clouds, the waterhole a pale circle gleaming dully. A hand banged on the cab roof, the corporal shouting instructions in a nervous, excited voice.

"Ndio," Karanja called back.

"What was that about?" I asked, the nervous tension mounting, my hands gripped tight around the camera.

"He wants him to drive straight to the guard post."

"Can't he drop us off first?" I was thinking of the film in my camera, the two reels in the camera case at my feet. But all she said was, "It would only make them suspicious."

And then Karanja was speaking, very fast, his voice high and uncontrolled: "Please. You see Tembo tonight. You tell him is not possible he come to the Conference. He think he has protection of delegates and newspeople. But I cannot guarantee. I know my Minister. Mr. Kimani is political man and very ambitious."

"He daren't have him arrested there, before all the delegates."

"No. No, he cannot do that. But when your father is gone, then he will instruct the Army to act. He will not have the alternative. Please, Miss Mary, you must believe that. Mr. Kimani is a hard man and such action . . . coming to the Conference, speaking to the delegates." He shook his head. "Is most extremely crazy please. Mr. Kimani then has his hand forced and he will act. He has not any alternative. You understand?"

"I understand," she said. "But do you? He'll still have those pictures and he'll use them." I was surprised at the hardness in her voice. "I think you'd better talk to your Minister."

We were already turning into the Lodge driveway, now overgrown and rutted, the welcome board on its timber arch half rotted away, its lettering unreadable.

"He will be stopped," Karanja said obstinately. "They do not let him reach the Lodge. His pictures will be taken. You tell him please."

A hand banged on the tin of the cab roof and we swung left. I was looking at Mary Delden, her lips tight shut and drops of perspiration clinging to the tiny hairs on her upper lip. Her features were tightset, the nostrils below the bony curve of her nose flared slightly. Pressed close together as we were I could feel her tension. The truck stopped and in a tight voice she said, "You can't arrest him. Not with all these delegates here. You tell Mr. Kimani that." The corporal jumped down and disappeared into an outbuilding. "Do you understand, Karanja?"

He didn't say anything, his hands gripping the wheel so tight his knuckles looked almost white.

"Karanja, do you understand?" She spoke in a fierce whisper as though he were a child who had closed his mind to reason.

He shook his head slowly, sweat shining on his face and a look of hopelessness. "He will be stopped. Not arrested, but taken to the airport under guard. I cannot prevent that."

The corporal came out with an officer, a big man, very black, with three pips on his shoulder and a walk that had a sort of swagger to it. He went straight to the far side of the truck and began talking to Karanja. I couldn't understand what was said, but it was obvious that he was subjecting him to an angry cross-examination, and his manner was truculent. The talk went on and on while we sat in the heat of the cab. Finally, Mary Delden leaned across and spoke to the captain in Swahili, her voice angry, almost petulant. Then abruptly she turned to me. "Open the door and let's get out. I'm tired and I want to wash." She picked up her camera, slipping the strap over her head. "Also I'm bloody hungry." The corporal moved to prevent us and she turned on the officer and said in English, "You've no right to keep me here. If you do I shall go straight to the Minister and demand that he gets the American Consul on the R/T." She reached past me, thrusting the door open. "Now, get out, Colin, and push that corporal out of the way. I'm not going to sit here and roast."

I didn't have to push him. The captain barked an order and the corporal stood back. I got out then, and she followed me. "Come on. A wash and lunch, then some sleep." She didn't speak to Karanja or the officer, she just walked straight off towards the main building and I followed her. "You think he understood you?" I asked as we entered the dark cool cavern of what had once been Reception.

"Of course. He understands English perfectly. Not speaking it is a matter of principle." The delegates were already at lunch. We could hear the roar of their voices, the clatter of plates coming from the dining-room. "Better get all your film into safe hands. Not your cameraman's. Somebody else. And if we're interrogated separately, then we went as far as the lugga, fell asleep for a time and finally made it out to the road, where Karanja picked us up just before midday." A flicker of a smile and then she left me, walking with long easy strides towards her room down near the empty shell of the swimming pool.

III

That night I saw Alex Kirby-Smith for the first time. He was seated a few tables away, talking to a group of Americans, a tall, heavily built man packed with a great deal of energy. His face as he talked was very alive, eyes creased by years of sun glare and a sharp aquiline nose that gave him a predatory look. His hair was long and fair, and it was swept back across his head as though blown flat by a wind. There was no mistaking him in that gathering. Even if I hadn't known it, I think I would have guessed he was a hunter, something in the sharpness of his eyes, the hard, bright gleam as he talked. His hands were in constant motion, emphasising his words, and one of those hands was gloved. It was the left hand and the brown glove was so incongruous in the sultry heat of the dining-room that my eyes were rivetted. It was some moments before the explanation dawned on me. It was an artificial hand.

The men with him at the table were all Americans and he seemed to be trying to convince them of something, leaning forward, his elbows on the table, a cigarette gripped in his right hand, talking energetically. But I couldn't hear what he said because Abe Finkel insisted on giving me his version of what had happened at the Conference. He was a good mimic and his account of the various speeches would have been very entertaining if my mind had not been on other things.

The Kirby-Smith table began to break up. He was still talking as he pushed his chair back and got to his feet. He was very tall, a striking figure in immaculate bush jacket with a red silk scarf at his throat, his heavy, cleanshaven face almost boyish with enthusiasm. And he moved with extraordinary lightness as though constantly poised on the balls of his feet. "It will be a hard trip," I heard him say. "But I think it might be arranged if you really want . . ."

"Don't you think that's great?" Abe Finkel said, tapping me on the arm. "Coming from old Willoughby-Blair. Wildlife is part of the pattern of total life and animals as important to man as man is to animals. Isn't that a laugh?" And he sighed and shook his head at me. "You miss the first day and you don't even listen while I'm giving you the benefit of my brilliant observational faculties. I don't believe you got lost."

"Nor do I," said Ken, grinning at me. "You spend a night out with the only good-looking girl in the place . . ."

"It was raining, my friends." Abe smiled. "Girls don't like having it off in the African bush in the rain, and even if there aren't any lions or rhinos there's still snakes and spiders—" He pretended for a moment he was lying out in the rain with soldier ants crawling over him, wriggling his body, his voice husky and complaining. "That a puff adder you got there?"

"Go to hell," I said, watching Kirby-Smith as he moved from table to table, talking to delegates.

"Not funny, eh?"

"No."

I had a clearer view of him, only two tables away, and there was something about his face—the tight hard mouth, the sharp thin nose, and the eyes alive, almost sparkling. She was right about the charm. He was one of those men with an attractive smile that can be turned on at will and though he was about fifty now he still had the engaging air of a much younger man. I wondered how he had lost the hand. A hunter with only one hand . . .

"You didn't get lost."

"What?" I turned to find Abe Finkel leaning close to me, no glint of humour now in his eyes. "What do you mean?"

"You heard me. It's a piece of nonsense, you and that girl getting lost. You went out on a job and you got something nobody else has got, right?"

"What makes you say that?"

"Do you think we don't check our equipment cases? You slipped three mags into the film carrier while we were at lunch. And what about Karanja? The story is he went out looking for you and got bogged down, that's why he wasn't in Conference this morning to introduce Kit Kimani. But this afternoon he was interrogating you and finally made off with the film from your camera. Why?"

"A precaution, I suppose. I don't know. He said he did it on the orders of his Minister."

"Sure, but why? What did he think you might have got in the can?"

"I don't know."

"You don't know! Hell, you're a poor liar. And putting the exposed mags in our case. Erd found them there right after lunch, while you were still feeding, and I slipped them into my pocket just in case." He stared at me, smiling. "Well, you going to share your dark secret?"

He was much too sharp and I didn't say anything, only shook my head.

"I might hang on to them."

I didn't know whether he meant it or not, his eyes watching me, full of devilment. "I don't think you'll do that," I murmured.

"No? You think a hardened old pro like me has any kindness for new boys, and a limey at that?" He was still smiling, his tone lighthearted, but the dark eyes watching me showed he was serious. "I want to know what you've been up to. Or would you prefer I asked the Delden girl?"

"You'll know tomorrow," I said, and got to my feet. I was feeling tired now and I wanted some sleep.

"Tomorrow—where?"

"At the Conference. When Kirby-Smith speaks." And I added, "You may want to do a deal then, so keep that film safe." His eyes were alight with curiosity, his face shining in the naked glow of the lights, but he didn't ask any more questions, and I knew he wouldn't talk, not with the prospect of a deal. The film was safe with him and I left them and went to my room.

Ken came in as I was stripping off my clothes. "You really got something, Colin?" He was frowning, his expression intent and puzzled. And when I didn't answer, he said, "Karanja took off in that truck shortly after midnight. I got that from one of the guards. I was up at dawn this morning. I was worried about you."

"You needn't have been." I poured some water into the canvas wash basin and began sluicing my face.

"There was a woman journalist wandering about, inquiring about Mary Delden. They share the same room and she was scared something had happened to her." He paused, waiting, while I dried my face on the towel. "Cornelius van Delden," he murmured. "I know something about him now and there's a rumour going around that he's in the country and and the Army looking for him."

"Who told you that?" I threw the towel down and turned to face him. "Have you been asking questions?"

He shrugged. "Not only me, but Abe and several others. We're all of us consumed with curiosity. And you out with that Delden girl. The same name."

"Why the hell start asking questions?" I demanded angrily, "I told you not to worry if I was late back."

"No need to get excited. I'm the only one who knew you were anxious to contact Cornelius van Delden and I kept quiet about that."

"Mary Delden is his daughter." I reached for my pyjamas. "That's all I'm going to tell you at the moment." I was thinking of that camp site down in the lugga and how he had bunks and supplies trucked in, Army guards acting as servants; two entirely different worlds, and tomorrow he would walk into this Lodge—into a trap by the sound of it. "These rumours. What exactly are they saying?" I asked.

"You've seen him, haven't you?" He was standing with his back to the window and at that moment the spots by the waterhole were switched on. His glasses glinted in the light. "All right. If you don't want to talk . . ."

"What are they saying?"

"That he hates Kirby-Smith's guts. That it's Burton and Speke all over again and somehow he'll manage to address the Conference."

"Burton and Speke?"

"It was Abe Finkel used that phrase. I don't know anything about it. All in the African books, he said. I'm not well read like Abe."

I had a vague recollection of some Victorian drama. The source of the Nile—that was it. A duel of words and Speke supposed to have committed suicide. And if the Lodge was buzzing with rumours that van Delden would make an appearance . . . "Who've you been talking to?"

"Just the delegates and the media."

"What about Kirby-Smith? Have you been talking to him?"

"No, but Abe has."

"What did he say?"

"Merely that Cornelius van Delden was a crank and personal non grata with the present Government. He's quite certain they'll see that he doesn't appear at the Conference."

So the trap was set and tomorrow it would be sprung. A man with a beard like that, so recognisable, couldn't possibly slip into the Lodge unseen. The whole area was closely guarded now, patrols out and sentries posted. I could see them moving down by the waterhole. I ripped a page out of my pad, scribbled a note, and gave it to Ken. "Take that to Mary Delden, will you? Tell her what you've just told me."

He hesitated as though about to ask more questions. But then he nodded. "Okay. I'll tell her." It was only after he had disappeared into the night that I realised I was still standing quite naked. I slipped into my pyjamas then and climbed into the bunk to lie awake for a time wondering how van Delden thought he could possibly get into the Conference. I was picturing him and Mukunga fighting it out with the Government guards, the sound of rifle fire echoing through the Conference room, and it was on this fantasy that I fell asleep, too dead tired to care what happened.

I heard an elephant trumpeting, high like a squeal, and shouts, and then I was awake, or thought I was, and there were voices whispering in the room, Abe talking softly, no light and shadows moving in the dark. A door closed and there was silence. I thought I must have dreamed about the elephant, that it was only the others coming to bed, and I rolled over and went to sleep again. The next thing I knew it was dawn and I wanted to relieve myself. At night we had been using the room toilet, flushing it out with a bucket of water in the morning. I climbed sleepily down from my bunk and crossed to the bathroom. The door was shut and when I tried the handle it wouldn't budge. Abe's voice behind me said, "Do it outside. The door's locked."

"Why?"

"He's sleeping in the bath."

"Who?"

"For God's sake! Who do you think? Go back to bed. It's not six yet." And he pulled the blanket over his head.

I went outside and peed over the edge of the verandah, staring out at the silent Lodge. The mournful note of the mourning dove called down by the waterhole and a stork stood like a sentinel on top of the main building. Dawn was just beginning to break and the air full of the murmur of insects and the hoarse croaking of frogs. Nobody was about, everything very still, almost breathless, and van Delden asleep in our bathroom. He must have arrived in the early hours, which explained why there had been no light anywhere when I had waked to the whisper of voices.

I climbed back into my bunk, but couldn't sleep, thinking about the script and what the climax would be, whether I was qualified to write it. I knew nothing about animals, nothing about Africa. I was London born and bred and all the things I had done so far had been in the UK, except for that one tanker film, and then the crew had all been British. I looked across at Abe Finkel, rolled up tight again in his blanket, at the litter of equipment under Lindstrom's bunk. They were in on it now, and though they had admitted they knew little more than I did about wildlife, they were so much older, some much more experienced.

Ken stirred in the bunk below me. "You awake, Colin?"

"Yes."

"Think we could get a picture of him sleeping in the bath? There's a window at the back."

"Is there enough light?"

"The sun's just rising and the window faces east."

Abe sat up. "You want to get yourselves shot? He's got a Colt strapped to his waist and a guy like that sleeps with one eye open." He swung his legs out of his bunk and slipped to the floor. "We'll set it up before we go to breakfast."

"He may not agree," Ken said.

"Oh, he'll agree. Didn't you hear what he said last night? We keep him here under wraps till Kirby-Smith starts talking and we'll get all the pictures we want. A guy like that, taking the risks he has, needs all the publicity he can get." He went outside to relieve himself and then he began to dress. "Our real problem is how to get the stuff out. I'm going to have a word with the pilot of that plane. I know where he bunks." He looked at me as he pulled on his boots. "How much are you prepared to contribute by way of incentive money?"

"I'm on a tight budget," I murmured.

"Aren't we all." He shrugged. "Never mind, leave it to me. We can settle up later." And he went out, carrying his shaving things as though he were going to the wash house.

He was gone about half an hour and by the time he returned we were all of us up and getting dressed. "He's flying the Minister out this afternoon, leaving about four, and he'll take our film with him."

"How much?" I asked.

"He's one of their mercenaries and he doesn't take risks for nothing. I gave him a cheque on a Swiss bank account for a thousand Swiss francs to be countersigned by the American Consul on delivery. That okay by you? Your people have no representation."

I didn't know. I was out of my depth, uneasily aware that I hadn't the facilities for this sort of thing. And then Mary Delden appeared on the verandah, looking fresh and neat. "Can I come in?" Her husky voice sounded nervous, her eyes darting around the room as she entered. "Is everything all right?" she asked me, and I realised she wasn't sure of the others.

It was Abe who answered her. "You might have warned us, Mary. Arriving like that in the middle of the night and your boy friend dead to the world—I might have screamed my head off." He was smiling, his dark face alive with the humour of it. "Had me scared."

"I'm sorry." She was smiling herself now, an expression of relief. "Where is he?"

Abe nodded towards the closed door of the bathroom. She went over to it and knocked. "It's Mary. You all right?"

The bolt clicked back and he opened the door, fully clothed, his bulk filing the gap and his eyes taking in the occupants of the room, a swift appraisal. They fastened on Abe Finkel. "Was it you I talked to last night? Good. And you've arranged for the pictures to be flown out."

"We'll need your co-operation."

"Yes, of course. I heard everything you said. What about the tape-recording?"

"That's taken care of. The cassettes will go out with the pictures."

"Excellent." He turned to Mary. "No change in the arrangements, I hope."

She shook her head. "Do you have to do it this way, in front of everybody?"

"How else?"

"They'll say it's because—you hate him."

He shrugged. "What does that matter, so long as I stop him." And he added, "So he starts speaking at ten-thirty?"

"About then. The Conference opens at ten as yesterday and there's one delegate to speak first, an ex-senator from Boston named Franklin. Karanja thinks Alex will talk for about half an hour, then after that there will be a discussion, with the Minister winding up just before lunch. In the afternoon we'll be taken to have a look at the area designated for the pilot scheme. Mr. Kimani will be promising us shots of rhinoceros, antelope, possibly lion, too."

"He's got it all fixed, has he?"

"Army scouts will be upwind and the game will be driven."

He gave a harsh laugh. "They've been collecting the poor brutes in bomas for several weeks now. It's one of the things I shall be telling the Conference." He looked at Ken and then at Lindstrom. "You're the cameramen, are you? Well, after I've had my say, see that you've got plenty of film in your cameras. You'll get a shot of an elephant then, and it will be something much more startling than anything Mr. Kimani can offer you."

"Was that what we heard last night?" Abe asked. "There was a lot of squealing and shouting from the barracks area. That's why we were awake when you arrived."

The big lion-like head nodded. "That was an elephant. The one you told me about, Mary."

"And you drove it into the Lodge area, in that condition?" The words trembled in the morning air, a note of anger and her face outraged. "How could you?"

"They posted guards so I had to distract them." And seeing the look of distaste on his daughter's face, he added. "It's doomed anyway. You know that very well, so don't be sentimental about it."

But she had turned her head to the window. "Karanja," she said. "I think he's coming here."

Through the window we could see him strutting across from the main building. "You'll come and fetch me, will you?" van Delden said to me. "As soon as he gets on his feet."

I nodded and he disappeared into the bathroom, bolting the door behind him.

Karanja made straight for our verandah. "Good morning, Miss Delden. Mr. Tait, everybody. I hope they do not wake you last night driving those elephants away." He seemed to have recovered some of his cheerful self-confidence.

"Was there more than one?"

"Oh, yes. They come for the garbage, you know." He hesitated, glancing uneasily at the two Americans, and then turning to Mary Delden. "I speak to you privately please. And you, Mr. Tait."

He took us over towards the swimming pool, and when we were out of earshot, he said, "You tell him please he is not to come here. It is no good for him. The officer in charge has guards posted all round the Lodge. After breakfast there will be more soldiers and there is no chance he will be able to slip past them, no chance at all."

"And how do you expect me to tell him?" she asked.

"I think you have some signal arranged. Please tell him. That is all I have to say. Except that my Minister is most anxious he does not make a fool of himself, not here in front of all the delegates."

"I can imagine." She was smiling sourly. "The Army arresting him and the news cameras rolling. That would really put Kimani on the spot."

"Please, Miss Mary. No cameras will be recording. It will happen away from the Lodge. You understand? He will gain nothing."

She nodded. "I understand. But you know him. Once he's set his mind to a thing . . ."

"That is why I ask you, as personal favour please. You must convince him is no good."

"You go and tell him. His camp is down in the lugga." And she told him exactly where. "I couldn't get through the guards, and anyway I have to be at the Conference."

He hesitated, then shook his head, smiling craftily. "I think he has left his camp now, otherwise you don't tell me where it is." And then, assuming the mantle of authority, he said sternly, "You will do as I say please. For his own good. To avoid trouble." And he turned and walked quickly away. He had done what he had been told to do and I had the feeling that his confidence was a thin shell and that underneath he was scared.

"What will they do to him?" I asked as I followed her to the main building.

"He'll be all right," she said. "He's a Kikuyu, and so's Kimani."

"Tribal loyalty?"

She nodded. "They'll both of them blame the Army and Kimani's a clever little man. If that doesn't work—" She gave a shrug. "Well, I guess Africa isn't all that different from Washington or London when it comes to politicians. Their main preoccupation is the same—the pecking order, and survival." She stopped there, glancing back at the waterhole, sniffing the air. "What a wonderful world it would be without politics. I always think of the Garden of Eden as a place devoid of politics. Even here, where we are supposed to be fighting for the survival of wildlife, it's all politics, each delegate with his own bloody axe to grind, his own image to project. Cornelius, he's the same—and Alex. They each have their own viewpoint and they're blind to anybody else's, a mental curtain. . . . Oh, well, you coming to breakfast now? I'm ravenous." She smiled and there was a sudden air of forced gaiety about her. "A full belly is the best sedative."

"I haven't shaved yet."

"Okay. I'll see you at the Conference then."

I watched her walk away, wondering what she was really feeling, brought up in a safari camp run by her father and Kirby-Smith, and now the two of them at each other's throats and about to come face to face. I was thinking of my own background, so orderly, so commonplace—and hers so explosive. Had she known what her father would do when she accepted the assignment? Had she realised it would be a confrontation and herself emotionally torn between the two of them? For that's what she seemed to imply—the two of them ruthlessly projecting themselves.

I went back to the room and got my washing case. Abe Finkel was there, neat and shaved, sitting on the verandah. "Ken and Erd are feeding now. We'll go later. Can't risk a guard finding him here before the balloon goes up, h'm?" His curly black hair gleamed and his eyes were alive like coals, a real professional newsman, knowing he'd got a break and keyed up to a pitch of excitement. "The pilot is in room 71. He'll wait for us there."

Right up until ten o'clock there were never less than two of us in the room or on the verandah. But the only guards we saw were out beyond the waterhole, where they had more sentinels posted and a detachment patrolling back and forth. It never seemed to occur to them that Cornelius van Delden might already be in the Lodge area.

Just before ten o'clock we all of us went over to the diningroom. The tables were stashed now, the chairs set out in rows, the room half full already. We found seats at the outer edge of a row and Ken set the Bolex up on its tripod. I had the Beaulieu with me just in case, but my main concern was the recording and I wondered whether I was near enough to the line of chairs and the lectern facing us. But once Sir Edmund Willoughby-Blair was on his feet and I had a playback of his opening words I knew it was all right. His brief resumé of the views expressed by the delegates the previous day was given in a clear strong voice. Concluding, he said, "I think we all recognise the problems facing the Government of the East African Federation. Our concern is the future of wildlife in this area, but anyone who listened to the Minister's speech yesterday and still does not accept that these problems must have a bearing on the animals who at one time occupied so great a part of the Federation's land area is not being realistic."

The Minister nodded and smiled. He was sitting next to the Chairman in a neat, rather too bright blue suit, the gleam of a gold ring against the dark hand resting on his knee.

"The problems, as I see them and as they have emerged in Conference, are threefold: First, the after-effects of an exhausting and protracted war. Second, the aspirations of a people on the move, natural aspirations of land tenure in an area of very high birthrate where population pressures have been increased by a flood of refugees. Whole tribes have been forced to move or expand their territories. Third, the resettlement of nomadic people from the drought-stricken areas of the north and the consequent switch from a pastoral way of life to the more efficient land use of husbandry. Those, gentlemen, are the three basic factors that confront us, and no amount of dedicated, even emotional argument will make them go away. Now today, the last full day of the Conference, we shall be concentrating on the practicalities, with a visit this afternoon to an area which I am told still has a concentration of big game that can, the Minister thinks, be preserved. In other words, a game reserve, or park, that is politically possible."

He glanced down at the neat blue figure beside him. "But we must not forget that Mr. Kimani still has to sell the idea to his Government colleagues and to the Army." He turned to his audience again, speaking slowly and emphatically to give weight to his words. "I would ask you, therefore, not to make it impossible for him by passing resolutions this evening, at our final meeting, that he cannot possibly support. I say this again, and most urgently, we have to think in terms of practicalities, of what is possible, given the circumstances. And to assist in this I have limited this morning's proceedings to two speakers, both practical men. One of them—Alex Kirby-Smith—has lived in the country all his life, is one of the world's scientific authorities on the management of game, both in the wild and in reserves, and, what is more important, because of his services during the recent war, he is acceptable to the present Government of the Federation."

During this part of his speech, the Chairman had been looking across at Kirby-Smith seated by the verandah, where the glare of the sun was like a spotlight on the large, tanned face, emphasising the sharpness of the nose, the keenness of those sun-creased eyes. There was applause from a little group sitting near him and he smiled his acknowledgment, a glint of gold teeth in the sunlight, the red scarf at his neck a casual splash of colour against the khaki of his bush jacket.

"But first," Sir Edmund went on, "I'm going to call on George L. Franklin of the Boston Foundation, a practical man in a different sphere—the world of finance. We have to face the fact that any wildlife programme requires money, for administration, management, protection. It cannot be self-supporting as in the old days when tourists came in their thousands. Those days are gone, perhaps for good. So, subsidies will be required. And now I call on George Franklin."

Franklin spoke for just over twenty minutes in that flat grating accent I had heard several times before. I think he was probably an accountant. Certainly there was no sentiment in his speech. He gave a breakdown of costs, facts and figures based on the old parks and updated to current rates of pay for wardens, scouts, roads, transport, and all the complex set-up for effective management of an area of about two hundred square miles. And he concluded by stating that the Foundation he represented was prepared to support such a project to the extent of twenty percent of the cost for a minimum period of five years.

I glanced at my watch. The time was just ten twenty-five and Franklin was now answering questions. Cameramen were moving unobtrusively towards Kirby-Smith, positioning themselves for the pictures they wanted as he moved to the lectern. Karanja was unrolling a map on the wall. Ken tapped me on the arm. "D'you want a shot of him as he starts speaking?" he whispered.

I shook my head, watching Abe Finkel as he moved quietly to the door. He was against the light then, in silhouette against the shattered windows, Erd Lindstrom beside him, and both of them had cameras. Mary Delden was already out on the verandah. She, too, had her camera, and from there she could see our room and keep an eye on the speaker. "You stay here," I told Ken. The light was too tricky for me to handle it. "I want a close-up of Kirby-Smith's face as he sees van Delden enter." I left the tape-recorder running, picked up the Beaulieu and headed for the door, the voice of Sir Edmund Willoughby-Blair following me as he thanked the speaker for his frank and detailed assessment and the generosity of his Foundation.

"Not yet," Abe said, gripping my arm. He was watching the Chairman. Erd Lindstrom was halfway to our room. "I've sent him to warn the old man. We'll signal him when the moment is right."

The Chairman was already calling on the next speaker and Kirby-Smith was on his feet, the cameras round him rolling and clicking. It was his moment and he made the most of it, even to the point of answering questions as mikes were thrust at him by men bored with the proceedings and in need of something more exciting, more colourful. "You ever ridden a wild elephant, Mr. Smith?"

"No, only rhinoceros." They didn't care that it was just a joke. They lapped it up. And he was cheerful, almost debonair, the charm switched on. He moved to the lectern, the cameramen followed him. "There's a rumour you're going north. Is that for the Government?"

"It's in my speech."

He was at the lectern now, facing his audience, smiling, his good-looking features alive and vital, brimming over with confidence, and Abe raised his hands. I saw Lindstrom acknowledge the signal and I watched the room, waiting. Kirby-Smith was talking now, about the war and the part wildlife had been forced to play. "An army on the march takes what it can. It feeds off the land, and in Africa that means game. I know there are people here who think this inexcusable, but to expect men to starve so that elephant or rhino, or gazelle, will survive is to ignore your own nature. There's not one of you, not a single one of you here, however dedicated to the preservation of wildlife, who, put to the test, would starve himself to death when he had the means to kill. Even those of you who think it all right to kill for the pot, in other words subsist off the land, abhor the behaviour of men like Stanley and Teleki, moving through with a vast retinue of porters and killing to keep their men supplied with meat. But they did it to save their expeditions from foundering, as I did it during the recent war to feed an army."

He paused, looking over the sea of faces, assessing the impact of his argument. "Some of you, I know, do not condone my part in it. But what would you have? I will tell you how an army marching on its stomach would have done it. . . ." Abe moved, raising his camera, and I turned, distracted from the speech, to see black guards running and Lindstrom walking backwards, his camera aimed at the leonine figure of Cornelius van Delden striding in battered sandals and dirty shorts towards us. Grey hair showed like a mat in the torn neck of his ragged shirt and there was a revolver strapped to his waist.

Heads turned, distracted by the shouts. The name Cornelius van Delden ran round the room. The newsmen, crouched in front of Kirby-Smith, cameras pointing, took their fingers off the trigger, leapt to their feet, and ran. In a moment the room was in an uproar, delegates crowding to the windows and out on to the verandah. I made a circling gesture to Ken and he panned over the scene outside, the camera closing in on van Delden, over the emptying Conference room, and then he moved in on

Kirby-Smith standing speechless and forgotten, on the Minister sitting dazed, and the Chairman banging an ashtray on the desk, and I switched off my tape-recorder and pushed my way out on to the verandah.

The little backwards-moving procession reached the verandah, backed up against the craning delegates, and halted. "How did you get here? . . . We heard you had been deported. . . . Mr. van Delden, will you be speaking?" And a very Germanic voice: "You vill make a stadement please. Ve vant to know vether is true there is nodding of vild animal from 'ere to ze coast." And somebody else, a Scandinavian by his looks—"Ja, we like a statement now."

The guards had halted, uncertain, black faces and khaki uniforms a crowded background to the bearded head of van Delden, and there was nothing they could do. They were faced by a battery of cameras and a solid phalanx of delegates.

"Gentlemen!" Sir Edmund's voice was no longer soft and persuasive. It boomed out like a sergeant-major's. "Gentlemen, your attention please. Will you now go back to your seats. We are listening to a very important speech. Now, please—immediately."

Slowly the scene dissolved as delegates began to resume their seats, but many of them hung around after they had made way for the Chairman, doubtless to see how he would greet this man come out of the bush like some prophet of old. They were not disappointed. Sir Edmund had a great sense of occasion. "Cornelius van Delden." His face beamed, his hand outstretched. "I remember you, back in '73 when half the scientists in the world, myself included, gathered at Lake Rudolf for that eclipse of the sun. Come along in. You were invited, of course, but I gather you were held up." And he turned, his arm round van Delden's shoulders, his bland, frog-like face beaming at the cameras as he said, "You know, we met before that, when I was serving in the KARs—the Mau-Mau troubles."

It wasn't the most tactful thing to say, bearing in mind that the Minister was a Kikuyu, but perhaps he meant it that way, for he must have known how van Delden had been treated at the airport, the search for him that had been mounted. But I don't think Kimani took it in. He had remained seated, his face blank, lower lip sagging and the whites of his eyes showing as though he had seen a ghost.

"The Minister I believe you know. And Alex, of course." And still standing with his arm on van Delden's shoulder, as though afraid if he dropped it he would be out of camera, he faced the room, his voice booming: "Gentlemen! I am sure you will all wish me to welcome the arrival at this Conference of a man who needs no introduction to you, at least as regards his reputation—Cornelius van Delden. He has unfortunately been delayed, circumstances beyond his control, but now that he is here, I know you will wish me to suggest that he gives us the benefit of his long experience—after Alex has finished speaking that is."

There was applause as he waved van Delden to a seat and then resumed his own. The Minister was conferring urgently with Karanja, but the room gradually settled and Kirby-Smith took up the threads of his speech, not as smoothly as before and not with quite the same control of his audience. Cornelius van Delden was too striking a figure, and the delegates were still craning to look at him. But Kirby-Smith was a good speaker and as soon as he came to his projected trip into the north he had their attention.

"I gather there has been a good deal of talk among Conference members about Ileret as a possible alternative to the pilot scheme offered by the Government and I believe most of you know already that I am leaving for the north very shortly to review the game situation on the shores of Lake Rudolf. Federation military aircraft overflying the region have reported considerable concentrations of game—" He turned to the map on the wall behind him. "Particularly in the Horr Valley area." He indicated the gap between the Nyiru and Ol Doinya Mara ranges below the southern end of the lake. "Also, on the slopes of Kulal. In fact, there appear to be above-average concentrations of game all the way up the east side of Rudolf." He came back to the lectern then, not to look at his notes, but because it was the most dominant position, standing there between the Chairman and the Minister.

"Ileret is close to the Ethiopian border. It is now part of the Military Zone and as you will have noticed from your maps all the area you will probably remember better as the Northern Frontier District is designated forbidden territory. I have to tell you that this is not only because the Army regards it as vital to the defence of the Federation's northern flank, but there has, as you well know, been a prolonged drought in that area. It is a pastoral region occupied by nomadic tribes, mainly the Rendile and Samburu. Their herds have been almost wiped out, even their goats and camels have suffered terrible losses. These tribes face starvation and though rain is now expected in the area, this can have no immediate impact. A few days' rain may save the last of their cattle from extinction; it cannot create new herds on which the people can live. The Government —and I am sure you will agree with this on humanitarian grounds—has accepted that this is an area calling for urgent relief. As Sir Edmund has told you, the preservation of wildlife is not something that can be considered in isolation. The people of the country have parallel claims. This, gentlemen, is a disaster area and the concentrations of game reported to be moving into it could destroy the last vestiges of vegetation, thus finally annihilating the Rendile and the Samburu."

The Minister nodded energetically, but a voice from the back called out, "It's their cattle and goats, not the game, that's destroying their environment."

"In the circumstances," Kirby-Smith went on smoothly, "you will appreciate that Ileret as a game reserve is not politically possible at the moment. But—and here I have some hopes for the future—the Government has asked me to undertake an expedition into the area. The objects

of this will be twofold: to examine the situation on the ground and to
take immediate action to relieve the threat of starvation." He held up
his hand as several voices were raised in protest. "Before you express
your quite understandable reaction, please remember this: here in the
comparative comfort of this Lodge you are being fed on tinned rations
that the Federation Government, with limited resources, has had to
import. The general population, however, has to live off the land. In
the north, there is almost nothing left for them to live off, except game
moving into their area."

"What game?" It was the same voice from the back.

"I'm talking about elephants mainly. There's other game, of course—"

"Have you any idea how many elephants are left?" And another delegate said, "Can't be many. They've been under pressure for years, the
forest burned up for charcoal, trees giving place to shambas and new
villages, the herds of cattle multiplying even faster than the population,
war, unrestricted poaching, finally drought. And now you want to—"

"Order. Order please, gentlemen." Sir Edmund Willoughby-Blair
banged with the glass ashtray he was using as a gavel and nodded to
Kirby-Smith.

"As I was saying," he continued, "I fully understand your reaction,
but when people are dying, as they are in the north, they will seek any
remedy. If it is left to them to take advantage of this extraordinary northward migration there will be wholesale slaughter and much of it will be
wasted, the flesh left to rot. I have equipment and men trained for the
task at hand. Nothing will be wasted. It will be a scientific cropping of
a natural resource and only a proportion of the animals will be killed,
sufficient to meet the needs of the moment and tide the people over until
their herds begin to increase again. I repeat, it will be scientifically done,
the animals cleanly shot, the meat fully used. The result, I hope, will be
a resumption of normal life for these tribes and viable units of wildlife
preserved—by which I mean that the numbers of each species will be
reduced to a level the country can reasonably support. Much of it is near-
desert and for the animals, as well as for the people, it is essential that
a balance be maintained between the available or potential vegetation
and the population it has to support. The result of this operation"—
here he turned to the Minister again—"when completed and a proper
balance struck, will I believe be the re-establishment of Ileret as a game
reserve. If this proves possible in the circumstances then prevailing, I
personally shall feel I have contributed both to this new country of the
Federation and also to the cause which is most dear to the hearts of all
of us here, the preservation of wildlife in East Africa."

He sat down then and in the silence that followed the Minister rose
quickly to confirm that the Government would consider sympathetically
the case of Ileret as soon as the present disaster situation had been dealt
with.

"I would like to put a question to Mr. Kimani." It was Cornelius van

Delden, his voice surprisingly gentle, quite different from his appearance, which contrasted so startlingly with the immaculate khaki of the previous speaker.

The Chairman nodded. "I was about to call on you to give your views on an area you were associated with for so long."

Van Delden was standing now, his head thrust slightly forward. "It is some years since I last visited Lake Rudolf. I cannot, therefore, comment on the situation as reported by Major Kirby-Smith. I can only say I'm relieved to know there is still some game left in East Africa. Here, as you have seen for yourselves—"

"There are many places like Lake Rudolf," the Minister snapped. "Even here, near to the largest battle we fought . . . delegates will have the opportunity of seeing for themselves this afternoon."

Van Delden nodded, turning and facing the body of the room, a big bear of a man in silhouette against the glare from outside. "Yes," he said. "I've no doubt you'll be shown some animals, but they will not be from anywhere near here. If any of you newsmen care to forego your lunch and can arrange to be taken to the area ahead of time, you'll be able to take pictures of the animals before they are released from their bomas."

Kimani leapt to his feet. "That is not true."

Van Delden shrugged. "Then take them. Straight from here. Before you can give Karanja or anyone else instructions to let the beasts go." He smiled, fixing Kimani with his hard pale eyes, staring him down, and it was obvious the Minister was at a loss. Kirby-Smith came to his rescue. "Next, I suppose, you'll accuse me of trapping them for the Government." The expression of amused surprise on his face produced a ripple of laughter. "It's well known, I'm afraid, among the older hands here that van Delden and I never hit it off. He's accused me of all manner of things since we broke up our partnership some fifteen years ago."

"Are you saying you didn't do the capturing? You gave no instructions?"

"Of course I didn't."

"But you don't deny the animals have been trapped?"

"This is ridiculous. You've only just arrived in the country—"

"It's what my scouts say. There's hardly anything left in this area larger than a warthog. The animals on show this afternoon will have been trucked in. And there won't be any elephants, not one, because full-grown elephants are too big to truck." He turned to the Minister again. "Your intention is obvious—clear the land of anything that competes with agriculture and cattle. So perhaps you would tell us now exactly what instructions you, or your Government, have given Kirby-Smith on this expedition to Lake Rudolf. Is it extermination?"

"No." Kimani banged his hand on the table, his eyes almost bursting from his head. "Of course it is not extermination. I have instructed Mr. Kirby-Smith personally and my instructions are exactly what he has told the Conference."

"Then another question. Did you personally instruct on the cropping to be done in the Serengeti during what is now I believe called the War of Federation?"

"No. The Government then was military."

"It was the Army that instructed me," Kirby-Smith said quietly. "Why?"

But van Delden ignored him, still facing Kimani. "But now that you are Minister of Lands and Resources, you can't be totally ignorant of what happened." He turned to the room, facing the delegates. "Major Kirby-Smith had the job of feeding the Army. Just as he now has the job of feeding the nomads in the Northern Region. Scientifically. It will all be done scientifically, he says. Do you know what the word scientifically means to him? It means extermination."

"Nonsense." Kirby-Smith's face was flushed, the smile and the charm gone. "You've accused me of all sorts of things. I've already said that. All of them without foundation. But to accuse me of exterminating wild-life, this is the most—"

"Then ask Kimani why he arrives so late that the opening of the Conference is delayed a day and the visit to the Serengeti cancelled. If delegates had gone to the Serengeti . . ."

"I take you tomorrow," Kimani said quickly, still on his feet. "Any delegate or newsman who wishes—"

"To Lake Lgarya?"

The man stood there, his mouth still open. Then he looked at Kirby-Smith and promptly sat down.

"No," van Delden said. "Nobody will be taken there, for if any of you saw it there would be such an outcry—"

"You know nothing about it." Kirby-Smith was no longer looking at the delegates. He had eyes only for van Delden, the two of them facing each other across the room. "Of course, animals were killed—"

"All the wildebeest, all the zebra, all the gazelles, the whole lot wiped out in a senseless orgy of killing."

"You exaggerate, Cornelius. You were in the Seychelles. You've no idea of what the war was like here. All the area south of here was a battlefield. The troops had to be fed—"

"A million animals slaughtered." Van Delden's harsh voice rattled round the room. "Wholesale, indiscriminate slaughter. Killing for killing's sake."

Kimani leapt to his feet again, ignoring the room to face van Delden as he shouted, "It is a lie. It was economic killing. Sufficient for the Army, no more." And he added, his voice high and very loud, "I know why you make these accusations. You are disappointed that the authorities do not let you stay, and since you refused to accept the air passage for return to your home, you have been hiding somewhere so you know nothing about it."

"I have seen it." Cornelius van Delden stared round at the delegates.

"I have seen what you will never be allowed to see—the graveyard of a million splendid beasts, trucks encircling droves of terrified animals, guns mowing them down as they milled in helpless masses, packed so close their bones lie heaped on top of one another."

"You lie," Kimani screamed. "I will have you arrested as the agent of the South African whites determined to destroy my country."

"I lie, do I?" Van Delden pulled a bundle of prints from his pocket and moving quickly along the rows of chairs distributed them to the delegates. "Pass them round, please. A man can lie, but not the camera. These were taken yesterday morning, using a Polaroid. They're not as clear as the human eye. They do not convey the vastness, the totality of his destruction of what used to be known as the Serengeti migration. You look at them. Just look at these pictures. That's what happens when there are no game laws and men are allowed to let their lust for killing run away with them. Extermination," he thundered. "And you sit there and let this man fool you into thinking it will be just a token culling. He has a contract and a freezer plant and you are condemning the last remaining herds of elephants to total extinction."

There was a stunned silence as delegates passed the pictures from hand to hand. One of them got up and asked Kimani if they could be taken to Lake Lgarya tomorrow "to see for ourselves," and the Minister shouted, "No. It is a damn lie. A trick."

There was a ground swell of talking, the cameras panning from delegate to delegate, and I saw Karanja watching Kimani and smiling quietly as though enjoying his Minister's discomfiture. Kirby-Smith stood up again, said something about conditions being different now. "In the Serengeti it was war." But nobody was listening, the delegates all talking among themselves. Sir Edmund banged the ashtray. "Order please, gentlemen. I suggest we adjourn now. Conference will open again after a quarter of an hour, in, I trust, a calmer atmosphere."

Chairs scraped. The newsmen closed round van Delden, grabbing at the pictures, thrusting them into his hand and taking close-ups of them as he held them. Pandemonium reigned and Mary Delden at my elbow said in a trembling voice, "He shouldn't have done it. Twisting it like that so they blame Alex . . ." She stopped there as Kimani thrust his way out on to the verandah, waving wildly at the guards leaning on their rifles. "Oh God! They've got him cornered now."

"Where's Karanja?" I thought Karanja might be able to help.

The corners of her mouth turned down. "He's no help. He's scared stiff, poor devil."

"No," I said. "He's enjoying it."

But she didn't hear me, drawing herself up, as though bracing herself. "I'll go and have a word with Alex. There's nobody else can stop them." And she walked quickly across the room, pushing her way through the crowd until she was standing at Kirby-Smith's elbow. He was talking to Sir Edmund and I saw him turn and bend his head to listen to her above the din of voices. It made me realise how tall he was, for she was my height, yet her eyes were only level with his chin.

Ken grabbed hold of my arm. "Can you get me some more film? I'm nearly out, and if you want good coverage when they grab him . . ." But it was too late already. Kimani had the captain with him now. He was shouting orders and guards were running to him from their positions around the Lodge. A shot cracked out, a flat whiplash of sound that silenced everybody for an instant. I thought for a moment it was some trigger-happy soldier, but there were shouts now from beyond the circle of buildings. "Ndovu, ndovu." Another shot, followed by a squeal, and a grey shape swayed into view from behind the last of the rooms. It crashed against the VIP verandah, scattering tiles and moving forward again, dragging one leg, its trunk raised. It stopped at the sight of us all gathered outside the dining-hall, the trunk waving as it searched for our scent, its ears spread like sails.

Suddenly I saw its eyes, small and sunken in great hollows behind the uplifted tusks. They were big tusks and the body behind the grey skull was all bone. I had just time to realise that the wretched beast was almost starved to the point of death when it trumpeted, the trumpet note ending in a squeal of fear, and then it was coming towards us again, its head and trunk swinging from side to side as though it did not know which way to turn.

That somebody wasn't trampled was due to Kirby-Smith's presence of mind. While he stood rooted to the spot, too surprised to move, he ran forward, grabbed a rifle from one of the guards, then, moving out ahead of us into the path of the elephant, he raised the gun to his shoulder, balancing it loosely on his gloved hand, waited a moment and then fired. The grey mass of bone came on without a check, then suddenly sagged at the knees, pitching forward, head lowered, tusks digging into the ground, scoring great furrows in the turf as it came to a stop and slowly keeled over on its side.

There was a great yell from the soldiers and in an instant they had fallen on it, knives appearing like magic in their hands, others using their bayonets as they hacked in a frenzy at the carcase, grabbing the meat they had been so starved of for so long. The tall captain was in there too and it was Kirby-Smith who finally forced them to some semblance of order, shouting for men who had once been game scouts and arranging for the orderly dismembering of the carcase. Then he called to the delegates, gathering them about him and pointing to the left hind leg, which had a length of thick wire embedded in the flesh. The whole foot was rotten, all swollen up and thick with flies, the smell of putrefaction hanging on the air. "That's what happens in Africa when the disposal of big game is left to men without rifles, men who are hungry for meat and have no feeling for the animals they prey upon."

I looked round for van Delden, wondering what his reply to this would be. But he was nowhere to be seen. "In the old days," Kirby-Smith went on, "this would be the work of poachers. But now there is no such thing as poaching. Anybody can kill. . . ." He hesitated, then went on quickly, "This is a wily old bull, who knows about humans and is not afraid to visit the waterhole here. Last night he was going over the garbage bins. He's probably the same beast the tourists used to photograph. But he put his foot into a wire noose attached to a log, an old poacher's trick, and a slow, painful death. Much better to deal with the problem cleanly with a rifle."

I saw Mary Delden standing irresolute, her eyes searching the crowd, and I went over to her. "Where is he?"

She shook her head, frowning, her mouth set in a thin line and tears in her eyes.

"What's the matter?" I asked.

She stared at me. "Don't you understand?"

"What?"

"Lord!" she breathed. "I told him about it. I told him there was an elephant around the waterhole, dragging a great log. Don't you remember? The dung beetle, the droppings. The rain had obliterated the marks, but in the night, that squeal we heard, the dragging sound. He used it to get into the Lodge and now he's used it to get out, the boys driving it here, a sacrificial offering and the diversion he needed. God Almighty! the callousness of it!"

I understood then. Not just how he had planned to get away, but how everybody, however much they were committed to the preservation of wildlife, still made use of animals for their own ends—van Delden to make his escape, Kirby-Smith to support his business, Kimani to increase his political standing, and the delegates, committed and dedicated men who had come from the ends of the earth, all here because animals were part of the position they held in life.

"While they're all bathing their heads in gore," she said hoarsely, "and disputing the rights of man and beast to live perpetually in a state of war, let's raid the kitchens and grab some beer. I want to get drunk. I want to get so drunk I don't have to think any more." She grabbed hold of my arm and turned in a stumbling run, crying silently in a blind rage against humanity.

PART TWO

THE SOUTH HORR GAP

I

It was Sunday before we finally got back to Nairobi, and like the rest, I was utterly exhausted, for the Conference had been extended a day, with disastrous results. Realising that the visit to the site of the proposed game reserve would be an anti-climax after the events of the morning, Kimani had insisted on personally conducting the delegates over the nearest battle-field, which was the one we had driven through on our way to the Serengeti. There he had lectured us in the pouring rain on the problems of an army fighting without lines of communication to any port and entirely dependent on the country for its food.

It had rained all that night and it was still raining on the Friday morning when we were huddled into wet hides for our promised view of wildlife in the reserve area. The animals had looked wet and bewildered, but by then the discomfort of our existence was such that nobody seemed much concerned about how we were able to see such a representative selection. Predictably, the Conference voted later that day in favour of the pilot scheme.

We had left that same evening, everybody glad to get away from the leaking misery of the Lodge. But by then the roads were almost impassable and it had taken us almost two days to reach Nairobi, trucks bogged axle-deep, floods in the Rift Valley and our food exhausted. The rain had not let up until our vehicles were struggling into the outskirts of Nairobi and by then I was so thankful to tumble into a dry bed that left to myself I should have gone home with the rest. Even here there was muddle and uncertainty. Flight schedules had been posted at Reception, all of them subject to confirmation, and on the Monday the place seethed with rumours of cancellations and delays.

We had been booked into the Norfolk Hotel, which was not the most convenient for finding out what was going on. It was away from the centre of town, nicely secluded in its own grounds, which was probably why it was the only hotel still open to visitors, all the others having been taken over by the Government either as offices or Army barracks. But the war had left its mark, a bomb crater gaping full of water in the middle of the central lawn, the glass of the surrounding windows all shattered and the phones in every room ripped out. With no taxis available, the only means of communication were the phones in Reception, and for these the newsmen had queued half the night only to find themselves cut off as soon as they tried to transmit copy that was considered in any way detrimental to the régime. All mention of Cornelius van Delden and the pictures he had taken in the Serengeti were banned.

The mood on that Monday morning was angry, particularly among the delegates. They were no longer guests of the Federation, meals were at black-market rates and the price of accommodation exorbitant. And with the first flight cancellation a rumour circulated that we would be billed for the extra night we had spent at the Lodge. For the media this was acceptable as being part of the pattern of a disorganised country in the aftermath of war. Men like Abe Finkel were accustomed to it, but for the delegates, conscious that their expenses had to be found from funds raised by voluntary subscriptions, it came as a shock. And there was no certainty how long they would have to wait. Only the Americans were sure of getting away that night. They had chartered a plane. For the rest of us it was a day of uncertainty, of waiting.

I spent most of it working on my script. I wanted to get it all down in outline while it was still vivid in my mind. Ken and I had been allocated one of the chalet rooms. Originally it had had big sliding glass windows opening on to the lawn, but now the glass was all gone and when darkness came the night pressed in on us, insects battering against the naked light bulb and an orchestra of sound, cicadas in the grass and frogs in the bomb crater. The first draft of the outline finished, I joined Ken in the entrance foyer, which was crowded with delegates and their baggage.

"Is Abe back yet?" I asked. He had set out to walk into the city centre immediately after breakfast.

He shook his head. "Erd's getting worried he'll miss his plane." And he added, "There's a rumour that we may get away tonight. A flight's due in from Tokyo around two A.M. and there may be seats."

My eyes searched the crowd. Now that I'd licked my script into some sort of shape there were questions I wanted answered.

"If you're looking for Mary Delden, I haven't seen her either."

"Was she here for lunch?"

"I didn't see her. But she may have had sandwiches in her room, same as you did."

The woman who had shared her room at the Lodge was talking to Franklin and I pushed my way through the crowd. But she hadn't seen Mary either. "We were booked in together, room 109, but I never saw her after we'd had dinner together on the terrace. I don't know what the hell she's up to, but she didn't sleep in the hotel last night."

"Have you asked at the desk?"

"They say she checked out about nine-thirty this morning, paid her bill and took her baggage. And it was an Army truck came for her." She stared at me, her eyes bright with curiosity. "I sure would like to know what she's up to."

I went in search of Erd Lindstrom then, but his only concern was for Abe. "I don't trust that pilot. He's one of their boys, a mercenary, and now he's got his money. . . ."

"You think they may have arrested him?"

"I don't know. Abe's pretty smart, but anything's possible in this crazy country."

There was a movement in the crowd, a surge towards the baggage piled by the door. Over their heads I saw a coach drawing up in the roadway outside. It was painted camouflage green and brown, the windows empty of glass. "Your transport's here."

He nodded uncertainly. "Looks like it."

The Americans were trooping out now and Karanja was there. "Please you take your place in Government bus for airport all people on flight to New York. You show receipted bills for hotel before boarding, please."

"What are you going to do?" I asked.

"Last Abe said to me was not to worry and get on the flight. So—" He shrugged and moved into the tail of the crowd, collecting his grip and his camera equipment as he reached the door. "He's done this on me before. Something's cropped up, I guess. His gear's still in the room, and I've left him the small camera with all the unexposed film. Tell him, will you. And I hope he doesn't get held up too long. The same goes for you. This is no place to have authority breathing down your neck." He was frowning as he turned and followed the others out to the coach. And after that they just sat waiting with the doors closed, Karanja leaning against the side of the bus with a sheet of paper in his hand and two soldiers standing guard.

There was tension in the warm night air and it crossed my mind that if Abe had been arrested, Mary Delden might be in trouble, too. After what had happened they might arrest all of us. I was wishing I could take Abe's place on the flight—New York, anywhere, so long as there was an end to this uncertainty of waiting. "Sont-ils certains de trouver un avion àl'aeroport?" It was the *Paris-Match* correspondent voicing all our thoughts and Karanja was talking to Erd now, questioning him. 'S'ils ne veulent pas que nous écrivons ce que č'est passé. . . .' Marcel Ricaud left it at that, his words hanging in the air and an icy chill running through the group left standing on the terrace, every one of us conscious of our vulnerability. We had been given a glimpse of the ugly side of war. We had been told things that the Government did not want known, witnesses to their failure to prevent van Delden speaking his mind, and so long as we were here the world outside could be kept in ignorance.

"What's the hold-up, Mr. Karanja?" It was Sir Edmund, his voice bland and reassuring.

Karanja didn't answer. He was still talking to Erd Lindstrom through one of the glassless windows.

"Mr. Karanja." The tone of command had its effect. Karanja turned. "I asked what the hold-up was."

"An American is not present." And Karanja called out, "Anybody know where is Mr. Finkel representing CBS, please?" His eyes rolled white in the lights and then fastened on me. He came over. "You are with Mr. Finkel at the Lodge. Where is he now?" His head was thrust forward, his manner slightly truculent, and I could smell the beer on his breath.

"I've no idea," I said. "And there's Miss Delden. She's missing, too."

"Miss Mary I know about. Is Finkel I am looking for."

"Where is she?" I demanded. "What have your people done with her? Is she under arrest?"

"No, is not under arreest." He looked surprised, almost offended.

"Then what's happened? Where is she?"

"She don't tell you?" He hesitated, then said, "Is gone with Major Kirby-Smith."

I stared at him. "With Kirby-Smith? Are you sure?"

He nodded. "Miss Mary okay. Now you tell me—"

"But why?" I couldn't believe it. "Why should she go with Kirby-Smith of all people?"

"Miss Mary good journalist, that's why. Now you tell me where is this man Finkel. All Americans present, only Mr. Finkel missing. You tell me where he is, please."

"I don't know."

"Then find him. He is not in his room and the bus cannot leave till he is found."

"But he's been gone since before lunch."

"I think," Sir Edumund cut in, "you had best let the coach go while you telephone the authorities. The Ministry will probably know where he is."

"Is too late for the Ministry now."

"Then phone the security police. Tell them to pick him up. He's probably in one of the bars. You might even try the old Muthaiga Club. But get those Americans away to their plane, now, before I ring Mr. Kamani myself."

I don't know whether it was Kamani's name or simply the long habit of obedience, but Karanja went back to the coach without argument and gave orders to the driver to proceed to the airport. The rest of us watched in silence as the coach drove off. I think, like me, they were all feeling a sense of abandonment as it disappeared down the heavily treed road, for the Americans had been by far the largest group at the Conference. There was a general movement towards Karanja, who was suddenly engulfed, a sea of anxious faces deluging him with questions about flights and departure times, and all he could say to pacify them was, "I will telephone."

It was Sir Edmund who rescued him, taking him by the arm and leading him through the flap of the reception desk into the manager's office behind. When they emerged again Karanja was smiling. "Everything arranged now," he announced. "You all leave by Government bus for the airport at twenty-three hundred." And Sir Edmund added, "I'm told there are two flights coming through during the night, one of them, a jumbo, is half empty, so there will be seats for all of you." The jumbo was bound for London via Naples, the other, a 707, for Frankfurt.

"Let's go and have a drink," Ken said. Everybody was moving towards the bar at the end of the terrace, a sense of relief showing in their faces, in the suddenly increased volume of conversation.

"You go ahead," I told him.

"Still worrying about her?"

I shook my head, feeling confused and not certain why it mattered to me that she had gone off with Kirby-Smith. A good journalist, Karanja had said. But it had to be something more than that. "I'll join you in a minute." And I went back through the foyer, climbing the stairs to room 109. But it was just as the woman had said, one bed still unmade, the other not slept in, nothing of hers left there, the wardrobe, the drawers, everything bare, including the bathroom. I stood there for a moment thinking about where she would be now, remembering the last time I had seen her, at the Lodge, lushed up on beer, her face puffed and shining with sweat, her dark eyes reflecting the violence of her feelings. She had looked older then, and I remembered how she had said, "He's always been like that—ruthless, egotistical, always disappearing into the bush. I never had a proper father." The tears had been streaming down her face. "How can I love a man like that? I hate him." And she had turned suddenly and left me, staggering blindly out into the rain, the beer not strong enough to drown the tide of her emotions.

And now she was with Kirby-Smith, who was everything her father was not, a commercial hunter. Where would she be now, at his house in Karen? Abe had said he had one of the old settlers' houses out on Miotoni Road. Or would she be camped somewhere on the road to the north?

I closed the door and went back down the stairs, wondering why I had bothered to check her room. It didn't matter to me what she was doing. Tomorrow I would be back in London, the whole episode nothing but material for a script. And yet . . .

I was still thinking about her, about the extraordinary love-hate relationship she had with her father, when I reached my room. But I didn't stay there. I went out on to the lawn, where the night was like velvet, all diamond-studded, and the older building, beyond the crater, a white blur in the starlight. I could see the balcony of Abe's room, but there was no light there, the whole building dark. So he hadn't returned and again I had that sense of uneasiness, the feeling that Africa hadn't finished with me yet.

A light beamed out from one of the chalet rooms, a man standing there, dark in silhouette. It was a moment before I registered that the light was in my own room. The figure moved, stepping through the glassless windows out on to the lawn. "That you, Colin?" It was Abe's voice. And he added, coming towards me, "Ken said you were somewhere around." His tone was quiet and relaxed, no trace of tension in it.

"Where the hell have you been?" He didn't seem to realize the trouble his absence had caused. "Karanja was going to hold the coach for you, but then Sir Edmund—"

"It doesn't matter."

"You should be on your way out to the airport with the others. Where have you been?"

"Checking on your film, for one thing." He took hold of my arm. "Come on, we'll go back to your room. We can talk there. And I've got myself a bottle of the real stuff.. Maybe that'll quiet your nerves." I started to protest that there was nothing wrong with my nerves, but his grip on my arm tightened. "Wait till I tell you what I've arranged."

"The thing you've got to arrange is transport out to the airport," I told him, my mind still on the problem of getting safely clear of Africa. "That charter plane is waiting there and if you don't get moving—"

"I'm not leaving with the others."

"What do you mean?"

"I'm staying on here. And so are you—if you want to. Now come on back to your room and I'll fill you up with something better than local firewater."

He wouldn't answer any of my questions until I was seated on my bed with a tooth glass half full of neat whisky. "Where did you get this?" I asked him. "It's bourbon, isn't it?"

"Right. A present from the American Consul." He lit a cigarette and flopped into the only chair, leaning back, his eyes half closed. "It's been a long day," he murmured, sipping at his drink. "That was the first thing I did, checked at the Consulate to see that the pilot had delivered your film safely. He had and the Consul countersigned my check." He stared out into the night, rubbing his hand over his eyes. He looked tired. "They picked me up as I came out of the building."

"Who did? The police?"

"Police, Army—I don't know. They weren't in uniform, just dark trousers and white open-necked shirts. They didn't ask me what I'd been doing at the Consulate, they just hustled me into an old Peugeot, gave me a thorough going over in the back of the car, and when they didn't find what they were after they drove me into town. I thought I'd land up in some damn prison or maybe an Army barracks. They wouldn't talk. They wouldn't answer any of my questions. And they weren't interested in my press pass or the fact that I was an American TV man. And when I insisted on their taking me to the Ministry, the guy sitting beside me in the back just gave me a broad smile and said, "You'll be well cared for, Mr. Finkel.' I figured that was a threat and I was in real trouble, but instead of landing up in jail, I found myself on Ngong Road on the first floor of a fancy black-market restaurant that turned out to be the old Nairobi Club. The windows were open on to a balcony and Kimani was sitting there in the sunshine with a drink in his hand, the pilot opposite him and another African, a man named Gethenji or something like that, a director of the new Federation Bank." He knocked back the rest of his drink and reached for the bottle. "Are you ready for another?"

I shook my head. "What did they want?"

"The film, of course. Kimani's no fool and he'd figured out what you'd got and how you'd got it. And by then, of course, I knew it was political dynamite. The Federation is pressing hard for full diplomatic recognition from the States. They want an American Embassy here, not just a Consulate. That's why they agreed to the Wildlife Conference. So in the end I did a deal with him." He smiled at me. "It was the least I could do after such an excellent lunch and those gorillas waiting for me downstairs."

I was thinking of that night drive through the rain, the incredible blazing dawn in the boneyard of the Serengeti. "What sort of a deal?" I asked bleakly.

"You want to get to Lake Rudolf, don't you?"

"If I could have persuaded van Delden to take me, yes. Where is he? Did they tell you?"

"They don't know. At least, that's what Kimani said, and I think he'd have told me if they'd picked him up. He said he thought he was probably working his way down to the coast and would get out that way, back to the Seychelles. Now, do you still want to go to Rudolf, or don't you?"

I shook my head, feeling Africa closing round me, scared of what he might have arranged. "Didn't they offer you money?"

"Oh, yes. That's why the bank director was there. I have the impression Kimani's position isn't all that secure. What he had in mind was a straight cash deal through the bank's representative in Zurich."

"Then why didn't you take it?"

"It wasn't my film, and knowing you wanted to get up north . . ."

"There are two planes coming through tonight," I said. "All I want is to be on one of them, out of here."

He laughed and I knew by the sound of it he had had too much. "So now van Delden's gone and the girl, too, you've lost your nerve." He thrust the bottle into my hand.

It was half empty. "You know about Mary Delden then. Did Kimani tell you?"

He nodded. "Clever girl, tagging along with Kirby-Smith."

"How do you mean?" The bottle rattled against the glass as I poured.

"She knows where there's a good story—drought, starvation, a culling operation. And Kimani wants it told. Savior of the starving multitude. That's political stuff in the Third World. So I guess does Kirby-Smith, provided it justifies him."

I slammed the bottle down. "So that's it. You're afraid you're missing out on a story. You trade my film of van Delden in the Serengeti for the chance of meeting up with Kirby-Smith and getting something for your own network."

He shook his head. "I had no choice. Just think for a moment how that film of yours could be intercut with the shots of van Delden's intervention at the Conference. Actual pictures of him standing on the Serengeti plain viewing the carnage. It could be damning for a man in Kimani's position, knowing the President was bent on full American recognition. Anyway, that's my reading of the situation, and it fits in with Kimani's willingness to do a deal. He wants the world to know they have a problem up there in the north. So you get your trip to Rudolf. That's what you wanted, isn't it?"

He was twisting it, trying to make it appear he had done me a favour. "You're not interested in Lake Rudolf," I said.

"No, but you are. Would you care to tell me?"

"No."

"Okay, but you have a reason." He reached for the bottle, pouring himself another drink as he said, "So do I. Not a spef—specific reason and I'm not after a story. It's not that at all." He put the bottle carefully down on the floor. "I'm a New Yorker, right? I was born and brought up in the Bronx, on the Grand Concourse. I'm a denizen of the concretest jungle in the world, and though I've been to a hell of a lot of countries, it's been mostly cities, or with mobs of people around—camps, mines, oilfields, anywhere there's a news story to cover. Driving out to that Lodge, the feel of Africa, the immensity, the solitude, and yesterday, coming back we saw a lion—a wild lion on the prowl for food." His voice had become a little slurred. "It was so thin and emanciated the ribs stuck out like a wicker basket and it stood there looking at us from the other side of the flood water where we'd bogged down. I'd never seen a lion in the wild before, only well-fed beasts in cages. So I figured just once in my life I'd cut loose, do something I wanted—not for money, not as an assignment, just for kicks. D'you understand?" He shook his head. "No, of course you don't. You're too young to have started worrying about what you've made of your life. But I'm close to fifty now, and seeing van Delden, his absolute commitment, his complete disregard of self—and the extraordinary impression he made . . ."

He paused there, staring down at his empty glass, his eyes half closed and a strangely sad look on his face. "Most of us, we live our lives, not believing in anything very much. But men like van Delden, they walk through life with God at their side, sure in the knowledge that they are here for a purpose." He put his hands up over his face, leaning forward as though in prayer. "Hell! I envy them, now, when it's too late. I'm just a spectator. That's all I've ever been, all I wanted to be. Not involved, not committed. A spectator." He spat the word out, contemptuous and sneering. "I've read a lot. Biographies mainly. A substitute for

the real thing." He let his hands fall, staring at me with his dark eyes.
"D'you know why van Delden went to the Seychelles?"

"He retired," I said. "His wife's family had a house there. . . ."

"Nuts! He's not the sort of man to retire of his own accord. He was
run out of Kenya—deported."

I didn't know whether to believe him or not. "How do you know?"
I asked.

"*The Nation.* After I left Kimani I had a look through the back
numbers. It was about a year before the war. A man named Enderby
disappeared up near Marsabit in territory van Delden had acquired as
a sanctuary. He was a white hunter collecting for zoos and safari parks
and specialising in baby elephants. The mortality rate was appalling. But
he didn't care, nor did the Government. Like the tourist traffic, it brought
in foreign currency. Only van Delden cared, and when Enderby started
moving in on his territory, he warned him—not privately, but in front
of the African game warden at a meeting in the warden's office in
Marsabit. He told him he didn't care whether he had a Government
permit or not, if he started using guns and thunderflashes on his land
he'd shoot him." Abe nodded. "I talked to the reporter who interviewed that game warden. He's still working for *The Nation* and he
told me the warden was quite certain van Delden had meant what he
said. He also told me it was common knowledge Enderby was involved
in the ivory trade, and Marsabit was known for its big tuskers."

"You think van Delden shot him then?" I was remembering that
wild old man in the blazing Serengeti dawn, the cold anger in his
pale eyes.

Abe shrugged. "A man like that, with his moral standards and his
love of elephants—it wouldn't seem like murder now, would it?"

"What about the reporter you spoke to, what did he think?"

"Served him right, that was his comment. He said everybody knew
van Delden killed the man."

"Then why wasn't he put on trial?"

"No body, no witnesses, and anyway they didn't dare. Think what
he'd have made of it with some of the most prominent people in the
country making fortunes out of ivory." He sloshed some more whisky
into his glass. "Where do you reckon he is now?"

I shook my head, wondering whether there was any truth in it. And
Abe's voice adding, "He's always been an elephant man, and with their
reconnaissance boys reporting herds of elephant moving north through
the Mathews Range and the Ndoto . . ." He was staring at me, his
eyes glassy bright. "There's a military post at Marsabit on the highway
north into Ethiopia and they report elephant for the first time in over
a year. Not much fodder for them there now, I'm told, and the springs
where the Rendile once watered their cattle all dried up, but I've a
feeling . . ." He shook his head, laughing at himself, a sound that re-

minded me of the giggle of a hyena. "It's just the way I'm made, I guess, but Marsabit was van Delden's stamping ground."

"You think he's trekking north, not heading for the coast?"

He shrugged. "How the hell do I know? It's just a feeling. What would you do in his place, knowing elephants the way he does? At *The Nation* they had the old 1965 survey maps. To the north of Rudolf there's the Molo River, all swamp and thick bush. Marsabit Mountain is over four thousand feet high, and to the west, overlooking the lake, there's Kulal, over seven thousand; two oases of virtual rain forest before the long desert march to the Molo and survival." And he added, "The Tsavo now—Tsavo East and Tsavo West. Before the Africans started fighting each other, those were the two largest parks, and some of the best elephant country left. Now I'm told they're almost empty of game. What the Tanzanian Army didn't kill, the Africans bordering these parks finished off. But not the elephants surely. Rhinos, yes, and buffalo, but I don't reckon elephants would just passively stay there to be slaughtered. Do you?" He stared at me as though expecting me to say they would, his eyes gleaming belligerently. "All I ever read about elephants . . . And game wardens. I've talked to some of them, interviews. . . . It all adds up to this—elephants live so long, always in family groups—they have this percip . . . they have the intelligence to differentiate between areas of safety and areas of danger. You understand? So, a family group may have safe-area knowledge going back two hundred years or more. Could be, even as far south as Tsavo, some wandering bull passed the word about van Delden's sanctuary. Too fanciful? Maybe. I don't know. So many hunters' stories, legends . . . difficult to tell what's fact and what's fiction." He downed his drink and got carefully to his feet, scooping up the almost empty bottle as he rose. "Well, I'm off to bed now. There'll be a truck here to pick us up about eight in the morning, and I've got Karanja acting as guide. If you want to go north—"

"You've got Karanja?"

"That's right. And I didn't ask for him. The Minister simply said Karanja would fix it and he'd send him with us."

"From what you told me I'd have thought his public-relations man is the last person he'd let you have."

"Maybe he wants to get rid of him. I don't know. Could be Karanja's not his man. If you'd seen as much of politics as I have . . ." He held the bottle up to the light, squinting at it and shaking his head sadly. "Don't reckon politics out here is much different from what it is back in New York. Just as rough, just as crooked, probably more so. Anyway, if you want to get to Lake Rudolf . . ."

"Marsabit is a long way east of Rudolf," I said.

He turned, the door half open. "Marsabit, Kulal, Rudolf—it's all one to me. So long as I meet up with some elephants."

"The Army will have killed them by the time we get there." I was thinking of what they had done in the Serengeti.

"I don't think so. They're not professional hunters like Kirby-Smith. And Marsabit is the most northerly outpost, less than a dozen men." He was standing there, swaying slightly, a sardonic smile on his face. "You think I've been talking a lot of crap, don't you? That I'm just a newshound on to another story. But you're wrong there." He shook his head. "It's not van Delden or Kirby-Smith I'm interested in. It's elephants . . . and Africa. The thought of all that space, the damn frightful emptiness of it." He focussed his eyes on me, holding on to the door. "You can come with me or not, just as you please. I don't care. Like the elephants, I'm following some strange compulsive urge of my own." And he added, "I don't expect you to understand. I don't understand myself." He nodded, smiling. "For once in my life I'm going to see what I want to see, film what I want to film. Goo'night."

He staggered out, closing the door behind him, and I was suddenly alone—alone and feeling scared. I was sorry then that he had taken the bottle. I could have done with another drink, remembering what I had read of Lake Rudolf in that faded typescript, the dessicated lava landscape, the volcanic cones and the hot winds whistling down from Kulal. Was it worth risking my life chasing an archaeological will-o'-the-wisp of that God-forsaken country? And Abe Finkel—trading my Serengeti film for the sight of a few herds of elephant—damn the man!

I moved to the chair he had vacated, sitting staring into the velvet darkness, my mind numb and the frogs croaking in the crater. Some strange compulsive urge, he had called it. Was I expected to share the problems of a man approaching fifty? I thought of London, trying to balance the life I knew against his offer of the unknown, the opportunity like a yawning void, a journey into space. Forbidden territory! I got the map out of my case and switched the light on, staring at it, trying to visualise what it meant, physically. I was hot and tired, exhausted after a day's work on my script, and I couldn't get van Delden out of my mind. Had he really killed that ivory hunter, or had Abe Finkel's imagination run away with him? An elephant man, and so sure they were being doomed to extinction. I remembered his words, the way he had faced the delegates, and then arranging for that poor beast to be driven into the Lodge area as into an arena so that he could slip away. And the tears standing in his daughter's eyes, her anger, her blazing anger at the callousness of it.

I was still sitting there, the map draped over my knees, when Ken came to tell me the bus had arrived. I didn't say anything, thinking of the aircraft flying through the night, back to England and normality, knowing I wouldn't be on it.

"You'd better get moving, we're on the first flight." And I heard myself say, "I'm not coming. I'm staying here." And I told him about the opportunity to visit Lake Rudolf, trying to keep my voice casual as

I arranged what he should take and what he should leave for me—the Beaulieu, all the spare film, and what cash we had left. It wasn't easy to convince him that I really meant it, but in the end he said, "Okay, if that's what you want. But rather you than me." And he began gathering up his things. It only took a moment, and then he was at the door, lingering there as though he half expected me to change my mind. "What shall I tell John?"

I had almost forgotten about John Crabtree and the BBC. I handed him the scribbled pages of the script. "Have that typed and give it to him, together with the film. He'll have to make what he can of it."

"And you'll be back—when?"

"How the hell do I know? Tell him I'm working on something else, outside of our assignment. I'll see him as soon as I reach London."

Ken nodded, standing there loaded with gear, waiting. "I'll tell him," he said finally. He wished me luck and then he was gone, the door shut and the room suddenly bleak and empty. I was alone again with Pieter van Delden's book and the old map, the frogs booming and my mind reaching out to the north, imagination running riot, my thoughts chaotic.

I must have gone to sleep there in the chair, for the next thing I knew I was shivering, a damp wind blowing into the room and the time almost one-thirty in the morning. I undressed slowly and crawled into bed, asleep almost as soon as my head touched the pillow.

Dawn woke me, the harsh cry of birds, and I lay watching the almost instant blaze of the sun, the shade lines darkening. None of the softness here of the English countryside, the birdsong, everything harsher, the grass coarse and the sun's heat not a life-giving warmth, but something to be afraid of. I looked at my watch. It was almost seven o'clock. If he had been on the first plane Ken would be landing at Heathrow inside of an hour, and I was still in Africa, committed to something for which my life had not equipped me. But at this hour of the day there was a freshness in the air, a sparkle, and suddenly I didn't care. Rudolf, the northern frontier, a new world . . . I threw off the bedclothes, stripped and showered, the tingle of my body matching the change of mood. And then Abe came in, looking bright as a bird and full of energy.

"You're still here then." He was dressed in khaki shorts and bush shirt, and he had all his gear with him. He smiled. "Just thought I'd check on my way to breakfast. I'll be out on the terrace."

I nodded, wrapping my towel round me. "I'll join you as soon as I've shaved. Order for me, will you? Has the truck arrived?"

"Not yet. But Karanja's here."

"You think they're really going to give us a truck?"

"If they don't, then your film remains at the Consulate." He turned to go, but then paused. "There's news of van Delden, by the way. A Land-Rover has been hijacked from a military post at Narok."

"How do they know it's van Delden?"

"You better ask Karanja. He's joining us for breakfast. Eggs and bacon okay for you? It may be the last decent meal we get for some time."

Ten minutes later I dumped my kit in the foyer and went out into the bright sunlight of the terrace. It was almost empty now that the Conference delegates had gone, a few Africans drinking coffee and Abe sitting at a table shaded by a thatched arbour. He was the only white man there and Karanja was sitting opposite him, dressed in a faded blue shirt and khaki trousers, a map spread out on the table between them. "Jambo," he said as I took the chair beside him. "You have good breakfast now, then we go."

"What's this about van Delden taking a Land-Rover?" I asked.

"The information come to Army Headquarters yesterday. There is a Land-Rover missing at Narok. Somebody steal it in the night."

"You don't know it was van Delden then?"

He grinned, a white flash of teeth. "You meet him. Nobody take a Land-Rover from the Army, only Tembo do a thing like that."

"And where's Narok?"

"That's the point," Abe said. "Narok is almost due west of here, about sixty miles." He swung the map round so that I could see, his finger pointing. "The scale is about thirty-six miles to the inch, so that puts him almost a hundred miles north of the Lodge." From Narok a gravel road ran north to Nakuru with a main road to Thomson's Falls and Nanyuki to link up with the highway north to Marsabit.

"He's not making for the coast then?"

"No, not if it's van Delden."

Our breakfast arrived—bacon and eggs, toast, butter, marmalade, coffee, yellow slices of paw-paw and half a lime, sugar if we wanted it. "No balance-of-payments problem here," Abe said, and Karanja grinned. "All black market for the rich men who run the rackets."

"And that doesn't include you?"

He shook his woolly head. "I am only here when I have guests of the Government. You are guests of the Government this morning. Mr. Kimani's orders."

Abe bowed his acknowledgment. "Most generous of him. And even more generous to spare you to accompany us."

Karanja laughed. "Mr. Kimani has his reasons."

Abe's eyebrows lifted, but he didn't say anything, and Karanja went on, "Those pictures at the Conference, some people think I engineer the whole thing."

"Is that what Kimani thinks?"

"I don't know. Maybe. But is good excuse sending me with you." And he suddenly burst out laughing for no reason that I could see except perhaps to cover embarrassment. "He don't want me here in Nairobi."

I think Abe had the same feeling as myself, that Karanja was in a very excitable state, his nerves on edge, for he quickly changed the subject. "That Land-Rover, how much gas was in it, do you know?"

"Nobody tell me." He was no longer laughing, his voice sulky.

"Could he get gas at Nakuru?"

"For petrol he must have a permit."

"What about the black market?"

"Maybe."

"At Nakuru?"

Karanja shook his head. "At Nakuru the police watch for that Land-Rover. At all towns, and there are Army patrols on the highway. I think he keep to the small roads." His finger traced a thin red line on the survey map running north from Narok to link with a network of tracks west of Nakuru. "Maybe some farmer sell him petrol to get to Baringo. But after Lake Baringo . . ." He shook his head.

"What about us?" I asked. "Where do we fill up?"

"At Samburu. That is Northern Army Headquarters now." He turned the map over, indicating a green patch just north of Isiolo. It was marked Samburu Game Reserve.

"And beyond Samburu?" Abe asked.

Karanja shook his head. "I don't know. Maybe they have some soldiers at Maralal or Baragoi. Is more probable Baragoi. You see Horr Valley between the mountains—there." He jabbed with his knife. "Is only way for trucks coming south from Ethiopia, that track and the highway through Marsabit. And where there are soldiers is petrol." He nodded emphatically. "We ask at Samburu."

I stared down at the map. Lake Baringo was at 3,300 feet with mountains towering all round it and only a single track running north, soon petering out into a broken red thread in the vast emptiness of the Rift Valley as it sloped down to Lake Rudolf. If he made it to Baringo, then he would have no alternative but to take the track eastwards into the mountains, and if he were heading for Marsabit, that meant swinging north through Maralal, Baragoi, and the Horr Valley. "Have you read von Höhlen's account of Teleki's expedition to Lake Rudolf?" I asked Abe.

He shook his head.

"Well, I have, and unless he can find enough petrol I don't see how he can make it, not to Marsabit, through the mountains and across the desert."

"Okay, so you've read about it. But he's lived there, remember. It's his country." He pushed his plate away and reached for the coffee. "What do you say, Karanja? You know the area."

"If he don't have fuel for the Land-Rover . . ." Karanja paused, his forehead creased in thought. "Very bad now for foot safari. Very bad drought, no water in Balesa Kulal." He pointed to a thin blue line on the map at the foot of the mountain's eastern slope. "And if Kalama waterhole also dry . . ." He shrugged. "Maybe there is some rain now."

But he said it without conviction. "Maybe Samburu don't eat all their camels. With camels it is not more than two, three days from Horr Valley to Marsabit."

"And there's water in the Horr Valley?" Abe asked.

"Yes, at South Horr. Always water at South Horr." He looked up as a soldier came to our table. They talked for a moment, and then he said, "The bus is here." He produced an envelope from his pocket and handed it to me. "You sign please and I leave it for Mr. Kimani at the desk."

It was a typewritten letter authorising the American Consul to hand over to the Minister of Lands the package containing my film, provided we had been transported to Lake Rudolf and returned safely to Nairobi. I looked across at Abe, but he was lighting a cigarette, avoiding my gaze. Outside on the road I could see a minibus drawn up in the shade, its dusty body still showing the zebra stripes of tourist days, but faded now and streaked with rust. Karanja was holding out a pen for me. "If you don't sign, then maybe Mr. Kimani think I engineer that too." And again he burst into laughter that was high pitched and without any humour.

I was still reluctant, but all the delegates had gone now, the time for refusal past. I took the pen and signed it, and Karanja went off with it to the reception desk. "I thought for a moment you were going to back-pedal." Abe was smiling, I think with relief.

"What would have happened if I had?"

He shrugged. "I guess we'd have been in trouble, both of us. Kimani's taking a bit of a risk as it is. The area we're going into is an Army responsibility."

I nodded, feeling the sun hot on my back, a flutter of nerves in my stomach. "I'd better get my things then and check out." Nothing else I could do now, and he smiled and said, "See you in the bus."

In the foyer I found Karanja still at the desk, chatting up the pretty little African receptionist, and when I asked her for my bill, he said it was all settled. "You and Mr. Finkel are the guests of the Government now. I show you what we do for our people, how the Government is helping them. Also very interesting country. Not many white men go where we are going and you get better film, very much better film, with shots of the lake and El Molo people." He said something to the girl, his teeth shining in a broad smile, and then he picked up my suitcase, leaving me to carry my camera, and we went out to the minibus.

Abe was already sitting in front beside the driver, two guns and a water bag beside him, cartons of ammunition at his feet. "We'll take it in turns," he said as I climbed past him. The body of the vehicle was a jumble of camping gear, sacks, and cardboard boxes, with jerricans ranged along each side and two soldiers sitting on the heap of stores, clutching their rifles, their heads almost touching the roof. Karanja joined me on the transverse seat, sliding the door to behind him. "Is more comfortable the minibus," he said, but without much conviction, and I was thinking a Land-Rover would have been better.

We drove out through the centre of Nairobi and took the road north-east to Thika, climbing steadily into old settler country of citrus fruit and tea plantations, jacaranda everywhere and the Cape chestnut trees in flower. There were plantation houses set well back in the shade of the trees, but they looked tired and neglected, their verandahs peeling paint, the gardens overgrown and littered with huts and rubbish, African children everywhere. The road was almost empty of traffic, its macadam surface pitted with holes loosely filled with gravel that rattled against the chassis.

Beyond Thika we began to catch glimpses of Mt. Kenya, its summit like a great medieval fortress, black rock against the crystal of perpetual snow and the hard blue of the sky. We were into more open country then, the Aberdares closing in to our left, and just before midday we passed the turning to Nyeri. There was a signpost there that still said Treetops, but when Abe asked Karanja whether there was any game left around this old tourist haunt, he said he didn't know. "The Outspan Hotel, where tourists stop for lunch, is now administration office for resettlement of Aberdare mountain region."

"And Treetops is abandoned?"

"Not abandoned. Is camp for hunters working with the Ministry."

"Your Ministry, eh?"

Karanja nodded.

Abe turned to me. "I was at Treetops once." His eyes gleamed behind his glasses. "I had been attending the UNCTAD meeting here in Nairobi, a United Nations conference to work out how the rich nations could best assist in the development of the Third World. Very boring, and after it was over I decided to take a break and get a glimpse of this wildlife people talked about. You ever been to Treetops?" He didn't wait for me to answer, but went on talking in that fast monotone of his that was sometimes hard to follow because it came in one continuous flow. "There was a white hunter with a rifle to meet our bus from the Outspan and we covered the last five hundred yards on foot with warnings not to talk and if we met a dangerous animal to slip into one of the hides provided. Good tourist stuff! I guess I was in one of my cynical moods. And then suddenly there was this rhinoceros less than two hundred yards away with a horn on him like a spike about two feet long, sniffing the air, his little ears cocked, and peering myopically in our direction."

He grinned. "I wasn't so sure about the tourist stuff then, but we made it to the stairs without him charging us and then we were back to the flush-toilet world we all knew. Treetops was no longer the original glorified hide in a tree, it was a comfortable hotel built on piles with a circular pool of muddy water in front of it and salt thrown down to attract the game. But nothing came, the rhino had disappeared and we had to be content with filming the baboons scampering about on the roof like clowns in a circus. At dusk some buffalo appeared, looking about as wild as a herd of black cattle; two of them had a wallow and that was just about the highlight. I was bored as hell."

"You got nothing out of Treetops then." I was wondering if that was the point of the story.

"Oh, but I did," he murmured. "That was the extraordinary thing. I got something so beautiful. . . ." He hesitated, staring at the road ahead, the long slope of the mountain, then turning to me again and asking whether I was a balletomane. He shook his head at my reply. "Then I'm not sure you'll understand, but I'm quite close to Lincoln Center—I live on West End and I see a lot of ballet. I love it, I really do." He shook his head, smiling. "It's difficult to explain if you don't appreciate the beauty of movement. We were still at dinner when somebody said, 'There's an elephant out there.' The long dining table emptied in a flash and there was this elephant, grey-white in the floodlights, surrounded by buffaloes. She just stood there, moving the tip of her trunk delicately over the ground until she finally fastened on the particular bit of salt she fancied. I'm sure it was a young female, she was so feminine, so dainty in all her movements, and the buffaloes stood glowering at her, disputing the ground. She shook her head at them, fanning her ears and taking a few tentative steps as though about to change. Then she wheeled abruptly and tripped off-stage like a ballerina who finds herself crowded by a bunch of yokels."

He twisted further round, gripping my arm. "You know, Colin, she was just about the prettiest thing I ever saw. No, that's not the word. I guess you can't describe an animal that big as pretty, but she was beautiful—so light on her feet, so graceful." He shook his head, laughing at himself, then reached into the pocket of his bush jacket and brought out his wallet. "I've always wondered whether I'd see her again, and when I got this assignment—" He produced the faded photograph and passed it to me. "I was shooting in black and white, of course, and that size I guess it doesn't look all that much. But the big blow-up I've got at home is really something. I shot three reels of her, so I had plenty to choose from."

It showed an elephant limned in light and ghostly white, the ears spread out like the wings of a butterfly, the trunk curled up, and it appeared to be dancing, one foot raised, the body twisted slightly as though caught in the moment of pirouetting, and to the left of the picture was a rhino pawing the ground in a scuff of dust, the head lowered so that the long horn was like a spear. It was a fantastic shot, every detail clear and the whole picture so perfectly balanced it was like an artist's impression.

"Nice, isn't it?" he said. "You know, I'm really proud of that picture. Compensation for all the dreary stuff I've shot in years of travelling around for the media." He leaned over, his finger pointing at the animal's left ear. "See that hole there. In the blow-up you can see it very clearly. It's a great tear shaped like a duck on the wing. That's how they recognise elephants. It's like a tag."

"What caused it?"

"The horn of a rhino probably. That's what I'm told, anyway. And she'll carry that mark to the end of her days."

"And you shot three reels in that one brief sighting?"

"Oh, no. I was up watching her half the night. She came back, you see. About midnight. There were rhinos then as well as buffs. And one of the rhinos began snorting and mock charging her. It was always the same place, the same bit of salt, and she'd just stand her ground, flapping her ears and laughing at him. In the end she'd shrug and stroll away as though she wasn't really interested, make a slow, stately circuit of the waterhole, and come back to the same spot. Then the whole ridiculous pantomime would start up again, the rhino snorting and Sally—" He looked at me, a solemn, sad look in his eyes. "That's what I called her—Sally. My wife's name, you see. She was in the Corps de Ballet when I met her, such beautiful balance, and so dainty." He was silent for a moment, the smile gone. Then he gave a quick little shrug. "Well anyway, this elephant, she flapped her ears at the rhino, standing tall and stately—just like Sally— her front legs close together so that she was slender and neat and statu-esque. Yeah, that's the word—statuesque. Then she'd drift off silently for another circuit of the waterhole, moving like a shadow in and out of the trees until she'd disappeared. And after a while, suddenly, she'd be standing there like a ghost again, absolutely still, waiting to make her entrance." He reached out and took the photograph from me, replacing it in his wallet. "All that patience, all that quiet determination over a little bit of salt, it was a lesson in animal behaviour and in deportment. The rhino, too, all that snorting and pawing and mock charging, it wasn't real aggression. He wasn't spoiling for a fight. He was just saying, 'For God's sake give me a little more room.' And though Sally could have picked him up in her trunk, all two tons of him, and slammed his body on the ground and knelt on it, all she did again and again was take a wander round the pool."

He had turned away and was looking out the window towards the mountains, where wisps of smoke showed blue against the dark of forest green. "That's what Treetops meant to me—the tolerance and beauty of big game animals. Also," he added in a whisper, "it gave me the urge the spend a few moments of my life in the company of elephants." He nodded towards the fires and the gashes where the trees had been felled. "There's going to be soil erosion there." He twisted round and faced Karanja. "Why doesn't your Ministry stop it? As well as soil erosion you'll have a drop in rainfall. Don't you ever think about the future? Or is that all our civilisation has taught you—rape the land, grab what you can, and to hell with tomorrow?" He stared at the puzzled Karanja, then looked at me, that sardonic little smile lifting the corners of his lips. "A long time ago now," he said, "since your Queen heard of her succession up there in that Treetops lookout. A lot has happened, the world gone sourer on the human race and everything more complicated." He said it sadly, then lit a cigarette and relapsed into silence.

We were just north of the equator then, close under the western slopes of Mt. Kenya. A white cloud had formed over its top and our talk was desultory, the heat increasing. At Nanyuki the broad main street was almost deserted, its shops all boarded up. We stopped outside one of them. Faded lettering announced it as The Settlers' Stores. "Maybe he have some beer," Karanja said. "Is only place till we get to Samburu." He remembered it as an Indian shop where safaris stocked up with wine and liquor, fresh vegetables and tinned goods, but it had been Africanised long ago and now the shelves were largely bare, only local produce sold, sacks of maize flour they called posho, melons over-ripe and crawling with flies, root vegetables I had never seen before. The beer was warm and flat from an old plastic container. We bought oranges and on Karanja's advice a bagful of local cigarettes, then we drove on.

I had changed places with Abe, but it was hotter in front and no more comfortable as we climbed into open country on the northern slopes of the mountain. "Much resettlement here," Karanja said, indicating the dried-up vistas of grassland below us. It was dotted with groups of huts and patches of abandoned cultivation. "After the settlers go the land is given to the Meru people and the Samburu." But there was no sign of life there, no people, no cattle, no game.

"Where are they now?" I asked, and I had to shout above the noise of the labouring engine and the rattle of gravel against the mudguards.

He looked unhappy and shrugged his shoulders. "Drought very bad."

He came to the high point of the road and suddenly we were on the brink of the northern frontier region, a burned brown plain reaching out to desert in which towering buttes of pale red rock stood like castles shattered by wind and sand. The survey map showed that we were at 6,390 feet, the road snaking down from the shoulder of Mt. Kenya and running out into an infinity of sand and rock. Dust devils whirled and there was no horizon, the deadness of the country losing itself in haze, land and sky the same opaque sun-blistered white, and away to our left the blurred shape of mountains rising like ghosts on the edge of visibility. It was appalling, breathtaking. Abe leaned forward, his voice in my ear. "The promised land!" He turned to Karanja. "You reckon elephants can cross that and reach the mountains?"

"Oh yes." He nodded. "Is not desert like the Chalbi. You look, you see trees, plenty of dry scrub, and they know where water is."

We coasted down into the oven heat of lower altitude, swinging north where the road from Meru came in, everything shimmering now, acacias lifting their flat tops above a glazed heat mirror, thorn trees standing on their heads, wisps of brittle scrub floating in the water mirages and butte tops trembling in the distance. The little township of Isiolo appeared as a glint of corrugated iron winking in the sun. The road passed it by and the macadam stopped abruptly. We were on to gravel then, the noise deafening and dust streaming out behind us, and that was where we saw our first sign of animal life, two giraffe standing by a thorn tree, their necks leaning sideways and a quizzical expression on their faces as they stared at us absolutely motionless.

It was the driver who saw them and he braked, shouting excitedly and pointing. The soldiers in the back reached for their rifles. The giraffe barely a hundred yards away, but by the time we had stopped they were already on the move, galloping off with that stiff yet graceful gait that enables them to keep their heads at a constant elevation. "They are reticulated giraffe," Karanja said as though he were courier to a group of tourists. "Is a species belonging to the north here."

"It's good to see something that's survived," Abe said sourly, his eyes on the two soldiers, whose disappointment showed in their faces as we drove on.

"Very difficult to shoot giraffe," Karanja said, as though he shared the soldiers' disappointment.

I was looking at the country now with a new interest, but we saw nothing else, only some ostrich, and ten miles further on we forked left on to a track that led to some round thatched huts that had once been the entrance to the Samburu Game Reserve. Now it was a military post. Karanja showed his pass and we were waved on, past some scout cars with their crews asleep in the shade of the armour, the track running out into open savannah country, a sort of plateau of sered grass bordered by a fine stand of acacia, dark umbrellas against a burning sky, mountains blue in the distance. The track had been pulverised to a fine grey dust and in the distance the dull green shapes of Army tents floated above the shimmering grass, a windsock hanging limp and the dust of a plane that had just landed lying like a pall of smoke over the improvised runway. Nothing stirred, the sun blazing down, the heat intense. "You want to swim?"

"In the river?" I could see it marked on the map.

"No, not in the river. At Buffalo Springs." He directed the driver at an intersection. "Very good water, very clear. No crocodiles." And he laughed.

"What about game?" Abe asked. "Any game left?"

"I don't know," he said uncertainly. "I think only Army now."

"How long since you've been here?"

"Four years, maybe five."

"And what was here then, when it was a game reserve?"

"Herds of eland, zebra, buffalo, also gazelle and oryx. There were bustards here in the grass, and lion, always some elephant down in the doum palm by the river." And then, brightening, he said, "Here is Buffalo Springs. You swim now."

The driver slowed. Two Army trucks were parked in the shade of some twisted trees. There were shouts and the sound of laughter, and when we stopped we saw the glistening black of naked bodies crowding a small rock pool. "Is very nice the water, very cool." Karanja's voice sounded uncertain, and when neither of us responded, he said abruptly, "Okay. We go straight to lodge now." And he spoke sharply to the driver.

The lodge had been sited close beside the river. It still possessed something of its original charm, but now that the Army had taken over, all but the largest trees had been cut down to make way for vehicles and a sprawl of tents and latrines. At the guard tent we dropped off our two soldiers and a corporal directed us to a stretch of the river bank where four large container trucks were parked. The river was very low, the trees on the further bank drooping in the heat and the head of a crocodile showing green in the sluggish water.

I climbed stiffly out and Abe followed me. "Those look like refrigerator trucks," he said. The grey slabs of their sides were painted with the Federation flag, an elephant on a bright blue background, and underneath in bold lettering were the words: K-S GAME CONTROL COY. A Land-Rover drove into the parking area, stirring the dust.

"We're staying the night, are we?" I asked Karanja.

He shook his head. "We are civilians, not Army. We cannot camp here."

"Then what have we come for?" Abe asked, the heat giving an edge to his voice.

"Is necessary we have military permit, also petrol. And I have business to see about, a matter of communications."

"Okay, and while you're doing that, you might enquire if Major Kirby-Smith is here. Looks like he's made this his base." He walked over to the nearest truck and stood staring up at it. "Game cropping must be quite a profitable operation," he murmured. "Those things aren't cheap."

The truck was much bigger than any of the Army vehicles and it looked fairly new, the design on its side brighter than the tattered flag that had flown over the Wildlife Conference. Flipflops sounded in the dust behind us and an Irish voice said, "Don't say we got tourists now."

It was the driver of the Land-Rover, a rather shabby little man with sandy hair and a rag of torn silk knotted round his throat. He held a battered briefcase in his hand and his bare toes were grey with dirt. "That your minibus? I haven't seen one of those in years."

There was a sudden gleam of interest in Abe's eyes as he looked at him. "You must be the pilot of that plane we saw landing."

The other nodded. "How do you like our new flag? Pretty, isn't it?"

"A golden elephant with ivory tusks?" Abe gave a sour laugh. "Very appropriate."

"Would you be a conservationist then?"

"Television," Abe said.

"Well, if you're looking for shots of the drought I can tell you this, there's plenty of material for you north of here, the carcases of dead cattle thick round every dried-up waterhole." His leathery face cracked in a grin. "But that's no reason why we should die of thirst, too. Come and have a drink. My name's Pat Murphy."

We introduced ourselves and Abe said, "You fly reconnaissance, do you?"

"Right. Bill Maddox and me, we take it in turns to watch over the northern frontier."

"And report on any unauthorized movements."

"Our reports cover everything—tribes, animals, the state of the water-holes." He stared at us narrowly, a nerve fluttering the corners of his eye-lids. "They're confidential, of course. You here on a story, or just for background shots?"

"Right at this moment I'm looking for Kirby-Smith."

"Then you're out of luck. He's not here."

"These are his refrigerator trucks."

"He left this morning. They'll follow when he gives the word. Now do you want that drink, because I certainly do and we got a truckload of beer in yesterday."

We left the driver in charge of our gear and followed the pilot along the river bank. At the entrance to the lodge, Karanja went off to find the adjutant and Pat Murphy took us through into the old tourist bar. It was now the officers' mess. There were several Africans there, very spruce in clean shirts and neatly creased trousers. He back-slapped his way through them and gave his order to the barman. "Did you come up through Nanyuki and Isiolo, or by way of Baringo?"

Abe did not say anything and when I started to answer, his hand gripped my arm, silencing me, a bright gleam in his eyes.

Murphy had turned back to the bar. He settled for the drinks, then handed us our beer. "Don't reckon you'd make it through Baringo." He laughed. "An old minibus like that, it's hardly the vehicle for the Baringo track."

The beer was ice-cold from the fridge and as we drank Abe said innocently, "You flew out that way this morning, did you? See anything interesting?"

Murphy hesitated, gulping the rest of his beer down and watching us. "Television, you said. We haven't had any television people up here before so you must have been at that Wildlife Conference." He put his glass down and lit a cigarette. "There was an old-timer, Cornelius van Delden, gatecrashed the Conference. That's what I heard. Care to fill me in on the details?"

Abe told him briefly what had happened.

"And now he's disappeared. Pinched an Army Land-Rover and took off into the blue." Murphy hesitated. "Is it Kirby-Smith or van Delden you're interested in?"

"Elephants," Abe said, and the Irishman laughed.

"Sure, and you'll find them, too. But you're here on a story and that means van Delden." He finished his beer and ordered three more. "I have been flying bush a long time now. Safaris, oil prospectors, Government officials—I met most people. Not many of them left now. White people, I mean."

"So you know van Delden?"

Murphy nodded. "Sure I know the old devil. I was the one who flew him down from Marsabit after the Enderby affair. You heard about that?"

"Come to the point," Abe said. "You saw the Land-Rover, did you?"

Murphy smiled. "I spotted a Land-Rover, yes."

"On the track from Baringo?"

"Could be." And he added, "Yesterday Bill flew Alex up to look at the South Horr Gap. So today I make my recce to the west along the edge of Suguta."

"And that's where you saw it?"

"Right."

"Abandoned?"

"Hard to say. Could be just parked." He had dropped his voice so that the African officers couldn't hear. "My report doesn't go in till the morning, if that helps, and I owe van Delden something."

"Could you show us the position on the map?"

He nodded and reached for his briefcase.

II

We were away from the Samburu Lodge by late afternoon and camped that night under Lolokwe, a great bald sugar-loaf mountain that stood up out of the plain just north of the cut-off to Maralal. The sheer sides of it were red in the sunset as we pitched our tent, Karanja showing us how the tubular framing fixed in to the canvas fly while the driver got to work with a panga gathering wood. Starlings watched us with inquisitive eyes, their metallic plumage iridescent in the slanting light, and colonies of weaver birds darted noisily in and out of nests clustered like small coconuts in the wait-a-bit thorns. The fire was roaring and the tea made by the time we had our bedding laid out under the rotten canvas.

The dusk was brief, darkness rushing in, Lolokwe a black mass against the stars and only the crackle of the blazing fire. Everything was suddenly very still, no sound of birds now. "Something I've always dreamed of," Abe murmured, his voice a whisper in the night. "Does it worry you, camping out like this in the middle of Africa?"

"No," I said. "No, of course not." But there was a tautness running through me, an awareness of the senses I had never felt before, my ears alert for sound, my eyes straining to pierce the darkness beyond the fire.

A faint breeze was coming off the mountain and Karanja sniffed the air, his face glistening black in the lurid light of the flames. "I think it rain tonight. Is why we sleep under cover." And he added, "You watch for scorpions in the sand here. Scorpions very bad."

"What about snakes?" I asked.

He grinned. "Snakes very bad, too, and we don't have snake kit. But here scorpions more bad than snakes."

The evening meal was posho and tinned stew, and while we were eating it, squatting round the fire, I told Abe about Pieter van Delden's book and the reasons for my wanting to go to Lake Rudolf.

"It seems," he said, "there is a certain dichotomy of purpose. Yours is practical. You want to confirm an archaeological discovery and capture it on film. I just want to absorb the quiet immensity of Africa and see how elephants solve the problem of survival in the hostile world of man." He lit a cigarette. "But for tomorrow I think we're both agreed, aren't we? We go take a look at that Land-Rover."

"I suppose so." I said it reluctantly, thinking of Lake Rudolf. I had a chance now to get to Lake Rudolf and I did not want to be side-tracked. "The pilot didn't say it was abandoned."

"He flew low over it and saw nobody."

"That doesn't mean it's van Delden's vehicle."

"All the more reason why we should take a look at it." He was sitting hunched up, his hands clasped round his knees, and in the firelight I could see the glint of curiosity in his eyes. A newsman on the scent of a story, I thought. And then he looked at me, smiling quietly, and said, "Have you thought about what we're doing here, really thought about it? We have moved back many centuries to a time when man was a part of the animal world. There are no garages here in the desert, and if we run out of gas, then we are as alone and vulnerable as those early men you've been telling me about who fired pottery on the shores of Lake Rudolf and marked it with the design of a pyramid topped by dwelling places. We are primitives now, huddled round a fire for protection, and for the future I can only think of the Arab word Inshallah. If it is God's will, then we shall find van Delden, and if van Delden is with us, then he is your best guide to Lake Rudolf. And for me—" He hesitated, staring into the fire. "He can teach me about elephants and how to live in harmony with this country where death and life are all one, an inevitable process that fascinates me because I've never felt it to be that way before."

"And if we don't find van Delden?"

"Then there's Kirby-Smith at South Horr. If we get a chance to see him at work I guess we'll both of us have a better understanding of Genesis and how the Tree of Knowledge made all creatures afraid of man." He turned and looked at me, smiling again. "This, my friend, is a journey back in time, and if I die as a result, then I shall die with some understanding, my body disintegrating to merge with the dust of the desert where it will give life. . . ."

"For God's sake!" I said. "You're not going to die."

"Of course not. But if I did—" He shrugged, still smiling, and now his smile was melancholy in the firelight. "I've never wanted to lie under the weight of a marble tomb in acres of headstones or have my carcase des-

patched to the crematorium because there's no room in the graveyards
of our over-population. Better my rotting flesh keep a jackal going for
another day or contribute to the soaring flight of a vulture, my bones
cleaned by ants—"

"What are you—a poet manqué?"

He laughed and shook his head. "I never learned to write that well."
He stared into the fire a moment, then added quietly, "All my reading
has been in search of knowledge, an attempt to understand. Perhaps here
—outside of books, outside of the experience of others—perhaps here,
in this solitude, I may discover the meaning of life, the meaning of God
even." He shook his head again, smiling and getting abruptly to his
feet. "I'm sorry, I talk too much. I'm going to bed now." And I was left
with the feeling he was upset at having let his tongue run away with
him, revealing an introspective disposition normally concealed from everybody but himself.

I sat on by the fire for a while, smoking a last cigarette and listening
to the stillness. And when I followed him to bed, I lay under the fly
staring up at the bulk of Lolokwe, unable to sleep. Sometime in the
night it began to rain and I woke to the sound of it on the canvas and
the drip, drip, drip on the sand beside my camp bed. I remembered
stories then of lions sheltering in safari tents and I lay curled up like a
foetus, my ears straining for the slightest sound beyond the patter of
the rain.

I woke again with the dawn and birds were calling. Looking out from
under the torn canvas, I saw the rump of a small bird whiter than white
against the black of a thorn and far in the distance an eagle nailed like
a cross against the sky. The rain had gone, the sky was clear, and in the
still-grey light the desert browns had a freshness of colour. Drongos, looking like jet-black flycatchers, flitted from bush to bush in the dry burned
scrub and I lay there watching the light grow fast until the sun came up
and the bare steep walls of Lolokwe turned blood-red. The driver threw
off his blanket, putting sticks on the fire, blowing life into the embers,
and Abe came strolling into sight between the thorns, slim and wiry-look-
ing in khaki bush gear, his head bent, his eyes on the ground. I thought
he was following the track of some animal, but when I called to him to
ask him what it was, he shook his head. "Only birds," he said. "The
sand's so soft after the rain the imprint of their feet is everywhere." He
came over to me, smiling. "You lazy guy, you've missed the best of the
day."

We broke camp and were away as soon as we had had tea, and by
eight-thirty we had passed the turning to Wamba and were on the road
to Maralal, driving towards the mountains. It was a dirt road, the going
sticky in places, and soon we were climbing in thick bush. Once, where
we stopped to relieve ourselves, we saw a pigmy falcon perched like a
small brown sentinel on the branch of a tree. The mountains were closing
in on us then and shortly afterwards we came across some old elephant

droppings. It was wild country, and just below Kisima Lake a track came in from the left and Abe told the driver to take it.

"Is not the way to Maralal," Karanja said.

"No, but we take it all the same."

"Maralal straight on," Karanja insisted.

"I know Maralal is straight on." Abe had the map open on his knees. "But I want to have a look at the escarpment running down into the valley of the Suguta."

"We look over the Suguta Valley from viewpoint beyond Maralal. You see river beds, geysers, volcanoes, everything you want from viewpoint."

The argument went on for several minutes while we sat there motionless, the engine throbbing and the heat trapped in the valley. I took no part in it, watching a bateleur, which I could now recognise by its distinctive cross-like shape against the blue sky. It was planing on the air currents high up where grey crags thrust clear of the dense bush that clothed the slopes of the mountains to our right. In the end Abe had to tell him about the Land-Rover. Karanja was suddenly silent. He was sitting with me on the front seat and there was sweat on his face, his body tense. "Is no good," he murmured. "They send patrol—"

"The pilot doesn't file his report till this morning." Abe leaned forward, gripping Karanja's shoulder. "Are you going to let them pick him up? You worked with him. You were one of his game scouts. You can't just drive on, now that I've told you."

"Is Major Kirby-Smith you go to see. That is what you say to me and what I tell Captain Ngaru. Our permit is for Baragoi. Also," he added desperately, "we don't have enough petrol."

"We have eight jerricans in the back."

"They are water."

"Four of them are water, four of them gas, so tell the driver to turn left."

"Let's go on," I said. "It only means trouble if we do find him."

"And suppose it isn't van Delden? Suppose it's some poor devil—"

"It's van Delden all right." It had to be, no patrols out on the Baringo track and nobody but the Army allowed in the area.

"Okay then, it's van Delden. And how do you expect to find your way in the lava wastes round Lake Rudolf without him to guide you? It's what you wanted, isn't it, for him to take you there?"

I shook my head, knowing he had made up his mind and unable to argue with him in the suffocating heat. All I could say was, "I'd rather drive on." I had a deep, instinctive feeling of unease, and it wasn't only because of that strange old man; it was Abe, too. But I couldn't put my feelings into words and with a sense of inevitability I heard him say, "Okay, Karanja, we turn left here."

Something in the way he said it, the quiet certainty in his voice, seemed to settle the matter. Karanja spoke quickly to the driver in Swahili and we turned on to the track that led back in a south-westerly direction into the Ol Keju Osera valley. It was thick bush all the way, the road steep in places and sticky with the night's rain, and half an hour later we had a puncture. It was hardly surprising, the tyres were almost bald, and while we were helping the driver change the wheel Karanja took the shotgun and went in search of game. He had heard the cackling call of guinea fowl.

"What happens if we do find van Delden?" I said. "There'll be a patrol out after him now. Karanja's scared of him, and so am I in a way."

We were pulling the spare wheel out of the back and Abe said, "Trouble with you is you think too much. Try taking things as they come. And don't worry about Karanja. A few hours in van Delden's company and I guess he'd be the way he was before ambition and the importance of being a press officer to a minister got hold of him." And then he went on to tell me why the pilot hadn't reported sighting the Land-Rover immediately. A dozen or more years back he had taken off from Loiyangalani airstrip after flying some tourists in for the fishing on Lake Rudolf and had been caught in a hurricane blast of wind from Mt. Kulal. "There's an island in the lake there, South Island, and he crash-landed on the lava slopes and smashed his leg up. Van Delden happened to be at the Mission and he went out at once, paddling across eight miles of water on one of the El Molo log rafts they use for fishing. The wind started up again in the morning and blew for the better part of a week, so if van Delden hadn't paddled out immediately Murphy would have been done for." And he added, "I got it out of him while you were on the terrace looking at that hippo. That's why he gave us time to get down here ahead of the patrol."

We had the spare wheel on and were tightening the nuts when two shots sounded in the distance. A few minutes later Karanja emerged from the bush, grinning and holding up a brace of helmeted guinea fowl. They were plump-looking birds, their dark bodies speckled with white spots, their heads strangely capped with a bony grey horn. He was very pleased with himself as he tossed the birds into the back. "You want we brew some tea, Paul?" The driver nodded, his white shirt dark with sweat, beads of perspiration on his forehead. "Okay, we have brew-up now, then we go find this Land-Rover."

Out here alone in the bush it was somehow comforting to see how quickly they got a fire going. In no time at all the water was boiling and the driver was stirring in tea and sugar. He sat back on his haunches and suddenly his eyes widened. "Ndovu!"

At first I couldn't see them, the bush hazed with heat, the light blinding. Karanja pointed. "See them? Elephants, beyond that big tree." The excitement in his voice vibrated in the air.

I saw the tree, a big euphorbia on a rounded shoulder of the hills, and suddenly a grey shap moved, and then another. I don't know how many there were. I only caught glimpses of them as they glided quietly across

a gap in the bush. "Cows," Karanja said. "They have totos with them."
They passed across the dirt road, up by the farthest bend, grey ghosts moving north along the contour line, and suddenly they were gone, merged into the shimmering grey-green foliage of the hillside. Abe stood staring after them. "Did you see, Colin? A whole herd of them. Kirby-Smith was right. There are elephants up here."

Karanja handed him a mug of tea and he sat down abruptly. "Meat on the hoof," he muttered, and a cold chill ran through me, the same sort of chill I had felt the day my uncle had taken his life. There had been other times, too. Over-sensitivity, that's what the doctor had said when I had played truant from school because I wouldn't share a desk with a certain other boy. The over-sensitivity of a boy who has lost his natural parents, but I had known something dreadful was going to happen, and a few days later he was found at the bottom of the cliffs. That was when we lived at Peacehaven and I had been on an easy pitch on those same cliffs the week before, prizing fossils out of the chalk.

"There ought to be some way we could communicate," Abe said. "Some language. Then we could warn them. But I guess elephant pidgin requires a deeper rumbling than I can manage on an empty stomach." His hands were clasped round his mug, his head bent as though reading the future in the tea leaves floating on the oily surface. "I wonder if van Delden can make himself understood. He's lived with them so long. . . ." He sipped his drink, his eyes fastening on me, the pupils slightly enlarged by his glasses. "All I know about elephants is what I've read since that visit to Treetops. They communicate by rumbling. But how much they communicate . . . ?" He took the plate Karanja passed him, cold baked beans and some slices of bread, and put it on the ground beside him. "Nobody knows how much they can say to each other, any more than we understand the language of dolphins and whales. For instance, this concentration of game up around Lake Rudolf. You heard what Kirby-Smith said, and he particularly referred to pilots having sighted elephants. I asked Murphy about that, but he doesn't fly to Rudolf. His job is keeping watch on tracks and waterholes. It's daytime flying, anyway, and the only place he's seen elephants is up around South Horr."

He reached for his plate, spooning beans into his mouth and gazing up at the slopes where the elephants had disappeared. "Now if I knew their language I'd go after that bunch and warn them. The way they were headed they'll finish up inside of those refrigerator trucks." He looked across at me, that sardonic little smile at the corners of his mouth. "A hardboiled media man and here I am, squatting beside a dirt track in the middle of nowhere, worrying about a herd of cows and expecting something to happen." His gaze switched back to the heat-hazed mountainside. "It's almost noon. The hottest part of the day. Those elephants should have been under the shade of the trees, fanning their ears to keep themselves cool. Do you realise an elephant can lower its body temperature by as much as sixteen degrees just by flapping its ears?"

"Then I wish I had ears as big as that." His words had made me uneasy again.

The driver rocked with laughter. "Him got big ears." He pointed at Karanja, leaning forward, still laughing, his teeth white. "You flap now, Karanja. Make cool."

"Time we got going," I said.

"No hurry." Abe leaned back, his eyes half closed. "We've been driving since first light."

"We can't just sit here on the off chance he'll pass this way." I reached for the map. "We're about fifteen miles from where Pat Murphy saw the Land-Rover abandoned and there's another track running direct to Maralal."

"Sure there's another track, but not suitable for vehicles and Delden needs transport. He's a long way from Marsabit, and a Land-Rover out of gas is about as much use to him as a load of scrap." He sat up suddenly. "I don't think you quite understand the sort of man he is. He'll have seen that aircraft circling and the patrol when it comes will take this road."

I stared at him. "He can't jump an Army patrol."

He shrugged, leaning back and closing his eyes again. Karanja moved uneasily, searching the bush as a dove went clattering through the branches above us. Away to the south, the cackling of guinea fowl came faintly on the still air. The heat was heavy after the night's rain and I felt drowsy, lying back and staring up at white drifts of cloud hanging over the mountains. "I think we go back now," Karanja said. He was getting agitated. "When the patrol come they want to know what we are doing on this road."

"It will be several hours yet before a patrol gets here." Abe shifted on to one elbow, listening as a bird whistled urgently in the bush behind us. A moment later it took flight, a metallic flash of blue. "Starling," Karanja said. "Something disturb him." The guinea fowl had ceased their cackling, everything very still and quiet as though the bush held its breath, waiting. And then suddenly van Delden was there, coming soundlessly out of the undergrowth behind us. Mukunga was with him and they both had rifles. Mtome and a very erect, very good-looking man I hadn't seen before appeared on the opposite side of the track. All of them had old khaki knapsacks, bandoliers stuffed with ammunition, blankets rolled and slung round their shoulders.

"Karanja."

"Ndio, Bwana." He had leapt to his feet, his eyes staring.

"You came to find me?"

Karanja nodded, speechless.

"How did you know where I was?"

"The pilot," Abe said.

Van Delden stood there for a moment, looking down at us. Then he came and sat beside me, placing his rifle carefully on the ground. "I was expecting a patrol."

"The pilot doesn't have to file his report till the morning," Abe said. "He stuck to his routine."

"Didn't he have orders to look out for the Land Rover?"

"He said he owed you something. His name's Murphy."

"Pat Murphy? Yes, I remember." He nodded. "So we've a little time yet before a patrol comes." He said something to Karanja, who moved quickly to the fire. "And you came looking for me. Why?"

Abe shrugged. "Not sure really. But we have a permit to go as far as Lake Rudolf. Thought you might need a lift."

Van Delden shook his head. "A vehicle, that's all I need." He looked from one to the other of us, his pale eyes watchful. "While tea is brewing maybe you'll tell me how you got hold of an old safari bus and a permit to enter the Military Zone." He gave an order to Mukunga and his three Africans squatted down by the fire, watching us. "And Karanja. What's Karanja doing here?"

"He's on loan to us as guide."

He laughed, that same harsh bark. "You have a way of getting what you want, don't you, Mr. Finkel. So what are you going to film now?"

"That depends on you," Abe said. "If we give you a lift—"

"No."

Abe gave a little shrug. "I guess you don't understand what television can do for you." He hesitated, then changed the subject. "I take it you're headed for Marsabit." Van Delden didn't reply. His eyes had shifted to the slopes above us and Abe said, "You saw those elephants?"

"They winded us."

"Is this their territory, or are they on the move with a definite purpose?"

Van Delden shrugged. "D'you know anything about the migration of elephants?"

"A little."

"Their normal range, for instance?"

"Scientific records suggest the limit is about eighty miles."

"Records—scientific records—" His emphasis on the word *scientific* was contemptuous. "The only official records are for park conditions. Elephants are quick to learn the limits of their protected area."

"And when it's no longer a protected area, what then?"

Van Delden shook his head. "Who knows? There were no so-called scientists recording data when the Cape elephants were wiped out by my father's forbears, or when British hunters eliminated the vast herds of southern Africa, shooting them for their ivory and for the fun of killing. Who's to say that some of those elephants didn't trek north, away from the slaughter area, north into Matabeleland, across the Zambesi? For all any scientist can tell you, man, those elephants you saw up there"—he nodded towards the green-brown slopes—"may be the distant descendants of elephants that came out of Cape Province more than a century and a half ago."

"So they go north, an inherited instinct. Is that what you're saying?"

Van Delden shook his head. "I've lived too long with elephants to be certain of anything. Like man, they're individuals, and, living almost as long, they are unpredictable, each according to his experience, some charging on sight, others fairly tolerant. At Marsabit they had a very restricted range. Just the mountain and its forest area and the grass of the slopes which they shared with the Rendile. They came down into the grasslands at night when the cattle weren't grazing. But there were others that came and went, bulls mainly, trekking from the Tana River, even from this area here. That was what the Boran said. But a scientist wouldn't accept that. He'd need to bug the beast with a bleep transmitter and follow it in an aircraft before he'd believe anything a tribesman told him."

Karanja handed him a mug of tea and he sat there, sipping at it noisily and frowning. "You've got your cameras with you?" Abe nodded. "And you're planning to film Alex Kirby-Smith with his gang of scientific exterminators."

"That wasn't the object," I protested.

But he was looking at Abe. "How did you get Kimani to agree to that?" And when Abe had explained, his eyes fastened angrily on me. "So you traded the film you got with me for the chance of an archaeological find." His voice was hard and unforgiving, the stare of those pale eyes almost baleful. "Mary was right. She said you had no feeling for animals." He turned to Abe again. "Where's Kirby-Smith now?"

"At Baragoi."

He nodded as though he had expected that. "He'll take them as they come out of the South Horr Gap into the near-desert country beyond." And then he was looking at me again. "You'll need a cold heart and a strong stomach, boy. There'll be totos of all ages, from new-born up to a dozen years, all with their mothers, and all led by an old matriarch, a complete family unit, anything from five to fifty strong. He'll bunch them by buzzing them with an aircraft, or maybe he'll use trucks and Land-Rovers to drive them on to his sharp shooters. The matriarch will be shot first, fifty, maybe sixty years of life cut down in a flash, the whole group wiped out in minutes, every cow, every calf." He turned back to Abe. "That way there's no survivor to pass the knowledge of fear and pain and death on to others coming through the mountains, no warning to the next unsuspecting family. Something for your captive TV audience to gloat over." He slung his empty mug at Karanja and got to his feet. "I'm taking your vehicle."

"Does it occur to you," Abe said quietly, "that the captive audience may feel the way you do, that the sight of such wholesale slaughter will sicken . . ."

"There won't be any slaughter if I can help it." He spoke quickly to

Mtome, who began getting our bags out of the minibus. "And if you were able to film it, do you think you'd be allowed to take that film out of the country?"

"Maybe not. But with your help we could smuggle it out." Abe got to his feet.

"Stay where you are." He was moving towards the minibus. "Dima." He motioned the tall African into the back. Mtome followed him, Mukunga standing beside the door, his rifle cradled on his arm.

"You're making a mistake," Abe said. "We come along with you now, we could film it all from your point of view. A great story. I could really make something of it."

"You'd make a lot of money. That's what you mean, isn't it? Like Alex, you're not thinking of the elephants, only of money."

"You're wrong. That's not why I'm here." Abe moved towards him. "What about it, van Delden? I'm offering you a world audience, the chance to make them understand the nature of elephants and what's happening to them in Africa."

But he shook his head. "What I have to do . . . I don't want anybody else involved." He had the door open and reached inside. "But you can have your cameras." He dumped the cases on the ground beside our bags.

I scrambled to my feet. "You can't just leave us here. We only turned down this track because we knew you were in trouble."

"Relax," Abe said. "He's not going to take us and the patrol will be here in a few hours."

Van Delden was moving round to the driver's seat and Karanja started forward, a tense, urgent look on his face. I thought for a moment he was going to try something desperate. So did Mukunga, but he was too late. Karanja was already on the far side of the vehicle, talking urgently to van Delden. He seemed to be pleading with him. Then van Delden did a strange thing. He put his arm across Karanja's shoulder, a gesture of affection almost.

They were like that for a moment, Karanja staring up at the other with a rapt expression, then he was nodding and van Delden got into the driving seat. He nosed the minibus into the bush, backed and turned it. "Karanja." He leaned out of the window, speaking quickly in Swahili. Karanja nodded, sweat on his face and his eyes wide. Mukunga climbed in and the bus moved off, a thick cloud of dust hanging in the air as it disappeared round the bend where the elephants had crossed the road.

I turned to Karanja. "What were you telling him?"

He shook his head, his eyes still on the dust cloud. "Is nothing."

"What was it?" I insisted.

"I offered to go with him." He turned away then, adding angrily, "But he don't want me."

"There was something else," Abe said. "Something about Kirby-Smith. I distinctly heard him mention the major's name."

"Is a message, that's all."

"What was the message?"

Karanja hesitated, then he shrugged. "I am to tell him if he kills elephants his men will die."

"Did he mean it?"

Karanja nodded unhappily. "He always mean what he say."

Abe looked at me, his dark eyes sombre. "There's a line: *Now he is treading that dark road.* . . ." He shook his head, the corners of his mouth turned down. "It isn't just a civilian outfit he's up against. Kirby-Smith has the support of the Army and in every African unit there'll be men who've been hunters or trackers all their lives." He turned to Karanja. "You going to pass that message on to Major Kirby-Smith?"

"Yes. I tell him." His eyes rolled, the whites showing. "You know I have to explain how we lose our vehicle and everything in it."

We went on talking about van Delden for a while, but gradually the heat overcame us and we lay there waiting as the sun slid down the brazen sky and the shadows lengthened. There was no wind, nothing stirring, no sound except the sleepy murmuring of doves. I was dozing when the patrol arrived.

They came in a truck, the driver slamming on his brakes at the sight of us, soldiers tumbling out of the dust cloud, deploying with their guns at the ready. They looked tough, battle-trained men, their camouflage green merging into the bush. Karanja called to them, stepping out into the road and walking towards the stationary truck where a corporal stood waiting. He talked to him for a moment, then orders were shouted, the soldiers climbing back into the truck, and it came on to stop beside us. "You get in now," Karanja said. "When we find the Land-Rover I talk with the corporal about transport."

"That Land-Rover would do us fine," I said.

But Karanja shook his head. "Is Army vehicle."

We slung our gear into the back of the truck and clambered up, the soldiers making room for us. "Looks like our only hope is Kirby-Smith," Abe said doubtfully. The black faces around us were covered in dust, watchful and unsmiling. About three miles down the road we rounded a rock outcrop and ran slap into a barricade of thorn, the truck slamming to a halt, enveloping us in dust. It was the ideal place for an ambush, the road blocked and rocks all round. Under a wild fig we found the blackened embers of a fire, the stripped remains of a dik-dik carcase lying on the ground beside it. The thorn barrier took some time to clear, so that it was dark when we reached the Land-Rover. The embers of another, larger fire, some blankets thick with dust, and two empty jerri-cans lying on the ground.

It was cooler now, the soldiers more friendly as a fire was lit and food prepared, the empty tank of the Land-Rover filled with petrol. Over the meal Karanja talked to the corporal, trying to persuade him to let us go on to Baragoi in the Land-Rover. I don't know whether it was the military permit or the need to radio a report of van Delden's movements that finally decided him, but shortly after eight we got into the Land-Rover and started back up the track, the corporal driving us.

It was a clear moonlit night and he drove fast. At Maralal he stopped at the old safari lodge, now a military post, to radio his report back to headquarters. The town itself was off the main road, but all round the junction leading to it rough shelters sprawled over the grass, a great concentration of tribesmen driven into the mountains in search of food and water. Beyond Maralal the road climbed steeply through a forest of trees and it became quite cold. "Soon we come to viewpoint," Karanja said. "Maybe we stop there."

The trees were a black arch in the headlights, their branches blotched with some growth that was pale like lichen. And then they ceased and we were out on to the top, in a burned brown scrub of moorland. Far away to our right the shadow of the Mathews Range stood against the sky and to our left the land dropped steeply down into the Rift and the valley of the Suguta. The moon was clouded now and we did not stop, driving on and on through desolate country, the dirt road gradually losing height as we wound our way down towards Baragoi. I slept fitfully, my head lolling as the Land-Rover bucked and jolted over the uneven surface, and then suddenly we were there, driving slowly down a street of grey dirt flanked by dukas, the village shops that had been built by Asians long ago. It was a dilapidated miserable place, the wood and daub buildings falling into ruin and sleeping bodies lying in the dust.

The military post was a huddle of tents and trucks on the edge of a landing field east of Baragoi. He stopped at the guard tent and while the corporal and Karanja explained themselves, Abe and I stretched our legs. The night was clear again, the moon set, and all around us, at every point of the compass, the jagged outline of mountains reared up like cut-outs against the stars. Abe nodded towards the north, where the Horr Valley showed as a black V. "I wonder if he made it through the gap there?"

I thought he probably had, but dawn would find him exposed on the semi-desert land beyond, and right beside us was a Cessna. It was the only plane on the field, and if it was serviceable, one quick sweep northwards would be enough, the dust stream of the minibus visible for miles. "How far do you reckon he'll have got by sunrise?"

Abe glanced at his watch. "Five hours from now, and he's about six hours ahead of us—that's eleven hours motoring from Baragoi." He shook his head. "He'll have run out of gas long before then."

"So he won't make Marsabit?"

"Not a hope." He looked at me, a sidelong glance. "Was he ever going there?"

"Where then?"

He shrugged, and I felt a sudden prickle of uneasiness. We were on the threshold now of country that van Delden knew better than anyone else. Karanja returned to say that Major Kirby-Smith was now camped about five miles beyond South Horr and the question of transport would have to wait until the morning.

We spent the rest of that night in the Land-Rover and woke in the dawn to the sound of voices and the movement of men as the camp came alive. I had never been in a military post before and my chief recollection of it is the open latrines, with African soldiers squatting and jabbering, dung-brown beetles crawling in human excrement, and the wood smoke smell of cook fires hanging in the still air. There must have been over a hundred Africans there including hangers-on and when the officer in command saw us shortly after seven he had already been in contact with Kirby-Smith's outfit and established that a vehicle had crossed the lugga near their camp about ten-thirty the previous evening. Captain Kioko was still interrogating us through Karanja when an orderly came in to say that Major Kirby-Smith was on his way to Baragoi.

He arrived about half an hour later. I was sitting in the shade of one of the trucks rereading von Höhlen's account of the Teleki expedition's first sighting of Lake Rudolf when the open Land-Rover roared into the camp. There were two of them in it, the windscreen folded flat and both of them wearing goggles. He stopped by the Cessna to have a word with the pilot, who was working on the engine, then he drove on to the command tent. Karanja was waiting for him there and when they had ducked inside the flap I returned to my book. We were so near to Lake Rudolf now that reading about it gave me the illusion that I had leapt the intervening miles of desert and lava and was already there.

I was reading again the passage that begins: "Almost at our last gasp, we hastened towards the slightly rippled sheet of water" when a shadow came into my line of vision and a husky voice said, "So it is you. Where is he, do you know?"

I looked up, recognising her voice, and for a moment I was too surprised to say anything. She was wearing the same faded safari jacket, the bush hat pulled down over her eyes. The book slipped from my hands as I scrambled to my feet, pleasure at seeing her again overcoming the sense of shock that she really was with Kirby-Smith. "I didn't realise it was you—in that Land-Rover."

"Where was he going?" she demanded, her face set, and no sign of greeting. "Was it Marsabit?"

"He didn't say."

"He must have told you something when he took your vehicle. What was it, a minibus? That's what we were told over the radio."

I nodded, conscious of the tightness of her lips, the strained look in her eyes.

"Was there enough petrol on board for him to reach Marsabit?"

"No, I don't think so."

"Just as well," she murmured. "Marsabit is no place for him now. Alex says there's hardly anything left of his sanctuary. It's been agronomised, most of the forest cut down to make way for shambas." She was staring at me, her eyes wide. "Why the hell didn't he make for the coast?"

"Perhaps if you'd been with him—"

"It wouldn't have made any difference." She bent quickly down, picking up my book and glancing at the title. "Still thinking about Lake Rudolf?"

I laughed. "Not far now, but it seems the last part is the most difficult. I need transport."

"I'll talk to Alex. Maybe he can help. You shouldn't have let him get away with your minibus."

"We had no alternative."

She nodded. "No, of course not. Did he say anything about Kulal?" I shook my head.

"Some years back he tried very hard to have the rain forest on top of the mountain made into a game reserve. He was very friendly with John Mallinson at the Mission there. Do you think he was making for Kulal?'

'No.'

She was silent for a moment, her head turned to the north. "So he's somewhere out there, waiting." And she added almost in a whisper, "God! If only he'd got out while he had the chance."

I had a feeling then that it wasn't her father she was worrying about, and the question that had been at the back of my mind from the moment I had seen her burst from my lips. I asked her why she had gone off with a man whose business was to kill the animals that had been her father's whole life. "I don't understand," I said. "I searched the hotel. . . ."

"You don't understand?" Her eyes blazed suddenly in the sunlight. "You saw what he did to that elephant. You were there. You saw Mukunga and Mtome drive it, with the snare still round its leg and the foot so rotten it was almost falling off. . . . Anyway, it's none of your business what I do." And she added fiercely, "At least Alex kills cleanly."

These words, the way she defended him . . . I stood there, staring at her dumbly, knowing now that it wasn't just for the story she was here. It was something else and I didn't want to think about it, remembering what she said about his charm. And at that moment the Cessna's engine burst into life. I could see the pilot sitting at his controls, running through his checks. "Is that an Army plane?" I asked, glad of the excuse to break the awkward silence between us.

"No, it's ours—part of the outfit."

"And it's being sent up to look for him?"

She nodded.

"Can't you do something?" I was thinking of the tough, wild African soldiers I had seen in the camp here and what would happen when the pilot reported seeing the minibus.

But all she said was, "If he'd seen what I've seen these last two days . . . the effect of this drought. As soon as you're clear of the mountains, all to the north . . ." The Cessna was moving now and a stream of dust enveloped us as it turned and began taxing out to the end of the dirt runway. "There's been no rain up there, no rain at all. Every well, every waterhole is dry." And she added, as though to justify her acquiescence in the search, "If we don't find him, that's something he'll discover for himself. There's no water out there."

"He has four jerricans full."

"That won't last him long in that heat." She turned to face me again. "How many are with him now?"

"Three," I said.

"Mukunga and Mtome. Who else?"

"A man called Dima."

She nodded. "Another ex-poacher. A Boran. All his best shots, except Karanja."

The plane's engine note increased. It had reached the runway end and we watched in silence as it moved towards us, rapidly growing larger. The wheels lifted clear of the ground and it banked slightly, roaring low over our heads as it turned northwards. In a moment it was no more than a speck flying towards the mountains that formed the South Horr Gap. "You should have stopped it," I murmured.

She shook her head, still staring after the plane. "Alex is afraid he'll try and do something stupid."

"And when that plane finds him and they send the Army in—what happens then?"

She turned on me angrily. "Do you suppose I haven't thought about that? But he's got to be stopped, somehow. He could have made for the coast. Instead he came up here, and I think Alex is right."

It was incredible, his own daughter. "You really want him caught."

She gave a little shrug. "Somebody's got to make him see reason, and the sooner they get him out of here—"

"You don't care what happens to him, do you?" I think I wanted to hurt her then. "You're not worrying about your father, only about Kirby-Smith."

"How dare you!" she breathed. "You know nothing about him, or about me. Nothing about either of them."

I could see Karanja waiting in the sun outside the command hut and I told her the message he had been given. "So you'd better make up your mind whose side you're on."

She was staring at me, an appalled look in her eyes. "So Alex was right."

"If Kirby-Smith starts killing elephants . . ." I hesitated, but what the hell? How else could I get through to her, through the thick skin of her apparent hero-worship of the man she was camped with? "When that recce plane gets back," I said, "you'd better arrange it so that you can talk to him. Talk to them both, or somebody's going to get killed."

She stood there for a moment, still with that shocked look in her eyes. I think she was near to tears, her lips trembling, her nostrils flared. But then she turned abruptly and walked away, back towards the open Land-Rover. I watched her go, feeling wretched, her figure tall and graceful in the blazing sun, and knowing the things I had said were better unsaid. I was still worrying about that when Abe appeared round the back of the truck. "What did your girl friend have to say?"

"Nothing," I snapped, angry at the glint of laughter in his eyes.

Kirby-Smith had come out of the command tent. The captain was with him and they were talking to Karanja. "She must have said something," Abe murmured. "You were talking with her long enough."

"She said the plane that just took off belongs to Kirby-Smith and is flying a search."

He nodded. "That was to be expected." He was looking at me curiously as he went on, "But they won't find him, that's for sure. He's too old a hand, and the zebra stripes on that vehicle are designed for sunlight and shade. "Did she tell you why she'd gone off with Kirby-Smith?"

I shook my head, not wanting to talk about it.

"She could be half in love with him." That sardonic smile and the dark eyes laughing at me behind the glasses. "You want some advice?"

"No."

He laughed. "I'll give it to you anyway. Lay her if you can, but don't get involved. She's a man-eater and you're too young for a girl who's half Italian and thoroughly Africanised." He patted my shoulder and turned away as Kirby-Smith came towards us, his face hard and his jaw set, the muscles tight behind the cheekbones.

"Is it true what Karanja says about my men being at risk when we start culling?" He was looking at Abe. "Is that what he said?"

Abe nodded. "Karanja was to give you the message."

"Do you think he meant it? Or was it just an empty threat?"

"No, he meant it."

"Then we'll have to find him. A man like that at large, he's dangerous." His shoulders straightened, his face loosening in that boyish smile. "Well, it shouldn't take long." He turned to the captain. "Once he's located, it'll be up to your boys. But no bloodshed. Get him surrounded so that he gives himself up."

Abe started to protest, but Kirby-Smith shook his head. "They're bush trained. They know their job. Now about your transport problem. You want to join me in my camp at South Horr, Karanja tells me." He paused, his eyes on Abe's face as though trying to gauge his motives. "I don't object to TV coverage of the way I operate, so long as it isn't slanted. We can talk about that later, but it'll be on my terms. Understood?"

"Naturally," Abe said.

His gaze switched to me. "And you?"

I nodded.

"Okay then. Get your gear into my Land-Rover. I'll be leaving just as soon as an Army plane arrives and I've had a word with the pilot."

About half an hour later we heard the sound of it diving down out of the sun, and then it was coming in from the southeast, a twin-engined monoplane with its undercarriage down. It landed in a cloud of dust and when the pilot got out I saw that it was a stranger. I had hoped it would be Murphy.

Kirby-Smith did not wait to see the plane take off and we were halfway to Baragoi when it passed over us heading north. It was a windy hair-raising drive, the wheels skidding on gravel, half floating in patches of sand, nobody speaking. Karanja had dropped his role of courier. Beside us in the back his flat broad-nosed features had a solemn, dejected look. Doubtless the captain had given him hell for turning on to the Baringo track and making van Delden a present of his vehicle, and I was quite certain Kirby-Smith had made him responsible for every foot of film we shot at his camp.

There were mountains on either side of us now, the country thickening as we entered the restricted gap of the Horr Valley. We were between the Nyiru and Ol Doinya Mara ranges then, towering pinnacles of jagged rock glimpsed through the branches of trees, and shortly after ten we ran into the dusty little village of South Horr. Mary turned to Abe. "This is the last village. North of here there's nothing, just desert till you get to Ethiopia." It was the first time she had spoken and by making the observation directly to Abe she made it clear she was still angry with me and not prepared to recognise my presence.

The village, which was little more than a single street, was packed with tribesmen, some of them armed with slender spears, their ear lobes hanging in loops, and many of their women had necks, arms, and ankles encased in rings of copper wire. They pressed so close around us that the Land Rover was reduced to a crawl, the ring of dark faces thrust close, hands reaching out to pluck at us and their speech importunate. Some of the younger men with elaborate hairstyles shook their spears at us, older men thrust cowrie shells into our hands.

"It's all right," Kirby-Smith said over his shoulder. He was talking to them all the time in their own language. "They want food, that's all." An old man, one of the elders, barred our way and we stopped while Kirby-Smith talked with him, everybody, even the young men, listening, silent. These were young warriors—the moran, Kirby-Smith called them —and they stood out like peacocks, slender, arrogant, almost naked, except for those with red blankets they wore like capes, and besides their spears, many of them carried a neck rest in the other hand so that they could lie down without disturbing the ochre plastering of their hair. Their elaborate hairstyles varied, some wearing it twisted in tiny plaits, long and swept back over the head, some in a fringe in front and falling halfway down the back, others in a bun or in two long pigtails, and all of them decked out with necklaces and headbands of seeds or shells.

Finally a way was opened for us and we drove on, and a moment later we were clear of the village, back in the emptiness of the valley. "It's this damned drought," Kirby-Smith said. "They'd never beg like that normally. That old man was telling me again how they'd lost all their cattle and their camels. They've trekked in from the desert on foot, depending on their moran for food, and those showy young men have just about killed everything that moves, except for the big game. That's the effect of hunger. They're an indolent lot normally." He laughed, a surprisingly high sound. "All the same, you don't want to tangle with them. They're a bit like the Masai, very proud, and they can be tricky."

The track snaked between thickets of bush, the trees mainly euphorbia and acacia, some leathery leaved evergreens and wild olives, all laced with the parasitic growth of rope-thick lianas. The air was hot and aromatic, and there were sunbirds flickering darts of colour. About five miles out of South Horr we dropped to a lugga where half-naked women were filling large earthenware pots and old kerosene tins. Clouds of insects that looked like mosquitos hung over the muddy stream. The Land Rover ground up the further slope, and after a few hundred yards we turned off to the right into a stand of giant acacia, where half a dozen tents were scattered round a clearing. Smoke drifted up from an open fire.

This was the base camp, a site, Kirby-Smith said, much favoured by safaris in the old days. "And by elephants," he added, indicating the trunks of the acacias, which all had polished bosses where the animals had rubbed themselves. He handed us over to a tall, very proud-looking African with a brightly coloured kikoi wrapped round his loins. "Eddie is boss-boy here. He'll look after you. The others are all out preparing the airstrip. Don't let the girls bother you." He looked to a little huddle of women squatting at the edge of the clearing. "See you later." And he and Mary Delden drove off, leaving us standing there beside our bags.

Abe looked at me, smiling. "If I've got my geography right, we're now within about thirty miles of your precious lake. And we're still in thick bush, trees all round us and a stream of fresh water close at hand."

"That thirty miles could be as far as the moon if the road is blocked and we've no transport." I wasn't prepared to let him read the typescript of Pieter van Delden's book, but I got volume II of Teleki's expedition out of my grip and handed it to him. "I've marked the passages. Read it and perhaps you'll understand."

Karanja called to us, "You like tea now?" He indicated some canvas chairs grouped around a table under the fly of a tent. "You sit there and I bring you tea." He came with three tin mugs as we were moving our gear into the shade of the tent. "That boy is Masai. I don't like Masai. They are very stupid people."

It was during the day we spent alone in that camp, with nothing to do but read and sit talking about the lake to the north, the lava waste that surrounded it, and about van Delden, that I first began to be really scared about how it would end, a sense of premonition that I tried to pretend was due to the heat and the strangeness of the place. Karanja had cut himself an arbour of shade under a bush and sat there like an animal in its lair, motionless, with his eyes staring at nothing, his face expressionless. The women had gone, driven off by their menfolk, and only the Masai made his presence felt, moving gracefully and doing little, sometimes standing, still as an ebony carving, watching us. The trees towered breathless, their leaves shimmering in the sun's glare, and occasionally, just occasionally, I caught a flicker of a bird. It was hot as an oven with the door open, releasing scents I had never experienced before. It was a heady, overpowering atmosphere and I would not have been surprised if some strange beast out of the past had presented itself before us or an early ape-figure masquerading as man.

Once Abe looked up from von Höhlen's book and said, "That typescript of yours, does it deal with Kulal in detail?"

"Yes, but he was attacked by the men of the rain forest, the Wandrobo. He never got to the top."

"Our friend von Höhlen says it presents 'a *terrible chaos of yawning chasms and ravines, with perpendicular brownish-black precipices, the general character and trend of which*'—he's not exactly my favourite travel writer—'*led us to suppose this to be a continuation of the same fissure as that in which our progress had been arrested during our march along the western face of Mt. Nyiro.*' That, I take it, is the dark fang of a mountain hanging over us now. If so, he says, then this fissure must extend for some forty miles." He let the book fall on his lap, staring at me sleepily. "Sounds pretty rough going. How do you propose getting to the top of it?"

"There'll be a track of some sort. Mary mentioned a Mission."

"Okay, so you get to the top, and it's forest something like we're in now. How the hell do you figure on making an archaeological discovery buried under five or six thousand years of decayed tropical vegetation?"

I shook my head. I hadn't really thought about it. I had been relying on van Delden. But when I told him this he laughed. "Van Delden has other fish to fry and his own safety to consider. He's not going to waste his time searching for pieces of pottery and the remains of an ancient civilisation." He picked up the book again. "Better give some thought to what you plan to do, now you're within striking distance of the lake. And save your film." A bird began a monotonous piping whistle from across the clearing as though calling for rain. Wet-wet-wet, it cried, trailing a long tail from one acacia to the next, where it sat on a branch watching us, its black wings folded, its tail hanging down and a large horned beak, bright red with an ivory tip.

I leaned back and closed my eyes, thinking about what he had said, wondering whether to show him the typescript. And still that feeling that it wasn't just Rudolf that was very close, but something more personal, more frightening. It would have been easy to convince myself that it was no more than the strangeness of my surroundings if I had not experienced this feeling before. Through my closed lids the sun shone red on my eyes, sweat on my chest, and that bird, which I later learned was a Van der Decken's hornbill, piping away, the murmur of insects, everything drowsy in the midday heat. I knew Abe was right. Van Delden wasn't interested in archaeological remains. I could almost wish that they'd find him and ship him out. But I knew they wouldn't, and as I dozed off I saw his face as he had stood looking at the remains of that wooden lodge at the edge of the Serengeti, tears in his eyes.

Dusk had fallen before Kirby-Smith returned, the Land Rover leading in two trucks full of Africans, its headlights cutting a swathe through the trees. They had shot a duiker, and while the carcase of the little antelope was roasting over the fire, we sat drinking warm beer with a pressure lamp hissing behind us and the night full of stars. The plane had been unable to make contact by radio, but the pilot had dropped a message over the nearly completed runway. No sign of the minibus. He had swept an area from the Suguta up as far as Loiyangalani and east across the slopes of Mt. Kulal. "From here to the lake, it's all open country," Kirby-Smith said. "Desert and lava, a few isolated trees. Nowhere he could hide a vehicle except at Loiyangalani among the doum palms. But Jeff says he flew low over the oasis several times. If the vehicle had been there I think he would have seen it. So it must be Kulal."

"The oasis or Kulal, what does it matter?" Mary said in a tight, controlled voice. "He's well clear of your operation."

Kirby-Smith hesitated, his cigarette glowing in the dark. "I'd still like to know," he said quietly. "I've a radio call—"

"Leave him alone, can't you." She got suddenly to her feet, paused a moment as though about to say something more, then turned abruptly and went to her tent.

Kirby-Smith sighed. "She's like her mother," he murmured. "Very emotional, and her mood changing from moment to moment."

"You knew her mother well?" Abe asked.

"Of course." He said it tersely, resisting any intrusion into that part of his life, and switched the conversation back to Kulal. "He may have made it into the great gorge on the eastern side. If he's attempted to reach the top, then there's only one track and it goes past the Mission."

The radio contact was for 2030 hours, but when he had spoken with Northern Army Headquarters he came back, shaking his head. "Their plane had no better luck than mine. Maddox flew from Loiyangalani across Kulal and halfway to Marsabit. Not a sign of him. No tracks visible, nothing." He sat down again and picked up his beer. "So that settles it, he's in the gorge on the eastern side of Kulal. Even Cornelius wouldn't risk foot-slogging it through the Chalbi in a drought."

But later, when Abe had joined me under the fly of the tent we had been allocated, he said, "If you were van Delden, what would you do—in a hijacked vehicle short of gas?"

I had turned in immediately after we had fed and was lying precariously balanced on the seat cushions of one of the trucks, watching a satellite move steadily through the stardust of the Milky Way, enjoying the solitude and thinking of Lake Rudolf, the acacias like a cathedral arch above me and the fire glowing in the night.

"Are you awake?"

"Yes."

He was standing over me rubbing at his teeth thoughtfully with the end of a green sliver cut from the bush the Samburu use to get the brilliant whiteness of their teeth. The toothbrush bush, Mary had called it. "Well, what would you do?" he repeated.

I shook my head. I didn't want to think about van Delden. I just wanted to lie there, pursuing my fantasy of an archaeological find that would be the talk of the academic world.

"Kirby-Smith starts culling tomorrow." He had stayed up talking to him, and now, as he prepared for bed, he was determined to pass on the information he had gleaned. A born newsman, I thought, as he said, "So this is where the action is. If I were van Delden, I know what I'd do. I wouldn't risk that vehicle out in open country. I'd drive it into the bush here and hide up within striking distance of the culling area."

"Too many tribesmen around," I murmured sleepily.

"Yes, but all of them close by the stream." He wrapped himself in a blanket and lay down on the truck seat they had given him.

"What happened to that hand of his? I bet you asked him."

"Sure I did."

"Well, how did it happen?"

"Snake bite." He smiled at me and I wasn't certain whether he was serious. "He was playing around with a mamba. It was when he was a kid and he thought he could handle it like Ionides. So you watch out for yourself." And then he suddenly asked me, "How much film have you got?"

"Not sure. Seven or eight mags. Why?"

"Take my advice. Don't be carried away with the excitement of the kill. Save your film for when van Delden comes on the scene."

"You think he'll carry out his threat?"

"I don't know. But if he does, you'll regret every foot you've wasted."

"Kirby-Smith expects us to film the culling. So does Karanja."

"So long as you've got a mag on your camera and they can hear it running, they won't know whether you're taking pictures or not. I've got about the same number as you, so maybe we'd better take it in turns. You want to save some for Rudolf—if you ever get there." He reached out, rummaging in his grip. "You taken your anti-malarial tablet?"

"I took it last Sunday. You only have to take them once a week."

"I'm told it's safer to take the daily dose." Something moved in the bush behind me. There was a snort, and then all hell broke loose, the crash of branches, the padded thud of rushing feet and a body like a tank hurtling past me. I was so close I felt the wind of it, smelled the musky smell of it, and then I saw it wheeling in the firelight, head lowered as it charged one of the tents, its long horn ripping the canvas, tossing it in shreds over its back. Suddenly the camp erupted, yells and shouts as the Africans tumbled out of sleep, and Kirby-Smith was there, a gun in his hand. But by then the rhinoceros had disappeared, leaving the wreckage of the tent scattered on the ground.

Karanja appeared, looking scared. Somewhere a man was screaming, a thin sound like an injured rabbit. "Lord God!" Karanja sniffed the air, the whites of his eyes gleaming in the starlight. "I never know that only once before."

"When was that?" Mary was suddenly there and her voice was shaky.

But Karanja shook his head. "Long time back," he muttered, and went to join Kirby-Smith by the remains of the ripped-up tent. Flames leapt as branches were dragged on to the fire, black bodies in silhouette. The screaming died away. "There's a breeze coming from behind us, off the mountain," Mary said as we moved to follow Karanja. "The camp was downwind of the beast, so it wasn't us that panicked that rhino."

Kirby-Smith was straightening up, a hypodermic in his hands. "Flattened," he said. "Not much I can do for the poor guy." He was staring past us at the dark shape of the mountain, black against the rising moon. "One of my best trackers, too." He looked at Abe, his face set. "Did you hear anything? You were close to where it came out of the bush."

Abe shook his head, and I said, "There was a crashing in the undergrowth, and then suddenly it was going past me like—"

"But before that. Did you hear anybody shout, any sound of voices in the bush?"

"No, nothing."

He turned to the ring of black faces crowding round us, questioning his men in Swahili. But they shook their heads, jabbering excitedly, their voices high in anger or fear—I wasn't certain which. In the end he posted sentries and went back to his tent. The camp gradually settled down again, but it was a long time before I got to sleep, and when I did I seemed to be waked almost immediately by the voice of the nearest sentry talking to his relief. The two Africans were sharp and clear in a shaft of moonlight. It was almost five and I lay awake until dawn began to steal over the mountains to the accompaniment of the chatter of some vervet monkeys and a rising chorus of birds. It was the dawn of a terrible day.

III

The dawn was cool, a freshness in the air, the mountains dark above the trees. I wanted to sleep now, but the camp had already come alive, full of the sound of African voices. Abe appeared, shaved and dressed, handing me a mug of tea. "Better get moving. We'll be off in a few minutes."

Two crows eyed me from a branch as I sat drinking my tea on the cushions to which I had clung during the night. "It's barely light," I muttered. "Do we have to start this early?"

"Elephants are sensible beasts. When the sun's up they move into deep shade."

"You got some sleep, did you?"

"Now and then, when you weren't snoring." He cocked his head, listening. "Sounds like the Army," he said, and I heard the drone of an engine coming from the direction of South Horr. "They're sending a patrol out with trackers."

"What for?"

"What do you think? Rhinos don't normally charge into a camp like that."

The truck's note changed as it ground through the lugga and Kirby-Smith came into my line of vision, neat in freshly laundered slacks and bush shirt, all khaki except for the bright splash of silk at his neck. Two Africans were with him, both with rifles.

"There was a man injured, wasn't there?" The whole episode was vague, like a dream.

"He's dead. Died almost immediately."

I remembered the hypodermic, the look of anger on Kirby-Smith's face. The truck bumped its way into the camp and came to a stop, spilling soldiers. A sergeant jumped out of the cab, went up to Kirby-Smith, saluting. Heads lifted to a roar of sound and a plane swept low over the tops of the acacias, heading north.

"Get dressed," Abe said, "or you'll be left behind."

The tea was thick and sweet. I gulped it down and reached for my clothes. "What's the plane for?"

"Spotter. The pilot is Kirby-Smith's partner. Name of Jeff Saunders."

Karanja appeared with two plates as I was pulling on my trousers. "Ten minutes," he said. "Okay? You take good pictures today." Two eggs each, some sausages, and a hunk of bread. I ate quickly, then went out into the bush rather than use the Africans' latrine. I thought of the night and that rhinoceros, feeling vulnerable despite the movement in the camp. Engines were being started up and through the leaves of a toothbrush bush I saw the patrol move off towards the mountains behind us, a tracker leading them. By the time I had finished, men were climbing into the vehicles. There were four trucks, all 15 cwt. J4s, open-sided with wire mesh guards over the radiators and handbars at the back of the cab. Kirby-Smith led the convoy out in his Land-Rover, Mary beside him and two Africans in the back.

We were in the last truck, and as we pulled out, the sergeant was posting guards round the camp. Karanja, standing beside me, gripping the handbar, pointed to a mound of freshly dug earth, the grave of the man who had been killed in the night. "One time that man serve with me as game scout. Tembo van Delden very hard man."

"What do you mean?"

But all he said was, "He is a Turkana same as Mtome. Abdoul and Mtome, the best trackers Tembo ever had." He shook his head. "Very hard man," he said again as we turned on to the main track and roared north into the choking dust of the convoy. The mountains fell away from us on either side, dim in that cold early light, and the thick bush dwindled, the only colour the flame of a shrub that was bright as a rose against the arid brown patches of sand. We crossed a deep-sided lugga, clinging tightly as the truck nosed down into the dry gravel bed, lifting its metal snout to the further side, gears grinding and the engine roaring.

It was then we saw our first manyata, a complete village of pigmy huts like up-ended wicker baskets. But no humans there. It was deserted, the boma surrounding it a withered tracery of thorn, thinned out by wind and sand so that it looked like dannert wire. The sand increased, the mountains dwindling away to nothing behind us, lost in the thorn scrub, and ahead, over the lip of the horizon, a lump began to take shape. A rock, a mountain? It was hard to tell in that pale light with nothing to measure it by, only the stunted trees, the stiff dried scrub.

"Kulal," Karanja said. "Kulal is where upepo is born. Upepo is the great wind that sweeps the lake."

"Have you been there?" I asked.

But he shook his head. "Only Marsabit. Kulal is very much bigger than Marsabit Mountain."

The dust cloud ahead of us thinned as the convoy turned off the track, driving fast over open scrub to where the Cessna stood parked beside a tent, a windsock hanging limp like an elephant's trunk. We came to a halt, the four trucks in line as though paraded for inspection, the drivers leaving their engines running and hurrying to the Land-Rover. The pilot was talking to Kirby-Smith, a younger man, black-haired with glasses and a pale blue shirt, his arm pointing back across the lugga as he leaned over the lowered windscreen. He made a circling movement, nodding, and then he hurried off to his plane.

From where we stood in the back of our truck we could see the flat expanse of the makeshift airstrip, scrub and boulders piled along the line of its single runway, and beyond it the thicker bush that marked the line of the lugga, acacias with flattened tops, and further still the greener growth spilling from the low arms of the mountains, the Horr Valley a sharp gash between cedar-dark slopes and the sky beginning to take on colour, the first rose tints of the rising sun. The Cessna's engine burst into life, streaming dust as it turned, the drivers running back from their briefing, everybody in a hurry and no time wasted.

The Land-Rover moved off, turning and coming alongside us. "Well, this is what you came for," Kirby-Smith yelled, his mouth stretched in a tight hard grin, goggles pushed up on his forehead, his left hand glinting silver in the sun, a metal split grip instead of the glove and the junction with the flesh of his forearm plainly visible now that he was in a short-sleeved shirt. "Watch your cameras and keep your heads down. I don't want anybody hurt and you haven't done this before. Okay?" He snapped the goggles down, gave a signal for the trucks to follow him and roared off down towards the lugga, driving one-handed and trailing a cloud of dust.

"You see something now," Karanja shouted in my ear. His teeth were white in his black face, his eyes shining. Suddenly I caught his mood and found myself in the grip of a wild appalling excitement, my blood singing as the dust and wind flowed past me. I called something to Abe, but he paid no attention, his eyes on the plane, which was climbing steeply from the strip towards the mountains.

A track had been cut diagonally across the lugga and we took it at speed, wheels thumping the mudguards, and then we were into scrub, bashing our way through the thorn bushes, branches whipping across us and the dust choking. The plane was ahead of us now, circling and diving into a green patch of trees, its wings brushing their tops as it banked. The bush thickened until we were jinking between trees in second gear. And then we were in a clearing and Kirby-Smith was out of the Land-Rover, the lead truck stopped and men with rifles running to take up their positions. The second truck peeled off to the left. The one ahead of us turned right and we followed it. The stout stems of a toothbrush bush reared up over the radiator and I ducked to the crash of branches and the strong scent of its shredded leaves and pulped stems. When I looked again we were on our own and driving slower, the man riding beside the driver standing now, holding something in his hand. A glint of silver and the plane passed over us, leaving behind the roar of its engines. A short sharp bang like a backfire was followed by a squeal and then a trumpeting sound. And suddenly I saw them, grey humps through the bushes, huddled close, and the driver slammed on the brakes as one of the humps swung round, changing in an instant to a menacing spread of ears, the trunk swinging forward.

I saw the small eyes glaring, heard the thin squeal of rage as it charged, charged like lightning, and without hesitation. The driver had the truck in reverse. We were crashing backwards through the bushes, and the man beside him was swinging his arm in a wild forward movement. Something sailed through the air, the elephant looming large, dust rising from its feet. There was a flash, the crack of an explosion, and the elephant stopped, bewildered. The driver stood on the horn. Karanja was yelling, we were all yelling, and the man who had thrown the thunderflash was pounding on the door panel. The truck was stationary now, the engine ticking over, and the great beast shook its head and turned, moving off to rejoin the others. The driver took his hand off the horn and said something to the man beside him, who nodded.

"They say it is the leader." Karanja's voice trembled with excitement. "They're all cows, cows with totos. You see, they begin to move now."

We sat there, waiting, listening to the others shouting and banging on the sides of their trucks. Then we were off again, swinging back on our tracks, moving slowly and glimpsing the grey shapes through the leafy screen of the bushes. We were riding the edge of the herd, ready to halt them if they broke our way. But they kept straight on, moving like ghosts, silently and fast in an attempt to get away from the smell and din of the trucks' engines behind them. And all the time the plane kept circling overhead. Suddenly we were on the edge of the clearing and my ribs rammed against the handbar as we stopped with a jerk, the engine killed. The elephants had stopped, too. I said something, I don't know what, and the driver hissed at me. "Please. No talk."

I counted five fully grown elephants, two with very small calves under their bellies. There were seven youngsters in all, some of them half grown. A total of twelve. The largest elephant was in the rear of the herd and she paused as though unhappy about the clearing, not sure which way to go. She turned and faced us, her ears spread wide, her trunk raised like a periscope, feeling the air. The sun was over the mountains, shining full on her, and I knew it was the one that had charged us. The trunk moved to and fro, testing and probing. There was a small breeze stirring the leaves above my head.

The whole herd had faced about, the cows' trunks waving, all of them undecided. There was no sound from the trucks now, but that breeze must have carried the taint of petrol fumes for the leader suddenly shook her head, turning and slapping one of the babies with her trunk, nudging it back under its mother. She laid her trunk for a moment across the other's neck as though to comfort her, then moved round into the lead and the whole herd started for the far side of the clearing, moving fast.

That was when Kirby-Smith shot her. The sharp sound of his gun was merged with the thunk of the heavy bullet smashing hide and bone. I saw the great beast check, watching the head sag, the ears folding back, and before she had fallen there were shots slamming in from all around the clearing. Three adults were down, another threshing wildly, then the little ones were falling in a cacophany of shots and squeals and trumpeted roars of pain.

In less than two minutes it was over, and all was quiet, only the great mounds of inanimate elephants lying like giant boulders in the slanting sunlight and the hunters coming out into the open, moving slackly like men who have drunk too much, their rifles across their shoulders and still smouldering with the kill.

The truck's engine sparked into life. We were moving out into the open and when we stopped Kirby-Smith was looking up at us, the goggles pushed up on his forehead, his eyes sparkling bright, his teeth showing between his lips. "Now you know about culling—short and sweet, not a lingering death like that poor beast at the Lodge."

He didn't have to give his men orders. They knew their business and they were already out of the trucks, axes in their hands, chopping away at the heads of the five adults, cutting out the tusks. The hunters exchanged rifles for knives, ripping into the hides, exposing the still-warm flesh. Kirby-Smith was back at the Land-Rover with the long antenna of an aerial up, the mike close to his lips. The cook-boy was scattering diesel from an old jerrican onto a pile of branches and in an instant a fire blazed at the edge of the clearing.

I had climbed out of the truck and was leaning against it, the excitement drained out of me, my mouth dry and my legs trembling. Abe was already crouched in front of the fallen leader, his camera levelled as the two Africans pulled one of the tusks from the axed socket. It came out, red at the root, and they stood it on its tip, laughing and talking as they measured it with their eyes, passing it from hand to hand to test its weight. Abe had straightened up and was standing quite still, surveying the scene, arms limp and the camera hanging at his side. He called to me and beckoned. They were working to loosen the other tusk now and I went over and joined him, gazing down at the great head lying still, the limp trunk with the gaping hole below the glazed orb of the eye, surprised to see that the lid had lashes of fine hair.

"Guns are like power saws," he said, speaking slowly. "I once filmed a redwood being felled. Four hundred years old, they said. Four hundred years to grow and it was cut down in minutes. Have you reckoned up the years of animal growth lying dead around us?"

I shook my head, staring fascinated as the second tusk was worked back and forth to loosen it from its socket. It gave suddenly and the two men tugging at it fell on their backs laughing.

"Twelve elephants. Could be a total of two hundred and fifty to three hundred years cut down in less than that number of seconds. That's progress for you, the march of civilised man. Enough meat to keep a hundred humans alive for another week. Maybe more, I don't know, but—" He gave a shrug. "So little gain for so much destroyed." He turned and looked at me, his glasses glinting in the sun. "You didn't take any pictures."

"No."

"Your blood was up and you were yelling. Did you know you were yelling?"

I didn't answer, remembering the exhilaration of the hunt, feeling ashamed. He smiled, patting my arm. "It's the Saxon blood, I guess. You're a barbarian at heart."

"And you?" I asked. "Didn't you feel any excitement?"

"No. We're an older, more sensitive race. City dwellers with a long history. I felt as though it were myself out there, as though I were this poor beast trying to lead my people away from the guns and persecution."

A voice behind us said, "We'll start with this one. How old would you say she is?" It was Kirby-Smith, and Mary was beside him, notebook open in her hand, her dark face streaked with dust and sweat, the mark of goggles still around her eyes.

"I don't know," she said. "But she was the leader, so she'll be on her last set."

"I wonder how far they've come. They're not in very good shape." Kirby-Smith bent down, tugging at the rubbery lip in an attempt to get the mouth open. The two Africans came to help, pulling the trunk clear and prising the jaw open with their axe handles. "New molars coming forward, but the eight in use well worn." His head was almost inside the gaping cavity of the mouth. "Say forty years approximate. List her as SH.1. I'll have one of the molars extracted for microscopic analysis." He gave an order to the two Africans, still feeling around the inside of the jaw. He straightened up, wiping his hand on his trousers. "A cross-section of the root gives us the age," he said, looking at us. "The layers of dentine can be counted, rather like rings on the stump of a tree. There's a study being made now of the age at which cow elephants become herd matriarchs. This one I think is younger than average. She may have just taken over as leader, possibly breaking away from a larger group, or perhaps the old leader was killed. It's an interesting field for study." And he moved off to the next adult, lying collapsed on its side, a gaunt grey mound.

"All done in the interest of science," Abe murmured. But I was looking at Mary Delden, standing notebook in hand and watching as Kirby-Smith worked to prise open the jaws, the gaping tusk wounds oozing blood. She hadn't said a word to me, hadn't even looked at me.

"For your information," Abe said, grasping my arm, "an elephant has six teeth on each of the upper and lower jaws, only two in use at any time, and these are replaced by new molars moving forward from the back of the jaw. In the full span of its life it goes through a total of six sets of teeth. You're not listening."

"Six sets," I said, staring at Mary's neat straight back and thinking of her father, wondering whether some tribesman would inform him of the death of these elephants. "Can't see how it helps to know their age." Could van Delden really carry out his threat—would he dare, against an organisation as efficient as this?

"Science, my friend. A lot of elephants have been killed over the years to prove this method of ageing them. We mustn't belittle the sacred cow of science."

Karanja called to us, coming from the fire with mugs in his hand, and I was suddenly conscious of my thirst. Work stopped, the place like a factory pausing for its tea-break, and, as we stood around drinking, the first of the meat trucks came in from our South Horr camp, the back of it full of Samburu tribesmen. They rushed at the carcases and had to be driven off at gunpoint. Guards were then posted and each man allowed to cut about a kilo from the flesh of one of the smaller elephants. More trucks were coming in, one of them so crowded with tribesmen they were clinging to the back of it like a swarm of bees. Others were beginning to arrive on foot and soon the clearing was a mass of half-naked Africans, all with long sheath knives of bright honed steel, their hide-covered handles worn with use. In an instant it seemed three of the carcases had been stripped to the bone.

Kirby-Smith had obviously experienced this sort of thing before. He was out there, standing guard with his men on the other carcases. He had a shotgun in his hand and when the first wild rush was spent he picked on a young warrior, red with ochre and splashed with blood, who was cutting out a huge chunk. He shouted at him, and when the man ignored his order, he raised his gun and fired into the ground at his feet. The moran screamed with pain, falling back and scrabbling at his legs, which were blasted more by sand than shot. The whole ant-like mass of Africans was suddenly frozen into stillness. He called the elders out then, and with their co-operation some semblance of order was established, so that each man got his share, and those who were willing to work for more helped load the trucks.

It was the sort of scene cameramen dream about, nomadic tribesmen, hunters with guns, and elephants being hacked to pieces, blood everywhere. Close-ups of men, half naked, armed with spears and knives, dark skins stretched over staring rib cages, faces drawn and shrivelled-looking, of dead elephants, of tusks and meat, of Kirby-Smith, the great white hunter, firing at a warrior with his red cloak flung back, his sleek ochred hair coming loose in coils like snakes and his knife flashing. Africa in Drought. I even had the title. But I had no build-up shots of cattle dead around the waterholes, of the Samburu abandoning their manyatas, and the scene in isolation would make no sense. But I knew I was only making excuses. I had missed the opportunity.

And then Abe said, "So you're taking my advice and saving your film. Funny thing," he added, "when it's an interview, just one guy and perhaps deadly dull, you've got a full unit every time. But get a subject like this, when you could throw the works at it, and you're lucky if you've got a single camera that's working, let alone a crew." He watched as the first truck moved off, loaded with meat and trailing a cloud of flies. "I guess we'll have to make a show of filming this evening."

Flies hung thick over the other trucks, crawling on the carcases. There was a smell of urine and a fainter, sweeter smell, the sun already high and blazing down into the clearing, the blue sky turning white with heat. "This evening?" I murmured.

"This evening there'll be another drive. There's a herd stalled in thick bush up on the slopes there and Kirrby-Smith suggested we stay with the hunters this time, show the world how neat and clean he does it. We got to earn our keep."

A second truck went grinding past. The loading was almost complete, the carcasses stripped to skeletal remains that gleamed white and red in the sun. The Samburu were beginning to drift away, clasping their bloody packages of meat wrapped in leaves. "The parable of the fishes, African style. You'll get hardened to it, and so will I, until it becomes just an operation—monotonous." The two last trucks pulled out and work stopped, the hunters drifting towards the fire, the cook-boy pouring out mugs of tea from a huge blackened kettle, and the men drank, their arms and bodies caked with dried blood, the smell of it sour on the shimmering windless air.

A Land-Rover had brought in Kirby-Smith's partner from the airstrip and the two of them were deep in consultation. Mary was sitting alone under the shade of a thorn bush, the branches above her hung with the nests of weaver birds. I had just made up my mind to go over and talk to her when the driver of the last truck returned on foot. He was bogged down in the lugga and we all piled in to one of the hunting vehicles.

The track through the lugga was now so badly churned and rutted that it was almost impassable. Trying to avoid the deep ruts of other vehicles, he had hit a soft patch of sand and was bellied down axle-deep. It took the better part of an hour to dig the vehicle clear, then winch it out backwards, and they still had to get it across the lugga. In the end they had to unload it, get it across empty, and then walk the meat across by hand and reload it on the far side. It was almost two-thirty by the time we were back at the clearing and being issued elephant steaks, fire blackened on the outside, raw inside. I was ravenously hungry, but by then I had had my fill of bloody bundles of meat crawling with flies and my stomach rebelled.

Mary was talking to Karanja and I saw her glance in my direction. She was holding a steak in her hand, tearing at it with her white teeth. She came over. "You're a carnivore, remember." She was smiling, a dribble of fat on her chin, and her fingers clasping the charred steak were streaked red. "Eat up or you'll run out of energy by the end of the day." Her eyes, shaded by the safari hat, were gazing towards the distant mountains. "You didn't film any of it this morning."

"No."

"Why not?"

"I didn't know what to expect."

"The light may not be so good this evening."

"It can't be helped."

"And that scene with the Samburu streaming in, hacking at the carcases. You won't get a repeat of that."

"Lord! A sickening sight like that. Do you think I want to see that again?"

She laughed. "You're all strung up still. But you'll get used to it, and it's what the public wants, isn't it? Plenty of blood, plenty of violence."

"I don't make that sort of film."

"Of course. I forgot. You like it to be remote, discursive, and only long shots of sea creatures dying of pollution."

"Elephants aren't the same as fish," I said. "They're mammals, and no viewer wants to see—"

"Dolphins are mammals, too. And whales." Her eyes glowed brightly, her face still flushed. "But here, it's different. Africa isn't remote like the sea. You're in the thick of it. That's the difference, isn't it?"

"Maybe." And I added angrily, "You're in no position to read me a lecture. What the hell are you doing here?"

Her gaze went back to the mountains and she was silent for a long time. We were both of us silent, eating slowly. "God knows," she breathed. "Something I've asked myself." And she added, "Hunting is in my blood. I guess."

"Elephant cows with young," I said. "Is that what you call hunting?"

She sighed. "Perhaps not. But it's all I'll get." And then, her voice suddenly practical, "Have you got enough film? Alex asked me to find out. He's always refused permission for cameramen to tag along. But now you're here, he's very anxious to have a proper record made of his culling methods. There'll be a truck going into Nairobi tomorrow. With a good supply of film you wouldn't have to be so careful of it."

"There's no film to be had in Nairobi," I said. "At least, that's what Karanja told us."

"The truck will be carrying ivory. If you're trading in ivory you can get anything in Nairobi." She looked at me questioningly. "Well?"

"I'll have a word with Abe," I murmured.

"Surely you're old enough to make up your own mind. There'll be no charge to you. He asked me to make that clear." She hesitated, then she said, "Alex is English, remember. It's the BBC he's interested in, a BBC 2 programme." She shrugged. "Talk it over with Mr. Finkel if you must, but let me know as soon as we get back to camp. I'll need a note of the make of film you require. Okay?"

When I told Abe of the offer, he smiled and shook his head. "Strings," he said. "He gets the film and pays for it, and then he has a say in what you shoot." He sighed. "I came here for the ride, to see a little more of Africa, and what happens?—I'm being pressured back into the business. I don't want to make a film for Alex Kirby-Smith. I don't want to be professionally involved. If I film anything it's the solitude and the beauty I want to film, not bloody massacres, however well-intentioned."

"You took pictures of the tusks being cut out."

"Yes, ivory. I may need that." He stared at me, his brown eyes sad. "You do what you like, Colin. It's a question of motivation. I know what I'm doing here. But do you?" And he added, "Better give it some thought. For all the chance you'll have of getting to Rudolf it might just as well be a thousand miles away."

The fire was already being put out. Orders were shouted and within minutes we were embarked and headed towards the mountains. We were the lead vehicle this time, the Land-Rover close behind us, the back of it piled with tusks and Kirby-Smith pointing the way by signalling with that gleaming metal hand of his as he navigated by compass. Whenever we were halted by a patch of bush so dense that we could not bash our way through, everybody would be out with pangas cutting and slashing.

It was almost five by the time we reached the edge of a dried-up stream bed. The Land-Rover went on ahead, feeling its way up the middle of the lugga, over banks of sand and round gravel beds full of rocks and boulders, until finally the lugga broadened out in a wide curve towards the mountains, which were sharp now against the westering sun. It was then that I used my camera for the first time, filming as Kirby-Smith stood on the seat of the Land-Rover briefing his hunters. Seen through the viewfinder, it was like a picture I had seen of Rommel in that desert war so many years ago, his face burned and creased with the sun, his goggles snapped over the brim of his safari cap. But this was a man briefing African hunters, equipped with .458 magazine rifles which they carried carelessly slung over their shoulders, not German panzer troops, and he was speaking Swahili.

A final gesture of the hand and then my camera was swinging as the Africans ran to their trucks and back again to Kirby-Smith, sitting now with the aerial up, talking into the mike. "So you're going to play along." How long Abe had been at my side I don't know.

"What else?" I asked, and he smiled and shrugged.

"The light's going to be tricky. Some cloud forming and it'll soon be dusk. If I were you I'd open up a stop."

"I know what I'm doing," I told him, my words half drowned in the roar of the Cessna as it passed over. It was so low I was able to trigger off a quick shot at it, its wheels almost brushing the trees on the opposite bank, its nose up as it began to climb. The engine note faded, to be replaced by the sound of the J4s as they fanned out, grinding and slashing through the bush.

"Four cows and about three calves." Kirby-Smith's voice was close beside me, high and sharp. "And Jeff says there's a young bull tagging along." He gripped my arm, his hand tight on my bare flesh. "Keep close to me and you'll be able to film the action as though you were seeing it over the sights of my rifle. I always fire the first shot. That's the signal—when I drop the leader. Got it?"

I nodded and he let go of me, moving quickly to the Land-Rover and backing it into a thicket of evergreens. Then he came back to the lip of the bank, carrying his rifle, a pair of binoculars swung round his neck. The rifle was a Rigby .416 with telescopic sights. He dropped to the ground, snapped the split grip that was his left hand on to the stock, settling himself comfortably on his elbows and slowly raising the gun to his shoulder. It was steady as a rock in the grip of that metal hand. He checked for wind, adjusting the sights, then his face became set in concentration as he swung the barrel across the broad open sweep of the lugga.

He must have heard the hum of my camera as I took a closeup, for he turned on me almost irritably and said, "You can do the personal shots tomorrow. For the moment just keep your mind and your camera on what's going to happen down there in the open curve of the stream bed. You missed a great opportunity this morning. I'm told you didn't take any film at all. In my outfit everybody has to pull his weight." He signalled to the others to get down under cover, then settled himself deeper into the hard sandy ground, took several deep breaths, and relaxed.

The plane swung against the clouds piling up over the mountain, a glint of wings in the slanting sun as it dived. The sound of its engine came to us faintly, and we could hear the trucks still grinding up the slopes as they maneuvered into position for the drive. "About ten minutes," Kirby-Smith said, and motioned Karanja to move further back. "But it could be sooner—you never know. Elephants move fast when they've a mind to." He turned to Mary. "Take the time from the first thunderflash. And then again from my shot to the last beast down. You've got the stop watch?"

She nodded, lying prone beside me. We were all of us lying stretched out on the ground, and after that nobody spoke, the only sound the monotonous call of a dove somewhere behind us. I checked my film. More than a hundred feet to go, almost three minutes' shooting. It should be plenty and I glanced at my watch. Five twenty-seven and the shadows lengthening every moment. The sun was only just above the trees, a bank of cloud below it to the west. If it went into the cloud . . . I was trying to decide what the setting should be if I lost the sun and then the first thunderflash went off. The sound of it was insubstantial, a distant bang. The birds heard it, the grey-headed social weavers setting up a squeaky chatter in a tree behind us that was festooned with their nests. A starling was chattering and whistling on the ground nearby. But the dove was suddenly silent. Far away across the lugga we heard the note of the trucks' engines change as they revved up. There was a faint breeze blowing towards us from the mountains, carrying the sound of shouts, and the Cessna was diving, closer this time. The drive had begun.

"Wind's right and the light's still good." Kirby-Smith's voice was quiet and controlled, no tension at all. "Just relax," he whispered, "and concentrate on the centre of the bank. See that sandbank with the shadow of a tree across it? I shall take the leader about there. The whole bunch will be out in the open then."

I saw the spot and checked the focus, the camera cradled on my arm.
I glanced at Abe, his camera showing above Mary's shoulder as he lay
stretched beside her, and I wondered whether he was going to film the
kill after all. Five twenty-nine and the lower edge of the sun almost
lipping the clouds. But the trucks were coming fast, the sound of their
engines growing, and when next the plane dived it was less than a mile
away. Another thunderflash, followed by squeals, and the sound of trumpeting and of men yelling and beating on the sides of their trucks, the
engines coming nearer.

"Very soon now," Kirby-Smith breathed, his eyes fixed on the far
side of the lugga, the heavy rifle pushed slightly forward, his good hand
on the butt close by the breech. It was a big strong capable hand, the
back of it sun-mottled and the hairs on his bare arms bleached almost
white. A truck appeared on the far bank and stopped abruptly, the two
men in it sitting motionless, watching. The plane came back, flying low,
its engine drowning the noise of the other three trucks, and suddenly
a grey shape appeared far up the lugga, moving fast. Out of the tail of
my eye I saw Kirby-Smith raise the rifle, snugging it into his shoulder.
The gray shape paused on the lip of the bank, trunk raised, scenting the
open space of the lugga. All was quiet, even the birds, a breathless hush.
Then the elephant started down the bank, moving slowly now, and
behind it the backs of others, ears spread, trunks waving.

It was at that moment that somebody fired. It wasn't Kirby-Smith.
The shot came from up the lugga. There was a piercing squeal and the
leader wheeled so fast I could hardly follow her as she plunged back
up the bank. I saw the others turn, all trumpeting and squealing, and
then Kirby-Smith fired, the crash of his rifle so loud my ears sang with
the noise of it. But the leader did not check and in an instant the grey
shapes had vanished from sight. More shots, the roar of engines starting
up, and suddenly a burst of flames from far up the lugga. It was there
for a moment, a great blossom of fire, and then it died to be replaced
by a pall of smoke, rising and drifting, thick and heavy in the breeze.

"God!" Kirby-Smith had dropped his rifle, the binoculars gripped in
one hand, levelled at the smoke. "It's one of the trucks." He leapt up,
seizing his rifle and running for the Land-Rover. I squeezed the trigger
of my camera, taking a wild sweeping shot as I jumped to my feet and
followed him, the others piling in beside me as he started the engine
and we went bucketing down the bank and roared off up the lugga
towards the dense pall of smoke still billowing over the bush ahead.

It was the far flank truck and as we rounded the bend we could see
it out in the open on a sandbank in the lugga, a blackened hulk half
hidden in an oily cloud. All four tyres were alight and burning furiously,
and when we reached it the heat was so intense we could not get near.
Nothing we could do anyway. No water, no fire extinguisher. We just
stood there helpless and watched it burn.

We couldn't even drag the bodies out. There were two of them in the front. We caught a glimpse of their charred remains as the smoke from the burning tyres rolled over them. "Why didn't they jump clear?" Mary's voice was taut above the crackle of the flames. "Surely to God they could have jumped." And Kirby-Smith, close beside her, said, "Wario could have been trapped by the steering wheel." He was tight-lipped and frowning. "But Jilo—he was a youngster, very quick, nothing to stop him jumping clear."

And Abe's voice, whispering in my ear, "Unless he was dead before the petrol tank caught fire."

I turned, saw the look in his eyes, and was suddenly appalled. "For God's sake," I breathed.

"There were shots, several shots." And he added, still speaking so low the others could not hear, "I started life as a newspaper reporter. Seen a lot of accidents and in cases of fire I never saw anybody burn to death without at least some evidence they had tried to get out. And this was an open truck." He nodded at Kirby-Smith, watching him. "Karanja warned him. And he's a hunter. He'll soon work it out."

Mary was staring, her eyes wide, her face pale under the brown skin. Abruptly she turned away, sickened at the sight. The stench of burning rubber hung on the air, and with it the smell of hot metal and blistering paint, the sizzling stink of roasting flesh. Nobody said anything more, even the Africans silent. I didn't know what to think, unwilling to accept Abe's observations, shutting my mind to the implication.

Gradually we all drifted away. Nothing we could do except leave the truck to burn itself out. The elephants were gone, the hunt over, and nobody wanted to talk about it, all of us, white and black, locked in on ourselves, silent. Surely to God it must have been an accident.

A voice spoke sharply in Swahili. It was Kirby-Smith ordering the men back to their vehicles. The sun had set, the short African dusk closing in on the lugga. Only Abe remained by the burning truck, taking stills with a tiny miniature camera. Then he, too, turned away. But he did not join me. He went over to where Mary sat alone on a boulder, her head bowed as though in prayer, her face devoid of any expression. He sat on the sand beside her, not saying anything, just sitting there as though sensing that she had a need for the silent companionship of another human being.

I wished then that I had his emotional perception. Kirby-Smith was against the Land-Rover with the aerial up and the microphone in his hand, his African driver, with Karanja, squatting on the ground nearby. One by one the engines of the three remaining trucks started up, the sound of them gradually fading as they headed back to camp. Nobody else but ourselves now in the open curve of the lugga, the dusk deepening and the first stars showing, everything silent.

I was standing on my own, feeling isolated in the utter stillness. There was no sound, not even the call of a bird. Nothing moved, only wisps of smoke from the still-smouldering tyres, and my thoughts in turmoil as I tried to come to terms with the possibility that somewhere, out there in the gathering darkness . . . But my mind shuddered away from the prospect.

And then I heard Kirby-Smith's voice: "Could be just the heat friction of a bullet passing through the tank." He and his driver were moving slowly towards me, a powerful torch beamed on the ground, and Abe was with them. "Or maybe he was using tracer. Did you notice what sort of rifles his Africans had?"

"I know nothing about guns." Abe's voice was a disembodied whisper in the night. "But he had a double-barrelled rifle. I remember that."

"A Rigby .470, that's what he always used. He must have had it stashed away somewhere." Silence for a moment, two figures bending down, searching the ground, and then Kirby-Smith straightened up and switched off the torch. "Looking for a spent bullet in the gravel here, it's hopeless." He was staring off into the darkness beyond the truck. "An old Lee Enfield firing tracer, that's my guess."

"Where the hell would they get tracer bullets?" Abe asked.

"Same place as the rifles. From the old battle areas. A lot of the game I've seen killed in the last year was shot with .303 and there's still plenty of ammunition lying around if you know where to look."

They were moving off towards the Land-Rover and Abe said, "You saw the driver's skull?"

"Of course."

They came back with a pick, shovel, and crowbar, and we set about digging a grave. We dug it on the top of the bank, working in the light of the Land-Rover's headlights, and by the time we had finished the truck was no longer even smouldering, the metal just cool enough for us to drag the remains of the two Africans out. It was a messy, unpleasant job, a roasted smell still clinging to the shrivelled tatters of flesh, the bones brittle from the heat. Karanja pointed to the driver's head, which had a hole drilled in the blackened bone just above the remains of the right ear, another larger hole on the other side. "This man shot dead." His voice was high and excited, trembling in the hot, stinking air.

"His gun must have gone off by itself," Mary said quickly. "The heat . . ." But she stopped then, knowing it wasn't that, for Kirby-Smith's torch was beamed on the rifle still clipped to its bracket.

Nobody said anything after that and we laid the bodies on a ground-sheet and carried them to the grave in silence. When we had shovelled back the earth and built a small cairn of boulders over the mound, Kirby-Smith drove us back to camp. He drove fast, crashing through the bush, swerving between the trees, tearing over the uneven ground, as though in fighting the wheel one-handed his powerful body found an outlet for the anger that showed in his face.

That night the tension in the camp was something almost tangible. Presumably Kirby-Smith had told his driver not to talk, but in a close-

knit group of men it is impossible to conceal a thing like that entirely.
It was in the air, a feeling of menace. And the patrol was back. They
had found the tracks of humans mixed with those of the rhinoceros and
further back the remains of a camp. Kirby-Smith's tracker and two of
the patrol, who were also expert trackers, were agreed that the camp
had been used the previous night. They had followed fresh tracks northwards in the direction of the morning cull, but had lost them where
the intruders had waded through the waters of the stream. They had
failed to pick up any tracks on the further bank, but the information
they brought back had convinced every African in the camp that the
rhinoceros had been cleverly manoeuvred into charging our tents, and
that somebody, ivory poachers probably with a vested interest in preventing an official cull of their source of supply, had been responsible
for firing on the truck.

All this we heard from Karanja as we sat by the fire eating a mess of
posho and elephant meat. And something else. The patrol had also
back-tracked the intruders on the approach to the site of their night
camp. Again they had lost the tracks in the stream, but the approach
had been made from the east, down the slopes of the Mara Range.
"Many years ago," Karanja said, "when I first work for Tembo and he
is game warden of this area, we capture a very bad poacher who is hiding
in secret hole in the rocks up there on the Mara."

The cook-boy was issuing cans of beer, one to each man, and the
patrol sergeant threw another branch on the fire. The flames rose, flickering on the black faces, everybody huddled in groups, talking, their
voices hushed. And close beside me, Abe said, "Do you think he's up
there, holed out in the same place?"

"Maybe." Karanja hesitated. "Maybe he is somewhere else now, but
is good place to hide. When we capture that poacher, if we do not
have an informer with us who know the place, we never find it." And
he added, "Also, there is only two ways to approach. We can climb up,
or we can climb down, and if we don't surprise him we are all dead.
He was bad man and he had a gun with him."

"And what happens in the morning?" Abe asked. "Is the patrol
going out again?"

Karanja nodded. "They will leave at dawn."

"Which direction?"

"Up on to the Mara."

"To search the other side of the stream for tracks."

Karanja shrugged, his eyes shifting in the firelight, his hands gripped
tight around his can of beer.

"Do you think they'll find any tracks?"

"Maybe."

There was something in Karanja's manner that worried me. He seemed
nervous and very tense, unwilling to continue the conversation. Abe
snapped the ring-opener of his can, threw it into the fire, and drank.

"Anybody else know of this hideout?" It was said innocently enough, but I saw he was watching him out of the corners of his eyes.

Karanja didn't answer, and when Abe repeated the question, he shook his head. "I sleep now." He started to get to his feet, but Abe pulled him back, his hand on his arm, holding him.

"I have told you what I know," Karanja said.

"Why?" Abe asked. "Why did you tell us about this hideout?"

Karanja shook his head again, the whites of his eyes gleaming in the flickering firelight. "Maybe you, or Mr. Tait, go with the patrol."

"You told Major Kirby-Smith about it."

"No, not Major Kirby-Smith."

"The patrol sergeant then."

Karanja was silent. Then suddenly he said, "There is a man in the patrol who is with the police when we bring that poacher in. He knows we caught him up in the Mara, but he don't know where."

"So you told them."

Karanja hesitated, then nodded slowly. "What can I do? If I don't co-operate—" He spread his hands in a gesture of helplessness, then caught hold of Abe's arm. "Why did he do it? Is crazy, to shoot men because they are killing elephants."

"You're certain it was van Delden then?"

"Who else? Who else but Tembo van Delden do a crazy thing like that?" And he added, "Once before, when we were at Marsabit—" He was suddenly silent, shaking his head. "But now it is different. Now, if he's taken by the Army . . ." He was staring at Abe and his eyes in the twilight seemed to be pleading.

"You don't want his death on your conscience, is that it?"

Karanja hesitated, then nodded, a reluctant, barely perceptible movement of the head. "If you were with the patrol—a newsman representing CBS—then I think they are more careful." And after a moment he said hopefully, "Then it is all right? I can fix it?" And he sat there, staring urgently at Abe, who didn't say anything for a long time, sitting hunched over his beer, sipping at it occasionally, lost in thought.

Finally he seemed to make up his mind. "I have a better idea." He finished his drink and got to his feet, dragging Karanja with him. "We'll take a walk, see where the night guards are posted." He turned to me. "You stay here. I'll tell you what's in my mind later." And, still gripping the unwilling Karanja by the arm, he led him out of the circle of the firelight. I watched them until they were no more than shadows against the bright gleam of pressure lamps hung outside the tents.

I leaned back and closed my eyes. The night was full of sound, the crackle of the fire, the whisper of voices, the incessant, strident cacophony of cicadas. Somewhere an owl was hooting, the first I had heard, a mournful, monotonous sound, and down by the lugga a nightjar was over-riding the croak of frogs with a shrill churring. I thought how wonderful it would be, camped here under the mountains, if this were just a photographic safari, no killing, no sense of something hanging over me. There was a shout, the click of a rifle bolt, and I opened my eyes, staring into the night. Abe and Karanja had been challenged by one of the guards. I could see a torch shining on their faces and I lay back again, watching a satellite, bright as a planet, moving steadily across the velvet sky.

Out of the tail of my eye I saw a figure move, flop down beside me, and Mary's voice said, "What does Abe Finkel think?"

"About what?" I sat up, leaning on one elbow. The fire was dying and I could not see the expression in her eyes.

"About what happened, who did it. God, you're slow. What else?" The husky voice trembled on the night air and I felt sorry for her. She knew there was only one man who could have done it and silence was the only answer I could give her. "You think I should have gone with him, don't you? You think I'm to blame. But it wouldn't have made any difference. He never listened to me." Her hands were clasped tight together, the fingers locked. "Well, say something, can't you?"

"What is there to say? You're here, and that's all there is to it."

"You don't understand, do you?"

"No, I don't," I said. "If you'd been with your father, if you'd gone with him—"

"He's not my father."

I stared at her, shocked as much by the tone of her voice, the emotional violence of it, as by the denial. "But when we were at the Lodge . . ."

"He gave me a name, brought me up—but he's not my father. Surely you must have guessed." And when I shook my head, she said, "Alex is my father. Now do you understand?" She seemed to expect some comment, but when I didn't say anything, she said angrily, "Well, don't just sit there staring at me. He's my natural father and I don't know what to do. A situation like this—I need help." She was staring at me, her eyes unnaturally bright. "Well, God! Can't you say something?" And then she laughed, a trembling note near to hysteria. "No, of course. Keep your mouth shut, don't get involved. Don't even bloody well think about it." Her eyes shifted to the forest. "All very well for you. But that man out there—you don't know him like I do."

She was silent for a moment, and then, in a quiet voice tinged with bitterness: "I thought—at that Conference—I really thought a confrontation would get it out of his system. I thought if they argued it out, the two of them, in public, before all those delegates—that would be the end of it. I thought he'd be satisfied then, feel he'd done all he could. But I was wrong. Instead, it seemed to fuel all the old resentment again, all the basic fundamental differences. The two of them, they're like two sides of the same coin, both of them obsessed with the rightness of what they're doing." The rush of words ceased abruptly, her voice trembling into silence. "But not this," she breathed, her nerves strung taut and a note of hopelessness. "Nothing can justify this." She was silent for a while, her fingers moving, clasping and unclasping. Then suddenly she rounded on me and said, "You've got to stop it—somehow."

"Me?" I stared at her, wondering what the hell she expected me to do about it.

"You and that American," she said, her eyes staring at me, large and wild in the dimming firelight. "You've got to do something. You're the only men here who can come between them."

I sat there, silent, not knowing what to say. There was no comfort I could give her. And then Abe came out of the shadows, Karanja beside him, both of them subdued. "The guards are on their toes," he said. "We were challenged twice." He glanced at Mary, then sat himself on the far side of her. "I think you could help." He stared at her, then hesitatingly, "That is, if you're willing. Karanja here knows of an old poacher's hideout—"

"I know about that," she said quickly. "The patrol leaves at first light."

He nodded. "Then it's a question of whether you're prepared to let your father be cornered up there without warning him."

"It doesn't worry you that he's killed two men?"

He smiled and shook his head. "I've seen too much bloodshed, too many people killed. . . ." He gave a little shrug. "Too many of us in the world anyway."

She turned to Karanja, speaking to him rapidly in his own tongue. And when he had answered her questions, she said, "He may not be there, of course."

Abe nodded. "Then we come back. But if he is . . ." He paused, facing her. "You realise they'll shoot him."

"I was hoping," she said, "that I could persuade you . . ." She glanced at me. "That's why I came to talk to you." Kirby-Smith called to her and she said she was coming. "He wants to dictate some notes."

"Will you create a diversion for us so that we can slip away unnoticed?"

She nodded slowly. "I—suppose so. Yes, of course. It's what I wanted —for him to be warned. But on one condition, that you make him realise it's useless to interfere. More troops will be arriving in the morning. He won't stop the culling and if he tries to attack the outfit again, then there'll only be one end to it. They'll track him down and kill him. Tell him that please, if you find him, and make him promise to head for the coast. It's his only hope."

Quickly they arranged the details between them. Just after midnight Mary would approach one of the guards, tell him she had an upset stomach, and go into the bush. She would stay there long enough for them to become anxious, then she would scream and start to run. After the rhinoceros episode of the night before, it would be sufficient to reduce the whole camp to instant turmoil. She got up. "That's settled then." She hesitated, suddenly bending down to Abe and kissing him on the forehead. "You're a very strange man. Thank you." And she turned and went quickly to the tent where Kirby-Smith sat at a table, his face lit by the bright light of a pressure lamp clouded with insects.

"Well?" Abe had shifted his position. He was close beside me now. "What are you going to do—come with us or stay and film tomorrow's cull?"

I stared at him, thinking what it would be like climbing up through the forest in the dark, up the densely covered slopes of the Mara. A night march like that, God knows what we would meet—elephant, rhino, and Kirby-Smith had said there were lions. And if we made it, if we found the poacher's hideout and van Delden there . . . What then? Would he do what Mary asked. "You really think you'll find him?"

He shrugged. "It's worth a try."

"So you'll go, tonight?"

He nodded. "Karanja says there's a track goes up from the South Horr side of the stream."

"And he'll guide you?"

"He thinks he can remember it."

I looked across at Karanja, sitting cross-legged, his hands clasping his knees, his face sombre. I didn't understand why the man was prepared to risk his life, his whole career, and when I asked him he simply said, "I must." His eyes shifted, staring at me, a helpless look. "If I don't then I am Judas." And he added, his soft voice in the night, "Many years and I almost forget how I love that man."

I thought of van Delden, trying to understand what there was in him that could endanger such a bond of loyalty and affection. But it was outside of my experience, something beyond my comprehension. And Abe —what made him take such a chance for a man he hardly knew? "Why are you doing it?" I asked. But he only smiled that infuriating little secret smile of his. "Do not ask," he murmured, "such knowledge is not for us."

"What do you mean by that?"

"Only that I don't know. You should read your Horace. He puts things very well. Probably better in Latin, but I was never taught Latin or Greek at school. I hadn't that sort of education." His eyes stared past me into the ember-glow of the fire. "If we find van Delden I don't think he'll do what Mary asks. He'll be warned, that's all, and shift his base. In which case I'll see something I've never seen before, a man in total defence of another species. To film that, so the viewer sees it all through his eyes —the elephants, the trucks gathering for the drive, the hunters waiting for the kill, the long barrel of the rifle, the sights coming up on to their target, and the target not an elephant, but a man, and then the truck a blaze of fire . . . But that was today." He smiled and shook his head. "I missed a great opportunity today."

"You'd have filmed it?"

"Sure I would. I won't get a chance like that again. Next time it will be different."

"There won't be a next time," I said. "Or if he tries it, then the Army will get him."

"Oh, I don't know. I guess he knows this country better than the Army." He laughed. "Anyway, I want to be with him when they start culling again. I don't want to be with the hunters. I'm on the side of the elephants, you see."

"You'll be in real trouble then." I was really concerned about him. I couldn't help it. I'd grown fond of Abe and to go off into the Mara seeking the company of a man who had put himself in such a terrible position seemed dangerous in the extreme. But when I tried to explain this to him he only laughed. "I may not find him anyway."

"No, but the patrol sergeant will know you were trying to warn him."

"So?" He looked at me, a strange expression in his eyes. "Does it matter?" And he added, "I don't mind all that much what happens to me, not now." His gaze had wandered back to the fire, and after a while he said, "I know what you're thinking, that van Delden has killed two men. But that's not the point." He paused for a moment, then he was looking at me and smiling again. "That shocks you, I suppose? But it shouldn't, not when you consider it in the context of all the senseless killings that go on in the world. You see, he believes passionately in what he is doing. To him it is justified." He stretched out his hand and gripped my knee. "I guess you're too new at this game to grasp what it is we've got here. This man is no ordinary man. He's something unique. He has so identified himself with the elephants that they are in a sense his own people."

"He didn't need to kill those men," I said obstinately.

"Didn't he? How else was he to stop the slaughter? How else protect them from extermination?"

"He'd only to turn the leader."

"That was today, but what about tomorrow and the next day and the next, the refrigerator trucks standing by, that freezer plant empty, and the word running like wildfire through South Horr to Baragoi and Maralal —all those tribesmen waiting to get their hands on the meat. One man against a bunch of professional hunters backed up by the Army." He was staring off into the fire again. "It's a damned odd story, the oddest I've ever come across."

It was stupid of me, but I thought then it was the story, not the elephants or van Delden's safety, that was driving him to this crazy idea of a night journey up the Mara. But when I put my thoughts into words, he turned on me angrily. "You fool! How can you understand my motives when I don't understand them myself? All I know is I'm going. There's nothing for me here. Kirby-Smith can't give me what I'm seeking here in Africa. But this man van Delden, I think he can." He got to his feet. "I'm going to get some sleep now. Whether you come or not—that's up to you."

PART THREE

THE LAST REFUGE

I

The moon was well up, but its light barely penetrated the leaf canopy. Evergreens and patches of thick impenetrable bush, the boles of tall trees, twisted ropes of lianas, and my heart pounding as we climbed, following the beam of Karanja's torch. We had been climbing for two hours without a break. I could hear Abe's breath coming in gasps, occasionally he stumbled. We were neither of us fit, but he kept going and I followed him, the camera and my grip becoming heavier, my shoulders aching. I no longer thought about the possibility of coming face to face with some nocturnal animal or even why I was here and not sleeping down at the camp. We had left it in a scrambling chaos of men shouting, but whenever we paused to listen, half expecting the sound of pursuit, we heard nothing, only the rustlings of the night, the occasional clatter of tree fruit falling or a nut.

We came at last to a stream, the same little river the road forded below South Horr. Now it was narrower, more of a mountain stream running fast over smooth boulders, a dark tunnel winding up through thick undergrowth. We waded up it, moving slowly, feeling for footholes, moonlight glinting on water and on the barrel of the rifle Karanja had taken from one of the hunters, everything black in shadow and monkeys restless in the trees, sharp barks of defiance. Something moved on the bank and we checked as it went crashing away through a thicket. "Nyati," Karanja said. "Buffalo." There was less bush now, the cedar beginning, and we left the stream, clambering straight up. We were no longer in the foothills. We were on the Mara itself. Exhausted, we reached the trail again. It was wider here and damp under the trees, the firm-packed earth marked with the footprints of elephants.

Abe flopped to the ground. "How much further?" he gasped.

"I carry your bag now," Karanja suggested.

But Abe shook his head. "You keep your hands free in case we meet something. All I want to know is how far from here?"

"An hour, two hours. Is long time since I am here."

"You haven't forgotten, have you? You know where it is?"

"Ndio."

"And this trail leads to the hideout?"

But all Karanja said was, "We go now. Maybe patrol wait for dawn, maybe is behind us." He reached down and picked up Abe's bag, and then we were on our feet again, following the trail as it climbed up through the cedar forest, clinging to the face of the mountain, winding round outcrops, the ground falling away below us.

It was not all clear. There were patches of green-leaved trees and shrubs, but these were now like clearings in the forest, the broken stems sticking up out of a trampled litter of branches, and only the largest trees left standing. For the first time I was seeing the role elephants play in the natural order of African ecology, but stumbling over broken branches with my feet slipping on the soft mush of elephant turds, and coming suddenly out into the first of these clearings, I was surprised to see the effect of such big animals browsing on forest growth.

Karanja had stopped. "Many elephants come this way," he said, looking cautiously about him.

"How long ago?" Abe asked.

He picked up one of the droppings and sniffed at it. "That is old. But this—" He put his foot on a smaller, softer ball. "This dung ball is fresh."

"How fresh?"

He bent down to smell it, then shook his head. "Maybe tonight. Maybe last night. I am not like Mukunga. Mukunga could say to an hour how old this is." He straightened up, staring across the clearing again. "Many elephants," he said again, his voice sounding uneasy. And then abruptly: "We go quickly now please. Is not far."

We went on, across the broken litter of branches into the forest again, our eyes searching ahead in the gloom, expecting any moment to see the dim shape of an elephant loom up through the trees. More areas of green-leaved devastation, and then we were under a wall of rock and Karanja had checked. The moon was low in the west, the light of it shining full on the mountain, jagged peaks pale against the stars and just ahead of us another clearing thick with a tangle of torn-off branches and trampled bushes. I saw leaves moving, heard the snap of a stem, a low rumbling sound, and Karanja was backing away, searching the cliff face. "Ndovu," he whispered. "Is best we climb into the rock." There was a crevice and as we scrambled up, the rumbling was nearer. There was a thin squeal and the crash of branches, then silence.

We waited, crouched in the gulley, listening. More rumbling, nearer now, and then suddenly a grey shape moved below us. Tusks glinted pale in the moonlight, a trunk lifted high, sniffing the air. The elephant had stopped and I realised it was a cow, for she had two calves following close behind her, one half grown, but the other so tiny it looked no bigger than a Shetland pony. It had a branch gripped in its miniature trunk and was trying to maneuver the leaves into its mouth, a puzzled, concentrated look on its small face. The cow turned, her ears spread in alarm, her stomach rumbling. She was so close I could see the way the top edge of her ears folded back, a sort of rubbery fringe, the bony outline of the huge head and the deep creases in her waving trunk.

The baby had caught the note of alarm now. It dropped the branch and vanished from my sight. She was guiding it under her belly with her foot and the older one was pushing past her. There was a shrill squeal as the trunk came down, slapping it into position against her gaunt flank. They stood like that for a moment, mother and child together and her trunk raised again, the prehensile tip of it feeling the air as though sensing our presence so close among the rocks, while behind her the rest of the family group came into view. They were cows with two or three half-grown calves bunched close around them as they stood filling the trail, alarmed and restless, their trunks moving from side to side, their feet scuffing the ground.

Karanja gave a short sharp whistle and stood up, clutching a sapling growing out of the crevice. Silence then and the grey tide of heads and hunched backs flowing past us. In an instant the trail below us was clear and not a sound anywhere. "Did you see it?" Abe breathed, his voice trembling on a note of surprise and wonder. "When she stopped right below us, her ears spread?"

"See what?" I asked, still thinking of that baby elephant, the only tiny one in the group, the impression they had given of a family fleeing through the night, and wondering how far they had come, where they were going.

"I guess it was just a trick of the light," he murmured. But as we scrambled down on to the empty trail I heard him ask Karanja how far we were from the Aberdares, and Karanja answered shortly, "A long way." He was moving out ahead of us, rifle gripped in his hand, head thrust forward, peering down the trail.

We passed the rock face and came in sight of the clearing again, Abe beside me saying, "She had two calves, and that little one, it couldn't have been more than a few months old. Did you see it?" He seemed to have an urgent need to talk, not caring that there might be more elephants ahead of us. "A baby calf like that, could it come all that way? And they were heading north. Do you reckon they were the same elephants we saw from the Baringo track?" And when I didn't answer him, my eyes fixed nervously on the far side of the clearing, he said, "Van Delden seemed to think it was some sort of inherited instinct. But north from here it's desert. Hey, Karanja!" And he caught him up. "All those tracks we've seen, they're all heading north, isn't that right?"

"Yes, all going north."

"So where do they go?"

"The major thinks Ethiopia, the Omo River maybe." We had come into the clearing and he was walking slowly, his eyes searching the forest on the far side. It was difficult to see ahead, for there was more bush here. Close beside us was a tree festooned with strips of torn bark like pale streamers in the moonlight.

"They can't cross the desert. They looked shagged-out already, and they've got calves with them. Those calves—"

Karanja silenced him with a sharp hiss. He had stopped and was staring intently ahead. We stood in a bunch, listening, but there was no sound, everything very still, the air breathless in the moonlight and the trail running ahead of us, across the clearing into the dark of the cedars.

And then we saw it, on the far side of the clearing, a dim shape coming towards us. No time to get back to the gulley and the bush thick on either side.

Karanja dropped Abe's bag, gripping his rifle. I heard the click of the bolt as he cocked it. The elephant heard it, too, its ears suddenly spread wide, the trunk curling upwards. It was out in the open now and I could see it quite clearly. It had stopped and was feeling the air, its trunk moving snake-like above its head.

Whether the elephant winded us or whether it actually saw us, I don't know, but its left eye was glinting in the moonlight and I had a sudden feeling it was focussed on me personally. My heart was thudding, my mouth dry, and as though he sensed what was in my mind Karanja hissed, "Stay still! Even if he charge, don't move." He took a few steps forward and stopped, the rifle gripped in his hands ready. The elephant was less than a hundred yards away.

I think it saw Karanja move, for it suddenly curled its trunk and let out a wild trumpeting that echoed and re-echoed from the rock walls above us. Silence then and the grey bulk coming towards us, slowly, almost hesitantly, so that I was reminded of that elephant at the Lodge, weak from starvation. It stopped again, its front feet on a log, its head up and its ears spread wide. It looked enormous in the moonlight, my gaze so concentrated upon it that I had the distinct impression that it filled the clearing. "Is bluffing," Karanja whispered. But his voice trembled and I didn't believe him. The beast was swinging its right forefoot back and forth, scattering leaves and broken bits of branch, its body rocking from side to side and its trunk coiling and uncoiling.

"I've read about this," Abe whispered. "I never thought I'd see it." He sounded excited rather than scared, and then the elephant tucked its trunk up under its tusks and charged. It was a slow, lumbering movement, yet it covered the ground all too quickly, and incredibly there was scarcely a sound.

I thought Karanja would fire then, and I stood rooted to the spot expecting any moment the sound of the shot. But instead he jumped on to a fallen log and just stood there, the rifle high above his head, both arms raised, facing the elephant. And when it was barely ten yards from him, the huge bony head, with the ears spread like sails, seeming to fill the sky and the tusks pointing straight at us, it suddenly skidded to a halt, shaking its head furiously and scattering brushwood with its flailing trunk. Then for a moment it was still, its trunk uncurled and hanging down, its head lifted until it seemed as though it were standing on tiptoe to look at something behind us. Again that shattering trumpet sound, and then it seemed to grow smaller, the skin of its flanks hanging in folds and its bones showing, its ears folding back, the trunk hanging down again. It shook its head as though disgusted at its failure to make us give ground, turning slowly and shambling off, head and tail up, sliding like a ghost into the tangled thicket of broken bush, going downhill and making scarcely a sound.

Karanja let out his breath in an audible sigh of relief, and I knew he hadn't been as sure of himself as he had pretended. "Long time since I see elephant behave like that. Tembo call it—" He frowned, laughing nervously. "I don't remember what he call it."

"Good for you." Abe was laughing and clapping him on the back. "But how did you know we weren't going to be trampled to death?"

Karanja shrugged, pleased with himself now and beaming all over his face. "Is a bull," he said, "and not certain of himself. You see him swing his foot and sway, and then trumpeting and making to stand big. Not often bulls make real charge. Cows, yes, 'specially when they have young. Not bulls."

"It is what they call a threat display then?"

"Ndio." Karanja nodded eagerly. "Threat display."

"Let's get on," I said, annoyed that Abe could stand there, quietly discussing the behaviour of the beast, while my legs were still trembling and weak from the shock of that charge. He seemed entirely unaffected, as though what he had seen at Treetops God knows how many years ago had convinced him all animals are innocent of any real hostility. I picked up his bag and went on across the clearing, wanting to get off that trail as quickly as possible, my mind still full of the memory of that great bulk skidding to a halt and the big domed head and the great ears blotting out the stars.

Behind me I heard Karanja say, "Is the word Tembo van Delden use—threat display. Where you learn it, eh?"

"Something I read."

"In a book?"

"Yeah. In a book."

Karanja shook his head. "Is difficult for me. I don't have enough books —no books like that." The cedars closed over our heads and we moved cautiously, the trail climbing steeply up through the forest. A lot of elephants had come that way, the trail marked by their great footprints, their droppings everywhere and a debris of leaves and discarded saplings. Once we disturbed a bird that went flapping past us silent as an owl. "Mountain eagle," Karanja said. "Mountain eagle very common on Marsabit." We were passing under a towering crag, almost a cliff, the face of it showing above the trees. "We go up into the rocks soon." We were on the level here, the going easier. I had got my second wind and I began thinking about the future, remembering the map and all the miles of semi-desert surrounding this range of mountains. The canopy thinned and I saw Abe's face looking drawn, his thin shoulders bowed and his breath coming in quick shallow gasps. "You all right?" I asked him.

"Fine," he said, and managed a smile. "Not as young as you, that's all, and CBS never gave us time off for physical training."

We were round the base of the cliff, the rock curving away to a dark cleft, and there was the sound of water. It came from the thin trickle of a stream falling over green-slimed rocks to a pool edged with ferns that elephants had trampled, the marks of their feet everywhere and lumps of dung. We waded into the pool, drinking the water as it came fresh down the rocks. It was clear and beautifully cool, and when we had finished drinking we splashed it over our faces, cleaning off the dried salt crust of our sweat.

Karanja drank only sparingly, then began searching the ground with his torch.

"Any sign of them?" Abe asked.

He shook his head and straightened up. "Too many elephants."

"How far now?"

"Not far."

"And you still think he's holed up on the mountain here?" Abe's voice sounded doubtful. "It's a hell of a way to the lugga where he stopped the cull."

"Eight miles maybe. Is nothing." Karanja was beside us, the rifle slung, his hands reaching for a grip on the slimy rocks. "We go up now." He began to climb, feeling for footholds. The rocks formed a slippery staircase that went up at an angle of about forty-five degrees. Burdened with cameras and our bags, it took us a long time to gain the top where it flattened out after about two hundred feet to a series of shallow rock pools in a steep-sided gulley. It was almost dark, the moon hidden by a black pinnacle of rock, the gulley narrowing to a cleft and the thin whisper of water falling. All round us were the shapes of fallen rocks, everything dark and no breath of wind.

Karanja, probing with his torch, suddenly bent down. "Angalia!" He was pointing, and though he had spoken quietly the whisper of his voice came back to us from the surrounding cliffs, an eerie echo in the gloom. It was difficult to make out what he was exclaiming over. "That stone— is dislodged. See the mark of his heel. There—is a toe." It required a good deal of imagination to interpret those faint marks in the gravel, but Karanja seemed satisfied. "One man wearing boots, another with bare feet. Now we know he has been here."

I stared round the jumble of fallen rocks, remembering how Mtome had materialised out of the bush the first time I had visited van Delden. Just over a week ago. It seemed an age, and Mtome had moved so silently. "Where?" I whispered, the hairs crawling on the back of my neck at the thought of a shot crashing into us from the shadows. "Where's the hideout?"

Karanja shook his head. "Is difficult," he breathed, staring off into the darkness. High above us a pinnacle of rock gleamed white against the stars and the moon-pale sky. But the cleft was a black abyss, shut in and full of the whisper of water as it fell down some hidden rock face. "Is higher, I think. When we capture that poacher we approach it from above."

"That's quite a climb," Abe said, staring up to where the V of the cleft showed on the skyline high above us.

Karanja nodded.

"But you brought him out this way."

"Ndio." He hesitated, then said, "You stay here please." And he left us, moving deeper into the cleft, his shadowy outline merging into the rocks until suddenly I couldn't see him any more. A moment later he called softly, the murmur of his voice whispering among the rocks, giving his name and ours too. I think he spoke in two different languages, for he repeated the names. After that there was a long silence.

"He's not there," Abe said wearily.

"Well, if he's not here," I said, "there's no point in our whispering like a bunch of conspirators." The place was getting on my nerves and only one way to settle it. "Mr. van Delden!" I shouted, and the cliffs were still repeating Delden as I announced who we were and why we had come. "There's a patrol coming to get you in the morning. We came to warn you. Mary asked us to." The echo of my words died away, then silence, only the sound of water. There was no reply.

"Pity," Abe murmured, disappointment in his voice. "If we could have gone with him—" A boulder moved in the stream bed behind us and I turned, my eyes strained into darkness. But nothing moved. A hand gripped my arm and Karanja said, "You make too much noise. Is dangerous if patrol is close behind us."

"What's it matter?" I said. "He's not here."

"For you, no. Is no matter. But for me . . ." The uncertainty in his voice and the shifting movement of his eyes in that dim light made me realise how much he had risked leading us up here. Abe realised it, too. "I'm sorry," he said. "You were hoping to join him, weren't you?"

Karanja nodded.

"And now?"

There was a long silence. Then Karanja said, "Now I must try to find him." And he added in a whisper, "Is nothing else for me to do."

"Where do you reckon he is then?"

He hesitated. "I think maybe he is waiting for tomorrow's hunt, out in the desert towards Kulal."

"That's quite a way." Abe sounded doubtful. "Perhaps if we rest here, get some sleep—"

Karanja shook his head. "Is necessary I go fast. In the morning there is more Army, more patrols. Is impossible for you."

Abe put his camera down beside his grip and sat himself on the rocks. "Okay, so you leave us here and go on alone. Is that it?"

He nodded, standing there, hesitant, staring up at the black V of the cleft. "Is what I must do." He said it reluctantly, unwilling to accept that van Delden had left and he had committed himself to no purpose. Then he turned to us again. "You will be safe here. In the morning, when the patrol come, tell the sergeant please I go back to Nairobi."

"Will he believe that?" I asked.

"Maybe." He sounded doubtful. "But tell him please." And then he said, "I go now. Goodbye, Mr. Finkel. Happy to have met you."

"I could say that I insisted on your guiding us here," Abe murmured.

"Is no good, not after I lose the minibus."

"That was my fault."

But he shook his head. "They do not believe that." He gripped Abe's hand, then mine, and a moment later he was gone. The flicker of his torch showed for an instant as he searched for the first footholds leading down over the lip of the watercourse, then it disappeared and we were alone. "Poor devil!" Abe murmured. "All those years with van Delden . . ." He shook his head. "And if he finds him, what then? What's the future for a man who abandons the position he has reached in the hierarchy of this new régime in Africa?"

His words reminded me of that night journey to the Serengeti, how scared Karanja had been. And now he was on his own, trying to make his way alone across a desert in search of the man who had been a sort of god to him long ago in another age. "Why do you think he's doing it?" I asked. "Burning his boats like that. It doesn't make sense."

Abe laughed. "You always want to know why."

"Don't you?" I asked irritably. "You're a reporter. You must be curious."

"Oh sure. But logic and emotion . . ." He smiled and shook his head. "Man is a crazy, mixed-up creature and I have long since given up trying to rationalise his behaviour. D'you think he'll make it?" he asked. "On his own, and no water."

"How the hell do I know?"

"You've read up on this country. You should have some idea. Have you brought that book with you?"

"Yes."

"I'd like to have another look at it when it's light."

"You'll wait here for the patrol then?"

"What else?"

"We'll be sent back under escort to Nairobi."

"Probably."

I sat there, feeling angry with myself. If I had stayed down there in the camp I could have been filming this morning. Something I could have sold, and like a bloody fool . . .

"Mr. Finkel." The voice, coming to us out of the darkness, was so quiet it was barely audible above the thin sound of water. "You're alone now, is that right?" A shadow moved, coming towards us. "Cornelius van Delden," it said.

The outline of his head was in silhouette against the stars, the beard and the long flowing hair showing white, the barrels of his rifle gleaming dully. He called softly into the darkness, giving instructions. "Now we must go out by a different route, and that will take longer." He glanced

at his watch. "I was intending to leave at three and it's already past that."
He hesitated and Abe got to his feet, facing him.

"Where were you planning to go?"

"There's a family of elephants must be kept moving or they'll be caught
in the culling area. We ran into them at dusk browsing on some wild fig
on the north shoulder of the Mara."

"And we met another bunch on the way up here," Abe said. "But
there's nothing you can do about it now. You've killed two Africans and
the Army is sending more troops."

But all van Delden said was, "Where did you meet this new lot?"

"Coming past the first outcrop about half a mile back."

"How many?"

"We didn't count."

"We've sighted thirty-seven so far. Three family groups with a few odd
bulls tagging along. All going north. Were yours going north?"

Abe nodded. "And the tracks we've seen, they're all going north, too.
But this is no time for you to be worrying about elephants. Your only
hope is to get out of here." And he added, his voice suddenly urgent,
"Make for the coast. That's the message Mary sent you."

Van Delden shook his head. "I've no intention of leaving now. Those
elephants need me and I want to know where they're going. If I can keep
them moving, get them clear of the culling area by dawn and then follow
them . . ." He turned abruptly away, calling softly to Mukunga. And
when the man appeared like a shadow at his side, fully equipped with
rifle and bandolier, he spoke to him softly in his own language. The
word *simba* was repeated several times, Mukunga nodding, a gleam of
white teeth in the darkness. Then he had gone, disappearing down the
rocks we had climbed, silent as a cat and moving fast. "Mukunga imitates
a lion very well," van Delden said. "Bulls don't mind so much. But cows
accompanied by their calves will keep away from lions. He'll get them
moving, and he'll do it better on his own."

"And suppose he meets the patrol?" Abe's voice was suddenly angry.
"Risking your own life, that's one thing, but sending a man out—"

"I know what I'm doing," van Delden said sharply. "It's you who are
risking lives, coming here. . . . Why? Why did you come?"

"I told you, Mary asked us—"

"She's a fool, sending two men up here who know nothing about Africa.
And Karanja, why did he come?"

"God knows, since you let him believe you weren't here. But he said
something about remembering the love he had for you, and because he'd
told the patrol sergeant about this poacher's hideout—"

"Said that, did he?" Van Delden laughed softly to himself, adding
harshly, "Silly bugger. He's Kimani's man now." He called to Mtome.
"We'll get moving now, if you're ready. I'm afraid you'll find it pretty hard
going. And we're out of grub. Have you got any food with you?"

Abe shook his head. "But you'll take us with you, will you?" There was a note of surprise in his voice.

"I can't very well leave you to tell the patrol Karanja was right. They're bound to have a good tracker with them." He started to move, but then hesitated, turning again to Abe. "About those elephants you ran into. They were cows, I take it?"

"I guess so. They had some young with them. But there was a lone bull following behind, a big gaunt-looking fellow." And Abe told him how Karanja had stood his ground when the bull charged.

"Damn fool thing." There was a grudging respect in his voice. "You could have been killed, all of you."

"I don't think so," Abe murmured. "He seemed to know what he was doing, and the bull wasn't sure of himself."

"You were lucky, that's all. At Marsabit, when I was there, you could do a thing like that and not much danger. The elephants were safe and they knew it. But here, after all that's happened—" He shook his head. "Here all the elephants are driven by a desperate urge to get away from man. I've been charged three times already. You were damned lucky." He paused, and then, as though merely voicing his thoughts: "A bull, you say. There were bulls hanging around the family group we saw at dusk, another with the herd we stopped them culling." He seemed about to say something more, but then he turned. "Wait here." He went back into the rocks, calling softly to Mtome again and issuing orders.

I looked at Abe. "You going with him?"

He nodded, and I caught a gleam of excitement in his eyes. "It's what I came for."

"But if he attacks Kirby-Smith's outfit again . . ." I was thinking of the elephant at the Lodge. He could use us, as I suspected he was using Karanja. "You realise it was deliberate. He deliberately waited until Karanja had left on his own."

"Sure. What else do you expect after you'd shot your mouth off like that?"

"How do you mean?"

"You shouted it all round this gulley, that the patrol was on its way, and he knew at once there was only one man who could have told them about this poacher's hideout."

"So I'm to blame—is that what you're saying? It's my fault if Karanja gets killed."

"It doesn't matter." He had sat down again, leaning back, gazing up at the stars. "Heading north," he murmured. "The only migration I've read about was between the Tana River and what used to be Tanzania. That was years ago when there were big herds. But whether it was just the bulls—bulls range wider than cows. . . ." He seemed lost then in contemplation of an enigma that had no bearing on our situation.

"You don't seem to care that you're risking your life." The echo of my words sounded high and uneasy.

He smiled at me. "Scared?"

"Yes, but you're not. That's what I don't understand."

"No, that's right. I don't care very much." He turned slowly towards me, leaning on one elbow. "You can still go down that watercourse, back the way we came until you meet up with the patrol. So maybe I ought to tell you. My wife died, just over a year ago. It was a long, slow, painful end, and we were very close. After that—well, I guess, my view of life changed. You've never been in love, have you?"

"Of course I have."

"But not with one woman, over many years." His voice trailed off into silence.

"Haven't you any children?" I asked.

"No. And if we had, I don't know that it would have made any difference. They'd have been grown up by now. That's how long we were together." He leaned back again. "Well, there you are—that's as near as I can get to explaining why I'm here, why I'll go on with van Delden. You do what you like."

But then van Delden reappeared, Mtome beside him, and I no longer had any choice. "Time we left." He picked up Abe's bag, feeling the weight of it. "What's in it, film?"

Abe nodded. "Some clothes, too."

"Shirt, spare trousers, socks, towels, pullover, that's all you'll need."

"My camera is no good without film."

"We're travelling light."

"I guess that settles it then," Abe murmured, still sitting there on the rock and his voice obstinate. "I'm not leaving without my camera."

Van Delden stared at him a moment, then pushed my bag with his foot. "More film?" And when I told him what was in it, he added. "All right then. One camera and one bag with as much film as you think you can carry." He was turning away, but then he paused. "Didn't that Austrian Count hunt elephant on the shores of Lake Rudolf? When was that? I can't remember."

"March 1888," I said.

"Just cows, or were there bulls, too?"

"Bulls and cows."

He nodded. "Interesting, providing he knew the difference. It's a long time since I read von Höolen's account of that expedition. If it isn't too heavy bring it along. And the map, too." He went back into the rocks then, leaving Mtome standing over us while we packed everything into the one bag.

"Which camera?" Abe asked me. "I've never used a Beaulieu before, but I think it's lighter so maybe we should take that."

"Whichever you like." I think he was being kind, knowing the Beaulieu belonged to me personally, but at that moment I didn't care. I was in a gloomy mood now, convinced that we would never have the opportunity of filming anything. How could we, in the company of a man waging a sort of guerrilla war? We would be lucky if we got away with our lives. And yet he had agreed to our taking a camera. First Kirby-Smith, now van Delden—it was extraordinary how publicity-conscious these men were. Each seemed to have a need for his activities to be recorded.

We left Abe's Bolex, and a bag with our discarded clothing, hidden under some stones in a crevice. Then we went up into the rocks, to a niche above the poacher's cave where van Delden and Dima were busy obliterating all sign of footprints. And when they had swept the ground clean with a leafy branch, we left, clambering up a rock face that brought us out above the thin trickle of the waterfall. The time by my wristwatch was just after three-thirty and the moon was lost behind the mountains across the valley.

It was all rock, the cliffs and peaks black above us, and we travelled fast, only the stars to light us, stumbling for footholds in the dark. The bag I was carrying became a leaden weight dragging at my shoulders. Once van Delden dropped back. "Want one of my men to carry it for you?" But I shook my head. They were already burdened with packs, blanket cloaks, water bottles, ammunition belts, and rifles.

"I'll be all right," I said, knowing that if we were going to make a film I would just have to get used to it. Abe, with only the camera to carry, was finding the going difficult enough.

Shortly after that we began to descend and soon we were clear of rock and into the cedars again, following some sort of a game trail. It was very dark, the descent steep as we dropped down on to the northern shoulder of the range. Here van Delden left us, taking Mtome with him. He gave no explanation, merely saying, "Dima will look after you now. He knows where to go." The forest swallowed them and we were alone with Dima, who said urgently, "We go quick now. In little time is day."

"Where are we going?" I asked him.

But he walked on, not answering, and Abe, beside me, said, "The question is, where's van Delden gone?"

"To join Mukunga, I imagine."

But he seemed doubtful. "If it was that, why didn't he go with him at the start?"

Dima hissed at us to be quiet and we stumbled on through the dark in silence. Gradually the forest thinned, gave way to a mixed growth that dwindled into bush as the first glimmer of light showed in the east. It was over half an hour since van Delden had left us and as the ground became easier Dima increased the pace. For a while I was barely conscious of the improving visibility, then dawn came in a rush and we could see the whole sweep of the Nyiru Range rearing peaks of bare rock on the far side of the Horr Valley. Ahead of us the land sloped to the desert brown of sand and gravel, and far ahead, where the horizon merged with the milk-pale sky, I thought I could see the top of Kulal.

We came off the shoulder of the mountain into dry scrub country dotted with thorn and acacia, and here we saw a zebra the moran had failed to kill. It was a Gérvy's zebra, the type peculiar to this arid northern territory. It had a large head and neck, and the stripes were closer. It stood watching us curiously until we came within its flight range, then it cantered off, pausing occasionally to look back at us. There was a sparkle in the air now and a freshness I had not felt since arriving in Africa.

We crossed a lugga fringed with trees and shrubs, their leaves drooping from lack of moisture. Probably the same lugga we had been in the night before, but further east. Dima had lengthened his stride, the going good over hard sandy gravel, and no sound except a few bird calls. We passed the thorn skeleton of an old manyata and I wondered what van Delden was up to and whether Mukunga would get those elephants past the culling area in time. Kirby-Smith would be leaving camp now and soon the plane would be in the air. "We should be able to see the plane when it takes off," I said.

Abe turned, looking back at me. "If we can see it, then the pilot will be able to see us." His face looked drawn and tired, dark shadows under his eyes.

"Maybe that's what van Delden wants."

He gave me a wan smile. "Maybe." And we pushed on, silent again, walking in a pale, cool light that was the interregnum between night and day. But it was brightening all the time and then suddenly the sun pushed a great shield of burnished red up into the eastern sky, and instantly the land flared with colour. From the flat sepia of desert gravel it turned to a dried blood hue in which everything glistened with light, scrub and thorn and skittering birds all brilliant with the great red glow of heat to come. It was fantastic, breathtaking, and all because I was seeing it on foot, not riding in the dust cloud of a line of trucks. And it was in that fantastic sunrise flare that I saw the neck of a giraffe stuck up like a post and peering at us over wait-a-bit thorn. I wanted to stop, enjoy this moment of startling beauty, but Dima hurried on.

The giraffe moved, became four, thin long necks and sloping bodies shining in panels of rich dark red separated by variegated lines of white as though a wide-meshed net had been flung over them. They stood in a bunch watching us, then trotted off with a rolling, camel-like gait that changed for a moment into a supremely graceful gallop that disturbed a family of ostrich. "Reticulata," Abe breathed as though making a mental note. He paused for a moment to stare after them, then trudged wearily on, his shoulders bent.

We were climbing now, the land sloping gently upward, the heat increasing rapidly. Blood pounding in my ears and both of us tired, walking on and on in a daze, gravel and sand glaring in the sun and dust devils beginning to form. And then, from the top of a rise, we had our first sight of the lava that lay ahead, a great wall of it like a railway embankment, black in shadow with not a tree or a shrub, nothing growing. Beyond it, bright in the sunlight, were what appeared to be slag heaps and old mining tips. "Is where we go," Dima said, pointing to the formidable embankment of lava. "We find spring there."

"It'll be dry," Abe told him, and the African nodded. "Dry." He paused, his face glistening black and frowning as he stared northward. "One day it rain again." He said it hopefully, but without conviction. "After rain desert very good."

The humped back of Kulal lay on the horizon like a stranded whale and in the clarity of that early light the green of forest showed a glint of emerald below the pink-white cloud suspended over the summit.

It was while we were still standing there, staring at the desolation ahead, that, faint on the morning stillness, came the sound of a shot. It came from our left, a sharp thin sound, followed by another and another. And then a wisp of smoke curled up as though somebody far to the west of us had lit a bonfire. I looked at Abe. "What is it, another truck?" Surely to God the man wouldn't have tried the same thing twice.

"Not a truck," Abe said quietly. "The plane, I think."

Dima seized hold of the bag, wrenching it from me. "We go quick." He said it urgently, shouldering the bag and breaking into a long loping stride.

"It has—to be—the plane," Abe grunted. "Those elephant . . ." But he was trotting now and had no breath for talk. I took the camera from him and as we went down the northward slope first Kulal and then the lava ridge dropped from view, our horizon closing in. Ten minutes later we encountered the first of the lava, an area of crumbled, perforated rock that forced us to a walk, picking our way and balancing precariously on shifting lumps of volcanic magma. More gravel interspersed with lava incursions, then the gravel became isolated patches and soon we were into nothing but lava, an incredible brown waste, all rounded boulders, through which we moved laboriously, the embankment black in shadow and rising up ahead of us like a slice of the industrial revolution painted by a madman.

Never in my life had I seen such a country, a hellish misery of moonscape rubble that looked as though great slabs of chocolate had been put through a grinder, then flung with wild abandon by giant hands across the face of the earth. And the embankment, when we finally reached it, was a crumbling wall of shattered metallic rock, so shot through with holes that it had the appearance of a fire-blackened row of office blocks badly shelled and falling into ruin. We moved slowly along the petrified base of it, feeling our way like crabs along the edge of a reef, and though we were in shadow the heat was overpowering. Twice Abe fell and it was only the fact that he had his hands free that saved him; the second time he grazed a knee, tearing a hole in his trousers. We were half an hour covering less than a mile, the shadows hardening as the sun struck with growing fierceness on the lava field to produce a blinding glare that hurt the eyes. Dima was well ahead of us then. I stumbled, just saving myself, and when I looked up again he had vanished. Far away to our left a stunted thorn tree stood on its head, the first mirage of the day's heat. He was nowhere to be seen and I had a sudden crazy feeling that the lava had swallowed him up. Then he was there again, beckoning us on, and he no longer had the bag in his hand, only his rifle.

It was a great cleft in the lava cliff and he was waiting for us at the entrance. "Stay now till Temo come." The cleft was deep, a dark gash in the fault line, and at the back of it brown grit like a very coarse sand overlaid the crumbled rock. It was cool by comparison with the temperature outside. Abe flung himself down, his thin chest heaving, his mouth open, panting with exhaustion.

"Where's the water?" I asked Dima.

"Dry now. All dry." He pointed to where he had dug with his hands in the grit. The hollow was cool to my touch, but bone dry.

"So what do we do now? Where do we get water?"

"Sleep now," he said.

I felt the dryness of my lips with my tongue, staring at the water bottle at his belt. But when I asked him to give us some, he shook his head. "No drink. When Tembo come—"

"We want a drink now."

"No drink," he repeated obstinately. I stared at the bottle thirstily, knowing it was no good. He had his orders and that could only mean van Delden knew bloody well there wasn't any water now between here and Rudolf.

"How far to the lake?"

He shrugged. "For this man—" He nodded to Abe, who was lying back, his eyes closed. "Too far, I think."

I sat down and leaned my back against the rough metallic surface of the rock. A wave of tiredness swept over me. And if I was tired . . . "You all right?" I asked Abe. There was no reply and I saw he had fallen asleep, his mouth open and his tongue showing dark and rough. I closed my eyes and in an instant I too was asleep.

I woke to the moan of wind and a gritty sifting of sand in the cleft. Dima was squatting in the entrance, his rifle wrapped in his cloak and his eyes slitted. Beyond him the lava glare was subdued, nothing visible, a sepia haze of windblown sand. The moaning died, the glare increasing as the sand subsided until the walls of the cleft framed an eye-searing glimpse of heat-hazed rubble. No shade now, the sun striking down almost vertically and my body parched. I glanced at my watch, surprised to find that it was already past eleven. I had slept for almost two hours.

The moaning started up again, but distant now like the faraway roar of an express train. "That damned wind," Abe murmured.

"How long has it been going on?" I asked.

"About an hour, I guess. It comes and goes."

I nodded, seeing his cracked lips, feeling dehydrated myself. God, the sun was hot!

"What's happened to van Delden?"

He shook his head, a minuscule movement as though even that was too much of an effort. I leaned back against the rock, trying to visualise what it would be like driving wild elephants into the teeth of a sandstorm, remembering von Höhlen's description of hurricane winds roaring down off Kulal. If only it would rain. I closed my eyes against the glare, hearing the murmur of his voice as he said, "In two hours we'll have shade again."

"You think he'll come?"

Abe didn't answer and when I looked at him again he had his towel over his head to keep off the sun. Through narrowed eyes I looked out across the field of lava to where the wind was spiralling sand high into the air. "This evening," I said, "when it's cooler and no wind, we'll have to try and make it to Sirima. There's a waterhole there."

"How far?"

But it wasn't a question of distance. I tried to explain the sort of terrain we would have to cross, but I couldn't remember how long Teleki had taken. Four hours, a whole day? I couldn't remember and I hadn't the energy to get the book out and look it up. "There's a moon," I murmured. "A night's march—"

"Forget it," he said. "It'll be dry like this place."

"There's always the lake."

"Forget it, I tell you." His voice had risen to a sharper pitch. "No elephants can live in this sort of country and I am not going where there are no elephants."

"There were elephants on Lake Rudolf when Teleki was there, lots of them."

"Bugger Teleki," he snapped. "You're always quoting Teleki. It's nearly a hundred years ago. The climate has changed. Everything has changed. And if van Delden doesn't come I'm going back."

I looked at Dima. "Are there elephants on the shores of Lake Rudolf?" I asked him.

He shook his head, frowning, and I didn't know whether it was because he didn't understand or whether he was saying there were no elephants. "We'll decide when it gets cooler," I muttered.

"Do what you like," Abe said petulantly, and hid his head in his towel again as another moaning holocaust of wind drove sand into the cleft.

I must have dozed off, for when I opened my eyes again it was with a jerk and the instant knowledge that Dima was gone from his watchdog post. I forced myself up and went to the entrance. No wind and the sun directly overhead. The reflected glare of the lava was worse than any studio's arc lights. It was eye-blinding and for a moment I could see nothing except sand moving a long way off and carrying with it the faint murmur of the wind. No sign of Kulal. It was hidden in a sepia haze. I shaded my eyes, straining south to where something shimmered in the heat. Bushes, trees—or were they moving? I wasn't sure. They merged and became one, separated into three—no five—all blurred, and then they started to run.

It took me a moment to realise they were ostrich, longer to work out that something had disturbed them. They were at least a mile and a half away, out beyond the lava where the first of the scrub showed as a wavering reed-like fringe. A man appeared, clear and sharp, and the shape of him was instantly shattered by the heat, a sand devil twisting up at the very spot where I had seen him.

"What is it?"

I turned to find Abe coming out into the entrance and when I looked again the sand devil was gone and there were two men, not one. "Van Delden," I said. "At least, I think it is. Dima has gone to meet him." I had seen Dima now, standing motionless at the far end of the lava wall, the dark of his body merged with the rock. A brown haze of airborne sand was flowing to the west of us and the sun bore down like a furnace.

"I wonder what he's done with those elephants," Abe murmured.

The figures moved in slow motion, crawling across the shimmering edge of visibility towards Dima and the lava wall. A breeze touched my face, the sand haze moving closer, the sound of it rising, and we went back into the torrid sun-trapped heat of the cleft, wrapping our towels round our faces. But this time it did not reach us, and when we went out into the entrance again I could see them quite clearly, Dima hurrying back ahead of them.

He was panting when he reached us, sweat glistening on his forehead. "Tembo say you go in." And he pushed us back into the cleft. A few minutes later van Delden arrived, Mtome close behind him. They flopped down, both of them exhausted, and I was shocked to see how deep the lines of van Delden's face showed under his beard. "What happened?" I asked.

He didn't answer for a moment, wiping his face on the sleeve of his bush jacket. Then he leaned back against the rock and closing his eyes, a pair of binoculars still slung round his neck, his rifle propped up beside him. "There was a guard on the plane, of course, and the damned fool had sat himself in the cockpit. Gone to sleep there and he didn't get out until he heard the Land-Rover coming in from the South Horr camp. It was Alex's partner, Jeff Saunders, and he had four soldiers with him." His voice was thick, almost a croak. "Didn't give us much time. We hit the plane and ran. We had to backtrack as far as the stream and wade up it. Only way I could be sure of shaking them off. A hell of a trek."

"Why wait for the guard to get out?" Abe asked.

Van Delden's eyes flicked open. "He might have been killed, that's why. The poor devil wasn't there because he liked it. He was a soldier, not a hunter."

Abe shook his head, smiling at such a fine distinction. "Where's Mukunga?' he asked.

"Still on the shoulder of the Mara with those elephants."

"Will they be all right?"

"I think so. With no plane it will take time to locate them. Too late to set up a proper cull. And if they do catch up with them it'll be dangerous stalking. Those elephants had Mukunga making lion noises at them all night. They'll be thoroughly roused and in an angry mood." He closed his eyes again, breathing deeply, his belly moving in and out in a controlled exercise of the diaphragm.

"There's no water here," Abe said.

"No. I hardly expected there would be."

"So what do we do now?"

"Wait for Mukunga. He knows where to join us."

"Yes, but what then? Where do we go from here?"

"Sirima, the lake, Balesa Kulal—wherever those elephants are going." He looked across at me. "Have you got that book? I'd like to check what von Höhlen says about the elephants they shot on the shores of Lake Rudolf. It was the east shore, wasn't it?"

"Yes, but when they discovered the lake, they were approaching it from the Nyiru Range, not from where we are now." I got the book out of the bag and handed it to him. "If I remember rightly they found two herds of elephants just south of the lake, then nothing till they were north of Mt. Longondoti."

He nodded. "Elephants would never move into the lava country under Kulal."

"Then how would they get up to the Longondoti area?"

"They would have come south along the lake shore from Abyssinia. But if they were going north, like the ones we've been following, then they've either got to cross Kulal or else follow the bed of the Balesa Kulal up the east side of the mountain. There's usually water there under the surface, but I don't think there'll be any now, not after the drought." He had opened the book and I watched him as he pulled a pair of steel-rimmed half-glasses from his haversack, marvelling at the man's stamina. He had been on the go most of the night and half the day and he still had the energy to check on von Höhlen's book.

The wind sound rose, sand driving against the lava edges of the cleft, and we lay curled up, our heads covered. This time it kept on blowing for a long time and even when the sound of it finally subsided I remained where I was, locked tight inside myself, wondering what the night would bring, where we would be tomorrow. I didn't dare think further ahead than that, committed now to the company of this old man and his strange obsession. Once, when I pushed the towel away from my face, I saw him still propped up against the rock, but his eyes were closed, book and glasses lying on the ground beside him. The others were asleep, too, and I dozed off to memories of Battersea Park in summertime and the shade of trees.

Surfacing at last, I found the sun had shifted, striking obliquely across the cleft, so that we were in shadow. Van Delden had the book in his hands again and was making notes. He looked across at me over his glasses. "You were right," he said. "Two herds of elephant just south of the lake on the edge of the lava country. After that, nothing till Longondoti, and then it was a young bull he encountered." He searched back through the pages. "That was March 17. Five days later Teleki refrained from shooting a herd of—'six females with five little ones of different ages . . . the Count brought down a rhinoceros and we heard lions roaring in the night.' That's on the shore of Alia Bay. Later the same day Teleki bags five elephants. He was firing so furiously he ran out of ammunition and had to send to camp for more. Two herds were involved, one of six cows with young, the other five full-grown bulls. As you said, bulls and cows, and both on the shore and in the water." He leaned back. "I can't remember ever hearing before of elephants browsing on seaweed."

I had shifted my position, for I found it difficult to follow him, tiredness accentuating his peculiar accent. "There was a bull browsing on weed," I murmured. "It smashed the canoe they'd carried up from the coast."

"He doesn't say it was a bull, and he doesn't say it was eating the stuff." He looked down at the book again. "He just says it was 'quietly rooting up seaweed'—he means lakeweed, of course. Later—" He searched the next few pages. "Later he meets up with 'a great many elephants—first two, then four gigantic beasts with huge tusks; then a herd of twelve bulls, four of which were very old; then three young bulls, with tusks reaching to the ground; and lastly, a herd of fourteen animals bigger than any we had yet met with.' And the only comment he makes at a sight like that is to tot up the value of the ivory!" He gave that strange laugh of his, half bark, half grunt, then turned the page and said: "Ah, this is what I was looking for: Wednesday, March 28—'During the afternoon a herd of female elephants with young ones went down into the lake near the camp, and remained for a long time standing still with water up to their bellies, rooting up seaweed with their trunks, from which they shook the water before eating it.'" He closed the book with a snap. "The man's too dull a writer to have made it up." And he added wearily, "But there's no weed in this part of the lake and Alia Bay is almost a hundred miles to the north beyond Mt. Longondoti and Jarigole."

"There's Loiyangalani," I said. "That's marked on the map as an oasis."

He nodded. "There's always water there. It comes down from Mt. Kulal, down the great gorge. There's a track runs from the Horr Valley to Loiyangalani built by the missionaries. But even if it has survived the war, and hasn't been destroyed by earth tremors, it's still no good to elephants. They wouldn't like it. Goes through the most Godforsaken country, nothing but lava and old volcanic vents." He stared out into the blinding glare. "No, my guess is they're going to pass Kulal to the east. They'll make for the dry bed of the Balesa Kulal and if they can't find water there, then the only hope is to try and drive them towards the track that leads up the shoulder of Kulal, past the Mission and into the forest." He shook his head. "Not easy, but we'll have to try it. Alex can't cull there, too far and the forest too thick. At least, it used to be thick. I don't know what it's like now."

"It's still green on top," I said. "You can see it."

He was silent for a while, then he looked at his watch. "Nearly two. Better try and sleep now. We'll have food and water in three hours' time, start moving again at five-thirty. See if we can find Mukunga before it's dark." He put his glasses away, laid the book on top of our bag, and, stretching himself out, was instantly asleep.

I sat there for a while, thinking about what he had said and gradually resigning myself to the certainty that I would never get to the great rock pyramid of Porr. So near. I picked up von Höhlen's book, unfolding the flimsy map at the end with their route marked in red and the dates of each camp. The closest they had come to where we were now holed up was March 5 and it was March 13 before they had been skirting the lake under Mt. Porr. I folded the map up again and threw the book down in disgust. A big expedition with a herd of cattle for food and it had taken them over a week to cover less than fifty miles.

I lay down then and the next thing I knew there were voices and Mukunga was there, squatting beside van Delden, talking urgently. The words ndovu and askari were repeated several times. "What's happened?" I asked. Van Delden shook his head impatiently and they went on talking. Finally Mukunga moistened his mouth from his water bottle, curled up, and went to sleep. Abe stirred and asked for water. "Lie still," van Delden said, "and you won't need it."

"Mukunga's had water."

"He's been on the run, that's why. The patrol that was sent out after you picked up the elephant tracks and if they hadn't been diverted by their desire for meat they'd have got him. They shot a full-grown calf and are camped beside the carcase."

We left at the time he had said, having had a sip of water. The wind had died, the sun low in the west. Behind us Mt. Kulal was a great reddening sprawl, the forest on its top showing green, the cloudcap gone. Everything was very clear in that evening light. There was a family of ostrich waiting for us as we came off the last of the lava into scrub. Ten minutes later we came upon the tracks of a vehicle.

The sun was setting in a red glow behind us, colour flooding the desolate landscape, lighting up the face of the lava embankment away to our left so that it was brilliant with purples and greens and sulphurous streaks of yellow. Faint on the evening stillness came the sound of an engine revving. Van Delden said something to Mukunga and he went on ahead, loping up a rise topped by the ragged shape of a thorn. When we reached the thorn tree he was far down the further slope, running for the cover of a thorn thicket, and in the plain beyond a Land-Rover was raising a cloud of dust and a group of elephants was milling around in confusion.

There was no doubt what the Land-Rover was doing, as it turned, then turned again. It was trying to head the elephants off by driving back and forth across their line of march. Van Delden had halted, standing with his head thrust forward, staring angrily. "Too late," he muttered. "Another hour and they—" He stopped there, his body suddenly rigid. "Who's that?" A figure had emerged from the thicket, a man no bigger than a speck in the immensity of the rolling gravel plain. But even at that distance I could see that he was an African, and he carried a rifle in his hand. He was running—running towards the elephants. "Who is it?" van Delden said again, and raised his binoculars to his eyes.

I turned to Abe, a sudden thought in my mind. He had the camera to his face and was looking through the eyepiece. "Can you see?" I asked him, but he shook his head.

"Can't be one of the hunters," van Delden murmured. "They'd never risk their lives on foot, not with all those elephants, and they're thoroughly roused now."

The Land-Rover had turned again, the sound of it overlaid by squeals and trumpeting. Then suddenly there was only the sound of the Land-Rover. The elephants had closed up in a tight bunch, several calves in the centre so that they were completely lost to view in the packed mass of grey backs and widespread ears. They were all facing the Land-Rover, and behind them the African was approaching them, trotting now and moving out to the flank.

The grip was suddenly wrenched from my hand and Abe zipped it open, burrowing around to produce the telescopic lens. "Light's not good, but worth a try." He was tense with excitement, his hands trembling as he changed the lenses. And at that moment the shot came, the sound of it clear in the sudden stillness, the silent, frightened herd, standing like sculptured figures, motionless. Mukunga was only halfway to the thicket, standing now, his rifle still slung across his shoulder, staring at the tight-packed elephants and the Land-Rover's dust stream. It could only be the unknown African who had fired, but I couldn't see him. It was as though the desert had swallowed him up. There was not a tree, not even any scrub in which he could have hidden himself.

Another shot, and then another, and suddenly the Land-Rover was swerving, half out of control.

The elephants had all swung round, trunks weaving, seeking the new source of danger. No trumpeting now, everything silent, even the Land-

Rover stopped. I saw him then, lying prone, the rifle out in front of him, his body merged into the sunset red of the desert gravel. In that stillness we could just hear the Land-Rover's engine ticking over. The elephants heard it, too, and it distracted them from the lone figure lying so close to them. They turned, the sound of the engine drawing them like a magnet, and suddenly one of them moved out ahead of the herd, trumpeting loudly. The next instant the dust was flying from its feet and it was charging with its head up and its trunk curled below its tusks. I heard the soft whirr of the camera and then it was lost in the revving of the Land-Rover's engine as it began to move, heading in our direction, but slowly, jerkily, its wheels spinning and throwing up streamers of red dust. The elephant was gaining on it fast, and it wasn't a mock charge. It was the real thing. "What the hell's wrong?" I breathed, and Abe close beside me answered through clenched teeth, "They've got a flat."

The Land-Rover stopped, I think to engage four-wheel drive, and Abe still had the camera turning when the elephant reached it, lowering its head and ramming its tusks into the rear of the vehicle. It pushed it forward perhaps twenty yards, head down and flanks heaving, the man in the passenger seat struggling to turn round, a rifle in his hand. The elephant lifted its head, tearing its tusks free, slamming them into it again and trumpeting in a fury of rage. Then it got a grip and was lifting the Land-Rover up off its back wheels, heaving and growling at it. For a moment I thought it would toss the whole thing over on to its nose, but the man with the gun at last managed to turn into a kneeling position and the crack of the shot seemed to stop everything dead, the animal standing there and the Land-Rover still up-ended, engine roaring and rear wheels spinning. Then the ears folded slowly back, the head and shoulders sagged, and as the elephant sank to its knees, the wheels got a grip and with a rending of metal the Land-Rover jerked forward.

The driver must have seen us now, for the vehicle was heading straight up the rise towards us, grinding slowly in four-wheel drive and bumping over loose stones, riding on the rim of a flat rear wheel. Through the haze of its dust I could see the dead elephant lying motionless like a great grey rock, and beyond it, the rest of the herd, half hidden in their own dust cloud, milled around, the sound of their squealing and growling coming to us as a distant, confused din, like the roar of a panicking crowd.

The Land-Rover topped the rise and in the last of the sun I saw Mary driving, and Kirby-Smith, beside her, with his hand on the wheel, trying to turn it away from us. Then it stopped, the engine gently ticking over, everything silent, even the elephants quiet. Nobody said anything, Kirby-Smith sitting there, his face caked in dust and sweat, and van Delden standing with his head thrust forward, staring.

"Leave your rifle and get out." Van Delden started to move slowly forward, Mary and Kirby-Smith still sitting there, watching him as though stunned. Her face was drained of blood and white under the tan. She pushed her goggles up, glancing at the man beside her, eyes wide and scared-looking. Her lips moved and in answer to the whisper of her words he shook his head, climbing slowly out and standing there, facing van Delden, his gun left on the seat behind him.

Slowly he pulled off his goggles, staring at van Delden, the white of his teeth showing in a smile, a conscious effort to appear casual. "You might have killed us."

"Maybe I will next time," van Delden said quietly. "But it wasn't any of my men fired those shots."

"Who was it then?"

Van Delden shrugged. He had reached the Land-Rover, his eyes on Mary sitting there behind the wheel. "After all I've taught you!" His voice was thick and angry. "Get out of there."

She shook her head, staring at him dumbly.

I thought for a moment he was going to tear her bodily out of the driving seat. "Get out," he said again, and it was obvious from the tone of his voice that he couldn't bear the sight of her sitting there in Kirby-Smith's Land-Rover. "Stop playing the fool with this man."

Her mouth opened, her eyes suddenly wide and appalled. "You think that? You think because my mother—"

"Shut up!"

The harshness of his voice was like a slap on the face, and she shrank back, her hands clenched on the steering wheel, her body rigid, the two of them staring at each other. Then he turned to Kirby-Smith. "I brought her up to respect life." He moved a few paces forward then, till they stood face to face. "Now I'm warning you, Alex," he said, speaking slowly. "I'll do anything, anything at all. . . ."

"You've done quite enough already." Kirby-Smith's voice was high and angry. "Yesterday it was a truck and two men dead. This morning you shoot up my plane. That can't go on."

"Why not? Do you think I'll give up?" And then he leaned his great head forward, his voice gentler, almost reasonable. "Even you must have realised there is something strange about this movement of elephants northward. You must have noticed their condition. I've seen two of them dying on their feet. And though they're exhausted, they don't stop. Even you and your hunters don't turn them back. They keep on coming, in family groups that are small and unbalanced. Haven't you noticed? Cows and bulls all mixed up. They've lost most of the very old and the very young. Only a few calves left. It's a pitiable sight. I've been following them now for three days, observing them. They're all converging here, so that I have the feeling this is some sort of gateway to a place they know about. Is that your observation? You've had planes flying. You must know far more about their movements than I do." He paused, staring at Kirby-Smith. "Well? Am I right? Are these the last sad remnants coming together in their effort to find a place of safety?"

Kirby-Smith hesitated, and I got the impression he was trying to work out in his mind how best to meet this long outburst. "They certainly seem to be converging—"

"Little groups from all over this part of Africa. All that's left."

"I wouldn't say that." And he added quickly, trying hard to maintain a casual reasonable air, "Really, you know, it's quite impossible to be sure of the exact distribution and numbers of the elephant population. There may be more left than you think."

Van Delden nodded, fingering his beard. "It's a nice, comforting thought. I'd like to think you're right. But I've lived in the company of elephants long enough to sense when something unusual is happening, and I tell you, Alex, what you're witnessing here is a quite extraordinary migration. It may be this is the last time these great animals will move over the face of Africa in large enough numbers for them to make a pattern." And he added, still speaking quietly and with great intensity, "They were nearly wiped out once before. It took the fall of the Roman Empire to save them that time—because the trade routes that took the ivory to the East were cut. Almost as though the country closed in to protect its own. But this time—"

"I think you exaggerate."

"I hope I do. But when the last of the bisons stood before the hunters, they didn't know it was the last."

"I assure you I have no intention of shooting them all. I made that clear at the Conference. I've always stuck to my quota—"

"Your quota!" Van Delden gave that harsh laugh. "You'll do what Kimani tells you and if I know that little man it's ivory he's interested in. Like you, he's a businessman, and when there's no more ivory, no more elephants, then you'll start in on any other profitable species that hasn't been wiped out, until one day you'll be down to a quota for warthogs." He stared at him for a moment, then said quietly, "You've a long walk ahead of you, so better get going."

It took a moment for Kirby-Smith to realise what he meant. Then his gaze shifted to the Land-Rover. I could see him measuring the distance, considering the time it would take him to jump in and get clear. Van Delden saw it, too. "Just stay where you are, Alex. I need a vehicle, so I'm borrowing yours. And I'm taking Mary with me."

"That's for her to decide." His eyes were still on the Land-Rover. "Taking my Land-Rover won't get you far," he said. "As for the culling, you can't stop me. I've got a Government contract and the support of the Army. You can't take on the Army.'

"Up here I can do anything." Van Delden said it slowly in a tone of absolute conviction. "I know this country. You don't." He turned then, calling to Dima to get the wheel changed, and then he reached into the Land-Rover, picked up the discarded rifle, emptying it of ammunition and throwing it into the back. He came back then to face Kirby-Smith again, saying quietly, almost conversationally, "I've nothing to lose, you know. Nothing at all. I don't set great store by my life in the Seychelles. I only went there when they kicked me out of Africa because it was handy, not because I liked it. But you . . . you've always managed your life so much more cleverly than I have. You've got plenty to lose, haven't you? Everything you've built up over the years."

Kirby-Smith gave a little shrug, and after that they didn't say anything, the two of them standing facing each other while Dima got the jack out of the back of the Land-Rover and slid it under the rear axle. The sun had set and down in the darkening plain the elephants had gone. Nothing stirred and there was no sign of the African who had fired those shots.

"Give Dima a hand, will you," van Delden said to me, not shifting his gaze from Kirby-Smith, and I got to work on jacking up the vehicle, glad of something to do. Mary was still sitting there, a lost, frozen look on her face. But in the end she got out and helped me get the spare wheel down. I think she felt the need of something to occupy her mind.

Dima had obviously done this many times before. It didn't take us long to get the wheel off, darkness already closing in as I hefted it up on to the bracket at the rear. Its rim was badly dented, the outer case cut to shreds. Behind me I heard Kirby-Smith talking to Abe, trying to persuade him to get van Delden to see sense. "More troops arrived in camp this morning and the Army now has two patrols out. They've already found the minibus and it's only a matter of time——"

"You could stop the cull," Abe said mildly.

"You saw what he did yesterday. Two men killed."

"I'm just a newsman."

"You saw it. You're a witness."

"They were shot, yes. I saw that. But I didn't see who shot them."

"I shot them," van Delden growled.

Kirby-Smith started to say something, then checked himself, turning to Abe again. "Tomorrow the Army are sending up another plane. He hasn't a hope——"

"Oh, sure," Abe said. "He hasn't a hope, as you say. But he'll do it, just the same."

"Then stop him. You heard what he just said. You're a witness to that."

Abe shook his head, smiling. "I didn't hear anything. You see, Major, I don't go along with what you're doing, so don't expect me to hold your hand."

We were tightening the wheel nuts and Mary was standing close beside me, just standing there, watching them, her eyes staring, the pale oval of her face devoid of expression, her body tense. I could guess what she was feeling, all hell let loose inside her in a conflicting tide of loyalties and emotions. From the rear of the Land Rover came the scrap of metal as Dima pulled the jack clear. Kirby-Smith heard it, too. "Be sensible,

Cornelius. All this part of the Federation is under Brigadier Osman and his Army Brigade." He was making a conscious effort to appear reasonable. "The old days are gone. They're gone for good. Taking my Land-Rover—" He hesitated, then said, "Tell you what I'll do. I shouldn't, but for old times' sake I'll tank up with fuel and drive you through to Marsabit. From there you should have a chance of reaching the coast."

"And what about the elephants?" Van Delden laughed. "No. You want a deal, you know my terms."

"I told you, I'm under contract. I can't break that."

"You mean you don't want to. That's understandable, since I hear you worked very hard to get it." He thrust his great white-maned head forward. "But it's a contract you can't fulfil. You tell them that." He stood like that for a moment with his head thrust out, and then he said, "I don't give a damn about my life. I've told you that. Or yours either. All I care about now is to see that enough of those elephants get through to wherever it is they're going. Then they'll be able to rest up, recover, breed, begin the long slow cycle all over again, building up their numbers. That's what's important, all I care about."

Kirby-Smith shook his head. "Your trouble is you've lived on your own too long. It's not what you want. Not any more." His voice had risen, the need for self-justification very evident as he said, "It's what the people want now. The people and the Government of this new Federation . . ."

But van Delden had turned his back on him. "Dima." He jerked his head towards the driving seat, and as the African slid behind the wheel and started the engine, he came over to Mary and said, "Get in the back."

She shook her head, her eyes unnaturally bright. "I'm not coming."

"Get in."

"I'm not coming, I tell you." Her hands clenched tight on the clips that secured the bonnet, and when he reached out and took hold of her arm, she flung him off. "I'm not. I'm not." Her voice was high, on the edge of hysteria. "I wish to God I'd never asked them to warn you."

To my surprise he turned to me. "Get her in the back and keep her there." His voice was surprisingly gentle. He looked at Abe. "I take it you're coming with us."

"Sure I'm coming with you."

"Then get in. It'll be difficult to see their tracks soon."

The first stars were already showing in the night sky. I tried to take hold of Mary's arm, but she drew back from me, half turning towards her father, staring at him as he stood there. The others were already clambering into the Land-Rover and I thought I was going to have trouble, but then she suddenly turned and walked to the back of it with her head up and her face set, climbing in and seating herself close by the tailboard. As I joined her I heard Kirby-Smith say, "What about my gun? I'm not leaving without my gun."

Van Delden looked at him. "Your gun. Of course." He reached into the back and picked it up by the barrel; then, standing back, he swung it

up and brought the stock crashing down against the hub of the spare
wheel. He handed it to him then without a word and got into the seat
beside Dima.

I didn't hear what Kirby-Smith said, his words lost in the revving of the
engine and the slam of the gears as we began to move. The lights came
on and for a second he was outlined in the red glow of the tail lights, a
solitary figure standing with the broken rifle in his hand. Then he was
gone, lost in darkness and the dust thrown up by our wheels. "He didn't
have to do that," Mary breathed, her voice barely audible and a shiver
running through her. "He'll never forgive that."

No point in reminding her there were evidently things van Delden
could never forgive. The man's pride had been injured, and I pictured him
in the morning limping wearily into camp with that broken rifle. To lose
face in front of his African hunters, in front of the Army, too—she was
right, he'd never forgive van Delden for that. I reached out and took her
hand. It was hot to the touch and I could feel her trembling. She let it
rest there for a moment, her hand in mine quite passive, then suddenly
her fingers tightened, gripping hold of me as though she was desperate
for somebody to cling to. She stayed like that, tense and rigid, as we went
roaring down the slope and into the flat land below. Then gradually her
fingers relaxed their grip and she let go of my hand.

The gravel plain was a narrow strip barely half a mile wide. Black outcrops of lava loomed away to our left. The southern cross showed faintly
above the outline of the mountains to our right. We turned eastward,
lurching and bucketing as Dima swerved to avoid patches of wind-bared
rock. And then we had slowed, searching the sand with our headlights
dipped for the tracks left by the elephants.

II

It seemed a long time before we finally found those tracks. We had been
casting back and forth over a wide area, driving slowly with Mukunga
and van Delden standing up in the front of the Land-Rover. It was Dima
who spotted the broken branch on the small acacia and after that
Mukunga went ahead on foot, tracking them by the light of our headlights. It was slow work and the moon was just rising when we sighted
them, dark shapes all motionless in silhouette. Dima cut the engine and
switched off our lights. Darkness enveloped us, the moon like a half of
an orange on the hard black line of the horizon.

Abe leaned forward. "Where do you think they're going?" And when
van Delden didn't answer, he added, "They can't survive in this waterless
desert."

"Don't talk. Just watch."

We sat there in silence as the moon lifted clear of the horizon, its
flattened orb changing from dull orange to white, its brilliance lighting

the desert, resolving the shapes of the elephants. We could see several half-grown calves huddled against their mothers, and ahead and a little to the left of them, a group composed entirely of adults moving restlessly. "Bulls." Van Delden had the binoculars to his eyes. "Strange to see half a dozen bulls herding with cows and their young." There was no wind, the aid completely still. Faint rumblings made a ghostly sound in the stillness. Gradually their ears were laid back against their massive shoulders and the trunks stopped testing the air; first one of the bulls, then another, turned their backs on us, and in a moment the whole herd was on the move, and we were following them, driving slowly through a pale white desiccated landscape with the moon hanging over the bonnet of the Land-Rover like a great lantern in the sky. Far ahead of us the elephants lumbered towards it as though drawn by its light.

Suddenly the Land-Rover stopped, van Delden reaching for his binoculars again, staring fixedly at the pale distant shapes. One of the elephants had paused, its trunk nuzzling at something on the ground, pushing at it with a forefoot. "Toto," Mukunga muttered, and van Delden nodded. All the elephants had stopped now, the cows bunching to present a solid front as they faced towards us, their ears spread, their trunks moving. They were about two hundred yards away, and I thought for a moment they were going to charge, they looked so menacing. The bulls, too, were restless, milling around, an impression of confusion and hostility.

"Have they winded us?" Abe asked, but van Delden shook his head. "It's the Land-Rover they don't like. That means they've already had experience of being hunted from vehicles."

Two of the cows detached themselves from the bunched family group, moving slowly back to join the distracted mother. She had got the calf to its feet and was standing there, head dropped, ears flat against its shoulders, the little trunk hanging straight down. The three elephants were close around it now, their trunks moving over its body as though to give it confidence, urging it forward. "Can't be more than a few months old." Van Delden sounded surprised. "That's the only toto we've seen. In fact, we've seen very few calves and most of those have been nearly full grown."

"Is that because of the drought??" Abe asked.

"That and the fact that calves are vulnerable to predators and man."

"And this is the only baby elephant you've seen. Strange that hers should have survived."

"She's probably the matriarch of this group. That might explain it." He shook his head. "Doesn't look as though it will last much longer though."

We had lost sight of it now, all three elephants close around it and moving slowly to rejoin the others. It was the signal for the whole group to begin moving again, but as Dima reached to start the engine, van Delden held up his hand. The mother had stopped again, and a moment later I caught a glimpse of the calf between her front legs and there was a bigger calf beside her, pressing against her flanks. She pushed the baby away, and Mary said in an appalled voice, "She's got no milk." The calf tottered to one of the other cows, pushed between her forelegs, attempting to suckle, then wobbled to one side and collapsed on the pale sand. Again the three elephants gathered round it, the older calf hovering in a restless, distracted manner, and the whole herd watching uneasily. This time the little calf did not rise and even at that distance I could sense the emotional disturbance affecting the whole herd, their distress obvious from their movements, some of them coming back to stand over the small bundle lying collapsed on the ground, moving their trunks over its body, the others either milling around or just standing distractedly, shifting their feet and swinging their heads.

Abe had found a pair of binoculars in the back and he had them glued to his eyes, leaning forward intently. Once I heard him mutter something about it being the same one, but he was only talking to himself and after that he was silent. We were there the best part of an hour while the little group round the fallen calf gradually broke up, leaving just the mother and two other cows trying to nudge it to its feet or lift it with their tusks. "Once at Marsabit," van Delden said, "one of my cows was wandering around three or four days carrying a dead calf in her tusks. But I don't think they'll be long now."

It was the bulls who moved first and I realised they had not the same close-knit family association. As soon as they had disappeared over the horizon the cows became very agitated, finally beginning to move off, uncertainly and looking back every now and then, sometimes half turning as though still unwilling to leave. Then the two remaining cows followed and only the mother was left, scuffing irresolutely at the ground, the older calf close against her as she continued to move her trunk over the body of her baby as though to fix it in her memory. Finally she abandoned it, turning and moving hesitantly after the others, rumbling and growling her distress, occasionally laying her trunk across the older calf's head and back. Abe let the binoculars fall. "She's very gaunt, quite different—she must be half starved."

Van Delden nodded. "They're none of them in good shape. Looks like they've come a long way, travelling fast."

"It's the same herd we saw last night." Abe was still staring after the retreating elephants. "They've come a very long way." He shook his head, his eyes strangely bright behind his glasses. Dima started the engine and beside me Mary's voice, high and urgent, cried, "You can't leave it—not like that."

"Why not?" van Delden asked. "It's not our job to interfere with nature, or have you forgotten?"

"But suppose it's still alive? You can't—"

"If you've got bitten by the silly sentimentality of the cities, forget it. As long as you're with me—"

"I didn't ask to come with you."

He nodded. "Nor you did. But you're here, so don't argue." And he told Dima to get moving again while she sat there staring sullenly at the back of his head. "You could have shot it," she muttered. "If it had been Alex . . ." But Abe turned on her angrily, almost shouting: "Isn't it enough just to have watched it? No need for a post-mortem."

The body of the calf was already merging into the moon-white landscape, the mother moving after the rest of the herd, the half-grown youngster still beside her. But her movements were slow and she kept on turning her head and looking back as though still expecting the calf to get to its feet and follow her. Finally she stopped beside a stunted acacia and began tearing at a branch. We stopped too, Abe picking up the glasses again and watching her intently as she wrenched the branch off and then went all the way back to lay it over the inert bundle lying in the sand. She remained there for some time, her head bent and her trunk constantly moving over it, then suddenly she turned and went lumbering off after the others already disappearing over a ridge dotted with a few thorns. Her feet made no sound and though she seemed to be moving slowly she covered the ground at surprising speed. We waited until she had disappeared, then followed, and when we sighted her again she was back with the rest of her group and they were bunched together with the bulls out ahead and moving quickly.

Gradually the moon shifted its position. From being over the bonnet it swung slowly to our right until it was above Abe's head. The elephants had changed direction. They were headed north now, and away to our left Kulal loomed, a pale cloud-capped sprawl.

I leaned across Mary, calling to van Delden. "They're making for the Balesa Kulal, aren't they?"

"Probably. The river bed isn't far now."

"Hey, but that's a dry watercourse." Abe seized my arm. "Didn't you say it was dry? Somebody said it was dry."

The Land-Rover slid to a halt. The elephants were standing in a huddle, so close they seemed to be in conference. I grabbed the binoculars lying by Abe's feet, thinking another calf was in trouble.

"How much water do they need? I read somewhere it's thirty gallons a day. Right?"

"That's about the normal intake for a full-grown adult," van Delden said.

"Hell! There must be twenty, thirty elephants there." He turned to me. "Are they clear enough to count? How many are there?"

Through the glasses I could see them quite clearly, all standing in a line as though they had come to some sort of fence. "I make it seventeen," I said, "but it's difficult to be certain. There are several big calves and they're keeping very close to their mothers."

"That's almost five hundred gallons a day. A lot of water, and in country as dry as this only a man like Aaron—"

Van Delden told him to be quiet. The elephants were moving again

and he signalled Dima to drive on. But we were too close now and
at the sound of the engine starting up several elephants whirled about,
ears spread as though about to charge, and the mother who had lost
her calf moved out in front, swinging her trunk and throwing sand in
the air. Van Delden leaned forward quickly and switched off the ignition.
In the sudden silence we could hear them, a low rumble of sound. They
stood there watching us for perhaps a minute, but with the light breeze
off the mountain blowing towards us, the Land-Rover still and no sound,
they gradually relaxed, finally losing interest and going off after the others.
Occasionally one of them looked back.

"Would she have charged us if we'd gone closer?" Abe asked as we
got moving again.

Van Delden nodded. "Probably. She's very distressed. The others certainly would. They're just about at the end of their tether, but cows in
defence of their calves wouldn't hesitate."

We could just see them now, heading north-east, and a few minutes
later we discovered what it was that had stopped them. It was a track
that still showed the faint treadmarks of vehicles, its edges bordered by
stones. Van Delden said it led through the Chalbi Desert to Kargi and
on to Marsabit. "In two or three miles they'll come to a crossroads.
There's a well just to the west of it."

"They can't draw water from a well," Abe murmured.

"It will be dry anyway."

"Can they make it across the Chalbi?"

"The bulls might. But not the cows with their young."

Sitting there, being driven through the stark beauty of that moonlit
night, the desert flowing white to the pale horizon and Mt. Kulal towering
high above us, I had a sense of unreality, as though it were all a dream,
the death of that little calf, the distress of its mother and her family
group, the whole macabre scene vivid in my mind, and yet everything
strangely remote. And the elephants out ahead of us, dim ghostly shapes
moving steadily towards a hostile, waterless desert. Looking at that desiccated scene, knowing that worse lay ahead of us if the herd tried to cross
the Chalbi, I was suddenly very conscious of the dryness of my mouth.
There was only a single jerrican in the back of the Land-Rover, presumably petrol, and nothing that looked as though it contained food. It was
twenty-four hours now since we had fed. "How far to the well?" I asked,
hoping he was wrong and there would be water in it. Mary laughed, her
teeth white in the oval of her face. "Haven't you ever been thirsty
before?"

I shook my head, not answering her. We had left the track and there
was scrub now, occasional thorn trees. We were heading cross country in
a more northerly direction, our speed gradually increasing, patches of soft
sand, the scrub thicker and more trees. Then suddenly we had stopped,
the engine switched off. In the stillness we could hear the elephants

rumbling to one another. We were closer than we had been before, but they ignored us, standing shoulder to shoulder in a ring.

They had found the well.

They remained like that, in a tight huddle, for several minutes. Two of the younger calves showed signs of exhaustion. One was sitting all alone on its haunches with its ears drooping like a dejected bloodhound. The other kept moving in on its mother, searching for a teat and being constantly thrust back by her trunk or a foot. And there were one or two almost fully grown who just stood waiting patiently, occasionally scuffing at the ground or feeling it with their trunks.

It was the cows that broke away first, drawn by the plaintive sounds of their young. They spread out uncertainly, searching the ground with their trunks and digging into it with slicing movements of their front legs, the toenails acting like a spade. One cow went on digging with her forefeet until she must have been down three or four feet. Two younger females came to help her, using the tightly curled tips of their trunks to scoop the loose sand out. But though they could smell water, they could not reach it.

The bulls began milling around, their trunks waving, their bellies rumbling. They were unsure of themselves and in a testy mood, the larger animals turning on the others if they got in their way. Finally one of them moved off. Others began to follow him, their backs towards us, a baggy-trousered shambling walk, the cows watching, some still digging at the soft sand. They took no notice of us, rumbling among themselves, and then, with much squealing and growling, the few young were marshalled and led away, out of the dry bed of the Balesa Kulal towards the great volcanic heap that towered above us in the moonlight.

Van Delden leaned back, lighting his pipe, the smell of his tobacco strong in the dry air. "There's a gorge," he said, "runs right back, almost splitting the mountain in two. Looks like they're making for that."

"Any water?" Abe asked.

"No. Not in a drought like this. Least I don't think so. But there's shade and enough greenstuff for them to browse on." He sat there for a while, smoking and not saying anything while the elephants disappeared from view over a rise that seemed to be a part of a long shoulder running up towards Kulal. "Well, we know where they're headed now, so no point in wasting good meat." He gave an order to Dima and we turned and started back on our tracks. We drove back until we reached the fallen heap of the baby elephant. I don't know whether it was actually dead, but it made no movement as Mtome plunged his knife into it and began carving out chunks of flesh. Blood was darkening the sand as I joined Dima in the Land-Rover to go in search of wood for a fire.

It was a strange, eerie meal, squatting there beside the carcase of the little elephant, the desert white in the moonlight and flames flickering from thorn tree branches hacked off with a panga that was part of the Land-Rover's equipment. At first Abe refused to touch the blackened meat, but when Mary said, "For God's sake, be practical," and began feeding him bits of her own steak, he overcame his revulsion. She watched to make certain he ate it, then asked me, "What happened to Karanja? Where is he?" And when I told her how he had left us the previous night, she nodded. "So it was Karanja." She turned to van Delden. "It was Karanja who fired on us, wasn't it?"

He was squatting on his hunkers between Mukunga and Dima, gnawing at a rib bone. "Could be," he said, working round the bone with his teeth.

"But why? I don't understand why."

He looked at her, holding the bone like a corn-cob. "Because he's back in a different world now, and in his way he's fond of elephants."

Abe shook his head. "If it was Karanja, then why did he disappear like that? He must have seen you standing there."

"He knows I don't trust him."

"But he wanted to join you."

"Maybe." He tossed the bone away and reached into the embers for a piece of meat. "He's an ex-Mission boy, you know. Clever as a vervet."

"And handsome," Mary whispered to me with an odd look on her face.

"After all the years I've known him I wouldn't like to say what goes on in his head. He's cunning and he never does anything without a reason. He's a bit of a showman, too."

"But a shot like that," Abe murmured. "Hitting the tyre on a moving vehicle. He wouldn't have risked that with Mary driving."

"He didn't know it was Mary, and there was no risk. He's a first-class shot. You know, when he left the Mission to join the Game Department he wasn't good for anything but office work. Most of my boys made fun of him, so he set out to become a better shot than any of them. I've seen him go into a thicket after a wounded lioness, no hesitation and grinning all over his face. Bravado, you'd say, but not quite that. He knew what he was doing, how sudden it would be. You see, a lioness doesn't growl a warning like a lion, the growl is instantaneous with the spring. I had a touch of malaria at the time, so I didn't dare risk it myself, too shaky. I let him have my .470 and he dropped the animal dead, right at his feet, with a single shot." He wiped his hands on his beard. "So long as he's got an audience . . . He must have an audience." He turned to Mtome. "Chai. Brew up some chai, and then we'll get going." And he added, "We'll drop Dima off to keep track of those elephants, then drive up on to the mountain. I've got a feeling that's where they're headed. There's always water on Kulal."

There was a goatskin waterbag I hadn't noticed before, a chargul hung on the side of the Land-Rover. Mtome produced a blackened tin from the back and in no time at all we were passing round an enamel mug of hot tea.

The moon was high in the sky when we finally left the white-boned carcase with a pile of red meat bloodying the back of the Land-Rover. We crossed the track again and stopped at the well, dropping the bucket on its frayed rope into the hole. There was no splash, no drop of water in it when we wound it up on the cumbersome wooden roller. Dima left us here, filling his waterbottle from the chargul and taking some of the meat with him. "Kambi ya mawingo," van Delden said as he got into the driving seat, and Dima, slinging his rifle over his shoulder, waved a hand in acknowledgment as he set off after the elephants.

Van Delden sat there for a moment, watching until the lone figure had disappeared from sight. Then he started the engine. "Kambi ya mawingo —that means the camp in the clouds. If we can get through to it, we'll stop the night there. I want to take a look into the western gorge." We moved off then, heading westward up the track that climbed the long shoulder of the mountain, and I sat there, feeling the hot air rushing past, thinking that at least I was going to get part of what I wanted. I was going up on to the great volcanic mountain that Pieter van Delden had written about with such awe.

It was a rough ride, and it got rougher as we climbed, the surface deteriorating until we were grinding up in low gear round hairpin bends flanked by crumbling banks of earth, the disused track falling away in places to the moon-white desert far below. High up on the shoulder, we rounded a bend and, suddenly, we were out on the lip of the world, looking down into a yawning chasm with the pale glimmer of cliffs and buttresses rising sheer on the far side. Ahead of us, the great bulk of the mountain filled the sky, half obscured by cloud, the gorge running back into it and lost in shadow.

We stopped there, all of us getting out to stand on a flat rock platform that seemed to hang in space. The bottom of the gorge was a good two thousand feet below and deep in moonshadow. Van Delden was scanning it through his glasses, Mukunga lying flat on the rock, his woolly head over the edge, peering down. "Fantastic!" Abe murmured, sucking in his breath at the sight of the world falling away into darkness below us. "Just fantastic! It must have been one hell of an earthquake to split the mountain open like this." He was staring down into the depths and he added sadly, "No way they could climb up out of that. No way at all."

"The Wandrobo had a way," van Delden said.

"You've been into that gorge, have you?"

"Once, but not right to the end."

"Then how do you know?"

"Jack Mallinson. He was the missionary here and he said the people of the forest used to come and go between this gorge and the one leading down to the lake."

Abe shook his head. "Mountain people maybe. But not elephants. They'll be trapped down there." The way he said it conjured a picture in my mind of elephants backed up against sheer buttresses of rock and the ring of hunters closing in.

Van Delden let his glasses fall, looking at him curiously. "Nothing we can do about that."

"And tomorrow, when Alex goes in after them—where will you be?" Mary's voice was a hoarse whisper, barely audible. "And there's Karanja. Karanja never liked Alex, and if he's down there—"

"You think he'd shoot him?"

She hesitated, staring at him. "There was that man Enderby." She said it slowly, almost reluctantly. "There was only you and Karanja at Marsabit when it happened. I know that now, so it was either—"

"You know nothing about it. You weren't there." He had gripped hold of her arm, silencing her. They stood like that for a moment, facing each other. Then he let go of her, leaning down and tapping Mukunga on the shoulder. "See anything?"

"Hapana, Tembo. Is too dark." He got to his feet.

Van Delden nodded, turning back to the track. "We'll get moving then."

"They won't have a chance," Abe murmured.

"Dima will tell us what happens."

Abe was silent then and my gaze shifted to the mountain, remembering the older van Delden, who had climbed Kulal, alone and on foot, all those years ago. But not from this direction. He had gone up from Lake Rudolf, spending six days exploring the mountain, finally driven down by starvation and the damp chill of the clouds. He'd found no traces of any civilisation, only the small black people who lived in the rain forest, the Wandrobo, and they had proved hostile. Now, looking up at the huge mass of the mountain, I felt it was hopeless, like searching for a needle in a slag heap. What possible chance was there of my stumbling on some vestige of the culture that had prompted a design on pottery that might be five, ten thousand years old? This was all part of the Rift Valley, shattered by volcanic upheavals; so much could have happened in that time.

The engine of the Land Rover started up and I turned to find van Delden already at the wheel. "Hurry up. We need some sleep and we've still got quite a way to go."

The two Africans were getting into the back. Mary lingered a moment, gazing down into the gorge, her face pale in the moonlight. Then she turned abruptly and I followed her. Only Abe remained, a slight, lone figure standing on the lip of the gorge.

"Mr. Finkel."

He turned as though in a dream. "I'm not coming," he said. "I'm going back." He spoke slowly, hesitantly, and I could see by the look on his face he was appalled at his own decision. "That gorge is nothing but a great rock trap. If somebody doesn't shift them out—"

"Don't be a fool man," van Delden said sharply. "You go down into that gorge, you won't shift them out—more likely you'll get trampled to death."

"I can at least try." It was crazy, and he knew it. To go back down the track and into that gorge, no gun, no food, and nobody with him. It would be the first time he had been on his own in Africa.

Van Delden shrugged. "Please yourself."

It was then that I started to climb out. I didn't want to, but I couldn't just leave him to go off on his own. Mary caught hold of my arm. "Don't be silly," she hissed. But it was van Delden who stopped me, leaning out of the driving seat and speaking quietly. "You scare them out of that gorge and tomorrow Alex will be able to run circles round them with his trucks. And if Alex doesn't kill them, then the heat will. It's hot like a furnace down there in the heat of the day. Now, for God's sake, man get in. Those elephants need time to recover themselves. Dima will tell us where they are when we pick him up in the morning."

There was a long silence. Abe standing there, irresolute, a small figure dwarfed by the immense bulk of the mountain behind him. Slowly he turned his head, looking back down into the gorge. "What is it?" Mary whispered. "Why is he so concerned?" But I couldn't tell her. I wasn't sure myself. It could be the ghost of his dead wife he saw trapped down there. Anything seemed possible in that weird light, and when van Delden turned to me and said sharply, "Go and get him," I shook my head. He revved the engine then, and the sound of it shattering the stillness seemed to break Abe's reverie. He looked round, his shoulders sagging, and as though still in a dream came slowly down off the rock and got into the Land-Rover without a word.

There were only a few more bends, then the track straightened out and we were approaching the Mission. Mary, close beside me whispered, "All my life I've wanted to come up here, but he wouldn't let me."

"Why not?"

She shrugged and the movement of her body so close against me was disturbing. "I was fifteen then." She gave a little giggle. "Perhaps he didn't trust me. It was a two-day journey from Marsabit to Kulal. It meant camping out in the desert. He sent me to school at Nairobi instead."

We had come out on an open stretch of grassland, the clouds low and casting a dark shadow ahead. There was no wind and nothing stirred as we turned off the track, driving out on to the shoulder of the mountain where a rock outcrop stood black against the moon like a ruined castle. Below it was a waterhole that had once been used by the Mission cattle. It was fed by a pipe and there was still a steady trickle of water running out of it, but there were no cattle now. Instead, the ground was marked by the feet of elephants, the dry sered grass trampled bare and the waterhole itself a muddy wallow. "So there is water here," Abe said, and van Delden nodded.

"It's the forest and the proximity of the lake," he said. "At this height the combination of the two tends to produce cloud."

"You knew that, and yet you let them go into that gorge when they

could have come straight up the track." Abe was staring at him accusingly.
"You could have herded them on to the track and up to the water here."

"Maybe." But he sounded doubtful. "Those elephants weren't in a
mood to be driven. And I didn't know what we'd find here."

"But you said there's always water on Kulal."

Van Delden turned on him angrily. "Look, man, a lot has happened
in this part of Africa during the last few years and Mallinson's been gone
a long time. What they did to Marsabit they could have done here. As
soon as I left Marsabit the bloody missionary there let the Rendile and
Samburu move into the forest. Dima was there about a year ago and he
says the whole mountain was bare, nothing but shambas, the lake we
called Paradise dried up, most of the waterholes too. And not an elephant
to be seen." He turned to Mukunga, who was bent down, studying the
ground round the pipe. "Any totos, Mukunga?"

"Ndio. Ndovu na watoto yao walikuwa hapa."

"He says cows with calves have been here." Van Delden sounded
puzzled. "I never saw any cows here before. Either they're staging through
on their way north, or else some of my elephants have moved in from
Marsabit."

"I thought you said they couldn't cross the Chalbi."

"Not now they couldn't. But once in a while it rains. They could have
crossed then."

Mtome had started to fill the goatskin bag from the pure clear water
running out of the pipe and I was thinking of all those tribesmen we had
seen, their cattle and their camels dead. "Why didn't the tribes move
up here?" I asked him.

"They're desert people and Kulal is cold and damp. Most of them are
afraid of the mountain anyway."

"But the Mission had cattle."

"The Mission was closed at the start of the African war." Mtome had
finished filling the waterbag and van Delden went over to the pipe, drinking from it in his cupped hands, then sluicing it over his face and neck,
and Abe, standing beside him and waiting his turn, said, "Would you
recognise your elephants if you saw them now?"

"Of course."

"After more than two years? It's at least two years since you had to
leave."

"Nearer three. But I'd still know them. And they'd know me."

"I'm told you can talk to them."

Van Delden straightened up, smiling. "You don't want to believe all
you hear, Mr. Finkel. I can imitate some of their rumblings, but the
vocabulary, if you can call it that is limited. I wouldn't be able to enquire
of a cow how she'd got here, for instance." He turned back to the Land
Rover. "Leave it at that, shall we? We'll know soon enough."

Abe followed him, his voice persistent. "And if they were yours, how
would you know? By earmarkings, or have you some other method?"

"Sometimes by the way they move, the tone of their rumblings, squeals and growls. But earmarks are the most reliable method."

"Those could have changed in three years."

"More rents and tears, yes. But the old marks still remain."

We were all back in the Land-Rover then and he had started the engine. Abe leaned forward, his voice urgent. "So if there was a big, very recognisable tear, you don't reckon it would have changed?"

"No, I don't." Van Delden glanced back at him, a gleam of interest in his eyes. "You've seen one of those elephants we were following before, is that it?"

Abe hesitated, then nodded reluctantly.

"Where?" van Delden asked him.

"At Treetops. It was a long time ago."

Van Delden looked at him a moment, then smiled. "So that's why you didn't want to eat from that calf. It was the mother, was it?" And as he let in the clutch, heading back to the track, he said, "That rent won't have changed much. Point her out to me if we come across her again."

The Mission was set on a rise above the track. The sprawl of wooden single-storey buildings had a dramatic appearance in the changing light, the moon coming and going as outlying veils of the cloudcap shifted. There was foliage growing through the roofs, no point anywhere, and the verandah of one building almost completely collapsed. Where the track bent round to the right, towards some store-sheds, van Delden stopped to sit gazing at what was obviously a staff cottage. It had been a pretty place at one time, but now the roof was sagging and all of one end of it had collapsed inwards. "Elephant," he murmured. Then turning to Abe, he said, "That was Jack Mallinson's place. He and the man before him were very conscious of the ecological importance of the forest. If the forest were cut down, then there would be no cloud over Kulal, no rain, just wind erosion, the sort of thing that's happened at Marsabit, at Meru and the Aberdares, all over the country. That's why the water is piped, so the cattle had no excuse to invade the forest. It was quite a job for a Mission to undertake, out on a limb here with supplies a major problem."

"And there weren't any elephants here then?" Abe asked.

"The odd bull, that's all Jack and I ever saw. I used to come regularly at one time to check on the greater kudu. It's a good place for kudus. But this mountain isn't like Marsabit. The altitude there is much lower and no storms." He turned his head away, staring at the black impenetrable shadow ahead of us. "Now we go into the forest. It's about six miles and if elephants have taken up permanent residence it may be slow going with a lot of tree shifting." He flicked the headlights to high beam and put the Land Rover in four-wheel drive as we ploughed left through the remains of a gate and down a vague track surfaced with the soft mould of forest humus, the moon suddenly obscured by the leaf canopy that had closed over us.

At first it was easy going, but in less than a mile we were bashing our way through a close thicket of reed-like stems. "Like driving through corn," Abe said as we crouched low to avoid the springing stems and flying debris. Twice Mtome got out to hack a way through with the panga, but after we had ploughed through the swamp of a stream bed, the track climbed again and we were slipping and sliding on mud-covered boulders. It was like that for perhaps another mile, our progress slow but steady, then quite suddenly we were into an area of forest that had obviously been browsed over by elephants. Their droppings were everywhere and as we laboured up the track, mud to our knees, clearing the fallen trees ahead of the Land-Rover, we became covered with mud and dung slime. Fortunately it was all fairly small timber we had to shift, but by the time we were through the area and back on to almost-clear track again, I was feeling utterly exhausted. Mary, who had been working just as hard as any of us, simply went to sleep.

Shortly after that we joined another track, turning left and climbing steadily along what seemed to be the crest of the mountain. The trees were taller now, the going firmer, less mud and no boulders, only elephant turds that sometimes looked like small boulders in the headlights. We stayed in four-wheel drive, but moving fast, for there were no trees across the track, just the brash of stripped and broken branches. It was very dark here in this high forest, dark and dank and no sign of the moon. We were into the cloud now and the contrast between this and the dry desert country far below was such that I had a feeling of intense anticipation. I don't know what I expected, but my tiredness was gone as I leaned forward, straining to see beyond the headlights, feeling that if I watched closely some marvelous revelation would leap into view.

I think perhaps I was a little lightheaded. The only thing of note we saw was one of the sacred trees. It was a giant of tremendous girth, and van Delden, pointing it out to us, said that the people of the forest believed that if ever those trees were destroyed it would be the end of the world. "It's a taboo that Jack Mallinson always respected. The Wandrobo would never survive the destruction of this forest."

"Have you ever met them?" I asked him, thinking that if I were to find the needle of that old civilisation it could only be through the people whose home this was.

But he shook his head. "Jack knew them, of course. He was always walking the forest alone. He loved it. Occasionally one of the few safaris that made it to the top of Kulal would report food or clothing missing, but never caught sight of the thieves. The Wandrobo know their forest and they move like shadows in the mist. They're a very secretive—"

The brakes slammed on, throwing us forward. And then we were roaring backwards, two grey shapes in the headlights, their heads up and their trunks tucked underneath their tusks as they charged us. They were gaining, the two of them shoulder to shoulder and filling the track. I could see their feet moving, but there was no sound, no trumpeting, only the noise of the engine. Rotting undergrowth cracked under our wheels and suddenly we were flung to the floor as the back of the Land-Rover smacked into the bole of a tree. We stopped dead, the engine stalled. Van Delden switched the lights off, everything black and no sound.

I didn't know what was going to happen and I just lay there, not daring to move. And then they trumpeted. The sound of it was startling in the stillness and very close, the most terrifying sound I thought I had ever heard. The lights came on and over my shoulder I could see the pair of them standing on the track with their trunks curled upwards and the eyes in their great domed heads glinting as they stared into the headlights. The starter whined, the engine came to life, and then we were driving straight at them, the horn blaring and van Delden swinging the wheel over as we hit the track. I had a glimpse of the two heads towering over us, the bright ivory of their tusks and their trunks writhing, then we were past them and driving furiously along the track.

Nobody spoke as we sorted ourselves out. I could see the black outline of Mukunga in the front, still with his rifle gripped ready in his hands. Van Delden turned his head and laughed. "All right in the back? You all right, Toto?"

"I'm okay, Tembo. We're all okay." She was laughing, too, as she gripped my arm and said, "You're trembling like a leaf. Wait till the engine doesn't start and they're leaning over you, ramming their tusks into the bodywork." Her grip was hard, her eyes glinting with excitement, and close beside me Abe's voice asked, "What were they, bulls or cows?"

"Cows," van Delden said.

"From Marsabit? Could you recognise them?"

"In that light and with them charging us?" He laughed. "Not a chance." And he added, "Cows don't usually charge like that, without any warning at all. Wonder where it was they got such a bellyful of man that it changed their nature." He was driving slower and both he and Mukunga were peering cautiously ahead. Once he stopped and switched off the engine, but there was no sound, the forest wrapped in its shroud of mist.

A little further on the trees fell away and we were into a clearing that was like a meadow climbing steeply up to the left of the track. Shadows moved in the mist and we stopped again. Beside us a pool of water had been trampled into mud and above it the grass of the slope was beaten flat. "Kambi ya mawingo," van Delden said. "But no good to us. It's already occupied." Vague shapes loomed beyond the headlights, their outlines blurred by the light drizzle that was falling. "We'll have to camp on the open slopes." The engine roared again and we shot across the clearing and into the dark tunnel of the trees on the far side, elephants moving like shadows and the track littered with broken branches so that we were crashing through a sea of half-dead foliage.

Gradually the debris thinned until finally the track was almost clear, the forest normal again and only the football-sized heaps of dung indicating that it had been used by elephants. The trees were smaller now and thinning out. Suddenly we were at the end of the track, a deep trench running across it. Van Delden backed the Land Rover into the undergrowth and switched off the engine. Darkness enveloped us and a great stillness, only the faint sound of moisture dripping from the leaves. "What now?" Abe asked, and there was a tenseness in his voice.

Van Delden got out. "We go on foot now. A few hundred yards, that's all. Put on all the clothes you've got. It will be a cold night."

It was a relief to get into our sweaters, for we were already chilled by the drive. Mary wrapped herself in a blanket he found for her under the front seat and then we skirted the trench, climbing through a tracery of thin-stemmed growth. It was, as he had said, about two hundred yards, and suddenly we were out in the open and there was grass beneath our feet. The cloud cover was thinner here, the moon's light filtering through. Just clear of the forest we cut branches and lit a fire, huddling close to it, grateful for the warmth and drinking scalding hot tea from a single tin mug passed from hand to hand. Incredibly, it was still only just after midnight. We seemed to have been travelling for hours.

But tiredness did not seem to have damped Abe's curiosity. "How long can the forest support that number of elephants?" he asked.

Van Delden shook his head. "To answer that requires a proper count, and we don't know how much of the forage is suitable. Not all of it, I suspect. Like I told you, Kulal has never been a natural habitat for elephants."

"It's a staging post on their way north, is that what you're saying?"

"Possibly." Van Delden took out his pipe and began to fill it. "That's what I need to know."

"And if they're just passing through, then they must have a way up and a way down. Isn't that right?"

"It's logical. But animals are directed by instinct, not logic."

"Are you sure? Would instinct alone be directing them north? It's a time of crisis for them and you said yourself they could be heading north because of some deep-seated knowledge. That's not instinct. That's something passed on from generation to generation. Or maybe it's imprinted in their genes."

"It's all speculation." A match flared, the hook-nosed, bearded face momentarily lit as he put it to his pipe. The tobacco smoke was comfortingly normal in the strangeness of that place. "There was an elephant at Marsabit—Ahmed. The biggest tusker anyone has ever seen. He was under the protection of Jomo Kenyatta. The one elephant whose ivory was safe. That was before the war, when Kenya was still a separate country. He was reckoned to be more than seventy years old when he died. That's a lot longer than most of them live. The average is about fifty years. But even fifty years, you go back three generations and you're back before the South African war, before Rhodes and the main drive of the English settlers." He was silent for a moment, drawing on his pipe. Then he said, "They can communicate, that I know. But what they can communicate is a different matter. The knowledge of safe territory is very abstract information compared with danger warnings, behavioural instructions, food satisfaction."

Abe nodded, taking out a packet of cigarettes and staring at it thoughtfully. It was his last packet and there were only three left. He put it away, sniffing the smoke from van Delden's pipe. "How many conversational sounds have you identified?" he asked.

"About forty."

"And they're all concerned with ordinary everyday things like food and behaviour?"

"Those I have identified, yes."

"What about extra-sensory perception?"

"I'm not an animal psychiatrist."

"Meaning you don't believe in it?"

"I stick to what I know, that's all. Things like telepathy . . ." He was staring into the fire, fingering his beard. "I just don't know. Anybody who's lived close to animals has observed patterns of behaviour they can't explain."

"So you've no idea why they're moving north, why there's this concentration of them up here?"

He puffed out a stream of smoke and shook his head. "Any observation I made now would only be guesswork. It could be that roaming bulls remember Marsabit as a safe area, nothing more complicated than that. But to switch to Kulal would mean they also know that Marsabit can no longer support them." He shook his head, silent then and gazing thoughtfully into the fire. "Inherited memory, a built-in survival instinct. I don't know what makes them head north, but that's what they're doing. And if there's a way up out of that gorge—" He tapped his pipe and got to his feet. "We'll see what Dima has to tell us in the morning." He said something about having used a lot of fuel on the way up, but by then I was so drowsy I could no longer keep my eyes open. Mary was already asleep, curled up in her blanket, and in the glow of the embers Mukunga lay on his back with his mouth open, snoring gently.

I stretched out on the grass, already half asleep, firelight flickering on my eyelids as Mtome added more branches. The sound of voices came to me as a vague murmur, but I was lost to the world and no longer heard what they said.

Maybe I dreamed. But I don't think so. I was too tired to dream. I woke with a piercing scream still ringing in my ears. My heart was pounding in my throat and I was shivering. The fire was glowing faintly,

but there was no warmth in it. A breeze was stirring in the trees behind
and it was cold, a damp chill. I knew instantly where I was, who the
bodies were stretched out around me. Nobody else had stirred. No sound
anywhere now and stars showing through a ragged gap in the clouds
above. Something moved in the shadow of the trees. The light from the
moon momentarily increased and I thought I saw a figure standing erect
and covered with hair. I sat up, fear clutching at me, my mind leaping
from the Wandrobo to yetis and all the stories I had read of wild
primitives found on mountains. Again that piercing cry, a scream of
rage and fear that made the hair crawl on my neck. The figure had
vanished.

I sat there, shivering and staring at the forest. But the gap in the
clouds had closed and all was dark again. "Baboon." The voice so close
beside me was quietly reassuring. In the glow of the embers I could
just see his bearded face, one eye open and his teeth showing in a smile.
"I should have warned you."

"It looked so big," I murmured.

"Yes, they're very big up here. They live in the gorge."

"I thought we'd left the gorge miles away."

"Kulal is full of gorges." The eye closed and I lay down again.

The next thing I knew dawn had broken and Mtome was trying to
rekindle the fire with wet branches cut from the undergrowth close by.
It was a grey dawn shrouded in mist, the grass beaded with moisture
and falling away from us in a smooth downland sweep that vanished
into a veil of cloud. I lay there clinging to the vast vestiges of sleep,
too cold to move. Somewhere the sun was shining, our opaque world
beginning to glimmer with a strange iridescence.

Mary came out of the bushes looking like a squaw with the blanket
draped round her shoulders and her black hair hanging damp and straight.
"There's a breeze," she said.

I could feel it on my face then. Flames flickered in the piled-up
branches and overhead the mist swirled, the sun's iridescent glow coming
and going. Away to our right a phantom pile of rock appeared in the
sky. It was there for a moment, a disembodied peak hanging in space,
then it was swallowed up again in the slow gyration of the clouds. Van
Delden sat up, beard and hair glistening with moisture. "What's the
time?"

"Past eight." The mist had lifted and she was standing looking out
across the grassy slopes to where they ended abruptly at a fringe of
small rock outcrops. "I want to see the lake," she said. "We'd be able
to see it from here, wouldn't we?"

"If the cloud shifts," van Delden said.

"It's shifting now and it's only thin stuff. The sun will soon burn
it off."

"Maybe, but Kulal is unpredictable, and it's the gorge I came to see."

Abe sat up abruptly. "You think those elephants could have made it across into this gorge?"

"It leads down to the lake, and if we get a breeze—" Van Delden glanced up at the thin layer of mist covering the sun. "Dima will be at the Mission now, but he can wait. We'll breakfast here and see if it lifts."

I got up then and went into the bushes. Abe followed me. "I didn't sleep much, did you?" His face looked thin and drawn.

"The baboon woke me."

"What baboon? I didn't hear any baboon."

"You were dead to the world. It practically screamed in your ear."

He laughed. "I guess I did get some sleep then. But I don't feel as though I did. I was worrying about those elephants, and about Karanja. You think it was Karanja fired these shots?"

"Van Delden seems to think so." A pale shaft of sunlight came through the branches. "Dima may be able to tell us something." And I went quickly out into the open again. It was warmer now, patches of blue sky and the mist blowing in the wind. The others were all standing by the fire, gazing down the grass slopes to where they ran out over the lip of a gorge. More and more of those grass slopes were slowly unveiled, the gash of the gorge smoking with mist, pinnacles of rock appearing and disappearing. Then suddenly the veil of humidity was swept aside and far below us Lake Rudolf emerged, a great expanse of water running north and south, bright in sunlight. There was an island, brown and bare, all lava, and the far shore just visible as a line of cliffs. The lake itself was pale blue and flecked with white.

"The Jade Sea," Mary murmured. "But it's blue, not green."

Van Delden nodded. "It's blowing like hell down there."

It was like that for a moment, an astounding, unbelievable revelation. Then the mist closed in again and it was gone, the glimpse so brief I could scarcely believe that what I had seen was real, clouds swirling over the sun.

"How far below us?" Her voice was still entranced.

"About six thousand feet," he said.

"Kulal is higher than that."

"The peak lies north-east of us, the other side of the gorge. We're a good bit lower here."

"And the gorge runs down to Loiyangalani?"

"It's the water from that gorge that makes it an oasis."

She turned, staring rapt at the mist rolling along the lip of it. "I'm going to have a look."

He nodded absently, fingering his pipe. The brew tin was boiling and Mtome, sitting cross-legged in front of the fire like a black priest at some primitive rite, threw in a handful of tea. Baby elephant steaks sizzled on their sticks, the embers blazing momentarily as the mist came down again so that Mary became a ghostly figure walking into an opaque void. "Last night," van Delden murmured, sucking at his empty pipe and looking sideways at Abe. "I was thinking. No elephant droppings on the track up the mountain. Did you notice any droppings?"

"Not till we got to the Mission." A sudden gleam of interest showed on Abe's face. "You mean there is a way up out of that eastern gorge?"

"A lot of elephants have been through the forest here and they didn't come up the Mission road." He nodded. "Yes, that's what I was thinking. This must be the route they're taking, all of them." He stared into the fire a moment, then slapped his hand against his side, turning to Abe again, the great head thrust forward, the pale eyes gleaming. "If that's the case, then elephants have a built-in survival sense that draws on the experience of previous generations. Exactly what you were talking about last night. I've never seen elephants on the shores of Lake Rudolf. There haven't been any there in my lifetime. But, according to von Höhlen, Teleki was shooting at them in the water there and they were feeding on the lakeweed. How could animals far to the south of here know there was weed in that lake, or even that Rudolf existed?"

"They couldn't," Abe said. "It's either intuition or inherited memory."

"Or else the sounds they make are capable of expressing more than I had thought. Some wandering bull . . ." Mtome handed him the tin mug full of tea and he passed it on to Abe. "A form of telepathy?" He shook his head. "That's getting close to your extra-sensory perception."

"I guess we have to accept," Abe said slowly, blowing on the tea, "that there are some forms of communication unknown to us. Or perhaps forgotten by us in our civilised materialism."

Van Delden grunted sceptically, his eyes shifting towards the gorge. The mist had closed right down on us, no sign of Mary, nothing but the damp green of the coarse grass. He called to Mukunga, who was dragging some more branches towards the fire, and he dropped them and hurried off into the mist. I followed him, hoping the mist would lift again. I don't think I would have risked it on my own, but I wanted to see down into the gorge. Behind me I heard Abe say, "Birds and migration, elvers, the young salmon—I guess we don't know so very much after all." But when I glanced back over my shoulder the two of them had been swallowed up and only the glow of the embers showed dull red through the thick cloud blanket that enveloped the mountain. From somewhere far away there came a faint cry. It fell away into echoing cries smothered by distance and humidity. "Nyani," Mukunga said, the wizened face grinning at me. But he moved faster after that, so that I was almost trotting. The grass ended, rock emerging, and he stopped abruptly, the ground falling away in a series of ledges and outcrops. The cry of the baboons was louder now, echoing up from below.

"Where is she?"

He raised his hand, listening, and then Mary's voice, away to the left: "Is that you, Colin?"

She appeared suddenly, her figure taking on substance as she climbed up out of a fold in the gorge edge. "Phlumps," she said, her eyes sparkling, her face fresh with exertion and the moisture in the air. "I'm sure I saw phlumps, then the bloody cloud clamped down."

A breeze touched my face, the opaque void at my feet shifting, the greyness glimmering. She pushed her damp hair back from her face. "They were on a sort of island, a mile, maybe two miles down the gorge. It was there for a moment only, floating in the mist and bright green in a shaft of sunlight. They were on the slopes, just grey lumps like rocks. But I saw them move—I'm sure they moved."

"Then there must be a way down." Or did this gorge link with the one we had seen last night? "Are you sure they were elephants, not baboons?"

"Don't be silly. I was brought up with them and I'm long-sighted." Her face was suddenly clouded. "Do you think they were the ones we were following? If it's all one great gorge, the mountain slashed in two—" I knew what she was thinking, that if the elephants could get through then so could the hunters. She lifted her head. "Look! The sun." And she turned to me, laughter lighting her face. "Now, at this moment, all I care about is that the world is beautiful. This mist, the gorge, everything—" She hesitated, looking at the mist flowing now like a river down the gorge. "Strange," she murmured. "Back down where we've come from it's all heat, sand, and lava, the harshness of life—reality. And up here—" She turned to me again, smiling. "Let's forget about reality, shall we? Just enjoy this moment."

I nodded, not sure what she expected, conscious of the mist flowing past us, brightening as the washed-out orb of the sun scintillated on a myriad airborne droplets, feeling my blood respond to the vitality that emanated from her. "Look!" She was pointing up the gorge and I turned to see the peak I had glimpsed earlier floating again, disembodied, high against a pastel blue sky. But this time it did not disappear.

The wind was strong now. I could feel the weight of it against my body, could see it blowing her dark hair back from her face. A shaft of sunlight swept across the grass, the slopes spreading further and further, a downward sweep of incredible, brilliant green. Mukunga moved, craning forward. He said something and then went scrambling down the rocks, sure-footed as a goat, to stand on a final outcrop, peering down.

"He thinks he saw somebody."

"A man?"

"He's not sure. Maybe a baboon." She had turned away from me, staring down the gorge, watching as the sun burned the clouds up and the wind tore them into fragments. "There!" Her island had appeared, a jagged pinnacle of rock and grass swimming in a white sea of cottonwool. "See them?" She was pointing. "Pity we didn't bring the glasses."

Grey shapes dotted the emerging slopes, but whether elephants or rocks I could not be sure. I was too busy searching the summit, where exposed rock topped the whole green pyramid like a castle or small walled city. But it was too far away to make out whether there were any vestiges of human habitation. The gorge was opening out further and further, the clouds breaking up into isolated wisps, the glimmer of the distant lake beginning to show through. Mukunga called to us, scrambling back up the rocks. "What's he say?" I asked.

She shook her head. "I couldn't hear."

Behind us van Delden's voice said, "So there are elephants down there." He had his glasses to his eyes and was chewing on a piece of meat. "Half a dozen at least, one or two half grown. What's Mukunga up to?"

"I think he's seen something," she said.

"Better get some grub," he told her. "Time we were moving."

The baboons were quiet now. No sound except the blowing of the wind, and the lake becoming clearer, a gleaming sheet of bright water on the edge of visibility. I could feel the sun now, grateful for the warmth of it. "Can I have a look through the glasses?"

He handed them to me, but though I searched every rock on the top of that tooth of worn volcanic debris I could see nothing that belonged to man. Two young elephants, bulls I think, were flexing their muscles, bodies straining to the thrust of head and tusk, locked in mock battle, and close beside them a cow suckled a half-grown calf. It was all very peaceful, a relief to watch after what I had seen near South Horr, and behind me I heard Mukunga talking quickly, explaining something in his own tongue. "He thinks he saw two men climbing up out of the gorge." And van Delden added, "Could be Wandrobo, or perhaps Samburu. The Samburu used to graze their cattle on the lower slopes." He turned to Mukunga, questioning him. The word *nyani* passed between them, and in the end he shrugged. "It could have been baboons. He's not certain. There was a lot of foliage and he only caught a glimpse." He turned to Mary. "Your tea will be getting stewed."

She nodded, staring down the gorge. But the wind was dying as fast as it had risen, clouds like wreaths of smoke eddying around the green sloped pinnacle, the elephants lost to view. We started back then, the sun already half obscured and the top of Kulal disappearing in a bank of cloud. "It was down there in that gorge," I said to van Delden, "that your father made some of his pottery finds."

"Where exactly?" But I could tell by the tone of his voice he wasn't really interested.

"I can show you on the map," I said. "It gives the position of all his finds." He didn't say anything and I asked him whether he could talk to the Wandrobo, if they had been Wandrobo down there in the gorge.

"I think Dima could. He's a Boran and familiar with the people of this area. But I certainly can't, nor can Mukunga." He strode ahead then, calling to Mtome, and Mary said quietly, "Pottery doesn't interest him and he hated his father."

"Then why did he ask me to lug the typescript and the map with me?"

She shrugged. "Perhaps he thought it could tell him something about Kulal, or Lake Rudolf—something he doesn't know."

"Such as?"

"Elephants," she said, grinning at me. "Or water. Some spring he doesn't know about, and elephants do."

We reached the fire just as the mist drove down over us again, thicker than ever, and I sat there drinking tea and chewing on a great hunk of meat, wondering why I hadn't the guts to walk off into the mist. There must be a way down into that gorge, and if I could meet up with the people of the forest who knew the mountain . . . I pictured myself being taken by little dark men to a peak of rock, the mist lifting like a veil to reveal some strange primeval stone wall, the sort of wall the Incas built. But it was just fantasy. I was daydreaming, knowing very well I would never survive without van Delden and his Africans. And so, when they started packing up and moving along the edge of the forest, back towards the Land-Rover, I went with them, carrying the bag with the film and the typescript in it.

"Why didn't you go and see what you could find in the gorge?" There was laughter in Mary's eyes, a glint of mockery. She guessed what I had been thinking.

"How did you know?"

"What else could you be thinking about with such a lost, dreamy look on your face? Well, why didn't you?"

"Because I don't have that sort of nerve," I said angrily.

"Suppose I got hold of a rifle?"

"And came with me?"

She nodded, her eyes bright, and I didn't know whether she was serious or just fooling. "I'm a pretty good shot. At least I used to be."

But we were into the forest now, slithering down the muddy game trail in single file. Through the small-stemmed trees I could see the trench. It was deeper than I had realised, a vertical-sided gash with a water pipe still visible at the bottom, the same pipe that served the Mission. Beyond it the bonnet of the Land-Rover gleamed wet behind its screen of leaves. We piled into it and got going, but we were hardly out on to the track when the engine coughed and died. The fuel gauge showed the tank empty and I asked van Delden what the reading had been when he had taken it over.

"More than half full, say ten gallons. He's sure to have had an extra tank fitted in place of the tool box."

We could hardly have used that much, and while Mtome unclipped the spare jerrican, I jumped out and crawled underneath, cleaning the mud off the tank with my bare hands. There was some rusting, but it was a dent in the side welding at the base of the tank that produced a reek of petrol on my fingers. "We snagged it on a branch or a piece of rock," I called up.

"I was afraid of that," van Delden said. "We were using too much on the way up." And he added, "More likely one of those bullets ricochetted."

We found some electrical tape in a toolbox in the back and bound it up as best we could. But I didn't think it would last and the spare jerrican was barely two thirds full, so we had only about three gallons. At kambi ya mawingo we had to wait for a big-tusked bull to finish showering himself at the spring. The sun was shining then, the grass slope glistening with moisture, steaming in the heat, and there were yellow swallow-tailed butterflies sunning themselves on the broken bushes close beside us.

It was very quiet as we sat watching the elephant syphoning the water up with his trunk and squirting it over his head and back, everything done in slow motion and time standing still. "Look! A touraco," Mary whispered. It was staring down at us from the branch of a tree, its body bright green with a splash of red on its wing, the black head cocked. Below it a sunbird flashed a brilliant emerald, its curved beak darting. It was a place of extraordinary peace. But then the bull began to move, ambling silently up the slope, and we drove on into the dark of tall timber beyond the spring.

Where the track forked, and we came off the spine of the mountain, it was all downhill and we made it to the Mission in about half an hour, thrashing our way through the debris of broken branches without any hold-up. There was no sign of Dima, the Mission deserted and nobody answering the blare of our horn. "Have a look at that tank," van Delden said, and he and his two Africans started up the slope to the Mission buildings.

The tape hung in tatters and I could smell the leak before I had even touched it with my finger. Mukunga was hallooing up the slope, and above me Abe said, "Maybe he went up to that clearing." I called to Mary to pass me a rag and the remains of the tape, and I was still lying there under the chassis, cleaning the mud off the fuel tank, when I thought I heard the sound of something far away. Mukunga had stopped calling, everything quiet again except for a distant bee-like drone. "Can you hear anything?" I asked.

There was silence, then Mary said, "Sounds like an engine."

"Coming up the road?"

"No. No, it seems to be above us."

I finished the taping, and when I crawled out from under the Land Rover I could hear it quite clearly, the drone of an engine high up on the mountain. "Must be a plane," Abe said. Van Delden had heard it, too. He was standing by the broken verandah, staring up at the sky. "There!" Mary was pointing and I saw it then, coming low over the forested slopes, its wings tilted slightly as it banked and headed straight for us, the sound of it growing until the roar of it was sweeping over us. It was so low I felt the rush of it through the air, saw the Federation markings and the face of the pilot looking down at us.

It was a twin-engined monoplane and as it zoomed over the Mission buildings, it tipped over on to one wing, sliding round in a tight turn. "Was that Murphy?" Abe was staring up, shading his eyes with his hands. "It was an Army plane and I thought . . ." His words were drowned in the noise of it passing low over the Mission. It climbed steadily above the forest, dwindling until it was a bright metallic speck glinting in the sun. "I'm sure it was Murphy."

And then van Delden was back. "Mary, and you, Mr. Finkel—quick, get out. I'm leaving you here, all three of you." He turned to me. "How's that leak?" And when I told him, he said, "It doesn't matter. It's all downhill now and what's left in the tank wouldn't get me back up again."

The plane was coming back, drifting down with its nose up almost at the point of stall, its engines throttled right back. And as it glided over us something white fluttered down from the open cockpit window and I saw Pat Murphy wave to us. Then he boosted the engines and went zooming up, turning and heading away down the line of the gorge. What he had dropped was his handkerchief, and tied into one corner of it was a message: *K-S plus Army support moving Kulal E gorge. Advise proceed Marsabit fastest. Radioing report abandoned Land-Rover Kulal Mission. Good luck. Pat.* (*Destroy*)

Van Delden read it out to us, then put a match to it. "I'll come with you," Abe said. He knew—we all knew—he was going down into the gorge. But he shook his head. Mtome was already unloading the remains of the meat, Mukunga checking the rifles and ammunition. "You'll stay here, the three of you. I don't know what's happened to Dima, but when he turns up tell him to wait for me here." He was already moving round to the driver's seat. "Get that meat cooked right away, then take it into the forest with you and hide up. They're bound to send a patrol."

"What are you going to do?" Mary was still sitting in the back of the Land Rover, and the tone of her voice, the frozen look on her face, the way she sat, bolt upright, her body tense, her hands clenched—I knew what she was thinking. "Please," she said. "Go back into the forest. Go back, before it's too late."

He stood there, looking at her a moment, his big head hunched into the massive shoulders, the grey hairs of his chest showing in the gap of his half-unbuttoned bush jacket. "I've never run away from anything in my life."

"But you can't do anything." The words came desperately, as though trying to break the barrier of his obstinacy with the strength of her own emotions. "Please. For my sake."

He shook his head, a slow, angry movement. "When he stops killing elephants, then I'll go. Not before."

"I'll come with you. I'll talk to him."

Again he shook his head. Then, in a surprisingly gentle voice, he said, "Nothing you can do. We are all of us born the way we are." He smiled, the smile creasing his eyes, lightening the hard lines of his face. "You stay and wait for me here. I'll be back by nightfall. Now get out, there's a good girl."

"I'm coming with you."

"No." He reached out, gripping hold of her arm, his voice harder now: "I'm in a hurry."

She shook her head dumbly, her eyes wide, her body straining back from the grip of his hand. "No. You're going to kill him."

"Not if I can stop him some other way." He was staring at her, knowing now that it was her father she was thinking of, not him, his pale eyes hardening, the softness gone from his voice as he said, "You'll do as you're told, wait here—and if I don't come back, then you can join him and hunt down the fleeing remnants of East Africa's elephants." He leaned forward, taking hold of her with both hands and lifting her bodily out of the Land-Rover. And when her feet were on the ground, he put his arm round her shoulders the way he had done with Karanja on the Baringo track and said gently, "It's not your fault, Toto. Just wait here, and pray for us. Pray for both of us." He bent his head down and kissed her forehead. "Whatever happens, you mustn't feel you're to blame."

﹘ He let go of her then, calling to Mtome and Mukunga and climbing in behind the wheel. The engine started, the two Africans piling in. "Deal with that meat now," he shouted. "Then watch for the patrol. And keep hidden." He gunned the engine and the Land-Rover went roaring off down the track, trailing a cloud of dust. She stood there, not saying anything, not moving, just watching as he disappeared round the first bend. She stayed there until the dust had settled, then turned slowly as though in a dream, her face pale and drawn, and in a small, vague voice she said, "It's always been like that, all my life." And I knew she was referring to van Delden going off and leaving her to wait.

"He'll get those elephants out of the gorge somehow," Abe said. It was meant to soothe her fears, but the lack of conviction in his voice only increased them.

"How?"

He shrugged, smiling vaguely. "I guess he'll find a way."

"And the Army? What about the Army?" She was still staring at us, her fingers twining nervously. And then she laughed, a high, uncertain sound, and she smiled wistfully. "The trouble is I love him. With all his faults, his obsession, his stupid, bloody obstinacy, his ruthless disregard for other people—I can't help it, I love him." She sighed. "Something he'll never know." And she added bitterly, "Even if he did, he'd never understand."

There was nothing Abe or I could say, no comfort we could give her, the three of us just standing there in silence. "Well, I guess he can look after himself," Abe said awkwardly.

"Oh yes, he can do that all right." She gave a false, bright little laugh. "He's over sixty and never suffered anything worse than a few knife wounds and his shoulder mauled by a man-eater, so why worry about him, or about Alex? What is written is written." She seemed to come to life then, moving quickly towards us, and in a firm practical voice she said, "Come on, better get that meat over a fire before it's crawling with maggots."

III

There was a strange atmosphere about the Mission, the wood of the buildings eaten away by termites and the forest moving in, the marks of animals and their droppings everywhere. As at the Lodge during the Conference, we were interlopers in a complex that had been built for a specific purpose, but here the sense of abandonment was overwhelming, our footsteps resounding in an emptiness that was full of the ghostly relics of a community dedicated to Christianity. And the disintegration of the fabric was not the result of war; it was time and the silent invasion of nature that had left its mark, so that I felt no sense of violation. But the sadness of all that hopeful endeavour wasted made it a strangely depressing place and I think we were all glad to get away from it, to the edge of the forest where we had a view of the road and the waterhole, and the Mission buildings were out of sight.

We got a fire going, and while Mary was dealing with the remains of the meat, I walked across the open grassland to fill the plastic water container we had found in the abandoned kitchens. The area round the pipe was so thick with mud and the slime of animal droppings that before wading into it I removed my boots and socks and rolled up my trousers. It was hot in the sunshine, and when I had filled the container I stripped off my shirt and ducked my head under the pipe, sluicing the clear cool water on to the stubble of my face, letting it run over my back, thinking how marvellous it was that there should be water up here on Kulal when all this Northern Region was dying of drought. And afterwards I ran barefoot up the slope to the ridge above. Crouched among the rocks, I had a clear view of the road running in hairpins down the ochre-coloured shoulder of the mountain to the plain below.

I lay there for quite a time, the sun drying my bare back and all that empty, desert-yellow country hazed with heat, the mountains of the Mara shimmering in the distance. But though I strained my eyes against the glare, there was nothing visible, no movement except here and there the dancing whirl of a sand devil. It was all emptiness, no stir of dust from a moving vehicle, the road up the mountain empty, too. And having satisfied myself of that, I relaxed, enjoying the solitude, the feeling of being raised up on a pinnacle of unbelievable remoteness, a world apart, untouched by man. And behind me, the mountain with its primeval forest, the source of water and of the storms that lashed the lake. Lying there, I felt I didn't care if I never returned to civilisation.

It was only gradually, and with a sense of reluctance, that I acknowledged the sound of distant shouting and turned my head. A small herd of buffaloes, black in the sunlight, stood motionless halfway between the forest and the waterpoint, their heads all facing towards the haze of smoke hanging over our fire.

I got to my feet, then sat down abruptly, conscious that I was alone and unarmed, cut off from the others. The calls had ceased, but the buffaloes remained with their heads up, all staring at the still figures by the fire. There was no suggestion of hostility, only an intent watchfulness, and they looked so ordinary, like long-horned cattle.

At last they moved, flowing in a black tide to surround the waterpoint, trampling the mud under their hooves as they jostled one another to get at the source of the water. There was nothing I could do except sit there and wait for them to go. One of them, having drunk its fill, moved on to where I had left the container, sniffling at it with a wet nose, nuzzling my boots. Something moved on the edge of the forest, a muddy shape pushing through the leaves, and an elephant emerged, moving slowly with that soft, silent tread that seemed to cover the ground without contact. It saw the buffaloes and paused, fanning its ears, its trunk exploring the grass irresolutely. Then it glided slowly forward, and with much snorting and backing the buffaloes made room for it. The scene reminded me of Abe describing the salt lick at Treetops, for though both the buffaloes and the elephant demonstrated, there was nothing positively aggressive in their behaviour. The elephant was putting the tip of its trunk to the pipe sucking at the water, and then transferring it to its mouth, and when it had drunk its fill, it began spraying water over its head and ears until all the mud was gone and the fore part of its body glistened darkly in the sun.

It was while I was idly trying to count the buffaloes, wondering how long it would be before I could retrieve my gear, that I seemed to remember more than two figures standing by the fire. But when I looked again the fire was almost out, only a faint flicker of flame from the pile of dead ash, and no sign of Abe or Mary, or of anybody else. I tried to recall exactly what I had seen on turning my head at the sound of their calls, but all I could remember clearly was the shock of the dark herd standing there.

My gaze switched to the buffaloes again. They were on the move at last, drifting back towards the forest. But the elephant remained. It was kneeling now, a picture of innocent enjoyment, sucking at the pipe, and each time it curled its trunk up over its head the prismatic colours of a rainbow showed momentarily in the sprayed water.

The fire died and nothing stirred, the sun burning my bare shoulders. At last the elephant finished its ablutions and got to its feet. It had one last drink from the pipe, then turned and ambled slowly off. The moment it had disappeared among the trees I ran down the slope, put on my boots and shirt, grabbed the water container, and made for the fire. The leafy fringe of the forest hung trembling in the heat, no animal emerged to face me, no sign of Abe or Mary when I reached the burned-out embers.

I stood for a moment, feeling deserted, but with the shelter of the trees to give me confidence I called to them, my voice loud in the burning stillness. There was an answering call from the direction of the Mission and then Mary appeared on the track, waving and walking casually towards me. "Where have you been?" I asked her. "Why didn't you wait for me?"

"We didn't know how long you'd be." She was laughing. "That bull might have stayed there all morning and we wanted to look at a map of Kulal made by the Reverend Mallinson. It's in the house back there." She took hold of one of the handles of the container, easing the weight of it as we walked down the slope to the track. "Karanja turned up while you were enjoying the view."

"Karanja?"

She nodded. "Karanja and Dima, they both arrived together." Her eyes were on the track leading down the shoulder of the mountain. "If we'd known about that map . . ." She turned to me. "You see, there is a way up out of that gorge. It's shown on the map, a game trail. Those elephants are safe on the mountain now."

So there had been no point in van Delden going back down into the plain.

"You must have had a good view up on those rocks. Did you see any vehicle moving?"

"No, nothing."

She shifted her grip on the container. "Well, I hope to God he finds out in time. . . . If he thought those elephants were still there and Alex was going in to get them . . ." Her voice trailed away. "Are you sure you didn't see anything? No sign of the Land-Rover? Most of the track we came up must have been visible—"

"I told you, nothing." I was still angry at having been left to fend for myself. "Where's Abe? Why didn't he wait for me?"

"As soon as Dima mentioned this map he insisted on seeing it right away. Now, of course, he wants to go off into the forest and have a closer look at those elephants." And she added, smiling, "You were in no danger from that phlump and I was keeping an eye out for you."

I asked about Karanja then. He and Dima had apparently stumbled into each other in the moonlight, following the elephants along a narrow game trail that snaked up the almost vertical side of the gorge. "Did Karanja say why he was following them?"

"I didn't ask him."

"But surely you must have—"

"He's rather full of himself at the moment."

We had reached the track and she turned left, walking towards the missionary's house, her head bent, lost in her own thoughts.

"Didn't you ask him why he'd shot up your Land Rover?"

"It wasn't my Land Rover and he didn't know I was driving it."

"What the hell's that got to do with it?" I said irritably. It didn't explain his motive, or why he had tried to stop the Land Rover from turning those elephants. But when I said it was important to know what was going on in his mind, she turned on me angrily. "So you don't care that I might have been killed."

"Oh, for God's sake!" I wrenched the container from her grasp and transferred it to my other hand. "All I want to know is why he did it. If the Army catches up with him he stands a good chance of being shot."

"They could make him Minister in place of Kimani."

I glanced at her, thinking she was joking. But she wasn't. "You're serious, are you? His motive was political, a gesture to draw attention to himself. Is that what you mean?"

"Anything to do with game in this country is political. I told you that before."

"But he's an African, a Government employee. It's one thing for van Delden to take the law into his own hands—"

"Is it? He's killed two blacks and he's South-African born. They'll never let him get away with that."

"And what about Karanja? Going off to warn van Delden, shooting at Kirby-Smith—"

"Karanja's one of them and Alex is a white hunter. In opposing him he'll have the support of all those who believe in Africanisation."

"But surely—"

"Oh, it's impossible," she cried, "talking to you about Africa." We had reached the gate of the missionary's house and she turned in quickly. "Ask Karanja," she said. "Maybe he can explain it to you."

The door of the half-ruined house was open and I could hear the sound of voices. They were in the room to the left, Abe and Dima standing in front of a map pinned to the wall. Karanja was seated at the missionary's desk, his rifle propped against the wooden arm of the chair, and as we entered he said, "No. I don't go from here until I talk with Tembo." There was a decisiveness in his voice, his manner indefinably different— more confident, almost authoritative. "Is important I talk with him." He saw us and swung round in his chair. "You, Mr. Tait, tell your American friend is dangerous for him to go into the forest alone."

"No danger, Karanja, if you come with me," Abe said. "You know almost as much about elephants—"

"I tell you, I not coming. I stay here and wait for Tembo." And he ordered Dima to the door to keep an eye on the track.

Abe turned to me. "Come and have a look at this map. And you, Mary. Right now this is where we are." He jabbed his finger on the paper. It was yellowed with sun and damp, the ink faded, but I could just make out the shape of the buildings and the track snaking up the mountain. All the gorges were marked, the tracks and game trails showing faintly, the broken line of the waterpipe, and right in the centre the peak itself, its height in feet written beside it. "The elephants came up out of the gorge on this trail." He traced the zig-zag line with his finger, and then he was pointing to a position due north of the Mission. "That's where Dima and Karanja left them. The scale is an inch to the mile, so it's only just over three miles away. Say we make it in two hours, that's nine hours since they left them. They won't have moved far."

"Perhaps they come down here for water," Karanja said. "In that case you see them without need to go into the forest."

"There's water at kambi ya mawingo," Mary said. "There'll be other places, too."

"Well, what do you say?" Abe asked me. "If we find the Wandrobo then maybe you'll get your archaeological mystery solved."

I shook my head, thinking of the elephant at the waterpipe and the two that had charged us the night before. "Van Delden asked us to wait for him here."

"He may not come."

"If Tembo say he come, he come," Karanja said.

Abe shrugged. "Okay, Colin, you and Mary stay here with Karanja, I'll take Dima—"

"No." Mary shook her head vehemently. "I'm not staying here while you go off exploring the mountain."

"It will only be for a few hours."

"I want to see those elephants, too, and now Karanja is with us—" She looked at me, her eyes sullen. "If Abe is willing to go into the forest on foot . . ." She hesitated, then said angrily, "What are you scared of? Dima will have a rifle with him."

I hesitated, unable to explain to her the sense of uneasiness the mountain gave me, or tell her about Abe's wife and the feeling I had that his addiction to danger was very close to a death wish. But in the end I agreed. "All right," I said. "I'll come."

Karanja got to his feet. "Is not good for us to split up."

We might have wasted more time arguing, but Dima suddenly poked his head round the door. "Patrol," he hissed, and in the sudden silence we could hear the sound of a vehicle coming up the track. By the time we had gathered up our things and reached the gate it had stopped and a dozen or more African soldiers were running up the slope towards the Mission buildings. Abe darted back inside the house, and when he joined us on the track leading into the forest, he had the map of Kulal stuffed into the front of his bush jacket.

We went down the track as far as the swampy stream with its thick cane growth and there Karanja left us, going back to check on the movements of the patrol. "You said there were no vehicles down on the plain," Mary whispered accusingly. "Nothing on the road."

"They must have been hidden by the shoulder of the mountain."

A few minutes later Karanja came running with the news that the patrol was close behind us, following the track into the forest. He had us moving fast then, along a narrow game trail that climbed steadily upwards through the trees. It was the same trail that he and Dima had followed on their way down to the Mission and shortly after noon we reached the spot where they had left the elephants. There was no sign of them now, only bushes and saplings freshly browsed and droppings that were warm to the touch.

Karanja paused for a moment, listening intently. But the forest was silent, a cathedral stillness, and he hurried us on, following the big footprints of elephants through a litter of broken branches that he hoped would make it more difficult for the patrol to follow us.

The trail broadened, the footprints increasing in number. And then the ground levelled out and suddenly we were in hot sun. It was a little glade full of butterflies and the quick darting of sunbirds, the grass falling steeply away, and across the green of foliage below we had a view eastwards into the Chalbi, the sand of the desert glimmering white like a great saltpan to a blue horizon hazed with heat. The tracks kept to the high ground and after that we were in thick forest again, among wild olive and other tall trees laced together with a liana tracery of rope-like strands.

"Where do you reckon we are now?" Abe stood with the map unfolded in his hand, holding it out for Karanja, who stared at it and shook his head. "We come to gorge soon," he muttered.

"And then?"

Karanja had his head cocked to one side, listening. "Maybe if we climb down into that gorge nobody follow us there."

"There's a game trail marked, but it zig-zags all the way, so I guess it's steep. Could elephants make it down a trail like that?" His mind was still on the elephants, not on the Army patrol following us.

Karanja shrugged. "We go on," he said tersely. "Not far now."

The trees became smaller, the forest thinning as we climbed, and suddenly there was light ahead, white and blinding. And then we were out of the undergrowth and on to a green strip of coarse African grass that went rolling down a shoulder of the mountain, cascading over rock outcrops towards the distant blur of Rudolf. Directly ahead of us it ended, vanishing abruptly into space, and, across the void beyond, a great peak of rock, all greys and greens and the black of shadows, rose naked against a blue-white background of cloudless sky. An eagle skimmed across the

face of it, poised like a speck of dirt on a colour slide, and in the fore-
ground, on that green grass sward, round elephant turds lay like footballs
on an empty soccer field. The eagle swooped and was gone. Something
died with a distant cry and we started out across the grass to the edge of
that gorge.

God knows how deep it was. Two thousand, three thousand feet? It
was impossible to gauge, for there was nothing to measure height or distance by as we stood on a rock platform staring down to terraces of grass
and undergrowth falling away into clefts of shadow, the bottom of the
gorge invisible. Abe shook his head. "No elephant could possibly—" But
Karanja was pointing away to our right where a tumbled terrace of rocks
had the brown earth of a beaten track threaded through it. "Game trail,"
he said. And then he was staring up at the peak opposite, his eyes slitted
against the glare. "Is there a trail marked up the far side?"

Abe pulled out the map. "No. There's a trail running along the bottom
of the gorge, that's all."

"Maybe it go up the gorge and round the other side of Kulal."

Abe shook his head. "Up the gorge it crosses the height of land, then
down along the shoulder of the mountain eastwards." He looked up at
the peak. "That's no place for elephants."

"I am not thinking of elephants, Mr. Finkel."

"What then—that we've got to go down and up the far side? Do you
really think that patrol would follow us down into the gorge? It will be
dark in a few hours."

Karanja didn't say anything and Mary murmured, "I wish Tembo
were here. He's no way of knowing where we are." She was staring at the
far side of the gorge. "Unless—" She turned to Karanja. "Do you think
he'd see a fire if we lit it high up, near the peak? There's no cloud. It
would be visible for miles."

Karanja looked doubtful. "Is how we signal before we have walkie-
talkie," he admitted. "But is dangerous." Whether he was referring to the
patrol or to the mountain itself I wasn't sure, but I could sense a deep
uneasiness.

"It's volcanic, so the rock will be bad in places." Mary was staring up
at the peak again, her hat pulled down to shade her eyes. "I'm not certain
about the last pitch, but up to that rock band just below the summit . . ."
She turned back to Karanja. "Do you think he'd see it?"

"Maybe cloud later."

"Then hurry." She was suddenly urgent. "We'll find a way up. And if
he sees the fire, then maybe it's not too late." Her voice trailed away,
his reluctance becoming apparent to her. "At least there's a chance," she
said. "If he's out on the shoulder of the mountain, clear of the forest."
And Karanja nodded uncertainly, his eyes troubled.

We started down then, into a tumbled litter of rocks, the trail falling
steeply, twisting and turning down the buttressed face of the first of a
number of ledges, and there were the slide marks of heavy bodies that

had come this way before us. As we wound our way down deeper into the gorge it became hotter, occasional thickets of undergrowth hung drooping leaves in the windless air and there was an increasing sense of being shut in. A squeal from the shadowed bottom of the gorge stopped us momentarily, but we could see no sign of any elephants and nothing moved. A few moments later, coming out of a thicket below a sheer buttress of rock, we had a view right down the gorge with the same "island" of rock we had seen the previous morning rising up out of the bottom, and the green of the steep meadow slopes was dotted with moving figures. Dima grinned. "Nyani." And as I focussed my eyes in the sunglare, I could see they were baboons, crouched and moving on all fours, and there were young ones clinging to their mothers' fur.

The island looked nearer than it was, for we were now more than half-way down and my impression was of a great rock and grass plug blocking the gorge. Mary was searching the opposite face, which now seemed to rise up almost sheer, the peak of Kulal hidden by obtruding bands of rock. "There's sure to be a game trail there."

"Not for elephants," Karanja said firmly.

"No, for kudu."

He nodded. "Is good place for greater kudu."

"To hell with kudu," Abe said. "You find me those elephants." And as if in response to his words a thin squeal came up from below us.

"Ndovu." Dima nodded. But the squeal was not repeated, everything hushed and still in the lifeless air, only the coughing grunt of baboons made faint by distance.

It took us another half hour to reach the bottom, but though we could occasionally hear elephants, we never saw them. There was water in the bottom, actual running water that flowed in a channel that was deep in shade and twisted like a tiny canyon among cliffs and buttresses, and there were sudden expansion chambers that were flat and full of the debris of lush growth. The humidity was very high and the sweat poured off us. Karanja sent Dima on ahead, then stood staring up at the precipitous trail we had descended. Abe and I followed Mary's example, took our safari boots off and dabbled our bare feet in a pool. Small birds flitted in and out of the rock face. There was no sign of any patrol and the only sounds were the faint rumblings of elephants and the snap of branches, from far down the ravine.

Dima came back after about ten minutes, his black splayed feet carefully treading the middle of the stream. He reported a well-used game trail with elephants on it, but not the elephants they had been following during the night. This was a small group of three cows and two almost fully grown calves, and he said there were more further down the gorge—he had heard them, but he had not seen them.

Abe wanted to go on, but Karanja had taken charge of us now and he was still worried about the patrol. The only way to be certain they were not following us down the gorge was to climb to a vantage point on the opposite side. We sat there, chewing on some of the leathery elephant meat and drinking all the water we could absorb while we discussed it. The ascent looked difficult, sheer cliffs of rock interspersed with clefts full of boulders and tangled vegetation, and Abe had the sense to realise it was beyond him. In the end it was Karanja who made the decision. Dima would remain with Abe and the two of them would head downstream, keeping to the water all the time. Mary and I would go with Karanja and try to scale the side of the gorge. If the patrol did catch up with us, then ours would be the only tracks for them to follow, and by then we should be well above them.

I left my bag and all the film with Abe and as we started up the gorge he called to me, "If you find an old city perched on the top, send word and I'll come and film it for you."

"If it has pearly gates," I shouted back to him, "I'll have them opened so you can ride your elephant through." It was a silly remark, nothing more, but I was to remember it later.

He was already splashing down the stream bed behind Dima. I saw him wave acknowledgment, then he was lost to view behind a buttress and we began casting along the north face, searching for a route up. But every cleft we tried proved impenetrable, all of them choked with fallen rock and vegetation. In the end it was the remains of stale kudu droppings that guided us. Mary spotted them, barely visible on a pile of detritus below a cliff overhang. The spill of rock and rubble led up behind the overhang, and after a few minutes' steep, almost vertical climbing from rock to rock we were out on a grass ledge with a melee of rock outcrops towering above us. It looked as though a demolition gang of giants had been at work on the mountain and if it hadn't been for the rare antelope that grazed there we would never have found a way. Their droppings were like signposts and both Karanja and Mary seemed to have an uncanny instinct that enabled them to follow the trail from one pale, dry-straw feces to the next.

We were in the sun's full glare, the climbing hard and exhausting, so that I was glad of the frequent pauses Karanja made to scan the far side of the gorge. Each time we stopped a new section of the trail we had descended became visible until at last we could see the lip of the gorge itself, a jagged line against the sun's glare. All this time we had seen no sign of movement anywhere on the trail.

The slope became easier for a while, our way winding through smooth battlements of rock, and when we paused again the sun was much lower and all the far side of the gorge was in deep shadow. Suddenly Karanja whispered hoarsely, "Soldiers. Don't anybody move." He would never have seen them if they had been on the trail, but they were on the skyline on the very edge of the gorge, figures moving in silhouette, climbing the rock outcrops and peering down.

We stood there, all three of us absolutely still, nakedly exposed in the slanting sunlight and very conscious that the gorge was so narrow we were in range of their rifles. Then Mary, who was standing only just above me, leaned cautiously down and gripped my shoulder. "See them?" she whispered. "Just starting down the trail."

"Of course I see them." They were leaping down the rocks, crawling out on to ledges, searching the trail.

"Not the soldiers, elephants—in the green of that first terrace." Her face was close to mine, the voice husky with excitement. "That's what they're all looking down at."

"Ssh," Karanja hissed from above us. "Don't talk, don't move."

I didn't see them at first. The sun was in my eyes and with the sides of the gorge all dark in shadow it was difficult even to detect the line of the trail.

"Almost level with us," she breathed, and slipped her hand over my shoulder, pointing.

I saw them then, on the trail we had come down, where it twisted among the rocks, dropping steeply into the gorge—brown-grey shapes plastered with mud, moving cautiously. A trunk waved above a low thicket, a great head thrown back, and there was an elephant sitting on its haunches as though performing some ridiculous act at a circus. It was sliding on its rump, two great leg stumps thrust out ahead. It checked on the lip of a sheer drop. Behind it, a youngster squealing miserably with another squatting adult holding on to it with its trunk.

We stood there transfixed, incredulous as the whole herd—seventeen of them—made that precarious descent to the sheer drop, made it safely and disappeared behind a buttress to lose themselves in a patch of forest thicket that clothed the next terrace. "I wouldn't have thought it possible," she breathed. "Tembo has talked about them going up and down steep mountain paths, in the Aberdares and the Ngorongoro, but I never saw it so I never really believed it." She was chuckling quietly to herself. "The patrol hasn't a hope of getting down into the gorge now, not with that herd blocking the trail. They'll have covered our tracks beautifully." The elephants had started to browse now and she whispered in my ear, "You counted, did you?"

I nodded, wishing to God I had my camera with me. If the sun had been behind us and that bloody patrol wasn't watching, what a picture it would have made—something unique, something I couldn't remember ever having seen on film before.

"I made the count exactly the same as last night."

I nodded. "Looks like Abe may meet up with his elephant after all."

"I hope not," she breathed. "They'll be frightened and exhausted, and when they see there's water there—"

Karanja hissed at us for silence again and after that we didn't talk, just stood there watching the African soldiers on the lip of the gorge and the elephants slowly moving down the trail. I was thinking of Abe, imagining him relaxed by the side of some pool with his trousers rolled up and his feet in the water and those elephants suddenly looming up in the last of the light. I wasn't seriously worried. He had Dima with him.

We were stuck there on the side of the mountain for almost half an hour. Then at last the patrol gathered together in a group and headed back into the forest. But even when they had all disappeared Karanja insisted on our remaining absolutely still until he was convinced they really were returning to the Mission for the night. At last he moved, coming down to join us. "Is getting late." There was an urgency in his voice as he stared at the lengthening shadows in the rocks that surrounded us.

"We've got to get higher," Mary said. "High enough for Tembo to see it. And the sky is clear. There'll be a moon later. We can come down by moonlight."

They stayed arguing for a while, Mary pointing out that the fire would not be visible from the Mission and Karanja still reluctant even though he was no longer in danger from the patrol. He was standing irresolutely, staring across the gorge at the trail opposite where the elephants were on the move again, performing their extraordinary circus act on the deep drop from one terrace to the next. Then he nodded abruptly, turning to face the mountain again, stocky black figure clawing his way up. Following close behind him, I sensed his reluctance, the tension building up in him, and I knew he was afraid. The sight we had just witnessed was in no way remarkable to him. His imagination operated on a different plane, the old superstitions of his race more deeply felt than any miracle of animal behaviour. And as we climbed higher and higher, the world dropped away below us, the gorge, the long grass shoulders of the mountain, the dark green cap of the rain forest that lay like a mantle across its broad back, all visible like a topographical map rolled out now that we were nearing the peak itself.

"Bad place," he muttered as I scrambled up to join him on a pinnacle of rock.

"How do you know? You've never been here before." My voice came breathless, the altitude pressing on my lungs.

"No. But is what everybody say. Nobody like Kulal. Cloud. Storm. Wind." His eyes rolled heavenward as though at any moment he expected a hurricane to hurl itself at us out of the cloudless sky. "Even Tembo don't like Kulal. Very dangerous mountain."

The sun was falling into the west, lighting the surface of Lake Rudolf to a deep jade green, the cliffs of the distant Turkana shore a faded line of brown, and no breath of wind. Another hundred feet and we reached a broad ledge close under the rock band. There were clefts and deep gulleys choked with vegetation and the stunted growth of trees. We rested for a moment, watching the sun grow in size and the sky turn to an incredible, brilliant green as the red disc dropped below the earth's rim. The long flat mountain ranges beyond the lake were turning black, puffs of white cloud over the Mara suddenly taking fire, the sky deepening to purple as we began searching the gulleys for dry wood, piling it on the ledge.

Stars were showing before we had finished, and when it was too dark to gather any more wood, Karanja settled down to the task of getting the heap to burn. At first all he achieved was smoke, for the wood was green and damp, but gradually the pile warmed through and flickers of flame appeared. We had less than two hours before the moon rose and we sat there feeding it sticks, nursing those feeble flickers until at last the whole pile suddenly caught.

It went up with a roar then, showers of sparks lifting into the velvet darkness, the glow of it lighting the rock face. Shadows danced and flickered, our faces red in the flames. Karanja had fashioned a long branch into a sort of pitchfork with the panga, and when the whole pile was alight and blazing red, he began to spread the embers westward along the ledge so that from a distance it would have the shape of an arrow pointing down the gorge towards the lake. I never saw the stars go out one by one over the Mara. I was like a kid on Guy Fawkes night, intent on the bonfire we had created, watching the sparks riding the heat upwards into the night, the red blaze warming the rock behind us, our shadows looming large. It was exciting, wildly exhilarating—a roaring fire on the top of a mountain peak where perhaps nobody had been before us.

And then it was done, the signal arrow made in glowing embers that must look from the distance like the red of lava flowing from a newly opened volcanic vent, and we sat there, the three of us, watching it, feeling the heat of it on our bodies, enjoying a spurious primeval sense of power, the mountain conquered, ourselves the masters sending out our message to the world. I can remember Mary's face bright with flame, her dark hair falling to her shoulders, her slim hands held to the blaze, sitting there, cross-legged, the firelight dancing in her eyes. And Karanja with his white teeth showing in a grin, and his face, with its broad flat nose, no longer black, but a dark bronze red.

"You think he'll see it?" she asked him.

"If he is looking towards Kulal."

"He must see it."

Far to the eastward the desert began to reveal itself in a soft light like the loom of a distant city. There were no flames now, only the charcoal-hot red of burning embers, so that we saw the moon quite clearly as it came up over the edge of the Chalbi, a huge great Hallowe'en lantern, its slightly lopsided pumpkin face glowing orange as though lit from within. Karanja went to gather more wood. The moon was an African moon and he was an African, taking it for granted, but to me it was a strange unearthly sight as it rose up out of the desert like some ghostly phoenix to turn the far-off sands the colour of dried blood. Mary saw it differently, sitting there beside me, hugging her knees and staring entranced. "It's beautiful," she breathed and I thought I felt the mountain shiver as though with laughter. A spark flew and I heard the sound of the panga slashing wood deep in the cleft behind us. "I wish he was here," she murmured.

'Who? Your father?"

"If you like."

It was on the tip of my tongue to ask which one, but I knew—knew also in that moment that she didn't think of him as her father. The heat of the fire that warmed our bodies was not for van Delden's safety, but only to draw him away from Kirby-Smith. I left her then and went into the cleft to help Karanja. There was something I had to ask him. And as we hauled at the branches of a half-dead tree, standing shoulder to shoulder in the dark of the cleft, I said, "You don't like the mountain, do you?"

"No."

"What are you scared of—devils?"

He looked at me and laughed, his eyes gleaming white. "Not devils, Mr. Tait. Only this mountain that is a volcano has exploded many times."

"Then why are you here?"

He turned, the panga hanging loose in his hand. "I don't want the Army to trap him in that gorge, and if he kill Major Kirby-Smith . . . either way is bad politically." He shook his head. "Is better I am with him."

"What can you do?"

He shrugged, the lift of his shoulders barely visible in the shadowed glow of the fire. "Maybe nothing. I don't know." He stood there, a dim shape, very still, and he was frowning, his thoughts turned inwards. "Is difficult for me. I am African and no influence outside of my country. I cannot write about elephants. But now that I have seen what is happening here, how they climb up out of that gorge, all together on this mountain and heading for Lake Rudolf . . ." He paused. "He and I, we think alike now, and I have friends in Government. When they know I am also trying to stop this killing—" He was staring out to the darkness of the gorge and after a moment he said, "Is part of our heritage and one day, maybe, I live to see those same elephants crossing Kulal again, but going the other way, going south into the lands they live in when I am young man, going to protected areas where the world can see them again. Quiet, dignified elephants living in peace and rearing their calves. Not fleeing half-starved and in terror, charging everything." He shook his head, smiling to himself. "Is a dream maybe, but that is what I hope."

I didn't say anything for a moment, surprised at his depth of feeling, the way his words echoed van Delden's. But it was one thing to declare himself against the killing of elephants up here in the fastnesses of Kulal, quite another to put it into practice, and if he started shooting at Kirby-Smith again . . . "You'll get yourself killed," I said. "You may have political friends, but they're a long way away."

"Okay, then I am killed." And he laughed, his teeth shining white. "But if I am killed, then it is reported in the press and everybody know that Karanja dies because he is opposed to the policy of extermination." He was still laughing, as though death were of no account, and when he saw I was shocked by his acceptance of it, he slapped me on the back. "No need to be afraid." He didn't realise that what appalled me was the harshness of this foreign world where everybody seemed to walk with death looking over their shoulders.

We finished breaking up the tree and dragged the branches to the fire, but the dead wood did not burn and it was the moon now that lit the rocks, its light white and brilliant, the desert turned to snow. "It's bright enough for us to find our way down," I said. But Mary shook her head, huddled close to the fire, staring at the moon. Karanja, too, seemed transfixed by it, and suddenly I realised there was a circle of light around it and the air was colder, a damp breeze blowing. And even as we stared the moon's halo intensified, a great circle filling half the sky. The desert blurred and vanished, the bright moon dulled, and in an instant the halo was gone and the moon itself had vanished, leaving only a vague translucence. A damp cold touched my face and suddenly we were in cloud and everything dark, only the fire glowing red on the eddying curtain of dampness that enveloped us.

"Does that mean we're here for the night?" I asked, and Mary nodded.

A blinding flash forked down the gorge, followed instantly by a crash of thunder that seemed to shake the whole mountain, and then the wind came, blowing out of the desert towards Lake Rudolf, and it began to rain. The rain was heavy for a moment and it was pitch black as we groped our way to the cleft. The noise of the thunder was incessant, flashes of lightning continually illuminating the rocks that sheltered us. Karanja curled himself up like a foetus, lying with his arms over his head, his eyes tight shut, moaning softly. The wind died and the air became charged with electricity. I could feel it tingling on my body as I crouched in the damp recesses of the rock, listening to the storm advancing on us from across the gorge. It was like an artillery barrage, the noise deafening.

I crawled to the entrance, lying there with the ground shaking under me, watching through slitted eyes the supercharged currents stabbing at the rocks in sizzling, blinding bolts of brilliant electric blue. And in their reflected glare I saw the black belly of the cloud hanging over the mountain, writhing and contorting. An eye-searing bolt struck just beyond the feeble glow of the fire, the thunder of it mingling with split rock in one gigantic crash. The ground shook and the acrid smell of pulverised rock drifted up on an eddy.

But that was the worst and I lay there, listening, as the core of that electrical storm swept over the peak above us, the noise of it gradually lessening to the grumble of a barrage battering the further slopes. I crept out then to tend the fire, my body chilled by the damp air swirling round us.

Mary joined me just as I had coaxed the embers into a blaze and we sat as close to the fire as we could, watching its glow reflected on the dense cloud mist pouring like smoke up out of the gorge. Lightning stabbed behind the peak above us, the growl of thunder reverberating through the rocks. She rolled over, staring up at me, her eyes wide and luminous in the firelight. "Frightened?"

I didn't answer, suddenly aware of her reaching out, her hand on my arm, pulling me down beside her. "Well, I am," she breathed, her face flushed, her lips parted, and the glow of the embers in her eyes. "Don't you know what to do when a girl is frightened?" There was a bubble of laughter in her throat, the hot glow of her eyes no longer borrowed from the fire, the passion of her nature overflowing. I felt the blood leap in my veins, the sudden appalling ache, and then her shirt was open, breasts bare, and she took my head in her hands, pulling me down, the open eagerness of her mouth reaching up to me. That kiss was like a flame running through me, the touch of her tongue, the feel of her hands tearing at my clothes, stroking me, and those breasts, the fullness of her flesh pressed against mine. Some residue of puritanical ancestry caused me to withdraw involuntarily, my brain flashing a memory of Abe's warning. "What about Karanja?" I breathed, my lips buried in her hair.

"Karanja?" The laughter bubbled again. "In Africa mating is normal." She suddenly drew back, staring at me. "You are normal, aren't you?"

"Yes."

"Well then—" And after that I didn't care as we sought the comfort and the warmth we needed, the reassurance of our physical existence. It wasn't love. It was something wild, primeval, totally primitive, our two bodies swept away by natural forces beyond control, and in the urge to imprint upon each other the fact of our survival we seemed charged with the same stabbing electrical currents as the air we breathed. It was as though the storm had entered into us. With passion we reincarnated the fury of it, and when we had spent ourselves and were lying on our backs, naked to the fire, there were stars overhead and the thunder was a faraway grumble fading into the distance.

For a brief moment the moon smiled down on us from a ragged gap in the clouds, but then it was gone and we were enveloped once more in a blanket of mist. I slept fitfully and woke with the dawn. There was a damp chill in the air, both of us lying fully clothed so close to the burned-out embers of the fire that the shoulder of my sweater was scorched brown. There was no wind and the mist hanging thick round our ledge made it seem as though we were imprisoned in an empty void, nothing visible except the rock behind us reaching up into clouds. I was lying there, my eyes searching the rock face, wondering what lay hidden behind that veil of mist, when Mary asked, "Did Pieter van Delden ever make it to the top of Kulal?"

"No," I said. "He never came to this side of the gorge."

"Well, now's your chance." She jumped to her feet, tossing droplets of moisture from her lank hair, her arms hugged round her, staring upwards. But then Karanja said, "We go down now." Sometime during the night he had come out of the dark womb of the cleft seeking the warmth of the fire. Now he was huddled close to the dead embers, shivering with only a thin shirt, his black skin blue with cold, and all he wanted was to get back down into the gorge. "You go on," Mary told him. "We'll follow."

He shook his head, arguing that we had better go down while we could. But there were currents of air swirling the mist around us, a faint glimmer of sunshine. "The cloud will clear soon," she said. He seemed to accept that, so we left him there, trying to get the fire going again, and climbed up the side of the cleft where erosions had fashioned footholds in the rocks. It was easier than I had expected and above the rock band the slope was gentler, a chaos of mist-enveloped outcrops and boulders, the shattered debris of a mountain shaken by volcanic disturbance. The cloud thickened as we climbed and in the end neither of us was certain that we had stood on the actual summit of the mountain, for it was a nightmare of rock castles and gulleys all dimly seen through a thick grey miasma of moving cloud.

"So where's your ancient city?" Mary stood laughing at me, with her hair blowing in the clouds and her face glistening with moisture.

"Well, at least we're on the peak. I've seen it for myself." I turned away, knowing now that no race of early men would be fool enough to build in such an area of instability. And since it wasn't Kulal, then it had to be Porr. It was the only other notable peak, and as we started down I was wondering whether I would ever get to that lone pyramid of a mountain halfway up Lake Rudolf. My mind on that, I lost all sense of direction. The cloudcap over the mountain had brightened now to a white translucent fog. It began to drizzle and we both of us stopped, realising suddenly that there was nothing to guide us in that tumult of dim-seen rock shapes. The only certainty was that we were on the slope leading down into the gorge, and so we went on, until suddenly we found ourselves on the edge of a void. We had reached the rock band, a vertical drop falling into nothingness. We stood there, calling to Karanja, our shouts lost in cloud and no echo of an answer. But a hundred yards or so to our left, beyond a pinnacle of shattered rock, we heard the sound of an answering call.

It was only when we reached the fire that we realised we were both of us shivering with cold. "Better we go down now," Karanja said, "before the mist clears." He was thinking of the patrol, which might well have started out from the Mission again at first light, but when I looked up at him and saw into his eyes there was a sudden flash of understanding between us. It wasn't just the patrol; we were both of us filled with the same urge—to get off that bloody mountain before it brewed another storm.

I think Mary felt the same, for she was on her feet at once, following close behind Karanja as he began the descent from that ledge. He moved fast, following unerringly the route we had climbed, and when we were about halfway down a breeze touched our faces, the mist lifting and brightening until it was a white intensity of trapped sunlight that was almost blinding. The far side of the gorge emerged first as a dark shadow, then as something visible but blurred. A moment later the mist vanished like smoke. The sun shone down on us and it was suddenly hot.

The abruptness of that transformation was startling, everything clean and fresh with moisture, and brilliantly clear as though we were looking at it under slight magnification. But the sun burned in a sky that was white, not blue, and it had a great circle of light around it. An ice halo, Mary thought. She had seen it once on Kilimanjaro.

We reached the bottom and turned downstream; no sign of any humans having been on the trail before us, only the tracks of elephants. We caught glimpses of that island of rock and grass coming gradually nearer until it seemed to block the gorge ahead, and every now and then the hot stillness was pierced with the cry of a baboon. We were right under that island with the wind on our back when there was a sudden roaring and squealing of elephants, a cry of pain, and then the crash of bodies in thick bush. Silence, and Karanja moving cautiously, his rifle ready in his hand. "What was it—baboon?" I asked.

He shook his head. "No, not baboon."

And Mary said, "It sounded human."

Outcrops of rock now, the trail narrowing and everything suddenly very still, the heat oppressive. Karanja called softly—"Dima! Dima!" We rounded a bend, the trail opening out again, a thicket of bushes on both sides of the stream, and suddenly there was Dima half hidden behind a rock, his rifle pointed at us. He stood up at the sight of us, calling urgently, and when we reached him there was Abe lying at his feet, his face ashen, blood streaming from a gash in his head and his right hand at a grotesque angle. His eyes were open, a glazed look, so that for a moment I thought he was dead. But then his lips moved in a whisper: "Is the camera all right, Colin?" He didn't seem to realise he still had it gripped in his other hand, cradling it on his stomach. And when I told him, he said, "Take it, will you. There's about a minute and a half exposed, all close-ups." He had closed his eyes, the sweat standing in beads on his face.

Mary came back from the stream, her neckerchief soaked in water. She bathed his head, then gently began rolling up the sleeve of his shirt. His arm looked as though it had been hit by a sledgehammer, the flesh all bruised, the bone broken just above the wrist. She straightened it with a deft, quick movement, the bone grating and his mouth open-

ing in a thin scream. "We'll have to splint it." He had fainted and
she looked up at Dima. "What happened, for God's sake?"

The explanation came in a flood of Swahili and when he stopped she
said to Karanja, "He could have shot it."

Dima shook his head obstinately. "Patrol come quick if they hear gun."

"Bugger the patrol," she said angrily. "He might have been killed.
And that patrol, wherever it is, is out of earshot."

"He don't know that," Karanja reminded her. "And if we are not
coming down the gorge—"

"The calf winded us, is that what you mean?"

Karanja nodded unhappily and I said, "What's this about a calf? A
calf couldn't have done that."

"No? Even at one year old they weigh about twelve hundred pounds,
and that big calf of hers must be at least five; that's the average gap
between births."

"But what happened?"

She stared at me, exasperated that I hadn't understood a word of
what Dima had said. "It was the elephant he called Sally. They were
holed up in the rocks there, waiting for us, and then this herd arrived
and she was in the lead. She was right there in that open glade and
he couldn't resist the opportunity. He crept down out of the rocks with
his camera. . . ." She turned to Karanja and asked him to cut some
sticks to use as splints. "Dima says he tried to stop him, but Abe
wouldn't listen. The cow came right down to the water and the odd
thing was she didn't seem to mind him. He was right there in front
of her as she started drinking and then spraying water over herself.
There was just the stream between them and he was crouched there,
filming her when it happened. Her ears suddenly spread out, her head
lifted, then she swung quickly round, facing up the gorge and trumpeting. That was when the calf came out of the thicket there, right
behind him. It was obeying its mother's orders, trying to get back to
her, and Abe was in the way. It sent him flying with a sweep of its
trunk, ploughed through the stream, and in an instant the whole herd
was crashing away down the gorge."

"It was my fault." Abe's eyes were open again, his voice urgent as
he struggled up on his left elbow. "I was between the calf and its
mother. I should have realised . . ." He sank back, exhausted, his lips
bared with pain. "I forgot—she still had a calf." And he added in a
whisper, "She was so quiet, so relaxed—until she scented danger. She
seemed to understand I meant no harm, that I was unarmed." He closed
his eyes against the glare. "I'm glad Dima didn't shoot," he murmured.
"You can't blame the calf." He reached out and gripped Mary's arm.
"Will it hurt much—when you splint it? I'm an awful coward."

"You'll be all right," she said cheerfully. "It will hurt for a moment,
that's all."

But it took much longer than a moment, the three of us holding

him down while he screamed and screamed. Then, thank God, he
passed out and she was able to finish the job without him struggling all
the time. She was covered with sweat as she sat back on her heels, staring down at the splint bandaged with strips of towelling. "I hope it's
all right. I've only done that with animals before, and usually we had
an anaesthetic." She looked round vaguely. "How far is it to Loiyangalani? There's an airstrip there, and if a plane came over . . . Where's
that map?"

I found it in our bag. The oasis camp of Loiyangalani was a good
six miles away. "He can't walk that."

"He'll have to. Or else we carry him. He has to be got to a hospital
somehow."

We started as soon as Abe recovered consciousness. I wanted to abandon all our gear, but Abe wouldn't hear of it and Karanja clung to the
camera and films as though they were more precious than the plastic
water container. Because of the elephants we were forced up on to a
shoulder of the mountain, clear of the gorge, which gradually petered
out below us. We moved slowly with many pauses, Abe lightheaded
and in pain, but doggedly staying on his feet, the heat increasing as
the day wore on and the lake drawing gradually nearer.

Coming down off the lower slopes was the worst. It took us over an
hour to cross an old lava field, the black rocks jagged and broken, the
late afternoon sun beating up at us, dust blowing and the temperature
in the high nineties. After that it was sand, long rolling dunes of it
with isolated patches of thorn and furze. By then we had finished our
meat and almost all the water, and Abe was barely conscious, stumbling
along with two of us supporting him. But we could see the broken
palms of the oasis now, the fire-blackened roofless buildings of the tourist camp, and the remains of the Catholic Mission that Dima said had
been run by Italians. And across the flat land beyond the palms, the
lake stretched flat as a steel sheet to the jagged volcanic outline of South
Island, the Turkana shore dim in the distance. There was not a breath
of wind and nothing stirred along the lake's edge, no elephants, not
even any sign of life around the huddle of cone-like dwellings that had
been the manyata of the El Molo.

All the way down we had reckoned on the El Molo supplying us
with fish, for this small lakeshore tribe has existed for centuries on the
teeming marine life of the lake, particularly tilapia and the huge Nile
perch. Now instead we would have to catch our own fish and Dima
went on ahead with Karanja, the two of them rapidly lost to view as
they loped off across the sands. We had glimpses of them later, after
we had reached the shelter of the doum palms. Abe had fallen into
a deep sleep, utterly exhausted, and Mary and I stood on top of the
shallow escarpment on which the palms grew, looking out across the
flats toward the sunset. Below us was the airstrip, the frayed windsock
still hanging from its pole, limp in the breathless air, and the green

line of a ditch carrying a trickle of oasis water out towards the deserted village, and beyond the manyata two tiny figures were hurrying towards the flat burnished circle of the port. And when they had disappeared from sight behind the jetty, there was nothing moving at all except birds flying in dark rafts close above the surface of the water.

The sun had set, everything very still, the sky a violent purple, and out across the pale, almost luminous waters of the lake, South Island stood black against the sky, a hideous, piled-up melee of volcanic vents and old lava flows. Years ago, I remembered, a British expedition had landed two men there and they had never been seen again. When I mentioned this to Mary she named them—Martin and Dyson. "Fuchs was leader of the expedition." And she added, "Tembo has been over there several times, once on an El Molo fishing raft. There's a herd of goats there and the largest crocs he's ever seen. He says it's just about the most desolate place on earth."

Night fell and with the stars came the mosquitos. We dozed intermittently, bitten to hell. A wind got up, rattling the palm fronds overhead, the moon leering down at us, more lopsided than ever, and then at last there were shouts and the two Africans were back with an old fishing net full of tilapia, all gutted and cleaned. We got a fire going and cooked them on sticks of thorn, holding them by the fins that fringed their flat bodies, and it was while we were squatting there in front of the blaze, sucking the flesh of the tilapia and trying to fend off the mosquitos, that a dark figure suddenly emerged from the palms. Karanja grabbed his rifle and we all leapt to our feet.

It was Mukunga and he held something out to us, wrapped in a palm leaf and all bloody. "Tembo send you present."

"What is it? Where is he?" Mary asked.

It was crocodile meat and van Delden was camped about seven miles to the north of us in what Mukunga called El Molo Bay. I remembered it from the map, a shallow inlet opposite the small El Molo Islands. "Me watch from hill of the dead. See smoke here." He had a 15 cwt truck with him. "You eat meat, then go with me. Loiyangalani no good —upepo now."

The moon had gone, black clouds overhead, and the wind in the palms was like the roar of the surf breaking on a reef. Gusts blattered at the fire, the meat sizzling and Mukunga talking fast in Swahili, gesturing and laughing. He was telling the story of how they had got hold of the truck, and I sat there, listening to the roar of the wind and thinking of van Delden. At one point Abe said urgently to Mary, "Ask him if he's seen any elephants along the lake shore."

"Ndovu?" Mukunga nodded, and after listening to him for a moment Mary said, "Yes. There are elephants in El Molo Bay, a whole herd and more to the north. He says they're feeding on the lakeweed, lots of them wading in the shallows all along the shore."

"Does Kirby-Smith know that?"

She nodded. "Yes. Alex knows." And she added, so quietly I hardly heard her above the shattering blast of another gust, "He's moving the outfit up to Loiyangalani." And she closed her eyes, sitting very still, not saying anything until finally Karanja dowsed the fire with sand and we walked through the palms to the truck.

PART FOUR

Wardens of the North

I

The moon was gone, black clouds hanging over the oasis as we headed north on a rough track, our own dust billowing past us in the gusts. We crossed a lugga, the track like the gateway in some ancient earthworks, and after that the wind was less. There was vegetation here, thorn trees mainly, and small birds rose up from under our wheels, skittering away like grasshoppers in the headlights. "Namaqua doves, I think." Mary was leaning forward, her hand on Abe's shoulder. He was in the front seat and he half turned to her. "This is one of the hunters' trucks, isn't it? How did he get hold of it?"

"Hijacked it."

"Yes, but how? Did Mukunga say?"

She nodded, silent for a moment. I don't think she wanted to talk about it. To talk about it meant thinking about what happened now. But in the end she told us what had occurred after van Delden left us at the Mission. He had coasted halfway down the shoulder of the mountain to a point where he had a clear view down into the gorge and could get the Land Rover off the track into the shelter of some rocks. Below them a party of hunters was moving slowly back to their vehicles parked in the flat scrub country where the cliffs widened out. Later, from a different vantage point, they had watched the vehicles crawl across the plain below, and at the well, where the elephants had dug for water, two of the trucks had turned off and started up the track towards the Mission. The first was the Army three-tonner carrying the patrol. "They let that pass," she said, "Then blocked the road with the Land Rover and ambushed the second vehicle, which was following some way behind to avoid the dust stream."

"What about the men in it—they were Africans, were they?"

"Yes, four of them. He dropped them off by the well."

The moon had come clear of cloud and I could see Abe's face, dead white and frowning. "At least he didn't shoot them."

"What happened to the Land Rover?" I asked.

"They ran it over the edge into the gorge."

The track had become harder, the shoulder of a hill rising black to the left, a glint of water far ahead. Abe was holding himself tight. "So what happens now, Mary? You said something about Kirby-Smith moving to Loiyangalani."

She nodded, that shut look on her face. "They were due to break camp at dawn this morning. At least, that's what the hunters said."

"To move up to Loiyangalani?"

"Yes."

"Then why aren't they here? There's no sign of them and it can't be more than a day's journey."

"The track, probably. Mukunga says it's very bad where it crosses the lava fields by Sirimar. Earth tremors have destroyed several of the concrete ways the missionaries built to get their trucks over the worst of the boulders. Maybe they couldn't make it."

Abe was silent then, knowing it was what she desperately hoped. We were running along the side of the hill now, close above the water, and it was shallow, more a marsh, with countless birds asleep like black stones. The headlights swung, the black stones turning to white, and three pelicans pulled pouched beaks from under their wings in slow motion. A goliath heron, still as a post, lifted its razor-sharp head and there were storks standing one-legged in the mud. On the edge of visibility grey outcrops of rocks moved. "Elephants?" But Mukunga shook his head. "Kiboko."

"Hippos," Mary said. And then we had reached the lake shore and the moon was clear so that we could see islands pale beyond the wind-whipped water. The track ceased and we were on the beach, the truck bucking as it ground in low gear up a long promontory dotted with the cairns of ancient burials. "Hill of the dead," Mukunga shouted above the noise of the engine and the breaking waves. Then we stopped and van Delden was standing there like some prophet in a hostile desert of rock, his white hair blowing, and a rifle, gripped by the barrel, lying across his shoulder. "That you, Toto? I was afraid we'd lost you." He spoke gently, a note of fondness in his voice.

"You didn't see our signal then? We climbed to the top of Kulal, lit a fire there." She was nervous, her words coming in a rush.

He shook his head, his eyes fastening on Karanja. "So it was you." He didn't ask him why he had fired at Kirby-Smith's Land-Rover and then gone after the elephants, he just stood there, smiling, his teeth showing white in his beard. "You stupid show-off man." It was said affectionately, almost admiringly, and he seemed on the point of saying something else, but Mary interrupted him, explaining about Abe's arm. "Has that plane been over here? We need to get him to hospital."

"Army planes have other things to do besides look for me." He went over to Abe, examining the splint. "A good job you did there. Anyway," he added, "nothing can land at Loiyangalani till the upepo dies down."

The truck had a first aid kit and he gave Abe an antibiotic injection. After that we settled down to sleep, building little stone windbreaks for ourselves. The ground was very hard, the noise of the wind and the lake incessant, but I was asleep almost immediately.

I woke with the first of the light to the sound of voices, Mary arguing with van Delden.

"It wouldn't do any good."

"You thought differently the other morning."

"I was afraid you'd kill each other."

"The situation hasn't changed."

There was a long pause. Then on a note of forced cheerfulness she said, "Perhaps he'll have turned back. Mukunga said the road was in bad shape."

"We got through."

"But with this wind blowing . . ."

"The wind won't stop him and he has enough men to rebuild the road where it drops down the lava escarpment to the shore."

"He won't risk those refrigerator trucks on a road like that."

"There's a back route. It was completed for the Mission early in 1973. One way or another he'll be here today."

Silence then. Finally she said, "All right, I'll try. But why is it always other people who must give way, never you?" Her words tumbling over one another, deep-throated and sullen. "It's always been the same. Can't you ever see another man's point of view?"

"No, not in this."

Another long silence, then he said: "You tell him. Tell him to pull his outfit back to the South Horr Gap."

"Why me? Why not talk to him yourself?"

That quick bark of a laugh. "We've nothing more to say."

"If you'd only talk to him reasonably. Not threatening, but trying to agree some limit—"

"You know that wouldn't work."

"Because you hate him."

"We don't speak the same language, that's all."

"You hate him," she repeated, her voice no longer sullen, but high and wild.

"That's enough, Mary."

"No. No, it isn't. You've always hated him, ever since—"

The smack of his hand on her face, her shocked cry brought me to my feet. They saw me then, their dark dawn figures turning away almost guiltily and van Delden calling to me gruffly: "Fetch some water from the lake, will you? I'll get a fire going."

I went down the hill, my mind still on that scene, past the heaped rock piles of ancient burials, the light growing all the time and the water glinting pale, wavelets whispering in the wind. Was she right? Was it the hurt pride of a man who had lost his wife to another man? Inland, the shallows of the marsh mere were a still pale expanse, coots bobbing and waders busy at the edge. The pelicans had all gone, the storks too, but the herons were still there, motionless. And then I was remembering the Serengeti and how he had stood there at the Conference full of a deep anger, and I knew it wasn't that.

The lake shore, when I reached it, was black lava shingle, the water tepid with an alkaline taste. I would have stripped off and waded in, but as I filled the jerrican something big swirled in the moving shadow of a shoal of fish and the surface of the water was whipped to froth, leaping glints of silver. The sky was taking on colour now, a faint blue with thin wisps of cloud drifting like fog patches, but the islands close offshore were still dark silhouettes. I left the can and walked along the shore towards what looked like a dug-out canoe drawn up on a stretch of dark sand. Three logs lay stranded close beside it, but as I approached them they rose up on short legs and went sliding into the water, hissing angrily. The sand was gritty and just beyond the straight furrows scored by the crocodiles were the great rounded pug marks of a hippopotamus. The canoe was a raft of logs lashed together.

The clouds took fire as I climbed back up the hill, the light intense and luminous, a brilliance that was harshly beautiful. A blackened tin of water was already boiling and Mtome was squatting beside the glowing oven of stones, kneading posho into a dough, Mukunga plucking two Egyptian geese shot the previous evening. Van Delden looked up from cleaning his rifle. "When the upepo stops blowing maybe I'll take you out in that raft."

I shook my head. "Don't bother."

"You want to see Porr, don't you? You can't see it from here."

"Not if it means going out into the lake on that thing."

"It's safe enough when there's no wind. The El Molo use them for spearing perch. Have you still got that typescript with you?" And when I told him I'd jettisoned it on the mountain, he said, "Pity. I'd like to have read it while we're waiting." He put his rifle down and fished something out of the pocket of his bush jacket. "This might interest you." He held it out to me, a broken piece of pottery, badly pitted, but still showing the dark brown marks of a design.

"Where did you find it?"

"On that first island, in a fissure, and there were marks on the rocks; too faint to make out what they represented. Did Pieter van Delden get out to those islands?"

I shook my head, turning the fragment over in my hand. "Is this part of a pot, do you think?"

"Keep it if you like. Take it along to the British Museum. They'll tell you. And there's more below the fissure, but all small pieces by the look of them. Maybe if you searched the other islands . . ." He stopped at a sudden outburst of bird cries and reached for his rifle.

We all turned, gazing down at the flat sheet of the mere where the birds moved restlessly. Something had disturbed them. Then, round the corner of the hill, an elephant appeared, moving slowly, its trunk exploring the mud and weed at the water's edge. It moved with a quiet, deliberate pachydermal dignity that seemed entirely at one with the primordial setting, and I had a sense of timelessness; I could be back a million, two million years, back further, perhaps, to a time when the first ancestor of man inhabited the shores of this ancient lake.

"A bull," van Delden said quietly.

Its back and head were plastered with mud and the sun, coming up over the hill in a burst of heat that coloured the land a fire-brick yellow, turned the animal from grey to pale ochre so that it merged into the background of sand and rock, barely visible as it shambled along the far edge of the marsh towards the lake shore, an ugly gash across its shoulders. More elephants made their slow weary entrance upon the scene. I counted seven of them, all adults, moving in a stumbling silent rush toward the lake, which was now a brilliant sapphire blue. The islands off the shore were no longer vague humps, but clear and sharp in that bright light, all browns and reds with a frill of white where the wind broke waves against their base. The bull, a distant tide-rock shape standing in the lake, was spraying water, its trunk lifting and falling, its body already glistening black, the wound showing as an open slash of red.

"A lost world," Mary murmured. And van Delden, looking at her sharply, said, "This is their last refuge."

"It can't support them."

"Always some specious argument . . ." He turned abruptly away, talking to Mukunga in his own language and shutting her out as though afraid of losing his temper with her again. We drank our tea and ate our breakfast, and all the time I was conscious of the tension between them. The fragment of pottery van Delden had given me seemed suddenly of no importance beside that little group of tired gaunt leviathans all standing now in the lake and drinking thirstily. How far had they come? I wondered. From the Aberdares where the forest trees were almost all cut down? Or Tsavo perhaps, across several hundred miles of hostile land peopled by man, their young all slaughtered, their numbers reduced? I picked up the piece of pottery and in a mood of sudden disgust I threw it on to one of the burial cairns, where it shattered into fragments. "You'd better show me how to use a rifle," I said to van Delden. "I've never fired one before."

"Later," he said. "If you wish." He was talking to Abe about the lake and its strange colouring, and I lay back, thinking about those elephants, the stones under me burning hot, the wind dying. Skeins of birds flew low over the lake, fish shoals dark like cloud shadows occasionally bursting into frenzied splashes of silver, and van Delden's voice murmuring gently in the heat: "They say it's the algae. When the surface is calm, then it really is a jade-green sea, all the mass of algae coming to the surface, a green skin of plant life. But with the upepo, it all sinks and the lake becomes hard and blue. Mostly, when I've been up here, it's been blue in the early morning, then the wind takes off and it turns green. You'll see—about noon it'll turn green."

Mukunga said something, getting to his feet, and Karanja also rose. "I go with him."

"No. One is enough."

But Karanja shook his head. "Is better I go with him. When the hunting trucks arrive I think they still have the support of an Army detachment. Maybe I know the officer." He shouldered his rifle, and without waiting for permission he went after Mukunga. The old man sat there, not saying a word, his eyes on the truck as it drove off, and I could guess what was in his mind. This was a different Karanja and he wasn't sure of him.

The truck disappeared beyond the line of the hill and he gave a little shrug, then turned to me. "Okay, if you want to try a few shots, we've spare guns and plenty of ammunition."

He had me firing at an old tin set on one of the burial mounds, and with the first shots the elephants were gone, lost to view behind a low rise. Van Delden, watching them, nodded his head in satisfaction. "The further north they go the better it will be for them. I'd like to get them all off that mountain and headed north." And he added, "They've a long way to go before they get to the Ethiopian border. This lake is all of 180 miles long."

I fired altogether about a dozen rounds, and with the last shots I hit the tin twice at a distance of fifty yards. "Calm," he said. "That's the secret. You have to keep calm. Whatever's coming at you, just hold your breath, aim, and fire, bringing the sights up on to the mark, steady and unflustered, just as if you were firing at that tin. Okay?"

The lake was already turning green, and not a breath of wind, the heat heavy and humid. Mary was splashing about in the shallows and I joined her, wading in with my clothes on. Her wet hair clung to her head, making it seem smaller, and I could see her breasts with the nipples poking at the thin wet khaki of her shirt. The water was tepid, the sun on it a blinding glare. Far to the north a toy elephant stood in a posture of levitation, its image raised by the lake's steaming heat. "So now you're a crack shot." She was grinning at me and I dived and grabbed her legs, tipping her up, and we played, laughing in the water till our eyes were sore and our heads burned with the heat.

I went up the hill then to see how Abe was, lying in the shade of the truck's canvas top, which they had rigged up in the lee of a burial mound. "Lucky devil!" he said. "I'd give anything to be in the water." It was airless under the canvas and he was sweating.

"Where's van Delden?" I asked.

"On top of the hill, keeping watch, and he's sent Mtome and Dima to guard the road. I don't think he trusts Karanja."

"How's the arm?"

"Fine. It doesn't hurt too much." He took off his glasses and asked me to wipe them. "What do you reckon is going to happen?"

I shook my head. It was something I didn't want to think about.

"You realise Kirby-Smith has lost a plane, two trucks, and a Land-Rover."

"He can always call on the Army for replacements."

He nodded. "If it wasn't for the Army I'd say van Delden was waging a pretty successful holding operation." I handed him back his glasses and

he said, "Sometime during the night he's going to dump me as close as
he can to the oasis. Mary will be with me. I think he hopes she can persuade Kirby-Smith to pull his outfit back. A truce, in other words—a sort
of modus vivendi. What's Mary think? Is that possible?"

"I doubt it. They were talking about it this morning and she didn't
think he'd agree."

"Nor do I." He eased his buttocks on the stones. "With luck I'll get
evacuated. What about you? If it's a shoot-out—" He was staring at me
and there was real concern in his eyes. "You'll have the camera, but if
you've got pictures they consider damaging . . . I don't know; maybe you
can trade the film for safe passage out of the country, but I wouldn't
bank on it." I thought I heard the sound of an engine, very faint and
far away, and I ducked out from under the canvas shelter. The road was
empty, but Mary was calling something from the lake shore, and then
the 15 cwt came into view with Mukunga driving, nobody else. It stopped
beside her, and van Delden, halfway down the slope, called out, "What's
happened? Where's Karanja?"

"Gone off on his own," she answered.

When I reached the truck they were still interrogating Mukunga and
I had to wait some time before Mary explained that the old oasis touring
camp had been occupied by an Army patrol and Karanja had gone down
to make contact with the officer in charge. "One of the trucks had a radio
aerial and he was very confident the officer in charge would let him contact Army HQ. The last Mukunga saw of him he was holding his rifle
up with a handkerchief tied to the barrel and walking straight towards
the building that used to be the bar."

"When was this?"

"About ten-thirty, just after Alex's outfit had established themselves
in the Mission buildings."

"Mukunga didn't wait for him?"

"Yes, but back at the truck, which was parked in the doum palms. He
waited about half an hour, then one of the hunting trucks started down to
the harbour and another headed out towards the airstrip. He was afraid
of being cut off, so he came straight back."

Van Delden was still talking to Mukunga, both of them gazing out
across the shallow expanse of water to the bare brown slope beyond and
the islands shimmering in the heat. Finally he nodded, looked at Mary,
and said, "Okay, we'll shift camp. You get your patient ready to move."
He called to Mtome, gave instructions to Mukunga, then turned to me.
"You want to try paddling an El Molo fishing raft? Take it up along the
shore there. We may need it."

The raft, when I launched it, proved more stable than I had expected,
but it had almost no freeboard and I hugged the shore, scared of deep
water. Also it was difficult to steer until I got the hang of it, kneeling
at the centre of balance and using the primitive paddle blade as a steering
oar at the end of each stroke. I was almost out of sight of the hill of the

dead before the truck began to raise its telltale dust stream. There was no wind now and in the passage between shore and island the water was flat, a dark, viscid green. Shoals of fish moved like cloud shadows and when I stood up, balancing myself carefully, I could see, far to the north, a heap of rock glowing white in the sun like the great pyramid of Cheops. And in a little bay about a mile away there were elephants standing in the water.

I began steering for the first of the islands, feeling free and full of a sense of exhilaration now that I was on my own in the immensity of the great lake. But I did not land, for as I glided into the shore long lizard shapes slid soundless and without a splash into the water. I had no rifle, no means of fending off the crocodiles, and I turned the clumsy craft and headed back towards the shore, the heat making the blood pound against my temples.

The hollow in which they had parked the truck was a mixture of sand and rock interspersed with gravel, and it was all the same colour, ochre yellow washed out by the glaring heat haze. From the top of a rise we looked out across the mere with its bobbing coots to the hill where we had spent the night, and half an hour later an open Land-Rover with African soldiers in it appeared in a cloud of dust from the direction of Loiyangalani. "They'll see our tracks," Mary whispered, and van Delden nodded. "So what happens then?"

"There are only four of them."

Nobody spoke after that, the Land-Rover crawling along below the shoulder of the hill until it came to the lake. It stayed there for a moment, one of the men in it standing and staring up at the hill. He was not in uniform, and van Delden, with his glasses to his eyes, muttered, "Karanja." The figure sat down again and the Land-Rover turned, moving back along the edge of the mere to the point where Mukunga had turned the 15 cwt off the track. It stopped there and we watched in silence as Karanja got out, stood talking to the driver for a moment, then turned and began walking toward us, his rifle gripped by the barrel and swung carelessly across his shoulder. The Land-Rover drove off, its dust gradually settling, nothing now below us but that solitary figure plodding steadily along the water's edge and up the slope, following the 15 cwt's tracks. Van Delden stood up, calling to him, and Karanja waved, coming straight towards us with something of a swagger, his teeth showing white in a broad grin. "So what have you been up to?" van Delden asked. "You look bloody pleased with yourself."

Karanja nodded, still grinning. "I think maybe the Army fly you out." He sat down, rubbing the dust and sweat from his forehead.

"You made contact with the military commander, did you?"

"Ndio. I talked with him by radio. There is report of a band of Shifta moving towards Marsabit, so he don't want any trouble here. But first he must speak with Nairobi."

"And what about Major Kirby-Smith? What about the elephants here on Rudolf? You know I'd never agree to leave without some guarantee they would be left in peace."

Karanja looked at him, not grinning now, just smiling quietly. "But if Ileret is made a game reserve, I think you leave then."

Van Delden gave that quick hard laugh. "With you as warden, is that the deal?" And Karanja went into a high peal of laughter.

"Would Kimani agree to that?"

"Kimani? Kimani is finished, I think. After what you do at that Conference." But he wouldn't even hazard a guess at Kimani's successor, still laughing in embarrassment and excusing himself by saying that he was not exactly the centre of things here on the shores of Lake Rudolf. And though van Delden questioned him closely, his answers were evasive. All he would say was that Pat Murphy was the source of the rumors, having just flown back from Nairobi, and that Major Kirby-Smith was worried that he no longer had full backing for his operation.

"He'll be ordered to stop it, is that what you mean?"

But Karanja shook his head. "That will depend on who is made Minister in place of Kimani." And he added, "Is only talk at the moment, you understand."

He wasn't being devious and his laughter seemed a cover for his own uncertainty rather than any amusement at the situation. His relationship with van Delden was a very strange one now, the old subservience overlaid by a pushful self-confidence, and yet underneath it I sensed that nothing had really changed, the bond between them as strong as ever, so that I wasn't surprised at the deep concern in his voice as he said, "Please, you take my advice. Do nothing. Perhaps tomorrow the major get a new directive."

"In this country," van Delden growled, "things don't happen as fast as that, and tomorrow he may kill enough elephants to fill those meat trucks of his."

Karanja shrugged, as though to indicate there were other, more immediate problems engaging his attention. "Is not the elephants," he muttered.

Van Delden reached out and grabbed him by the arm. "What do you mean by that?"

But Karanja shook his head, wrenching himself free and getting to his feet. "The Army don't want any trouble," he said again. "I am to tell you that and I have told you. They have mortars and machine guns and they know where you are." He turned to Mary. "You talk to him. Maybe he listen to you." And he walked off, down towards the lake shore, a suddenly impressive figure, solitary against the flat immensity of that jade sea.

"He's right." Mary was leaning forward, her dark eyes pleading. "Wait and see what happens."

Van Delden said nothing, sitting there, his rifle across his knees, staring after Karanja, and I wondered what he was thinking. He was seeing Karanja as I saw him, symbolic of the future here in Africa? Or was he resenting the passage of time, the change in attitudes? And Abe said quietly, "If the cull is called off, then I hope to God he's stopped in time." And I knew he was thinking of that elephant making her way down the gorge.

There was nothing for us to do now but wait, and after we had fed the afternoon passed slowly, a somnolent interlude, the heat intense and the lake a shimmering, blinding glare. We kept watch in turn from a crumbling outcrop, but no vehicle came down the track and nothing moved except the waders probing the mud at the mere's edge. I lay dozing, conscious of dehydration and the burning power of the sun, and all the time that sense of waiting heavy on my mind. At one point I remember studying van Delden through half-closed lids and thinking of Lear—that gnarled face burned brown by the sun, the long white hair lank with sweat. For Lear there had been nothing but disaster, and I wondered, my mind dulled by the heat and full of foreboding as the sun swung slowly across the brazen sky and sank towards the Turkana shore. And still nothing happened.

The sunset that evening was a purple flare like rich blood spilled across a pale blue-green ceiling. The lake turned red, then faded to the dull sheen of beaten metal, and with the dusk the birds came, pelicans, storks, geese, all manner of birds singly and in flights. Two shots gave us a meal, and while Mtome prepared it, the rest of us laid out the net in the shallows and hauled in more tilapia. On the shore there, looking across to the fading shapes of the islands and thinking of the people who had inhabited this world thousands of years ago, I had a sense of frustration: to have come so far, and in van Delden's company, everything I had planned, and now I knew instinctively that this was the end of the road. Mary, standing barefoot in the water, caught my mood: "You should have explored those islands while you had the chance. I'd have come with you."

"We'll go tomorrow," I said. But I was certain we wouldn't. And so was she. She shook her head, staring out across the lake to where the first star showed in the dying green of the sky. "Tomorrow I'll be at Loiyangalani," she said, her voice a whisper, her face a pale oval against the dark of her hair. And suddenly I knew that deep down inside she was afraid.

"You could refuse to go."

"No." She shook her head, silent for a moment. Then she said, "But there's nothing I can do. Nothing anyone can do." And she turned abruptly away, heading back towards the fire that now glowed brightly in the dark outcrop of the rocks. I stopped to slip on my boots, wondering that she could walk barefoot over stones and gravel, and as I neared the fire I had a picture of dark African faces lit by the flicker of the flames and the old man sitting cross-legged, his great bearded head ruddy in the glow. It was a very Biblical scene, but Old Testament, not New. No man camped on Lake Rudolf could think in anything but Old Testament terms. This was eye-for-an-eye country, intensely primitive.

That night we took it in turns to keep watch and when Dima woke me, just after midnight, the moon was up and the lake was so still it was difficult to tell where sky and water met, the reflection of the stars equally bright. The hill of the dead was almost white in the moonlight and below it the pale shape of the mere was dotted with the paler shapes of birds all fast asleep. It was a dead world, and lying in the hard hollow of the rocks, I had a sense of unreality, a feeling almost of disembodiment. There was no sound, no movement, everything frozen into immobility, no breath of wind and the air hot and heavy. I had time to think then, all the time in the world, but my mind seemed disorientated, incapable of concentration.

Time passed and gradually I became aware that the night was not entirely lifeless. Behind me, down the lake shore, shapes were shifting position almost imperceptibly. A hippo had its snout just clear of the water and there were crocodiles slithering on the dark volcanic sand. And towards the end of my watch several elephants appeared over a rise to my left, pale prehistoric shapes moving soundless through the moonlit landscape. They passed within a few hundred yards of where I lay, moving in a straggling line towards the lake. It was like a slow-motion film with no sound track, and as they disappeared from sight a voice behind me said very quietly, "If this could ever become a safe place you could walk among those elephants as you would among friends."

"Was that how it was at Marsabit?" I asked, looking back at him over my shoulder.

He nodded, his white hair gleaming silver in the moonlight. "I knew them all, and they knew me. Some I could go right up to and they'd touch my face with their trunks." And he added in a hushed voice, "It's a wonderful thing when an animal as big as that, and wild, gives you its confidence. It's like a revelation. Can you understand?"

"Yes, of course."

"Hmm." He sounded dubious. "To understand that is to understand the relationship of man to beast, the need they have of each other." He was silent then, watching as the last of the elephants slowly disappeared into a shallow dip between two pale rock hillocks. "Have you checked your camera?"

"It's okay."

"You realise nobody has ever shot a film of an elephant kill being stopped." He was staring at me, his voice suddenly urgent. "It means a great deal to me, that it should be on record. And the future of these animals could depend upon it."

"I've still got to get it out of the country."

"Yes, well, we'll have to think about that. But after you've got the pictures." And he nodded. "Better get some sleep now. We start at four."

But after what he had said sleep eluded me, my mind on what the day would bring. The world I knew seemed very far away, the harshness of this near-desert country all about me and the memory of those elephants gliding silent through the moonlight very vivid. Elephants. I could hardly remember when I had not been following their big footprints. I

tried thinking about the night on Kulal, and romping in the warm waters
of the lake, but it was all ephemeral. And that glimpse of Porr, the broken
piece of early pottery I had discarded, nothing had any significance now,
except this ghostly congregating of elephants. This was the day towards
which we had been steadily moving, Abe and I two outsiders, spectators,
caught up in a confrontation that was an extension of the arguments we
had heard at that Conference. So long ago it seemed with the lake gleaming pale under the stars and Karanja snoring gently, his broad nostrils
quivering.

Dozing, I was vaguely conscious of Mtome fanning the embers of the
fire, of dark figures moving against the stars. The moon was half across
the sky, lighting a bright path from South Island to the shore below us.
No sign of dawn yet and I sat up and looked at my watch. Just after four
and van Delden sitting on a rock, his beard limned in light, his head bent
over an old Lee Enfield rifle, checking the magazine. Below me, Mary was
stooping over Abe and I heard her say, "A few hours now and you'll be
able to get it properly set."

"I'm okay," he murmured. "It's just stiff, that's all." But his voice
sounded tired. "Any elephants passed during the night?"

I didn't say anything, nor did van Delden, and nobody spoke much as
we sat there among the rocks, drinking tea. By the time we had finished
breakfast and loaded the truck, the first faint glimmer of dawn was showing behind the bulk of Kulal. Flights of birds were circling the mere as
we drove round the edge of it, back on to the track, Mukunga at the
wheel and van Delden sitting beside him. Karanja leaned across to Abe.
"When you see the major, ask him whether Kit Kimani is still Minister.
If he does not know . . ." He hesitated, then added firmly, "Is important
he does not do anything without authority. Tell him that."

Abe nodded, but his eyes looked glazed and I wasn't certain he had
understood. We were driving without lights, the bumps in the track
unavoidable, and he was obviously in pain.

It was about six miles to the lugga and as we approached it the truck
slowed. Van Delden had the glasses to his eyes, searching the line of
drifted sand and rock outcrops. We ground our way through the empty
stream bed, past the twin hillocks that formed a natural gateway, and
then we were out in the open with the raised line of the doum palms
away to our left, and all ahead the land stretching flat like a salt pan to the
El Molo manyata and the port. There was grass here, dry wisps overlaying
a carpet of fresh growth, and above us the stars were paling, the dawn
light growing.

We were about five hundred yards beyond the lugga when the truck
slammed to a halt. A light had appeared at the furthest extremity of the
palm tree ridge. Mukunga switched off the engine and in the sudden
silence we could hear doves calling. A hyena whooped up among the
sand slopes we had crossed coming down off Kulal, the sound very faint
and changing to an ugly chuckle. There was the snap of branches, some-

thing moving on the doum palm escarpment, then we heard the sound of an engine and headlights swung across the shape of the Mission buildings. Van Delden turned to Mary. "Looks like they're on the move, so I'll have to leave you here."

"He can't walk that far."

"Then you'll just have to wait for one of their trucks to pick you up." He had the glasses to his eyes, watching the headlights flickering in the palm tree boles. "Hurry now. I can't wait here."

She got out then and Karanja and I gave Abe a hand. His face looked very pale, his glasses owlish as they caught the dawn light. "Okay?" I asked him.

He nodded, standing with his head up and his mouth set. "I'll make it."

A thin squeal sounded from the doum palms and we all turned our heads towards the ridge, but nothing moved and the sound was not repeated. Van Delden leaned out of the truck, his head turned to Mary. "Try to make him see sense. Because if he doesn't . . ." He bit the words off short and told Mukunga to get going. "Goodbye, Toto," he called softly. Her answer was lost in the sound of the engine and all I caught was the emotion in her voice. It was in her eyes, too, staring at him, very wide. Abe, standing beside her, his arm in the sling she had made for him, said something and she darted a quick glance towards the palms. Only then did she look at me, but our wheels were already stirring dust as we swung round to head back the way we had come and she turned away with a casual wave of her hand.

I was still staring after them, wondering why I had not insisted on going too, when Dima shouted something, pounding on Mukunga's shoulder and pointing towards the lake. A boxlike object which could only be a truck was moving against the pale glint of the water, and there was another almost hull down beyond it. They were both moving parallel to us, feeling their way slowly without lights. Our speed increased and we scuttled for the protection of the lugga, bucketing across it and swinging sharp right to skid to a halt behind an outcrop. Van Delden jumped out, swearing softly. "Get your camera."

"It's too dark," I said.

But he brushed my words aside, giving orders to the Africans and clambering up into the rocks, his rifle in his hand. "Take them a little time to flush those elephants out of the palms," he said as I joined him, lying in the shadow of an almost perpendicular rock. "Dawn will come fast now and they need the light for accurate shooting."

"You mean they're going to cull—now?" My mouth was suddenly dry.

"Yes, what else? Dawn's a good time."

"What about Mary?"

"I tell you, it takes time to set up a big kill. They'll have reached the Mission before anything happens."

But as the light strengthened and the hunters' trucks began to take shape in the flat country towards the lake, we could just see Mary, with Abe beside her, still standing on the track almost exactly where we had left them. Van Delden nodded towards the dim-seen figures. "What are they waiting for?"

I shook my head, unwilling to tell him what was in my mind.

"Silly little fool," he growled. "They'll be in the way if they don't get moving."

Karanja slid along the rocks towards us. "What you do now?" But at that moment lights blazed behind the escarpment and we heard the roar of engines, headlights flickering on the tree boles. Trucks were moving on the sand slopes beyond and we heard the distant sound of men yelling, banging on door panels, horns blaring, followed by squeals and trumpeting—a terrible hunting-cry noise that ripped the peaceful stillness of that lakeside dawn to shreds. And down on the flats towards the lake the trucks we had seen moving into place in the half light were closing in, slowly, menacingly, the sound of their engines lost in the uproar.

For a ghastly moment I thought van Delden was going to do nothing. He lay there, shaking his head as though willing it not to happen, his gazed fixed on the doum palm escarpment. Dark shadows drifted through the tall curved stems, and then they were coming out, a whole herd with calves of various ages, sliding down the escarpment to the flat arid grassland below, not trumpeting, not making any sound, but moving swiftly, almost purposefully, to their appointment with death. And in the lead, as they headed straight for the lake and the waiting hunters, was a large tusked elephant with a single calf beside her, tripping daintily—like a ballet dancer. The words flashed into my mind, Abe's words, and in that instant, my gaze switching to the two figures still standing on the track, I saw him start forward and Mary trying to restrain him. "Oh, God!" I breathed aloud. And van Delden, beside me, muttered, "What's he think he's doing?"

But by then Abe's figure had detached itself and was running awkwardly. I thought I heard him shouting, but I couldn't be sure, there was so much noise, a thunderflash exploding and the trucks racing for the end of the palms where they could come down into the flat and complete the drive. Abe was still running forward and Mary had almost caught up with him, two tiny figures running in the pale dawn, and the lead elephant had sighted them. She had stopped and was standing, stiff-legged and uncertain, her head moving from side to side, one foot scuffing the ground. The calf moved ahead of her and she laid her trunk across its shoulders, edging it into safety behind her as she faced the two humans hurrying towards her. The rest of the herd were bunching up behind her now, adults presenting a solid front, the calves pushed in behind, all of them alert to danger, thoroughly roused.

I knew what was in Abe's mind. He was remembering what Karanja had done, up there on the Mara, hoping to turn them towards us before

the trucks came down off the escarpment and began the final drive to
the killing ground. Van Delden knew it, too, and he was already on his
feet, running for the truck. And as we piled into it, the engine bursting
into life, I had a feeling of panic, a dreadful certainty; Abe knew nothing about elephants, only what he had read in books.

We came out between the twin hillocks, the wheels churning gravel
as we hit the dip of the lugga, and van Delden had the Lee Enfield
instead of his double-barrelled rifle gripped in his big hands. I was
standing in the back, holding on to the handbar, the cloud hanging over
Kulal glimpsed out of the corner of my eyes, tinged with red, and away
to the right the hunters' trucks raising streamers of dust. Abe was
motionless now, about fifty yards from the elephants, one arm raised
above his head, and Mary had also stopped a little way behind him. I
saw it like that, the scene set as in a still, very clear in the rapidly
increasing light, everything motionless. And then the two trucks came
belting round the end of the palms. There was an eruption of noise,
the crack of a shot, flat and hard, the sound of it coming from a Land-
Rover moving in from our right, and in the same instant the herd
matriarch charged, not trumpeting not making any sound, just covering
the ground at great speed, the dust flying from her dancing feet. And
behind her half a dozen others, big beasts with their trunks curled underneath their tusks and their heads high.

I saw Abe flung aside and Mary trying to run, engulfed in a grey
mass. Another shot sounded, and another, a whole ripple of fire. One
elephant checked, another down, but the rest of them kept going, driving straight for the Land-Rover and the two trucks now stopped and
in the direct line of their charge. And it was in that moment I grabbed
the camera, a reflex action, the need to do something, to blot out the
scene I had witnessed. By the time I had it to my shoulder the elephants
were in among the trucks and all was confusion, my impression blurred
by the din of shots and the squeals of rage, the camera whirring and
everything seen through the eyepiece. Another elephant went down,
rifles blazing and drifts of smoke, and one of the trucks backing away,
but not fast enough. A thunderflash burst, but the elephants swept on,
a grey tide engulfing it and the matriarch's flailing trunk smashing
down on the driver's head, splitting his face open like an over-ripe melon.
Tusks drove into the body of the vehicle, heads lowered, grey flanks
heaving, and then the truck was on its side, with the wheels spinning
and spurting sand, men running.

The cows stood there for a moment, bayoneting the truck with their
tusks and trumpeting in fury, then broke, roaring and screaming, as the
Land Rover drove in furiously and bullets slammed into their hides. A
shot right beside me, deafening, tracer streaming out on a flat trajectory
to strike at the Land-Rover. More shots and the Land-Rover stopped,
two men jumping out of it as an elephant bore down, raising it with
her tusks, and another, a big bull, I think, coming in from the other

side, and the men running as it bore down on them. One man was picked up, flung in the air, the elephant suddenly on top of him, kneeling on him, crushing the life out of him, and then it rose, shaking its head at the bloodied pulp on the ground at its feet.

I ran out of film then, standing there dazed and shaking, realising suddenly that we were stationary. Van Delden and Mukunga were firing over the bonnet, shooting lines of tracer, and the others had scattered, lying flat on the ground at either side of us. One of the trucks from the escarpment was on fire, the other backing away with a flat tyre. More thunderflashes went off, but the elephants ignored them. They had regrouped around their young and they passed within a hundred yards of us, taking no notice and moving swiftly northwards towards the lugga. By the time I had changed the magazine in my camera they were gone and only the dead remained, lying like low tide rocks, all still except one, which was thrashing its legs and trying to lift its head. And in the silence I could hear the gurgle of breath coming laboured from its wide-open mouth.

I sat down then on the tailboard edge, my knees shaking, my legs suddenly weak. The cloud over Kulal had thinned and was now a canopy of violent red. The sun was up behind the mountain, the palms a brilliant green, the earth blood-red and the lake blue, all bright, brittle colours in the sunrise, and van Delden walking slowly with bent head towards the curled-up khaki heap lying in the dust ahead of us. Exhausted, and moving like an automaton, I scrambled out and followed him. Mary lay in a fallen heap, her head at an awkward angle, the neck broken. But for that she might have been asleep. All those elephants passing over her and no mark. It was unbelievable, and only the flies clinging to her eyes to show she was dead.

Van Delden knelt down, brushing the flies from her face. "That fool American." He closed the lids with his fingers, his hand quite steady and nothing else said, no expression of grief. It wasn't callousness. I knew that. It was just acceptance. The man who had been a father to her and had never really known her. . . . "You realise she loved you— very deeply?" My voice was hesitant, under compulsion and sounding strange.

He looked up. "What do you know about it? About love and the pain of love?" And he added quietly, "She was very like her mother— tempestuous, hot-blooded, full of vitality and grabbing at life with both hands. Do you think I didn't love her?" He stared at me, no trace of emotion in the pale cold eyes, and his voice hard as he said, "She's dead, and that's that." He got to his feet, his big head turning to watch Kirby-Smith as he came limping towards us, and I saw his hands clenched on the gun he was still holding.

I don't know what he said to him because at that moment I heard a groan and a voice, very faint, calling me. It was Abe. He was about forty yards away, lying twisted against an old ant-heap. "Is that you,

Colin?" The blood bubbled in his lungs as he forced the words out, his eyes staring up at me, glazed and not seeing. His thin chest was so badly damaged he might have been in a road accident, the rib cage stove in, the white of shattered bone protruding through a dark mess of congealing blood that buzzed with flies. "Is she all right?"

"Yes," I said. "She's all right." I knew it wasn't Mary he was thinking of.

"They were shooting."

"She got away."

"It was those trucks, the skunks! She was charging them. Not me." His voice was suddenly strong and he tried to sit up. "Sally. I can't see her. I can't—" He fell back with a gurgling cry, blood frothing in his mouth.

"Just lie still," I said. "Save your strength."

But he didn't hear me, his lips moving, framing his wife's name, but no sound coming. His eyes closed and he gave a bubbling groan, his mouth spilling more blood. I think he died in that moment, but I couldn't be sure, never having seen anybody die before, and I called to van Delden. But he didn't hear me, his mind shut to everything else but the man facing him with one trouser leg ripped open at the knee and a lacerated arm. ". . . your own child. God help me, I can't shoot you in cold blood—"

"You dumped them there deliberately."

"Don't be a fool, man. Finkel had busted his arm."

"You were using them."

"He was injured, I tell you."

"But Mary—to leave Mary there. Right where I was going to cull. You knew what was going to happen. You knew." His voice was high, almost out of control, the two of them facing each other, ablaze with anger, the body at their feet forgotten, and van Delden saying, "You could have stopped it." His voice was hard and full of menace. "Instead, you fired. You fired at the lead elephant."

"To turn them."

"No. To start the cull."

"If I hadn't had to shoot from a moving vehicle—"

"You'd have killed that cow, but it wouldn't have stopped the others. Don't you understand what those beasts have been through? They're so desperate now they'll charge any vehicle on sight."

"We'd have stopped them if you hadn't interfered. Firing on our vehicles—"

I saw the gun come up, the flash of the barrel in the sun, and I shouted something. But Mukunga was already there, his hand on van Delden's arm, and the old man suddenly came to his senses, turning angrily away. "Get out of my sight," he growled, shaking his head like a big bull uncertain what to do next. "God Almighty! I should have killed you long ago." He glanced briefly at Mary and his eyes passed on

as though she were nothing now, his gaze fastening on a truck raising
a cloud of dust as it came down the track from the Mission. It was an
open 15 cwt. Kirby-Smith had seen it, too. His Land-Rover had been
righted and one of his men drove it up to him, rubber flapping from
the front tyres, which had both been ripped open by the thrusting
tusks. Mukunga was talking urgently to van Delden, Mtome and Dima
gripping their rifles, eyes watching nervously as the Army truck approached. The hunting vehicles were sorting themselves out, one of
them already under tow, and overhead the red of the sky was beginning
to fade.

The Army truck slowed as it approached Mary's body, a young black
officer standing up beside the driver, holding on to the windscreen. It
stopped and he stayed there for a moment, his gaze switching from
the dead girl to Abe's body lying at my feet, and involuntarily I thought
of Fortinbras, expecting him at any moment to make a speech. Instead,
he shook his head, at a loss what to do in a situation like this. Slowly
he stepped down from his vehicle, turning to Kirby-Smith as though
seeking a lead. He said something in Swahili and Kirby-Smith nodded.
Then suddenly they were all talking and Kirby-Smith's partner, Jeff
Saunders, drove up in one of the hunting trucks to join in the angry
exchange. Everybody was talking at once, all except van Delden, who
stood there, not saying a word, just waiting.

Finally the officer turned to him. "Where is Karanja?" he asked in
English.

It was only then that I realised Karanja was not there, that he had
not been with us in the truck when we had driven out from the lugga
in our abortive attempt to head the elephants off. Van Delden shook
his head, turning and looking back. The others also turned and following
their gaze I saw a lone dark figure halfway along the track from the
lugga, walking steadily towards us.

The officer got back into his truck and went to pick him up. When
it returned Karanja got out. "Very bad business," he said, addressing
Kirby-Smith, his voice high and trembling slightly, either with tension
or suppressed excitement, I wasn't certain which. "There will be no
more culling please and you will withdraw your outfit to South Horr
to await further instructions." And when Kirby-Smith started to argue,
Karanja cut him short. "Those are the orders of the Military Commander." And the officer beside him nodded.

It was Saunders who said quickly, "Brigadier Osman doesn't control
this operation. It's a political matter and Kit Kimani has given us—"

"Mr. Kimani is not any longer Minister. There is a new Minister
of Resources, Mr. Abbas. That is what Lieutenant Elmi has just told
me." And he turned to the officer beside him, who nodded his head
again and said, "Ndio."

"So you don't shoot any more elephants, not until I have spoken on
the radio with Headquarters." He turned to van Delden. "I suggest you

go back now to your old camp beside the lake and wait there. I will make endeavour to arrange safe passage for you out of the country. Okay?" And he added, "I am sorry—about this." He made a gesture that embraced the two sprawled bodies, then indicated the truck. "This detachment is leaving now in support of the Army post at Marsabit. Maybe I arrange for you to go with them." He turned to me. "You took some film. I would like it please." He was looking straight at me, his tone commanding, and when I hesitated, he said, "Is not good that what happens here is shown in the West, so you will hand it to me, please."

I glanced at van Delden, but he didn't say anything, his gaze turned inwards, his eyes blank. And as I turned away to get the film I heard Kirby-Smith say, "Abbas. There was a Tanzanian called Simon Abbas, took over Tsavo East just before the Ugandan Army moved across the frontier. Is that the man?" And Karanja nodded. "Is why I tell you there will be no more culling without his authority. He has great interest in elephants."

I got the film and when I came back with it Kirby-Smith was talking urgently with his partner. "If they won't loan us a plane, then see if you can persuade Brigadier Osman to have Pat Murphy fly me to Nairobi. The sooner I talk to Abbas . . ." They were already moving away and van Delden, still standing by Mary's body, suddenly lifted his head and called out, "Alex!" And when the other paused and turned to face him he said quietly, "Where are you planning to bury her— here or in Nairobi?"

"How the hell can we bury her in Nairobi?"

"You could fly her down."

"There isn't room in a Cessna."

"Use one of your refrigerator trucks then."

"No." The suggestion seemed to upset him.

"All right then. Where?"

"It's nothing to do with me."

"She's your child."

"I tell you, it's not my responsibility. You brought her up. You caused her death. You bury her."

Van Delden stared at him for a long moment, then he nodded his head slowly. "All right. If that's the way you feel."

We loaded both bodies into the 15 cwt and drove back to the hill of the dead. We buried them there on the stony slope that looked out over the little bay to the El Molo Islands. "Dust to dust, ashes to ashes . . ." Van Delden knew the relevant passages of the burial service by heart, and seeing him standing there, white-headed and bearded, intoning the words of committal, I knew he had done this many times before. The dust we tossed into the shallow graves was volcanic dust, and the sun shone out of a clear sky, the heat blistering.

It took us the rest of the day, working with wet towels over our heads, to build the two cairns, and in the evening, when it was done, we sat over a brew of tea, watching the birds fly in to roost on the mere below us, the sun falling below the Turkana mountains and the first stars showing pale in the rapidly darkening sky. Nobody spoke, van Delden sitting silent and withdrawn, the three Africans squatting round the embers, a stillness settling on the land, and I found myself remembering Abe's thin, sallow face, the dark worldly eyes, and the little twisted smile. I hadn't been brought up to believe in anything very much, but now, in this wild place with the stone cairns shadowy above me, I knew there must be something—something to reach out for. He had possessed an inner strength. He had talked of love, and suddenly I envied him, his peace, the certainty of his beliefs.

Sometime during the night Karanja arrived. He and van Delden were talking for a long time, but I couldn't hear what was said, only the murmur of their voices. I went to sleep again, and when I woke it was dawn and van Delden had gone.

I got to my feet, looking wildly round, realising I was alone, the two cairns outlined against the sun rising behind Kulal. And then I saw them, four dark figures splashing through the shallows of the mere, and north along the shore a solitary figure kneeling on a log raft and paddling it across the still, calm surface of the lake towards a small group of elephants standing up to their bellies in the water. I stood there for a moment, staring at the white of his hair shining in the early morning light, the paddle flashing drips of water and fish breaking the surface ahead of him in glints of silver. It was something I shall always remember, that lone figure on the El Molo fishing raft paddling slowly up the shore of Lake Rudolf, heading north like the elephants.

By the time I had reached the bottom of the hill the four Africans were waiting beside a Land-Rover parked on the track above the mere. Karanja came to meet me, smiling and with something of a swagger in his walk. "You sleep very deep, Mr. Tait." And on his shoulder he carried van Delden's double-barrelled rifle.

The sight of it, with the picture of that lone figure still vivid in my mind, shocked me. "You let him go—unarmed."

He shrugged. "Plenty of fish. He live like the El Molo now." And he added, "He is Tembo van Delden and he is back with his own people. With the elephants." Then, with something of a flourish, he said, "The new Minister has appointed me Warden of the North. I look after all game in this region now. That is what I came to tell him, that he and his elephants are safe."

Six hours later Pat Murphy landed me at Wilson Airport, Nairobi, and that same evening I boarded a flight for London. Since then I have been scripting a documentary, *The Building of the Canals*, and in my spare time writing this account of the fortnight I spent in Africa. I have had no news of Cornelius van Delden, though I have written twice to Karanja, once care of his Minister, and have made enquiries at the E.A.F. Embassy. I have, therefore, no certain information as to his present whereabouts, or even whether he is still alive. But in my mind I see him still as I last saw him, paddling alone along the shores of Lake Rudolf against a background of elephants belly-deep in the water. My guess is he will remain there till he dies, a forgotten man, lost to anything but the world he knows and understands better than any other human being.

THE END

FILMI, FILMI, INSPECTOR GHOTE

BY

H. R. F. KEATING

Published by special arrangement with Doubleday & Co., Inc.

The Deputy Commissioner was reading a *filmi* magazine. There was no mistaking it. Inspector Ghote had come hurrying into his big airy office in response to a crisp summons on the intercom and he had caught him in the act. The head of the Bombay Police Crime Branch was leaning back in his chair reading a trashy magazine devoted to huge pictures of film stars and the gossip of the *filmi duniya*.

Ghote stood there stiff with dismay.

If only he had had the sense to have taken one quick glance through the little square of glass in the door. But no. It had been a long while since he had received orders direct from the Deputy Commissioner and the thought of what he might hear had swamped everything else in his mind. A big case perhaps, influential people involved, a chance to put himself in good standing with the most senior officers. And now he had caught the Deputy Commissioner out.

What should he do?

He decided on a small cough. And as soon as the sound—it had unfortunately come out rather more like the strangulated bellow of an affronted bullock—had broken the quiet of the room he swung round and pretended to be occupied in closing the door with proper care.

"Ah, Ghote. Yes. Come in, man."

He turned and walked smartly towards the enormous desk with its telephones and its neatly arranged files, its big blotter and its presentation pens. And the *filmi* magazine was still open in the Deputy Commissioner's hands, the star's face on its cover plain to see—it was the famous cutting profile of Ravi Kumar, the No. 1 Superstar of them all—as well as the advertisement on the back for Somebody-or-Other's Suiting.

Ghote placed himself at attention behind the four chairs drawn up in front of the big desk.

"Yes, sir?" he said.

The Deputy Commissioner laid down the magazine, sat forward and regarded him steadily through liquidly intelligent eyes.

"Ghote," he said, "I have a priority case for you. Just been notified. Emergency call from Talkiestan Studios."

For a moment he paused, as if the news was almost too big to break.

"Dhartiraj has been killed," he said.

"Dhartiraj? The star?"

Ghote, whose knowledge of the film world hardly extended beyond an adolescent admiration for the top stars of that day, was not altogether sure what kind of an actor Dhartiraj was. He even wondered whether after all he was not a well-known wrestler.

But, no, he had been killed at the famous Talkiestan Studios, one of the all-India known names in the great Bombay film industry. He must be a star. Killed in suspicious circumstances plainly, and he, Inspector Ghote, put in charge of the investigation.

Suddenly his heart beneath his open-necked checked shirt began to thud in awed delight.

But, as quickly, other thoughts rose up. Incredulous, doubt-tinged thoughts.

"But, sir," he said. "Sir, is it me only that you are putting in charge?"

Then, feeling abruptly that he should not have voiced any fears about his own ability to tackle any case, however influential the victim, he hastily found a reason for his words.

"Sir, I am not at all knowing the *filmi duniya*, sir. I am not at all a film world person."

"I should think not," the Deputy Commissioner said with a trace of tartness. "I would not expect any of my officers to bother their heads with this sort of thing."

And he jabbed his finger straight down on to the sharply handsome face of Ravi Kumar.

"Had to send out for this myself," he added. "Just to get my bearings, find out that Dhartiraj was a great player of villains and so forth."

"Yes, sir," said Ghote, as if he had never for a moment wondered why his chief should have been going through such frivolous reading matter.

"Yes," the Deputy Commissioner went on with a faint sigh, "I suppose I shall have to let it be known that I am taking a personal interest in the case. But—"

His eyes came up and he looked Ghote inflexibly in the face.

"But I want it clearly understood, Inspector, that it is you and you alone who are investigating the affair. If it comes to the Courts eventually, it will be you and you alone who would be chief prosecution witness."

And again from Ghote's heart rich thuds of pride and pleasure began to beat out. But this time he did nothing to silence them.

"So it is definitely a question of murder, sir?" he asked, putting into his voice all the seriousness and purpose he could command.

"Yes, Ghote, it is a question of murder."

When Ghote approached the Talkiestan Studios, his head still full of the Deputy Commissioner's promises of technical backing and with the sight of him sitting, as he himself had clicked heels and left, looking at his telephones almost as if one of them had particularly told him whom to select to take charge, he found the studio gates besieged.

Plainly the news of Dhartiraj's death had begun to leak out. Through his car windscreen, only the tops of the tall iron gates, with the legend "Talkiestan Studios" in huge white letters above them, could be seen for the backs of dozens of eager Bombayites intent on pushing, scrambling, edging or even crawling their way to a view of the studios' compound.

Ragged shirts and laundered ones, bare backs and sari-clad ones, flowing kurtas of purest undyed white *khaddi* and workaday uniforms of messengers, postmen and peons in all shades of green and khaki jostled and elbowed and struggled for place.

"Horn through," Ghote snapped out to his driver. "Push on, push on."

On the far side of those gates, which he saw now were being defended by a couple of harassed-looking Gurkha chowkidars and a tall fancifully turbaned Pathan, lay his case. There somewhere would be the body of the dead star. There the witnesses. The suspects. Even perhaps the murderer.

"Horn through, man, horn through."

With savage little klaxon blasts reinforced by shouts, fierce and commanding as they could make them, through each of the open windows, inch by inch they crept forward. Then, when at last the heavy bumper of the car was in actual contact with the rusty iron of the gates, Ghote leaned yet further out, selected the chowkidar who looked most in control and barked at him the two words: "Police. Open."

The man, one of the two short-statured stubby-faced Gurkhas, gathered his two partners and then with a key painfully extracted from his pocket undid the heavy padlock, keeping the gate chain tight. At once the pressure of the crowd outside began to force back the two tall gates. The chowkidars pushed against them with straining backs. Ghote's driver, needing no instructions, eased the car forward so that it never ceased to block the slowly increasing gap. The moment the gates were wide enough the chowkidars redoubled their efforts and held them steady. The car scraped its way through.

Inside the compound it was clear that the tragedy had brought all normal activity to a halt. People of every sort were running excitedly here, there and everywhere in search of some new tidbit of rumour. Small groups came momentarily together, their voices rising to a wild clacking, only suddenly to break up again. Others shouted across to friends the cream of what they knew. Yet others yelled orders for quiet. Ghote, leaving his driver to help the chowkidars at the gates, stood looking on at them all, determined to get his bearings as quickly as he could.

Extras. Some of these people would be film extras. He felt a quick rose tinge of pride at working that out, the unexpected readiness with which the word had come into his mind. Yes, definitely those at first unplaceable men and women, looking like idlers who should not have been inside the compound at all, would be film extras. And that huddle of women under the big gul mohar tree, somewhat better dressed, though their saris were flashily bold, would be extras of a better class or small-part actresses. Yes.

And others in the spate-eddying crowd were easier to account for. The clerks, the smartly dressed stenos, the peons and messengers. Studios would need those as well as any other business. And coolies, even if in this strange world it was not easy to say exactly what their tasks would be. But simple enough to pick them out in their loincloths or tattered shorts as the necessary labour to move whatever had to be moved in the business of

film-making, to haul things up and lower them down. There were a fair
number of Ghati women about too, dark-skinned creatures from the hills
with their coarse-coloured saris drawn tightly over their hips, even less
skilled labour for even simpler unknown tasks. A sudden waft of the smell
of new-sawn wood told him that a trio of excited gossipers beside a grotesque shape of papier-maché moulding, once bright, now washed out
from lying too long in the sun, were carpenters. A film studio would need
plenty of carpenters.

Yes, and there, those two men in heavily embroidered kurtas, standing
nose to nose and talking with deep resonant voices and wide gestures,
they must be proper film actors. Proper film actors.

For a moment he felt a sinking. Those would be the sort of witnesses
he would be having to deal with. And they were not the sort he understood.

But he would deal with them. Just let them try any of their tricks.
When it came down to it, people were people, whatever their high and
flighty claims. And people could be made to tell the truth, or be caught
out in their lies. They could have their wild talk and their prideful over-
claims held down, if there was someone determined to do it.

He swung round and went back to the tall Pathan chowkidar, standing
puffing beside the re-closed gates.

"Who is in charge here?"

"In charge, Inspector sahib? There are many *burra sahibs* in Studios."

"I want whoever can tell me what happened to Dhartiraj. *Ek dum!*"

"Oh, my God, yes. Yes, Inspector sahib. I am thinking it is Production
Manager Sahib you are wanting."

"Then take me to him, *jaldi, jaldi.*"

He followed the tall, loping Pathan through the turbulence. The whole
compound was a jumble of different single-story buildings, mostly wooden-
built with deep verandas in front, almost as confusing at first encounter as
the excited crowds milling this way and that wherever they went.

"Dance rehearsal room, sahib," his guide said suddenly, as they passed
a tall construction in dirty white slabbing. "Air-condition. Very good."

"Yes," Ghote said.

He spotted among the jabbering clerks and extras and coolies a man
carrying a curious plastic tray in front of him, as if he was some sort of
vendor, and an unaccountable recollection of something he believed he
did not know told him that the fellow was a make-up man. He felt a new
spurt of confidence.

Perhaps he was not as incapable as dealing with the *filmi duniya* as he
had told the Deputy Commissioner.

Here and there, as they made their way through the crowd and past the
confusion of buildings, cars were parked, mostly familiar and dusty Ambassadors or Fiats. But one or two, in the shade under trees, were magnificent
and foreign. Stars' vehicles, he said to himself. Yes.

Posters on the trees, fixed high up and protected with transparent plastic, with the names of films that stirred faint memories in his mind, shone down at him with the words across them in huge letters "Silver Jubilee". Yes, films that had run in their original cinema for an uninterrupted twenty-five weeks. And there, a title he doubly recognised because he had taken his Protima and little Ved to see it, was one with the coveted words "Golden Jubilee" plastered across. Fifty weeks of continuous showing.

So that had come from these very studios.

He felt obscurely that he had taken another firm step into the mysterious world ahead of him. Yes, he might have to make guesses from time to time and there would be things he did not at first understand, but he would be a match for it all. He would be. He must be.

Two or three chickens fled squawking from under the Pathan's heavy sandals. Above, the crows, infected by the human agitation below, cawed and croaked even more noisily than usual. And, as they approached a low brick-built structure, a degree more impressive than the other offices they had passed, a new note was added to the encircling din, the shrilling of many telephones.

The news of the calamity must be getting out. Reporters by the score would be checking on the rumour. Before many minutes, indeed, they would be swarming down to the studios, bribing their way in, asking questions, taking pictures. He would have to be pretty damn sharp with them. See that they kept well out of the way.

The tall Pathan led him up on the veranda of the brick-built building and flung open one of the cabin doors.

"Production Manager sahib," he said loudly, "it is the C.I.D. Inspector."

The Production Manager, a grizzled stumpy man wearing a bright orange shirt with Bombay scenes printed on it, the Taj Hotel with its tall crowned Intercontinental tower, poor old chopped-down Flora Fountain, the dazzling upspringing skyscraper of the Overseas Communications Building, was attempting to answer two telephones simultaneously. To Ghote's quick gratification, he slammed them both down at once.

"C.I.D." he said. "Thank God, you have come."

Ghote drew back his shoulders.

"All hell is being let loose here," the Production Manager went on. "We are badly needing police co-operation."

"But there are men from the local station here already, aren't there?" Ghote said.

"Oh, yes, yes. But such fellows are no good at all. What we are wanting is some tough C.I.D. to clear out all these extras and riffraffs so we can deal with the mess to the best of our ability."

"The C.I.D. does not carry out crowd control," Ghote said with sharpness. "I am here to investigate the death of Mr. Dhartiraj."

"Yes, yes. You can see Studio Publicity Manager and fix up with him what story is to be put out. With all these damned phones ring-ringing all the time the sooner we have agreed statement the better."

"Listen to me," Ghote shouted with sudden ferocity. "I am not here to help with studio publicity. I am here to carry out investigation. Were you yourself on the scene when the tragic occurrence took place?"

"No. No."

The Production Manager was startled into silence. Ghote jumped quickly into the pause he had created.

"Well, then," he said, "who was at the scene? That is the fellow I am wanting to see."

"But— But that would be Director Ghosh. Bhabani Ghosh, twelve jubilees in five years. He is the one who is directing *Khoon Ka Gaddi*."

"*Khoon Ka Gaddi*?" Ghote asked.

It must be the title of the film they were making. But the Production Manager had spoken the words with such awe, as if they were bound to be rich with meaning for whoever heard them, that he felt abruptly lost again. *Khoon Ka Gaddi*. It meant *Cushion of Blood*. No, surely not. Ah, yes, *gaddi* in the sense of a Rajah's seat of honour. A throne. Yes, *Throne of Blood*, that sounded more likely.

"Yes, yes," said the Production Manager, rapidly regaining his former bounce in face of this ignorance. "The mightiest historical ever made. *Khoon Ka Gaddi*, screenplay by Dr. Arvind Bhatt, Litt. D., from *Macbeth* which is by William Shakespeare."

"I know *Macbeth*," Ghote stated sharply.

He was not going to let this fellow walk over him. And, besides, it was almost true. The play had been one of his set books for Inter, until the syllabus had been unexpectedly changed. And, as he had always liked to be well in advance with his work, he had read most of it. Well, Acts One and Two certainly, and perhaps more.

"Yes," he repeated. "Well I am knowing *Macbeth*. But where is Mr. Bhabani Ghosh? If he was the principal witness, then it is him I am wanting to see."

"But he is there," the Production Manager answered. "There. At the scene of the crime."

"The scene of the crime? Then take me to him straightaway. Take yourself, if you please. I have no time for hanging about."

The scene of the crime. That was where he ought to be. There. Where it had happened. Seeing for himself. Investigating. Taking charge. Taking the case by the scruff of the neck, by God. At the scene of the crime.

II

Marching out behind the once more subdued Production Manager, Ghote felt a pulsing of pleasure at the speed with which that stumpy orange-shirted figure was trotting down the veranda steps. To talk about the

Studios' publicity, what self-centred madness. A murder had been committed. And its perpetrator had to be found. What was needed was—

"Production Manager Sahib."

The bellow through a jerked open window behind them was so loud that, though it was not his name that had been shouted, he came to a total halt on the top veranda step. The Production Manager froze as if he had been struck solid by the hand of God himself.

When, after a second of statue stillness, he turned cowedly round Ghote saw that his face bore an expression of such abjectness that it really seemed as if he was indeed confronting a god of man made flesh once more. His lips chewed hard at nothing as he endeavoured to get out a single word.

"Sethji?" he pronounced at last. "You called, Sethji?"

Ghote followed the direction of his cringing stare, wondering at the effect that the head of the studios, the Producer, the man of money and power could have. It was certainly very different from the way things went in his own world. There, if the Commissioner himself should address him he would certainly come to attention and answer with plentiful "Sirs". But he would not touch any feet. And that, in all but actual fact, was what was happening here.

At the jerked open window the god himself looked out, his name painted in large letters of gold under a plastic panel on the door just beside him, "Mr. Chagan Lal." Seth Chagan Lal. A face of hard and solid fat with two small unyielding eyes and the straight slit of a little closed-up mouth. Above, a hard black boat-shaped cap, and below, the top of a pudgy body in a coat of white silk ornamented with pure gold buttons, pushed to popping point by the hard pressure of the flesh beneath.

"Production Manager Sahib, you are taking away the C.I.D. wallah they have sent."

It was an accusation.

The Production Manager looked suddenly, inside that orange shirt with its bold black designs, like a too small shop-window dummy.

"Sethji." A small sound emerged from him. "Sethji, I— I did not know. It was . . ."

"If they are sending to investigate the murder of one of my stars, I am wanting to see, isn't it?"

The voice came in sharp successive small bursts of thunder.

"Sethji, he is here."

The Production Manager pushed a chopped-down gesture towards Ghote. It said, in so far as it dared, that he should go in at once and talk to the Seth.

Ghote debated in himself whether he should decline. He was after all not someone to be summoned. He was in his own person the chosen representative of the law, here to investigate the death of a nation's idol, a star.

At the open window Seth Chagan Lal remained unmoving.

Perhaps, as in any case sooner or later he would have to be interviewed, perhaps this was as good a time as any.

He crossed the broad veranda and opened the door with the Seth's name on it.

The office in which he found himself, stepping at once into an air-conditioned coolness that was instant luxury to the skin, was enormous, far larger than the Deputy Commissioner's back at Headquarters, larger than that of the Commissioner himself. All along the wall at the back ran a deep sofa, evidently the place where the outermost circle of the Seth's suppliants sat when at last they were admitted to the great man's presence. It was covered in a flower-patterned material. A large area of dark red wall-to-wall carpeting had to be crossed next before coming to a small array of chairs, very modern-looking in black leather and gleaming chromium tubing. And between these and the great man's desk there was another five or six feet of uncrossable red carpet.

But what a desk it was. In a wild comparison that abruptly invaded his head, Ghote reckoned that it was only a little smaller in area than the whole of the bedroom in his own home. Its top was a single sheet of heavy glass, supported some six inches above the great dark and gleaming wood of the structure itself. Under it could be seen posters for films that must have achieved some special honour. On the top of the glass there was, on the right, a magnificent table-lamp crowned by a shade of heavy red silk with beside it, like a fleet of small ships at anchor underneath a huge lighthouse, a dozen thick pens and pencils in dull and solid gold. To the left, there were seven telephones.

On the wall behind there could be seen the golden grille of the immense air-conditioner and the battered green-painted door of a very large safe.

Seth Chagan Lal waddled stiffly round to the huge chair behind the desk and sat down. Only then did Ghote take in that at one corner of the enormous piece of furniture there was sitting, perched on a very small stool-like chair, a very small secretary, an Anglo-Indian girl to judge by the skirt and blouse she wore and the lengths of shapely, but small, legs dangling down.

The Seth thrust a mess of papers and documents in a green leather folder towards her.

"Take," he said. "Write some nice answers. And ring them also at Cotton Exchange. Say to cover New York without fail."

The diminutive girl took the folder, contrived in one rapid movement to reduce to order its this-way-and-that confusion, tucked it under her arm and minced past Ghote to the door, leaving behind a momentary fragrance of flowery talcum powder.

"Sit," said the Seth, giving Ghote a single sharp look.

Ghote marched across to the chair nearest the great desk and lowered himself stiffly on to its very edge, though he was unable not to acknowledge the padded give of the leather beneath him.

"Mr. Lal," he said firmly. "My name is Ghote, Inspector Ghote of Crime Branch C.I.D., and I have been put in charge—"

"*Khoon Ka Gaddi* must go on. That is the first thing to be said."

The Seth's little eyes in their hard encasing of fat bored straight into him.

"I realise, Mr.—"

"In India there are two crores of people buying cinema seat each day. Twenty million sums of, let us say, rupees three each. I am not going to let the distributors think that my film will not take its share of them."

The glare from the fat-encased eyes did not slacken by so much as a pin's width.

"Did you know that there are four hundred-five hundred films made here each year. Every one of them set to make money from mine. That is why *Khoon Ka Gaddi* must not stop."

"Yes, Mr. Lal, I well realise that—"

"It is not arty-warty films I am making. It is not Best Direction I am worrying about next week when it is Filmfare Awards. No, I am well knowing what it is that people are wanting, and that I am giving."

Abruptly he inclined forward across the huge glass expanse of the desk top, cutting short Ghote's intervention even as it came to his lips. A look that might have been a smile fixed itself on his face.

"I was a poor boy once," he said. "Poor. Poor. And to my native-place near Hyderabad there came one day a touring talkie. Then it was that I saw what a different world it could bring. And that is what is wanted in film line. That. A different world. With jewels. With far, far places. With music. With some really sexy scenes. And that is what still today I tell my directors to give."

"Yes, yes. And I understand that the death of—"

"When I was beginning I did not have the money even to buy one story. Just enough for a song only. But I bought what I knew was good, what I knew the people would like, would sing, sing, sing themselves. And I persuaded a star, a big star then, to sign, though I had almost to drag him there for the *mahurat* shot so that I could say that the film had been blessed and had begun. But when I played over that song to the distributors I began to get my money. Little by little. Three years it took to make that film. Three years, and then house-fulls all the first ten weeks. A real box-office grosser from the start."

Ghote decided it must not go on any longer. He jumped to his feet and leaned in his turn across the great glass expanse.

"Mr. Lal. I am the Investigating Officer in the case of Mr. Dhartiraj deceased. Deceased upon your premises. Sir, it is because that death took place on these premises that I decided to hear any statement you had to make first. But I am not going to be delayed from visiting the scene of the crime."

"The scene of the crime?"

The Seth's fat-hard face had darkened.

But at least, Ghote thought, he listened to what I said.

"Inspector, this is the scene of the crime. This."

And the Seth's clenched little fist came down so hard on the big sheet of glass that it gave out a deep booming note and even bent a little under the impact.

"Inspector, today it is very different matter with a Fifteen Arts production. Today I am not having to go round with one song only to the distributors. Today I can demand and get twenty-five lakhs of rupees per film per territory. Inspector, for *Khoon Ka Gaddi* it will be more. That film is a very-very big investment. And with Dhartiraj dead and eight reels in the cans only the situation is very-very serious."

"Yes, Mr. Lal, but—"

"Inspector, I am not wanting any scandals. That is the point, Inspector. Very well, very well, we shall have quickly quickly to find a new star. And, very well, new shooting there will have to be, though that must be kept to a minimum-minimum. But nothing else is to go wrong. *Khoon Ka Gaddi* is going to be finished on schedule. And it is going to be an all-time hit film when it is finished. Touts at every cinema will be asking more-more for tickets than has ever before been demanded. Do you understand that?"

Ghote sat back in his chair again carefully. He had felt the Seth's sheer will flinging itself against him like a wild but deeply powerful monsoon sea. And he knew that he must not let it overwhelm him.

"Sir," he said slowly, "I am having to make one thing clear. A murder has taken place, and in due course there will be a person to be charged under Section 201 of the Indian Penal Code. Sir, if that person comes to hand—and I will be sparing of no effort to achieve that eventuality—then that charge will be made, whatever effect it may or may not have upon the progress of your film or upon Fifteen Arts Private Limited."

For long seconds Seth Chagan Lal sat perfectly still. His blubber-hard face betrayed not a jot of surprise at his having been addressed in such terms. The little eyes expressed no flare of resentment.

"Very good, Inspector," he said at last, "you have had your say. I do not know whether you had thought before you have spoken, thought that a person of my interests would have also influence. But you have spoken."

He put out a pudgy hand and minutely straightened one of the thick gold pens that lay beside the tall table-lamp.

"And now," he went on, his voice still at the same low pitch, "now I will have my say. Inspector, I am a man who gets his way. It is not without hurting people that I have risen up from a poor clerk first coming to Bombay to where I am today. And I still have a long way to go, Inspector. A long-long way. And nothing and no one is going to stop me."

He leaned back a little bit.

"Inspector, it would be best if you were not one of the people who stood in my path."

Abruptly he reached under the glass of the desk top and pressed a bell-push that sounded a discreet buzz somewhere behind Ghote. At once the little Anglo-Indian secretary came in, carrying her shorthand notebook.

Ghote got up and made his way out past her. He did not feel it was necessary to say goodbye to the Seth.

But, as he stepped from the luxurious coolness of the big office into the dry and dusty sunlight, his mind was hard at work.

He had had a warning. That much was more than plain. Seth Chagan Lal had interrupted his busy routine, busier no doubt by far now for having to deal as quickly as possible with the consequences of Dhartiraj having been removed from the role he had had in that deep-sucking investment of a film, in order to speak with him before his investigation had even begun to get under way. He had summoned him to warn him. But what exactly had that warning been of?

There had been all that talk of the amount of money involved, but not a word that was direct. Black money, could it be that? Everyone knew that films were often made with funds that were never put on paper for the tax man to see, money raised through smuggling and in half a dozen other illegal ways and converted through the profits of film-making into sums that could be used in the open. Stars too were often paid in black. Again that was something everybody knew. It was common gossip that they got two fees for everything, for signing a contract or as shares in a film's profits if they were high-enough ranking stars, one sum paid by cheque and entered in the books, the #1 money, and another, larger sum paid in cash, in huge wads of big hundred rupee notes, the #2 money. Yet it was hard to see how the murder of Dhartiraj and some dubious black money transaction on the part of Seth Chagan Lal could be connected.

No, there must be something else which he had been warned about. He had been as good as told not to find out certain things, things that would add to the delays in making *Khoon Ka Gaddi*. But what exactly? What on earth could—

"Inspector."

He blinked.

The Production Manager was standing at the foot of the veranda steps, stumpy and bright-shirted as he had been a few minutes before. Why then did he seem so different? Why did everything seem changed, as if a whole new factor had been introduced into a situation that had seemed, just those few minutes earlier, crystal clear?

But whatever it was it would have to be thrust to the back of his mind now. He could not delay an instant longer. He had been on his way to the scene of the crime and it was there that he must go. And surely it was at that scene, among the simplicities of real and actual clues, that the path lay. There he could apply everything he had learned over the years, the taking of statements, the making of measurements, the checking and the counter-checking. And from those the truth would emerge.

What had happened. And then the arrest under Section 201. And be damned to Seth Chagan Lal.

Yes, the Seth might be a great man in his own world. But here, in the police world, a star was rising in the heavens. His star. He had been put in charge of this case, this all-India important case. And he was going to bring someone to court at the end of it, charged with murder.

"Yes, Production Manager Sahib," he said. "Take me to the scene of the crime."

It was a tall corrugated-iron building standing at the very far end of the Studios compound with a high entrance door opening on long rails top and bottom. But this huge door had a small door within it, hardly five-foot high and proportionately narrow. Above this a thin enamel notice-plate, streaked with rust, announced "Sound Stage No 2".

"Inspector, it is here."

The Production Manager pushed at the narrow door.

At once an angry voice bellowed out at them in sharp Marathi.

"No entry. No entry."

The faintly stubbled face of a long-service police-constable appeared briefly in the sunlight.

"It is the C.I.D. Inspector. He has come."

The constable stepped back at the Production Manager's words and flicked up a salute. Ghote stooped a little and followed that orange shirt inside.

It was blackly dark. Partly this was the effect of stepping in out of the bright sun, but partly too it was due to a single very powerful light shining downwards somewhere in the middle of the tall building and cut off from them by tall screens reaching nearly up to the roof.

Scenery. Yes, of course, those would be scenery.

Ghote felt a renewed comforting sense of security at having known once again, almost instinctively, what was going on. He followed the bright orange shirt confidently into the thick dark, neatly avoided tripping over a great fat black cable snaking over the floor, succeeded in not knocking into any of the thin sloping struts supporting the scenery, and suddenly, with an effect of extravagant drama, found he had emerged into the pool of strong white light he had glimpsed above the tall scenery screens.

He might, he thought abruptly, be in some actual film. Under the glare of the light a rough circle of people, ranging from the most ordinary to the most extraordinary, stood unmoving as if caught for a still. A still, yes. That was the word.

It was at once plain which of the group was Director Ghosh, in charge of the shooting when Dhartiraj had been killed. It could only be that tall, swaying-bellied Bengali with the bold features and the long curling hair, dressed in a flowing white kurta and pyjama, a gold locket to be glimpsed hanging from a chain round his neck.

Next to him was a uniformed Assistant Inspector of Police, no doubt the fellow who had come in response to the first call made to the nearest police-station. Then the lanky chap standing next to the black, complicated-looking camera, which itself seemed one of the silent circle, must be the Cameraman who had been at work on the scene, a Gujerati by his looks.

But then, at the far side of the circle, was a face he recognised. A face indeed. A face in a million. Nilima. Nilima, star of countless films, there herself. How often, though he was no cinema-goer, had he seen painted on hoardings those voluptuously beautiful features spread over almost a square yard of surface. Nilima, a legendary figure. Here, and standing struck as speechless as the rest of them.

Yes, and he would have to find out and quickly just who they all were. That fellow in the gorgeous red rajah's costume standing a little back from Nilima. He ought perhaps to know him too. Yet there was an odd downward-looking air to him that seemed very different from the radiating assurance of the star. Who would he be?

"Director Sahib. It is the C.I.D."

At the Production Manager's words, spoken with a jarring loudness, Bhabani Ghosh had turned and stepped back a pace from the close circle. And the gap he made showed the sight they had all been standing silently looking down at, so many different forest animals hypnotised by a mighty snake. There, sprawled on the floor, harshly illuminated by that blinking white light, lay the heavy, red-robed body of a man. The murdered star.

III

There was surprisingly little blood. A single dark rivulet ran congealed over the floor and a few heavy spots showed up on the white pages of two or three clipped together sheets of paper lying nearby. More evident were the diamond-like fragments of glass scattered everywhere in thick pieces, debris from the big black lighting lamp whose fall must have been responsible for the star's death. It lay close against his shoulder, almost as if it had been propped up against a sleeping man.

It must, Ghote thought, have killed him at a stroke, probably snapping his neck as he had sat, leaning forwards, on the richly embroidered regal cushion just behind him.

But such matters would be for the police surgeon to decide. At this moment his information must come from the silent circle of onlookers.

He stepped forward and tersely introduced himself to the big Bengali director.

"You were here?" he asked. "You saw what happened?"

Bhabani Ghosh looked at him with darkly brooding eyes.

"My God, Inspector," he answered, "I was directing him. Such a movie we were making."

He lifted up his large head and stared into the distance. It seemed to Ghote that he must be very much aware how nearly his long locks resembled a lion's mane at that angle.

He put his next questions with considerable sharpness.

"You were directing him, telling him what to do? And then what? That big light fell? Did you look up? What exactly did you see? What did you see up there?"

He pointed to the blackness above.

Director Ghosh brought his gaze back to earth and blinked.

"Inspector," he said, "I saw nothing."

"Nothing? Nothing? That light fell on your star, Mr. Ghosh. How can you say you saw nothing?"

"Inspector, I was not there."

"Not there? But you said—"

"Inspector, let me explain, I beg of you. Film business is a very complicated and difficult business, Inspector. It would not be possible for someone like you, an outsider only, to have any idea of what it is that happens."

Ghote felt a faint chill stir in his mind. Was he after all bound to find himself always wandering in a strange country?

"Go on, Mr. Ghosh," he said, with a touch of grimness.

"Inspector, it was like this. Today I was able to have Dhartiraj for the morning shift. You understand the shift system, isn't it? We are having at present for *Khoon Ka Gaddi* an eight-day session of morning shifts. That is to say that for eight days I am able to film Dhartiraj from 8 a.m. till twelve noon. At that time he goes to another studio shooting another film. I suppose he is—he was, I must say now—he was shooting at present some fifteen or sixteen films, and, of course, he has signed contracts for many more. Perhaps as many altogether as—"

"But, excuse me."

Ghote felt he had to interrupt. If he was not careful this word-torrenting Bengali would drown him in a huge lecture, a deluge of public facts. And the man behind them, the man who might have seen something vital to finding the killer of Dhartiraj, something he did not even know that he had seen, might escape.

He interposed the first question that came to his mind to give himself time to think how best to get inside underneath the torrent.

"But, excuse me, to make a film in bits and pieces only, is that truly possible?"

And it seemed that this mere holding question had itself gone home under the gush. Bhabani Ghosh's expression of grand pourer forth of impressive information disappeared from his large-featured face like steam blown away by a sharp chill wind. His big brown eyes looked directly at Ghote for the first time.

"Yes, Inspector," he said, speaking now on a quiet note of intimacy. "Yes, you have gone to the heart of it. It is impossible to make films, true films, in such conditions. You have heard of *Chaka?*"

Ghote had not, recognising only that the word was Bengali for "wheel".

"No," Bhabani Ghosh said with an underlying bitterness. "Of course you have not h_ard of *Chaka*. It was only a true film, the story of a man's rise and inevitable decline. It was only my masterpiece."

He smiled. A smile that was for himself.

"The film that I made," he went on, "before they asked me to forget I was a new-wave wallah and come to Bombay to make films that people would see, films using always a sneering villain, a weeping mother, a bullying mother-in-law, stories with twin brothers parted in childhood or with fights on the cliff edge when the hero wins against even a dozen *goondas* all wearing leather-jackets, backgrounds chosen because the studio had them on film already. Yes, and I came. And I made these films. Twelve jubilees in five years, and one a gold."

He glared down at Ghote. But Ghote knew that the animosity was not directed at him.

"Oh yes," he went on in the same low intense tone, "I made films that people would want to see, films with everything in them all at once, films to make people dream they are living wicked Western ways—nightclubs and discoes and all the time wearing jeans—and then to wake to find they are pure Hindus still. Yes, in bits and pieces I made such films."

There was a glinting tear on one of his big flabby cheeks. And, Ghote thought, it is a tear not made of glycerine and placed with infinite care.

Glycerine. Where had he read that this was how tears were produced in the film world? No matter where. He knew it. He knew more about this world than Director Ghosh had given him credit for. And he would find out whatever else he needed to know.

Now was the time, too. When he had got his witness looking at the truth.

"Please," he said quietly. "Please to tell me who were the people who actually saw Dhartiraj's death."

"But I was explaining, Inspector. There was no one."

"No one?"

He looked incredulously at the circle still gathered round the big red-robed recumbent body of the murdered star.

"Inspector," Bhabani Ghosh said earnestly. "By a curious chance there was in fact no one at all near Dhartiraj at the moment of his death. As I was telling, we were shooting this morning a scene where Dhartiraj, who is playing Raja Maqbet, was—"

"But—"

Ghote cursed himself for breaking in when the information was beginning to flow like this. But he could not help himself.

"But Dhartiraj is a great actor of villains, isn't it?" he asked. "And Macbeth is the hero of Shakespeare's tragedy."

Director Ghosh sighed.

"Oh, Inspector, Inspector," he said, "you have a lot to learn. You know Shakespeare's play?"

"Yes, yes."

"Very well, in that Macbeth is killed in the end, isn't it? He is killed by Macduff. Now, do you think that anyone could make a Hindi film in which the hero is killed? And by a side hero only? No, no, the one who is left the winner must be the hero. So in *Khoon Ka Gaddi* is Maqduv who is the hero, and he of course is played by the great Ravi Kumar himself. Dhartiraj was the villain, Maqbet."

"I see," Ghote said.

"Very well." The big Bengali resumed his explanation. "The scene we were about to shoot was the one in which Maqbet seats himself upon the *gaddi* that he has wrongly usurped from Maqduv and—"

"But— No, no. Excuse me. Please go on."

"Where Maqbet is seated upon the *gaddi* meditating upon the promise he has made to his mother that he will not harm Maqduv, the son she has borne out of wedlock, only as it will come out in the end it is Maqbet who was born out of wedlock and Maqduv who is the rightful rajah."

"I see."

"Well now, I had gone through the dialogues for this with Dhartiraj and we had agreed at what moment he was to rise to his feet and beat at his breast. So it was next a question of the lighting, and for that I was using a stand-in. But when the fellow comes he is wearing the turban that Dhartiraj himself will wear in the shooting, and as soon as Dhartiraj saw it he realised that there was something altogether wrong. It had not nearly enough jewels for an artiste of Dhartiraj's stature, that is to say for a rajah of the stature of Maqbet."

"Yes, yes, I see."

"Very well. So Dhartiraj sent the stand-in to obtain more jewels from the Property Department, and in the meantime he sat down on the *gaddi* to go through his dialogues while I went out of the set to have discussions with my cameraman where—"

"Bhabaniji, Bhanbaniji. Directory of Photography, if you please."

It was the Gujerati beside the craning-forward camera who had been listening with avidity to every word the Director had been saying.

Bhabani Ghosh's bold features took on a look of swift contempt.

"Very well, I went into conference with my Director of Photography about what orders it would be necessary to give the Lights Boys. You know that each light is operated by a coolie up on a catwalk?"

"Yes, yes," said Ghote, who had not known.

"Very well, so Chandubhai there and his assistants came with me and the Audiographer also, what you would be calling the sound man."

"I see."

"And Dhartiraj's make-up man knowing it was too soon to correct his make-up went to the canteen, leaving Dhartiraj alone on the set."

Ghote thought he had grasped the situation.

"And then?" he asked.

"Then? Then, quite soon after we had begun our conference, there was, I am almost sure, a sudden whistling sound and the Five-K came—"

"Excuse me, the Five-K?"

"The five-kilowatt light," Director Ghosh explained, a little testily. "We are using a great number of different lights for different purposes in filming, Five-Ks, Two-Ks, Sunspots, Solars, Babies. But, as I was trying to tell, I am almost certain that I actually heard the whistle of that light coming down. And then there was a sickening crash. Perhaps one moan only from Dhartiraj. And silence."

"Silence. Then what?"

"Why, then we all rushed back to the set and we saw just what you yourself can see now. Believe me, Inspector, I at once ordered that nothing, but nothing, was to be moved. The thought that it was an accident for which the Studios might be blamed was the first thing that came into my head. And at once I sent a Lights Boy up to see what had happened up there, and to report to me personally. If it had been a rope that had frayed, then it was important to hide— Then it was important to keep the evidence, you understand."

"I understand. But it cannot have been a frayed rope that the Lights Boy reported."

"No, it was not," Bhabani Ghosh said sombrely. "He told me that the ropes holding the Five-K had been severed. Cut clean through with an abominably sharp knife."

"And that was when you knew it was murder and telephoned for the police?"

"Yes, yes. And in double quick time this gentleman here, Assistant Inspector— Assistant Inspectorji, I was never hearing your name."

The Assistant Inspector clicked his heels.

"Assistant Inspector Jahdev."

"You arrived on the scene at what time, A.I.?" Ghote asked.

"10.37 ack emma, Inspector."

"And at what time did the light fall?" Ghote asked Bhabani Ghosh.

"I was altogether too overwhelmed to note the time, Inspector. But it cannot have been longer than fifteen minutes before Mr.—er—Mr. Jahdev arrived."

So, Ghote thought, there was every chance that nothing material had been altered. He could see the circumstances just as they had been at the moment someone had cut those ropes, watched the Five-K—yes, the Five-K—crash down on to Dhartiraj and had then slipped away in the darkness above.

But that someone had a body. He was not the invisible man. He must have climbed up to that catwalk immediately above the set and have hurried down again. He had not been seen up there, but the chances were that he had been seen elsewhere although plainly no on here had spotted anybody running from the scene.

Questioning, thorough and precise questioning, might well make it absolutely clear however that someone was unaccounted for. THE someone.

It would be a matter of hammering at them all. Of forcing from people's minds things they did not know were there. And he would do it.

He turned back to Bhabani Ghosh.

"You were telling that you were about to arrange the lighting for the scene of Dhartiraj meditating upon the *gaddi*," he said. "And you said also that each light up there has a Lights Boy to look after it. How many of them were up with their lights then? Where are they now?"

Too frightened to talk. If he knew anything.

"But, no, Inspector," the Director said. "For this scene I intended to have one spotlight only. Maqbet was to be haloed in light. It was an effect I had used in my *Chaka*."

For a moment a look almost of desolation came into his eyes. But he hurried on.

"So, you see, there was no one on the catwalk directly above the set. Indeed, all the Lights Boys had gone to the canteen. And the single light we were using had the effect of making everything up there even more dark than usual."

"I see. So it would not have been at all difficult for the person who cut those ropes to do so unobserved?"

"Exactly, Inspector."

There was a note of sombre satisfaction in the tall Bengali's voice. The very impenetrability of the affair seemed to give him deep pleasure.

Ghote felt a sharp surge of white-hot determination.

"Nothing could be seen up there?" he barked.

"Nothing, Inspector."

"Nothing from down here perhaps," he came banging back. "But what about the one light that was on? And the lights coolie for that? He was up there. What did he see?"

Inside him a fountain of brightness spurted high at Director Ghosh's instant look of acknowledgement. No, the Deputy Commissioner had chosen well. A new bright light was needed to shine into the darkness the *filmi* people delighted to wrap round themselves. And he was it. Despite every doubt, he felt it now. A new light to penetrate that dark.

IV

An unexpected intrusion, however, prevented Ghote getting at once to the lights coolie who might well turn out to have seen, not the man who had cut the ropes of the Five-K above Dhartiraj's head, but something, even some already forgotten tiny incident, that could put him firmly on the trail of the murderer. He was, in fact, a little delayed by the arrival of the rest of the team from Headquarters, the men from the Fingerprint Bureau, a photographer, a stretcher party to take the body away eventually to the Police Surgeon. But it was while he was dealing with them, his determination kept just beneath the surface like a powerful film-studio light itself ready at a flick to throw the whole of his life into a new brilliant brightness, that the real interruption occurred.

The Bombay corps of Press reporters came clamouring loudly to the sound-stage door.

He decided it was his bounden duty to see them. After all, this was no ordinary crime. A star had been murdered. A man known to millions all over India. It was right that the Investigator himself should tell the world what there was to be told.

He held his conference just outside the big studio, discovering as he stepped out that the sun had mercifully gone behind a big sailing white cloud so that there was no reason not to stand out where they were.

Some twenty or more reporters were gathered there and for almost half an hour they banged question after question at him. He had never before experienced an encounter with the Press at this pitch and he was bitterly conscious that on occasions he floundered.

There was even one moment when he was reduced to prolonged and hopeless silence.

It came just after he had dealt particularly well with a query from a man with whom he had had talks more than once in the past, the crime reporter of the *Free Press*. He had asked the sort of question that he himself felt ought to be put, a simple request to know exactly what forces the C.I.D. were devoting to the case, and it had not been difficult to produce in reply an impressive list of almost every facility they had, right down to naming the police dogs who might possibly be of use, Caesar, Akbar, Moti. Then, a tall beaky-nosed woman at the back, whom he had not previously noticed, an angular creature in a sari of tiny green squares, abruptly called out.

"Miss Pilloo Officewalla, chief gossip writer *Film Femme*. If your investigations should lead you to believe a famous star has murdered Dhartiraj out of mad jealousy, what steps would you take?"

It was not that it was difficult to answer. It was simply that he could not believe what he had heard. And for second after second he had stood there mentally repeating the words.

Miss Officewalla, who he discovered to his surprise when he mentioned her afterwards to his *Free Press* acquaintance, was considered to be Queen of the Gossip Writers, had actually begun to put the whole question again before he banged back the only possible reply.

"Madam, if I had arrived at such a conclusion I would proceed to arrest the gentleman in question."

"Or lady?" Miss Officewalla shot out.

Again he felt a sensation of obliterating bewilderment. What world was this that he had entered?

But he managed to reply more speedily.

"Is it likely, madam, that a lady would be involved? You have heard me outline the circumstances of the crime."

One of the reporters at the front did then ask, plainly only out of a sense of duty, whether he did in fact have reason to suspect a male star and no one had seemed disappointed when he had reminded them that he had been at the Studios for less than an hour. And then someone asked something which gave him a splendid final chance of expressing his determination "to solve this beastly crime with all possible speed and to see that justice is meted out to the person, or persons, wherever they have chosen to hide themselves, who have done to death such a star as the late and the great and the greatly lamented Dhartiraj." And how the pencils had raced across the tilted notebooks at that.

It was a rich moment. And there would be others for the man who had cracked the Dhartiraj case. They would crowd round him, the reporters, in the years to come just as they crowded round the stars of the *filmi duniya*.

But they were leaving now, hurrying away to telephones and typewriters, and he turned to the sway-bellied figure of Bhabani Ghosh.

"Now, what about the coolie who was up on the catwalks—it is catwalks, isn't it?—at the time the Five-K fell?"

"Yes, Inspector. It is old Ailoo. He is our oldest Lights Boy. He was actually the fellow I sent up to see whether the ropes had frayed, an altogether reliable fellow."

They went back in and once more Ghote threaded his way through the thick darkness of the big studio. He stopped when they reached the throne-room set again to make a rapid check on the Headquarters technicians at work there. It was important to show them that there was someone in charge who was right on top of every least thing. Then he set off following the tall white-muslin clad back of Director Ghosh, along narrow corridors formed by the tall canvas frames of other sets, peering hard in the faint illumination that came from two or three low-powered bulbs high in the ceiling of the tall building. Glimpses of strange, over-bright scenes caught his eye, a paddy-field painted on a wall stretching back in row after row of neat cones of rice-straw, a prison-cell composed only of a wall of metal-painted wooden bars. It was stuffily hot, with the occasional huge fan standing idle.

And at last they came to the rough representation of a country drinking-shop, a black-doored hut with a crudely carved table and bench outside it, dotted with squat bottles.

"Where Maqbet and Banko discuss the witches they have seen," Bhabani Ghosh explained.

Ducking under the green-paper branches of a squat palm-tree, Ghote felt a small jab of pleasure that at least the witches had been left in Shakespeare's play by—what was his name?—yes, by Dr. Arvind Bhatt, Litt. D.

But it was the man sitting on the ground, his back resting against the canvas wall of the drinking-shop, who claimed his attention. He did not need the Director's murmured "This is old Ailoo" to tell him that the gaunt figure—he must have been anything between fifty and seventy with short cropped grey hair and a grey stubble on his lean face—wearing only a pair of tattered khaki shorts was the person he wanted.

He had scrambled to his feet at Director Ghosh's words and the moment that the tall Bengali left them Ghote tackled him.

"Now, you were the Lights Boy operating the only light that was being used for the scene of Dhartiraj upon the *gaddi*?"

"Yes, Inspector sahib. Light No 12, Inspector sahib."

Well, at least the fellow seemed intelligent.

"Good. Now, I want you to tell me exactly what you saw over in the darkness above where Dhartiraj was. Exactly, mind."

"Sahib, I did not see."

Rage spewed up inside him, sudden and overwhelming. To meet with stupid obstinacy now. He did not deserve that.

"What do you mean you did not see?" he shouted. "You were there, isn't it? Up there on the catwalks? And there was someone else up there too, not so very far away. How dare you say you saw nothing."

"Sahib, I saw nothing."

Ghote raised his hand to bring the taut palm slapping down across the old man's face.

Old Ailoo stood there, impassively waiting to receive the blow. And at the last moment Ghote checked himself.

This was not the way to deal with a witness. It was not the way he had dealt with witnesses in other investigations. He must not allow the overwhelming importance of this case, those whisperings of the great things that would come from it, to make him forget himself. For better or worse, he had always tried never to lose his temper except in pretence, during an interrogation. And he must stick to that.

"Come," he said to the old man, "you and I have much to talk. This is not the place. Where can we go where we would be more comfortable?"

Old Ailoo's grey-stubbled face lost none of the calm acceptance with which he had awaited the blow.

"Sahib," he said, after a moment's grave consideration, "there is the Recording Room. It is very small, sahib, but it is air-conditioned. And since there is no more shooting it would not be in use."

"Good idea," Ghote said. "First-class idea. Show me the way."

The old coolie did not react to this praise in the way he had hoped. But nevertheless he set off at a good pace into the mysterious darkness of the huge studio. Ghote followed his spine-jutting back past painted village—there was a well, looking exactly like the one he had known in boyhood, wide and friendly, but when he idly touched one of its grey stones it proved to be no more than hollow plaster-of-paris—past prison cell, past grimy city wall, until they came to the Recording Room.

This turned out to be no more than a largish grey-painted booth filled with various pieces of apparatus, all dials and knobs. But it was certainly pleasantly cool after the musty heat of the big studio. Ghote moved a pair of headphones and sat himself on the audiographer's stool and old Ailoo stood, at as respectful a distance as the little booth permitted.

"Well now," Ghote begain again, "you say that, although you were up on the catwalk beside your light—Light No 12, wasn't it?—you did not see anything or anybody over the place where Dhartiraj was killed. Tell me, how did that come to be?"

"Sahib, it is very easy. I was working the light."

"But, no," Ghote said. "Surely not. Director Ghosh was discussing still what exact lighting to use. There was nothing for you to be busy over."

"Sahib, no. It is more more than that. When you are at your light it is what you are doing. You must always be ready. Ready for the sahibs to call up 'Tilt left, No 12. Tilt right. Pan up, pan down. Make harder, make softer. Silk diffuser, quickly, quickly. No, glass diffuser, you idiot'."

Old Ailoo reproduced the words, no doubt daily shouted at him, without the least trace of resentment. And Ghote got a sudden glmpse of the life he must lead up on the catwalks, with the world below reduced to voiceless bawling up at him to make his lights do this or that as if he were no more than a piece of machinery. And there would be a precariousness, too, about his existence. The catwalks he had glanced up at as he had threaded his way here and there through the fantastic world of the studio had looked appallingly narrow, two planks wide only, sometimes one, secured with tangled lengths of frayed-out rope, swooping and swaying all across the high roof of the huge building. Did coolies ever fall?

He put the question to old Ailoo.

"Oh, yes, sahib. Light Boys falling from catwalk sometimes. We had one in this very studio who broke his back, not one month ago. He was moving a Baby. You know what is a Baby, sahib?"

"Yes, yes. Well I am knowng such things."

"Yes, sahib. Well, when Benwa had untied the rope of the Baby it slipped from his hand as he was moving, sahib. He swung out to catch and he fell. In hospital still, sahib, and what is his wife to do and his four children?"

Ailoo stopped abruptly, seemingly feeling that he must have said too much. Ghote quickly sought for another question to ask. If he could get the old man to talk freely he might yet remember something he had half-seen in the darkness when that Five-K had been cut down.

"Lights falling like that, is that something that happens often?"

"No no, sahib. Not so often as coolies falling. Lights very very costly, sahib."

Again old Ailoo relapsed into uncomplaining silence.

"Was anyone else hurt when that Baby fell?" Ghote asked, determined to keep this forthcoming vein of talk alive.

"There had been a man almost underneath," Ailoo resumed. "A stand-in wallah called Sudhaker Wani. But Benwa had called out, so he was not truly in danger even though afterwards he cursed him as if he had done that on purpose."

"He ought to have been grateful," Ghote contributed.

"Oh, but he is a terrible fellow, that one. Always doing things to get himself money, fetching and carrying and obtaining for whoever will pay."

The old man's disgust at a way of life so different from his own single-minded devotion to his light was almost laughable.

"But the Baby that so nearly killed him," Ghote asked now, glimpsing a way of bringing the talk round to what he wanted to know. "It was purely an accident that it fell?"

"Oh, yes, sahib. Benwa is a good and careful fellow. That day in the studio it was very very hot and he was sweating very much. That is why the Baby slipped."

"I see. But the Five-K today, that was a different matter, eh?"

"Oh yes, altogether, Inspector. Those ropes had been cut."

"How many ropes?"

"Two. Two only, Inspector."

"Two quick cuts, and then the Five-K would fall straight on to Dhartiraj?"

Old Ailoo looked at him with an expression of the utmost seriousness.

"Inspector, I am certain of that. Certain."

"So someone cut them," Ghote said softly. "Someone did that. And did you see nothing of them?"

"Sahib, no."

"Not a glimpse of the colour of a shirt? Not the whisk of the tail of a *dhoti*?"

"Inspector, I wish with all my heart that there had been."

The old man laid a thin work-scarred hand on the rib cage of his chest.

And Ghote believed him. What he had said rang true. He was one of life's truly simple people. He had his job. He did it. He had no aspirations beyond what that job called for. No glancing always elsewhere for him to see if a better chance was to be grabbed. No, he had seen nothing.

"There is just the question of access," he said to him at last.

"Access, sahib?"

"Of the way the man we want could have got up to the catwalk above Dhartiraj."

"Oh, that is quite easy, sahib. There are iron ladders here and there round the walls of the studo, and that is how we get up to our places. The one for the catwalk over Dhartiraj would be the one in the corner nearest the big door."

"Would it be easy for someone to get up unseen by that one?"

Old Ailoo thought carefully.

"Yes. Yes, sahib, it would. That ladder is in a very dark corner with the sets they are having just now. Unless someone was standing there, and there is no reason for anyone to do that, it would be altogether easy to climb up with no one seeing."

Ghote pursed his lips.

"But that is not the ladder for your place, for Light No 12?" he asked.

"No, no, sahib. Mine is the next ladder along. The two catwalks are not joined together at all. You would have to go down and up again to get from my place to that one. So I did not kill him, sahib."

The old man was completely unresentful of the accusation he had heard in Ghote's question.

"You can swing across on a rope, sahib," he added in the same placid tone. "But only a young fool would do that. It is dangerous, and there is no need."

"I see," Ghote said.

He sat in silence reviewing all that he had learnt. And the more he thought the more certain he became that the situation was by no means as simple as he had hoped when it had occurred to him that someone working Light No 12 should have at least glimpsed something of the man who had cut the Five-K's ropes.

"No," he said at last, "I do not think there is anything more I have to ask you, Ailoo. I had hoped you would have seen something. But I see now that you did not. No, strange as it may seem, I really believe no one at all saw whoever was up there."

He sighed.

"So it looks as though I shall have to go about my business another way," he said. "A longer and harder way."

V

It was while Inspector Ghote was up on the narrow and swaying catwalk examining for himself the Five-K's two sliced-through ropes that he fastened on his decision. It was a decision which had lurked under everything he had done since questioning old Ailoo had proved that, for all the number of people inside the #2 Sound Stage at the moment Dhartiraj had been done to death—and he had had an almost panoramic view of them all by the time he had climbed three quarters of the way up the ladder—it was almost certain that there had been no one who had seen the murderer.

He had climbed up with Assistant Inspector Jahdev—a fellow, it had turned out, of an almost impossible talkativeness, once freed from the constraints of mingling with *filmi* people—and all the while that he had listened at interminable length to explanations of every step that had already been taken and every step it was intended to take in the primary investigation to which his own inquiries were, in the official word, "parallel" he had been aware dully that the case would now be a question, not of the almost instant triumph which such a dramatic murder seemed to call for, but of days and even weeks of patient exploration of the dead star's life. It would be a matter of unearthing any motive which anybody close to the star might have. It might all too easily peter out in a tangled mass of vague possibilities and there would never be that dazzling moment when the prosecution would call its chief witness and he himself would step into the box, a star, to tell the world how he had tracked down a star's murderer.

So at last he had made up his mind to it.

"A.I." he had said, breaking it on a dissertation on the various types of knots that could be made with ropes, "I suggest that you go at once and find Miss Pilloo Officewalla, chief gossip writer of *Film Femme*, if she is still in the Studios. I would like to pick her brains on this *filmi duniya*."

But, waiting in the Production Manager's cabin which he had managed to secure for his own use, for the arrival of Miss Officewalla, he could not help experiencing a certain trepidation, despite the sheer fantasy of the question she had put to him at the Press conference. The beaky-nosed gossip writer represented, he felt, all the unknown and even unknowable complexities of the *filmi duniya*. She was, if what he had learned of her was only half true, in her own person the high priestess of a world that seemed to be conducted on entirely different principles from his own everyday existence. And, besides, those questions of hers had been put with a terrible sharpness.

How he would have liked to have done what he had planned while he was still on his way to the Studios, to have visited the shop of some *raddi-wallah* and have bought from his store of old newspapers acquired at one-third of their published price a good pile of film magazines from which he could have extracted at leisure a whole background of knowledge. It was the sort of work he liked best. To be tucked away steadily amassing knowledge, working through quantities of material that might be dull but were yet pregnant with the possibility of some startling result.

But such a slow but steady method was no longer right. If he was to bring the murderer of Dhartiraj to justice as quickly as his thousands of fans would require, then he must act with speed. And for that it would be necessary to secure the total collaboration of Miss Pilloo Officewalla.

The constable whom Assistant Inspector Jahdev had placed on duty outside tapped loudly at the door.

This is it, he thought.

"Come in, please. Who is it?"

As if he did not know.

The door was held open. Miss Officewalla, tall, her softly green sari swishing silkily, her big thin beaky nose preceding her, entered.

He asked her to sit. He offered tea. He accepted its refusal. Briefly as he could he explained his needs.

"Well, you have come to the right person, Inspector," she said, leaning forward across the desk that separated them until it seemed her nose was about to dip experimentally into the piles of papers he had collected.

"Yes," she went on, "*Film Femme* gossip is the best in India, though I am saying it. Who exposed the cleavage photos scandal? Who was first with the news of Kundan's midnight decision to marry? Who, and who only, had the full story of Nilima's life from her earliest moments balanced as a baby on a tall bamboo already earning her keep in her simple entertainers' family to stardom and her torrid affair with Ravi Kumar. Who first—"

Ghote held up his hands to stem the flood.

"Miss Officewalla, I am thoroughly knowing your achievements in journalism line," he lied. "But it is incumbent upon me now to proceed with minimum waste of time. Assistant Inspector Jahdev is preparing for me a list of all those who might have connection with the late Dhartiraj who were in the compound here at the time of the crime. But doubtless you already know many of those names. What I am asking is that you should go through them making whatever frank comments you like. In that way I may learn what motives people could have for ending Dhartiraj's life."

Miss Officewalla shook her narrow head.

"Ah, Inspector, I see that you do not at all know the *filmi duniya*," she said.

Ghote felt affronted. After having lied so neatly about her journalistic achievements it seemed quite unfair to be told promptly that he knew nothing of the film world.

"No, Inspector," Miss Officewalla went on. "This is the whole point about Dhartiraj. He was the star without an enemy. He was a kind man to everybody, always ready to be chief guest at a charity show or to make a friendly appearance in another star's film. He was the universally loved member of the *filmi* community. A happy man always, bluff and hearty in every way. No one in all the time he has been a star ever accused that man of creating mutual rifts and tensions. Except, of course, Ravi Kumar."

"But—"

Ghote bit the question back. Ravi Kumar was, after all, the #1 Superstar and it would show appalling ignorance not to know why he, of course, was the only person who would ever have accused Dhartiraj of creating rifts and tensions.

But, luckily, it appeared that the Ravi Kumar-Dhartiraj clash was another of Miss Officewalla's particular triumphs. Without being asked, she proceeded to enlighten him.

So he listened, patiently as he could, while she unfolded her long tale. Ravi Kumar, it seemed, had years ago taken Dhartiraj's wife from him. And ever since he had refused to have Dhartiraj in any film with him— what pride the fellow must have, Ghote thought, when it was he who was in the wrong. But it had been Miss Officewalla, and Miss Officewalla alone, who had learned that Seth Chagan Lal had when casting *Khoon Ka Gaddi* at last persuaded the Superstar to relent.

He longed all the while to get back to matters that were relevant to the case. But he no longer dared interrupt. He had begun to feel that if he was to be a star investigator then, should he once betray ignorance of the film stars' world, luck would instantly repay him by withholding some vital fact he would need to get his man.

"And who," Miss Officewalla demanded suddenly, "was the first to print that Ravi Kumar had lost his keep?"

"Keep?" he asked at once betraying his new resolution almost before it had been formed.

But it seemed Miss Officewalla was prepared to condone a degree of ignorance for the sake of the full retailing of such an extraordinary professional success. Perhaps fate would be as kind.

"Keep? Keep is the old joke, Inspector. What does a producer get when he has first hit film? A jeep and a keep."

She leaned forward and her beaky nose twitched.

"A keep. A mistress."

"Oh, yes. Yes, of course," Ghote said hurriedly.

"What a story," Miss Officewalla went on happily. "To have your latest keep stolen from you by the very man whose wife you had stolen in the first place. And then she too, that little Meena, was in the film at that time."

Suddenly the implications of what she had been saying struck home to Ghote. Was she not laying out, when you came down to it, a classic motive for murder?

"Please," he interrupted. "Please, tell me more about this Miss Meena. She is a star?"

He made no effort now to pretend that he already knew.

"A *bachchi* star, yes," Miss Officewalla said. "She had not yet taken any role, but she had been cast as the Rani Maqbet in *Khoon Ka Gaddi*. Of course, this was the influence of Ravi Kumar. The girl was a decent extra only when he took her. But as his mistress naturally had a chance of stardom. And she would—"

"Excuse me."

Ghote felt that once again he had to break in. It was worth any loss of esteem to get all the details of this quite clear.

From behind Miss Officewalla's beak of a nose a look of brief contempt did appear now. But she paused to explain.

"A decent extra is one that can be used in top society scenes, as guests in night clubs, that sort of thing. They have decent clothes they can wear, a suit or a sari of something more than cotton. Though they are often extremely flashy."

She glanced down at her own sari with its subdued pattern of small green squares.

"They would be paid at the rate of Rupees 25 a day," she went on. "Instead of the Rupees 100 per mensem that the ordinary extra would be pulling down."

"Yes," said Ghote, "thank you."

"Now, as I was telling. That Meena—heaven knows what her name was originally—although she was a *bachchi* star only, was also altogether a sex-bomb. At parties she would wear her sari so low that it revealed not only the navel but the beginning of the curve of the buttocks also as if she was all the time playing the vamp in a film."

Miss Officewalla looked severe.

"So of course," she went on, "the girl was beginning to make a name for herself. *Film Femme* had to recognise her with a cover. Even established stars were having to take notice of her so as not to be accused of jealousy. We ourselves had a very good photo of her being offered a glass of cane-juice by Nilima herself. She was altogether rising fast in the estimation of the fans."

Ghote felt puzzled still as to how this could be when the girl had not yet ever been seen on the screen. But he decided he had better not put forward this view.

"Yes, yes," he murmured encouragingly.

"Yes, she would have done very well, even though she did not know acting, if it had not been for her so-called illness."

Miss Officewalla put such meaning into the last words that Ghote felt obliged to say "Ah ha" as significantly as he could.

"The illness," Miss Officewalla triumphantly added, "that, as I said and said in my page, was no more than the simple effect of the strain upon her love loyalties."

"Ah," Ghote repeated, though he felt himself to be sadly floundering.

"Yes, yes. Although they continued to put out medical reports that the girl had wasted away from some disease, they were never able to put a name to it at all. And the fact remains that soon after she had given up the role of Rani Maqbet, because she had got too thin to be a star, she left Ravi Kumar to go to Dhartiraj. My revelation she had done that was the greatest sensation ever to come out of Bollywood."

"Bollywood?" Ghote asked, experiencing yet another surge of bewilderment.

Miss Officewalla's thin face sharpened instantly into a totally scandalised look.

"Do you not read at all, Inspector?" she demanded. "The Bombay film set-up is called Bollywood in simply every film magazine. I had thought that Crime Branch C.I.D. were at least educated."

That had been a bad moment. But Ghote, though shot through with darts of despair at the thought of how much admitting such ignorance could have turned luck against him, would not let himself abandon the prickly business of learning from Miss Officewalla every bit he could about

the *filmi duniya*. His grim determination had been reinforced by her brisk
dismissal of his interest in Ravi Kumar. The superstar, she had said wither-
ingly, could not possibly have been inside the Talkiestan Studios compound. A superstar did not go about anywhere unnoticed, least of all at
the gates of film studios.

He had sent out to Assistant Inspector Jahdev to check on this, but he
had known that it was a vain hope. And so it had proved. Assistant Inspector Jahdev had brought in his list of all the people known to be
within the high walls and guarded gate of the Talkiestan compound at the
time Dhartiraj had been killed, and of course the name of Ravi Kamur
was not among them.

So bit by bit he had extracted from the gossip queen a few names of
those in some way close to Dhartiraj optimistically to put down on a large
sheet of paper he had headed "People to See". There was the star's personal pandit—a notoriously saintly and very aged astrologer. There was
his personal make-up man who had been with the star for years and was
well-known as his chosen confidant, even if he was also, as it emerged, in
Miss Officewalla's pay. There was his secretary who was new to the job,
and it was certain that Dhartiraj, busy with his new keep, had not made
any advances of a sexual nature to her. There was his former secretary
newly and happily married to an account executive. There was his Personal Assistant but he too was tried and trusted, though not in the pay of
Miss Officewalla but in that of one of her rivals, even if what he told her
was "not at all reliable". There were his *chumchas*.

"*Chumchas*?" Ghote asked.

He knew that the word meant "spoons" in Hindi, but he could not exactly produce its *filmi duniya* meaning. *Chumchas* were something to do
with stars, but what?

The look of sheer disapproval returned to Miss Officewalla's face—
Ghote felt that at any moment he might feel the sharp peck of her nose-
beak—but she answered his question, in an icily chilled voice.

"A *chumcha* is the follower of a star. He feeds his star with whatever
he is needing, laughter for his jokes, praise for his performances, revela-
tions on his rivals and scorn for the gossip writers. And in return the star
feeds him, with food at the posh hotels of Juhu, with drink from his bar,
with a small part in a film sometimes. And they vie who can serve him
best, make him laugh the most, however ridiculous they have to make
themselves, find him the best girl, tell him the dirtiest stories."

"Yes, yes," Ghote said rapidly. "All this I am of course well knowing,
though it is kind of you to remind. But what I am wanting to find out is:
would not one of these fellows very likely bear a grudge against Dhartiraj?
What are the names of Dhartiraj's *chumchas*, if you please?"

He poised his ballpoint, which only then did he notice was an altogether unsatisfactory shade of bright pink.

"It is of no use," Miss Officewalla briskly replied. "You see, his
chumchas—"

But he felt he had to re-assert his authority now, the authority of the C.I.D.'s top investigator.

"Please, madam, the names. I require."

Miss Officewalla heaved a sigh.

"Very well. Khwaja Abbas, Khrishan Chander, Jayawant Dalvi, Suresh Joshi, Adil Jussawalla, Manohar Malgonkar, Ashok Mitran, Mangat Rai, Partap Sharma, Baldev Vaid. And I suppose you might put in with them, young Kishore Sachdev."

Ghote scribbled, recognising that to produce such a list in one long breath, and in alphabetical order too, was tremendous confirmation of Miss Officewalla's command of her profession.

"Kishore Sachdev?" he asked, at last looking up.

"Oh, he is a well-off boy Dhartiraj brought from Delhi to try his luck in films after he had met him two-three years ago at the big Stars Charity Cricket Match. You know, the time Billy Banker went on the field dressed as a Western ballet girl."

She gave him a sharp look.

"Billy Banker is a famous comedian," she added.

"Yes, yes, I am knowing."

Ghote felt the sting. Everybody knew Billy Banker, perpetual broadly grinning joker on and off the screen.

He glared down at his list of names.

"Very well," he said. "I will investigate each and every one of these fellows. And pretty thoroughly, I can tell you."

"But, Inspector," Miss Officewalla said, cool as ever. "It would be of no use. I was explaining. Each of those people depends entirely on Dhartiraj. Some he was buying from other stars even. Any he could sell, though he did not. It would be killing the golden goose altogether for them to attempt to murder him."

He looked at her with suspicion.

"You are certain?"

"Inspector, I have my reputation. You can check easily. Any one of my rivals would confirm."

"Well . . ."

He was unhappy to let them go. They had extended his roll-call of possibilities marvellously.

"But these other names you have given me," he said, feeling a definite sense of grievance. "None of them is exactly a one hundred percent possibility."

To his surprise Miss Officewalla looked abruptly irritated.

"That I am giving?" she said. "But I am not at all giving. It is you who have been asking. If you are wanting my advice, that is another matter altogether."

He looked up.

"You have advice? There is someone you believe might have killed Dhartiraj? Someone who was here?"

"Inspector, am I to get your maximum full co-operation?"

"Yes, Miss Officewalla," he said.

There seemed to be no other reply he could make. A #1 investigator had to get results with #1 swiftness. And so far he was getting nowhere at all.

Miss Officewalla drew herself up and looked at him hard down her beaky nose.

"Jagdish Rana," she said.

"Jagdish Rana, he is a star. Yes, he is a star."

A bright little flame of triumph sang in him. Jagdish Rana was a name he knew of old, one that he had seen on posters and in advertisements by the hundred here and there about Bombay over the years.

"Yes, even you would know him," Miss Officewalla said. "Until four or five years back Hari Ram—as he was called at birth—was a really sizeable marquee name, one you would see on the front of half a dozen cinemas at a time. He was the villain in every film there was, hit picture or flop picture. Until Dhartiraj came from nowhere and topped him from his place."

Was that motive enough? Ghote's first instinct was to reject it as nonsense. But then the weight of all the various things he had been learning in this long, long morning about the way of the *filmi duniya* came home to him. No, perhaps to be toppled like that was motive enough for murder, in this world.

"Yes," said Miss Officewalla, seeing the thought harden in his eyes, "he had reason to hate Dhartiraj all right. Dhartiraj who was a Punjabi just like him, Dhartiraj who had reduced him to playing side heroes only, like Banko in *Khoon Ka Gaddi* and lucky even to get that. Dhartiraj who was on the point of pushing him out from being a star altogether. Inspector, if I were you I would go at once and talk to Jagdish Rana."

VI

Ghote was at the studio gates on his way to the beach at Juhu where, so Miss Officewalla had told him, Jagdish Rana, the fading star, was shooting on location, when the Pathan chowkidar came running up. He thrust his fanciful turban in at the car window, bringing with him a blast of highly spiced breath that made him realise that he had gone without a midday meal himself.

"Inspector," he said, "we had orders not to let you leave the Studios."

"What is this?"

The fellow cleared his throat with a tremendous solemn rattling.

"Sahib, it is Miss Nilima. She is wishing to see you."

He spoke with awe. And Ghote in his turn experienced much the same feeling.

Nilima, the great star. Even as infrequent a cinema-goer as he was, he had seen Nilima on the wide silver screen at least some dozen times over the years. A distant figure of marvellous beauty, of charged sexuality, a dream. True, she had never obsessed him as in sober fact she obsessed the thoughts of thousands and thousands of men all over India. But there had been moments, watching her in enormous close-up from far away across the dark spaces of a cinema, and able to examine her as he never could have examined anyone like her in reality, when certain thoughts had lodged for a time in his mind.

She was, after all, exceptional. Her figure had a fullness rare to see in such perfection, and was always seen to the utmost advantage. Soft saris clung caressingly to her hips. Or, portraying some simple Rajasthani peasant girl in *ghagra* and *choli*, the latter was always at stitch-straining point across her bosom. Or, wearing Western clothes, her shirt was so low-buttoned that it looked as if at every instant the last rules of decency were to be burst apart. Her face, too, was composed of everything that might rouse the sensual, a seemingly flawless skin of infinite touchability, poutingly full lips, enormous melting eyes, a continuous teasing play of expression.

And she had summoned him to see her? Why? Impossible to tell. Except that—the thought came to him late—he was now, suddenly lifted up, a person who could talk to Nilima, with any other star of the high world of the films.

But, if he was such an investigator, ought he not be to be going out to crack this case, to bust it wide open? Should he obey the summons?

A battle raged within him.

It was decided only by the look of total assurance on the fierce sweat-streaked face thrust in at the car window. If it was so much assumed that he would at once go to Nilima, then had he not better go?

And, besides, he could deal with whatever business it was she wanted to consult him about in double-quick time. That would be the way, yes.

With the tall turbaned Pathan loping along at his vehicle's wing, they went once more through the crowded confusion of the Studios compound —a little less excited now, a little more purposeful—until they came to Sound Stage #1, a building much like the one that had been the scene of the crime.

But at its door they met with a check.

"Shooting. Shooting."

A whole little crowd blocked their way.

But the chowkidar knew the true importance of his errand.

"It is Miss Nilima who has asked the Inspector Sahib to come," he proclaimed.

Ghote stood as tall as he could and contrived an air of lofty patience while the huddle blocking his way took in this news.

"But it is Nilima they are shooting. Nilima."

The Pathan utterly ignored this objection and in less than a minute Ghote found himself inside the building, creeping along in the dark following the chowkidar's broad back towards the set where the great Nilima was at work. It was very much reminiscent of his approach to the scene of Dhartiraj's death, except that hardly had they advanced ten yards than there was a sudden shout of "Lights" and a blaze of whiteness struck out from some twenty or more lights high above them. It was followed at once by another shout of "Music," a blast from a buzzer and then a blare of sound from some huge unseen loudspeakers, so noisy it immediately drowned every thought in his head.

The Pathan turned to him and leaned down to whisper, though with all the noise that could hardly have been necessary.

Ghote stoically received again the blast of spiciness that told him how well the chowkidar had eaten.

"Sahib, they are picturising on her."

The fellow sounded as if he could not have had a bigger piece of luck than to come into the studio at this time. But what Ghote felt with fury was the familiarity with which he had used the English word "picturising", all the more galling because he himself was not at all sure what it meant.

But that question at least was soon to be answered. The Pathan beckoned him to follow again and in a few moments they turned a corner and were able to see the whole process going on.

In effect Nilima was being filmed, Ghote quickly realised, as if she was singing the song that, after an orchestral introduction full of the rippling of the *jal-tarang* and much swooping of many violins, the loudspeakers were now feeding in the voice of a highly skilled playback singer. Yes, he knew about those. At home whenever his son got control of the radio it was the *filmi* songs of playback singers that poured out in honeyed lilting sweetness.

Nilima was evidently taking the role of a beautiful woman trying to make up her mind what to wear for some very special occasion, perhaps her wedding, perhaps to meet the man she loved. Ghote could not decide whether the song would be part of the Macbeth story or come in some other film altogether. Certainly the setting was not a modern room and Nilima was already wearing a sari, of tremendous richness, that could have come from any time together with quantities of equally timeless silver jewellery. The *almirah* too, from which she was to choose the new sari, was a large richly carved piece that could have fitted in with almost any period of the past.

Nilima half danced, half swayed from it, her mind not at all made up, over to a huge gold-framed mirror towards which she yearningly leaned, her hips moving in time to the sugary—and blaring—music.

Ghote noted that she did not look quite as magnificently beautiful seen close to as he had remembered her from the screen. It was evident, for one thing, that she was no longer in her first youth. It was evident too here that the goddess was a human being, if only because she was beginning to sweat. And certainly with the glare of the lights above them it was appallingly hot in the shut-up studio, despite the big fans that had been wheeled up to blow into the set.

"Cut! Cut! N.G.! N.G.!"

The loudspeakers whined into silence. The Pathan at his side bent his head and whispered.

"It is a No Good because of the sweat, you see, sahib."

"Yes, yes, of course," Ghote whispered crossly back.

A man with a make-up tray had hurried across to Nilima. Ghote wondered if his ministrations would last long enough to give him himself a chance of hearing from Nilima what it was she wanted. He glanced at his watch. Time was getting on. And the fading Jagdish Rana, the only man, it seemed, with a reason to hate all-popular Dhartiraj, was still unquestioned.

But the make-up man did not take long to dab at Nilima's face with powder, spray it with rose-water, carefully wipe it dry and make some tiny final adjustments with a long brush to her eye-shadow.

"All ready?"

"Silence. *Choop chaap*. Silence."

A hush fell.

"Lights!"

"Music!"

The buzzer blasted. The loudspeakers sprang into blaring sound.

"Camera! Action!"

A man with a clapper board, the Clapper Boy—Ghote knew what he was called, but only now realised that the scrawled chalk figures on the black board must indicate which scene and "take" this was—stepped forward and clacked the board's bar down on to its base. Nilima began again her swaying, dancing progress towards the mirror.

This time no human beads of sweat interfered with the fantasy. Nilima leaned yearningly into the mirror. She stepped back and turned. She began to sing.

Her voice was not beautiful, Ghote noted. But he saw that this was not at all important since she was singing only so that her lips would synchronise with the words of the playback singer. And yet . . .

Yet, even with the sweat beginning once more to penetrate the heavy layers of make-up, Nilima was magical. There was no other word.

"Cut! Cut!"

Again the loudspeakers whined down to nothingness. And again the make-up man went to Nilima's assistance, not without sharp words being said about the delay his failure to deal with the perspiration problem was causing.

The delay, Ghote thought.

When would he get to Jagdish Rana at this rate? What could Nilima want with him? Would it affect the case? Was it more important than getting quickly to the fading star?

But she wanted to see him. She had sent messages specially to make sure he did not leave the studios without coming to her. The great star.

The scene began again. And stopped, this time for some reason even the chowkidar could not understand. Then it was started once more. And stopped. And began again.

Can I believe your sugar-coated words? How many times now had he heard Nilima sing that? Always in the same slightly croaky manner?

Could such a line, sung in a song, fit somehow into the tragedy of Macbeth?

He sighed. In the film world it almost certainly could.

But suddenly loud voices were shouting and echoing "O.K." "O.K." and he realised that the whole business was at last over.

"Come, Inspector."

His Pathan guide led him into the set itself and to Nilima. The fellow made her a low salaam and told her that this was the C.I.D. Inspector.

At once she took half a pace towards him and held out both her hands, palms open as if in supplication. He saw her eyes were shining with a warmth that seemed to caress him from head to foot.

"Bring chairs," she said to the Pathan in a swift aside. "And, Inspector, you will take something to drink? Cane-juice, Coca-cola?"

"Yes. No. No, thank you, nothing to drink."

He made an effort to pull himself together. It was ridiculous, really, that anyone should offer some sugary cane-juice or a cold drink in a way that sounded as if she were putting a rich pearl on a cushion of velvet before a lover. He had come to see her on a matter of business. It was possible she had information which would lead to the apprehension of a murderer. That was why he had come. Otherwise he would have been out at Juhu beach by now interrogating his most likely suspect. It was ridiculous she should make him feel like this. But she did.

"Madam," he said, croaking out the words, "if you are wanting to see me, I am altogether at your— Madam, I am here."

The chowkidar returned carrying two canvas chairs, one in either hand. Ghote saw that one had printed on its back the word "Nilima" and the other the word "Director." The Pathan placed Nilima's for her, his face foolishly radiant at every move. Ghote took the other chair from him and put it facing the star's.

He sat down. "Director".

Nilima leaned forward towards him. A wave of deep and disturbing perfume reached him. He breathed in.

"Inspector," she said, in that richly cooing voice he remembered from the darkness of all the cinemas he had seen her in. "Inspector, I have asked you to come to make to you a plea."

A clammy flush of sweat sprang up on the front of his thighs.

"Madam."

He felt a tremendous urge to deliver himself of a pledge to help to his utmost, whatever request it was that she made to him. An overwhelming purposefulness seemed to emanate from the goddess sitting looking at him, not two yards away. There was something in him, deep down, that was able to attempt to analyse that purposefulness, to record coolly that it sprang no doubt from the mixture of sheer physical perfection—even if he had noted that time had had its effects even here—combined with an uncheckable confidence in herself and in her power of securing instant attention. Yet with all his conscious mind he wanted simply to agree in advance to whatever demand she might make.

The huge almond eyes were softly beaming.

"Inspector, the death of poor Dhartiraj, it was not an accident, was it, like when that Baby fell in the studio a week or two ago and nearly killed that fellow?"

He swallowed.

"No, madam. Today's incident was in no way accidental."

"Yes, that is what I had heard. So now I tell you, Inspector. You must solve the mystery. You must do it at once. They have been saying in the Studios that no one was seen up on the catwalk. Is that so, Inspector? Is it so?"

"Yes," Ghote replied, his voice throbbing with emotion. "Yes, it is so. I can tell you that."

He had been going to add "with all my heart" only some tiny voice inside him warned that it would be an unjustified extravagance. He contented himself instead with leaning forward as earnestly as he could.

Nilima stayed silent, as if to take his words and breathe on them the stamp of her own being.

"An invisible man," she said at last. "An invisible man, Inspector, and you will find him. I knew it the moment I saw you. 'Here, here', I said, 'is one to do it.' And you can. You can. Inspector, do it. Solve this mystery."

She moved a tiny way towards him. He felt a surge, not of desire—how could you desire a goddess?—but of willingness, of utter willingness to do anything asked of him because Nilima was asking it.

The deep-down cool voice repeated that this was only the famed aura of the film star affecting him as it had affected hundreds of thousands of others, only more closely, more intimately. But the willingness did not slacken.

"Madam, I hope— I hope to solve the myst— the matter. But let me tell you it will not be easy, not at all easy."

Was he making it sound even harder that it was so as to please her the more? There was Jagdish Rana out at Juhu. Perhaps, had he declined to come to Nilima, he would be making the arrest even at this minute. But, no matter, if he went from her and found the murderer straightaway, what a tribute that would be to lay at her feet.

"But you would do it, Inspector."

The pigeon-soft cloud of sound enveloped him. He felt a renewed urge to make the task sound altogether impossible.

From the pocket of his shirt he extracted—his fingers were appallingly sweat-sticky—the bundle of notes he had made during his talk with Miss Officewalla. He sorted through them scramblingly.

"Madam," he said, as at last he found what he had been looking for, "please to glance through the following. It is a list of those close to Mr. Dhartiraj who might have had reason to want him dead. Please understand, it is not a matter of accusing any of the persons mentioned. But I wish you to see how very many people it may be necessary for me to interrogate, and even then the murderer may well not be among them."

He thrust the list to Nilima. Their hands did not quite touch, but it seemed to him, it distinctly seemed to him, that at the tips of his fingers he had detected a tiny warmth that came from hers. There had been an exchange between them. The slightest of exchanges, but an exchange. Between Ganesh Ghote and Nilima.

But Nilima did not look at the list. Instead she held it out back to him.

"No, Inspector," she said, the words wafted towards him. "No, you would read it to Nilima."

He took the sheet. He gave a small cough to clear his throat. He began to read. He stopped. His throat had remained implacably dry. He coughed again. He managed to get to the end of the list.

"Inspector, that was wonderful. Wonderful. And Nilima's name is not there."

He felt a little shock of dismay. That Nilima should be stupid.

"But— But, madam, your name could not be on this list. It is the names only of those who had some direct link with Dhartiraj, his family, his employees, his servants, his—er—*chumchas*."

"Inspector, you have made such a list, and so soon. Inspector, now Nilima has even more faith in you."

She rose from her chair. There was a tinkling of silver ornaments, a stream chuckling in the hills.

Ghote, too, leaped up. The chair with the word "Director" across its canvas back teetered dangerously. He wanted to salaam, to pour out an assurance that he would not rest till he had done what she had asked.

But some almost totally buried rational instinct told him suddenly that Nilima had not, when you thought about it, ever said to him why exactly she had asked to see him with such urgency.

"Madam," he blurted out. "Miss Nilima, what I am not at all understanding is why you have asked me to do this, which is after all my simple duty only?"

She turned back to him. There was a hint of disappointment on her wonderfully womanly face, the faintest pout of the lips. He felt with a jab of pain that he had failed her. He should somehow have known the answer to that question. He was not the man she had believed he was.

"That is—" he stammered. "That is—"

A hint of a smile appeared on her face, the moon almost breaking through dark clouds. It was forgiveness.

"Inspector." Her voice conveyed that she was repeating a simple lesson to a child who had failed childlishly to learn it at first telling. "Inspector, the film. *Khoon Ka Gaddi*, the mightiest historical ever made. It stars Nilima. Inspector, the making of that film cannot be delayed."

VII

All during the drive across to the sea at Juhu, Ghote sat contemplating his interview with Nilima as if lookng at a brightly painted picture—or even, he thought, like a film, a film in Technicolor.

Nilima, the great Nilima, the darling over the years of millions, had begged him, had called to him and begged him, to solve the mystery of the death of her fellow star. She had made him feel he would earn her ever-present gratitude. He saw it all. As soon as the arrest was announced she would ask him to come to her. More. She would tell him he was welcome to visit her whenever he wished. He would become one of her circle, her golden circle. He would mingle with her and her fellow artistes. The man who had solved the Dhartiraj mystery and the brilliant stars. As one. At one.

By God, Jagdish Rana had better watch out. If the truth of it lay there, then he would have it out of him if he had to prise it away with his bare hands.

"Sir, this would be it."

His driver had pulled up in front of a two-story bungalow, all new in shining pink paint, overlooking the wide yellowish beach with its scatter of bathers and picnic parties, its camels giving rides, its chiropodists and ear-cleaners and fortune-tellers, its families of acrobats performing daring feats on their long bamboo poles for the benefit of small circles of onlookers.

Inside the bungalow, which proved to have a huge staircase winding up from its hallway to the modest floor above, Ghote found that Jagdish Rana had just finished shooting his scene—he was playing the brother of the villain—and that there was nothing to prevent an immediate interrogation. Except the finding of a place to hold it. Most of the ground floor of the house was devoted to the hallway and an enormous lounge, complete with grand piano, where the remainder of Jagdish Rana's scene was then being filmed. In the only other two small rooms the owners of the house, who had, it seemed, built it for the sole purpose of renting out to film companies, were living a cramped existence and were to be seen peering discreetly at the *filmi* goings-on, two fat and moony faces, one above a multi-coloured shirt, the other above a pale pink chiffon sari. Only the enormous master bedroom on the floor above appeared to be free of actors or technicians.

But is was by no means an ideal setting for a probing interview with a murder suspect. It was altogether too soft. It was ridiculously soft. To begin with it was carpeted, not tiled, carpeted from wall to wall in a soft creamy white such as would have shown forever the least mark made by the accidents of everyday living. Then there were mirrors everywhere, mirrors in heavily ornate golden frames throwing back increasingly soft reflections of the whole room in endless perspectives. It was dimly lit, too, with the thick pink velvet curtains almost completely drawn and lamps in pink silk shades casting soft pools of light in unnecessary places. And finally there was the bed. It was round and it was huge and it stood up on a circular platform of its own, covered by a great puffy pink circular quilt.

The quilt alone, he thought, would make even the hardest of floors more than comfortable enough to sleep on. And to sleep underneath it at any time would be an impossibility, even on those winter mornings when the water in the shower struck cold.

But the room had another enormous disadvantage as a place in which to conduct an interrogation. There was only one chair.

It was not much of a chair either, a stool-like object covered in very deeply padded pink silk standing in front of the expansive built-in dressing table. But, except for the bed, it was the only thing on which to sit. He jerked it round, banged it down and lowered himself on to it, his back as straight as he could make it.

He indicated the bed to the failed star.

"Sit, Mr. Rana, sit."

Jagdish Rana stepped up on to the low platform and sank down on the puffy pink quilt at the edge of the big round bed.

Ghote peered at him in the dim light. He very much wanted to haul back the heavy velvety curtains and let the sun flood sharply in. But to do so would alert his suspect.

Yet, despite the soft dimness, he thought he could see enough. It was plain he was facing a man on the downward slope. Under the eyes there were heavily obvious pouches. The lips below the thin line of the sharply black moustache, which he remembered now from the times he had seen this lean face painted to three or four times its true size on dozens of huge hoardings over the years, were pursed in tenseness. And no sooner had he sunk into that circular softness on the bed than the tension manifested itself.

"Inspector, I am agreeing to this interview under protest. I have already told an Assistant Inspector I saw back at Talkiestan all I know about the death of Dhartiraj. I am not to be hounded in this way."

The pencil-thin black moustache twitched.

"I have contacts in the Police Department, Inspector. I must warn you, if you detain me for one second longer than is necessary, I have telephone numbers in my little book that I can ring."

With lean nervous fingers he tapped once sharply on what looked like a small address-book in the top pocket of his wild-silk shirt.

But Ghote, his pledge to Nilima still ringing in his head, was quick to counter this.

"Mr. Rana," he said. "Or should I call you Mr. Hari Ram?"

He saw with a stab of pride that this piece of out-of-the-way information, culled from his long session with Miss Officewalla, had paid off. Into the fading star's eyes there had come a quick look of sullen defiance. He would know now that he was not dealing with anybody who could be kept in their place by threats. It was level fighting between them, at the very least.

"Mr. Hari Ram, a great star has been murdered today. Anybody who knew him and was near the scene comes under suspicion. You equally among them. Perhaps even more than equally."

Again he saw the tired eyes flick in instant response.

"But, Inspector, why me more than others? Dhartiraj and I were the best of friends, I assure you. Co-artistes and the best of friends."

"Yet he had shaken you from your place at the top of the tree of villains," Ghote replied flatly.

The thin lips tautened.

"Inspector, I am thinking you do not know so very much about the film world."

Ghote almost leaped up and flung back at him that this was not at all the case. Was he not the chosen emissary of Nilima herself?

But he sat where he was on the softly yielding little pink stool-chair.

"Inspector," Jagdish Rana went on, measuring him with his every word, "Dhartiraj was a great artiste. That I would be the last to deny. But there are other stars who have had success also. Perhaps from the well-known fickleness of the front-seat wallahs they have lost for a while some of their status. But they are still stars. Top stars."

In the pinky dimness it was clear to see that suddenly control had snapped.

He leaned forward from the plump bed, his tired eyes wide.

"I am one of those stars," he went on in a voice somewhere between a snarl and a whine. "In my day I have made *chhutti* of every other villain actor there is, and I will again. I will. There is life enough in this body. Yes, I can act them down to the ground, I can fight with the best, I can sing."

And he bounded to his feet, and struck a swaggering pose as if about to launch into some song that would toss verses from hero to heroine changing with each one to some new and more marvellous location, at one moment calling across from one Kashmiri peak to the next, then sweeping down a broad Bombay road sitting up on the back of an open sports car driving with two nonchalant fingers and no feet at all and then as suddenly in the romantic deserts of Rajasthan, he mounted on a white horse, she coyly amid the branches of a lone tree.

He even tossed off a few steps. Ghote waited till he had one foot high in the air and then shot in a sharp question.

"But just how long since you were in a jubilee film?"

The dance collapsed from one beat to another. Jagdish Rana's face flushed a deep and ugly colour. He plunged forward towards Ghote on his little pink chair.

"Listen to me," he yelled. "Why do you think I told you I cannot waste time here with your ridiculous questions? Because at any minute I must go to see Seth Chagan Lal to sign for the role of Maqbet in *Khoon Ka Gaddi*. That is why."

The moment the words were out of his mouth he must have realised what a motive for murdering Dhartiraj he had let slip. He stepped backwards away from Ghote, stumbled at the edge of the circular bed platform and almost fell.

"But— But, Inspector," he babbled. "But please understand. I am second to none in my admiration for Dhartiraj. Yes, he ought to have played that part. He would have been a Maqbet in a thousand. But— But the film must go on, Inspector. We are all agreed on that. Someone must play the role."

He gave Ghote a quick little look from under his eyebrows. It reminded him of a schoolboy who had been caught out in some really serious offence, had bluffed to the hilt to get out of it and was looking up at the teacher to see if he had succeeded.

Well, he had not.

The scent of success rose suddenly in his nostrils. Perhaps the case would not after all be the long drawn-out business he had feared. Perhaps he was going to fulfill his pledge to Nilima almost as soon as he had made it. And then . . .

For a moment he allowed a vision of himself as the affair came to its climax to hang brightly lit in his mind. The hushed court, the learned judge looking like some flapping-cheeked character actor leaning intently forward to catch the least word of the evidence, himself in the box with the spotlight playing down on— No. Not a spotlight, of course. But it would be himself in the box and he would parry with calm the last frenzied assaults of the defence pleaders. An unanswerable case. A swift and decisive verdict. And the cheers.

"Please to resume your seat, Mr. Rana," he said, chilly as water from a mountain stream.

Jagdish Rana, eyes bloodshot from the wildness of his actions, looked for one instant as if he would refuse to obey. But then he turned back to the big bed and slumped down, pushing the round feather-puffed pink quilt askew.

Drawing in a long breath, Ghote began systematically questioning him. At what time exactly had he arrived that morning at Talkiestan Studios? What had been his shooting schedule for the morning shift? Had it been kept to? What had he done while he was waiting to go before the cameras? When had he had his make-up done? How long had it taken? Who had he talked to? Who had he seen? And each answer he checked carefully against the timetable he had made out on the longest sheet of paper he had been able to find in his pockets.

Yet before long it became increasingly plain that only indefinite evidence was emerging against the fading star. True, it was possible that he could have killed Dhartiraj. During the period of only five minutes or so for which it was strictly necessary for him to have established an alibi he had not, so far as he was able to prove, been in anyone's company. Like Dhartiraj he had been learning his dialogues, and he had retired, so he said, to his car to do so.

He made a couple of attempts to claim that he had been under observation at the time. But when Ghote telephoned Assistant Inspector Jahdev at Talkiestan both the people he had named, small-part actors, had not been prepared to say they had seen him.

On the other hand nothing emerged to disprove his contention. Assistant Inspector Jahdev put a whole squad of men on to looking for anyone who had been anywhere near the place where the villain player's car had been parked at the time of the murder. But he had been able to find no one definitely in the right place at the right time.

Yet motive Jagdish Rana undoubtedly had and Ghote felt loath indeed to give up the hunt. And before the interrogation was over the case against him was abruptly strengthened.

It seemed that he might too have possessed the means of committing the crime.

Assistant Inspector Jahdev had telephoned to ask for an urgent word. Ghote took the call on the extension telephone in the big bedroom, an instrument covered in its every square centimetre with tiny mosaic fragments of purple and gold Rajasthani enamel work.

He was at once assailed by a breathless account of what someone called a setting coolie did at a film studio. It was apparently to move sets as and when required.

"A.I.," he broke in eventually, "I am quite familiar with the film world. Please go on."

"Yes, yes, of course, Inspector." Assistant Inspector Jahdev sounded very crestfallen. "But— But, Inspector, what I was about to tell was this. You remember when I telephoned last I said that there was one fellow missing who might have been near where that car was?"

"Yes, yes."

"Well, he was this setting coolie by the name of Mangu. And when I just now got hold of him it turned out that he was missing because he had tried to hide. He was altogether afraid, Inspector."

"Yes, yes, man. Afraid what of?"

"That was what I was telling, Inspector. He was afraid because he had been given the job of taking back to the Property Department—you know that that is that building that is just beside the #2 Sound Stage, right up against the back wall of the compound, it is a long—"

"A.I.!"

"Yes, Inspector?"

"What was the fellow taking back there? The coolie, what's his name?"

"His name is Mangu, Inspector. Shall I spell that? It is—"

"A.I., what was he taking?"

"But I was saying, Inspector, he was taking back a long, curved-blade dagger. It seems that there is a scene in this film where the villain sees some sort of a ghost of a dagger or something of that kind. I am not—"

"Never mind, the ghost. What did this Mangu tell you?"

For a long moment the line was silent while Assistant Inspector Jahdev patently tried to advance his narrative in his own mind to a point that was likely to interest the Headquarters wallah. Ghote waited with what patience he could collect. If ever this chap has to give evidence from a witness-box, he thought, he would lose his audience in no time at all.

"Yes," came his voice at last. "Well, the thing is this. Mangu had not taken back that dagger. He had altogether forgotten, and he remembered only when he heard about the murder. It seems that at first he thought the deed had been done with this identical weapon. But, of course it—"

"A.I.!"

"Yes, Inspector. Well, he found when he went to look for this dagger, which is, I am understanding, a devilishly sharp affair, he found it had been moved. To begin with he thought that somebody had—"

"A.I. I do not want to know. Just tell me where the dagger is now."

"But I was saying. It is back in Property Department. The fellow Mangu took it there as soon as he had found. It was lying—"

"He carried it to the Property Department by the handle?"

"Well, I expect so, Inspector. It would be the way that you—"

"His hands, A.I.? What are the condition of his hands?"

"His hands? But— I will look, Inspector. The fellow is standing right beside me now. I will look."

It was only a few seconds later that a chastened voice said: "They are covered in grease and dust, Inspector. It is very unlikely that there would be fingerprints, I suppose."

Ghote banged out a few more questions to see if it had been established at just what times the dagger had been left for anyone to pick up. But the answers were unsatisfactory. The table where it had been was well out of the way. Jagdish Rana could easily have taken the weapon on his way to cut the Five-K's ropes. But so could dozens of other people.

"Thank you, A.I.," Ghote said at last.

He went back to the little squabby pink chair and faced Jagdish Rana once more. He was determined not to let the least discrepancy or obscurity in anything he had said go unexamined. If there was even a hairline crack into which he could prise his way he would find it. But the interruption had not been helpful. There was a new, faintly obstinate note in the way the replies came.

And then abruptly his growing fears were realised. Jagdish Rana broke off half-way through an answer.

"Inspector," he said, "what is the use of you going on and on like this?"

Ghote looked at him coldly.

"I am inquiring into a case of murder," he said. "The murder of a great star."

"Yes. And what have you done? Just because I have been offered the part— No, because only Seth Chagan Lal will be discussing with me whether I can play the part of Maqbet, you have got it into your head that I and I alone could have killed Dhartiraj. Well, that is ridiculous."

Ghote, from down on his low chair, tried to hold him with his eyes.

"Mr. Rana," he said, "you are altogether mistaken about the manner in which a murder inquiry is conducted. Let me tell you, a really experienced officer does not just pick on one suspect and try to his level best to make out a case against him. Not at all. He makes rigorous inquiries in each and every direction, and only when these are properly concluded does he make an assessment of the evidence to hand."

"But all the same you are going on and on asking and asking me the same questions, hoping only to catch me out."

"I am not," Ghote shouted in fury.

But a tiny twist of knowledge inside him asserted that what the star— the failing star, curse him—was saying was true. He even had words ready in his memory to rebuke him from the great criminologist, Dr. Hans Gross, whose book, edited in 1924 by J. Collyer Adam, Police Prosecutor, Madras, in its mildew-marked dark blue binding was always to hand in his office. "The Investigator must advance step by step, making use only of such definite opinions as may be prudently formed from events as they arise." But, fired by Nilima's appeal, he had plunged like a madman at the first indication of a possible lead.

Yet, even now, he fought to suppress that wriggle of disquiet.

"Mr. Rana," he said, "it is up to you to realise that you are in a very serious position. You yourself have admitted to me that you had the very strongest motive for wishing Dhartiraj dead. You have no alibi at all for the time in question. And, let me tell you, the knife which was almost certainly used to cut the ropes of that Five-K, was easily available to you. It is altogether a damn poor outlook for you."

"But, Inspector, I am not the only one with a motive."

"No? No? Well, what others are there?" Ghote raged.

He ferreted out furiously the list he had made with the help of Miss Officewalla. It was looking more than a little battered now and he hated its creases and crossings-out.

And Jagdish Rana, he saw, was leaning back on the bed now, pillowing his head on the heaped mound of the puffy pink quilt, his legs dangling idly.

"If I must teach you your job, Inspector," he drawled.

"Teach—"

Ghote spluttered. He knew that he was spluttering. His vision of himself going to Nilima before the sun had set on Dhartiraj's killing and telling her that the mystery of her fellow star's death had been solved was fast vanishing. And its going was bitter.

"Yes, Inspector," Jagdish Rana said, all the more effortlessly cool for his own rage. "There is certainly one other person who has a motive that is a great deal stronger than the heap of nonsense you have tried to put on to me."

"And who is that? Who? Who?"

Jagdish Rana allowed himself the luxury of a slow smile. It was the smile he must have used in countless films playing a villain outsmarting the hero in the early part. And Ghote, from his faint memories of posters and hoardings, knew it. It was gall to see.

"Who are you trying to name?" he shouted. "I must warn you that—"

"Inspector, have you considered the fellow, Sudhaker Wani?"

"Sudhaker Wani? Who the— Well, yes, naturally, he is one of the names . . ."

He rapidly spread out his tattered list on his knee, though he well knew that this was not a name Miss Officewalla had even mentioned. Yet it was vaguely familiar. He tried hard to think where he had heard it recently.

Jagdish Rana lounged back against the quilt, one eyebrow raised.

Was it the name of some star? Would a star's name be so utterly unknown to him? He brought himself to acknowledge that it might. But if the name Sudhaker Wani—it certainly hardly sounded like that of a star —was one he ought to have recognised and had not, then . . . Then the only thing to do was to admit his ignorance and ask.

He cleared his throat.

"Please be so good as to tell me about him," he said.

And he pulled a fresh sheet of paper out of his pocket and poised his ballpoint.

"Sudhaker Wani, as you know," Jagdish Rana said with a thin smile, "is a stand-in at Talkiestan. Today he was working for Dhartiraj even. But he is also more than a stand-in."

Ghote remembered at once where he had heard the name. Sudhaker Wani was the person who had nearly been killed when that Lights Boy had let the Baby fall. He had even seen him, dressed in a *filmi* rich rajah robe, when he had first gone to the scene of the crime.

"Yes?" he said.

"Inspector," Jagdish Rana said, stepping from word to word, "have you ever come across fellows who, though they are in some fifth-class position only, occupy much higher places in reality. Sometimes they are big union-wallahs holding down no more than a peon's job. Or it may be a man who works as a clerk in some office but who is also a pandit to whom everybody goes for advice."

"Yes?"

"Well, Sudhaker Wani is such a man. He is not a pandit, far from it. Prayers and advice are not at all his line. Or not the sort of advice a pandit would give. Because Sudhaker Wani will give advice all right on such matters as erotic powders and charms against this and charms against that. He has an old aunt only who makes such things, and, believe me, he is very popular around the Studios on account of her."

He came to a halt.

"Go on," Ghote said.

"Inspector," the fading star continued, almost wheedlingly, "there are other things also that man does. If, for instance, anybody is wanting to go to a blue film show somewhere around Colaba or in some empty flat in Pedder Road, it is to Sudhaker Wani they go to ask where they can find."

"Well?"

Jagdish Rana smiled very slightly.

"Well, tell me, Inspector, why should Dhartiraj be having a secret conversation with such a man as that?"

He let the question hang in the air.

"If Dhartiraj should have wanted some of these erotic powders," Ghote suggested at last.

"Pah. A man like Dhartiraj to go to a hole-and-corner fellow like him. No, Inspector, if Dhartiraj was wanting such things he would pay one thousand rupees or more and go to a genuine sexology specialist. Doesn't he throw Rupees 125 per peg to drink Royal Salute whisky? Isn't that a well-known fact?"

It was not to Ghote.

"Yes, yes," he agreed. "That is well-known."

"Well then, why should Dhartiraj be talking to such a fellow?" Jagdish Rana leaned sharply forward. "I will answer that one, Inspector. The fellow must have believed he had a hold over Dhartiraj. It has been said often enough that if you buy from that old auntie of his, you pay twice. Once for what you get, once to keep his silence. Well, he is just the sort of fellow to have found out some secret of Dhartiraj's. And then he would try to get money out of him. Isn't it? Isn't it?"

The fading star was leaning well forward now, his feet planted on the creamy carpet of the round bed platform, his body tense and urgent.

"But Dhartiraj was not at all the sort of chap you could do that to," he went on. "He would laugh only. Or more likely, much more likely, he would tell the fellow straight out 'It is the police for you, bhai' or 'It is straight to the Production Manager I am going, and out of the Studios for you altogether.' That was the sort of fellow Dhartiraj was."

Jagdish Rana leaned another inch forward. The very pouches under his eyes seemed to have been pulled away to nothingness from the intensity of his effort.

"Well, Inspector, what is Sudhaker Wani to do now? He is threatened in every direction. He will be turned out of the Studios where he is making so much money, and every anna of it in black. Or he will be handed over to the police. He is a desperate man."

"Go on," Ghote said.

"It is simple, Inspector. Today he comes to take his place as Dhartiraj's stand-in. He is sent away to get more jewels for the turban. And, just as he goes, he sees that Five-K hanging in the darkness over the man's head like a sword only. He snatches up that dagger. He runs up the ladder. Cut, cut. He slices through the ropes. The Five-K falls. He is saved."

And he gave a mighty kick as he brought the accusation to a finish.

The giant round bed, to his utter surprise and even more to Ghote's, shot away on its central pivot and spun round and round in a mad whirl of triumph.

VIII

The cry came high in the sun-baked air, just beginning to lose its hard brightness with the onset of evening, as Ghote, the urgency of his mission sprawling over his mind, hurried from his car parked just off the rutted and dusty road towards the silhouetted outline of the old ruinous building.

"Pack up. Pack up."

He almost broke into a run.

Was he going to be too late? Would his man have finished his work and have gone off by the time he reached the Haunted Palace? And was that really what the place was called?

Striding over the tussocky brown-dried grass of the uneven ground rising up from the tranquil tree-fringed expanse of Lake Powai—seemingly a totally country scene, though the huge belching mills of North Bombay lay not so far away—he strove to remember exactly what had been said to him at the Talkiestan Studios when he had raced back there from his interview with Jagdish Rana at Juhu. It had taken infuriatingly long to track down anybody at the Studios who could tell him anything about Sudhaker Wani, stand-in and go-between, even where he was to be found. Often enough, though, a certain evasiveness had made it clear that many people in the Studios knew the stand-in all too well.

It was from the Production Manager's secretary, a big blowsy Goan girl, whom he had first passed over in favour of going straight to her boss at the top, that he eventually got his answer.

"That man."

There had been stormy washes of emotion in the way she had spoken of him. Of fear. Of revulsion.

He had wondered briefly whether there might not have been a history of something like an abortion, performed, in disgusting conditions, by the fellow's aunt. But he had much more important matters to deal with.

"That man. He is at Haunted Palace this shift. Sethji has said that shooting on *Khoon Ka Gaddi* must not be halted. So they are carrying on out there with the scene where the Banana Grove comes to Dehra Dun."

But was it really called the Haunted Palace, this ruin of a building gradually emerging as he hurried forward through a screen of low heat-stunted trees? He did not want to make a mistake, if the name was only one of those *filmi* jokes. Miss Officewalla had said that film people spent much of their time joking. But it would not at all do for the investigator of the murder of Dhartiraj to look a fool.

He hurried through the trees, and the ruin stood plainly before him, a substantial building which well might once have been a nawab's palace endowed with a peaceful lake view. On the smooth grass of what must once have been a garden there was a group of twenty or thirty people standing idle. Some he recognised. There beside his camera was the Cameraman—No, Director of Photography—and those must be his assistants beside him. And there was the Audiographer fellow. And now, emerging from the ruined house, there was Director Bhabani Ghosh, swaying-bellied in his flowing white muslin kurta. And it was plain that most of the others standing about among the tall reflector screens on their long thin black legs were actors or extras, busy disrobing themselves of the costumes of foot-soldiers from some historical time. And there were coolies too and, sitting on the ground with a pack of cards, technicians of some sort. On the fringe there was the usual collection of urchins. Some were trailing dusty and broken blade-shaped banana leaves.

Yes, "till Birnam Wood do come to Dunsinane." But where was Maqbet? Where was Dhartiraj's stand-in? Dhartiraj's murderer perhaps?

He scanned the group almost frantically for the somewhat hang-dog figure he remembered all too vaguely from the circle of people standing round the body of Dhartiraj. No. No one he could recall.

Had that Goan girl, the Production Manager's secretary, been lying? Was that why she had seemed disturbed?

He broke into a run and thrust himself without ceremony between Director Ghosh and the Cameraman who had just embarked on an earnest conversation.

"Sudhaker Wani," he burst out. "Sudhaker Wani, the stand-in? He has been here? He is here somewhere now? I demand to see him."

The big Bengali director stepped back a pace.

"Why, it is the Inspector," he said. "Inspector Ghote, isn't it?"

"Yes, yes. But Sudhaker Wani, where is he?"

Bhabani Ghosh's bold-featured face broke into a wide, easy smile.

"But, Inspector, he is right beside us. Here. This is him."

He gestured towards the two men Ghote had taken for the Cameraman's assistants. And it was true. The one on the left was surely the fellow he had seen in the morning. Then he had been wearing, rather sheepishly, a rich red rajah's robe and now, whatever costume he had had for the shooting taken off, he was dressed just in a pair of dirty khaki trousers and a dull blue shirt on which at some time a right-angled tear had been mended not very skillfully. But it was the same man.

Ghote stopped to take a long hard look at his face. It was not one that would ever be easy to remember. The trick was to seize on the most notable feature and let it soak into the mind while repeating as many times as possible the name. But Sudhaker Wani—Sudhaker Wani, Sudhaker Wani, Sudhaker Wani—did not seem to have any one really distinguishing mark. Mouth, ears, chin, eyebrows were all smallish and totally regular, seeming to retreat into the neither light nor dark flesh. His body, too, was as average as could be, neither fat nor thin, not tall nor short. Ordinary.

And the fellow's eyes, when he at last addressed him, hardly moved up at all to look at him.

"Sudhaker Wani, I am an officer of Crime Branch C.I.D. investigating the death of Dhartiraj and I wish to ask you a number of questions."

"Very good."

It was a low, characterless murmur.

Excusing himself to Director Ghosh, Ghote took a quick look round and decided that as good a place as anywhere to conduct the interview would be the interior of the Haunted Palace.

Inside the ruin, an empty shell, its floor strewn with brick dust and fragments of white stone, the trapped air noticeably muggier than the now cooling out-of-doors and smelling acridly of bird lime, there seemed to be only one room that was almost intact, though it too was open to the faintly darkening sky. Ghote led the way into it and sat down on the ledge of the single tall frameless window.

Sudhaker Wani stood in front of him, waiting impassively.

He had intended to begin by asking him directly exactly what he had been doing during the few minutes when Dhartiraj had been alone on the *gaddi* learning his dialogues. Jagdish Rana's vivid account of how the fellow must have seen the poised Five-K as he had gone to take away the turban to be more ornately jewelled, of how he had snatched up the waiting dagger, of how he had climbed the ladder in the darkness, had slipped along the catwalk and had sliced through the ropes in two quick cuts, was so clear in his mind that he had thought he could not wait one instant before testing its reality. But, cooled perhaps by his ridiculous mistake in not at once recognising the man he had pursued so hotly, he sat for some while just looking at him, and when he did put a question it was one that was almost totally irrelevant.

"Tell me, when you wear those rich clothes with all the jewels on them, what do you feel?"

But even the oddity of the question was powerless to affect the immobile figure standing in front of him.

"Inspector, I do not mind," he answered, without a single flicker of those steadily downward-held eyes.

"No," Ghote said, "I am not asking if you mind. I am asking: does it make you feel different, to be dressed as a rajah?"

"No, Inspector."

Again there was not a flicker of interest in the answer, not even the tiniest hint of surprise.

"But, look, I am asking out of interest only," Ghote persisted. "I have not seen very much of filming, and I wondered what it does to people to wear the clothes of someone else. It is something that affects me, you know. When I have to wear a uniform I feel altogether different from myself in shirt and pants only. Do you follow that?"

"Yes, Inspector."

But he might equally well have said "No".

"And you tell me," Ghote said, with a spurt of exasperation, "that to wear the clothes of a rich and powerful man does not put into your head what it must be like to be such a one, to order men about, to turn them out of their homes, to put them to death even?"

Just for an instant then the downward-held eyes did flicker. But it was so little that he doubted what he had seen.

"Inspector," the fellow answered in the same uninflected voice in which he had replied to every question, "I am stand-in only."

"But you are not stand-in only."

The fellow had given him an opening and he seized on it. Was it the first step of a path that would lead to heights which only a few hours ago, at the start of this extraordinary day, had been utterly inconceivable?

"Inspector?"

"You are not stand-in only, Sudhaker. You also perform many different services for people in the Studios, isn't it?"

"Inspector?"

"Do not pretend with me. I know already a great deal about you. You have an aunt, isn't it? An aunt who makes mixtures of herbs and secret ingredients which people buy for large sums? Is it from her that the stars get their bed-smasher *paans* which to chew only is said to increase the potency like a bull's? Those and other such things? Is it? Is it?"

"Inspector, I do have auntie."

"And through you she sells such things."

He hammered it at him.

"Inspector, there is no harm. The things they buy do not truly harm those they are given to. Maybe they are sometimes making a girl thin or some such thing. But, Inspector, in the West many girls are wanting all the time to slim."

Ghote trod down this hint of rebellion as if he was squashing an unpleasant insect.

"Listen to me, Sudhaker. In Vigilance Branch they are keeping a file on you only. You are damn lucky not to be in the lock-up already."

At last there was a clear reaction in those downward-looking eyes. A side-glancing flick of fear.

"Now, the blue films," Ghote plunged in, feeling coiling up inside him the possibility of complete success and the heady scent of all that it could lead to.

His ferocity with the one hint of information he had about the fellow's activities seemed to pay off. Though information came in driblets, it came. It was necessary whenever there was a pause only to tap impatiently with his foot on the fragments of brick and stone on the floor to get the flow started again.

There was, it came out, not only the sessions of blue-film viewing for which the stand-in acted as organiser, but he was also involved in their making. He found technicians who would be willing to shoot them at an out-of-the-way bungalow at Dahisar and he found girls and men from among the Decent Extras willing to act in them. He even contacted smugglers to take the finished prints by sea to the Arab countries where they were especially popular.

"No, no, Inspector, I am telling you. The films we are showing in Bombay are different. They are from Sweden-Denmark. The girls we are having to use to make them here are mostly too thin. Only the Arabs are liking."

At this new sign of returning confidence Ghote tapped his foot with more than usual sharpness. Let the fellow understand he was not dealing with anyone who could be trifled with.

"Inspector," the stand-in promptly admitted, "it is because there is too much risk. If they seized any films in Vigilance, they could recognise the girls and lead from them to everybody."

"And the girls?" Ghote asked, taking a small chance so as to keep his ever-speeding initiative. "You make use of them in other ways for people who can pay?"

"There is that demand also, Inspector."

Another quick tap of the foot.

"Rupees 500, Inspector."

Tap, tap.

"Sometimes Rupees 1,000. But that is lucky. I am not making so much, Inspector. There are many, many expenses."

"But no tax returns. Every anna of it in black for you, Sudhaker."

He felt a spasm of anger zig-zag through his head. The claims the tax man made on his own limited pay and the slow way in which Dearness Allowance was screwed up rupee by rupee against the ever-leaping cost of living. But he brought himself under control. Only clear thinking would keep this flow of answers running.

"But the girls are not all," he said levelly, certain from the mere attitude of the man in front of him that the well had yet to be emptied.

"Yes, I am getting people things also. Things that are hard to get."

Smuggling. Of course he would be a distributor of smuggled goods as well as concerned with taking blue films out.

"What things, Sudhaker?"

Get as many details as possible, get him to feel he was in it so deep he could only keep on telling the truth.

"Inspector, you know what it is film people are always wanting. It is big foreign television sets now, and watches with digital face."

Digital face? Oh, yes, no hands but little numbers instead.

He tapped his foot once more.

"But, Inspector, when they can afford and afford. To a star what is a thousand bucks even? It is nothing, less than nothing."

This is it, Ghote thought. Now is my chance. Push on to the heart of it now.

For a moment he almost saw a glittering panorama spread out in front of his eyes.

But in fact in the little room the light had become plainly bad. Above the roofless ruin the sky was now a dark blue, the colour it would hold for only a few minutes before darkness swept over it.

Nothing for it, however, but to seize the opportunity.

"Yes," he said. "A thousand rupees is less than nothing to a star, especially a star like Dhartiraj."

He leant forward sharply in the failing light to catch the least change of expression on the stand-in's impassive face. But there seemed to be nothing. Nor were there signs more tell-tale, any alterations in the way the hands were held, or the weight on the feet distributed or in the posture of the body.

But he had not answered.

"Well?"

"Dhartiraj?" the stand-in repeated tonelessly. "Yes, I suppose he could pay better than anyone else, except Ravi Kumar."

For a moment Ghote was tempted to pursue this fleeting mention of the superstar who had, after all, a strong motive for killing his rival in love. But he had not been in the Studios when the murder had taken place and he must therefore be left out of account. Nor must this fellow be let for one instant off the hook.

"You suppose that Dhartiraj could pay well," he said, jabbing the words out. "Then, tell me, what did he pay? What did he pay you for?"

"Inspector, nothing."

"I know better than that. You have been seen talking to Dhartiraj when no one was near. Why would he talk to you unless it was to buy?"

It was taking another chance, to presume so much from something Jagdish Rana had said almost in passing. But the guesses he had made up till now had paid off handsomely.

"Well?"

"Inspector, no."

Yet the fellow did not seem to be denying it with much emotion. And he must have realised that the question was leading to an accusation that he had killed the star.

"Do not lie to me, Sudhaker. You were seen, I tell you."

"Inspector, no. Dhartiraj was not the sort of man who buys from Durga Auntie. A man like him would never want anything to harm— would never want a love potion, Inspector. And if he wanted, he would go to a big sexologist fellow. He had that much money."

Ghote saw the force of that. But he was determined not to be checked.

"Yes," he said, "Dhartiraj was rich. But he cannot always have been so. He rose to fame. So, when he was not so rich, what was it that he bought from you?"

It was almost dark in the little ceilingless room now. Inwardly Ghote cursed.

"Well? Answer. Answer."

"Inspector, nothing. I have said."

"Not things to harm perhaps. He was not the sort of person to want to harm. But something to be ashamed. Did he buy that, Sudhaker?"

"No, Inspector."

"Something not at all harmful in itself, but something that now he would not like the *filmi* magazines to know about and to print? Yes, Sudhaker? Yes?"

Still the fellow stood there impassively in front of him. But surely he must realise that the question hit at him deeply.

It was almost impossible to see his face any longer. Ghote realised at the back of his mind that he had been aware the sounds of the film crew departing had ceased some time before. The last car had gone revving and bucketing along the un-made up track back to the road.

"Sudhaker Wani, when you were told by Dhartiraj this morning to take Maqbet's turban and get more jewels put on it, what did you do?"

"Inspector, I took it to the Property Department."

"Straightaway, Sudhaker?"

"Yes, Inspector, straightaway."

Ghote strove to analyse the totally placid tone of the fellow's reply. It surely could not have meant that he had indeed gone straight to the Property Department and talked with someone there the whole time that the murder had been done. Then there would surely have been a tinge of boasting in it. And, if he believed that he had succeeded in setting up a false alibi, there would have been a trace of defiance. Or, if the reply had been merely the best he could think up, there could certainly have been a hint of tenseness.

And there had been none of those things. Just a seemingly blank indifference. As if there was something altogether more important to the fellow than his questions. And that could not be. What was the fellow after all? A stand-in only, a man in a job that required only the endurance to stand where he was put for long, long periods. All right, he had his other activities too. But, though no doubt they brought him a good deal of money, there could be nothing in his life that could make him careless of the threat of a murder charge.

Yet he seemed totally unaffected.

A streak of despair shot through his head. Why was he faced with this? He ought at this instant to have begun to get from this sullen figure a confession to murder. A confession to murdering Dhartiraj, the star. The first steps on an ever-widening path that would have brought him to that almost unimaginable moment of dazzle-lit recognition.

With heavy weariness he put the next question.

"You say you went straight to the Property Department with that turban. Is there anybody who could swear to that?"

"Inspector, I was there."

"But who will swear to it?"

"There must be many people, Inspector."

Must there? Not if the fellow had not been there at all.

"Who, Sudhaker, who?"

"Inspector, there will be many people."

He pushed himself to his feet.

"That we will see," he said.

IX

It did not take long to get Sudhaker Wani put in the lock-up at the police-station nearest to Talkiestan Studios under Assistant Inspector Jahdev's charge. Ghote felt happier when it was done. With every passing minute he was beginning to feel more and more sure that the charge that would eventually be brought would come under Section 201 of the Indian Penal Code: murder.

Nothing the fellow had given away so far could lead to the charge, though there were things that needed explanation—if only his comparative willingness to talk about his smuggling and offences against Section 292 (Obscene books and films) compared with his later blank indifference. But no doubt some sort of answer to that would emerge. And perhaps the contrast just did not matter. If he could be shown to have been lying about what he was doing at the time Dhartiraj had been killed, then the whole situation would look different.

"Get a move on," he snapped at his driver, who was finding it hard to work his way through the last of the evening traffic rush.

The man glanced round to him as if surprised at his impatience.

He glared straight ahead, determined to offer no explanation.

Get to the Studios, get over to the Property Department, pin down whoever was there. And then, if it emerged that Sudhaker had been lying . . . Then tear the fellow apart. Get him down to Headquarters and make him talk if it took all night. Because what a morning it would be after. The dawning of what a day. The beginning of an altogether new life.

But at the Studios gate he met a check.

As his car approached two chowkidars—different men from the ones he had seen before—came running out into the roadway, holding up their hands to stop the traffic. One came right up and stood there bang in front of his vehicle.

A flare of rage ripped across his mind. What the hell was the man up to? What did he mean stopping him like this?

But a moment later he saw what it was all about.

From out of the widely opened gates there slid, smooth as a python, a huge limousine. And, seated at the back, all alone and looking like a maharajah in his durbar hall, there was Seth Chagan Lal.

If anything Ghote's rage fanned up yet higher.

Oh, yes, Seth Chagan Lal was a Producer, a man who held even the fortunes of stars in his hand. But what right had he to take priority over an investigation into the murder of a man who was the idol of millions? He had half a mind—

But already the long limousine was gliding round his own battered vehicle. He slumped back in his seat.

And then, with a bouncing jerk, the limousine came to a halt exactly parallel with him. He saw the Seth jabbing crossly at some buttons. He must at last have hit the right one because the window directly between them slipped suddenly down smoothly and a waft of air-conditioned coolness reached out to him on his hot leather seat.

"Ah, Inspector, it is good I have seen."

"Yes, Mr. Lal? Yes, sir?"

He wished he had not sounded so much like a clerk or a servant even.

"What so far have you found out?"

He hesitated. Should he tell him that what he had found out was a police matter and that no one, whoever they might be, had any right to know?

The tight blubber face was looking at him with unwavering intensity, eyes stone-like, slit mouth closed. It was no more than two feet away.

Well, there were people who, if they asked a question like that even out of casual interest only, got some sort of full answer. Influential people. People you wanted to have on your side, the police side.

"Sir, we are making progress."

"Progress, progress. Inspector, I have publicity managers, one, two, three, to tell people things like that. But I am asking you what has happened in the case. Seth Chagan Lal is asking, Inspector."

"Sir, we have pursued several lines of inquiry."

A glint of anger showed in the little stone eyes.

Ghote swallowed.

"And— And already I have one of the Studios employees behind the bars."

There was a moment's silence. Then the hard voice came again.

"But you are not charging him with the murder of Dhartiraj."

"Yes. Yes, that is true. Most sagacious of you Sethji. It is an employee whose other offences have come to light."

Why did he do it? "Most sagacious of you, Sethji". And he was meant to be the star investigator, the match of any man.

"But why is the fellow not charged with murder? Why, Inspector?"

"Sir— Sethji, we are not having adequate evidence."

"Evidence, evidence. You have got there behind the bars a criminal, isn't it? You have found a criminal in the Studios. Well, then, it is likely-likely, I am telling you, that he can be found guilty of the murder. Charge him, Inspector, charge."

"No, sir."

He drew himself up straight on the scuffed leather of the car seat.

"Inspector, what are you meaning 'No'? I am saying, Inspector, that it is altogether best if someone is charged. The murder of Dhartiraj is a damn serious matter, Inspector. Serious for Talkiestan Studios, serious for Fifteen Arts Films. You have got a man there. Charge him."

"Mr. Lal, not only is there no firm evidence against him but it is possible he may prove to have a good alibi. No question of a charge can arise."

"No, Inspector? Perhaps we would have to see."

The blubber face was hard as tyre-rubber.

Ghote found himself, almost without realising what he was doing, making a peace offering. After all, Sudhaker Wani was not the only man he had under suspicion. If the case against the stand-in did after all fall down when he came to make his inquiries, then there was still something that Jagdish Rana would have to answer.

"On the other hand, Mr. Lal, there is the possibility of a case against another individual. I am talking in strictest confidence, please understand."

"Inspector, when you are talking to Seth Chagan Lal you are talking at V.I.P. level. Always."

"Yes, sir. Of course, sir."

"Then who is this man?"

Damn. Damn. Damn.

He had not intended to name a name. He had succeeded after all in keeping Sudhaker Wani's actual name out of it. But now, thanks to trying to butter Seth Chagan Lal with talk about "strictest confidence", he had got himself faced with the direct question. Was there no way out?

None showed itself.

"Sir, it is— It is a star that I am having to name, sir."

The blubber face, so close to his own, darkened in an instant with massive emotion. The stone eyes glared like twin sports-car headlamps set beside the everyday orange glow of Ambassadors and Fiats.

Of course, film stars were the Seth's great stock in trade. To lose one would be like a diamond merchant in the Zaveri Bazar losing one of his precious gems. But such searing rage as this . . .

"Who is it, Inspector? Who?"

The voice compelled with all the willpower that had taken the man from a scraping clerk's existence to his present riches and esteem.

"Sir, it is Jagdish Rana."

The Seth's face changed in an instant.

"Jagdish Rana," he exclaimed, his voice crackling now with mere exasperation. "You were talking of stars."

Ghote felt sharply offended. Once again his assessment of some aspect of the *filmi duniya* was being scorned. But Jagdish Rana was a star, however firmly on the downward path. He was. Not only had he claimed it himself with much drama, but *filmi* people still called him a star. Miss Officewalla even had done so. It was unfair.

"But sir," he burst out, "you yourself are even considering him for the role of Maqbet in *Khoon Ka Gaddi*."

And then the hard blubber face split open in brief laughter.

"Jagdish Rana, Maqbet. Maqbet, Jagdish Rana. Oh, Inspector, Inspector, you have no idea. You are having no idea at all. Arrest Jagdish Rana if you like. Arrest him three-four times and there is nothing to care. Nothing at all to care."

The big air-conditioned limousine had shot off into the darkness, leaving Ghote with one final glimpse of the Seth pushing and jabbing happily at his buttons to get the window to go up. He himself had not ordered his driver to go on into the Studios. Instead he had sat there letting the traffic whiz by and had thought.

There was a lot to think about.

First, there was the fact that Seth Chagan Lal's derisive permission to him to arrest Jagdish Rana had precisely cleared the failing star. If there was no chance at all of the fellow stepping into Dhartiraj's shoes in the part of Maqbet, then he hardly had a motive for wanting to get Dhartiraj out of the way. What the fellow had said to him out at Juhu had been only the wildest of boasting.

So, if when he made his inquiries at the Property Department here he found that Sudhaker Wani's offered alibi did in fact stand up, then he would have no real line to pursue. So that alibi must be false. He must get his hands on Dhartiraj's murderer. He must. That was what it was all about. The vision.

"Go in, man," he snapped at the driver. "What for are you sitting about here all night? Go in."

But as the car went on up to the Studios gates something else that he knew he ought to think about emerged like an iron rock in his head. It was

Seth Chagan Lal's whole attitude. It was not somehow what it ought to be. It had been much too concerned all along, both just now and this morning.

Yet why that should be defied guessing. And they were through the gates now and making their way through splashy pools of light to the Property Department.

Well, there his answer would lie. Must lie. Sudhaker Wan's alibi must be broken.

Only at the Property Department he found that he had forgotten in his absorption in the importance of the case one simple thing. That ordinary people had ordinary lives to live. None of the staff in the Property Department were the same as those who had been there first thing in the morning.

He stood feeling foolish. Damn it, he ought to have realised when he had seen that different chowkidars were on duty at the gates. A film studio, working three shifts a day, could not have the same personnel there from start to finish.

For a few minutes he planned furiously how he could get a list of the home addresses of everyone who had been on duty in the Property Department that morning from Manager to humblest coolie, how he would go all over Bombay finding them one by one, dragging what he wanted to know out of them.

But before very long he realised that even a whole night would not be time enough for that. And—he asked and they confirmed it for him—before eight o'clock next morning every one of the people he wanted to see would be back in the Studios.

Slowly a cold greyness rose up in him, blotting out the fiery ambition that had lasted him ever since he had had that interview with Sudhaker Wani and before. No, there was one way to conduct an inquiry and one way only. That was systematically to interview everybody who might have any light to throw on the circumstances, whether they seemed likely suspects or not.

He had people he ought to be interviewing on these lines. The names on the list he had compiled with Miss Officewalla's help. None of them was a very likely murderer of the dead star. Miss Officewalla had made that quite clear. But in logic they might have killed him, and it was his duty to check on their whereabouts at the time of the crime. If it took him all night.

It did take him most of the night.

Dhartiraj's personal astrologer—that saintly old man—proved to be much concerned to explain how the star's horoscope had accurately predicted that this was a most inauspicious period for him, and had incidentally mentioned that he had been conferring with fellow pandits at the time Dhartiraj had died. The dead star's former wife, now the embittered Mrs. Ravi Kumar, had taken a long while to track down but then had said convincingly that she had not seen Dhartiraj for many months and that she had been under the hands of her hairdresser at the time he had died. The as yet unfilmed new star, Meena, Dhartiraj's keep, looking every bit as thin as Miss Officewalla had said she would, had been in floods of tears. But eventually she had remembered that she had been in bed that morning till very late and there were two of her servants to prove it. He had questioned them thoroughly, just as he had questioned Mrs. Kumar's hairdresser and, just as with him, he had eventually satisfied himself that what he had been told was true.

Dhartiraj's make-up man had been, he claimed, in vigorous dispute with Nilima's make-up man at the time of the death on the relative merits of home-produced and foreign-smuggled cosmetics. And Nilima's make-up man, who lived in a particularly crowded area in Dadar and who had not at all liked being waked in the middle of the night, had eventually agreed that this had been so. Dhartiraj's secretary had been busy with the star's mail at the time of his death, and luckily had had to consult his Personal Assistant over much of it. So eliminating them had not taken as long as it might have done.

But it was in the very early hours of the morning that Ghote managed to get home at last for an hour or two's sleep. And he had done so with the additional depressing knowledge that none of the people he had spoken to had been able to suggest anyone who had even remotely disliked the ever-popular player of villains enough to have wanted to kill him for any reason whatsoever.

When the alarm clock on the little shelf above the bed clangingly woke him next day his mood had not changed. He saw only a long slog before him. Even the prospect of being able within an hour or so to check Sudhaker Wani's alibi with the people who had been in the Property Department the previous morning did not fill him with yesterday's enthusiasm.

Thank goodness, he thought, that I missed the Press last evening. If I had told them that someone had been "helping with inquiries", what would they have expected? A brilliant solution to the killing of a brilliant figure?

He arrived at the Studios as early as any of the employees and tackled the business of checking on Sudhaker Wani's presence in the Property Department filled with a premonition that he was going to find that the stand-in had at least a reasonable alibi.

And if that proved so, he thought, it would be the painful round of examining every less and less likely possibility until in the end there was none left and other routine tasks would assert their claims even over the case of the murdered film star.

But, quite soon, he found that the stand-in hardly had an alibi at all.

True, he had brought the Maqbet turban to the Property Department and had handed it over with Dhartiraj's instructions. But as soon as he had done so he had left.

"Where did he go? Did you see? Where?" he asked the Department Manager, who had taken charge of the turban himself.

"Inspector, he might have gone to a hundred and one places. He might have wanted a *bidi* only, and smoking is strictly forbidden within the walls of my department."

"But Sudhaker Wani did not smoke," the Department Sub-Manager, hovering helpfully, put in.

His superior rounded on him at once.

"I dare say, I dare say, Sub-Manager. But a man has many other reasons for not wanting to stay. There is always the call of nature, you know."

"Yes, Manager Sahib," the Sub-Manager dutifully replied.

But, as Ghote left, he heard him mutter, "But I think Sudhaker did not have those even."

He wondered briefly at the words. They confirmed his own feelings about the stand-in as a man somehow different from the human majority. But the thought faded.

What was important was that, once more, he had a strong suspect. Sudhaker Wani had not stayed inside the Property Department, as he had implied the evening before. He had lied about that. And if he had not stayed there, there was plenty of time for him to have hurried back to Sound Stage #2—it was only a few yards—to have quietly taken the curved dagger from its table, to have slipped across to the ladder up to the catwalk, to have made his way swiftly to the dangling Five-K, to have slashed—once, twice—at its ropes, and easily in the ensuing confusion to have got back to the Property Department, replacing the dagger more or less in its original position on the way.

He could have done it all. He must have done it. He must be made to confess that he had done it. It was still less than twenty-four hours since the crime had been committed. To have solved the mystery in that time would be a star performance. A true star performance.

X

Sitting fuming with impatience in his Headquarters office, Ghote saw with pouncing pleasure when at last a couple of Assistant Inspector Jahdev's constables brought Sudhaker Wani in, that he was looking a good deal worse for his night in the lock-up. A spell in such a place, narrow, high-walled, probably no bigger in area than the veranda outside, ventilated only by its tall barred gate, pungent with the combined stink of as many as a hundred prisoners stripped to undershorts and sandals, was a pretty good way of splintering almost any shell of pride.

Had it then been only pride that had sustained the fellow during his previous interrogation? Would it be no more now than a question of using rather tougher methods than he had employed the day before? It certainly looked, if only just, as if the fellow was not after all so hardened against attack as he had seemed.

So, be that little more tough and perhaps before even half an hour was up the confession would be pouring out, the first step on the upward rising path to such blazing heights it was not possible to think about.

"So, Sudhaker, last night you told me that you went from Dhartiraj to the Property Department and that there were plenty of people who saw you there. Suppose that now you give me their names."

"Inspector, I cannot."

Those eyes were fixed, obstinately as ever, on a spot just a foot or so below his own.

"You cannot, Sudhaker?" He put a plainly jeering note into his voice. "You cannot? Not even one? Not one person who saw you in the Property Department?"

"Inspector, I gave the turban to Manager Sahib. Sub-Manager Sahib was there also."

"Yes, you gave. And then you went straight out."

Silence.

"Well, yes or no? You went out?"

"Yes, Inspector."

"That is better. Now, outside the Property Department there are often coolies sitting on the ground waiting for orders. There are clerks also, coming and going?"

Silence.

"Are there? Are there? Yes or no?"

"Yes, Inspector."

Yet still not a flicker in that face.

"You often go to the Property Department?"

"Sometimes, Inspector."

Plainly a half-truth. Safe enough to risk contradicting that.

"But this morning only Manager Sahib and Sub-Manager also were telling me something very different. They were saying that often and often stars are sending you when you are their stand-in to have changes made in their costumes."

Still that downward-cast face.

"Yes or no? Yes or no? Answer up."

"Yes, Inspector."

A hint of a dry mouth in that whispered reply? Keep it up.

"Very good. So you are often going to the Property Department and the many coolies sitting outside know you well. Yes?"

"Yes, Inspector."

That was better. That came quicker.

"And you know these coolies?"

"Some. Perhaps."

It seemed as if under this grinding the fragments of fact were becoming smaller and smaller. They were hard little nuggets still, but surely the possibility of at last breaking them down till they hid nothing was there.

"You know more than one of those fellows out there by name, isn't it?"

But no answer now.

He brought his hands up on to the top of the desk and bunched them loosely into fists.

"Yes, Inspector. Yes."

That had been an instant reaction. His spirit must have taken a battering during the night in the lock-up. There were raw areas there.

From the scatter of flat little metal paperweights on the desk top he selected the heaviest, and holding it in his right hand he brought it smacking down into his left palm. The sound was loud in the quiet of the little office, with only the occasional cawing of a crow or hoot of a motor horn outside.

In the stand-in's downward-held eyes a tiny side glance betrayed that the pantomime had had its effect.

"Now, Sudhaker, it is time that you and I got down to business."

No reply to that of course.

"Well, Sudhaker, do you agree? Yes? Yes?"

"Yes, Inspector."

Hah, the fellow no longer knew what he was saying. In we go.

"You did not stay near the Property Department after you had taken in that turban, did you, Sudhaker?"

"Yes, Inspector. Yes, I did. Yes, yes."

That was panic. Press in, press in.

"How dare you lie to me, my friend? How dare you? Now then, where did you go when you had left the turban? Where? Where? Come on, out with it."

"Inspector, nowhere."

"Nowhere? Nowhere? You have a body, Sudhaker. You have legs and arms and a trunk. Legs and arms and a trunk that can feel pain too, let me remind you. Now, where were they those legs and arms of yours? Nowhere? Nowhere? I do not see how that can be, my friend."

"Inspector. Inspector . . ."

"Well, speak up. Speak up. Where did you go when you came out from leaving the turban? Dhartiraj's turban, Sudhaker? Dhartiraj's turban that he was not wearing when that Five-K crashed down on to him? Where did you go when you had left it?"

"Inspector, to make water only. Only that, I swear."

"Oh, so you swear now, do you? You swear to your lies, to add to it all?"

"No, no, Inspector. I did that. I did. I did."

He knew at that moment—all his experience of criminals and witnesses lying and wriggling under questioning told him so—that in this at least Sudhaker Wani was telling the truth.

It crossed his mind that the Property Department Sub-Manager had ironically proved wrong about the man's need to answer Nature's calls, however much he believed him to be right about some secret core in him that seemed impervious to ordinary human weaknesses. But had he now penetrated to that core, found it was not so remarkable after all?

Certainly he had the fellow at his mercy now. And he could hold him there, just by keeping his eyes fixed on him, while he thought over the implications of this small piece of fact that he had, with disproportionate effort, pulled out.

All right, after taking in Dhartiraj's turban for its richer encrustation of jewels he had gone out to relieve himself. Where would he have gone? No doubt round some corner, perhaps up against the high surrounding wall of the Studios compound. So how much of the quite short time needed to get into Sound Stage #2, up that ladder and across to the Five-K would have been taken up? The distance involved was not long and the handing-over of the turban had taken only at most two minutes. How long to go and urinate? One minute? Perhaps a little longer. But that would still leave him enough time. It plainly would.

He felt the nearness of the kill run like a fiery spirit through his veins. A promise of heady intoxication soon flooding over him.

Abruptly to be stopped.

With absolute suddenness he saw that the picture he had been constructing, a picture born when Jagdish Rana had described the murderer realising what the hanging Five-K meant and returning to the scene to take the curve-bladed dagger, scramble up the ladder, make his swaying way across the catwalk and slash at those ropes, was not true. It did not fit the sober facts of life.

Quite simply, a man who had decided to kill Dhartiraj would not have been able to stand somewhere and quietly relieve himself. It would be possible, yes, that Sudhaker had not wholly made up his mind to kill Dhartiraj when he had seen the dangling Five-K and that, torn by indecision, he had actually gone round some corner as if to urinate and had counted on his answer manifesting itself then according to some code of luck. The human mind could work like that. But it was not possible that Sudhaker had actually urinated and then hurried off to cut down that Five-K.

And, though there was nothing in the way of proof, he himself had no doubt at all that what Sudhaker had told him was the simple truth. He had gone to a corner somewhere and had urinated.

And so he had not murdered Dhartiraj.

But there was some mystery there still. The fellow had done something that had justly put him into his present state of fear. Best find that out before anything else.

"You made water," he said, not letting the pressure slacken by the least amount. "And what else did you do after? That was not all. What else did you do?"

The stand-in did not answer.

"Come on, man, you have more time to account for than that. What did you do?"

Still there was no reply. But the silence was quite different from the silences that had gone before it. Ghote could feel it. It must have been evident in some tiny difference of stance or perhaps even in the rate of breathing, though he would have been hard put to it to pin down just what it was. But he knew quite clearly that this was no longer the resolute indifference of the Haunted Palace interview and neither was it at all the evasive silences of the beginning of this interrogation. It was the silence of desperation, pure desperation.

It would not take long to break.

"Where, Sudhaker? Where?"

And that barked demand was enough.

"Sahib. Inspector. I was talking with Salim Ali. He is a young fellow, Inspector, who is working as extra and is also sometimes a musician with a hotel band. And, Inspector, he writes songs. They are very good— That— That is, Inspector, they may be quite good. And I wished to buy one."

"To buy a song?"

He felt himself slithering helplessly, deprived of all sense of direction. Only the fact that the stand-in had checked himself after saying that the young Muslim's songs were "very good" had told him that, however unlikely it might seem, Sudhaker believed himself to be revealing a secret that was valuable indeed. And this was enough to keep him hammering.

"To buy a song, man? What is this? Speak up, speak up."

"Inspector, for a film."

The stand-in spoke the words in such a tone of beaten-down confession—they had hardly been audible at all—that Ghote knew at once that he had penetrated to the fellow's innermost secret.

"Go on," he said simply.

"Inspector, this is for what I have been making every anna I could. This is why I was selling Durga Auntie's spells and mixtures. This was why I was helping to run blue-film shows and selling smuggled items and hanging round the stars' *chumchas* making black-money deals and listening for little things to sell to the gossip writers. Inspector, did you think it was to get cash for spending only? No, to make a film you are needing capital outlay. Enough at least to buy something good going cheap, like Salim Ali's songs when he is wanting always money for *bhang* and other drug— Enough to buy, if you can, a good song, Inspector, so that you can borrow enough to make six-eight reels to show to the distributors and in that way make a beginning."

Ghote blinked in astonishment.

"You are aiming to be a Producer, a film producer?" he asked.

His evident incredulity roused the stand-in.

"And why not?" he spat out. "Why not, please? Did not Seth Chagan

Lal begin from nowhere himself? And is he not a true *crorepati* now?"

"Yes," Ghote said slowly, his exchanges with the wealth-oozing Seth clear in his mind. "Yes, I see that you may be right."

He saw more. He saw, with this explanation of the stand-in's behaviour, that the path he had been following in his eager hunt for Dhartiraj's killer had finally come to its destination. And that destination had nothing at all to do with the murder.

He had been on a long, long detour. And, worse, now that he had retraced his steps and come back to the place he had turned off wrongly, there was, with Jagdish Rana's motive brutally removed by the laughing Seth Chagan Lal, nowhere else at all to go.

Life had flicked off the switch of the great stairway of light up which he had thought he was climbing. And there was suddenly no upward path left. Only blackness.

He sat on at his desk after he had ordered Sudhaker Wani to be taken away and let the dismal grey clouds sweep endlessly across his mind, barren of even the least drop of life-giving rain.

Every hope had dwindled to extinction. Sudhaker Wani had turned out to be no more than a mixed-bag petty criminal with ridiculous ambitions. Jagdish Rana's once naked motive had been shrivelled up by Seth Chagan Lal's dismissive laughter. And with the ever-friendly, everliked Dhartiraj as victim there were, unlikely as it might seem, simply no other suspects. His long talk with Miss Officewalla had shown him that. If anyone had ever known anything to the detriment of a star, Miss Officewalla would have told him of it. That was something certain in a world of fantasy.

But no one she had told him about—except, of course, the great Ravi Kumar, who had not been in the Studios when Dhartiraj had died—appeared to have had the least motive for the murder.

For a few hallucinatory moments he toyed with the notion of somehow proving that, after all, Ravi Kumar had entered the Studios. In disguise? But he was a star and could not possibly have passed the scrutiny of the chowkidars unnoticed. At tremendous speed? But the gates were shut, and however fast a star flashed by in his Mercedes or big Buick he would be seen and saluted. By some other entrance? But there was none. A high wall surrounded the whole Studios compound and there was only one way in, and besides a star could not enter in stealth. No, in saying Ravi Kumar was a star, a superstar, everything was said. A superstar did not commit murder, could not commit murder. The two ideas just did not belong in the same world. A superstar up in the Court of Sessions on a murder charge. You might as well bring a civil action against one of the gods.

So what was left? Nothing.

What had become of all his hopes? Where was the promise of stardom as a detective? What had happened to the fiery pledge he had given

Nilima, Nilima brightest female ornament of the starry heaven as Ravi Kumar was its brightest male ornament? That burning promise had died into nothingness. Utter nothingness.

Sitting at his familiar desk, staring at the door in front of him, he could feel that word echoing and mocking through the empty spaces of his head. Nothing, nothing, nothing. Until quite suddenly he realised that there was in that desolate terrain one tiny contradictory form.

In the rolling hills reverberating with that empty thunder there was one small upright figure. It was duty. Routine. The insignificant yet undeniable demand of his calling.

He had a report to make out.

He heaved his typewriter on to the desk, took paper and carbons from their drawer, inserted them, checked that the carbon was the right way round, poised the forefingers of either hand to type and began.

There were, at least, all the technical aspects of the case to deal with. The Police Surgeon's conclusions from the post-mortem, though they added nothing to what he had conjectured himself, the painstaking findings of the scene-of-crime technicians, for all that they did no more than confirm what had been perfectly evident at first sight, even the fact that there were only the fingerprints of the correct Lights Boy on the remains of the smashed Five-K, all had to be incorporated in their proper order.

He sat for a moment then and wondered whether he ought to move on to give an account of what had actually been his first step in the case, his interview with Seth Chagan Lal. Surely not. What the Seth had had to say had been nothing really to do with the matter.

Yet the thought of the Seth filled him with a sudden inexplicable disquiet. He pulled out a handkerchief to dab at his abruptly sweat-damp neck.

Well, at least what the Seth had said about Jagdish Rana was relevant. He battered furiously at the typewriter keys setting it out.

But at last the whole course of his investigation up to that minute was there on paper. And not a single conclusion had emerged. Not even the hint of some new lead.

There was only one thing to be done. Go through the whole pile of banged-at sheets and smudgy carbons and correct all the typing errors.

He took an old blue ballpoint from the little brass tray in front of him and set to work.

It was only when he had got right through to reading over what he had written about Sudhaker Wani and the stand-in's unimpressive features rose again in his mind's eye that a chance remark the fellow had made suddenly jutted up in the smooth run of the routine like a little jagged thorn.

It had been when the fellow was finally admitting the many ways in which he raised money towards his extraordinary aim of becoming a producer. He had mentioned gathering little scraps of gossip to sell from the stars' *chumchas*. And it was just this thought of *chumchas* that turned

his own mind now to considering Dhartiraj's leaderless crew. No doubt
Miss Officewalla had been right in telling him that for any one of them to
have murdered Dhartiraj would have been killing the goose that laid the
golden egg. But had there not been one name in that list she had brought
out with such impressive speed which was a little different from the others? Had there not been a young man attached to Dhartiraj, but not one
of his regular *chumchas*? A well-off young fellow the big star had met at
a charity cricket match up in Delhi and had brought back to Bombay?
Had brought back with promises of stardom in his turn? Promises which
had not been kept.

But how much had Dhartiraj really tried to fulfill those promises? Had
he not perhaps promised everything and done nothing? So was there not
then in his circle someone with a grievance against him, a strong grievance?

What was the young man's name?

He dived into his piles of notes. Sheets of paper rose into the air,
slipped to this side, slithered to that, fluttered down on to the floor. His
hands padded and clutched.

And then he had the list he wanted. And there at the end of it was the
name.

Kishore Sachdev.

Yes. That was it. That was him.

And, as he stared at the two words scrawled on the battered sheet of
paper, creased and crumpled from its long sojourn in his shirt pocket, the
whole idea of the youngster as Dhartiraj's murderer grew and flowered in
his mind.

He saw the whole situation. A young man in Delhi, well-off but bored
in the sterile atmosphere of the capital with its endless concern over
status, its intrigues, its small circle of people meeting and meeting each
other at parties and receptions, at clubs and restaurants. And then into
that never-ending round would have come the splendid rosy promise.

Stardom. A life of glamour. Of renown. Of recognition through all
the length and breadth of India. Of adulation.

It would seem like a dream happening in reality. There would be the
flight to Bombay sitting beside the friendly already established star and
the heart beating and thudding over every mile of the journey.

And then in Bombay over the months and the months there would
come the slow fizzing-away of hope. Disillusion. Then bitterness.

Yes, by God, that young man might very well long to kill Dhartiraj.
But had he been in the Studios at the time of the murder?

Even Assistant Inspector Jahdev had not yet been able to produce a
complete list of every person whatsoever who had been inside the high
walls of the compound when Dhartiraj had died. There were dozens of
coolies and Ghati women it would take days to trace and account for. But
it was so unlikely that any one of them would have killed Dhartiraj that
the effort was hardly worthwhile. A person like Kishore Sachdev, on the

other hand, would almost certainly be recorded as having been present if he had been there.

Once more the papers on the desk rose and fell.

And then there it was. The name on the list. "Kishore Sachdev, model".

Dhartiraj had not been accompanied to the Studios on the morning of his murder by many of his entourage. But this young man had gone along. Perhaps to make one more plea to the influential star for a small starring part of his own. He had been there.

Rising like a waterspout gradually mounting far out to sea, Ghote felt within him the increasing pressure of excitement. He was on to something. And it was something that no one else had in the least thought of. Not Miss Officewalla, for all her knowledge of the *filmi duniya,* though it had been from her that he had learned the key fact. Not Assistant Inspector Jahdev, for all his lists and inquiries. Not Seth Chagan Lal, for all his onward-rushing determination. Not Jagdish Rana, for all his efforts to get himself off the hook. Not Sudhaker Wani, for all the little pieces of knowledge he dug for round the Studios.

No, he himself, the star investigator, had picked out this tiny thread when all the others had gone blindly looking everywhere else.

Yes, Kishore Sachdev. He had picked him out. And where was he? Where was he now?

He reached for the telephone.

XI

It took more than a little telephoning, however, to locate Kishore Sachdev. But to Ghote it seemed now that every fresh obstacle was there only to be smashed down. The man who had been selected above all the officers of Crime Branch to investigate the death of a star was not going to be prevented from getting hold of his suspect by any difficulties. Eventually he tracked down one of the young man's *filmi* friends who was usefully talkative. Yes, Kishore had gone to the Nataraj Studios at Andheri. He had gone to ask the great Ravi Kumar for a side-hero's role in the huge new multi-star mystery movie *Grand Trunk Express men Hatya* which the superstar had just signed for, not only as leading player but also "to make his bow at the megaphone", since he had seen the original in the U.K. and could, with the help of a cameraman "to look after angles and things like that", make a shot-for-shot hit out of it.

So it was not until well into the afternoon, after another distinctly exhilarating encounter with the Press—"I am actively pursuing an important new lead"—that he found himself at last at the Nataraj Studios.

Somewhere in the back lot he emerged unexpectedly from a clutter of buildings very similar to those at Talkiestan into what he at once realised was a typical Indian village. All down the slope of a small hillock a beaten-earth village street had been created. On each side little mud-built houses looked out, their doorways none the less dark for the fact that they backed on to either the high wire fence of the Studios compound or on to the walls of a sound stage. Artfully arranged freshly-cut branches ingeniously blocked out the intrusive corners of other buildings and at one point a whole mock palm rose up especially to conceal—Ghote felt a jab of pleasure at realising this—the top of a telegraph pole.

At the foot of this immemorially typical street stood a camera on a tripod. It was backed by a large row of canvas chairs occupied by the Director of this film—Ghote had not been able to find out what it was called, but he had learned from Kishore Sachdev's friend that it was one of twenty-seven which the great Ravi Kumar was at present engaged upon —and other prominent actors, including at the far end none other than Nilima again, sitting beside an elderly lady who from her proud looks and considerable amplitude could only be her mother. At the star's feet a tailor knelt stitching furiously at sequins round the hem of her peasant skirt.

Nilima, he thought. Nilima here. Nilima here to witness the arrest. My pledge to her kept right before her eyes. And then . . . Then when the trial had been brought to a successful end amid the full dazzle of nationwide publicity, then Nilima's gratitude, Nilima's friendship. A new and totally different life. It could be. It would be. It must be.

He directed a probing, furious glare at the small crowd of people standing behind the chairs. Kishore Sachdev should be among them. But he did not know what the young aspirant to stardom looked like and abruptly too much was happening elsewhere for it to be possible for him to make inquiries.

Never mind. He could wait. What he had come here for was worth waiting to achieve.

What had caused the sudden flurry of activity had been the appearance at the top of the little hill of the great superstar himself, mounted in full glory upon a superbly bejewelled riding saddle fixed to the back of an ancient sports car. He was dressed in a richly embroidered kurta and his head was held high, the famous cutting profile, which Ghote had seen on hundreds of huge hoardings and on thousands of bright-coloured posters, looking down proudly on the scene below. Almost under his nose another cameraman crouched on the front of the car, held in place by two straining assistants. On either side, appallingly insecure, coolies clung on holding wide sheets of reflecting metal to catch and intensify the light of the sun.

"Silence," yelled the director.

"Silence, silence," a score of voices clamorously echoed.

And, when at last silence was achieved, "Camera," the director shouted.

A Clapper-Boy jumped forward and held his board in front of the camera's nose. It clicked resoundingly. "Action."

The old sports car slid forward down the hill, skilfully maneuvering between the house fronts on either side of the narrow earthen path. Ravi Kumar rode with marvellous dash, reins held with contemptuous looseness, whip crackingly flourished. Two-thirds of the way down the little hill he pulled up with a magnificent toss of his head. He turned a little in the saddle and haughtily regarded the dark house doorway on his left.

"Cut! Cut!"

A look of mean rage flashed on the famous profile.

"Raviji," the director called out. "You must not come so far down before you see the girl in the doorway of that hut. Otherwise when we shoot Nilima there the background would not be the same."

Ravi Kumar brought his whip thwacking down on the front of the car.

"Directorji," he shouted. "You have made me start too far forward. Am I having to teach you your business also?"

The Director hopped to his feet and hurried a little way up the hill.

"It is that damned setting coolie, Raviji," he explained. "He was altogether misplacing the mark. You. You there. Where are you?"

From the darkness of one of the doorways up against the high outside fence of the compound a bare-chested coolie emerged.

"Adjust the stone of Mr. Ravi Kumar," the director ordered in a voice of thunder.

The coolie trotted up the hill to a joint where a large white stone appeared to have been carelessly left by the roadside. He turned.

"But— But—" he could be heard to mutter.

The director straightened himself to his full height. Rage contorted his every feature.

"Are you daring to tell that that stone was put where I ordered?" he yelled. "If Mr. Ravi Kumar is saying it is in the wrong place it is in the wrong place. Move it. Move it."

"But—"

"Move it or never enter these Studios again."

The coolie stooped and picked up the stone. He set off step by step down the hill, pausing at each one to see whether it was the spot where he ought to lay down his burden.

"More. More. Idiot. Idiot."

The director actually jumped from the ground in the wildness of his rage.

At last the coolie put the stone down.

"No, you fool," the director yelled yet more loudly. "Not so far. Back. Back. Up. Up."

The coolie picked the stone up and climbed back up the hill.

"There."

Ravi Kumar himself had pronounced the word.

"There, there," the director yelled. "There, where I was all along saying."

He walked backwards till he reached his chair and flopped into it in utter exhaustion.

Then, with much shouting of directions and counter-directions, the old car was carefully reversed up the little hill till once more it was at the crest.

"Silence," called the director with what was left of his voice.

"Silence!" Ravi Kumar shouted from the hill-top.

"Silence," respectfully echoed voice after voice.

And the shooting of the scene began again. The old car started to glide forward. Ravi Kumar sat up straighter in his saddle. He flourished his whip.

But hardly had the car advanced ten yards when it became clearly evident to everybody that the marker stone at which Ravi Kumar was to begin to bring his horse to a rearing halt was in the wrong position altogether for him to look into the correct house doorway at the end of the maneuver.

"Cut! Cut! Cut! Cut!" the director yelled, as if by sheer repetition he could somehow obliterate the plain fact that the stone was ridiculously too far down.

But his yelling did nothing to avert the superstar's wrath.

He jumped down from his high saddle in one lithe bound. He strode down the rest of the hill towards the director in ominous silence. And then he exploded.

"Please be so good as to tell me how it is possible for an artiste to perform in conditions like these. How can he? Where is his art? How can he build up a truly great performance when all the time people are doing things like this to him?"

The director very slowly rose from his chair, crouching a little as if to keep under a line of fire.

Ravi Kumar planted himself right in front of him.

"You are doing it so as to make my role a failure!" he shouted. "They are bribing you because they cannot stand somebody having six-seven hit-films one after the other. But I am not going to let it happen. I am not staying here to be insulted. I am going. Yes, going. Now. Now. Now."

But he did not go. He stayed long enough to repeat all he had said previously and to add one or two more observations. And only then did he turn on his heel and march away.

From behind the row of chairs a whole flock of men hurried forward, chattering like so many sparrows, and set off in the superstar's wake. The *chumchas*, Ghote thought, pleased with his quickness. Yes, they would be following to add their agreement to everything the enraged Ravi Kumar said, to suggest what they could to make his fury burn yet higher, even to offer themselves as targets for its side blows. He saw it all.

And then he saw that a well-dressed young man was following the chattering flock at a slight distance, looking anxiously towards the striding superstar almost as if he was a foreign-exchange tout waiting a favourable opportunity to descend on some rich tourist.

Kishore Sachdev.

It could be no one else.

Swiftly he set out after him. He felt, as he rapidly closed on him, the throb of the hunter's excitement. The unknown they had all left out of account, the one person who had a good motive for wanting to kill the all-popular Dhartiraj. And he had him under his claws.

"Kishore Sachdev."

The young man wheeled round, the very picture of guilt. Almost there and then he put him under arrest.

But no. Question him. Get the facts out of him. Get, if it looked at all possible, a confession. And then the path of glory could begin. The making certain of the case, the trial, the final sentence, the acclaim.

He looked closely at the young hopeful whom Dhartiraj had brought from Delhi with such empty promises. He was, he saw, at most twenty-two or twenty-three. Tall, handsome enough, with good strong features and a well-fleshed face. Yes, the basic equipment for stardom, to judge by what the accepted stars looked like. And the eyes. They were large and a limpid brown, reflecting at this moment, clearly as the still surface of a jungle pool, all that the fellow must be feeling, bewilderment, fear and—surely—guilt.

He watched his every least reaction like a crouching panther.

"Mr. Sachdev, my name is Ghote, Inspector Ghote, C.I.D. I am in charge of the investigation into the death of Dhartiraj."

Would there appear something new in those large pool-reflecting eyes? The dull acknowledgement that a daring plan had not after all been successful?

He had to record that nothing of this sort appeared. Perhaps the boy was a tougher customer than he looked. But one good long hard session across a desk, and he would be finished. He had the marks of soft living all over him, the just thickening roll of flesh at the neck, the beautifully kept fingernails, the well-oiled hair, elaborately cut. Yes, he would snap all right. Snap at a touch.

"I have a number of questions to put to you, Mr. Sachdev, in connection with my inquiries."

The boy licked at his thick sensuous top lip.

"To me? To me, Inspector? But . . ."

"Yes, to you, Mr. Sachdev. And why not? Can you tell me that: why not to you?"

Kishore Sachdev swallowed.

He could trace it as if in a slow-motion film, the nervous jerk of the Adam's apple.

By God, he would get him here and now, just where they were. No need of the trappings of an official interrogation.

He turned and gave the hastiest of glances back to the row of chairs at the foot of the little hill. Nilima, was she there still? She was. But she was listening, head gracefully bent, to something her mother was saying. Laying down the law, by the look of it. What could he do to attract her attention?

He could think of nothing.

He turned back to Kishore Sachdev. To be confronted by the calm and easy look of the well-off, of the people for whom the police were respectful protectors, if not simple servants.

Inwardly he cursed himself. If only he had struck while he had the running . . .

But it was no use wishing. That moment of truth, with Nilima first among the audience, was not to happen now.

"Mr. Sachdev," he said, making his voice as stiff and unyielding as he could, "I must ask you to accompany me to Headquarters. I have reason to believe you can be of material assistance in my investigation."

The boy looked back at him calmly. He guessed that he was weighing up whether he should pretend to assert himself with all the arrogance of the rich or to be falling in with this little policeman's whim. He would, damn him, be coolly working out which of the two attitudes was most likely to help him conceal what he had to hide.

Well, let him choose whichever he cared to. The realities of an interrogation would soon produce an altogether different story.

"Inspector, I will happily answer your every question. But I have important business here at Nataraj, so could we not go somewhere quiet here?"

What was this? What was he trying? Was it no more than an attempt to make things easier for himself by choosing a favourable setting? Or was there some other reason?

In any case there was no question of agree—

He checked himself.

No, better to let the young upstart think he had gained something. Then when the chips came down he would be all the more disconcerted.

"Very well."

"Let me think . . . Ah yes, there is Mr. Kumar's dressing-room. I was with him there before the shooting. He will certainly not come back to the Studios for a little now, so we can go there."

"Very well," Ghote said again.

He felt nevertheless quite put out. The casual ease with which the young would-be star proposed to make use of the dressing-room of such a distantly high figure as Ravi Kumar made him feel acutely the difference there was between the two of them. He himself, he knew well, would never have dreamed even of asking permission. Yet this well-off youngster had just assumed the right.

He followed him through the confusion of huts and buildings that made up the studios.

Yet Ravi Kumar's dressing-room proved to be not at all what he had expected. It was small. It was very untidy. It did not even smell very pleasant, even though a bottle of Yardley's after-shave stood with its cap off on the cluttered dressing-table.

The dressing-table, with its square mirror surrounded by bare light bulbs, was altogether a terrible mess. Ashtrays full of butts lay here and there on its glass surface mingled with half-empty teacups and squashed packets of cigarettes, Dunhill and other expensive foreign brands. A three-quarter melted bowl of ice had had some chewed *paan* spat into it.

On the floor there were even two or three gnawed chicken bones among the empty and half-empty Limca, Coca-Cola and Mangola bottles and the full ashtrays. And plainly no one had bothered themselves to heed the painted notice on the bathroom door saying "Please Try to Leave Clean." That strong sour odour was all too apparent.

There were, however, plenty of chairs in the confined space. Ghote took one and indicated another to Kishore Sachdev. And he found, as he sat down, that something—it was most probably the atmosphere of the sordid little dressing-room—had taken all the fizz out of him. He addressed the young man opposite soberly.

"Please be so good as to tell me where you were yesterday morning between the hours of nine and eleven ack emma."

"But, Inspector, you must know. I was at Talkiestan Studios. I went there with Dhartiraj. There were times when he did not want a whole crowd with him, and then often he would ask me only to come."

A little surprised by this frankness, Ghote went on resolutely.

"He asked you only. Why was that, Mr. Sachdev? Were you very close to him?"

The large limpid eyes clouded, as if the boy found the question particularly difficult to answer.

"Well?" Ghote prompted carefully.

"Inspector, I think it was because I was different. I was not one of his *chumchas*. From me he could expect true answers."

He had been about to press in with another question. But some faint extra look of anxiety had come into the boy's eyes with those last words, and he restrained himself.

"Well, no, that is not exactly correct," the boy said.

Ghote waited.

He was not sure where these hesitant answers were leading—they were certainly not going in the direction he had expected when he had first told the young man he wanted to question him—but it was clear that there was something here bursting to be said. And that was worth any amount of patient waiting for.

The silence grew.

Then, with a look of overwhelming trouble welling up into his telltale eyes, Kishore Sachdev came out with it.

"No. When you got down to it in the end, I was altogether no better than any of them. I also wanted what Dhartiraj had in his gift, and in my way I did as much as any of those *chumchas* who were hoping to be given a little flat or a car or a good dinner at the Taj even. I also told him lies.

I also said what I thought he would want to hear, and I did not mind if there was nothing of the truth in it at all."

Ghote stamped hard on the twinges of pity that had grown responsively in him. The scent of the hunt was beginning to rise from the ground ahead again and he was not going to let it go.

"You lied to Dhartiraj!" he barked out. "You cheated him. And that must mean that you hated him. You hated him, isn't it? You hated Dhartiraj."

He glared hard at those pool-eyes. In them now he was going to see an admission. An admission that, yes, the boy had hated the dead star. And after that would come the beginnings of a confession. A confession to seizing on that suddenly appearing opportunity, to snatching the curve-bladed dagger, to running up the ladder to the catwalk, to cutting the ropes of the Five-K and watching it fall.

And, just as he had counted on, it came, the look in those eyes that said clearly as any jabber of gabbled-out words, "Yes, I hated Dhartiraj".

"I wanted to hide it," the boy whispered. "I feared that I would be asked, and I wanted to hide it. But you have got it out of me, Inspector. Oh, God, so soon."

Ghote felt it singing and singing inside him. The triumph. Yes, he had got it out of this boy quickly. But then he was the man to do that. He had been chosen for just this task. This was his case and he had cracked it, and soon there would come the courtroom, the listening judge, the gowned pleaders and the star prosecution witness. And after that . . . After that the flash and dazzle of the photographers' light-bulbs and then the long newspaper articles. "How I Brought A Star's Killer to Justice, by Ganesh V. Ghote."

XII

Ghote sat straighter on his chair amid the clutter and mess of Ravi Kumar's little sour-smelling dressing-room. Kishore Sachdev, opposite him, was sitting heavily slumped, his well-fleshed shoulders sagging, his pool-limpid eyes clearly signalling the turmoil within.

Ghote spoke decisively.

"Just tell me everything."

His notepad was ready. His ballpoint poised.

Again it was the wretched pink thing he had bought in a hurry one day from a pavement vendor's array. But no matter. Soon it would be nothing but proper fountain-pens carefully chosen in proper pen marts.

"Come, tell."

Kishore Sachdev raised his head a little. His eyes shone with a pure desire to unburden himself.

"Inspector," he said, almost as if he was only half-conscious of the words beginning to pour out, "I met Dhartiraj first when I was in hotel management line in Delhi. You know my parents are rich. My father wanted me to follow him in contracting business. But I did not at all like that idea. So he persuaded me to go into hotel line. And I met Dhartiraj when he stayed in the hotel where I was. He allowed me to take him to dinner, and after I saw him again and again. And I told him that it had always been my ambition to be a star."

He paused. In his limpid eyes Ghote saw all that was conjured up for him by the word "star". An existence in another world, free from all the dust and trappings of that everyday world in which children, however pampered, are brought up and go to school and meet with disappointments, and where young men, however much money there is at their disposal, encounter the snags and difficulties of ordinary living, the constant failure to achieve what the eager mind has foreseen. That was what "star" would have meant: a wonderful world of nothing ever being less than what it might have been.

For a moment his attention focussed on the untidy sour-smelling mess that surrounded them. The spat-out *paan* had coloured all the melted water in the ice-bowl now, a pale rusty red. And this was the actual world of the biggest star of them all. But that was a thought to be pushed aside.

"Go on," he said, curbing his urgency with difficulty.

Kishore Sachdev began again, in the same dreamy voice as if he was hauling up buckets of remembrance from a deep well.

"When—when I told him I wanted and wanted to be a star, he at once invited me to come to Bombay. He was very warm. We shall be brothers, he said. So I told my father that I wanted to go and there was a terrible-terrible row, and my mother was in tears also. But I left. And in Bombay at first it seemed to be as it had been in Delhi. Always there was a role for me just around the corner. Always Dhartiraj was repeating I was altogether handsome enough for a star, that my voice was very good, that I dressed very well. But then the right chance was never quite coming. Each time there was something wrong. And in the meanwhile I am entertaining that man. I am giving him daily a thousand salutes. I am taking him to the Taj, to Sheraton also. Wining and dining, booted and suited. The only thing I was not doing was getting girls for him. And it was a long, long time."

The flow hesitated and stopped. The boy sat brooding on some inner vision.

"How long altogether?" Ghote prompted.

"How long?"

"Yes, how long since you came from Delhi?"

"Oh, that has been more than two years."

"And what have you been doing all this time?" Ghote asked, stung into curiosity. "Nothing but entertain Dhartiraj?"

"No. No, I did other things."

He paused, still inward turned. Ghote was on the point of giving him a push when he began again.

"No, I am taking some modelling work. They also say I am very good and will one day become a star."

"But you did not get any acting roles at all?"

"Well, you must understand that, if your ultimate aim is to reach the grade—top one, if God is willing—then it is not right to take any small parts. Then you would become an actor only. But one side-hero's part I got, the villain's brother. It was not very long ago. The film has not been shown yet."

"I must go and see it when it comes out," Ghote said.

And underneath he thought, "What a hit it will be, with a murderer playing in it".

"There is nothing to see," Kishore Sachdev said, with a flicker of fire. "In the cutting-room every foot of that part was taken out. I had thought that my break had come, that for once a star was not using an actor beside him that he knew would not make an outstanding impression, that for once a star was not using his nephew or his son."

The pool-eyes were burning now.

"But, Inspector, he sat there in the cutting-room telling the director what to take out. He had seen the rushes, Inspector. I also. And I was too good. That was a rich field to project my histrionics. And he would not have."

"But I thought he was always very friendly," Ghote objected.

"But he was a star, Inspector. He would not have another role eating into his own. And he was friendly all the time, too. He said it would spoil the film having two villains. So my part must go and another song be put in instead."

The boy sank into silence, a silence seething and bubbling underneath with pricking resentment.

"You hated him for that," Ghote stated, "and so you killed him."

"No."

For a few instants Ghote truly believed that he had misheard the single syllable the boy had spoken. He was even about to prompt him to expand on the one word of his confession to the murder when the realisation of what had actually been said came home to him.

"No?" he said. "No? You are denying that you killed him? Come, what is the use? Already you have told me so much, make a clean breast of it all now. It is the only way."

"But I did not kill him," the boy repeated.

Then Ghote felt the anger surge up in him, a great black monster power-driven through the sea, on the point of breaking through and destroying.

He hurled himself to his feet, thrust his face down at the handsome boy's.

"I know very well you killed Dhartiraj!" he shouted, his face right up close to those well-fed features. "I know it. You need not think you are going to get away with this. I tell you, I know too much. Now, answer up. You killed him?"

As near as he was to the boy's big brown eyes he could see the least flicker in them. And it was plain that his shouting was having its effect. The boy was frightened, scared out of his wits.

He waited for the confession.

The boy's tongue, thick and pink, came out and licked quickly at his lips.

"Inspector, I did not. I did not."

"You dare lie to me? I will have you stripped to nothing for this. To nothing. Do you understand? Do not go thinking anybody or anything will protect you. Now, out with it. You saw that Five-K hanging, you went up there, you cut the ropes. Out with it."

"No, no. I tell you a thousand times 'no'. I did not do it. I hated that man, yes. I came to hate him, and I hated him all the more because he was my only hope. But I did not kill him. I did not."

The rage bucked and jumped in Ghote's mind, strong, heavy, thwacking.

"You will not get away with this, young Sachdev. I am going to make it hell for you, double hell. You think you can lie and wriggle your way out of this. But let me tell you one thing. Not all the money you can bring, not all the lawyers, will help you one little bit. This is the murder of a star. A star. The whole damn world is against you and I am at the head of it."

He saw the face, still within inches of his own, cringe and crumple.

"Now!" he shouted, "the details. Each and every detail, and quick about it."

"No. No. No. No."

The boy was shouting back now, shouting back desperately. Flicks of spittle came up and spattered against his own face, frothy and faintly cool.

And in those large limpid truth-telling eyes he saw that what he was shouting was so.

The boy had not murdered Dhartiraj. He knew that now at last, with as much certainty as if a hundred witnesses had lined up in front of him and each had repeated that they had seen the boy ten miles from the scene.

He sat back in his chair and let a long sigh whistle out.

"Were you near Dhartiraj at Talkiestan?" he asked, careless almost of the answer.

"Inspector, I was with him up until he sent that stand-in fellow to get more jewels on that turban. Then, when he said he would go through his dialogues, I left."

"You did not hear his dialogues for him?"

A little spark of hope had come back to him, flickering delusively.

Surely it would be the duty of whoever was with a star to do that for him? Was there something here after all out of character?

"No, Inspector. That I did not do. His *chumchas*, yes. They knew that going over dialogues was one of the things that they had to do because he did not read well."

"But if he did not read?" Ghote said, the flickering light still dancing and faltering in the darkness ahead.

"Inspector, it was not that he could not read. It was just that he did not like. When he nearly knew his dialogues he could follow them without trouble."

A sudden memory rose inconsequently in Ghote's head, empty and purposeless as it was now rapidly becoming. Another star who had had difficulty over reading something. Nilima. She had asked him to read one of his lists aloud to her. Disillusionment swept across him.

"Nilima also?" he asked before he could stop himself. "She cannot read?"

The boy looked up at him, a little surprised.

"Yes," he said, "Nilima can read. With her it is that she refuses always to wear specs."

Ghote thrust away this new lost illusion. He ought to be pursuing that flickering hope of there being something not quite explained in what the boy had told him.

"But all the same," he said, "it might have been what you would be asked to do, to hear Dhartiraj's dialogues for that scene upon the *gaddi*?"

"No," the boy answered. "I never did that. I was his friend."

A sudden look of bitter self-hatred sprang into those limpid eyes.

"No, that is not so. It was that he believed I was his friend."

With that, the last flicker of hope died. Wearily, Ghote completed his questions for form's sake.

"You left him then when he began to learn his dialogues. Where did you go?"

"Inspector, to get a cup of tea. But . . ."

"What but?"

"But when I got outside I knew that I did not want tea. I had wanted only not to be with Dhartiraj."

"So what did you do?"

"I went and sat in his car, Inspector. It was parked well in the shade. I could be alone there."

"Yes, I see. And did anyone come up and speak with you while you were there?"

"No. That car is air-conditioned. I left the glasses up, and they are of blue glass. No one would see."

He looked at Ghote again.

"Inspector, I realise I am not able to give you any alibi for myself. But, Inspector, what I have said is so. I did not kill Dhartiraj."

No, Ghote thought soberly, you did not. Certainly, you could have done. You could even have slipped out of that car, suddenly unable to resist the temptation that had come to you when you had realised how easily that Five-K could be cut down. You could have run back to Sound Stage #2 and climbed up to that catwalk. You could have done. But you did not.

He pushed himself to his feet.

"All right," he said, "that is all. I hope I have not prevented you from seeing Mr. Ravi Kumar."

The boy raised his shirtsleeve and looked at the thin gold watch on his wrist in an almost casual manner, as if those few normal words of inquiry had at once lifted him back into his ordinary life.

"Well, if I have missed him now," he said, "I can see him tonight. There is a big birthday party for Billy Banker at the Taj. He will be there. Everybody will be there."

He sighed.

Ghote sat on when he had left, thinking almost idly about the interview. Really the way the boy had failed to produce any alibi was another point in his favour. If he had been doing what he said he had, sitting behind the blued-glass windows of Dhartiraj's big car, then no one would have seen him. He should not have been able to produce an alibi. Indeed, the very fact of not having an alibi was yet another bonus point for him. When a murder was committed it was not really very likely that everyone who might have some reason for wishing the victim dead should have an incontrovertible alibi. And of the three people he had interviewed as likely suspects only Kishore Sachdev had simply said that he was on his own at the time Dhartiraj had died. Both Sudhaker Wani and the failing Jagdish Rana had tried in their different ways to wriggle themselves out of such a situation.

With the stand-in that was perhaps to be expected. After all, he lived on the edge of the law scraping together the money he needed to start off as a producer. But Jagdish Rana was different. He should not have tried to pretend there were people who had seen him when there had not been.

He jumped up and began to pace up and down the little room, steering clear only by instinct of the ashtrays, the gnawed bones and the bottles on the floor.

Jagdish Rana had gone further than trying to make up for himself an alibi out of nothing. He had gone out of his way to suggest that Sudhaker Wani was the murderer. Now, why? Why?

In his excitement over discovering Kishore Sachdev, this had not occurred to him. But it had been an act of the basest kind. The fellow had deliberately suggested that Sudhaker Wani, who although he was no innocent was not in fact guilty of murder, was someone who ought to be investigated, someone who ought to be arrested, tried, even in the end found guilty and hanged.

It was foul. Despicable.

The man who had done a thing like that might well indeed have done it only to avoid finding himself on trial and convicted. Convicted of murdering Dhartiraj, not so as to open the way for himself back to stardom through getting the part of Maqbet in *Khoon Ka Gaddi*, but for some other reason. Yes, some as yet undiscovered reason which he had foolishly risked having brought to light when he had uttered that, as it had turned out totally ridiculous, boast about Seth Chagan Lal.

He swung on his heel and went out. His vehicle was where he had left it, the driver lying dozing across the back seat with both doors open to give himself air. He woke him with a tap on the thigh.

"Home now," he said. "But come for me again at eight pip emma. I shall be going to the Taj Hotel. To a party. A *filmi* party, where everybody will be coming."

XIII

As the car zipped through the night along the sweep of Marine Drive, the coolness of the air from the sea a sheer treat, Ghote found that he was possessed by nothing of that almost insane excitement which had gripped him when he had been on his way to wrench Kishore Sachdev from among the great Ravi Kumar's *chumchas*. Then, convinced that he was on the very point of seizing the murderer of Dhartiraj, he had felt himself a king. Now, the different disillusionments of that interview well in his mind, he was no more than a man with a discrepancy to clear up.

There was something unsatisfactory in what that failed star Jagdish Rana had told him. It was worth getting hold of him, even if it meant approaching him in the middle of a party at the Taj Hotel, to clear the matter up as rapidly as possible.

Yet it was conceivable that, pressed over what exactly he had been doing at the time of the murder, the bitter star would reveal that he had indeed tried to direct the hunt on to the dubious Sudhaker Wani because he saw it getting too close to himself. It was conceivable.

When the car came to a halt under the deep portico of the hotel's high tower Ghote told the driver to park within sight over by the Gateway of India in case there might be someone to take to Headquarters later on.

In the white marbled lobby with its fountains and cool magnificence he spotted at once the person he hoped he would see, the hotel security officer. He went over and had a quiet word.

Yes, Billy Banker's birthday party was being held tonight, and, yes, if Inspector Ghote wanted one of the guests the best thing would be to mingle with the crowd, appear at his man's side and take him off without fuss.

The security officer led him up to the big reception suite where the party had just begun. He left him at the door.

"Good luck, Inspector."

"Thank you."

"And no disturbance?"

"None at all."

Plainly the party was in its earliest stages. There were few enough people in the big room to be able to see at a glance that Jagdish Rana was not among them. At the far end under a cluster of bright paper lanterns the guest of honour, Billy Banker, looking just as he did in photographs and on posters, a great teeth-splattered grin all over his face, stood vigorously embracing whoever came up to him. Two or three garlands were round his neck and on his head there was a little green papier-maché bowler hat. Happily there were enough guests between him and the doors—Was that fellow the play-back singer? And those two fat men with even fatter wives in gaudy saris with all that jewellery were undoubtedly nouveau-riche film distributors—for there to be no question of going across himself to offer congratulations.

A bearer came up with an enormous tray of glasses of whisky and gin lined up in neat ranks and presided over by tall jugs of water and soda. Ghote waved him away. But he felt a flush of pure relief at having been so quickly marked down as a pukka guest. At home he had had grave fears about the smartness of his best shirt and trousers.

But he would have been even more pleased had Jagdish Rana been there already.

He told himself that his absence at this early stage of the affair by no means meant that he was not going to come. He would have to come. For any star on the edge of toppling into being only a figure from the past, to be seen at a party where "everybody" was expected was an absolute necessity.

As a precaution, however, against his man arriving and running off at the sight of this policeman, he moved cautiously deeper into the huge room, already noisy with a score of different conversations under its glittering chandeliers. It was important to time his descent on the failed star just right. Suddenly the fellow would find him at his elbow, *Mr. Rana, I would like a word, if you please.* Quiet, but firm. He would see then that there was no hope of getting away.

Around him the party was minute by minute gathering impetus. He glanced back at the doors. No sign of his man.

"Well, bhai, what sort of a stunt movie are you taking now?"

"No, no, it is not at all a stunt movie. Stunts it will be having, yes. But it is a folklore. Strictly a folklore."

The voices were loud in his ear.

"Folklore, ha, ha. A flop picture before there is one reel in the cans."

"No, no. What you are just signing for will be the flop picture. A Muslim social. Never has a Muslim social really clicked at box office."

"But it is not at all a Muslim social. It is a Hindu picture, a devotional. You have heard altogether wrong story. I tell you, bhai, they will be going and kissing the screen when it is shown. No tout will dare sell tickets even though there are queues miles long. They will be garlanding the posters for this, garlanding the posters."

He moved away. With all that back-slapping and shouting he would never spot Jagdish Rana if he came slipping quietly in.

The large alcoves opening off the main room were as yet mostly unoccupied. He went and stationed himself at the edge of one of them where he could get a good view of the doors and settled down to make a thorough study of the whole party. The more familiar he got with what was going on, the easier it would be when the time came to slip through the chattering gesticulating crowd and come up behind his man, quietly and efficiently as any of the bearers deftly sliding through even the most packed areas, their big trays of drinks held miraculously steady, the equally large trays of assorted snacks as adroitly balanced and twirled.

But one or two of those snacks would be nice now.

At home, a prey to anxiety over shirt and trousers, he had had little heart to eat the quick meal his Protima had prepared.

He must not forget, too, that he had promised her a full account of the function. But how was he to know which of the guests were stars? Those three gorgeously dressed women who had just arrived, with their heavy make-up and clustering jewellery, surely they must be stars? But which?

Through a sudden gap caused by a photographer clearing himself a space he caught a glimpse of the face of one of them. Yes, surely she had been the vamp in the last film he had seen. Certainly the cleavage of her Western-style blouse and that pair of clinging gold-threaded pants, was very like what the vamp had been wearing there.

Well, that would have to do for Protima.

But, if those stars had come, had Jagdish Rana as well? Had he missed him?

And if he was here it was unlikely that he would have collected the sort of admiring circle the three newcomers had gathered. Really, some of the men there were making utter fools of themselves, smiling and boasting and elbowing to get into the photographer's shots.

A bearer came by with his tray fully loaded with snacks. Their smell was deliciously mouth-watering. Oh, to take up one of those little plastic sticks, dip the morsel on the end of it into some of that spicy-looking sauce and put it into his mouth. But the bearer did not seem to notice him and he lacked the courage to call.

He pushed himself up on tiptoe to get a better look at the doors over the heads of the now quite dense crowd. A man was just entering whose appearance seemed familiar.

With a little sinking of awe, he realised that it was no less a person than the Chief Secretary of the State Government, the civil servant who had ultimate control over himself. Such guests came to honour a star. And he was here under false pretences.

But Jagdish Rana was not here. Was he not going to come after all?

And if he did not, how difficult would it be now to get hold of him? Had he already realised that, since no announcement had been made about Sudhaker Wani being arrested charged with the murder of Dhartiraj, his ruse must be rebounding on his own head? Had he decided to cut and run?

Ah, there was Miss Officewalla coming in, dressed in another light green sari though one lacking the business-like pattern of squares she had been wearing the day before. He watched her stop just inside the doors and give the whole scene a slow careful survey, much as he had done himself. She was, in fact, employing just the technique he had been taught at Detective Training School. *Start from your immediate left and proceed methodically in a clockwise direction.* Yes, there was a professional all right.

And how long would it be before he had to beg her aid again in finding Jagdish Rana? And this time would he be as easy to locate as he had been out at that absurd bungalow at Juhu?

He watched Miss Officewalla advance into the crowded room, greeted every now and again with shrieking claims of deference, that plainly hid a good deal of real awe. They must come, he realised, from her colleagues, or rivals, acknowledging the star of their own world. One or two of the men he had picked out earlier because of their trick, when a bearer with drinks came up, of taking one glass and swiftly tipping the contents of another into it. Miss Officewalla, he saw without surprise, was greeted knowingly by a bearer with a tray of fruit juices, and took tomato.

Well, he would let her ply her trade for a good while yet before going to ask her for help. Say a full half hour.

He looked at his watch. Already a quarter past nine. Time had been flying.

All right then, give Jagdish Rana till ten exactly. And if he had not appeared by then, go and humbly consult the gossip queen.

People were arriving in swarms now. Men who could only be stars from their air of total assurance, though he could not even guess at their names, were greeting each other with loudly exuberant shouts, giving each other fancy left-handed handshakes, embracing with much slapping of backs. There would be no opportunity now of standing at the doors after coming in. People like those two Westerners, the one with the shirt open down to the navel and the other wearing that big straw hat—really was that correct at a party?—would push anybody trying to stand there right out of the way.

It was certainly altogether a very Western occasion. Now that he thought about it, he had hardly heard a single word not in English from any of the people going past or beginning now to fill the alcove behind him. Above the clamour there had risen time and again loud cries of "Darling" and "Darling, how lovely". And there had been public kissing.

A bearer with a freshly loaded tray of snacks, wafting a tongue-tingling

odour, was working his way round on a path that would bring him within
striking distance at any minute.

He salivated.

And then a sudden great movement through almost the whole of the
loudly talking, self-intent gathering caught him up. It was like a sharp
gust of wind sending uniform ripples all over the wide surface of a huge
lake. Heads turned, voices dropped, there was even something like a
single concerted gasp. He followed the direction of it all, to the wide
double entrance doors.

There, in a space which had in a few instants somehow cleared itself,
stood the two great ones of the *filmi duniya*. Ravi Kumar had arrived
escorting Nilima.

Photographers' bulbs broke and flashed. Here and there some of the
more naive of the gossip writers actually took notepads from their pockets
and began to scribble. As one, the whole assembly turned to each other
and spoke.

He has come with her.

She has come with him.

They have come together.

What exactly was said it was impossible to hear. But the meaning was
clear enough. Two giant astral bodies had entered temporarily the same
orbit. What it portended, if anything, none could tell. But that it mysteri-
ously affected every single soul in this fragile world was plain beyond
doubt. And had to be acknowledged in mere exchanged statements of the
facts.

He has come with her.

She has come with him.

They have come with each other.

It was a tribute to the superstars from all the galaxies that swung and
glittered beneath them.

Ghote, like all the others round him, looked and looked for the minute
or two—it can hardly have been longer—that there was a space round the
newcomers. Ravi Kumar was standing, eyes directed to some far, far
point, carriage proud, profile clear-cut and poised to conquer. He wore a
sportingly cut orangey-buff suit seemingly designed to set off a shirt of the
most dazzling peacock blue, in itself created to be no more than a background for the most vibrant psychedelic tie Ghote had ever seen. Only
vaguely did the superstar seem aware of Nilima beside him, although her
arm was lightly linked in his.

But, to Ghote, Nilima was the sight to feast on. If she had seemed a
figure of goddess-like opulence when she had summoned him to her at
Talkiestan Studios, she now looked a dozen times more marvellously
glamorous. He felt overwhelmingly that the combined imaginations of
every ever-dreaming man in all Bombay could not have conjured up the
vision that she was.

She wore a sari. A green sari. But it put such a green silk affair as

Miss Officewalla had on into the category of a garment stitched out of wilting leaves. Gold threaded it and underlay it and stiffened it and shimmered it. And its own green was so dark and lustrous that it would not have needed even a particle of gold to enhance its beauty and its glow. And Nilima wore it, so it seemed to him standing there at this distance, mouth falling open in mere admiration, as no sari had ever before been worn in the whole history of the world. It clung to her. It embraced her. It hid and revealed her. It promised and it forbade. It was everything. It was all that could possibly be needed.

But there was jewellery also.

Gold lay thick in her hair. Gold cascaded from her ears. Gold lay on her neck, thick, rich and softly giving out its unchangeable message. Gold for a golden one. The earth's most precious ore fit tribute to the earth's most precious person. A goddess. More than a goddess.

The thoughts moved in slow procession through his head in the brief period before renewed movement in the dense crowd blotted out his view. And to think that he himself had talked to. that goddess. That it had been only yesterday that she had sat within a yard of him. His fingers had nearly touched hers. He had felt that tiny heat coming from the tips of hers to the tips of his.

And into that world she daily inhabited he might himself gain entrance. He had only to solve this case. That was all. Simply to find the murderer of Dhartiraj, her friend and co-artiste, and he would be welcome in the circle in which she moved. She had asked him to do that, for her. And the means to do it was within his grasp. Only let Jagdish Rana come here tonight, only let him not have fled but be at this moment on his way to flaunt himself at this party and he would have him.

The bearer with the tray of succulent, lightly steaming snacks came and stood right in front of him. A dumpy woman guest was inquiring from him with sharp anxiety whether the contents of the little crispness-covered rolls were truly vegetarian.

"Yes, madam."

"You are sure?"

"Yes, madam."

She took one. Popped it into her little round mouth. Swallowed it in one soft gulp and took another. He could easily help himself now.

But the little brown and yellow rolls on their gay plastic cocktail sticks were as ashes to him. Hunger had left him. Consuming ambition blotted out everything.

Jagdish Rana where was he?

XIV

Suddenly panic beat up in Ghote's heart. What if the failed star had come creeping into the party while all eyes had been on Nilima and Ravi Kumar? While he himself had been gazing, lost, at the golden star? The fellow could be somewhere in the big room at this moment. The crowd was certainly so thick that he could be going about unobserved. He could perhaps stay here as long as necessary to show himself as being defiantly in circulation and then quickly leave.

But, no. Jagdish Rana would not enter in the wake of the truly great ones. He would not permit himself to suffer that eclipse. No, had he been on the point of coming in, he would have quietly gone back downstairs and have waited a little, lurked perhaps in those luxurious lavatories down there with their heavy appointments and almost palace-like air. He would wait until the great wave had rippled into quiet. And then he would make his entrance.

And that might, then, be quite soon now.

Oh why were there so many chattering, laughing, gesticulating people between him and the doors?

He put one foot on the top of the substantial skirting board beside him and by hooking his fingers behind a pillar up against the wall he managed to heave himself some nine whole inches higher.

It was uncomfortable. His ankle was appallingly cricked. But he did not have to stay there long.

There was a good clear space in front of the doors now with the party plainly at its peak and bearers beginning to load immense supper dishes on two huge tables nearby—one "Vegetarian," as a bold black-and-white notice proclaimed, the other "Non-Veg"—and into this space there stepped, quite unexpectedly for all the length of time that he had waited for him, the failed star.

The fellow had chosen his moment well. His entrance could not have failed to catch some eyes, even though people were beginning to move away from the doors down towards the huge platters of pilaus and lobster curries, of mounded kebabs and dark swimmy vindaloos. But the eyes that turned to see who had entered so late flicked away again almost as swiftly as if some leprous beggar had wheeled or poled his way into the big chandelier-glittering room.

Within two minutes of that dramatic and well-contrived entry no one at all was within hailing distance of the newcomer.

Ghote saw him square up to the rebuff. He could imagine from the sudden sharp tilt of the head the look of resolution that must have come on to his face and how it would for a minute or so pull taut the pouches that sagged under the eyes. He felt a dart of admiration for the fellow's courage. He himself, he suspected, would have turned tail and crept out meeting with such hostility. But Jagdish Rana was braving them all, thrusting into the crowd now determined to be talked to.

But the fellow was nevertheless his prey. The man he intended to see in the dock on a charge of murder. The murder of a star.

He moved off into the crowd himself. No point in leaving the fellow to find someone at last to greet him or to meet with further rebuffs. His courage might break after all and he might make a bolt for it. The sooner that *Mr. Rana, I would like a word if you please* was spoken the better.

But it was not at all easy to approach him. Down from that uneasy perch at the corner of the alcove, he could no longer see his quarry and the tide of people going towards the supper tables was flowing strongly now so that he was having constantly to push his way through.

"Excuse me."

"I beg your pardon."

"Excuse, madam."

"Sorry, sir."

He was making infuriatingly slow progress, and leaving a small trail of resentment behind him. But Jagdish Rana must be somewhere at the other end of the room. And that would be all too near the entrance doors.

And that man was his passport to the world above awaiting him. Nilima's golden world.

He thrust and pushed at the noisily talking guests streaming down towards the supper tables.

A bearer came up and offered him a large plate and a napkin-wrapped fork. No fingers-eating here.

He curtly waved him aside.

Then a notion flashed up.

He darted forward and caught him by the elbow.

"Sahib?"

"I am needing the toilet, quickly."

He hardly had to contrive a look of acute anxiety.

And the idea worked.

"This way, sahib. Follow me."

The fellow had absolutely mastered the knack of threading through the press. The slow buffeting progress of a minute earlier was transformed behind that white-jacketed back into the easiest of sliding motions. Sometimes they seemed to be going sideways. Once even they actually went back towards the supper. But all the time the end of the big room grew nearer and nearer.

And then there was Jagdish Rana.

He was standing all on his own where the crowd had thinned, a half-empty whisky glass in his hand, quite evidently trying to look like someone pondering over which of his friends to go and talk to next.

But—maddening stroke of ill-luck—he was standing facing exactly in the direction in which he himself and his bearer guide had just emerged from the thicker throng. And the consequence was plain to see on the fellow's face. The sudden look of puzzlement and then the swift dawning of recognition. Recognition, realisation and flight.

Ghote experienced a sharp blaze of self-directed rage. If only he had not been so hot in the chase. What had happened to his idea of coming quietly up behind the fellow?

But no time for that now.

Jagdish Rana was walking rapidly away.

Mercifully he was on the other side of the long room from the doors and had a good long way to go to them, but there was almost nobody to block his path.

"Mr. Rana," he called out, loudly as he dared.

It was worth a try. But, as he had really expected, it had exactly the opposite effect from what had been intended. Jagdish Rana simply quickened his pace.

At something not far short of a run, though still decorously enough not to draw attention, he set off to get to the doors first if he could.

Should he actually run? He felt that it would really be very wrong. And, besides, there was a fair chance that he could cut him off.

But then he saw what Jagdish Rana must have already noticed and what had kept him a little unaccountably on the inner side of the room. Behind a wide white-clothed table on which trays of snacks had earlier been put for the bearers to take up there was an unobtrusive door. Unmarked and in the same pale green colour as the big room's walls, it must lead to a service staircase of some sort.

And Jagdish Rana now had only to slip round the end of the wide table to reach it. And beyond it there might well be three or four different escape routes.

He had broken into an undisguised run before he had had time to think. But the sound of his feet thudding on the polished floor must have alerted the escaping star, because he too sprinted a few yards and now had almost reached the service door, his right hand held in front of him to bang it open.

Running full out, Ghote decided in a single instant what he had to do. Hardly decided, rather simply acted.

He dived forward, slid a yard or two across the floor as if on ice and zoomed under the wide white-clothed table.

He felt the heavy damask cloth brush across his head and shoulders. Under the table, it was for one instant cavernously dark. Then he was out, paddling himself with his hands up into a crouch.

And colliding with Jagdish Rana at the opened service door.

He wrapped his arms firmly round but the fellow fought back like a tiger and, anxious to make as little noise as possible, it was all he could do to hold on.

At one point the heaving, jerking star contrived to bang the heel of his shoe hard on his shin and he let out an involuntary yelp. From the corner of his eye, as he wrestled, he saw faces turning towards them and two or three bearers cautiously approaching.

But in his time he had dealt with too many unwilling arrestees not to know how to tackle them, and it was less than two minutes before he had Jagdish Rana neatly held in front of him, one arm twisted securely and even a little viciously behind his back.

He pushed him hastily through the doorway in which they had fought and found, as he had expected, that there were service stairs leading down. In a very short time he had emerged into the guests area of the hotel again and was marching his captive without ceremony across the gleaming white foyer, conscious of the raised interested eyes of the visitors and guests always to be found there and of the efforts of his friend the hotel security officer to interpose his tall frame between them and the inadmissable sight of the sagging-eyed star being hustled out.

Well, he would have to do something some time about putting relations there back on their former good footing. But no. No, he would not need to. Where his life was going at this very moment he would soon be beyond the need to maintain friendly relations with hotel security officers.

The tall glass doors swung open before him as he pushed Jagdish Rana through.

"My vehicle," he snapped to the magnificently turbanned white-uniformed chaprassi on duty, giving him its number.

The car came up with satisfying promptness at the chaprassi's loud call. He pushed Jagdish Rana in at the back and slid in after him. There was no need to give an order. No sooner had the chaprassi slammed the door closed behind him than they were off.

Sitting in grim silence beside his captive, he allowed himself to jump ahead to the point where he would have him on the other side of his desk at Headquarters and, preliminaries over, they would be getting down to the meat of it. He would teach the fellow to send him on a fool's errand. He would make him pay for every minute spent hunting for Sudhaker Wani, questioning him and finding in the end that he had been negotiating over buying his film song at the time Dhartiraj had been killed. Yes, he would pay.

He would pay by having his real motive for killing Dhartiraj ripped out of him like the inside rottenness of some animal being torn out by some filthy butcher. And he would be made to confess. To confess with every possible detail of circumstance so that the evidence when it came to court would be beyond any doubting. And then, when sentence had been pronounced, there would follow his own golden hour as the day the night.

Seen across his desk, there was no doubt that Jagdish Rana, once the first choice of every producer as villain till the up-and-coming Dhartiraj had displaced him, was a man in a corner. The eyes showed it, flicking whitely from side to side. The face showed it, patched with sweat. The very smell of him, the sweat mingling with the sharp noxious odour of a stomach rebelling in acid-swamped fear, showed it to the hilt.

"We are meeting now in altogether different circumstances," Ghote banged out at him.

He offered no reply.

But it was plain from the sudden quick biting of the lips that he too was recalling their former encounter and how he had planted his dart of suspicion and sent that big absurd circular bed spinning round in his triumph. Was seeing that moment and contrasting it with his situation now, hauled out of a big *filmi* party and bundled up here like the lowest of pickpockets or pimps.

Ghote decided to rub it in.

"We meet in different circumstances. Isn't it?"

Still no answer.

"Speak up, man. Speak up. You are under interrogation now. We meet in different circumstances from the last time you answered my questions. Yes?"

"If you say."

An ungracious mutter.

"Under what different circumstances, Mr. Rana? Under what change of circumstances exactly?"

No reply.

Ghote bounced forward in his chair in simulated rage.

"Because you brought me here," Jagdish Rana jerked out.

"Yes, brought you here after you had tried to run away. Well, why did you run, Mr. Rana? Can you tell me that? Why did you run when I called that I wanted one word only?"

"I did not run. I was leaving. It was a pretty rotten party."

Ghote produced a good hollow laugh, leaning back in his chair.

"Such a rotten party that you were leaving by servants' entrance? And as fast as you could go? Not the way for a star to behave, Mr. Jagdish Rana."

"I remember. I felt ill. Yes, that was it. How do you know that I was not feeling ill?"

"Oh, but, yes, Mr. Rana. I am sure that you were feeling ill. Very ill. At the sight of a police officer."

This was easy. It was a pleasure. To play with the fellow like this till the moment came to plunge in the hook and drag the stinking truth to light. And the truth this time it would be. The end of the investigation was in sight. It had gone astonishingly well, but there were times when things did go right. And this case, his biggest by far, for all that at the start it had frightened him as a child is frightened by distant thunder, had really gone wonderfully. He had had his bad moments. He had gone off on the wrong track. But that was almost all the fault of this rat sitting here in front of him. And, that small error dealt with, things could not have gone better. And they would go on going well, right up to the trial and the verdict.

"Oh yes, Mr. Rana. Anybody would feel ill at the sight of a police officer when they had on their conscience a murder."

Now. This was it. Now rip it out.

"But— But, Inspector, you are making a very great mistake."

"Oh, no. Before I was making a mistake. When you did your level best to make sure that I would. Before I was wasting time chasing here, there and everywhere after an individual known by the name of Sudhaker Wani. But now I am not making any mistake at all."

"But, Inspector, if you were not able to pin anything on that fellow, is it my fault? Inspector, I told you only a few facts that were altogether self-evident."

"Oh, yes, Mr. Rana? And what was it you were telling? Exactly how the murder was committed, isn't it? Exactly how. How the murderer saw the Five-K hanging in the darkness over Dhartiraj's head like a sword. How he caught hold of that dagger. How he went climbing up that ladder. And how, cut, cut, he sliced through the ropes that held that light. So tell me, Mr. Rana, how did you know so exactly, exactly how that murder was done? How? Eh? How? How? How?"

And it looked as if he had got there. The face in front of him with its pouchy eyes and that pencil-thin moustache had gone greyer and greyer as each item of his catalogue had smacked into him. Step by step greyer and greyer. Step by step an admission of guilt.

"But, Inspector, it was— Inspector, believe me, I do not know."

"But I know, Mr. Rana. And I know, too, that for the time of the murder you had no alibi whatsoever, that you tried to put one together and altogether miserably failed. So, come, what have you to say now?"

Would it be now, the moment? Now that the words he had pushed and struggled and fought to get at would fall to him like a big succulence-packed jack-fruit falling from its stalk close up to the trunk of the thick tree?

Jagdish Rana's face was dripping with sweat. The smell of his foul breath was strong in the air.

"Inspector, I admit it."

Hah.

"Inspector, I admit I did not have any alibi. And I agree I told you as if I had been there just how the murder was done. But, Inspector. I had to do that. I had to make you believe that someone else had killed Dhartiraj."

"Oh, of course, you had to make me believe. You had to make me believe anything rather than that you were the murderer. But do you think I am a fool only? Do you think they would be putting someone who was a blithering idiot on the Dhartiraj case? Oh, no. And, though your damn lies may have put me on the wrong track for a few hours, by God, in the end I—"

"Inspector."

The failed star's voice rang out with desperation.

"Inspector, it was not me. It was not me, I tell you. But how could I have told you then what I knew? How could I be the person to have to tell? I am no more a favourite of the fans, I admit, but what if I had been the one to betray that, unknown to all, who had gone slinking into Talki-estan Studios by climbing the back wall just at the time of the murder but Ravi Kumar himself?"

XV

A sense of sky-wide awe filled Ghote's mind. Ravi Kumar. Ravi Kumar, the unchallenged superstar, the man watched by millions all over India from the towering slopes of the mighty Himalayas to the distant southern-most tip of the sub-continent and beyond, too, as far as Hindi films ever went, to England, to the Arab world, to Turkey, to Africa, to Russia. Ravi Kumar had been given him as the true murderer of Dhartiraj, the man who had motive enough in having lost his mistress to the popular player of villains and who now, contrary to every belief, had been seen within a few yards of the place where the murder had happened at the very time of the crime. Ravi Kumar. It was as if the President of the United States of America had been shown up as the killer in some squalid quarrel over a woman of the streets belonging to the British Foreign Secretary. It was as if one god had stuck a knife into another, and he himself, a humble serving police officer, had to make the arrest.

How plain now were the reasons for Jagdish Rana's wrigglings and writhings. Easy to see now how the fellow would have done almost any-thing, told any lies, pointed to any other possible suspect, to avoid this appalling betrayal and the total sentence of banishment from society that would follow. To be the man who had denounced Ravi Kumar, it was worse than being the man who would have to arrest him.

No. As bad. As bad as being the officer who would have to carry out the arrest of Ravi Kumar. And that was himself, Ganesh Ghote.

He sat in utter silence. Opposite him Jagdish Rana sat equally without making the least sound. Only the lingering odour of his stomach-ravaged breath—no wonder that he had been in such acute internal distress—hung in the trapped air.

For long long seconds there was room for nothing else in Ghote's mind but the stupendous fact he had learned. But at last, and still without a single word or even a sound being uttered, a new feeling began slowly to grow up inside him.

It was a thought of such daring that at first he could not credit his own head with having formed it. But little by little it took root and grew and flowered with at last an abundance of blossom. It was the thought that, if Ravi Kumar had to be arrested, then there was after all a man fit for the task. If the superstar had to be led away to a common cell, then Inspector Ganesh Ghote was, strange though it seemed, the man to do it.

He had been chosen. Inconceivable as the idea had been once, he could accept it now. For the superstar there had to be a super-detective and he was that person.

And no sooner had he, in all but actual fact, spoken aloud that immense thought than his mind, as if released from an obliterating weight, began to work in lightning jumps of activity. If Ravi Kumar was to be charged with the murder of Dhartiraj, the facts of the matter must be discovered and collated. If, before, he had been determined to present a foolproof, a lawyer-proof, case against Jagdish Rana, how much more necessary it would be to assemble a perfect case against Ravi Kumar, the man all India would demand to see freed.

So every fact of what the superstar had done would have to be brought to light. But in doing that—he saw in an instantly lucid flash—he would have to act with the greatest caution. No one—not even a super-sleuth—could go about asking questions, checking alibis, making observations, taking measurements which would be seen as incriminating a figure of such magnitude until the time had come to make the arrest. No, he must proceed testing each step, one at a time.

"You saw Ravi Kumar inside the Studios at the time Dhartiraj died?" he abruptly asked the failed star sitting in front of him.

The breaking of the silence in his little office seemed even to him an outrage. There should have followed after Jagdish Rana's accusing words a hushed silence lasting hour upon hour. And could it be no more than half a minute since he had heard them?

"Yes," the failed star answered, as if he too felt the desecration. "Yes, Inspector, I saw him."

"And where exactly was it that you saw?"

Keep it calm. Just as if it was any ordinary interrogation.

"Inspector, it was over the back wall that I saw him climb."

"The back wall? There is a way of entering the Studios compound there? Where exactly is this?"

"Inspector, I could show you the place. There is a narrow space between the wall of Sound Stage #2 and the end of the Property Department. Often they leave properties there that are too big to be stored inside. And a few weeks ago they put, right up against the compound wall, the keys from a giant typewriter they had used in a dance sequence when then had one girl on each key. They are piled one against the other and they make it possible to come down from the top of the wall—it is about fifteen feet high, you know—as if by a sort of big staircase. On the other side, you see, there is a banyan tree growing quite close to the wall."

"And how was it that you came to be there yourself?"

"Because when I am working at Talkiestan that is where I leave my car."

A swift bitter smile appeared under the knife-edge of his moustache.

"There was a time," he added, "when I could leave it right in the front, under the big gul mohar tree."

"But now you leave it at the back in such a position that you can see the gap between Sound Stage #2 and the Property Department?"

"Yes. And I was sitting in the car learning my dialogues when he came over the wall. I noticed first when he was cutting the wire at the top."

"Cutting the wire?"

"Yes, there is an extra fence on top of the wall there because otherwise it would be possible to get over by climbing the banyan. You sometimes see boys up there, looking in. And I noticed a man there with wirecutters. I was going to call some security fellows. But then I recognised Ravi Kumar."

So the superstar had gone to so much trouble to get into the studios unobserved. There could hardly be any doubt left about why he had done so.

"You recognised?" he asked, feeling the weight of the burden grow and blowing up his determination to shoulder it.

"Yes, I recognised even though he was wearing a headcloth pulled low so that the end covered almost all his face. I could not at first believe what I had seen. Ravi Kumar never wears any sort of a hat so that he can always be recognised by the fans."

"But you knew who it was?"

"Well, yes, Inspector. It was something in the way that he jumped down from the wall on to the top one of the big typewriter keys. Otherwise I would not. He was wearing a long old white shirt as well, with its tails down to his knees almost. Ravi Kumar who is the smartest dresser in the whole film community."

Ghote felt he could see exactly the man who had jumped down so lithely from the high saddle of the old sports car to rebuke his director at Nataraj Studios.

"Why was it that you did not speak with him?" he asked.

"Inspector, almost I did. Almost I came out of my car and made a joke with him. Until I remembered."

"You remembered? What did you remember?"

"That I was no longer making jokes with Ravi Kumar. That he would no longer speak with someone who soon was not at all going to be in the same circle."

The fading star spoke with such simple bitterness that for the first time Ghote felt pity for him. To have been in that golden world and to know that its doors were slowly closing against you forever.

"So you stayed in your car and you watched him?" he asked.

"Yes. I had the glass up on the side which faced outwards so that people would not see me there, and so I was able to watch him."

"And what did he do?"

"He walked up to the corner and then he looked out. And, when he saw that there was nobody near, he darted."

"He darted? Where?"

"Into Sound Stage #2, Inspector. And after ten minutes only he came out and left by the way he had come. And quite soon after that people came running everywhere to say that Dhartiraj was dead."

"I see."

One thing Ghote could do to check Jagdish Rana's story without giving anyone an idea that he actually suspected Ravi Kumar of having murdered Dhartiraj. And that was to go and have a good look at the place where the failed star had said that Ravi Kumar had got over the Talkiestan Studios' wall. But for this he needed daylight.

So at the late hour at which he finished questioning Jagdish Rana all that he was able to do was to have him taken back to his home and order a guard to be kept on him. It was not that he suspected that what he had been told had been another attempt to send him off on a false trail. There had been altogether too much anguish in the telling for that to be possible. But, when it came to the trial, Jagdish Rana, willing or not, was going to be one of his principal witnesses.

But, that done, he found he could not at all face going home to get a few hours' sleep. The small routines and circumstances of home life seemed insupportable with all the mountain-looming heights so close in front of him. Everything that until now had been comforting, the small size of the rooms, the familiar smell, taste and consistency of the food his Protima cooked for him, even the awkward heavy dribble in the spray of the shower that always struck just at the same spot on the left-hand side of his head, seemed suddenly intolerably confining and mean.

He decided "to doze it" on a bench just outside the office, as he had done on numerous other occasions when a case had kept him most of the night.

But he was up and awake well before dawn, standing under a shower that was much less comfortable than his own at home, despite its dribble, getting himself a shave that, for all the expert hands of the barber, was plainly more sore than his own work with his own razor, drinking a single cup of tea and not enjoying it.

At last, however, it was nearly light enough to start on his examination of the studios' compound wall.

He drove himself, guarding against the least possibility of what he was doing coming to any ears that might draw the correct conclusion. And as he went through the almost traffic-free streets, just springing to view with the coming of the light, excitement began to stir in him at the thought of what the next half-hour might bring. The everyday early morning sights, people emerging bent double from pavement shacks and making their way to the roadside taps, vendors beginning to arrange their goods, oranges or padlocks or pairs of socks, in elaborate piles, a man sitting up suddenly from his spread-out sleeping mat, getting to his feet and rolling up the mat all in almost one movement—each passed in front of his eyes like a cinema film flicking its grey images on to the screen while real events went on elsewhere.

In a few minutes he was at the Talkiestan gates, still closed and silent at this early hour. But he paid them no attention and instead drove carefully all round the outside of the big compound until he came to the long narrow street that ran parallel to the high back wall.

Here he abandoned his car just in the entrance to a lane and set out cautiously on foot.

People were waking into life in this back-street area, too. A taxi driver had begun to give his vehicle a careful wash. A solitary youth on a bicycle made his way along the middle of the empty street, weaving this way and that as if still half-asleep. From the far end, where he remembered there was a mosque, there came the high pleading sound of the muezzin's call.

It did not take long to find the banyan tree whose branches overhung the compound wall. It grew at the end of a short and very narrow lane formed by the fact that the two buildings on either side, a small blue-painted temple and an establishment called the Moon Winding Works, a business specialising in rewinding burnt-out electric motors, did not butt up against each other, perhaps to allow access to the holy banyan.

The little lane—it was hardly wider than four feet—had, however, also plainly found another use. To judge from the stink, it formed a convenient public lavatory and was also used as an unofficial rubbish-dump.

Ghote made his way over two or three squelchy mounds of discarded paper and rags, sending a scrawny chicken squawking and flapping out of the way, and came up to the tree whose long brown dangling rope-like roots fell to the surface of the lane itself, on to the roof of the Moon Winding Works and down inside the high blue temple wall.

It was easy to see how anybody with some agility—and Ravi Kumar certainly had that—could have swung himself up by those thick roots into the body of the tree and from there on the top of the high studios' wall. And up on the wall the sprung-back lengths of barbed wire, plainly freshly cut, provided final evidence that Jagdish Rana had been describing something that had actually taken place.

Standing back at the corner of the Moon Winding Works, leaning against the cupboard-like stall of a cigarette vendor, its doors fastened for the night by a cheap padlock, Ghote gave himself to considering exactly what must have taken place at this spot shortly before, in the Studios on the other side of the high wall at the end of the lane, Dhartiraj had died.

There was nobody very much about at this moment, though at that later hour of the morning there would have been at least a few people passing by. A car would have driven up and have been parked, perhaps just inside the very lane opposite, where his own vehicle was. It would certainly not have been Ravi Kumar's ivory-coloured Mercedes, the one he had seen on his visit to the Nataraj Studios. It would have been instead some other deliberately chosen nondescript car, an old Ambassador probably, the like of thousands and thousands on the Bombay streets. It would have been borrowed, without asking, from one of the superstar's *chumchas*.

Its solitary occupant, dressed in a common white shirt with long dangling tails and a headcloth artfully arranged to cover most of his face, would have sat waiting until there was no one at the entrance to the lane. Then he would have slipped out of the car, have hastily locked it, rapidly crossed the narrow street and made his way down to the old banyan at the end of the rubbish-piled lane. One glance back to make sure no one had entered behind him, and then a quick heave upwards and in a few seconds he would be on the wall. Then out with his wire-cutters and to work.

Yes, that was how it must have been.

It would be necessary to check his own recollection of the lie of the land on the far side when the Studios opened for the day, but there could be little doubt of it now. Ravi Kumar had entered the Talkiestan Studios. It would have been a slightly risky thing to have done but not until that dagger was lifted to cut the Five-K's ropes would anyone who had spotted him have had the least idea what it was he was intending to do. And if he had been spotted he could have called the whole thing off. No, it was risky but not too risky. And to commit a murder without taking any risk would be expecting altogether too much of life, even for a superstar.

So now there was only one thing to do. To confront Ravi Kumar, superstar, with the reality of the deed he had done.

XVI

Ghote found the superstar at his home. Not without difficulty.

Asking the encyclopedic Miss Officewalla where he was likely to be had, of course, been out of the question. The least hint that he wanted to see Ravi Kumar might have had a special issue of *Film Femme* on the streets with the words blazoned across its cover "C.I.D. Accuses Ravi".

So he had had to find his way through the *filmi* jungle on his own. It had not been easy. On the telephone he met from film Studios and film companies a series of rebuffs. *Is Mr. Ravi Kumar working there today? Who is that calling, if you please?* And that was a question he dared not answer. He was tempted many times to say that Inspector Ghote of Crime Branch C.I.D. urgently wanted to interview Mr. Kumar. It would come to that in the end, he felt almost certain. But not so utterly certain that he could afford to have the whole world know the gigantic fact that a superstar was to be accused of murder.

It was only when, in mere desperation, he simply looked up Ravi Kumar in the telephone directory—it was like finding one of the gods listed among a whole column of simple Mr. Khrishnas or as one of any number of businesses styled Lakshmi—and rang his house that he began to get anywhere.

Yes, someone had answered, Ravi Kumar is at home. He was going to Talkiestan for the morning shift but he had not left yet.

He looked at his watch.

"But it is already ten o'clock," he said. "Isn't it that the morning shift begins at eight ack emma?"

"Ravi Kumar does not get to the Studios before eleven," came the lofty response.

At that he banged down the receiver and hurried to his car.

But, up at the big house on Pali Hill, looking down from the sea-jutting promontory on to half the teeming insect world of Bombay, he met with a whole new bristling crop of difficulties. He had seen himself arriving, ringing at a bell beside a gate—a superstar would have to ensure himself privacy—handing in a letter saying that "Inspector G. V. Ghote, C.I.D. wishes to see Mr. Ravi Kumar in connection with the unfortunate event at the Talkiestan Studios" and very soon after than being respectfully shown to see a cautiously apprehensive superstar.

But things did not at all turn out like that. True, there was a gate, ornate, filling every inch of the archway in the high white wall that surrounded the property and firmly locked. And there was a bell. And, when he had thrust his way through the small group of onlookers waiting to catch a possible glimpse of their hero and had rung at it, a chowkidar did appear, eventually.

He handed him his letter, which he had taken the precaution of making sure was thoroughly sealed, but the man, a surly-looking individual in a dull red cotton uniform, simply took it and tossed it, in full view of all the watchers, on to a bench just inside the gate on which there were already lying a dozen other letters, mostly looking very grubby, and three or four small parcels tied with many windings of fine cotton string.

This was something he would not stand for. Damn it, he might end this visit by taking away the fellow's master under arrest.

He called him back.

There was no answer.

He put his finger on the bell push and kept it there. In a minute or so the fellow re-appeared.

"Go away or I will be calling the police," he shouted.

"I am the police."

The fellow laughed.

Ghote felt rage compacting itself inside him. Oh, to yell back that not only was he the police but that he was the one policeman ready to arrest Superstar Ravi Kumar. But the time was not yet. Not just yet.

Bitterly he dug into his pocket and brought his hand out clutching an impressive handful of notes.

"That letter is Number One urgent priority," he said.

The chowkidar put a broken-nailed hand through a gap in the ironwork of the gate and took the money.

"No 1 priority, *jee* sahib," he said insolently.

But he did take away the letter.

And before very long he came back once more, hauled a long key from the pocket of his red uniform, put it in the lock of the gates and opened them just wide enough for someone to slip through, provided they were prepared to turn a little sideways, and beckoned to Ghote.

Ghote, despite his stoked-up inner knowledge, was prepared to turn a little sideways.

Inside, the chowkidar pointed to the door of a large white-painted house across a garden as big as a small public park and Ghote set off.

He walked slowly, going over in his mind the interview ahead. But he could not help noticing the garden: it showed so many signs of extraordinarily lavish care. Not only was every patch of grass finely mown and miraculously green but the whole area had been worked at till there was room for nothing more. There were raised flower-beds and there were sunken ones, and each was not only brilliant with flowers but its earth was teased into the merest granules. There were walls by the dozen, running here and there, and there were ponds and fountains. And on every available surface there stood a statue. The whole world appeared to have been ransacked to provide them. Not only were all the Hindu gods there, and many more than once, but there were Buddhas by the dozen and whole regiments of European figures, funny little men in bright red conical hats with tiny grinning faces engaged in such occupations as fishing and raking. Enormous sums of money must have been spent on the place. But no doubt that was the object.

At the house itself there was another bell to be rung. It came in the centre of a formidable wooden door studded all over with large black bolt heads. After a shorter wait than at the gate it was opened by a bearer attired in a white uniform with a full magnificent red turban and broad red cummerbund.

Ghote felt he was getting near the heart of it all.

"Mr. Ravi Kumar is expecting me," he said sharply. "I have sent a letter."

Without a word the bearer ushered him into a spacious hall, its floor flagged with black and white marble, its walls hung with the superstar's innumerable trophies of fame. Through an open doorway Ghote glimpsed the dark interior of a projection theatre.

Well, this was it. The superstar's home. His citadel. And the invader had entered it.

He made himself taller.

The bearer showed him into a room that he supposed was the dining-room and left him, still in silence. There was a long table glinting with so much polish that it looked like a pool of still water. Drawn up to it were a dozen upright chairs with ornately curved backs painted a glossy white and seats of deep red velvet, very highly sprung. They would not, he thought, be pleasant to sit on if the air-conditioning was not working at full blast. In the middle of the table there were four many-branched silver candle holders, the tall twisted red candles in them almost matching in colour the velvet of the chairs. On the walls were similar candle holders, though these had dummy candles with little electric light bulbs in them.

Something about the candles on the table caught Ghote's eye and he peered forward and inspected them. They showed no sign of use, their wicks were white and they were covered in a faint layer of dust.

Not surprising, he thought. The heat from them all would be intolerable.

But after this discovery he found nothing more to do. He went over in his mind once or twice more what he hoped to learn from Ravi Kumar, but there was nothing else to be done there. He peered through the slats of the window blinds at the enormous garden and watched the shadow of a cloud slowly pass across it.

The minutes went by.

It was not acceptable to keep a police officer working on a case of this importance waiting like this.

He went to the door and peered out. The big black-and-white flagged hall was still and empty.

What if his letter had alerted the superstar? Was he at this instant making his way by fast car out to Santa Cruz to take a plane to Europe or America? Or, more likely, was he busy arranging himself at huge cost some unbreakable alibi?

He was on the point of marching out, going into whatever rooms presented themselves, shouting and demanding till he located the superstar, when he heard the slap of bare feet coming from a corridor at the far end of the hall. Hastily he stepped back inside the dining-room and pulled its door quietly closed.

A few moments later the door was opened again. An old servant stood there, barefoot, gnarled of face, almost black of skin.

Ghote guessed at once that this must be Ravi Kumar's personal servant. No one else would have dared to be dressed the way he was in a baggy pyjama with an old shirt at the top, its long tails dangling down.

And that shirt. He knew, strongly as if he had seen it all with his own eyes, that this had been the very garment that the superstar had worn when he had climbed into the Talkiestan Studios. There would have been not the slightest difficulty in borrowing it off this fellow's back. And it would be next to impossible ever to gain an admission that this had happened. The fellow would, in all probability, have been Ravi Kumar's servant even before his film days. Someone bound to him and his family before him. And his confidant now, sometimes disapproving, but hearing everything and never, ever, telling anything.

"Come," the man said.

Ghote followed him, out into the trophy-hung hall, round the corner and along a wide corridor. He went over, for one last time, the way he meant the interview ahead to go.

It would be tricky. There was no denying that. For all that it looked certain that the superstar had disguised himself and entered the Talkiestan Studios in secret just before Dhartiraj had been done to death, the case was not yet proven. And, if by some extraordinary chance the supposition he had made turned out to be wrong, then to have accused a figure as colossally influential as Ravi Kumar of a crime as terrible as killing a fellow star, why, it would be worse than suicide. But if, on the other hand, he really was on the point of coming face to face with the man who had cut loose that Five-K light to fall on the hapless star below, then he had to tread even more carefully. What he had to do was to get the superstar to betray himself. To say something that he should not have known, could not have known. That would give him the final conclusive proof that the extraordinary task that seemed to have fallen to him was indeed what it appeared. And then he could act.

But he must not put his opponent on his guard.

The long-shirted servant pattering along in front of him had swept open the door at the end of the corridor and was standing aside for him to go in. This was it.

"It is Ghote Sahib."

He registered that the superstar had apparently not told even this confidential servant that his visitor was a C.I.D. inspector. Then his eyes took in the huge room in front of him.

Huge though it was, it was apparently the superstar's bedroom and it reduced to mere nothingness that other luxury *filmi* bedroom he had seen, the one with the absurd turn-table bed where he had first interviewed Jagdish Rana out at Juhu. The bed here was on a scale as big as the room and the superstar lay in it flopped on a heap of fifteen or twenty pillows, each covered in a smart chocolate-brown striped material matching the sheets. Spread here and there over the deeply-valanced gold-threaded bed-cover were newspapers, carelessly discarded, almost a dozen different magazines, a scatter of glossy photographs, a transistor radio, many-knobbed and playing *filmi* music, a big hand-mirror in the shape of a lotus leaf, two different trays with cups and plates on them, and heaps of letters, opened and unopened.

He looked for his own among them. But, though its official buff envelope would have stood out among all the ones he saw, he was unable to spot it. Was it somewhere hidden among all those striped pillows?

He stepped forward.

Ravi Kumar was regarding him carelessly. Or was he? The nearer he got the more it looked as though the superstar's gaze was directed not at him but at perhaps a crowd somewhere in the distance behind him.

Almost he turned to make sure there was not a small group standing admiringly in the doorway he had left.

He crossed the soft carpet, glancing a little this way and that at the huge mirror-hung room. Beyond its windows, out on a veranda, he saw there were four or five men lounging in wicker armchairs, reading magazines and playing cards. The superstar's *chumchas*, no doubt. Well, with the noise of that transistor they would hardly be able to hear that the two of them were talking at all, let alone what was being said.

But even when he got right up to the bed the superstar was still looking loftily at that imaginary crowd in the doorway.

He cleared his throat, noisily as he could.

Ravi Kumar seemed not to have heard. But perhaps the unceasing flow of honey-sweet music from the transistor was to blame.

He tried again. A whole consumptives' chorus of phlegm-rattling.

And this time the superstar did at least raise an inquiring eyebrow.

Well, that would have to be enough introductiton. The man knew who he was, and he knew who it was in front of him. His opponent. Then get ready for battle.

"Mr. Kumar, I have come to ask you when it was that you last saw the late Dhartiraj?"

For second after second the superstar did not reply. He lay back on his great mound of striped pillows with the many-knobbed transistor pouring out its honey-music somewhere by his knees and he looked into that far distance where a crowd was adulating him.

But under a steady gaze he proved unable to keep the pose up indefinitely, and abruptly he reached forward, picked up the first magazine that came to hand and started to read. It was *Star and Style* and there was a picture of himself in colour on the page where it had been open.

But the gesture was all Ghote needed.

"Mr. Kumar, where?" he jabbed out.

"How should I know?" the superstar answered with give-away promptness. "Yes, certainly I would talk with Dhartiraj. But it is a well-known fact that he and I were not friends. I probably saw him last at some party or other."

"You did not see him shortly before his death? Where were you that morning, Mr. Kumar?"

And the look in his eyes then was almost enough. They showed a quick but unmistakable glint of a buried fear being unsettlingly confirmed.

It was almost enough. But not quite. He felt he had to have words to back it up. Words that could eventually be incorporated in a report. *In answer to the question Witness said . . .*

But Witness said nothing that helped.

"Inspector, I refuse to answer all these ridiculous questions."

And he heaved himself off his pillow mound, leaned forward with effort and, twisting one of the transistor's many knobs, made the outpouring of music that had surrounded them twice as loud as it had been and more.

There could have been no more effective way of indicating that the interview was at an end.

XVII

For perhaps ten minutes after Ravi Kumar had so brutally obliterated his interrogation with the thick treacle of blaring *filmi* music Ghote tried to continue. Once he began to slide his arm across the rich bed-cover towards the almost quivering transistor with the aim of reducing its volume by just a little. But the superstar spotted his maneuver long before it was near success and snatched the many-knobbed machine to his chest, where he actually contrived to increase yet more its honey-blare.

Soon after that Ghote gave up. He turned and marched out of the big room.

It came as no surprise to find the superstar's black-skinned draggle-shirted servant standing just outside the door waiting to escort him to the gate.

He left furiously plotting how to overcome the breath-taking opposition he had met with. He must show he was the man's match. Plainly, though, he would not get to see him again just by asking. He had been lucky to get as far as he had. No doubt, the superstar must have decided, probably not without misgivings, to see whether the request for an interview meant that the police were in any way suspicious of him. And then, when he had at last got in to see the man, that single question about where he had been at the time of Dhartiraj's murder had been quite enough.

Driving slowly southwards through the northern suburbs of the city towards Headquarters, lost in these thoughts, he suddenly almost brought the car to a halt.

By golly, if Ravi Kumar had been so alerted by that one question, it added a powerfully strong link to the chain of reasoning that said he was indeed Dhartiraj's murderer. If only there was one more witness to that climb-in at Talkiestan beside Jagdish Rana. It was only too easy to imagine what a clever defence pleader would make of the bitter failed star in the witness-box. *Mr. Rana, had you any reason to be jealous of my client, Mr. Ravi Kumar?* It would need only that to make his foundations crumble.

If only there had been, inside the compound or outside it, someone about at the time Ravi Kumar had got over that wall. A simple *mochi*, sitting on his haunches at the street corner making a sandal while he waited for some passer-by to offer him a repair. Anything.

But there would not have been. For one simple reason. If there had been anybody there to see, Ravi Kumar would have stayed sitting in his anonymous borrowed car till the coast was clear. The street there was never so busy that there would not be short periods when it would have been possible to slip into the lane between the temple and the Moon Winding Works unobserved.

Yet—he was now jockeying the car round by Opera House: there was a hell of a queue for the morning performance at the cinema, must be a real hit-film—if only, say, that cigarette vendor with the stall on the corner of the Moon Winding Works had been there. At round about ten in the morning he ought to have been. But he must have left his post for some reason. Ravi Kumar would never have walked right past him into the lane. Perhaps he had gone for a skimpy cup of single tea somewhere, or perhaps he occasionally made use of the services of a doorstep barber nearby. But might he not have been back at his stall when Ravi Kumar crossed over the wall on his way out?

It was a chance. Just a chance. But perhaps a chance worth looking into.

The turning to the left into Charni Road was there. He swung round into it and headed north once more. It was a long way back. But it might, it just might, be worth it.

But getting to the narrow street behind the Talkiestan Studios took exasperatingly long. As always when he was in a hurry, every other driver, not to speak of every other innumerable cyclist and roadway-walking pedestrian, seemed to be bent on frustrating him. And with every fresh hold-up the importance of seeing that cigarette vendor seemed to grow. There was no reason to suppose he would hold a vital clue, but the notion that he did so became minute by minute more firmly fixed in his head.

It was nearly an hour later that he at last turned into the long street behind the Studios.

Though by no means blocked by traffic, it was very much busier than when he had seen it at dawn. Cars, lorries and the occasional yellow-topped taxi, their progress complicated by slow-moving bullock carts, horse-drawn victorias, long heavily-loaded two-wheel pushcarts and bicycles by the score, slowly jostled their way along. On the pavements, where their narrowness and pot-holed state permitted, people were drifting from one dark little shop to another, pausing to look at the arrays of foods or sweetmeats, standing to bargain over a sale or stopping to ponder deeply which number at the lottery-ticket seller's was likely to be lucky that day.

He halted at the first lane he came to and abandoned the car. It would be quicker on foot.

But again his very haste seemed to create obstacles. He could see over the slowly-moving heads the blue-painted roof of the temple at the corner he was making for. But first a boy occupying all of one flat area of pavement to lay out his mother's newly-cooked chapatties to cool, hopped right under his feet and nearly sent him sprawling. Then a slightly mad leper, for some inexplicable reason, selected him as his target and would not get out of his path, even when he had given him all the small change he had. Next a pickpocket he knew of old came up and made a performance of claiming his acquaintance. This last delay so irritated him that he began to imagine seeing, down by the blue temple, as totally unlikely a figure as Ravi Kumar's shirt-dangling servant.

But when, battered and bad-tempered, he at last reached the corner of the Moon Winding Works the cigarette vendor was at least there, the doors of his cupboard-stall open, busy selling two Chaminars from a crumpled packet to a clerk from some nearby office.

He could hardly wait for the transaction to be completed.

"Police," he said to the vendor, flashing his identity card, as soon as the clerk had turned away.

The man immediately looked panic-stricken. But he was not so much so that he was unable to answer questions.

No, he said simply, three days before at ten in the morning he had not been at his stall. He had gone to the hospital, to get something for his chest.

He coughed prodigiously to show how necessary that had been.

Ghote was turning away, unable to believe his idea had proved fruitless, for all that his reason told him that nothing had been more likely, when the vendor, coughing completed, added something else.

"But, Inspectorji, if you are wanting to know what went on in the lane at that time, you could speak with old Kesar. She is always here in the morning."

"Old Kesar?"

Hope was spuming up in him again.

"She spends the morning picking over the rags and paper she has gathered," the vendor explained. "And it is here that she sleeps also."

He laughed, and coughed again at length.

"You would be saying she looks like no more than a heap of rags herself," he said, as soon as he was able. "Often when she was lying there I have not known until she moved."

Ghote peered along the narrow lane down lowards the dangling roots of the banyan. He could see no one.

"But it is still morning," he said. "Where is she?"

If the old rag-picker was really as inconspicuous when she was lying down as the vendor had said, what would be more likely than that Ravi Kumar had walked right past her on his way to climb the tree? And, in a lane so narrow, was it not also more than likely that he would have disturbed her? Enough to have made her look up? And perhaps remember him?

His other witness. At last.

"Inspectorji, she is not here any more."

"Not here any more? What do you mean? What?"

"Inspector, just ten minutes ago some men came and took."

"Took? Took? What are you meaning 'took'?"

"I was thinking they must be her family, Inspector. But I did not know she had family. I was thinking that they had come at last to take her to hospital. God knows she needs it more than I even. A thousand things she must have wrong with her, old Kesar."

"But what men? Which way did they go?"

"Inspectorji, I am not knowing. All I am knowing is that first a fellow came looking down the lane till he saw old Kesar. And then he was calling to some more fellows, and they came and they did not say a word but they picked up old Kesar and left, carrying her like a bundle only."

"The fellow who came first," Ghote asked, horrible suspicions rapidly confirming themselves in his mind, "was he a fellow with a long dangling white shirt and a black face, a shirt down to his knees?"

The vendor lifted up his bare skinny arms in open amazement.

"Inspector, it was he."

"Which way? Which way did he go?"

But the vendor had not seen them after they had turned down the street out of his view. And, although Ghote ran out at once in pursuit, he knew even as he did so that it would be useless. They had had too much of a start, Ravi Kumar's personal servant and the *goondas* he must have hired.

And so it proved. An exhausting jostling run all along the remaining length of the road produced not the least glimpse of any party of men carrying an old rag-picking woman like a bundle. But it would have been all too easy for them to have taken her down some lane to be lost at once among a maze of buildings or to have had some sort of vehicle waiting and to have taken off in that.

Ghote at last came to a halt, panting and with every limb slithery with sweat.

He felt sick, too.

Sick, not so much from exertion, though no doubt running and dodging through the street crowd at full pelt for a good quarter of a mile under the heat of the sun had had some effect on him, but rather sick from ill-success.

Once again he had been thwarted by the superstar. First, that blank defeat in the huge bedroom of the house on Pali Hill. And now, when with a little more quickness of thought and decisiveness of action he could have jumped one step ahead, he had been beaten again. No doubt Ravi Kumar, going over everything he had done in getting into the studios to cut down that Five-K over Dhartiraj's head in the light of the clear C.I.D. interest in his movements, had remembered the old rag-picker he had seen or half-seen in the lane and had decided not to risk her realising, unlikely though it was, that in her dirt-engrained old hands she held a vital clue against him. And, once he had made that decision, he had acted. With superstar speed.

Ghote, leaning against a battered red black-domed post-box, gave himself to thought.

At least now it was clear beyond any remaining shadow of doubt that Ravi Kumar was his man. The fellow had shown that he had something to hide that was worth taking a considerable risk over. But, this one weakness dealt with, he must now believe himself altogether secure. Up there on his superstar's pinnacle, he must think that he was beyond the reach of the law.

But he would find out differently.

Very well, perhaps he himself as a simple inspector might have some difficulty in reaching him on his own. But he could be the force that saw that those powerful enough to get to him reached up there and let him pull him down.

If Ravi Kumar was very, very influential, so was the Commissioner of Bombay Police. And so was the Deputy Commissioner in charge of Crime Branch.

The Deputy Commissioner had said that he would have to let it be known he was taking a personal interest in the case. Well, it would be necessary for him to do a little more. To accompany his inspector to that big house up on Pali Hill to effect the arrest.

Yes, by God.

He pushed himself away from the support of the post-box, turned and marched off in the direction of his car.

The Deputy Commissioner agreed to see him without the least delay. Looking into his big office through the square of glass in the door before entering, Ghote could not help recalling the days and the days that had passed with him thinking he was never going to get work of sufficient importance to get his orders direct from here. But now all that was changed. A high fate had all along been reserved for him, and now that it had come he was equal to its claims, to the last one.

He pushed wide the door.

"Ah, Ghote, yes. What can I do for you?"

The words were certainly welcoming. How extraordinary they would have seemed less than a week ago. But somewhere behind them was there a hint of caution? But why should there be?

No, he was imagining things. He must learn to get rid of such phantom suspicions. He was above worrying in that petty way now. He must start behaving with all that unthinking assurance of the stars. Yes, he must behave like a detective star.

He pulled out one of the four chairs lined up with precision in front of the big desk and sat down.

"It is my investigation, sir," he said. "It has taken an altogether most serious turn."

But now there could be no mistaking it. The Deputy Commissioner's face had registered, if only for a moment, dismay. Or more than that: the confirmation of something long feared.

No time now to work out what the look could mean. Just time to note that it had been there and to feel a sudden bottomless disquiet.

"Sir," he said, suddenly able only to push the words out as best he could. "Sir, I have proof. Sir, not necessarily a case ready to go to court, sir, but altogether enough to act on. To act on with your assistance, sir. Sir, I shall need that most definitely. It is Mr. Ravi Kumar, sir."

And, yes, on to the Deputy Commissioner's mobile and quick-darting features there had not come the look of intense astonishment that there ought to have done at those words.

Instead he had pursed his lips in recognition of a plainly expected calamity.

"Yes, Ghote, Ravi Kumar," he said.

"Sir, in the course of my investigation I questioned a certain film star, or rather a certain ex-film star, a Mr.—"

"Ghote."

"Sir?"

"Ghote, there is no need for you to go over the whole course of your investigation. It is enough for me to know that you have good reason to believe that Ravi Kumar himself killed Dhartiraj. You have good reason?"

"Yes, sir."

"Then act on it, Inspector. Act on it. It is your simple duty as Investigating Officer in the case."

"But— But, sir, I think I shall be needing your support, sir. Ravi Kumar is a great star, sir. A superstar and—"

"I do not need you to tell me what Ravi Kumar is, Inspector."

The Deputy Commissioner was, beyond doubt, irritated. It was something he himself had never heard from him before, nor expected to hear. Angry he could be, on occasion, when anger was justified. But never peevishly irritated. Never.

"Sir," he ventured nevertheless, "your assistance and support, sir."

"Ghote, let me spell it out for you. Almost as soon as I had been informed of the murder of Dhartiraj I received certain other intelligence, vague and doubtful intelligence"— his eyes flicked to the direct-line telephone beside him, and Ghote saw failed Jagdish Rana sitting on that absurd circular bed and tapping with too much pride on the little book of telephone numbers in his shirt pocket—"but enough to make me realise that what you have discovered in the case was a possibility. I had to consider, then, how the affair should be handled in the light of what might happen. And in due course I decided that what was necessary was an investigation by an officer who would get at the facts—if what I feared turned out to be the facts—but who was sufficiently low-ranking not to compromise the whole department if the worst came to the worst. It seemed to me, Ghote, that you were the man for the job."

The Deputy Commissioner was looking at him full in the face. The liquid, all-seeing eyes saw all.

"Ghote, the case is yours and yours alone. Pursue it, man. Pursue it wherever it leads you. But pursue it yourself."

XVIII

Inspector Ghote left the Deputy Commissioner's office like someone staggering in the midst of a violent rainstorm. He was hardly able to think.

He stopped in the cool dimness of the winding stone staircase leading down to the entrance of the building and stood looking sightlessly out of the narrow window slit in front of him at the quiet activity of the sun-bright compound outside. Floppy-uniformed constables were making their way here and there, wives were standing chatting to each other, children were playing in the dusty gravel. It was a placid scene. And inside his head there was turmoil. Whenever he tried to think about any one of the facts that he had just learned it seemed as if two others, as force-driven, as oppressing, would come battering down at him. He felt himself tottering helplessly, unable even to fight his way to any sort of shelter.

Yes, it was confirmed now that Ravi Kumar was indeed the murderer of Dhartiraj. Yes, the Deputy Commissioner had feared as much all along. Yes, above all, his investigation had by no stretch of the imagination been the star-shining ascent he had seen it as. No, he had not been selected as the man best capable of bringing to a successful conclusion the biggest case the department had had to face for years: he had been picked out as the one officer the department could afford to lose.

And there was no way out of his situation.

Like rain-filled gusts of tormented air his thoughts continued to batter this way and that.

No way out. He had been told that it was his duty to pursue the case to its logical conclusion. And that must mean the arrest and indictment of Ravi Kumar. The indictment of a god. Those court scenes he had seen so delightfully in his mind's eye, the spotlight full on the chief prosecution witness, Inspector G. V. Ghote: they would take place right enough. But the spotlight would be illuminating a figure to be reviled. The #1 villain of all time. The man the whole nation would rejoice in hating, for whose downfall a million eyes would eagerly watch.

A star ascending. No. No, what he had been chosen as was to be the Fall Guy. That was what they called it. The Fall Guy.

The goat tethered to the jungle tree for the tiger to smell out, for a whole nation of clawing tigers to smell out. While up above, in the *machaan*, the sportsmen looked down.

Yet what else could they do? He could see their dilemma. That was the worst of it. He could see that for the sake of the Department someone had to be sacrificed.

But, no, that was not the worst of it. Everything was the worst of it. That Ravi Kumar was a murderer, that Ganesh Vinayak Ghote was the Officer Investigating, that he had been chosen not for his as yet unrevealed abilities but for his defects, that his investigation had been successful in spite of those defects, everything.

Oh, and God, now it was clear why such a powerful figure as Seth Chagan Lal had taken such a close interest in the inquiry. Jagdish Rana must have hinted to him as well that the murder had been committed by the one impossible person. The Seth had wanted to make sure this little police iuspector was keeping well away from the truth.

Well, at least he had got at the truth. At least he had done that.

He placed his hands on the rim of the big flowerpot that stood just under the window slit in front of him and gripped it.

Yes, he had at least succeeded.

Though the price of success was abject failure.

He stayed clutching the big pot as if it was some great stone that he had to lift up and fling down on to besiegers below in long ago Mahratta times, as if all depended on him to save the fort from sacking, looting, rape.

Down in the compound an open police truck came to a halt under the shade of the big tamarind tree opposite and half a dozen armed police jumped down with their rifles and set off in a motley group in the direction of the armoury. A chicken went dust-scuffling along beside them. In the sunlight the shadows were dense and still.

And he found that, underneath all the chaos that had whirled storm-like through him, one resolution had revealed itself.

He had been put in a position from which there was no drawing back. Very well then, he would not draw back.

Pursue, the Deputy Commissioner had said. Then pursue he would. If Ravi Kumar was the murderer of Dhartiraj, then he would arrest him under Indian Penal Code Section 201 in the proper form. He would arrest him, do what he would to stop him. And then he would strive to his utmost to see that, when the case came to the courts, it was as good a case as could be made.

Quite probably he would never get a conviction. The whole might of the best legal representation that could be secured, and the dirtiest, would be arrayed against him. Public opinion would loom like an electricity-charged sky waiting to break into thunder and lightning against him. But do what they all would, he would go on with it. He would put in front of the court, and the world—it was his duty—the very best case possible. And somewhere the truth of it would be recognised.

It was in his own office, under the familiar groan-creak-groan of his own fan, at his own desk with its familiar little defects, that he began the fight.

The first thing was to secure another interview with the suspect, and one at which he would not be able to refuse to answer questions.

But here at least life had become easier for him. If he was going, before long, to arrest Ravi Kumar—and he was—then no longer did he need to conceal his intentions at all costs.

He picked up the telephone and dialled.

"*Film Femme*, your favorite film magazine, good afternoon."

"Miss Officewalla, please."

She was there.

"Miss Officewalla, it is Inspector Ghote. There is yet one more thing that you can do to help me."

"Inspector, I am very busy—"

He cut urgently across the languid and haughty voice.

"Miss Officewalla, I am wanting to put questions concerning the death of Dhartiraj to Mr. Ravi Kumar."

There. It was done. Nothing now could stop the whole worshipping nation from knowing soon that this obscure C.I.D. wallah was accusing the greatest superstar of them all of a most dastardly crime. Well, all right, let them know. Let them do what they would.

At the far end of the line there was a holy silence. It was broken at last.

"Inspector? Inspector Ghote, is it that you are still a member of the C.I.D.?"

"Please ring on another line and make fullest inquiries."

Another silence. But a shorter one.

"Well, Inspector, I will not conceal from you that I will be doing that before I set a single finger to my typewriter. But in the meanwhile may I ask some questions?"

He drew in a breath.

"Miss Officewalla, in due course I would answer each and every one of your questions. But, madam, first there is what you can do for me. And perhaps also what I can do for you."

"Well, Inspector, what is it? What is it?"

The vibrant eagerness contrasted sharply with the *I am very busy* of a minute or so ago.

"Miss Officewalla, you would not be altogether surprised, I think, to hear that when earlier today I attempted to put questions to Mr. Kumar he refused to pay any attention whatsoever."

There came a dry chuckle down the line.

"So this is my problem, madam. I am wanting to meet him where I can speak with him without his preventing. Some sort of a public place, if you please. And, madam, I would be very happy for you to be a witness of what occurs. The sole and solitary witness, if you are liking."

He heard the indrawn breath. The gulp and grab of the big fish taking the bait.

"Inspector, I will fix it, even if it has to be bang in the middle of the Filmfare Awards themselves."

"The Filmfare Awards?" Here at least was some part of the *filmi* world he knew something about. The huge annual prize-giving ceremony called for traffic arrangements of such elaboration that even Crime Branch had to take cognisance of them. "Yes, when are they taking place then?"

Miss Officewalla's hiss of dismay came clearly over the crackle and buzzing of the line.

"Inspector, they are next Sunday only. Everyone knows that."

"Sunday. Of course, Sunday. I had not realised it would be Sunday so soon. And, of course, if that is the best occasion to confront—"

"No."

"No, madam?"

"No, there is a better occasion. I have just seen on my desk diary here. Inspector, I take it you can wait till at least the day after tomorrow?"

"Yes," Ghote said, "I can afford to wait."

"Very well then. The day after tomorrow at 11:13 a.m. exactly, the time fixed by the astrologers, the *mahurat* takes place for Parvati Films International's new mythological. It is going to be a very big affair. They are paying the priests who will conduct the ceremony more than has ever been given before. None other than Baby Pinkie—the little shortpants horror—will be turning the camera. And who will have the honour of acting as Clapper Boy but Ravi Kumar himself?"

"Yes," said Ghote. "That would do very well."

In the time that led up to the *mahurat* ceremony officially starting Parvati Films International's new mythological Ghote hardly ate or slept. He could think of nothing but that grim moment ahead when, with Miss Officewalla representing the eyes of all the world on him, he would have to pin down Superstar Ravi Kumar and would almost certainly end by arresting him on a charge of having murdered Dhartiraj. Though he went through the pleasures of a day off-duty as if it had been any other, the customary comforts of his home life hardly existed for him. It was not now that he despised them, as he had done when he had not been able to endure the thought of going home when he had believed he was the chosen star detective of the whole Bombay force and was heroically on the track of the greatest murderer of all time. It was simply that the task ahead, to which he was inescapably duty-bound, was so awe-inspiring, now that he had to tackle it as one simple unsupported investigating officer.

His Protima, of course, pressed him in a wifely way to take food and he had to rouse himself enough to invent a stomach upset, bad but not so bad that she would go hurrying off to borrow the neighbours' thermometer. He submitted, however, to the concoction she always made at such times and endured its mouth-wrinkling bitterness with his thoughts concentrated on the hour of 11:13 a.m. next day.

He arrived for the ceremony ridiculously early, holding in front of him the *mahurat* card which Miss Officewalla had persuaded Parvati Films to send him by messenger, a splendid piece of stationery with a folded outer cover of crisply crinkled deep red secured with a little golden tassle and inside an ornately printed thick sheet of purest white giving not only the time and the place but heart-arousing descriptions of the stars of the new film, its producer, its director, its song writers and even of its story writer.

For almost an hour he wandered round the studio where the ceremonial filming of a key scene from the new film was to take place, already gnawed at by anxiety in case Ravi Kumar for some reason failed to appear to perform his honorary function of acting as Clapper Boy or in case, when he did, that he would somehow still succeed in avoiding being questioned. He watched setting coolies labouring over the final erection of the set, a lavish temple with gigantic pillars and a huge flight of steps mounting up to an enormous statue of the goddess Kali—it all seemed to have been left appallingly late—and he experienced a jab of real disillusionment when that figure of weight and majesty was revealed as feather-light plastic when a carpenter toppled it with an accidental poke of his sawing elbow. Nor was it any compensation when the assistant director insisted on the lights in the goddess's jewel eyes being tested after the accident and he was able to see them glow a magnificent red.

But gradually the studio took on the look proper to the occasion. Scores of folding chairs were hastily set out. The garlands for the camera and the sound booms were hurried in, bringing with them a cool fragrance of frangipani amid the hot dust smell. Then the priests, saffron-robed, bespectacled and seemingly far distant from their surroundings, were shown up on to the marigold-hung platform built for them and the music began, the light and insistent rhythm of the drum and the throaty piping of a *shenai*. Soon the priests were chanting too.

The studio was beginning to look reasonably full at last, though none of the people arriving in a steady stream appeared to be the V.I.P.s he was looking out for as heralds of the arrival of Ravi Kumar. A Parvati Films executive was, however, going round to various actors in costume and to the technicians handing over, with much attempt at being discreet, wads of notes from an enormously bulging wallet.

The black money payments, he thought, feeling very much an old hand at *filmi* ways now. Twenty percent of the paper sum as extra non-accountable payments. But, of course, a much larger proportion for the stars. And what was that story Miss Officewalla had told? About the producer who was unwilling to pay up when the moment came and covered his whole head with bandages and pretended to have been in an accident so that he could not talk to the star who came to demand his money? Something like that. It seemed right for this world he had got himself into. But the killing of Dhartiraj, that had not been a matter of easy-come easy-go. That had been real. And Ravi Kumar would find out just how real before many minutes had gone by.

He looked over at the big clock that had been hung on one of the walls so that everyone could see when the auspicious moment for the starting of the film had come. Nearly eleven o'clock. Surely when that first shot, even if it was not, as Miss Officewalla had explained, the first scene, was due in only fourteen minutes time Ravi Kumar and the other notables had left their arrival rather late. This was worse than when he had waited for Jagdish Rana to arrive at the party at the Taj.

But those people coming in now, they were stars, surely. Yes, that was Billy Banker, grinning like a monkey. And there was the Minister who, Miss Officewalla had said, was to switch on the camera. And there was that dancer— What was her name? Everybody knew it—the one who had notched up no fewer than six hundred films and was still to be seen in every cabaret or night-club scene. Well, if she had come, Ravi Kumar should not be long coming too. After all, he was, so to speak, here on duty. And, look, that must be the other star with a duty to perform, Baby Pinkie, in those pink satin shorts.

Ah, there at least was Miss Officewalla, with her beaky nose scenting and seeking this way and that. And there was another face he knew, young Kishore Sachdev. Come to see if he could get a word with the great Ravi Kumar, of course. Well, he would miss his chance. A more important matter had to be brought to the attention of Mr. Kumar than any film role.

And there was Director Ghosh, come to wish his colleague at Parvati Films good luck, but not too much. And there was Seth Chagan Lal, looking richer than ever. Were those diamond buttons on that white sharkskin coat of his? Perhaps, when not only the villain of his *Khoon Ka Gaddi* but its hero also was swept off the scene, he would have to retrench a little.

Suddenly, from up in the high roof of the studio, a whole battery of lights plunged their hard beams down on to the set. They would be beginning at any minute. But where was the Clapper Boy?

He looked at the big clock.

Ten past eleven. The long minute hand swept to the time just as he looked.

Where was Ravi Kumar?

In a sudden sweat-drenched panic he pushed his way through the

crowd—already one or two people were standing up on their chairs—
to the place where he had seen the gossip queen. Careless of the fact
that she was in full flow of a joking conversation with the joshing Billy
Banker, he went up to her and broke in.

"Madam. Miss Officewalla. Where is he?"

She was not put out. With a quieting gesture of her thin long-fingered
hand, she gave him a rapid aside.

"He will come. Do not worry. A great star is always late."

She turned back to the grinning comedian.

"A fan," Ghote heard her explain briefly, as he retreated.

They were rehearsing the two stars up on the set now for the scene
to be filmed. Another of the assistant directors was crouching in front
of them on the huge temple steps under the stern gaze of the illuminated Kali reading over and over the lines they would have to say. *What
you have done will bring dishonour to us all. It was for you that I did
it.* Here the female star practised her reaching-forward gesture that conveyed how much she loved him. And he practised his stern rejection
face. *For this I will cut your nose.*

They went over the little scene time and again. Miss Officewalla had
said it was a key part of the story. Neither of the star's Hindi was very
well pronounced.

But suddenly there was a commotion over by the entrance doors. He
swung round. His eyes took in the big clock as he did so. 11.12. Surely
there would hardly be time now even if— But it was not Ravi Kumar.
It was Nilima.

He turned away. It no longer mattered whether Nilima saw him make
the arrest or not. It would not be the first big step up into that different
world of hers. It would only be a matter of duty, with universal execration following it.

His eyes flicked back to the clock. Still 11.12. But that long minute
hand must be going to move on to the auspicious moment at any instant. The chanting of the brahmins had risen to a holy clamour.

And still no Ravi Kumar.

Baby Pinkie had been standing up on a chair by the camera for some
minutes, the Cameraman at his side demonstrating just what he had to
do to turn it. The Minister who was going to switch the camera on
had been there for even longer, standing on the other side, Ministerial
finger on the switch, a slightly bewildered-looking figure in his plain
white jacket and white Gandhi cap.

He looked at the clock again. How truly terrible if the moment was
missed. How like Ravi Kumar to bring about such a disaster.

But the long minute hand still pointed firmly to 11.12.

And there, as he gazed and gazed, it firmly stayed. The *filmi* world
knew how to cope with the inexorable progress of the heavenly bodies.
Clocks could be fixed. Time could be made to stand still.

*   *   *

It must have been only five minutes after the appointed hour that Ravi Kumar arrived to perform his allotted function. And he performed it very well. Bar the fact that it was not actually taking place at the correct moment, it went without a hitch.

"Ready for Take," an Assistant Director called out.

"Sound start," the Director boomed through his megaphone.

Two sharp whistle blasts came from the sound booth, the exact replica of the one in which Ghote had heard the solid facts of the murder from old Ailoo. How long ago it seemed, that talk when he had come to learn of the old coolie's undeviating devotion to the exact limits of his task, of the younger Lights Boy who had been so badly injured when the Baby had slipped from his hand and nearly fallen on to Sudhaker Wani and all the details of what must have happened when the Five-K had been slashed from its place.

Of when Ravi Kumar, as it had now turned out, had slashed the Five-K down.

And there he was now, looking so debonair and carefree, stepping forward at the Director's shout of "Camera" and "Clap," holding the clapper board unnaturally high so that everybody could see, as well as the lens of the camera, the film's title neatly written on it and in large letters the word *Mahurat*.

"*Mahurat* shot," he called out, his voice confident and easy. "Good luck to Parvati Films International. Fresh laurels, fame and glory to our stars."

And CLAP.

It was done. Hero and heroine spoke their lines and got them right. "Cut," bellowed the Director in high good humour.

Clapping broke out everywhere and there were shouts of "*Shabash*" "Good luck" and "Jolly well done." Bearers swooped down with huge trays of snacks and drinks, and discreet words to the more important guests to indicate which glasses of fruit juice held the gin that the visiting Minister ought not to know about.

Ghote moved with purpose through the crowd. He saw that he would not need to signal to Miss Officewalla. She was approaching the smiling, laughing Ravi Kumar as steadily and swiftly as himself.

He felt a swift stab of hunter's joy at the way he eventually contrived the moment of confrontation. He succeeded in keeping himself screened from the superstar by the busily eating and drinking guests until the very last moment. He must have risen up beside him like an avenging spirit.

And for a moment—for just one moment—the handsome, confident face showed a tiny spasm of fear. It went as quickly as it had come and the cutting profile was calmly turned away, as if by looking elsewhere his own whole existence could be blotted out. But the telltale look had been there. And it gave him renewed heart.

"Mr. Kumar," he said, thrusting himself forward until his face was within three or four inches of that much photographed profile. "Mr. Kumar, am I to speak in front of all?"

The superstar turned at the words. Not quite so impossible to touch him then.

"Mr. Kumar, I have enlisted the aid of Miss Officewalla here. No doubt she is well-known to you. She has agreed to act as if you were giving her interview so that we can go somewhere quiet together."

The superstar plainly took in what he had said. He clearly was working hard to make up his mind what to do.

A sense of slowly growing achievement was there to feel inside himself, like a seed little by little bursting its hard shell and forcing its way to the light. He was going to beat this man. Heavy as the dense weight of the earth his power might be, immeasurably heavier, so it might seem, than the tiny seed underneath. But that seed had its force. And it would push through.

"Well, Mr. Kumar? Is it?"

"Very good."

The fellow still kept his debonair look. But no dramatic breakdown was to be expected. The thing was that he himself was the one with the initiative now.

Miss Officewalla asked, loudly for all to hear, if Raviji would give her a short interview and, with smiling apologies to the adulating circle round him, the superstar left in her wake.

Ghote brought up the rear, knowing he would be unnoticed.

Not for the first time he thought of Miss Officewalla with gratitude. She had known at once where in all the confusion she could find somewhere to go and talk undisturbed. It was the Publicity Manager's cabin here, small and stuffy, its walls covered with posters of past triumphs, and exactly what was needed.

He positioned one of the chairs on the near side of the desk for Miss Officewalla, indicated to Ravi Kumar that he could take the Publicity Manager's own seat and made no attempt to sit down himself.

"Mr. Kumar," he began without preliminaries, "I have evidence that approximately ten minutes before the murder of Mr. Dhartiraj you were seen entering the compound of Talkiestan Studios by climbing over the back wall thereof. Is there any comment you wish to make on that?"

He kept his eyes fixed on the superstar's arrogantly handsome face as if his very life depended on his never once blinking. But he was aware that, at his side, Miss Officewalla had drawn in a quick breath as if to say, "Good God, is it that strong against him?".

He waited for his answer.

"What evidence, Inspector?" The superstar sounded totally cool. "I am telling you it would have to be pretty remarkable to contradict the known facts."

And his smile, the smile that had time and again enraptured a million female hearts, flashed out like a scimitar.

"I am not at liberty to reveal the names of witnesses at the present time," he said stolidly.

At his side he felt Miss Officewalla's faith begin abruptly to seep away like water from a cracked *chhatti*.

"But," he added, without too closely considering what he was saying, "I can assure you, Mr. Kumar, it is the evidence of a man who knows you well and it is altogether circumstantial."

"Of a man?" the superstar asked sharply.

"Yes," he shot back, a hot sweep of triumph running through him. "Of a man, Mr. Kumar. Not of a poor old woman rag-picker who saw what she should not and was paid for that by being carried off to God knows where."

"What rag-picker, Inspector? Really, you seem to be talking sheer madness."

It was coolly said. Said with diabolic coolness. A coolness that contrasted all too clearly with his own flush of raucous heat.

He swallowed hard and tried to regain his previous dominance.

"Mr. Kumar, all that is neither here nor there." But the words did not somehow sound as authoritative as they ought to have done. "Mr. Kumar, I have asked what you were doing at the time."

"At the time poor Dhartiraj was killed, my dear fellow?"

"Yes, sir. At that time."

He should not have said "Sir". Damn it, he should not.

"As it happens, Inspector, I can give you an answer to your question. I have only just this moment realised it. We are at a *mahurat* now. I was at a *mahurat* then."

"At a *mahurat*?"

He had sounded damnably confident.

"Miss Officewalla can confirm even," the superstar said, with enormous laziness. "She was there also. And about two hundred other people."

"Why, yes," Miss Officewalla said. "Yes."

She stood up with disconcerting suddenness and turned towards the door.

"Yes," she said. "I had quite forgotten that *mahurat*, Raviji."

XIX

Raviji. The term of familiarity struck Ghote like a cold knife. Miss Officewalla had lost faith in him. Ravi Kumar had with a few careless words slashed his whole case into ribbons.

But he could not have done. It was impossible. Bitter though Jagdish Rana was, he had not been lying in his description of the superstar climbing the back wall at Talkiestan Studios. He had seen him do that.

And so had the old rag-picker. Or why else had she been made off with?

His mind whirred round like a slipping gearwheel. And then clicked home.

"Mr. Kumar," he said, "at what time exactly were you at that *mahurat* where Miss Officewalla saw you?"

"That would be easy to check," the superstar answered, as cool as ever. "The time for every such ceremony is invariably well-known."

"And," said Ghote, swinging round to address not Ravi Kumar but Miss Officewalla, her long thin fingers already on the handle of the door, "certain great stars consider it is their right always to be late, isn't it? Isn't it, Miss Officewalla?"

She let the door handle go and turned to look at the superstar with eyes already hardening against him once more.

"Yes," she said. "Of course he was late. How foolish of me not to think."

Ghote turned back to Ravi Kumar.

"I am suggesting," he said, "that you left the Talkiestan Studios by the same way that you had entered. That you dropped in the borrowed, car you were using the old long-tailed shirt you had been wearing over whatever smart clothes you had on and that you took a taxi to the *mahurat* so as not to be seen coming in an old, old car which might make people talk."

"Yes," Miss Officewalla broke in, her voice showing her mounting excitement, "it was by taxi that he came. Someone sent us a photo of him arriving, and I remember thinking it was unusual for Ravi Kumar to take a taxi."

"Well, Mr. Kumar?" Ghote said.

He had not expected the superstar to break at the beginning, but he thought it was well possible that he would now.

And it seemed that he was going to.

He lifted his head in a quick challenging look.

"Yes," he said, "I did go into the compound at Talkiestan over the back wall."

The slow beating of triumphal music began to sound in Ghote's head. To bring the great Ravi Kumar to court in the face of a million adoring fans would be terrible. But at least he would be doing so now with an admission in his pocket, however easily that might be withdrawn in the witness box. Yet it was something that he had not really dared to count on achieving. And now he had it.

"Yes," the superstar repeated, "I entered that place like a thief in the night."

He rose from his chair behind the Publicity Manager's untidy desk.

"But I did not go there to kill Dhartiraj," he said. "I admit even that I had reason enough to hate him. But I did not kill him, and I will refuse altogether to say why I entered those Studios."

So this is the line he is going to take, Ghote thought at once. Clever enough. To admit to what there was ample evidence against him for, but to deny absolutely anything that must still be supposition. It was really the superstar way. This arrogant claim to be above questioning. This calm assumption that he could not be brought to trial like a common murderer.

Well, let him see what it felt like to be arrested. To be kept in a cell and to know that all the time everything about you was being investigated. Perhaps that would break the superstar shell and show the man beneath.

But would it?

An uneasy suspicion grew in him that it would not. There would be lawyers demanding the release of such an obviously innocent man. There would be messages going in and out of that cell, whatever precautions were taken, when it was Ravi Kumar, with all his wealth and with all the admiration that existed for him, who was needing information.

He scrabbled for some way of countering it all. Briefly despaired. Renewed his determination. And found a possibility. A daring, almost ridiculous possibility, but a possibility.

"Mr. Kumar," he said, "I require you to accompany me straightaway to Talkiestan Studios where we will go through together all your alleged actions on the morning of Dhartiraj's murder."

The superstar had, at once and without the least protest, agreed to the proposal. It was, Ghote realised after a little, the course that must have seemed to him to be in his own best interests. He must still hope to come out of it all, not just unharmed, but to advantage. He would have shown himself willing to indulge the police in whatever they wanted and he would have given away nothing. He would see himself as playing in the real world the role of hero unjustly suspected but bound to be triumphantly vindicated in the last reel.

Well, they would see. Under real pressure, as intense this way as it could be made to be, he might crack.

Words from the great Hans Gross's mildew-marked volume, long ago committed to memory, came back to him. They were from the pages headed "When the Witness Does Not Wish to Speak the Truth" and they seemed to fling a bridge for him all at once to the days of simplicity before the notion had got into his head that he had been somehow chosen to be a star detective. "The Investigator is the calmer of the two. For the Witness is playing a dangerous game while the worst that can happen to the Investigator is once more to be made a fool of." If only he could hold on to that, then perhaps, even with all the superconfidence of the superstar, Ravi Kumar would yet betray himself.

So they went, superstar, investigator and, representing in her beak-nosed person all watching India, Miss Officewalla, once more to the Talkiestan Studios. And, such was the influence even without a word

being said of the great Ravi Kumar, that shooting was halted on Sound
Stage #2 and the set for Maqbet's throne room was hastily re-installed
while up above on the plank-wide catwalk a new Five-K was fitted at
the exact spot where the one that had fallen to kill Dhartiraj had been.
Even the curve-bladed dagger that had been used to slash those ropes
was brought by Assistant Inspector Jahdev from its safe-keeping. A small-
part actor was found to take the murdered star's part, eagerly volunteered
indeed, and the red robes Dhartiraj had been wearing were brought out
again for him to wear.

Swaying-bellied Director Ghosh, Cameraman—no, Director of Photography—Chandubhai, his assistants, the Sound Recordist, old Ailoo were
all summoned to take their former places. Even Nilima, at work elsewhere in the Studios, hearing of what was going on, presented herself
ready to play her part. And Ghote, with the new realism that had come
to him ever since he had learned that he was no star but more a convenient extra, thought to himself that no doubt she was determined to
steal the scene if the least opportunity arose.

At last all was ready. Ghote turned to the superstar.

"Very well, Mr. Kumar," he said, his voice as grimly matter-of-fact
as he could make it. "We will go to the start now and proceed."

Ravi Kumar turned without a word and followed him. The car was
waiting just outside the narrow door of the studio. They climbed in,
himself, his witness and the necessary Miss Officewalla. In three minutes
they were in the long street at the back of the compound. Ghote told
the driver to park just inside the lane on the far side from the blue-
painted temple. They got out and stood in a little awkward group under
the slow stares of the proprietors and customers of the little dark shops
at the lane entrance.

"It was here that you waited in that borrowed car?" Ghote asked the
superstar, though he hardly made the words into a question.

Ravi Kumar gave him a suddenly sharp look.

"Yes, it was," he said, sounding just a little put out.

"Very well," Ghote said brusquely, "we will assume that whatever
time you waited till you thought the lane opposite was all clear has
gone by. Please proceed accordingly."

Without any comment Ravi Kumar set out across the street, dodged
just behind a slow bullock-drawn big-barrelled water-cart, its dangling jug
clank-clanking as it went and headed for the narrow entrance between
the temple and the Moon Winding Works.

The cigarette vendor, perched up on a thin stone shelf under his
stall, watched them go by, coughing hard, his eyes darting with curiosity.

Ravi Kumar strode down the lane ahead of them, setting a pace that
seemed to reflect a certain nervous tension. Ghote saw that he gave just
one quick glance to a heap of paper scraps, doubtless the place where
the old rag-picker Kesar had been lying, unnoticed by him as he first
went down towards the banyan.

Good, he thought. Keep up the pressure.

They reached the tree.

"Go in under," Ghote said, pressing hard.

Ravi Kumar stepped under the rope-hung shade of the big old tree.

"Go up. Just as you did before."

Without a word, the superstar seized one of the dangling roots and hauled himself upwards. In a few seconds he was on top of the high wall. The coiled-back strands of the barbed wire he had cut before vibrated a little as he arrived.

Ghote turned to Miss Officewalla.

"Madam, would you care to go back round in my vehicle?" he asked. "I am intending to accompany Mr. Kumar all the way."

"Yes, very good, Inspector."

She sounded subdued, more so than he had ever heard her. He welcomed it. It was a sign that the intangible pressure he was trying to build up really existed.

He turned, stepped under the banyan, caught hold of the same dangling root that Ravi Kumar had done—fibrous and harsh to the touch—and swung himself up as easily on to the broad top of the wall.

"Now," he said, "how long exactly did it take to cut these wires?"

"I don't— About two minutes. Two minutes, or less."

He pushed his shirt-cuff clear of his watch.

"Then we will wait," he said.

He stood beside the superstar in silence. Down in front of them in the Studios compound they could see the tree underneath which Jagdish Rana parked his unimpressive car. A dog went ambling along in the sunshine and smelt at it. Around them was the old sharp odour of bird droppings.

He allowed three full minutes to go by on his watch, and then another half. He saw that there was a sheen of sweat on the superstar's forehead although they were well shaded from the sun.

"Very well. Show me the way you got down."

But it was not difficult to see how it would have been done. The keys of that gigantic, pink-painted typewriter, peeling here and there now, led down like so many rock steps to the ground below. Ravi Kumar jumped down them with every appearance of casual ease.

But he put a foot wrong on the lowest one and for a moment had difficulty keeping his balance.

Close behind, Ghote leaped right over the last two of the keys to land with a neat thump just at the superstar's back.

"So," he said, "you then went quickly up to the end of this passage and at the top you looked this way and that. Then, since there was nobody about—or nobody that you could see—you went quickly along to the door of Sound Stage #2. Please carry out the same procedure again."

Ravi Kumar turned his head, as if to make sure that any sign of stress that might show on his face would not be observed. But he set off at once.

At his heels Ghote saw, when they came to the head of the passage between the Property Department and the side of Sound Stage #2 that Miss Officewalla was already there. She watched the superstar hurry along to the narrow door into the studio with the eyes on either side of her beak of a nose positively glinting.

"You went in," he said sharply when the superstar hesitated for a moment at the door.

They all three entered. Inside it was as black as he remembered from his first visit coming to investigate the circumstances of Dhartiraj's death within an hour of its occurrence.

"Please do as exactly as possible what you did before," he said to the superstar.

"Certainly."

Was there a little relaxation, now that he guessed that his actions on the previous occasion had not been observed beyond this point? The pressure must be screwed up again.

He followed the superstar's pale blue silk shirt through the darkness. He was led directly towards the corner, not far away, from which the ladder led up in the dark to the catwalk where the Five-K hung. The route took them quite close to the table with the curve-bladed dagger on it. "Is this a dagger that I see before me?" Yes. He could just spot it there. It would be the work of a second only to dart aside and seize it.

But Ravi Kumar did not so much as glance at the faintly glinting shape on the table. Instead he went straight to the foot of the narrow iron ladder.

"Mr. Kumar," he said sharply, "have you followed exactly the path you took before?"

He had wondered briefly whether to accuse him directly of having avoided going to the table with the dagger. But he felt it vital at this stage not to risk pretending to more knowledge than he had. If the superstar had, for instance, come this far and then gone back for the dagger, to have claimed to have known otherwise could well let go like steam from a suddenly pierced vessel the pressure he hoped he was keeping up.

"Well? Have you?" he jabbed out, in face of the superstar's silence.

"Oh, yes, Inspector. I have."

Was there a tiny note of mockery there? It must not be.

"But you did not just stand here," he snapped out. "Please go on and do just what you did before."

The superstar turned to the ladder in silence. He began to climb up. He seemed not to be going as fast as he might have done.

Ah, the nerves strained again.

And then the pale blue splodge of colour up in the darkness ahead ceased to move.

"Well, go on, go on. You did not just go three-quarters of the way up that ladder and then stop. Go on, Mr. Kumar."

"But, Inspector, that is just what I did do."

The voice coming down from the darkness was openly mutinous.

He glared upwards.

That attitude must be crushed. Crushed at once. Or he would lose him altogether.

"So this is to be your story, is it?" he said to the dimly-seen figure. "Very well then. If you say that you stopped where you are, from now on I require you to do what I say."

He wheeled round, darted over to the table where dagger was, seized it, was back at the ladder's foot in two bounds and up half a dozen rungs as quickly.

He thrust the dagger upwards, handle foremost.

"Here," he said. "Here. Take. Take this and do exactly what I direct you to do."

"Certainly, Inspector."

He was losing him. Damn it, he was losing him. But why? Nothing for it but to press him and press him still.

"Go on up," he ordered.

He turned rapidly to Miss Officewalla.

"Madam, I am going up too. But I do not think a catwalk is a suitable place for a lady. Please wait here and watch closely from below."

"Very well, Inspector."

At least she was still subdued.

He started up the ladder behind the superstar and the moment he had reached the top he directed him sharply to cross the catwalks to the place where the new Five-K hung. The superstar seemed to take the creaking and the slight sway of the planks beneath their feet very much for granted. Was this just that the man who had bounded down so easily from that ornate saddle on top of the sports car when they had been shooting that village scene was naturally well-balanced? Or was it that the rocking groaning path they were taking was one already familiar to him? Surely he had made this journey holding that dagger in this way before.

They reached their destination.

The superstar stood directly above the new Five-K.

"Well, Inspector," he said, his voice distinctly mocking now, "am I to cut the ropes? It won't do that chap below much good, but if you insist."

Thinking hard how to snatch back the lost initiative, Ghote stood looking down at the brightly-lit figure on the red *gaddi* below. Damn it, how was he to regain the grip he had had not so long ago? And he must. He must.

And abruptly he knew what might do it.

He looked up and faced the superstar boldly.

"Yes," he said. "Yes, Mr. Kumar. Do just that. Stoop down to use the knife on those ropes. Do everything but actually cut them. Go on. Kneel and use the blade. Now. Do it now."

It was what the fellow had surely done just those few days ago. Make him do it again then. Test him. Test him to the very limit. And see if he would break.

Very slowly, without another word being said, Ravi Kumar turned and knelt on both knees on the narrow catwalk. Below him it was just possible to make out the ropes holding the dangling Five-K. The blade of his curved dagger caught the light as he moved it towards them.

And then it stopped.

In the darkness Ravi Kumar swiftly straightened up. He swung round. The knife blade was glinting in front of him.

"No, Inspector," he said in a voice little above a whisper. "I will not do it."

Had he got him now? Had he?

The glinting blade moved suddenly, lunging nearer.

In a single instant his mouth went parchedly dry. He found himself swaying urgently backwards on the narrow plank beneath his feet.

And stopped himself.

He must not show fright. He must act as if fear was an impossibility.

"You will not do it, Mr. Kumar?" he asked.

His voice sounded extraordinarily level. He marvelled at it.

"No, Inspector," the superstar's voice came back in the darkness.

It seemed more tremor-filled by far than his own.

"No, Inspector, it turns out that I would rather tell you the truth."

So this was the moment. He had done it after all.

"Go on," he said, hardly breathing the words.

"Inspector, I did not know I was so weak-stomached. But to go through doing what that fellow must have done. It's ridiculous. But I cannot."

"That fellow". The implication was clear: some other person. But had he not pushed him up to the edge and over?

"Go on, Mr. Kumar," he said, quietly again.

"Inspector, it is not an easy thing to tell. But I— I was here that morning for a private reason, Inspector."

He leant forward in the dark as near as he could get to the superstar's face. He wanted to see, if he could, its exact expression. The voice had certainly betrayed some deep inner trouble. But what exactly? Would some contraction of the features in that cuttingly handsome face betray it?

The dagger blade glinted terribly near to his unprotected stomach. But he must behave as if that simply did not exist.

Should he murmur some encouragement to go on? No, it was coming again.

"Inspector, you are a married man?"

"Of course."

"Did you fall in love with your wife, Inspector, after you were married? In love? Really in love?"

"Yes," Ghote said, remembering a strange, almost hallucinated time. "Yes, I did."

"Inspector, I am in love."

Meena, Ghote thought. That thin, ill creature he had interviewed, the "keep" Dhartiraj had stolen from the all-conquering superstar who had once stolen his wife from him, the *bachchi* star who was to have played Rani Maqbet in *Khoon Ka Gaddi* before Nilima took over the role. So that, after all, was his motive.

"Go on," he said. "Tell me. Tell me everything."

"I love her, Inspector. Ill or well, thin or not, I love her. I tried that morning to telephone her at his house because I knew he was on the board to be shooting here. They said she was not at home. I did not know if they were lying to me. I had to see her. I thought she must have come here with him. But I did not want anyone, not one single soul, to know that I, Ravi Kumar, had come down to chasing that girl wherever she was. So I took my servant's old shirt and a headcloth, and I borrowed a car from one of my *chumchas*. I drove to that place by the back wall that I had happened to notice, and I came in here. To see if she was here, Inspector. With him. And I climbed that ladder, Inspector."

Now. Now it was finally coming.

"But, Inspector, only to where I showed you. From there you can see all the studio. And she was not here, Inspector. So I left. I left just seconds before that fellow cut the ropes over Dhartiraj. I heard the noise of it as I crept towards the door, but I did not know what it was. And that is all, Inspector. That is the truth."

XX

To believe Ravi Kumar or not. Ghote stood in the darkness, at the very scene of the crime, feeling the roped plank beneath his feet still swaying a little from the force of the superstar's gestures as he had confessed his secret, and set out to weigh all the circumstances in equal pans.

First, was this no more than an attempt to pull the wool over his own eyes? Was Ravi Kumar, increasingly desperate at the unexpected closeness of the hunters, attempting to tell some just likely story, and one that had a good deal of feeling in it, so as to secure his sympathies? To blind him to the truth? It would be a superstar's answer: relying on that magnetism of his. Yet on the other hand it could not but have cost a man of his pride, a man up there, more than it was easy to realise to have to admit that he had been beaten by a rival in love and that he was even reduced to the meanest stratagems just to make sure that the girl was not in his company.

It was not difficult to imagine how having all this come out in open court, to be printed in the papers and the *filmi* magazines, would be almost death to him. Yet had it not perhaps been risked just so as to escape precisely from a sentence of death?

But what if in fact Ravi Kumar had not killed Dhartiraj? What if he had done no more than what he had said?

Then someone else must be the murderer.

The superstar had not utttered a word of his plea. In the dark he was awaiting judgment. Standing, still and spent.

Ghote looked down again to the very spot where Dhartiraj had died. Nothing had changed there. Ravi Kumar's confession, delivered in that low intense voice, could not have penetrated to anyone on the ground. They were standing or sitting simply waiting to know if anything would emerge from this reconstruction. No doubt most of them were puzzling pleasantly about the superstar's presence. But only Miss Officewalla would have had any idea that the great man had been undergoing trial. Trial by ordeal.

But what if he had not been enduring that ordeal? What if he had been only concerned to avoid a terrible embarrassment? Why, if Ravi Kumar was not the murderer of Dhartiraj, then Inspector Ghote no longer faced the prospect of appearing in court accusing India's most popular idol.

A burden, an almost intolerable burden, would have been lifted from his shoulders.

And it could be so. Ravi Kumar's story could be true. There was not a single fact that contradicted it.

He smiled wryly to himself in the gloom. Yet another suspect believed totally to be guilty and found after not so long to be innocent. First Jagdish Rana, the murderer from thwarted ambition. Then Sudhaker Wani, seen as a threatened blackmailer striking back. Next young Kishore Sachdev, seen as reacting against brutally crushed hopes. Was Ravi Kumar just one more in that shameful parade?

No. No, he was not. His was a different case. With the others that absurd ambition so suddenly sparked up in him when he had believed himself chosen as a star investigator had led him into ridiculously seized-on judgments spurred on by the hope of achieving a star-like and startling success. But with Ravi Kumar it had been truly different. There he had discovered someone with a real motive for killing the victim who had no actual alibi but who had tried with every trick he could produce to fabricate one, someone who had all but been in the very place where the killer must have stood at the moment of the crime. No, there was no shame in having tracked down Ravi Kumar.

And still there was only his word for it that he was not in fact Dhartiraj's killer.

Yet that word had carried a lot of conviction. There was something that could not be denied. And, if it was so, it would lift the burden. It had lifted it. Rightly or wrongly, at this moment he was feeling nothing but a tremendous sense of relief, a balloon lightness.

Unseeingly he looked down at the red-robed figure below of the actor playing the part of Dhartiraj.

And a totally new consideration was borne in on him. One that abruptly turned everything about the case upside-down.

If Ravi Kumar had been telling the truth, then at the time Dhartiraj's killer was supposed to be climbing that ladder to get to the catwalk the superstar himself had been three-quarters of the way up it. It was impossible as a route to the Five-K hanging like a convenient doom over Dhartiraj's head. And—the image of the hanging light brought this to him—here was a sliver of confirmation for the superstar's claim: surely the murderer must have been in the studio earlier so as to see that the Five-K threatened the figure on the *gaddi* below, and Ravi Kumar had not been there.

So it seemed very possible that the picture he had had of the crime all along, a picture shared by everybody he had talked to, was simply not so. No one had climbed that ladder. They could not have done so.

But, if that was the truth, how had the Five-K come to be cut loose? Because it had been. Nothing was more certain than that. A knife, almost certainly the curved dagger Ravi Kumar was still holding towards him, had sliced through those ropes. And that must have been done with the intention of killing Dhartiraj. He would, from this point of view, have been an absolutely clear target. Looking down at that actor there now, that much was totally evident.

But how had the murderer got to the Five-K then?

The answer came to him.

Old Ailoo had told him it. At the very beginning of the inquiry. You could, he had said swing dangerously on a rope from one catwalk to the other. And that is what the murderer must have done. He must have crept up another ladder, gone behind old Ailoo as he sat concentrated entirely on the light that was his charge, and have daringly swung across.

He looked. It would be possible, at least for a lights coolie used to these heights and the precarious holds, or for some sort of acrobat. A lights coolie? He considered the notion. Well, by some barely imaginable chain of circumstances, true, there might be a Lights Boy who might have some grudge against Dhartiraj, the all-popular, that would have made him want to kill him. But it was highly unlikely, and nothing that any of Assistant Inspector Jahdev's minute inquiries had turned up had showed the least sign that such a person existed.

But then no one, it seemed, would have wanted to kill that friendly figure, with the single exception of Ravi Kumar.

Now if it had been Sudhaker Wani sitting down there on the *gaddi* then dozens of people might have had a motive. The stand-in with his dubious activities of all sorts must have made plenty of people fear and hate him. Was it possible that the killer had thought Sudhaker Wani would be sitting on the *gaddi* and not Dhartiraj? It was. As far as anyone down on the ground was concerned since, until Dhartiraj had suddenly demanded extra jewels for his turban, it had been expected that the stand-in would take his place. But no one up on the catwalk could have mistaken the two. It was totally plain from here at this moment that it was the small-part actor sitting there now. No, if it was to turn out that someone had swung across to the Five-K wanting to kill Sudhaker Wani, then it would have to be a figure as laughable as a short-sighted acrobat.

And then he realised that the notion of a short-sighted acrobat was not laughable at all. Such a person existed, had been in the studio, had a strong motive.

He stood still on the narrow, slightly swaying plank beneath him, frozen with awe at his discovery.

Nothing seemed to have changed. Yet how much had. He was still staring downwards. Ravi Kumar was still, only seconds in fact after he had ended his admission, awaiting his verdict. What had made the idea flash in on him, showing him in an instant all the facts that he had known all along? What had tumbled the wall after high wall of prejudice that had prevented him seeing?

First of those walls, and most appalling, had been the one built up by his idea of himself as superstar investigator. It had simply deterred him again and again from using the old and well-tried ways of his craft. He had attempted, ridiculously, to hit on a super-solution instead of patiently discovering the facts, carefully testing them and eventually quietly seeing the conclusion that they led to. Next he had been blinded by the notion, shared by everybody, that the murder had been committed by someone taking the route to the spot that seemed most obvious. Well, they had not. And, once he had seen that, everything had begun to look different. And lastly, perhaps excusable but a grave error all the same, there had been the idea that the murderer had to be a man. He himself, not ten minutes ago, had even said to Miss Officewalla that a catwalk was no place for a lady.

But there were women who played with heights as a child plays with its toys. Women, indeed, who had as children played with heights. Professional acrobats, members of entertainers' families.

And there was a woman, in the studio at the time of Dhartiraj's death, who had begun life as just such an entertainer, a fact that was well-known to every reader of *filmi* magazines, a fact he himself had been told by Miss Officewalla. And he had seen with his own eyes that that practised acrobat was extremely poor-sighted.

Nilima.

Nilima, the aging Nilima, who had gained the coveted role of Rani Maqbet at the expense of the young Meena when the *bachchi* star had inexplicably lost her youthfully luscious curves. Nilima, who had been photographed even handing Meena a friendly glass of sweet and sugary cane-juice. And had not Sudhaker Wani himself admitted that his old aunt make up mixtures which, while not fatal, did make people thinner as they liked to be in the West? What a hold on a rich star the money-hungry stand-in must have thought he had. And, when that Baby light had fallen some weeks before and had so nearly killed him, what ideas it must have put into Nilima's head. And then suddenly to have seen the dangling Five-K when she had already heard Director Ghosh say he wanted the stand-in to sit on the *gaddi* to be lit. It all fitted together so conclusively.

Yes, Nilima was the murderer.

And the world-heavy burden of indicting a nation-popular superstar had come on to his shoulders once more. The golden Nilima. The burden was yet heavier.

She had gone by the time he got down to the ground. He had had first to tell Ravi Kumar, however briefly, that he accepted his version of events, and that his secret would be safe with him. In the confusion of it all, he was a little worried that he had even indicated why he had changed his view of the whole affair. But, all too soon, the superstar would know in any case.

It seemed, however, when he at last got down and began asking for Nilima, that as soon as everybody had dispersed to their places for the reconstruction—and how stupid it had been, looking back, not to have properly accounted for Nilima when that dispersal had taken place at the time of the murder—the golden star had simply left the studio. She had, in fact, left the compound altogether. The chowkidars eventually reported that her Mercedes had gone through the gates, her driver at the wheel as usual.

But from there on she seemed to have disappeared. He had gone immediately to her home, only to be told that she had not arrived there. Her mother said she had had no other engagement after her shift at Talkiestan and that she had been expected to come home.

So then it had been a question of telephoning, with the advice of Miss Officewalla, every place she might have gone to. It had been a time-consuming search. And it became all the more baffling when, some two hours later, her driver was reported as having returned to the house with the Mercedes, but no Nilima. He had taken her, he said, to a big block of flats off Altamount Road where she often went to visit a former female star, now almost forgotten. But she had not come out to the car again and, when he had inquired, he was told she had never visited her friend. Miss Officewalla confirmed the likelihood of all this. The ex-star was much relied on for advice, she said. And there were also a good many different ways out of that particular block.

But she told him not to worry. Nilima had disappeared in this way before. She made almost a habit of rushing off to shrines all over India to seek spiritual guidance at what she felt were tricky points in her career. Only last year she had caused a great sensation by disappearing in much the same way as this, and it had turned out that she had gone in secret up to Jammu to learn whether she should retire or not. The answer had, of course, been "No."

"It must be the same this time," Miss Officewalla assured him. "And, if you will promise me to a keep a secret of the greatest importance, I can tell you without fail when you will see her again."

He promised, with all the solemnity he could muster.

Miss Officewalla considered.

"Very well then," she said eventually, "I will confide in you, Inspector, what I have pledged myself to tell nobody else in the whole wide world."

"Yes?"

"Inspector, I know who is to receive 'Best Actress' at the Filmfare Awards Night on Sunday. It is Nilima, Inspector. And, believe me, nothing that there is will prevent her being there for that."

With this hope he had to be content.

The moment had almost come. The time when he would have to step out from the darkness at the side of the stage at the Shanmukhananda Hall, biggest in Asia, and, under the beating-down glare of all those lights, go up to Nilima, while she was still clutching the statuette of Best Actress, still all radiant smiles, and arrest her on a charge of murder.

The idea came into his head of simply leaving, of pretending that he had never experienced that sudden coming-together up there high above Sound Stage #2 at Talkiestan Studios, of simply slipping away. But he squared his shoulders and pushed the thought firmly down.

Nilima had murdered Dhartiraj. He was the officer in charge of the inquiry. He would arrest her under Indian Police Code Section 201.

Looking out at the rows of stars and dignitaries on the stage in front of him, wilting and sweating on their upright chairs under the heat of the lights, he found himself quite unworried by the fact that Nilima had not yet come to take her place among them. A lot of other top stars were as late. Miss Officewalla, flitting here and there through the huge hall— proudly boasting itself the biggest in Asia—busy gathering flavoursome titbits for her brew of gossip, had told him that she had no doubts whatever that the golden star would come to claim her award, and he was content.

He had plenty of time. They were still handing out the statuettes for the Technical Awards, best cinematography (colour), best cinematography (black-and-white), best audiography, best screenplay, best dialogue. The huge show had been going for little over an hour. It was only half-past ten. And he was going to wait to play his part in it, which would be as undramatic as he could make it, but more dramatic all the same by far than any of the tears of joy and the embraces that greeted each award as it came.

He was going to let Nilima receive her prize. He felt that he owed her that. It must mean so much to her when she was in the last years of her career, in its last months in all probability. There would have had to have come a time when she could no longer appear before the cameras as the most glamorous creature of all. The inexorable wrinkles could not have been held back for ever. Not by all the creams and oils. Not by whatever magical mixtures she could buy, at whatever cost, from people like Sudhaker Wani's old aunt. Not by all the electronic and hormone treatments that the ingenuity of Europe and America could provide. The time would have to come when she would have to submit to the oblivion of being unfilmed. This was, and Miss Officewalla had confirmed it, almost certainly the last chance she would ever have had of receiving a Filmfare Award. He would let her take it, and have one short moment of joy from it.

Then he would step into that glare and do his duty.

He felt a sudden flutter in his stomach. And quelled it.

No, if it meant shrieking mobs of fans hounding him every day, if it meant that his name would be remembered longer than Nilima's as the man who had tried to pull down the airy edifice of light that was the *filmi duniya*, why then it would have to be so. No doubt he would have the very greatest difficulty in securing a conviction against her. It would be as difficult as he had imagined it was going to be over Ravi Kumar. More so, in that he could so easily be made out to be cruelly attacking a defenceless woman and India's darling. But he would bring his case. He would make his arrest. Nilima was the murderer he had been ordered to find. And that was that.

He looked out from the comforting darkness at the brightly lit platform.

But what if, in spite of Miss Officewalla, she did not come after all? What if she had somehow—though it was not possible—heard something down below there at the Talkiestan Studios when he had listened to Ravi Kumar's confession of hopeless love? What if, when he had at last told the superstar that he believed him, she had—but it was not possible—somehow gathered that he now knew that she was the person he wanted. He had almost certainly mumbled her name to Ravi Kumar in his confusion and haste. What if even now she was in America or England or Germany on the way to being beyond his reach?

The burden would be lifted. He would not have to step out there under the glare. He would not have to put himself up as a target for all the vilification and abuse that the golden star's countless defenders could find to hurl at him. It would be a release.

But, no, it would be a worse fate than what he would have to do in a few minutes' time. He would then be to the public the man who had failed to avenge Dhartiraj, and to himself he would be a man who had failed to carry out his duty.

No, it was the lights for him. It had to be.

In the dark someone blundered into him. He turned. It was Ravi Kumar, Ravi Kumar coming to take the empty chair reserved for him out there.

"I am sorry, Mr. Kumar," he apologised.

The superstar looked at him. He flashed out a smile, the smile reserved for nameless fans. He turned and walked on to the stage, with that swagger that said, "I know a thousand eyes are on me". There was a great storm of applause, thundering up to the platform like surge after surge of the sea. Ravi Kumar raised his clasped hands over his head in acknowledgement. He beamed. He breathed in the adoration. This was his element.

Briefly, watching from the dark, he recalled that, not so long ago, he had held for a few mad days, the notion that he too could live in a similar element. Could be an adulated detective. How absurd.

But now surely the moment before him could not be long away. If Ravi Kuma had come, could Nilima be far behind? The Minister who was handing out the awards—no mere State office-holder, but the Minister of Defence from Delhi himself—was picking up the statuette to go to the Best Supporting Actress and the roll of nominations was being sonorously proclaimed. Even the Hollywood star who was a guest of honour—What was he called? Those American names were all so hard to remember—was sitting up and looking more alert than he had managed to do for many minutes. It would not be very long now. No doubt Nilima had kept her entrance until after this award. She might be waiting somewhere in the darkness behind him now. But she would come.

Then, just as the name of the winner was read out and the explosion of applause followed, a figure did come sliding up behind him in the darkness. For an instant he thought it was her. Was she coming to speak to him? To appeal to him? As she had appealed once before—but that must have been mere cunning, mere making sure that this policeman was not getting anywhere near her.

But it was quite a different figure that emerged from the shadows. Miss Officewalla, tall and beaky.

"Inspector."

"Yes? Yes? What is it? She has gone? You have heard something?"

"Yes, Inspector. I have just had a telephone call."

"She has fled away to Europe? To America?"

"No, Inspector. She has not fled. Perhaps it is worse. Perhaps better."

"Yes? Yes? What?"

"Inspector, you know that big circus that there is at present on the Oval Maiden by Churchgate?"

"Yes, yes."

What was this? Circuses?

"Inspector, it seems that she went in there just half an hour ago. I do not know whether she persuaded them or what. But she climbed up to the very top of the tent. And then she threw herself to death, Inspector."

It was a shock. But it was a shock that sent his mind racing. He seemed to know for certain everything that had happened. Yes, Nilima had gone to consult some shrine when she had left the Talkiestan Studios so suddenly. She must have wanted guidance badly. But she had come back to Bombay, just as Miss Officewalla had said she would, to collect her Award. And before setting out for the hall she must have rung up Ravi Kumar to find out if anything had happened in her absence. And he had told her what he had guessed from those mumbled words of his own up above the scene of Dhartiraj's death, that she was certain to be arrested for the murder. And so she had taken that way out. The woman who had begun as the child of the family of poor acrobats and had risen to such heights had decided to end her life in the circus, climbing high as she could and then falling, falling.

It was a fitting end. A fitting *filmi* end.

He stood thinking about her for a little longer, not formulating any ideas that could be expressed in words, simply feeling what it was that she had been and the sadness of it.

Then the thought of what this had done to his own situation rose up. Well, the answer to the riddle of Dhartiraj's death would never now be more than a confidential entry on the files. No execration for him as the persecutor of a golden heroine. And no glory as the man who had broken the case of the murdered star. Some public blame for an apparently unsolved mystery. Some recognition for what he had done from his superiors perhaps. A quiet end to it all.

Well, perhaps it was best. Perhaps that was a fitting end to it for him too.

THE END